TIME OF DAUGHTERS II

BOOKS IN THIS TIMELINE

INDA

THE FOX

KING'S SHIELD

TREASON'S SHORE

TIME OF DAUGHTERS I & II

BANNER OF THE DAMNED

TIME OF DAUGHTERS II

SHERWOOD SMITH

Book View Café

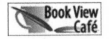

Time of Daughters II
Sherwood Smith
First Edition December 3, 2019
ISBN: 978-1-61138-846-6

Production Team:
Cover Design: Augusta Scarlett
Beta Reader: Debra Doyle
Copy Editor: Debra Doyle
Proofreader: Sara Stamey
Print-Formatter: Chris Dolley

Book View Café

www.bookviewcafe.com

Book View Café Publishing Cooperative
P.O. Box 1624, Cedar Crest, NM 87008-1624

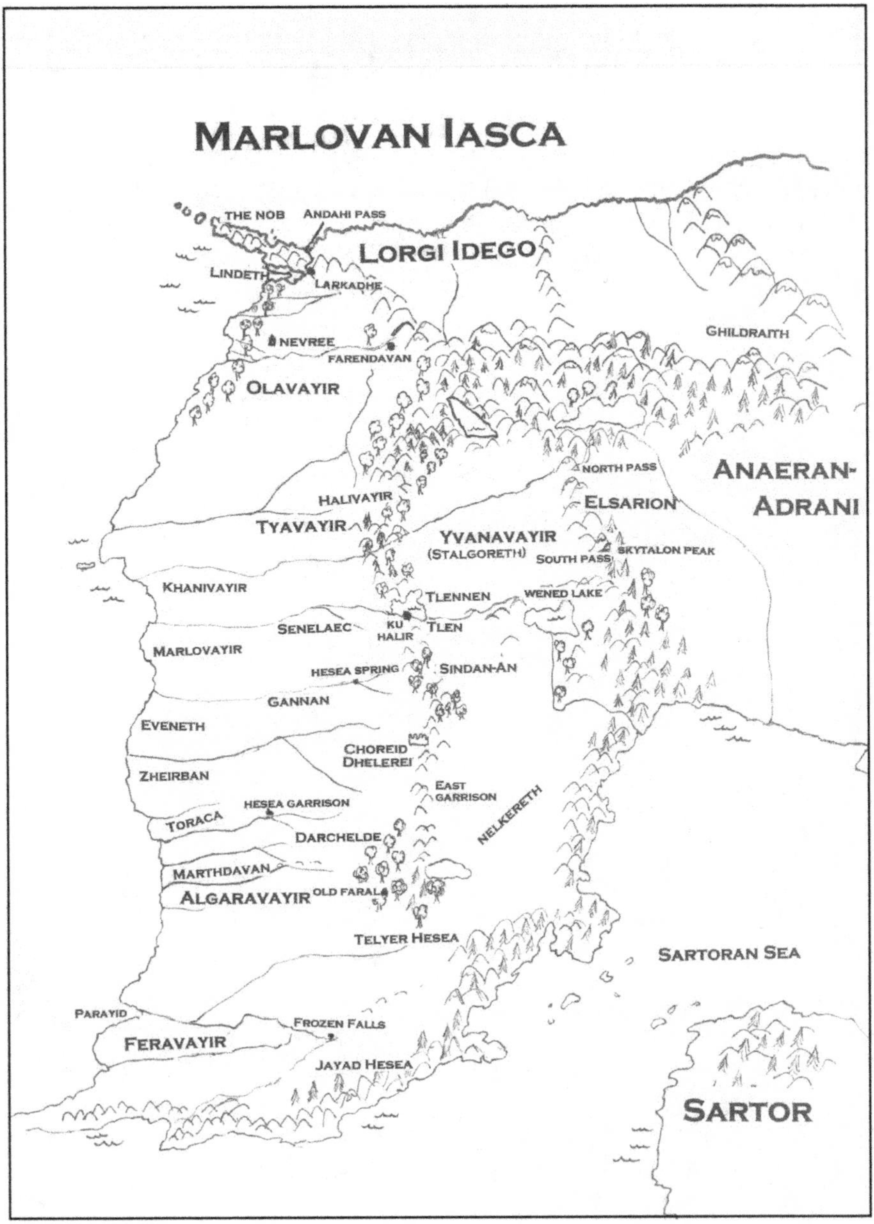
MARLOVAN IASCA
THE NOB
ANDAHI PASS
LORGI IDEGO
LINDETH
LARKADHE
NEVREE
FARENDAVAN
GHILDRAITH
OLAVAYIR
NORTH PASS
ANAERAN-
ADRANI
HALIVAYIR
ELSARION
TYAVAYIR
YVANAVAYIR
(STALGORETH)
SOUTH PASS
SKYTALON PEAK
KHANIVAYIR
TLENNEN
WENED LAKE
SENELAEC
KU
HALIR
TLEN
MARLOVAYIR
HESEA SPRING
SINDAN-AN
GANNAN
EVENETH
CHOREID
DHELEREI
ZHEIRBAN
EAST
GARRISON
NELKERETH
HESEA GARRISON
TORACA
DARCHELDE
MARTHDAVAN
ALGARAVAYIR
OLD FARAL
TELYER HESEA
SARTORAN SEA
PARAYID
FROZEN FALLS
FERAVAYIR
JAYAD HESEA
SARTOR

A VERY BRIEF PREFACE

The second half of this record begins five years after the end of the previous. Arrow (Anred-Harvaldar) and Danet still rule Marlovan Iasca. Their three children have reached adulthood.

A list of Who's Who can be found at the back.

PART ONE

ONE

Spring 4083 AF

There were no fanfares for the merchants, artisans, and runners riding in and out the city gates, after being holed up as a frigid storm swept through.

Bunny, now a riding master in the queen's training, had just brought the new arrivals to the stable, splashing two by two through the wide, sky-reflecting puddles as Lineas walked at the back of the group.

A lone horseman rode in through the gates. Princess, royal runner, and girls turned to stare at the comely young man riding easy in the saddle, his dark blue royal runner's coat water-dappled. Familiar? Dark hair queued back, sharp cheekbones so familiar, though planed by the past five years—

"It's Quill!" Bunny shouted, forgetting that as a master, she was supposed to model proper discipline. Her fingers swooped and dived, the equivalent of shouting in Hand as she cried, "He's *back!*"

Quill laughed, his gaze flicking from Bunny's happy smile to the lone bright red head among the various blond and dark haired crowd. Nearly six years of carefully cultivated emotional distance vanished like smoke as he gazed down into Lineas's equally happy smile, her wideset eyes crinkled in friendly welcome. Without a vestige of heat.

"You're back, you're back," Bun crowed, then belatedly recollected herself as the staring sixteen-year-old girls whispered together.

"Quill is a royal runner," Bun explained, hands still signing. "And a friend from when we were all small. He's been gone, doing the magic renewals all over the kingdom." And to Quill, "Was it fun?"

He laughed. Only Bun would ask that. What was she now, twenty-one, twenty-two? He was glad to see all her old enthusiasm, with no hint of longing. As he'd hoped, her teenage crush had died long ago.

He slid from his horse and relinquished the reins to the waiting stable hand. "It was." And because it seemed that Hand was now a part of everyday speech, he signed as he said, "Have things changed much while I was gone?"

Bun turned to Lineas, rolling her eyes. "Where to start?"

"I'll show him, if you like," Lineas said, her long, slender fingers graceful and dragonfly-quick in Hand.

"Do that. We'll be starting with the hooves, so take your time," Bun added with meaning, remembering the state some of the horses had been in on certain girls' arrival.

And so Quill's plan to slip back into castle life unnoticed also went up in smoke, leaving him to face the one person he'd wanted time to prepare for. But time, as well as desire, were not his to command.

"Thank you," he said to Lineas as he hefted his travel bag over his shoulder. "Lead on." And in Old Sartoran, "Class in basic horse care?"

"Yes," she answered in the same tongue. "Many of them arrived with runners having done all such care. They'll learn fast." She smiled up at him. "Congratulations on your new sister. Oh! Did you know about her?"

"Camerend has been writing to me all along." And because it was Lineas, "I could see his happiness in the way he formed his letters."

Lineas's smile brightened, then dimmed, her gaze direct, an echo of grief in it and in her voice as she said softly, "I'm sorry about Shendan."

"I saw her at the beginning of my journey," he said. "She was content."

"Content," Lineas repeated, and as she stepped onto the landing, she turned to face him. "Content. What did she mean by that? That she was ready?"

"She didn't want to face another winter, but mostly it was contentment at the current of our lives. The kingdom at peace, or as much as it ever is. I stopped in Darchelde on the way back, but didn't see your parents. Your mother was reported to be somewhere near the western border, and I was told your father volunteered to serve in the king's call."

"Yes. He's been up in Ku Halir, helping build the new garrison." Lineas opened her palm northward.

They reached the second floor, which led to the royal residence. The ring of boot heels caused them both to look up, and then to step to the wall when they recognized Connar. Lineas's face brightened as Connar's blue gaze flicked from one to the other.

"Quill is back," Lineas said in Marlovan.

"Quill," Connar said equably, and to Lineas, "We saw one another at Larkadhe."

Lineas smiled. "I'm going to show him around, since everything has changed since he left."

"Someone else can do that," Connar said.

"I don't mind. Bunny truly doesn't need an assistant for today's lesson, and I want to hear all about his journey. He's been everywhere."

Then she stepped close to Connar, standing on tiptoe. He leaned down as she said softly, "The gunvaer was called to the barn." She backed away again, her expression grave.

Connar's eyes shuttered. His hand rose to touch her cheek in a gesture equal parts tender and possessive. Quill felt it like a kick in the gut.

Then the prince ran down the steps three at a time.

Lineas said to Quill, "The stable people will keep Bun in the courtyard with her class. It's Firefly," she added with a compassionate glance toward the stable. "She made it to thirty-three. The gunvaer doesn't want Bunny to know that the mare is dying. Even when animals live quite long for their kind, Bun always takes their deaths so very, very hard, as if she were at fault. And Firefly is one of her favorites."

Lineas thumbed away the sting in her eyes, reminding herself that Firefly was not writhing in pain. And not alone.

Before Quill could find words that didn't sound forced or sickening, she started up the steps to the third floor and began enumerating the alterations to castle life. " . . . so the middle wings have all been reassigned, out to the garrison, the barns, and the pottery. Here we are."

They topped the last step at the third story landing—they had reached the floor belonging to the royal runners, called the roost.

She indicated the slit window looking into the castle's interior structures. "Those roofs are now the queen's training. They drill in the courtyard below the queen's suite, exactly as they did in the old days. All those carts and the pottery clutter we used to hide in and under is all gone, and what can't be used or remade shifted out to the other side of the north river."

She waved eastward, and started down the hall. "But at least you'll find things mostly the same in the roost. We'll go straight there, because the schedule is so different now. Tell me about your travels! I know you were renewing the magic, but surely you had time for other things. Connar said you were at Larkadhe. Did you hear the windharps?"

"I did. I stayed on an extra week against a prospective wind change." Memory assailed him, sound, smells, sense: sitting high on a mountaintop with Vandareth as they shared a packet of fresh-picked cherries while Vanda reeled off the galloping rhythms of poetry in Old Venn against the wind's threnodies.

" . . . I saw the great trees in Shingara . . ." *Lying on an ancient Dawnsinger platform, rain tapping on the front-woven roof as singers wove complicated triplets in singing up the sun.*

"And was there for the Feather Dance up above Khanivar, which the locals call the Roof of the World." *High, crystalline voices of children in air so cold it seized the throat, but the light there was so pure, so brilliant it hurt. They sang and sang, yet the Fire Dragon of the Flying People still did not come, and so the singing changed timbre to lament, leaving him wondering what story lay behind a myth, and ritual, clearly ancient.*

" . . . A triple rainbow over the ocean after a storm while I was on a houseboat below Parayid Harbor . . ." *As a mysterious trader posed three riddles to Quill in Old Sartoran before he would permit him to see the statue of an egret taking wing carved of silverwood from the walking tree people of the east.*

"I planted rice in a terrace farm all the way south . . ." *As a flock of long-tailed jezeels crossed the sky, calling to one another, until they vanished beyond the mountains above the Sartoran Sea.*

Which he climbed over the next three weeks, having gone off the right trail. He'd nearly frozen to death, with scant food left in his pack, his gloves ripped and palms bleeding from the jagged rocks when in desperation he followed a little white goat into a village built straight into living rock, whose people, dark of skin and clever of fingers, carved their history into a glistening moon-white stone, their work so fine and intricate you'd take the long narrative screens for paper.

Kings would pay a kingdom's ransom for the smallest of these, he'd said to the daughter who served him almond-flour cakes and spiced goat milk. She'd shrugged as she retorted mildly, *What use is that to us? We live as we live.* To which he said, *I trust unscrupulous thieves never find you.* She chuckled, replying, *Ah, but the fogs hide us from wicked hearts.* And as he'd made his way down the mountain, he had looked back, but could not find the trail among the dappled shadows and drifting mists . . .

"Quill?"

He blinked into Lineas's face so close to his he could see his own reflection in her widened pupils.

"Are you reliving a memory?" she asked, a pucker of concern in her brow.

He forced a laugh. "I was. Forgive me! It's just that most don't want to hear a very long tale of travel, weather, and people without fame, or doings without blood or steel."

"I would," she said, too gravely and too gently for rebuke. "That's my favorite kind of tale. But I'm certain you're tired and travel-worn, and hungry at the least. And the seniors will be so glad to see you. I'd like to hear the tale of your journey, if you ever decide to tell it."

"I'm afraid that would take as long to tell as it was to live."

She ducked her head, hiding her expression, and he would have cut out his tongue if it meant he could take the words back. Dolt! He'd managed to forget how quick she was, how sensitive to deflection. And once again he saw Connar caress her.

"Forgive me," she said, hands together.

"No, forgive *me.* Lineas—"

"There you are. At last!" Mnar bustled down the hallway toward them. Other than looking a little grayer, she seemed unchanged. "Lineas, on your way downstairs, send a fledgling for a meal, and Quill, I'll fill in anything you've not already heard through your notecase."

Lineas flitted off.

Mnar said, "Was it good, your journey?"

"Very," he said, fighting the urge to run after Lineas. He made himself turn away as Mnar clapped her hands together.

"Excellent," she said. "Later on I'd like to hear all about your journey. Right now, let me go over the changes since you left. As Lineas probably told you, they're considerable, beginning with putting together a staff for Noren, who the queen is preparing to take over the queen's training when she's had a year or two more. . ."

Quill actually knew more about the schedule than Mnar assumed, having received a long letter that morning while both he and Camerend waited out the same massive storm at opposite ends. But he sat politely, assuming an alert look, while resolving to smother all the questions arising from that single touch from the prince's hand to Lineas's cheek—out of all the news he'd received, there had been nothing personal, of course. And he had stupidly, *stupidly*, not asked her to write to him while he was gone, for oh, such sterling reasons.

As Mnar talked, people showed up, smiling and welcoming Quill back. The most startling changes were in the former fledglings, now runners, and in the former fuzz, nearly unrecognizable with over five years' steady growth.

He discovered that though he'd considered carefully what he could tell and what not to, no one had time to hear much of it. They really wanted to be heard, for all their interest was bound up in the constantly flowing river of castle life. As it should be, he told himself.

At the end, Mnar paused, pointed at the cooling food that had been waiting for him all this time, and said, "Any questions?"

"None."

"Excellent. Get that meal into you, then go straight to work on the map with any emendations you've noted . . ."

After Lineas's warning about Firefly, Connar changed his route, and his intention. He waved off his first runner, Fish, who stood in the courtyard with Connar's practice weapons, and noted Bunny in the courtyard, busy with a line of girls laboriously learning the rudiments of horse grooming on the oldest and most placid of the animals.

It looked like the conspiracy to keep Bun from finding out about Firefly was working so far. A relief. Connar found Bun entirely incomprehensible, especially her passion for fixing whatever broken animal came her way and descending into wild grief when she couldn't.

He slipped into the stable, a vast building more airy than some of the best rooms in the castle. Foreigners who scorned the Marlovans and barbarians sometimes said that they treated their horses better than they did each other. It was often true. The royal horses had the largest stalls, roomy, always clean, whatever the time of year.

Connar's steps slowed when he saw his mother's old mare lying on her side on fresh hay, Danet sitting at Firefly's head, stroking slowly and gently, her profile long with the grief she didn't try to hide.

The stall stood open. Firefly wasn't going anywhere—she had lain down for the last time, as horses will do when they know the end is near.

Danet looked up at the footfalls, and when she saw Connar, her lips parted, and her eyes sheened with moisture. Connar, seeing the sob she swallowed, hurried the last few steps. "Lineas told me," Connar said as he knelt beside Danet.

Firefly's ears flicked, and she heaved a snorting sigh, but otherwise accepted Connar's presence; it was on her back that all three royal children had had their first ride.

Connar watched Ma's slow, gentle hand stroking Firefly's face, and when a tear splashed on her knee, he said, "Don't be sad. Firefly had a good long life."

"I know. And it's good to be here with her." Danet took a deep, shivering breath and said huskily, "But it still hurts to say goodbye." She tried a wry smile, crooked and trembling. "And I admit I'm feeling sorry for myself, a little. Because Firefly is the first of what I'll be facing. I never think about it, but I'm getting old, too."

"No. You're not," Connar said fiercely.

"Your Da's got white hair coming in. The other day I saw him from the back and was reminded of his father . . ." She gazed off, and sighed.

Connar had slept little, or he might not have spoken, but the words he wrestled with from time to time made their way out, there over the horse that breathed so slowly.

"If. Something happens to Da. What if Noddy doesn't want to be king?"

Danet looked up, startled out of grief, and stared at Connar. He gazed back through those thickly fringed blue eyes, as beautiful as the summer sky. She wasn't sure when he had learned to mask his emotions; she had only become aware of it the year after he took that terrible beating.

Her first impulse was to retort, "Then he'd be smart." But Connar's question, so sudden, unsettled her. She stroked Firefly's soft nose as she tried to reach past that blank gaze for the impulse behind it. Then said slowly, "Since this is actually a subject that becomes important only after your da dies—"

Not my da, came the thought, and Connar, as always, hated that thought, hated Lance Master Retren Hauth for putting it there—hated the way his own mind twisted back and forth during those nights when he couldn't sleep.

Danet leaned toward him over Firefly's head, her hands gripping her elbows, and gazed straight into his eyes, her pupils huge. "Since it's just you and me here, I'll tell you the truth. I don't care which of you becomes king. As far as I'm concerned, you can settle that between yourselves. But it would kill me—I mean it, it truly would kill me, it would faster and more merciful if you took a knife and cut out my heart—if you two fought over that throne. The single pride of my life is how good you boys have been to each other. *For* each other."

Connar heard the ring of truth in her husky voice, and leaned over to put his arms around her. She always seemed so strong, he was surprised how thin and bony she was. Hugging her gently, he said, "Mine, too."

He only realized how tense she was when he felt some of that tension went out of her body, and he let go. "You know Noddy," he said quickly, easily. "Says one thing, then another. I just wondered—you were talking about age, and so forth. I'll forget it by tomorrow. The way he does."

He shifted the subject to Firefly, reminiscing about how Danet put Bun on her back for the first time, and she'd clung to the saddle and wouldn't let go. He went on to other good memories of family rides, speaking in that warm, silvery voice that never failed to have an effect.

At the sound of footfalls, they both looked up, and there was Noddy.

"She's down." Noddy stated the obvious, as usual, and dropped to his knees beside Connar, his long face unhappy. "I checked on her last night, and she was still standing. But she hadn't eaten." He stroked the mare's face and gently fondled her ears in the way she liked it. "Connar, if you want to go out with Second Wing, I can stay here with Ma."

"Ma, do you want us both here?" Connar asked.

"The fact that you asked is enough for me," she said, and then her breath hitched. "In any case, she's gone." For it had happened peacefully while the boys spoke.

She laid her hand gently between Firefly's closed eyes, then lifted her head. "Sage, you can lift the perimeter. If Bun comes in, let her say her farewell before the Disappearance."

Connar got to his feet "I'm going. I know this will be bad."

Noddy rose, too. "I'll go with you."

"Thank you, boys," Danet said, her hand still resting on Firefly's forehead.

Noddy walked out, using his sleeve to wipe tears.

Vanadei, his first runner—assigned after Noddy left the academy—saw his expression. "It's over?"

"Yes." Noddy sleeved his eyes again, then his expression eased incrementally. "Connar was there too. Ma was glad."

All morning, Lineas thought about Firefly. Late that afternoon word spread that Firefly had died. Lineas braced for Bunny's tears as she carried her dinner tray upstairs at the watch change bell.

Noddy intercepted her at the top of the stairs, his eyes ringed with dull flesh. "Lineas," he breathed, "there you are. Bunny's got Connar cornered. I'm afraid . . ." His big hand gestured widely.

Lineas heard Bunny in the distance, almost unrecognizable in shrieking fury. "I'll do what I can," Lineas promised as she set the tray down inside Bunny's door and sped toward Connar's suite.

She found Bunny in Connar's outer room, trying her hardest to hit him as she screamed, "You knew! You knew and you didn't tell me! You stupid shit, both of you, you should have told me! You're all liars, it *wasn't* fast, just like that—"

"Bun," Connar said, fending her off with forearm blocks, his hands stiff with frustration.

Bunny whirled and kicked out, catching the edge of his knee.

Fish was standing against the wall. He started toward Bunny, whose head jerked. Glaring at him with red eyes, she screamed, "Touch me and I'll *kill* you!"

"Fish, back off." Connar raised an arm to block Bun's flailing fist; though she wasn't a fighter, her daily drill each day at best perfunctory, she was quite strong from lifting saddles and carrying wounded dogs, goats, and sheep almost as large as she was.

Annoyance flared in him along with pain from his knee, and the words *It's just a dead horse* were right there, wanting to be spoken. Then his gaze lifted as Lineas rushed in.

"Bunny. Bun." And when Bunny burst into angry tears, screaming imprecations, Lineas said distinctly, "Hadand-Edli."

Bunny whirled around, snot and tears smeared over her red face. "Did *you* know?" she demanded.

Connar thought, *Lie,* and then grimaced when Lineas said, "I did."

Bunny stopped short, her eyes distended in fury, her mouth working.

Lineas met that fierce gaze and said softly, "We all knew. The queen ordered us not to tell you."

Bun's mouth dropped open. Then her face crumpled and tears flowed again as she screamed, "Why would she betray me like that?"

Lineas advanced, reaching for Bun's hands.

Bun evaded her reach, but stopped trying to hit Connar. As she sobbed, Lineas said, "I can tell you why, but you have to listen."

Bunny gulped down a sob, and glowered at her as she wiped her sleeve over her face. "If you say it was for my own good—"

"No. It was for hers." This caught Bunny's attention, and Lineas said calmly, "Think about it. Yes, Firefly was your first ride, and you loved her. You love them all. But she was your mother's when she was a girl. She trained with Firefly, she was there when Biscuit was born. And you're the gunvaer's daughter. She couldn't bear to see you trying to heal Firefly, *and* see Firefly die. She knew you'd try, because you always try, you do your best, always. But this time it wasn't going to work."

Bunny was breathing fast. "I could have . . . I could have," she said in a small voice.

"No." Lineas said it softly, and tears gleamed in her eyes. "No."

Bunny gulped. "I kept checking her. I *knew* something was wrong, but yesterday she was perky. When I left she was nosing her feed."

Lineas said, "I'm told she only did that while you were there. She knew what you wanted, but she couldn't manage it."

Bunny choked on her sobs, as Lineas spotted Sage and Loret at the door, the queen's runners clearly sent by her. She made the sign for *Wait,* and they withdrew out of sight.

Lineas took Bunny's hand, sweaty and slimy with snot as it was, and drew her away from where she'd backed Connar against a wall. "I wasn't there, but Dannor told me your mother was with Firefly. It was as peaceful as it could be."

"We were there, too," Connar said. "Noddy and me. It was."

Bunny's chest heaved in a huge, crashing sob, but this time all the anger was gone, leaving desolate grief. She dropped Lineas's hand and ran out. Lineas walked out more slowly, pausing when she saw Noddy lurking in the hall.

"I think it'll be all right," she said softly as she passed into the princess's room, leaving Noddy in a mixture of relief and sadness at his mother's and Bunny's grief. He glanced toward Connar's suite, and heard the clatter of wood as Connar kicked upright the table that Bun had knocked over.

Connar was mad. He'd get over it fast—his temper was a little like thunderstorms, Noddy thought as he retreated to his own suite.

"It was just a horse," Connar said, alone again, then caught himself: he was only alone in the sense of his family being elsewhere. He had trained himself not to talk about anything but immediate requirements in front of Fish, who he was certain blabbed every detail of his life to Hauth.

So he regretted the outburst, but only for a heartbeat. This was a *horse,* among the hundreds they dealt with. "Horses die. Everything dies. At least she wasn't killed," Connar said, dipping a cloth in the fresh water jug and wiping Bun's slime off his hands.

Fish remained silent, knowing after five years that Connar would shut up immediately if he tried to start a conversation. Then Connar turned his way, his expression expectant.

Did he actually want an answer for once? Fish's mind caromed from his own feelings—he liked animals, and hated the thought of losing his own mount, earned when he was promoted to first runner to the prince—and

"But the boys," Danet said, meaning Connar, "listen to Lineas. She speaks Iascan, she gets along with everyone. And Connar in particular has only that garrison runner."

Mnar did not like the idea of sending Lineas to Larkadhe, though she couldn't think of a reason against it. Maybe it was just that it was so unexpected. Also, Lineas hadn't had proper training for such a post. But it was the queen speaking—Danet hadn't asked their opinion, she'd said *I want*.

"It surprised me, too, when Connar-Laef chose young Fish Pereth, but the garrison runners are well trained, especially in military niceties, which is Connar-Laef's future concern," Mnar said. "Whom would you like for Hadand-Edli?"

"Let her pick her own. She's certainly old enough—"

And here were the girls flocking in to add their well-meant noise. Danet set herself to appreciate the generosity she recognized behind it, and presently they all left.

Danet closed her eyes, grateful for the silence, but her mind promptly wrenched her back to Firefly, silent and still.

When she opened her eyes to the fresh, herbal scent of listerblossom, here was her beloved, Garrison Commander Jarid Noth, quietly holding out a cup. She set it down, and relaxed into his arms with a deep sigh.

TWO

That first year after Connar was sent to East Garrison for his initial training season, Lineas had resolved firmly against expecting any attention from him once he returned ten months later. That way it would hurt less when he inevitably moved on to another favorite.

To her surprise, the first night he returned he asked for her to rub lavender and carrot-seed oil into his scars, as she had every night after the bandages came off that terrible summer previous. And he asked her to stay with him for the night. He continued to ask for her until he was sent to winter training at Hesea.

Because he hated any kind of personal talk, she had no idea how much he'd come to appreciate a favorite who didn't expect to keep things in his room, who didn't assume she had a right to his time, who followed his moods without a lot of the yammer he loathed. And who he didn't have to hide his back from.

He assumed this was probably why he didn't have nightmares nearly as often when he was with her. And if he did have one, she didn't pester him with questions or coos of pity, she just rubbed his shoulders and back until he slept again, her fingers soothing away the shards of remembered pain, the images of his own blood dripping on the parade ground, and beneath it all, Cabbage Gannan's shrilly gleeful voice when they were both thirteen, *You're not a real prince.*

As for Lineas, to be with him made her sublimely happy, and she had no experience with anyone else. She didn't want anyone else.

When he rode away for his second year, he was impatient for variety, always within certain limitations, such as never permitting any of his partners to remain the night. Once the sex was over, he couldn't sleep until they were gone, and too often, whether he'd had sex five times or not at all, sleep was broken by nightmares mirroring the frustrations of the day: garrison life was very much like academy life, with captains replacing masters. *They* still held command. Not him. When his sleep was broken he got into the habit of rising, and going to the torchlit practice yard to drill until his muscles trembled, in hopes his mind would release him to sleep.

By the end of that second rotation, he was longing for the royal city again, and the sheer relief of Lineas's light touch and calm mind. Being with her was like floating in a forest pool balanced between sun and shade, warmth and coolness.

And so they established a pattern: when he was away, Lineas lived a single life. She was too self-conscious to flirt, and anyway could not be intimate where she didn't love, so she kept herself busy until Connar's return. And on his return, he always sent for her and she always came.

After Ranet's arrival at the palace, Lineas became more scrupulous about retiring to her room, for she believed it would be right and proper for Connar to turn to the person he was expected to marry. Ranet was the prettiest of all the royal girls, kind, and hard-working. She also adored Connar, but in his eyes she was still too young. The idea of marriage with her belonged to a hazy future. So he kept asking Lineas to come to his larger, more comfortable room, warmed by firesticks in the fireplace those winter weeks.

The night after Firefly died, he went looking for her, and found her standing in the hallway with a couple of the queen's runners. At his approach they laid fingers to chest—Lineas included—as they broke up, she with a bemused expression. "What's wrong?"

"Nothing!" She turned her wide eyes up to him. "It's . . . just now I was given new orders. I've been assigned to serve as second runner to you and your brother, when you—we," she conscientiously amended, "go north."

That surprised a laugh out of him. "Good plan!"

She smiled to see how pleased he was, and they retired, she with her quiet, polite "Good night," to Fish, who responded with the Hand sign for good night, a perfunctory politeness at best; at least when Connar was with Lineas, he knew that he would not be needed until morning, and left for his own rest.

"I wonder what they're thinking," Connar said presently, as he and Lineas lay in bed, limbs entangled in the blissful aftermath of passion. "Sending you instead of one of the other feet." That being the academy slang for royal runners. "Or Quill, back today and stinking of horse. It must be your Iascan. I remember hearing a lot of it when I got my tour through Larkadhe. Or," he turned to smile, his eyes reflecting the dancing flame of the one candle, "they don't think we can defend ourselves, and we need an extra-tough bodyguard."

He attacked her then, and they wrestled. Every so often she managed to flip him when he wasn't expecting it, or got a lock on him—as she did that night, causing him to laugh.

Their usual method of surrender was a kiss, and presently they quieted again, sleep stealing over them both. For some reason, that image of Quill lingered in his mind, sliding him back into wakefulness.

The last time Connar had seen Quill, he and his escort had ridden out of Larkadhe to the mouth of the Pass to take a look at the famous water-carved passage through the mountains. A lone figure in a dark blue runner's coat rode down from the north, a sword strapped to his back and knives in the tops of his boots, with a bow slung at the saddle. Connar had stared in surprise when he recognized Quill, who he was used to seeing among the modest, blue-robed, unarmed feet around the royal castle. The academy boys had had a wide range of insults about the cosseted feet, who—as everyone knew—didn't compete in the arts of war, didn't wear weapons, and (this earned their especial scorn) didn't get caned for defaulters.

That day in the Pass, nobody seemed to notice anything amiss as Captain Basna said to Quill, "They sent you to the Idegans? I thought you were redoing the water spells."

"I was. I am." Quill tapped his saddlebag. "But the long runners were all elsewhere, so I said I'd run a message over the Pass to Andahi."

"Any news from up there?"

"The only item of import was some crowing about having chased the Skunk's gang into the southern mountains."

"No doubt pushing him down onto our side." Captain Basna made a spitting motion, then raised a hand in salute, and clucked at his mount as they started up the Pass.

"Skunk?" Connar asked, glancing back at Quill's solitary figure.

"Jendas Yenvir, a horse thief. They say he's part morvende—he's got the white hair and fish-pale skin, but no talons. And he has a black stripe going from brow to the back of his head, the way that some part morvende do. He's tried to get his gang called after white hunting cats, but the locals all call him Skunk."

Connar scarcely listened to the talk about Jendas Yenvir and his striped hair. He was still thinking about Quill. Of course the runners would carry weapons—they could encounter anyone in those mountains, most often various types of brigands or run warriors escaping punishment for crimes, who certainly wouldn't respect those blue coats.

It's just that no one had ever seen the feet training with weapons, though it was stupid to think them incapable. Even Fish could carry his own weight—Connar had gone to watch the garrison runners' drill one morning before his first garrison posting, to discover it wasn't much different than what he'd done as an academy senior, except more hand to hand, and of course no lance training.

After reflecting on these things, he turned his head on the pillow, and said to Lineas, "Do you think Quill could take me down?"

She opened heavy eyes, looking confused at the abrupt question when she was so used to his habitual silence. Her voice husky with sleep, she murmured, "I think he would risk his life to defend you."

Connar accepted that, turned over, and neither woke until the dawn bells.

By then word of the new orders had spread along the residence; when they rose, Lineas to retreat to her room to fetch clothes for the baths, there was Fish with coffee for Connar.

On her way to the door, Lineas was about to give Fish a polite good morning, but met such a narrow-eyed, white-lipped glare the words froze in her throat as she stopped just inside the suite door.

His gaze flicked to the shut bedchamber door, then he said in a low, venomous voice, "You think I'm incompetent, is that it?"

"What?" she said.

Fish's lip curled. "You seemed to have weaseled your way into going north. Well, you're in for a surprise if you think you've got him by the prick."

"The orders came from the queen. I didn't—"

The latch rattled as Connar began to open the door, and Fish turned away, his hands stiff with tension as he began to uncover Connar's breakfast tray.

Lineas did not understand the tension between Connar and Fish, but she'd learned to glide silently between them. She was gone before Connar emerged into the room.

She met the queen's third runner Sage and Noren's Holly going down to the baths and joined them.

"You look sober," Sage said to Lineas.

"It's . . . I don't understand the rivalry with the garrison runners," Lineas said, unwilling to mention Fish's name, as that felt like gossip.

Holly relished gossip, being as curious as she was lively. She'd been the first of the newcomers to master the complexities of relationships among castle staff, and she had not endured the years of lessons the royal runners were given about circumspection. "Fish get nasty with you?"

Lineas looked startled as Sage said, "I should have guessed. He's in a snit over your being transferred to the princes, right?"

Bitterness, Lineas had learned early, usually stemmed from the kind of disappointment that seemed unjust. But she had never done anything to Fish. So it had to be due to something older. "I don't understand—we're all dedicated to service."

Sage gazed into the middle distance, then said finally, "It's not you, Lineas. It's us. Fish Pereth was a fuzz same year as me. He's smart. Very. But he liked mean games. When he got caught, he said everything he was supposed to, but as soon as the seniors were out of sight, he went right back to it. So they sent him over to the garrison runners. He's hated us ever since."

Lineas recollected her first year. Fish had been derided as a snitch by the garrison boys in their never-ending feuds and stalking not-quite-games, that the fuzz (first year royal runners in training) had been strictly forbidden to stay out of.

"Did they tell him why when they put him out of the royal runners? Oh, but they must have," Lineas said.

When she was fourteen, two of her fellow fledglings had been released from training, a boy and a girl, both of whom had spent time closeted with the masters before they went elsewhere—one to the scribes, and one sent all the way back to Feravayir. The first one, she remembered, had wanted to go. He preferred the scribe life. The second had been a bit more mysterious, but then life was generally mysterious to her then.

Sage eyed her. "You're thinking of Liet Genda. Maybe you didn't know that she turned out to be what the military would call a spy. Her loyalty belonged to Lavais-Jarlan of Feravayir, not to the kingdom." She sighed. "This is what Camerend said to me. The senior staff can explain as carefully as is possible, but people are going to hear what they wish to hear. I believe Fish Pereth heard only that we didn't want him."

Holly's hands flung wide, then she said with a wry face, "I'm not surprised, considering how horrible everyone says his mother is, and that uncle that everyone says is a drunk—"

Sage cut that off, as usual, saying in a scolding voice, "I *wish* you wouldn't spread about 'what everyone says' without telling us who said it first, and what proof they have. Retren Hauth is an excellent master, that's what I've heard from Headmaster Andaun . . ."

Lineas didn't hear the rest, as she scarcely knew who Master Hauth was. Instead, she was contemplating what she had observed as a small child in Darchelde, how anger begets anger. Fish was angry over something, so she resolved to be kinder to him, as on the other side of the garrison, in the cramped, stuffy quartermaster's office, Fish complained with pent-up resentment about the interloper royal runner.

His father listened with scarcely hidden disinterest, and Retren Hauth with the close attention he paid to anything that remotely touched the true king.

At the end, "Lineas said she didn't weasel her way into those orders, but I don't believe it. Of course she did. She had to. When has anyone ever taken women on military posts?"

"She's a royal runner," Hauth stated derisively, for he loathed whining. "They go *everywhere*. The garrison trains men as runners for the military captains and commanders, but the royal runners have never made a gender distinction, since they don't fight, and are excluded from the chain of command. One of the reasons why we only assign male runners to captains and above is that they sometimes earn side-promotions in the field."

Fish knew that, of course: runners were sometimes commandeered into logistical support. He had no interest in such a promotion.

Hauth went on. "But that won't happen with that girl, so why are you complaining? They probably need another paper-weasel up north. Has she ever lied to you?"

"She doesn't talk to me. I make sure of that."

His father, the garrison quartermaster, lifted his head at that, and said mildly, "Might be a mistake."

Hauth snapped his palm down and away. "If royal runners gossip, it's always in one or another of those old languages no one uses anymore. She won't jabber with Fish." And to Fish, "Nothing I've heard about her indicates that she lies. Have you ever considered that Connar asked for her? It's probable, if they're exclusive."

"But that's just it," Fish exclaimed. "He's not. While he's here, she's convenient, but the day we ride out, he's got his eye roving. Male or female, it's rarely the same one twice. They come at him everywhere we go, and some days, it feels like they're lining up at the door," he finished with disgust.

"He's young." Hauth shrugged. "And he's still at that snotty defiant age. He's not the only one," he added.

Fish flushed with mortification, and muttered, "The only person he talks to is Nadran-Sierlaef. And that's mostly telling him what to think."

Tired of Fish's habitual trail, Hauth resorted to his own equally habitual trail. "This next post is their first taste of command. You'll see. It'll make all the difference. Connar won't be able to miss how stupid the heir is when it's them giving the commands for the first time. He'll get tired of doing all the thinking, and when he does, he'll need allies. You are in place to be the first."

Fish sighed.

Hauth added, "As for the girl. If you can, listen to the two of them."

"Shit," Fish uttered with heartfelt revulsion. "It's bad enough being around them without trying to ear in on their headboard banging."

Hauth hissed out a sigh. "Before. Or after. We need to know what's in his mind, and remember, whatever he's telling her is surely making its way to the king and queen in that girl's regular reports."

Hauth left after a few more exhortations, leaving Fish alone with his father. "I don't think Connar tells anybody anything," he groused.

His father, aware that his son hadn't come out with that opinion in Hauth's hearing, retorted, "Your job is to make sure of that."

Fish left, disgusted with everything and everybody. The only thing he was sure of was that riding out of the royal city, once his greatest pleasure, had been ruined. He slunk to the garrison drill court to work off his temper while Connar was scrapping with the rankers.

Passing in the other direction, Quill at last had a chance to visit Hliss, now officially Aunt Hliss, as she was wearing a ring on her heart finger, matching the one Camerend wore. Her work chamber was heady with the pungent scent of flowers used in dyes as they talked.

Quill looked down in delight at Blossom (given the name Danet on her Name Day, but that altered rapidly through a series of sickeningly sweet nicknames until Blossom was settled on what everybody agreed was the cutest baby ever born) as she toddled about, chattering. Quill had so little family that every added person made him happy, especially as he had always liked and admired Hliss, and Blossom, so far, had the same even temper as Andas, Hliss's son by the king.

Hliss watched with pleasure how careful Quill was with Blossom's eager lurches and wild battings of dimpled hands, then he looked over her blond, curly head to ask, "How is Andas?"

"Flourishing. Even though your father's mostly at Darchelde now, he still sees to it that I receive regular letters. Also, ever since Andas learnt writing, Arrow's been sending his own runners, or asking the ones going to and from Larkadhe to ride to Farendavan before taking the south road." Hliss's gentle face curved into a sardonic smile that brought the gunvaer sharply to mind for a moment before she said, "He knows I won't let Andas return until he's too old for the academy, but I suspect Arrow can't help hoping. However he might wheedle, Andas is with my mother. She won't let him go."

"The king can't help but hope, I suspect," Quill said. "He's proud of his army."

Hliss's dimples were back. "Oh, I know. And we don't argue about it anymore. He comes over at least once a week, sometimes more when he can, Noddy often with him, to share his letters and read mine. Things are—"

They looked up at the shadow in the open door. A fledgling whose name Quill hadn't learned yet touched fingers to chest and said, "Quill, summons to the roost."

Quill bent down to kiss the top of Blossom's curly head. He flicked a quick farewell to Hliss, who continued sorting flowers for dye, and crossed the court toward the main castle as the fledgling ran on with the rest of her messages.

He reached the roost, where Mnar was waiting. "We haven't a lot of time," she said. "I've written to Camerend. He says he'll write you when he can—he's in a blizzard at the moment—but right now he wants you to tutor Lineas in the protocols of state runners."

"Lineas?" Quill repeated.

"It will mostly have to be by letter. We're making her a golden notecase now, as you know she's unable to do magic. An initial set of studies that she can take along—"

"Where?"

"To Larkadhe."

"What?" He didn't realize he'd yelled the word until he saw Mnar's mouth tighten. "Why?" he said more quietly.

"Ask the gunvaer," Mnar retorted, and Quill flushed, listening to the rest of her instructions without comment.

He left, wild with the urge to demand answers to questions that he had no right to ask. Sharpest was regret that he had not asked Lineas if she would like to exchange letters while he was gone. Five years of silence, meant to cure him of his infatuation, was proving to be the worst decision he could have made. All it had accomplished was to create a divide in their old easy communication.

Now that he was losing her presence, he would simply have to bridge that distance by letter.

THREE

The entire castle and a good part of the city turned out to watch the two princes depart for the north. Fish relished the attention, the clatter of horse hooves and rattle of weapons as the chosen wing formed up into column, banners snapping in the fresh spring breeze.

The king and queen came down to say goodbye to the young men they would always think of as boys, off to their first command.

As everyone assembled in the great stable court (except the supply carts, which were already on their way out of the city gate), Arrow walked up and stood at Noddy's stirrup.

He smiled from Noddy to Connar. Strictly speaking Noddy, as heir, ought to ride at the front, but Noddy insisted they ride together, just as they'd share command.

"So you're wearing the captain's flash now," Arrow said, pointing to the new silver chevron that Noddy and Connar each wore on their right sleeve, below the flare of the coat shoulder cap.

Both princes suppressed the urge to touch the symbols of real command, though they were highly conscious of them. "That's what the heir traditionally wore when doing his two years at Larkadhe," Arrow said, having thrashed this much out with Danet over an early breakfast. "You also know I didn't do that two years. But I've told you everything my Da told me, when he used to ride there on inspections. Only now you've got your share of tax money up in the north again, which he rarely did, so they shouldn't be griping too much. Ah, people always find something to gripe about," he said, turning his hand flat, and then aware that he'd rambled from his point, he sighed. "Use good sense up there, right?"

"Right," they said, both at the same time. They'd grown up knowing the complexities of Marlovan chain of command: they shared the wing lined up behind them, though Noddy, as heir, had seniority. When they arrived at Larkadhe, they would be able to command the garrison there, but they were under Commander Nermand at Lindeth, and he was under their uncle Jarend at Nevree.

Noddy didn't think about any of it. Connar had been unable to think of much else.

"Then ride out." Arrow stepped away.

those soul-sucking royal city guards, he said, "I know what will please Noddy. And if he's pleased, the king will be."

"What's that?" the jarl asked.

"Lance exhibition, then a competition. With something fun as a prize. He'll win, so we can choose something he'll like. Something that won't cost anything," he added in haste.

His brother, known as Blue, leaned over to smack the back of his head, but Cabbage—experienced as he was—saw his brother's arm cocking back and shifted to evade.

The jarl scowled at Blue. "It's an excellent idea. Costs us nothing and buys us good will."

Cabbage was careful to keep his expression neutral, but inwardly he gloated: not only was his father pleased, and his brother thwarted, but Connar would *loathe* it because he wouldn't win—not against Gannan's heavies.

A little later, Cabbage caught his da when they were alone, for he didn't want Blue beating him for bragging. He said, "One thing for sure. After bunking with Noddy for all those years, I know him. I can find a time to suggest I ride north with them, since I have orders to report to Lindeth. If I tell Noddy I have to get there soon, he won't want to stay camped here long. *And* you won't have to spend anything to send me to Lindeth."

The jarl's frown eased. "You do that, and I'll give you enough to buy the horse you've been pestering me about."

'Pestering' was asking once last year, and once after New Year's, but Cabbage knew better than to respond with anything besides "Thanks, Da."

And so it was.

Noddy was offered the best chamber in the castle, far from the mingy room his parents had stayed in with him as an infant a few months after he was born. He had a delightful time, competing in bruising lance rides with the jarl's two big sons and his heavier Riders. The Gannans kept larger mounts than most, as the family tended to run large, and they had provided kings with heavy cavalry for several generations.

Cabbage also convinced his father that hand to hand and sword practice would be too risky—the last thing they wanted was the king's sons being hurt in their castle—so there was no opportunity for Connar to demonstrate what he was good at; Cabbage knew that Connar had become extremely adept with sword, especially on horseback.

Noddy didn't notice what was missing because he was having so much fun. The second night, he was awarded the prize for the competition, which was a choice between three young women popular with the younger members of the Gannan household. All three, who liked the big, genial prince despite the fact that he was no prize to look at, had not only volunteered with enthusiasm, but even offered to go with him as a group, which caused Noddy to blush crimson.

Before he could go off to a night of fun, Cabbage caught him by the arm and said casually, "I'll have to leave soon. You know I was assigned to Lindeth."

And Noddy, predictably, gazed with widened eyes and said, "Cabbage, why don't you ride with us?"

"But I'm already late for reporting in. It was that black frost."

"We should be going ourselves. Tell you what. I'll give the orders to ride out tomorrow, and you come with us. How's that?"

Everyone was happy with this except for two people. Connar was furious, partly with Noddy but also with himself for not having foreseen that and committed Noddy to a long stay.

The second angry person was Kendred, Cabbage's runner, who had just —after weeks of flirting—found romance. He'd looked forward to a few more days of enjoying the fruits of his labor while the roads dried out, when the order came down: ride out at dawn.

He stomped down to the stable at the single clang of the pre-dawn watch, loaded with gear. His rage was incandescent with ill-use after his flirt, the previous night made aware that he was about to ride off for the rest of the year, cut her losses and went off with someone else.

Kendred flung the gear onto the ground outside the stalls and slammed his way in—almost bumping into a short figure in a coat, saddling a horse directly in front of the stall he had to get to. In the flickering orange torchlight he only saw an anonymous dark coat on what appeared to be a small boy. Then he saw the braids. A girl. That made him madder.

He grabbed one of those frizzy red braids and yanked hard, smiling with grim satisfaction at the girl's yelp of pain. He shifted his grip to fling her out of his way, but a heartbeat later he found himself sitting on the stable floor, his knee on fire with agony.

Lineas stood over him eyes wide with fury.

Before either Kendred or Lineas could speak or move, a voice roared in ill-humor from the stable door, "What's going on here!"

Lineas saw her assailant blanch with terror. Her neck throbbed—she knew the pulled muscles would torment her by noon—she was as angry at herself for being unobservant as she was at her assailant.

But when his anger transformed in a heartbeat to terror, her emotions reeled. She remembered the Jarl of Gannan from Convocation, recognizing the tight mouth and narrowed eyes of an angry nature. Her mind flitted from her assailant's wretched expression to the huge man entering with a threatening tromp, and Auntie Isa's voice whispered in her mind, *Anger is the easiest poison to spread.*

She forced herself to salute the jarl, and to say, "I was clumsy. It's so dark —I ought to have lit another lamp."

The jarl's expression was not made any more pleasant by being side-lit in torchlight, all the harsh grooves of habitual ill-temper carved the more deeply. But the anticipatory relish eased, and his fist unclosed. "Easily done, easily done, royal runner. Kendred! Get on your feet, and give the princes' runner a hand."

Because of course he'd recognized her bright red hair from the previous evening as she served the princes along with the other royal runner. The honor of Gannan House must be preserved—and the princes ushered safely on their way.

Kendred scrambled to his feet, hand to his chest, and put as much weight as he dared on the bad leg.

The jarl whirled about and bawled out the name of one of his own runners as he demanded a progress report on the preparations, leaving Lineas and Kendred staring at each other.

"If I'm not supposed to be here," she said softly, "you might have spoken."

Kendred made a noise in his throat that could have meant anything. He was thoroughly in the wrong, and knew it. He also knew he'd unaccountably been saved from a bloody thrashing by the very same person who had just taken out his knee.

Her gaze fell from his face to the way he stood, and she said, "I did hurt you. I'm sorry . . . Kendred? Let me give you a hand."

Later, crouched on her mat over her journal between two flickering lamps, as rain pattered on her tent roof, Lineas wrote:

He said nothing, so just did it. We were finishing as the rush crowded in, which I'd hoped. After I got his saddle onto Cabbage's mount, he still would not look at me. His ears sticking out at angles were bright red as he said, "If you're going to hold it over me, take yourself off."

I said what would I get from such behavior and he said something under his breath about ratting him out and I said I don't rat people out.

He still wouldn't look at me, and refused to let me help him wrap up his knee, though I could see how swollen it was and felt very bad when I watched him trying to mount. I saw that he didn't want to tell Cabbage Gannan, who I had that scuffle with on my first day. So far I've only seen him. He's almost as large as N but much blonder.

I still don't understand why Kendred attacked me. What I did wrong. Is this another invisible rule that everyone but me knows? I thought I knew them all, but I always think that. Or maybe I did nothing, but was just in his way.

I didn't tell Q in my letter. I don't even see C or N so there is no reason to tell them. It is my own problem to deal with, and so I help Kendred as much as I can, getting two of things early in the morning and leaving one of them outside his tent so he doesn't have to see me, and hasn't the double walk. Each day I see him walking with less of a limp I feel better. I don't know if he notices that my neck is less stiff. Maybe he doesn't care. I'm still annoyed with myself for being unaware, and consider it an excellent reminder, and I do my Fox drills in my tent every night, in the dark. Until now I never really thought about the origins, how you can do an entire drill in one confined place—which was a necessity in the confines of a ship, so very long ago.

As to Q's newest letter, it is about the justice system in Larkadhe, which is actually two justice systems, side by side, with a guild council at the top, parallel to the commander. Which claims authority over what affair is brought before them is complex, and I am surprised he knows all this, as all he told us about his travels there was listening to the windharps.

I wish he had said more about his travels, but there must be a reason he did not. Or it might be that he shares more with other people, and somehow over the five years he was gone I lost his friendship, which I thought always to have, and now I'm merely a peer to be friend-LY to.

That aside, he says it is important that between military and civilian chains of command there be communication, and Q thinks that this is why I was assigned to the princes, to take charge of this communication. So I had better memorize this list of individuals and their positions. . . .

The princes rode through Marlovayir (where they were royally entertained by Knuckles, who was very much like a jovial uncle), then Khanivayir, and by the time they crossed the great Tirbit, the northlands were in spring bloom. On both sides of the road they frequently passed farmers busy planting, and singing as they worked.

These songs, Lineas reflected, were not Marlovan, though some were adapted. They were far older, from before the restless outcasts from the Venn moved in to take this land.

The accent changed as they traveled northward, interesting to her sensitive ear. Meanwhile Kendred recovered apace, doing his work so fast that Lineas withdrew, sensing that her help had ceased to be useful and was deemed intrusive. She saw nothing of him after that, as Cabbage Gannan prudently kept himself and his runner well clear of Connar, except when Noddy oversaw lance practice and asked for him.

And so, at length, the cavalcade spotted the three hills of Nevree.

They camped out on the plains where the Olavayir Riders usually drilled, and the two princes rode in alone to visit their cousin Tanrid.

They were duly presented by the jarlan, their Aunt Tdor Fath, to the senior jarlan, their grandmother Ranor, who was now partially blind; they missed meeting Tanrid's wife only because she was at Lindeth. But Tanrid urged them upstairs to observe his son, a sturdy toddler with his father's short upper lip. He was at that moment concentrating fiercely on smashing small pebbles with his fat, dimpled hand through the tiny hole on top of a noise-box, to watch them clatter on the hidden mechanism that caused tiny paper flags to whirl.

They were then taken to meet their Uncle Jarend—who, they were amazed to see, made Noddy look short and slender. Though Connar knew Da didn't lie, there was always a question in his mind, the result of Hauth's poison. As Jarend made conversation, his voice a low rumble that sounded like a rockfall, Connar looked at his huge hands, thinking that one blow from that fist really could have dropped Mathren Olavayir like a rock.

But it was also clear that Uncle Jarend was aging a lot faster than the king. Jarend asked after Arrow (saying that he received regular runners, but he liked hearing from them, too), chuckling in deep, genial rumble as they spoke. He told them that they should find the north peaceful and easy, "And my son tells me they make excellent barley-wine up there, where the winters are fierce."

They thanked him, and when Aunt Tdor Fath made surreptitious motions toward the door, they said they had to get back to their camp before dark, and bade him farewell.

Tanrid walked them out to the stable. "Thank you for coming," he said. "Da tires fast these days. But he's been looking forward to your arrival ever since we got word you were destined for Larkadhe. What he doesn't know is that there's been trouble up the peninsula at the Nob, and occasionally horse thieves along the hills east, as always—though we're not sure if they're Jendas Yenvir's gang or not."

"Jendas Yenvir," Connar said. "I heard that name last year."

"No surprise." Tanrid made a spitting motion to the side. "He's the boldest of the gangs of horse thieves. Price on his head from four kings, last I heard. Including ours. There's also been trouble up the Andahi Pass, though the Idegans seem to be dealing with it, according to the merchants who come down. The timing of the trouble on our side seems suspicious, as if someone wants to divide us between too many distractions. You only brought a wing?"

"We've got two companies coming," Noddy said.

Tanrid looked relieved. "That's good. Two with what you have at Larkadhe won't strip Lindeth too badly. If you take the east patrol, then that frees Lindeth to deal with the Nob, specifically Ovaka Red-Feather attacking our supply wagons going north. It takes a full company out of rotation for that long journey up and down the peninsula, just to protect treaty-mandated supplies, while their own people attack us from behind masks. And then dare to squall if they don't get their stuff . . . but I'm sure you already know the Nob complaints."

This, both princes assented to.

"Oh. Last thing." Tanrid flashed a grin at Noddy. "Neit asked to be transferred to Larkadhe as one of your long runners while you're there. She knows Lindeth well, and can serve as liaison with Nermand."

Noddy blushed. "Neit," he repeated, grinning shyly. "I haven't seen her for an entire year, I think."

"You seem to have made quite an impression—it was her idea."

Noddy laughed. "Thank you, Cousin."

"What Da said about the barley-wine is true. I'll visit when I can. Save some for me."

He flipped up a hand and retreated toward the castle. The princes turned away, Connar thinking about Jarend's huge fists. Hauth had dropped hints that he believed Mathren had been murdered unawares, as he had always been as alert as he was fit.

Connar didn't give a spit about Mathren, much less Mathren's son Lanrid, Connar's progenitor. But he felt a sharp urge to locate that boy runner who had been witness (no boy; Tarvan had to be in his thirties now) just to satisfy his own mind.

He thought about Tanrid's slow voice, his lazy but watchful gaze. Connar still didn't completely trust this cousin, so he wasn't going to ask about that runner Tarvan. He'd find a way on his own. After all, he had two years.

FOUR

Though the north was that much closer to the warm belt of the world, Larkadhe, lying in the shadow of great mountains during winter, did not feel the effects of spring until the sun had risen high enough on its daily trip from east to west to thaw the sloping lands below.

Then the weather warmed quite rapidly. It was a ripe spring day when they arrived in Larkadhe at last, and Steward Keth Dei (known to everyone simply as Steward) took Lineas and Vanadei through the castle.

Lineas had met him ten years before, when she was brought as a beginning magic student. He looked mostly unchanged, maybe a little whiter at the temples. He was a tall, weedy, pleasant-faced man, descendant of the Dei family of the south, and a connection to the Montredavan-Ans of Darchelde—Quill's family

Being royal runner trained, he spoke to Lineas and Vanadei in Old Sartoran as he whirled them through spaces Lineas recollected in vivid bits, always from the vantage of a very small child. The castle seemed larger than she remembered, but the rooms looked smaller—she remembered them as vast, cold caverns.

Then they entered a tower built of a different stone than the usual honey-brown. This milky white stone felt older, separate somehow from the rest of warren of levels and rooms that comprised the rest of the castle.

They toiled up another spiral of steps worn gently in the middle by uncounted generations of feet, and paused on a landing. On the other side stood a pair of doors carved with flowering trees.

Lineas gasped, and turned to Vanadei, who grinned—he'd visited once before as a teen. "This is it, the famous morvende archive. Or, was."

"Storage," Steward said, palms up. "The morvende moved everything out in my grandda's time, or at least, that was when someone came up here and discovered the doors standing open, and nothing inside. Now we put all the winter gear in there. Lineas, I put you directly above," Steward said as they climbed to the next landing. "It's a pleasant room, you'll find, and it puts you conveniently between the residence down *that* passage—" He pointed off to the left "—where the princes will stay, and Yvana Hall, a collective name for the civilian wing of governance."

"Yah," Vanadei repeated, his bushy brows rising. "You said Yah-vah-nah, not Eee-vana."

"Well, that's how they pronounce it up here," Steward said, winged brows slanting up. "You'll get used to the accent. Like treacle, someone once said. The Hall was named for the hero Hawkeye Yvanavayir by his brothers, each of whom governed here. It was they who knocked out the ancient, moldering walls, which some said never truly dried out after the Great Flood, and rebuilt those rooms to be more comfortable. Though the Idegans among us insist that Marlovan-style can never be called comfortable."

"It's a beautiful room," Lineas said, looking at the round chamber with its slit windows that viewed the mountains above, the valley sloping away below, and in the west, a thin strip of winking light on dull blue—the sea.

Steward chuckled. "We're told that the great Evred-Harvaldar preferred this room so that he'd have access to the archive, before it was closed. The princes will of course have the grand suite."

Lineas gestured acknowledgment, aware of that internal sense of misstep. She had nearly forgotten her disastrous magical studies, which now rushed back with all the old intensity, making the inside of her head feel as if it didn't fit.

Steward started downstairs, saying, "Now, for the civilian side . . ."

He led them back down the spiral, talking rapidly. Lineas had already memorized the lists of guild representatives, runners, and auxiliaries, which steadied her as they passed down a hall with windows cut into a wall.

She glanced out to see Connar and Noddy being led across a court, Connar striding along, princely and handsome. The princes' clothes were made by the same tailor, but Noddy always looked sort of bulky in his coat, whereas Connar's sash at his trim waist contrasted with his straight shoulders, the skirts swinging with every stride of his glossy boots, his blue-black hair swaying down his back.

The sound of his voice rose, warm and golden. She couldn't make out the words as he was walking in the opposite direction, but she could see people turning to watch him.

Despite the decorative words of poets and balladeers, few of us beam like the first sunny day after a long winter, when we are happy. Some turn brick red. Others gasp and stutter. Connar was one of those few who seem to radiate warmth and light, on this, what he considered the happiest day of his life. Command at last, with Ghost Fath and Stick Tyavayir—the best seniors of his year—on the way, under his command. The only thing that could make the day more perfect would have been Stick and Ghost already arrived, their picked men with them.

But he was happy enough to spark all in reach of his voice, kindling a general sense of celebration. The castle servants had already begun putting together the expected banquet when the two-day scouts arrived, but now everyone set to with renewed enthusiasm.

She looked back over her shoulder, surprised to see his surprise. "Yes, all guild people. To oversee anything that has to do with trade up and down the Andahi Pass."

"Do these spies live here in the city?"

"Spies! Well, I suppose they could be considered spies, in that they live here and must report everything they see, but Connar, there hasn't been any trouble with Idego's king since the slaughter in the Pass, before we were born."

He looked into her earnest face. "I know, I know," he said. "I'm not looking for trouble. Go on."

She explained that expert witness was expected to be heard by all before anything was decided, she detailed who had votes, who didn't, under which circumstances . . . and by the end he only heard the sound of her voice, always so pleasant, but his internal dialogue took all his attention: this wasn't command at all. It was more of what the king did, only in one city instead of an entire kingdom, and what sounded like far more fussing with details.

And everything fell into place, a heady sensation. He startled Lineas, interrupting her scrupulous explanation by taking hold of her shoulders and kissing her soundly.

She reddened with pleasure as he exclaimed, "Lineas, you're so good at this. Look, I won't be able to report it to Noddy half as well as you. Do you mind repeating it all for him?"

"I don't mind at all," she said softly. "That's what I'm here for."

"Then wait here. So you won't have to run all over the castle. I know where he is, and I don't think you've been over to garrison-side yet, am I right? Thought so. Wait here for him."

Connar kissed her again, elated with certainty. Damned Hauth! Just because that shit Lanrid got himself killed up Andahi Pass, that was no reason to stick Connar with the tedium of Yvana Hall. As crown prince, Noddy *should* be presiding over there, disentangling squabbles over money exchange, trade, and the value of kind and time. Connar, as second prince and future commander of the army, had a *duty* to hunt down soul-eaters like Yenvir the Skunk!

At the garrison, he spotted Noddy's head above all the others, and men melted to either side. Connar reached Noddy, grinning in surprise when he recognized Ghost Fath's pale hair at Noddy's right. "Finally!"

"Arrived at dawn," Ghost said. "We were way off where we thought we were on our map—camped last night thinking we had another day of travel, woke, looked through the field glass to see that white tower sticking up. So we're here in time for breakfast."

They all laughed, then Noddy said, "I was just about to get us started on double-stick drill. Work up an appetite."

"I can do that," Connar said. "Lineas is waiting up at Yvana Hall to take you through that side of duty."

Noddy blinked, having to mentally disengage from the clear line of today's duty, and substitute another duty, one he was uncertain about. He hated uncertainty. But he knew this was duty, too, and so he took off, leaving Connar to the heady pleasure of commanding what would soon be a full garrison.

After a day of drill and scrapping, he mounted the stairs in that pleasant state of tiredness, thinking that he could divide them into patrols as soon as Stick Tyavayir arrived. One he'd lead himself, once he found out more about the trouble Tanrid had mentioned.

But when he got upstairs, it was to find Noddy with that brow-furrowed expression that meant trouble right before them. "What's wrong?"

"I don't think I can manage Yvana Hall. Alone." Noddy studied Connar with the pleading expression Connar knew well.

"You have Lineas," Connar coaxed. "Surely she'll explain everything. That's why then sent her along, that's her duty."

"I know." Noddy opened his hand. "But she's a runner. Can't, what's the word, preside."

"But you can."

"Not if I don't understand." Noddy's craggy brow furrowed more, and Connar saw the little signs of the immovable rock Noddy could become when he was convinced of something.

So he said, "Tell you what, let's get Lineas in here to explain more. How's that?"

"Yes." The furrowed brow eased. "Good idea."

"I can send Fish—wait. He might not know where they put her. Vana, do you know?"

Vanadei had been quietly setting out the dishes from the supper tray. "I do. Shall I fetch her?"

Connar opened his hand toward the door.

Noddy stayed silent as they began eating supper. Vanadei returned when they were halfway through the meal, Lineas at his heels, both breathing fast as if they'd run all the way.

"What can I do?" Lineas asked, turning her wide-set gaze from one to the other. "Did I not explain well?"

Noddy swung around to face her. "You explained everything. I think I have most of it. I know I can ask when I don't. But there's one thing." He turned his guileless gaze from Lineas to Connar. "I don't, that is, I can't preside, when I don't really understand. What justice *is*."

That's because there is no such thing, Connar thought, but he knew that was the sort of words you couldn't say outright. Like calling poor, silly Bunny stupid or ugly.

"It's difficult to say what it is," Lineas said slowly. "There is a good library downstairs. I've been reading as much as I can, since the gunvaer gave me orders to help you. It's almost easier to say what it *isn't*." She saw from their twin frowns of perplexity that that was no help.

She tried again. "One thing I learned from a scroll Mnar sent me with—I can share it with you, if you like—is that most of the time justice, true justice, in which everyone is satisfied, isn't a single action. It's more likely to be a lot of small actions and decisions."

Noddy's brow cleared. "Oh," he said. "So it's not justice, that is, not always justice, when the king, or a prince, or a jarl, says a thing and one side is happy but the other isn't." He heaved a sigh. "I don't mean where one side did a murder, or suchlike. Even then, sometimes they think they were right, do you see?"

'Justice' is what power says it is. Connar's lip curled, and he looked down at his hands until he knew he had control of his face.

Then Lineas startled him by saying, "I've also read that too often what the powerful regard as justice made at the height of emotion, especially anger, isn't truly just, and can be regretted when the emotional tide recedes."

Connar knew better than to think Da, or even Andaun, had condemned him that terrible day out of anger. It was their rules that seemed mere convenience.

Lineas said, "The scroll asks you to remember situations in your own life when someone decided against you unjustly, and then how right it felt when there was justice. Or how you felt in a situation where judgment wasn't clear, but whoever was in charge chose on the side of mercy or generosity." And when the brothers still looked uncertain, she recollected what Quill had written to her when she had expressed a similar uncertainty, and quoted, "All of these get remembered, but it's the last two that build the trust that brings people to choose to follow the law."

Connar leaned his elbows on his knees. "Whose scroll was this? Because it seems to me that another word for generosity is giving in. Which is seen as weak."

Lineas couldn't mention Quill because of the secret of magic transfer. So she made the mental shift back a step, and said, "The scroll was written by a Sartoran queen, translated by Joret Dei and sent over to Hadand-Deheldegarthe in the last century. I don't think anyone ever thought of either of those women as weak gunvaers."

Noddy and Connar exchanged looks. No. Though most of the history they knew about that time pertained to the Venn War, they'd heard how Hadand-Deheldegarthe, at a younger age than any of them were now, had defended the throne against the Jarl of Yvanavayir, knives against sword. Nobody ever said a word about her being weak.

Lineas went on. "I can share my copy, but what she said was, if you know there is a clear wrong and you give in to please someone, or because you're afraid of what might happen if you pronounce truly, then yes, everyone will see you as weak. On both sides. Even if the favored side is full of praise. If they knew they did wrong, and they are rewarded, they were really bought off. And that isn't justice."

Noddy said slowly, "So what that means is, if you're not sure about one part of a judgment, then only decide on what you're sure of."

Lineas's lips parted. She began to say, "But that's not what it meant." Then she caught a sharp glance from Connar that caused her to freeze.

Noddy's expression eased. "I can do that."

"I knew it," Connar said, clapping his brother on the shoulder, and Lineas figured he'd stopped her because she was only making things more confusing. She reminded herself that she had plenty of time to explain things more clearly.

Over the next few months, as spring ripened into summer, Lineas was so busy helping Noddy that her letters to Quill, already shorter, arrived less frequently.

At his end, Quill dropped everything to answer as swiftly as possible, either from the roost archive, or occasionally he endured the sharp jolt of transfer to Darchelde when the roost did not have what he thought she needed to read. He copied out quantities of information in a tiny, clear hand, to make it easier to her to read by candle light, as her rare responses invariably came very late at night.

He and Vanadei, as offspring of royal runners, had been the only two small children brought in to be raised at the roost. The adults thought it better to give them to each other for company, so they'd shared a room until they turned fifteen. After that, though they had separate rooms, they continued to regard one another as brothers.

When they reached the age of interest, the fact that one was drawn to his own sex and the other to the opposite enabled them (so they decided) to be sympathetic without any of the jealousies they saw in many of their peers as they all navigated the shoals of attraction and sex.

After a week of no letters at all, Quill wrote to Vanadei to ask if Lineas was all right.

Vanadei to Quill:

Of course Lineas is fine, or you would have heard. I know you really want her state of mind, but I can't tell you that with any more success than I could when we were fledglings and she a fuzz. I can tell you that while the gunvaer's reasons for her being attached to the princes seemed mysterious to us at the time, I have to salute her insight, as no one, not even Mnar, seemed to predict how good she's been for the crown prince.

In my five years with him, I've seen how much better he does when someone has the patience to answer all his questions, and listen to him work his way through the answers a piece at a time. I do that for him. You know that. But I've learned in watching Lineas's endless patience, her tentative suggestions that never hurry him, her ability to go over details repeatedly the way he likes, he does better than anybody expected.

He's learning. I'm learning by watching him learn. But you didn't ask about him.

Lineas still works hard, and still has that cat habit of staring at air as if seeing things invisible to the rest of us. And while I'm certain that if I asked her what she was looking at, she would no longer pipe up that she was looking at nothing because normal people see nothing and she is very normal, it seems an insult to ask a peer I work with every day if she is well, as if she were incapable of reporting it if she weren't.

In short, if you want to know what's in her head, you'll have to ask her.

Since Vanadei had never been to Larkadhe previous to this assignment, he didn't perceive how the city's attitude toward their Marlovan governors began to alter from wary distance and scrupulous politeness to cautious optimism. All he noticed was that the civilians, especially Idegans and Iascans, were gradually more forthcoming, but he ascribed that to his getting better at the local accent and idiom.

Both Lineas and Noddy were used to laboring to figure out what everyone else seemed to know. Over meals, when Vanadei was busy with other aspects of Noddy's life, Lineas and Noddy talked out the knottier questions brought before them as Noddy assembled his mental architecture, and Lineas struggled to comprehend what lay behind every conflict, no matter how small.

Noddy always listened, which led them in some surprising directions, more witnesses called, more evidence assembled, even in cases considered by everyone to be minor or even minuscule. But the extra time furnished judgments that evoked the words 'lenient' and 'far-sighted' and finally 'astute,' after a couple of situations in which enterprising souls attempted to practice upon the formidable-looking crown prince looming in his wingback chair with the unblinking stare. Some had labeled him stupid and credulous because of his habit of slow, repetitive speech, but so far, the judgments being passed down were far from either.

What they didn't know was that Lineas had learned as a child to discern ill intent. When she twigged to someone wasting Yvana Hall's time and resources with false testimony, and clarified it to Noddy, the cleaning and laundry crews gained new labor, for restitution was Noddy's favorite sentence. He'd never liked seeing thrashings during their academy days, even the minor ones, and had still to recover from his sick horror at standing there with the entire academy watching Connar being caned bloody. He knew that flogging, the most customary punishment, was even crueler. He flatly refused to hand it out. Instead, the worst offenders found themselves repairing the road to the Pass, in all kinds of weather, including those who would much rather have dealt with the flogging, as it would at least have been faster. But Noddy remained firm: someone's blood all over the ground was no use to anyone, whereas the treacherous road was daily becoming much easier to navigate.

Connar heard about Noddy's successes from runners going back and forth as he did what he loved most, riding in the wind and air at the head of a hard-trained column.

He began his Larkadhe command in better spirits than he'd been in since he was small. Those few times the old nightmares came back he rolled out of his camp bed and rousted everyone to what was known as a night raid drill —and since he fought alongside the others, seemingly tireless even midway through the night, no one voiced any complaint. They admired the prince too much for that, an admiration bolstered by their awareness of themselves as fit, ready for action . . .

And nothing happened.

Connar's primary goal was to lay the horse thief chieftain Jendas Yenvir by the heels. Everybody from Halivayir down to Tyavayir knew the man's general description: tall and well made, long white hair with a dark stripe down the middle, and very pale skin that he kept shrouded, as he was part morvende, the cave dwelling people. Their skin burned in mild spring airs that no one else minded. And so he preferred to attack by night.

Connar and his company rode back and forth along the east, dealing with the occasional small crimes or conflicts, but of Yenvir the Skunk, there was no sign.

It was a beautiful summer, those heavy spring rains having brought all the berries and fruits to ripeness. So far north, near the belt of the world, gave them access to varieties of citrus that were much rarer in the midlands.

As Midsummer Day approached, Connar became steadily more restless. The most they'd accomplished was intervening in a squabble over the ownership of some wandering sheep. Nothing a patrol of scouts couldn't deal with—certainly nothing worth notice by an elite company of King's Army, led by a prince.

The sun, now overhead from rising to setting, brought hot weather, when everything except the bees seemed somnolent. One morning Connar woke sweaty and grimy, sick of tent living, bedrolls, and bathing in streams no longer cool. "We're riding for Larkadhe," he said, to the unspoken relief of many.

Nothing had been said about Midsummer festival so far, and it had been a long time since their last liberty. The only one annoyed at the new orders was Fish. He hated castle life, but no one was asking his opinion.

Late that day they galloped, war banners flapping, into the main courtyard at Larkadhe's castle. Connar leaped off his steaming horse, tossed the reins to eager hands and strode inside.

He looked impatiently around, realizing he'd forgotten where everything was in this stone warren. He remembered the white tower, and ran up the stairs. It was empty.

He ran back down and cut along a hallway, knowing he was lost. He spotted a passing runner. "Where's Nadran-Sierlaef?"

The runner saluted. "Probably in the residence." The young man cast a glance at the sunset azure in the slit window, then added reflectively, "Though he might still be over at Yvana Hall."

Connar followed the runner to the main staircase, and recollected where he was. He dashed to the royal suite and banged through the doors, to discover only Fish, in the midst of dealing with laundry. "Where's everybody?"

"Vanadei's in the kitchen," Fish said. "Sierlaef in Yvana Hall."

Connar banged out again, and had to ask someone which way to Yvana Hall. The hall itself was empty, but he saw light under a doorway on the opposite side of the vast chamber. He crossed the hall and opened the door to an antechamber containing not much more than a low table, two mats, and two walls of some sort of books.

Noddy and Lineas sat across from each other, heads bent inward, almost touching as Lineas used her quill to point out something on one of the many pieces of paper scattered over the table between them. It was a curiously intimate moment.

"There you are," Connar stated, aware that he spoke louder than necessary.

Both heads jerked up, then identical smiles lit their faces, utterly without self-consciousness. Still, Connar was unsettled at that first image, which insisted on lingering.

He walked in, forcing his voice down. Forcing a smile. He knew his reaction was boneheaded—he and Lineas had spoken no exclusivity. "They're keeping your supper warm down in the kitchen. Are there that many criminals lined up?"

Lineas leaped to her feet, face lengthening in dismay. "Oh, I did not know how late it was—I don't mean to make extra work for anyone—" Muttering disjointedly, she dashed out.

Noddy launched into a rambling, detailed report of what he had been doing, so disjointed that even if Connar had been interested, he would have had difficulty following.

As it was, he waited until Noddy paused to rethink a tangled sentence, and said easily, "Sounds as if all's well, then." And lest Noddy decide he wanted a crack at commanding the patrols, he added in haste, "You're doing much better here than I ever could."

"It's because of Lineas," Noddy said. "She translates everything."

"Does she?" Connar was too hungry to ask why Larkadhe's justice system didn't demand everyone speak Marlovan, and swept Noddy off to supper.

Lineas had run to the kitchens to beg them not to disturb themselves over her portion, but she hadn't gotten five words out before Fish showed up, with Vanadei right behind him, wanting their respective princes' supper.

Lineas backed up to let them speak, then looked down in horror at herself in her creased clothes, her inky hands. Surely she smelled as terrible as she looked, and what if . . .

She sped along the back routes to fetch fresh linens and her second robe, and retreated to bathe. While she plunged gratefully into the water, upstairs, Neit arrived straight from the stable, expecting to find Noddy alone.

She stopped short on the threshold when she saw Connar sitting across from Noddy.

Noddy looked up, his sudden smile lighting his face. "You're back from Lindeth," he said, stating the obvious as usual. She thought the habit one of his chief charms.

"Back indeed," she said. "Here's what Nermand sent. Judging by what he told me in handing it off, nothing of moment." She tossed a sealed letter onto Noddy's end of the table. Ordinarily she would have dropped down beside him unasked, but because Connar was there, she waited.

"Come, sit," Noddy said. "Vana?"

"I'll bring another plate," Vanadei said.

"Bide, Vana," Neit responded with a wave of her hand. "Ate on the road. Too hot for more." She saluted Connar, saying, "What brings you back?"

"Boredom," Connar said, interest mildly flaring at the cool look she gave him.

But she looked away again immediately, addressing herself to Noddy. "Entire rope walk in Lindeth is being decorated. You really ought to see the lantern sail once, if you can."

Neit had favorites in nearly every northern city, and liked men, large or small, quiet or noisy, but the one characteristic she found unattractive was anger. Maybe because she'd grown up avoiding the tempers, and on the practice field a brutality scarcely this side of actual war, practiced by many of what her da had warned her was part of the disbanded Nighthawk Company. The worst of those was Halrid Jethren, but as he was the best of all the lancers, Jarend, the kindly jarl, had always said, "Give them time." As soon as Neit saw in mouths, eyes, shoulders, hands the signs of hidden anger, any attraction doused instantly. Even in boys as pretty as Keth Jethren, Halrid Jethren's son, or the ice-eyed, silent boy everyone called Moonbeam, Keth's shadow.

Connar was angry. She sensed it, and found it all the more unsettling because she didn't *see* it.

Noddy set his cup down. "Vana told me, no one works on Midsummer Day as well as the Restday before it."

"True enough," Neit said. "So ride down to Lindeth! There's music, and dancing, and games, and the eats are prepared weeks in advance, excellent brews of all kinds. You'll love it. I promise."

Though none of that sounded particularly inviting to Connar, he was restless enough to give in to impulse. "Why don't we both go?"

Noddy beamed. "Yes." Then his brow puckered. "How many do we take?"

Connar shrugged. "A wing, for the two of us? Same as we came?"

Noddy thumbed his bottom lip. "Are we riding back at night, then?"

"No! Why would we?"

Noddy had learned a great deal during these weeks that he had not given a thought to before. "I think landing nearly a hundred extra on the garrison during this festival, with no warning, is going to be rough on Nermand. Might even take insult, I don't know. I haven't met him direct."

Connar was used to camping in the field, and had never had any interest in logistics. That was Fish's business. "So we quarter 'em on the town!"

"During a festival? When everyone within a week's ride is crowded there?" Noddy turned his hand down flat. "They'd gouge us a year's pay for the entire garrison."

Connar stared, reflecting that Noddy would never have fussed about such things before. "So?" And at Noddy's grim look, he remembered that someone would be reporting to the royal city. Suddenly they were boys again—with someone over them, watching in judgment.

Then Neit said, "Why don't I ride for Lindeth and ask? I can get there and back by morning."

Noddy said, "You've already ridden it once today."

Neit snorted. "Lindeth? Eh. I go twice that far on a long ride. I've got most of a moon tonight. You could read by it."

Noddy fell into a brown study, and Connar glanced at Fish. "Where's Lineas?"

And laughed inwardly at the tightening in Fish's face as he said, "I'll find her."

Down in the baths, while her hair dried in the warm wind ruffling down one of the tunnels, Lineas washed out her other outfit and carefully laid it over a spoke on one of the clothes trees to dry.

Fingering her hair into braids, she walked slowly upstairs, aware of her growling stomach. But when she reached the landing outside her room, there was Fish, leaning against the wall, arms crossed.

As she topped the last step, he glowered her way. "He wants you." And ran downstairs.

She paused long enough to finger the last of her frizz into its braid, then slipped down in Fish's wake.

She found the princes together in the reception room of their suite, the remains of their supper being carried out by Vanadei. Neit sat with Noddy, sparking a smile of welcome from Lineas, which caused a grin and a flip of fingers in salute from Neit. Noddy's slow voice rumbled in various contingency plans, if Nermand could not accommodate a wing.

Connar was still in his dusty riding clothes. When he saw her, he got to his feet, unaware of interrupting Noddy. "I'm tired—been up since long before dawn."

He held out his hand to Lineas, who laid her palm in his, smiling happily as she followed him into his room.

Neit watched them go, waited, and when Noddy (used to being interrupted) didn't pick up the thread of his discourse, asked, "Did she get any supper?"

Noddy glanced her way, and she sensed that he'd noticed, too, but all he said was, "She might have eaten in the baths."

Neit bent down to kiss Noddy. "I'll ride out now, and see you in the morning."

FIVE

Neit was back before they woke. "The Commander said to thank you for sending me ahead, and he can take in a wing, but it'll be hot cots."

Connar grimaced. Then reflected that as commanders of Larkadhe, he and Noddy wouldn't be expected to sleep in beds night-duty men had just gotten out of.

Neit went on, "He said that the night duty men will do half-watches through the night at the sentry stations along the boardwalk, as most trouble is from sailors on liberty. Your wing will have until dawn."

"Then it's settled," Noddy said.

Connar agreed to sit with Noddy in the hereto empty wingback chair in order to help dispatch as much business as they could before the festival day. Connar found the elaborate ritual confusing, the stilted language tedious. He could see that it all worked—no arguments burst forth—but by midday, he would have welcomed a duel breaking out in preference to the mind-numbing succession of chalked-up slates and papers and beads of the stringers, whose exact accounts of moneys in several values everyone but him seemed vitally interested in.

Connar was ready to set fire to the entire room by the end of the long day, and stared in disbelief as Noddy and Lineas (who was so quiet Connar scarcely noticed her over in her corner, scribbling away) packed up papers and withdrew into that inner chamber, ready to spend yet more hours in going over, again, minutiae of testimony and long lists of numbers.

Hauth wanted Connar to murder Noddy, Da, and who knew how many others in order to call himself king and deal with this kind of shit! As Connar downed a few swallows of cellar-cold, dark brown ale, he reflected that if Hauth walked in right then, he'd smash the ale tankard over his head and use a shard to cut his throat.

The only improvement was that Connar had slept better in those few days. Lineas's presence somehow returned him to that calm forest pool. He slept, he woke refreshed.

So, that last night, when the two princes met for dinner, Connar told Noddy that Lineas should accompany them to Lindeth, an unexpected declaration that thrummed through her, igniting the white fire of joy all through those next few days.

That dimmed somewhat the next morning, when she found Neit next to her, looking unwontedly sober as they saddled their horses in the light of lanterns, the sky bluing in the east.

They hefted saddles, Lineas's loose sleeves falling back, exposing her wrist knives.

"You go armed, I see," Neit said with approval. "Better to have than want to have." She patted the sword in her saddle sheath.

Linet blushed. "I promised Quill I'd always wear them if I rode away from Larkadhe."

"Good man, Quill. Maybe a little too much of that Old Sartoran foolery, but everyone has at least one bad habit." Neit added in an undervoice, "I know it's none of my affair, but it might be good for Connar to snap his fingers once, just to find you busy with another lover."

Lineas dropped her hands from the saddle girth and stared, her wideset eyes round. "I don't understand."

Neit glanced to either side, and finding no hovering ears, said, "I guess we're all different, but I wouldn't put up with any man, even an emperor, expecting me to be at his beck and call without ever asking."

Lineas flushed bright red. "I love Connar," she whispered. "Always have, ever since I was small. And I don't want to . . . I can't be with someone I don't love."

Neit whistled softly. "Oh. You're one of *those*." Her face was mostly in shadow, but Lineas made out the lineaments of pity before they separated to finish their work, leaving Lineas wondering if once more, she'd stumbled into Not Normal.

Except, what was the problem? Connar had thought of her, wanting her to enjoy the festival, which was so much better than this other idea Neit seemed to be suggesting, that she ought to get lovers just because *he* had them. Her skin crawled at the thought of being intimate with somebody she didn't love.

She had told herself repeatedly over the past five years that she would accept it if Connar found someone else to love, for there should always be more love in the world. But she knew it would hurt terribly if he shut her out. As he must if he made a ring vow . . .

Noddy gave the signal and the trumpets blared, jolting her to the present. Foolish, to let such thoughts start to ruin a festival day! Her favorite festival in a new place, with new people and maybe new customs.

They rode out, leaving Ghost Fath and his company in command of Larkadhe.

Lineas's joy was back, mixed with anticipation—and the sight of Lindeth, decorated with garlands everywhere, proved to be everything she'd hoped for.

They rode to the garrison first, where the animals were stabled, and the men dismissed for a day's liberty, with orders to be ready to ride in the morning. Then the princes and their runners set out on foot for the boardwalk, as the streets were thronged with people.

She'd seen the sea once before, the spring she accompanied the gunvaer to Algaravayir. She and her twin cousins, Noren and Hadand, had accompanied the gunvaer and the Iofre to the harbor, but it had been windy and cold, with rain coming. She remembered the ocean as gray. So she was unprepared for the vastness of sparkling blue reaching all the way to the horizon, the tang of salt on the fresh breeze, the cry of shore birds overhead as below, people gathered in knots of hilarity and anticipation to watch the games, or dance, sing, eat, flirt, and chatter.

Central along the boardwalk, giving the best view of the ships floating in the harbor, was a structure with a sunshade, to which they were directed. Here, they were met by Tanrid Olavayir's wife Fala, daughter of Commander Nermand and his Iascan wife. Fala, a comely young woman early in her second pregnancy, and equally comfortable among Iascans and Marlovans, welcomed them with the easy friendliness that made her so popular.

"Come, sit and have something to drink! You must have had a hot ride," she fluted in a high voice. "Tanrid is off judging one of the games. I'd introduce you to my little boy, but he hates any change in his day as much as his da and grandda, so I'm here quite alone, and would love the company."

Connar and Noddy returned a polite answer, Connar refraining from pointing out that they'd already met Fala's and Tanrid's son, who was not nearly as fascinating to anyone else as he obviously was to his besotted parents.

"Go ahead," Connar said to Noddy, whose hand was unconsciously tapping his thigh as he watched a group of drummers finding their rhythm for a group ready to sing ballads. "I'd as soon stretch my legs." And as Fish made a motion to follow, he waved him off, saying in an undervoice. "Do what you want. If I can't defend myself from a bunch of drunks, I deserve to be gutted."

Fish, expertly assessing his mood, saluted and backed away, gazing out to sea as he counted under his breath. When he reached ten, he set out, and soon spotted Connar's glossy blue-black horsetail as the prince made his way southward down Lindeth's main street, parallel to the boardwalk.

Connar and Noddy had chosen to wear their riding coats rather than their distinctive blue and gold House tunics, but even so, Connar was never going to be anonymous. Fish knew what his slow and painful fate would be if anything happened to the second prince and he was not there.

Fala gave a mental shrug and, including Vana and Lineas in her friendly gaze, said to Noddy, "We have an extra drum if you'd like to join the singers over there." And to everyone, "Who wants something to drink?"

Out of sight, out of mind.

Connar forgot them all as he strode along, his impatient gaze skimming the crowds, the brightly decorated booths before many of the shops, and the strolling hawkers and performers. He was in the mood for a scrap or a screw, either would do—both would be better.

His eye caught on a curvaceous young woman perched in a low window. She strummed some kind of stringed instrument as she sang a ballad. Connar paused, his gaze roaming appreciatively over her ribbon-tied curls and down her voluptuous form, which was enhanced by pink and azure filmy stuff tied with a lot of silver ribbons. He slowed, taking in the half-circle of husky sailors vying to catch her eye; when she finished the song, she glanced down at a cap set at her feet.

Promptly the would-be swains jostled one another in their haste to cast coins into it. The bright glint of gold shone against silver. The woman's lazy eyes took in the pile, her generous lips curved, dimples deepening at either side, and she started another ballad, as Connar imagined untying those ribbons one by one.

When she finished the second song, again the audience scrambled to please her. Connar stood alone, arms crossed, daring her to look at him.

She did.

After the third song, and he hadn't moved, she said in a sultry voice, "Don't like my singing?"

"Would I be here if I didn't?" he retorted, being expert by now in avoiding all questions about music.

"But . . ." she prompted, glancing at the coin-filled cap.

"I had another reward in mind," he said.

"Which would be?"

"A kiss."

Scoffing comments rose around, but not too heated when the other men took in Connar's stance, and the muscle evident in those crossed arms.

"Oh?" she asked. "Would that be worth more than a tinklet?"

The avid watchers laughed as she named the lowest piece of coinage common along the coast.

"You'd have to decide that," he said.

She strummed idly, watching beneath her eyelids. She had an idea who he might be, and wondered if a prince's wandering interest could be parlayed into better earnings than usual. Setting aside her instrument, she crooked a finger. "Let us assay," she said.

Two of her most persistent would-be swains cursed, and she suppressed a smile as Connar advanced. He closed, they kissed.

He knew what he was doing.

He let her go, and whispered into her lips, "Well?"

She was ready for a break anyway. Wondering how deep his pockets were, she inclined her head toward the inn across the street. "Let us discuss it over a meal. You pay," she added. And to the others, "I'll be back."

"In two turns of the little glass," one fellow cracked as she took Connar's arm and towed him across the street.

The woman drawled over her shoulder, "Do you think I'd let that happen?" Her laughter floated behind.

A very agreeable interval later they lay side by side in a room miraculously cleared after Connar offered a handful of gold to the proprietor. She considered how she could benefit further, then said idly as she twirled a lock of his hair around her finger, "I almost hate to say it—professional pride—but your voice is easily as good as mine. Shall we essay a duet or two?"

He had been considering whether he was ready for another round. "I don't sing," he said.

"You don't? Or you can't? I don't believe the latter. You have a singer's voice." He still hadn't told her who he was. She was ready for this to go either way.

"Can't. Don't. What does it matter? The truth is, music to me is just noise. To both of us, actually—my brother and me." (Which he believed was true, without considering that Noddy had followed him in this as in many things; left to himself, Noddy enjoyed a rousing ballad, though not with any passion.)

She couldn't prevent a little gasp. "Really?"

Connar sighed. "It's not like we're missing it. I hate that reaction—either pity, or a look as if I've broken some kind of rule."

She rose on an elbow, and dropped the languishing manner. "You really can't hear music as . . . *music?*"

He shrugged, already losing the mood. Time to move on. "A rhythm, yes. I love the drums. But the rest, it's always been noise. I thought that was the same for all. Put up with it the way you put up with traditions, because that's what we do." He got up to splash himself clean in the lukewarm basin of fresh water he'd asked for when the proprietor cleared the room.

She saw that she wasn't going to keep him, and shrugged off her plans. "I think I'd almost rather give up a leg than give up music," she said as she rose and shook out her tumbled under-gown.

"That's because you're a musician." Connar kissed her again, quick and valedictory. "Thank you."

"Mmmm, I thank you in my turn," she responded. "A poignant interval, from which I believe I feel a ballad forming. I'm not quite certain if it ought to be a lament."

"And that," he said, shoving his feet into his boots, "is as good a signal as any to be on my way."

He shut the door on her laughter, and left her to sort her ribbons. As he ran downstairs, he was aware that the good mood she'd given him had soured. He made an effort to shake it off. It wasn't as if the general prejudice in favor of music was any surprise, especially from a musician. He'd walked into that ambush on his own by admitting to it instead of keeping his mouth shut.

He got outside, to discover the hubbub increasing to the pitch of drink-loosened hilarity. The shadows had melded, and in the western sky the magentas and oranges were fast fading as stars emerged overhead, snuffed again by the stronger light of lanterns being lit up and down the street.

He glanced down narrow alleys toward the harbor, unaware of Fish, straightening up from his distant vantage and falling in at a circumspect distance. Out in the harbor, ships rocked, their geometries lit by clusters of colored lanterns.

Connar had seen ships lit by lanterns in the harbor at Parayid. Once was enough. He moved farther down the street, into an area with bigger and more elaborate houses, many with husky guards guarding the tables out front, with apprentices in their festival best handing out samples, or selling small items. From open windows above, voices drifted down, laughing, singing.

Fish, having stood on the street the entire time Connar was with the singer, frowned back at the crowded street. This was the worst sort of terrain with only one person on guard: shadowy except for the rings of golden light, broken here and there by colors from dyed lanterns. Thick crowds moving in and out of the shadows. Was he being followed, or was that just his imagination? It might even be one of Stick Tyavayir's scouts, thinking the same thing Fish had. If only he could see better!

He brushed his fingers reassuringly over the knife at his belt, remembered the ones in his boots, then stopped short; Connar had halted in the middle of an intersection, heedless of arm-linked, tipsy dancers staggering in one direction, and in another some apprentice-aged girls stalking snickering boys, while all around people strolled, talked, laughed, and commented over the wares, the stars overhead, the lanterns hanging from ship-spars out at sea.

Connar, an island in an ocean of movement, stood very still, staring up at a painted sign:

Lindeth-Hije Shipping

SIX

Hije. Where had Connar heard that before? Then he remembered. Hije was the founder's name of the company his birth mother had come from.

He glared at the arched, golden windows of the store. He had ended up a prince, amid people who loved him. He loved them back. And he wouldn't want to become a shopkeeper, or shipkeeper, or whatever "shipping" meant.

And yet right here, in this building, lived the people who had thrown him away.

He walked through the open door, his lambent gaze lancing straight to a fellow leaning on a display table, but when the fellow looked up, the awkward knot in his throat bobbing and his mouth open, Connar recognized this was a gangling snot of no more than sixteen.

Behind the counter stood a girl about the same age, dressed like Connar's musician in filmy layers of green with yellow ribbons tying the sleeves and bunched all down the front.

The only other people in the shop were a pair of old women, ogling some long, curved porcelain vases that had to have come from overseas.

The pair of teens stared at Connar.

"May I help you?" the girl asked. "Are you lost?"

Connar uttered a sharp laugh. Lost. Good one. "Who runs this place? I want to talk to him."

"Her," the teen corrected politely. "I'll fetch my mother." She shot a glance at the boy, who lifted his hands and walked out, casting a quick, uneasy glance back at Connar.

The girl whisked herself behind a hanging curtain woven in patterns of orange blossoms and pale blue birds, then came out again, followed by a dark-haired, dark-eyed woman who stumbled to a stop when she saw Connar.

He stared back. The woman, whose hair was shot with white, had his winged brows, which rose nearly to her hairline.

"Well," she said, and swallowed audibly. "Please. Come back to the private room. Sese, bring some wine punch and shipcakes." *Seh-seh,* she'd said, an Iascan name.

"I don't want any," Connar said curtly.

"Well, I do," the woman retorted frankly. "The wine, anyway."

There was no heat in her voice, only a slight tremor.

Connar's mood shifted from anger to wariness as he followed the woman down a short hall with crates stacked on either side, to a small room fitted out with tapestries of a kind he had never seen before—no battles or heroes, but patterns of stylized shapes that drew the eye.

He wrenched his gaze away, as she sank down on the other side of an exquisite bluewood table carved along the edges with intertwined laurel leaves. She gestured toward the guest mat on the other side as she said, "You have to be Fini's son."

He stood before her, arms crossed, ignoring the implied question. "And you are?"

"Hije sa Vaka. Fini's sister. We shared a mother." *Hee-jeh.* More Iascan.

"Not a father?" Connar asked.

"No." She shook her head, a gesture that looked odd to Connar, until he realized she wasn't shaking something loose, but emphasizing the negation. "Fini's father was a ship captain. Some said privateer, some said pirate. He trades in luxuries. Mother met him in Brenn, where she lives, running our fleet there."

Connar brought his gaze back. "Where is he now?"

"I guess at sea. We haven't seen him for twenty years." She lifted a hand that trembled a little; she made a fist and dropped it. "Your blue eyes come from him."

Sese came in then with fine porcelain in what looked to Connar like tiny, narrow-mouthed cups. He was used to the wide, shallow wine cups that Marlovans used, that required two hands. Harder to cut throats when both hands are busy, Da had said to Connar and Noddy once, laughing.

The girl set down the tray, and Hije began to pour out wine into two cups. As she lifted one to her lips, Connar said, "So you know who I am."

The cup lowered. "The moment you walked through the door," Hije said. "Though your bones are different. They must belong to the father I never met. Your coloring is my sister's."

"Tell me about her." Connar began to prowl the perimeter of the room as he took in the objects. A feast for the eyes, every one.

Hije said. "Very well. But you have to realize first that I hated Fini. Really hated her, though we are related by blood. So regard what I say in the light of that. She was older than I by two years. Grandmother spoiled her rotten when she was small. So did Mother, on her rare visits from Brenn. Until she was about fourteen, Fini's father used to sail in every year or two, bring her fabulous gifts—that golden cup up there, with the swans etched on the side is one of them—and tell her she was born to be a princess. She was careless about lessons, but she certainly stuck to *that*."

Hije drank some wine, then lowered the cup. "Remember I warned you about my dislike. Do you want me to go on?"

"Go on."

"Fini knew how to coo and simper—but as soon as Mother or Grandmother were out of sight, she'd pinch and slap me into doing all her work as well as my own. Enough?"

"Is there more?" Connar asked.

"She was smart. Sang like a bird, and played the tiranthe. But as soon as she got old enough to catch the eyes of the boys, she threw those aside and went after them. She liked making them fight over her. After she caused trouble up at the Marlovan garrison, Grandmother sent her to Nevree. She was supposed to be learning the business. But she wanted to marry someone with a title, as high a one as she could find." Hije's voice husked, and she drank off her wine. "Fini wanted someone to make her a princess."

Connar turned around, and in a sudden movement dropped down onto the guest mat. Hije hid a sigh of relief. She still felt that back-of-the-neck grip of threat, but there was a matter of family justice here. He had a right to ask, and she owed him the answers.

She forced herself to meet that unwavering blue gaze. "I was a year younger than Sese out there when you were born, right after your father was killed, and everyone expected there to be war as a result. Either from the Idegans coming down here to destroy us after burning Larkadhe, everyone said, or from the Marlovans. We were all scared. Some ships refused to land, and prices . . ."

She saw the tightening of impatience in his expressive brow and waved a hand. "Well. Anyway. I was running both shops, young as I was, Lindeth and Nevree, which is where all our Marlovan trade is handled—I had to ride twice a week, because Fini refused to help me. Then she had you. Grandmother was very old, and knew her time was coming. Sending you to the Marlovan capital was one of the last things she did."

Hije paused, and wiped a strand of hair off her damp forehead. "There was no way I could raise a child, much less a boy. All our boys go to sea, and we hadn't anyone to take you in to train up. But there were all those mighty Olavayirs at Nevree. Grandmother thought, surely there'd be a place for you, but *they* said there was political trouble, and there was no marriage. Before he was killed, the father was supposed to marry someone else, and they also said the old jarl had just died, and the family grieved. Grandmother knew the truth, that they all hated Fini, and so she sent you to them at the capital."

Connar said, "You didn't tell me why she abandoned me."

Hije looked away. "It was shameful. It still is, really. She had you, threw a tantrum that you weren't a girl, which meant she couldn't secure the heirship away from me. She gave you a king's name, said you deserved a king for a father, but any time you cried, she left you to me and my cousin, who was thirteen at the time. One day she put you in a basket in the front room right out there, told the new apprentice that she was going to find a better nanny goat for milk, took the best gems, and never came back. We don't know if she's a princess somewhere—in which case she would probably invent the sort of family a princess would have—or if she's dead."

Hije took another sip of wine, then said in a cautious voice, "Were they good to you, the Olavayirs?"

"Very," Connar said dryly, but he decided against pointing out that she could have asked any time in the past twenty-four years. Though Hauth had had nothing but disparaging words to say about this half of his birth family, Connar found this Hije far less objectionable than Hauth. Maybe she'd been afraid. She and her daughter were certainly very Iascan, right to the accent.

He swung to his feet. "If she ever turns up again, and asks for me . . . no, on second thought, let her show up." His teeth showed, and his pupils, large and black, reflected the lights in a cold glitter. "Thanks," he said, and walked out.

Hije let out a deep breath, as Sese tiptoed in, her eyes round. "Was that really him, Prince Connar?"

"Oh, yes," Hije said.

She sipped again, deciding what to say. Though he was gone, the simmering atmosphere lingered—very like Fi's tempers, but deeper, far more dangerous. She wasn't certain if that sense was fancy, knowing that he'd become a prince, and so he could make worlds of trouble for them with a wave of his hand, or because he looked so martial in that tight coat with the knife in his sash. She decided safest was as little said as possible. "He wanted to know about our family, which is his right. I told him, and he left. All very polite."

Sese went out again, a little disappointed that there hadn't been more drama, but thrilled that she'd met a prince. At least that much she could tell everyone on the street.

Connar headed back, followed by Fish, who was now certain that someone was shadowing them. It could be Stick Tyavayir's men, for the same reason Fish was there. If it wasn't, the streets were reassuringly full of roaming armed guards from the garrison. He wasn't afraid of attack, precisely, but it was unsettling to sense someone pacing him, remaining skillfully out of sight in the way that Fish had learned as a boy. It was the way they didn't want to come forward, if for nothing else, to trade watching so he could risk getting something to eat and drink. He was desperately thirsty.

At least Connar didn't stop moving until he reached the pavilion again.

Noddy beamed. "You're back! Come. There's plenty to eat here."

"Looks good," Connar said, hauling himself easily over the rail and dropping onto the bench beside Noddy.

Fish caught up, heart hammering. He had to report. Maybe doing it in public would deflect some of Connar's mood.

"You were followed," he said to Connar.

Connar's head jerked up. "By?"

"I didn't spot them. It was dark by the time I—"

"So you're saying you followed me after I told you not to?"

Fish was about to point out that he'd not received orders, only a general suggestion of liberty, but he knew how that would be taken.

Then Neit, leaning on the rail, snorted. "Of course he did. He'd be first against the wall if anything happened to you, because that's general runner orders."

"That's right," Vanadei spoke up unexpectedly. He almost never talked in front of Connar, unless asked a direct question. "If Fish hadn't done his job, I would have had to go."

"Did you see who it was?" Connar asked, his tone a jot less hostile.

"No."

Fala, daughter of the garrison commander, had grown up around military thinking. "It might even have been on Da's orders. Same reason."

Noddy opened his hand. "I've counted at least two patrols in sight all afternoon."

Fish relaxed incrementally as Connar stared out at the harbor, at which time Lineas started blithering on about how beautiful the lanterns on the ships were, bright as stars reflecting in the water, yadoo laloo, and did he chance to see them?

Fish didn't like royal runners on principle, but lifted his hand in thanks when Vanadei offered a cup of cold ale, and a bowl of rice balls and cheese crisped in cabbage leaves. As Fish wolfed these down, he wondered how Lineas could be so blind as not to notice Connar wasn't listening to a word she said.

He was wrong.

She kept talking, filling the silence, as Connar ate a few rice balls and drank some spiced wine. There were times, especially in their early days together, when he was still healing, when she had been able to talk him into a calmer mood. She could see in his tight profile that something had disturbed him, but as she went on about how beautiful the parade of ships around the harbor had been, with all the lights up the masts and in the yards and rigging, she heard his breathing slow. If it was only her tone, or the sound of her voice that soothed him, that was all right.

The last Midsummer game commenced with a blaring of trumpets and a shout from the crowd along the boardwalk below their stand. Out on the water, rowboats raced out to a line of ships in competition to be first to raise a banner to the highest mast. As Connar raised his head to watch the end of the race, Lineas brought her sentence to a natural close.

The boats arrived, people scrambled aboard, and a banner, too dark to see, jerked up to the top of an elegant schooner. Shrieks of triumph carried across the water like gull cries, to be taken up by the spectators.

And the festival was over—all except for the private fun.

Along the boardwalk the crowd stirred, breaking up into clumps and wandering off.

Noddy stretched, saying, "It's late, and we have to be out of the garrison before the last night patrol gets in." With a hopeful expression, "While you were exploring, Cabbage Gannan came by at the end of his duty patrol. He said they've been tied to the city for weeks, preparing for today. He gets a day free tomorrow, so early, before the heat, he's taking his riding and anyone who wants to come from West Company out to the North Bend to run lance drills. We can come watch, he said. Or even run with them, if we like. It's only garrison first-years, nothing official. Since we don't have a long ride back to Larkadhe, I thought we could do that."

Connar muttered, "You can if you want. I've been doing nothing but drill for the past couple months, and I don't need to ride out of my way just to watch Gannan prancing around sniffing your tail."

Noddy's voice dropped a note or two in disappointment. "I don't like to split our escort."

They walked in silence.

It seemed to take much longer to get back, partly because the darkness, the long day, the warm sun, and the spiced wine left them all tired. But at last they spotted the torchlit towers, and soon were inside.

The princes and their first runners were conducted up to the commander's offices, where it was clear they were to share a room. Connar was annoyed, but he knew it couldn't be helped. He could see the castle was crowded.

Neit, who had gone off on her own at the end, reappeared and beckoned to Lineas. "You can bunk with us runners," she said, an invitation Lineas welcomed with relief.

It seemed no sooner had she laid her head on a flat pillow than Neit was shaking her awake. "Come on, we don't want Prince Crabby to have to wait."

"Crabby?" Lineas whispered, aware of her dry throat. She'd obviously been snoring. Well, so had everyone else; she'd fallen asleep to the sound.

"Did I say Crabby? I meant Connar," Neit said, laughing as she fingered her sun-bleached hair into fast braids. And then, "Don't fret, Lineas, I poke fun at everybody. Especially when I've had half a watch of sleep."

Lineas smiled back. "Do we have time for a bath?"

"Nope. But we'll all soon be stinking of horse. The ensorcelled bucket is over there. You can plunge your head into the water, which will make your face and mouth feel clean, at least."

Lineas did. The magic purification spell fizzed briefly over her face, mouth, tongue, and teeth, a pleasant, refreshing sense, and as she walked back, her head and yesterday's braids dripping. she wondered if Quill's hand had been the one to renew the spell on the bucket. She yanked on her boots, strapped on her knives, and Neit led the way out.

They had their horses saddled by the time the last of their escort crowded into the stable, most looking frowzy and crapulous, others moving with the curious, careful rigidity of apocalyptic hangovers.

As the column started out of the stable yard, Lineas turned her mount toward the back, but Neit leaned out and caught hold of her reins. "Oh, no, you don't. You ride up front with me. I'm not going to be the only reasonable one amidst four pricks after a short night, too much drink, and no sex."

Lineas blushed, not certain whether to laugh or apologize, but she perforce followed Neit up the column, smiling in thanks as the banner bearers prudently dropped back to make space for them.

Trumpets blared, causing at least half the escort to wince. In silence they rode through the gates and turned northward toward the hazy mountains, the pewter-colored ocean at their left.

After a time Vanadei silently produced a bag of leftovers from the night before, and broke out of line to offer food to Noddy, then Connar. In silence the princes each took something. Vanadei dropped back to share out the rest among the four runners, the escort having their own provisions furnished by the garrison.

Cold and soggy as the cabbage roll was, Lineas began to feel a bit more awake after eating half.

The food seemed to have a general good effect. Before long, Noddy said to Connar, "If you're truly tired of riding the field, I'll trade with you. I don't mind."

Connar sighed. "I'm not at all tired of it. Never mind what I said, Noddy. We're not yet into Lightning Season, and you know how hard heat is on you. Let's stay as we are."

"I forgot about Lightning Season. Do they have it this far north? Ah, matters not. I'm content keeping on as we have." A pause, then, "Have you reconsidered heading for the river? It might be cooler."

Connar bit down on the flare of annoyance; he knew what would happen if Noddy saw Gannan prancing about with lances. "According to the map, this is the straightest line back to Larkadhe, and it will take us within reach of the cliffs where Great-Da Olavayir turned the tide of the battle with the Venn."

Neit opened her mouth to interject a comment, but Noddy, unaware, exclaimed, "I'd like to see that! Let's go that way."

Neit sat back, unwilling to contradict Noddy before the entire escort.

Vanadei and Lineas noticed her frown. They knew she was the most traveled in this area, and as the sun slowly rose, they began to perceive why. Though a bird might be able to fly straight to Larkadhe, humans and horses had a succession of rocky ridges and forested cliffs to negotiate, the beginnings of the great mountains still shadowy in the thick haze.

Connar's head throbbed as he scowled straight ahead, willing them to cover the distance faster, as huge chalk cliffs appeared behind the rocky hills.

Noddy gazed northward, wondering if this was the very road their ancestor had ridden during the Venn war, and which of those ridges was the one they descended to wipe out the west end of the Venn invasion.

Lineas stared at the slowly roiling mist above the ridge, wondering if the silvery shades flickering in and out were ghosts, or some other . . . thing? Being? Living or dead, or did those two distinctions not matter to magical races?

Neit stirred uneasily, watching the horses' ears, which twitched westward frequently enough to disturb her. The horses were a long way from panicking—everyone would notice that—but they smelled, or heard, something out there.

Twitch. It was like a signal, too swift for clumsy humans; these boys were excellent riders, but their horses were mere mounts, not partners in the way you were when you rode alone, watching everything.

Time to speak. Better to get yapped at than stay silent and walk into some kind of trouble. She fell out of line and rode up on Noddy's other side as she said, "We're too far north. Need to cut east as soon as we can. This is a bad area."

"Bad?" Noddy squinted up at the ranks of mountains thrusting up northward; the rising sun had begun burning off the mist, throwing back a murderous glare. "Road, or riders? Should we send the scouts ahead, with whirtlers?" He whistled briefly, the sound of the signal arrows.

"Better a company," she stated. "The distance looks short on the map, but it's rough terrain to ride. This road here, it's going to bend west by midday, taking you straight up the coast to the Nob. Nobody rides it with fewer than a full company. Those mountains that way are full of Bar Regren as well as all kinds of rough riders."

"Bar Regren?" Noddy said.

"What the folk of the Nob peninsula call themselves. Don't like Marlovans. Don't like Idegans. Don't like anyone but themselves—"

This time they all saw their horses' ears twitch westward, and felt the subtle shift in the animals' muscles that signified awareness.

"There's no east road," Connar said.

"There's a trail on that ridge. See? Two by two, we can ride it." Neit pointed into the hillock below the rising sun. They shaded their eyes, making out a winding pathway between clumps of birch and alder.

"Let's do it." Noddy raised his fist, then flattened his hand, fingers pointing eastward.

That's when Fish yelled, "To the left!" at the same time as the scout riding a short ways in front whirled his horse, bellowing, "Ware west!"

Above the rocky ridge to the left, silhouettes popped up, at least a hundred of them. The breeze beginning to stir carried a guttural shout down the slope.

At the back of the column, Stick Tyavayir fumbled for his field glass, then dropped his hand as the silhouettes topped the ridge, roaring a war cry as they charged down the gradient.

Or began a charge. As the princes and their escort ripped free their swords, they took in details of the enemy: most on foot, some riding, a variety of weapons and armoring, mostly chain mail. And a ragged, jolting mess of a charge making it clear that whoever these attackers were, they had never actually drilled charging down a rocky incline. Two fell, and a horse stumbled.

But another hundred topped the ridge, and another.

Noddy turned to Connar who shouted, "Stick! *Line!*"

Stick Tyavayir had begun to gallop up the column toward them to get orders. When he heard that, he wheeled his horse so fast the animal reared, forelegs pawing the air as he roared *"Line!"*

The trumpeter blew the chord reinforcing the order, and adding the quick double blast that meant *west* as the escort formed up shield to shield in front, back row tightening bow strings.

Connar and Noddy watched the enemy leader, a big, gray-bearded fellow bellowing at the front of a pack.

"Vanadei, what's he saying?" Connar demanded.

"Two languages." Vanadei squinted. "One I don't know. The other's dialect—something little-king . . ."

"'Princes first, kill the rest, catch the horses,'" Neit translated, her gaze unwavering on the advancing menace as she quickly looped up her long braids to get them out of her way. "Can't speak Bar Regren, but I know North-Tongue."

No game, then. The sense of unreality vanished, hearts beating hard. Noddy's big mount sidled under him as he watched Connar.

Connar kept his gaze on the attackers, heartbeat crowding his throat. *Just like drill, just like drill.* "Wait for it, wait . . ."

The column stilled, except for gazes twitching between the bellowing, roaring enemies and the princes.

"Arrows ready," Connar called, when the foremost attackers reached a hundred paces.

"Arrows ready," Stick snapped, and the trumpet tooted a single note. Bows creaked as the company loosened their arrows in their quivers with a practiced motion, drew and aimed.

Stick watched Connar, who waited until the advancing wedge was fifty paces away, then flung up two fingers, meaning one shot, one man. And brought his hand down.

Arrows zipped through the air in a blur. Most found targets—four arrows dropping one man, while the man next to him got none—others clattered off various types of shield. The enemy wavered, until those coming behind forced the front ones onward, leaping over the fallen.

As Stick roared, "Shoot!" and bows twanged, Lineas's shaking hands clenched on her knife hilts. Like Neit, she carried no shield. Unlike Neit, all she had for a weapon was her knives; Neit carried a sword as well as knives in forearm hilts. Lineas felt exposed. Her stomach roiled, and she wished she hadn't eaten.

Stick gave the signal for shoot at will.

"Noddy." Connar spoke without moving his gaze from the advance party. "When I say, charge. Take out the leader."

Noddy said, "Keth?"

Kethedrend, the banner scout behind Lineas, had already loosened the ties on the heir's banner in case. With a swift motion he wound the banner around one arm and chucked the lance past Lineas's mount's hindquarters.

Noddy slung his shield back on its saddle hook and caught the heavy wood out of the air with the ease of long habit. He locked his heels down, and muttered, "Say when."

The graybeard, a huge man wearing chain mail over his clothes, raised a thick wooden shield studded with spikes, a spear clutched in his armpit, point too high, as he forced his horse into a gallop, fifteen paces, ten—

"Now."

Noddy's big horse, which had performed this drill countless times, sprang into a gallop. The lance came down, the two animals charged the last distance. Graybeard aimed his shield—then screamed as the sharp iron of the lance head shattered the shield and drove through his body.

The enemy wavered in shock, then roared in rage and closed with the Marlovans.

Lineas had drilled with horseback fighting six years before, as part of her training as princess's first runner, but not since. Most of her training had been in hand-to-hand defense on foot. All her focus narrowed to the big, sweating, roaring man coming at her as her heart thundered frantically. Slash! Whoosh! Too slow—too weak—her breath clawed her throat as she blocked and twisted, blocked, twisted, blocked.

Awareness widened in lightning flashes: they wanted her out of the way; *they wanted to kill the princes.*

At first she only blocked, but desperation drove her to strike back, though she couldn't make herself kill. But she could slice tendons, and here was the inside of a wrist as a cudgel whizzed past her head. Her left hand ripped across that wrist, sending the man howling as the cudgel dropped from nerveless fingers—and he was muscled away by another with a sword, as a man on foot darted at her from the other side.

She sliced down to the right, then threw her weight into a slash to the left, binding the sword and using her whole body to force the blow just off her shoulder. She nearly fell, and wrenched herself upright as a sword blurred toward her head from the right.

Crash! Clang! Vanadei's horse plunged between Lineas and her attacker, giving her a heartbeat to recover her balance—to look—Noddy striking a horizontal blow with the lance that knocked two men off their horses, splintering the wood. He tossed it away. Next blink there he was, a sword in his right hand, his shield in his left, battering another enemy. Connar swung from the shoulders, his sword making a downward sweep the steel was a glinting blur. A man's head spun away, an arc of dark splash through the air.

Shadows boiled the edge of her vision.

"Watch out!" Neit shouted.

Lineas turned her head, and raised her knife to block a wooden pole descending to force her off her horse. She twisted—the wood smashed against her forearm—white pain sheeted through her. She fell back on the horse, her good hand scrabbling at the saddle. She caught the edge of the pad in a death grip and fought for consciousness.

A clang a hand's breadth over her head shocked her into alertness as Noddy fought off steel blades slicing over her head, deadly with both sword and shield. A warm splash hit her face, and she tasted the tang of someone's blood. Her stomach revolted violently, and for an agonizing eternity she struggled against the deadly giddiness as nausea clawed its way up her throat. She whispered the Waste Spell over and over, trying to spit out the horrible acid taste.

A hand jerked her reins and pulled her horse out of the fray. Lineas could not use her left arm. Both her knives were gone as Neit crowded up on her right, bleeding from her shoulder and a thigh.

"Wake up. Wake up—are you awake? Good girl. Go get help."

"What?" Lineas tried to talk but no sound came out.

"We're too far for whirtlers. Ride over that ridge yonder, you'll find the river. Gannan and a good part of the new recruits in Lindeth West Company are there, drilling. Get them. Lineas, do you hear me? Go, go, go!"

Lineas righted herself, catching the reins with her right hand an instant before Neit smacked the horse's rump. *"Go!"*

Lineas bent over the horse's neck. "Don't faint, don't faint, don't faint," she muttered over and over as she concentrated fiercely on the winding trail that Neit had indicated.

The will doesn't always win over the body; she slipped into fugue, but old drill and habit kept her in the saddle until she found herself leaning backward instead of forward. The horse was now picking its way down a goat trail.

Lineas lifted her aching head. Silver water gleamed in the sunlight as the river flowed toward the sea. On the bank, dust hid a myriad of figures . . . fugue again, then she found herself surrounded by gray-coated riders.

And there was Gannan. Who once, as a little boy, tried to get everyone to call her Pimple. The stray thought somehow steadied her, and she gulped in air. "Attack," she said. "The princes—"

Gannan took in her blood-splattered robe, her broken arm that was already swelling, and her chalk-white face under the freckles.

"How many enemies?" Gannan snapped. Though he'd only been captain of a riding—nine riders—for two months, many of the other young men had been with him at the academy, and they'd gladly followed him for this exercise.

She shook her head. "More than us."

"Which direction did they come from?"

Lineas uttered a disjointed report, miserably aware that she was making little sense, but Gannan turned away and issued a stream of orders, then added, "And somebody bind that up."

He pointed at Lineas's arm. Once again little stars shimmered across her vision, shadows roiling at the sides. When she'd fought that back, a fellow younger than she said, "Hold out your arm."

What followed hurt nearly as much as the original break, but he got it set, bound it across her stomach, and then said, "You'll do now. I'd better catch up with my riding." And he galloped away.

She looked wearily at the dust of Gannan's company vanishing around a bend.

The princes' escort was holding its own, though barely; fired by the sight of their princes fighting like madmen, the wing fought savagely. But they were outnumbered four to one, with more enemies cresting the ridge. It was beginning to look bleak, which maddened Connar into launching into the thickest groups of enemies, laying about with sword and long knife, his lips drawn back over white teeth in a savage grin. Those nearest flogged tired bodies into renewed effort at seeing their prince slaughtering enemies at either side, backed by his older brother, who was slower, but powerful enough to knock attackers right out of the saddle.

But sheer numbers began to press tightly around them—

Then trumpet notes from behind, and Gannan's young lancers burst between clumps of alder and charged. Heads turned, terror striking into the Bar Regren at the high, harrowing shriek *Yip! yip! yip!* a heartbeat before the lances smashed that tight-packed mass into bloody wreckage.

What Gannan lacked in imagination he made up for in strength and skill. His company thundered from both sides in the academy's much-used two-prong flank attack, Gannan—filled with angry joy—in the lead. All his life he'd longed for the chance to prove himself, and here it was.

Though Gannan's scratch company was only equipped with practice lances—that is, regular lances, but without sharpened steel tips—a blow from one of those at full gallop was lethal enough. Their attack was so fast and savage that most of the surviving Bar Regren fled, leaving a cluster of them caught between the Marlovans. These threw their weapons down, hands high.

Gannan was ready to strike them all down, too, but caught himself up when Noddy raised his hand, fingers open, and Stick Tyavayir shouted, "Fall back!"

The trumpet blew the halt.

Hard-reined habit squelched bloodlust, barely: no one wanted to be caught in action after orders, and the trumpet patterns they had responded to for over a decade were as good as spoken commands.

Gannan's company joined the remains of Stick's escort in circling what was left of the attackers. What now? The question semaphored between the young captains. There was little provision traditionally for the taking of prisoners. In battle Marlovans fought until either everyone was dead or driven off. But here were these men standing with their weapons at their feet, faces stricken with terror.

Stick turned to the princes, question in his blood-splashed, bony face, his expressive mouth a thin white line. Connar was poised to cut the enemies down where they stood, but Noddy—after two months in Yvana Hall—said, "They will stand trial. That's the law."

Puzzled looks turned his way. *Law.* Like *orders,* that was a powerful word. Everyone knew what happened if you ignored orders. "Do we march 'em back to Lindeth, or go on to Larkadhe?" one of Gannan's captains asked.

Connar's mind had leaped from law to executions, deliberate and drawn out. Lindeth was Nermand's command, but Larkadhe belonged to them. He smiled. "Larkadhe. We'd just have to come back, wouldn't we? Why should we sweat back here for their convenience?"

Bleeding from three nasty wounds, Stick tried to count how many of his men—every one of them known to him, and some he'd grown up with—lay on the ground, he hoped wounded, probably dead. Fury rose in him, and he met Connar's grim, humorless smile with one of his own. Then he turned his head. "Fall in," he said to his men, swaying in the saddle, then jerking upright.

As his runner urged his mount near so he could bind the worst of his captain's wounds, Gannan roared at the prisoners, "March."

Vanadei said in an undervoice to Noddy, "Shall I find Lineas? She went for Gannan, but she was riding with a broken arm, and I don't see her anywhere."

Noddy opened his hand. The young medic got the nod from Gannan, and cut out a couple of ridings to see to the wounded and Disappear the dead. At a twirled finger in the air, another riding began rounding up all the riderless horses.

Vanadei left them to it. He rode up the path that Neit had sent Lineas along. Mindful of his horse, as they hadn't brought remounts for so short a journey, he took it slow, figuring he'd encounter her along the trail.

She wasn't there.

He rode all the way to the riverbank, and looked around in dismay at the pocks made by West Company's horse hooves during their drill. There was no chance of finding her horse's prints in that mess.

He peered along the river, which was mostly hidden beyond the bend by several different types of willow. Complicated terrain. In the other direction, the river widened out from the bend as it headed toward the sea, the slope gentle as it led down toward the ocean. But she wouldn't go that way, surely?

With a broken arm, how clearly would she be thinking?

He found her drooping over her plodding mare an hour or so later, going in the wrong direction. When he caught up, she raised a feverish face and squinted as if trying to bring him into focus. He swallowed the words he'd been preparing, took the reins from her lax right hand, and said only, "Let's go home."

The sun had begun sliding down behind them when they caught up with the princes. Stick Tyavayir's first runner supported his captain, whose face had gone paper white under his tangle of dark red hair. Gannan had sent a scout to report to Lindeth, and stayed with the princes as escort to them and the prisoners, the latter of whom were stumbling with thirst and exhaustion by the time Larkadhe's white tower emerged from the hills, glowing in the slanting late-afternoon rays.

Vanadei led Lineas up to the front. Noddy's tight expression eased when he saw them. Connar glanced over, and flashed a quick smile at Lineas before they turned toward the open gates, trumpets blaring.

The echoes were dying away when Lineas raised huge, feverish eyes, and said, "Why is Evred here?"

"Evred?" Neit asked, as Connar and Noddy slewed around to stare.

Lineas' face lifted, pale except for hectic red in her cheeks, and her too-bright eyes. "His ghost," she said. "Right there, on the wall. With the others."

SEVEN

"She's delirious," Connar said. "Let's get her inside."

Lineas lifted her good hand. "He's so bright! How could you not see him?"

She did not see the worried look Noddy sent her, or Connar's wary skepticism. She stared at the ghost, whose blue gaze stared out into eternity. How could he be *here?* Lineas was quite certain Evred had never left the royal city.

"I'll take her," Neit said.

"You need a healer yourself." Noddy reached over, laying a gentle hand on her arm, between dirty bandages tied in two places.

Vanadei said, "I'll take Lineas to Healer's Assistant Inda."

They had dismounted by then. At Noddy's gesture Vanadei guided Lineas through the lower region of the castle to the wing connected to the garrison, where the elderly healer lived with his assistant, tall, long-faced Healer Assistant Indevan Janold.

At the sight of Vanadei, the assistant's somber countenance changed as he smiled.

"Inda," Vanadei said.

"Never mind explaining. I can see," Healer's Assistant Inda murmured, raising a hand to cup Vanadei's cheek. "Go. Get yourself cleaned up. Or do you have anything I need to look at right away?"

"Bruises only," Vanadei said. "She's hallucinating," he added over his shoulder.

He would have liked to stay—he and Inda had been exclusive since they met—but stronger right now was the longing to rid himself of dirt, sweat, and Bar Regren blood. He knew Lineas was in safe, gentle hands.

When he returned, clean and in clean clothes, the aches had begun to seize his muscles. He knew everybody had to be feeling the same, if not worse.

He found Lineas sitting on a mat, staring fixedly into space. "Green kinthus," Inda said. "I suggest taking her upstairs now, while she's free of pain."

"It was a clean break, wasn't it?"

"The secondary fracture wasn't. And the joint in her elbow wrenched badly. The fracture and break are spelled, but you know the magic just holds the bones together. It takes time to heal, and magic cannot take away pain."

Vanadei promised to return as soon as he had liberty, which earned one of those brief, sunlit smiles. Then he coaxed Lineas to her feet, careful to avoid the new sling cradling her left arm.

"I was clumsy," she said in a dreamy voice as they walked toward the stairs. "Slow."

Vana said, "Not trained for battle. You stayed alive, which is all anyone would ask you to do."

"I was useless," she whispered.

Vana wondered how to get through to her, or even if he should try while she was under the influence of green kinthus. As they started up the stairs, the approach of a hasty step caused Vana to pause, ready to pull Lineas back against the wall if a superior came down.

It was Fish. "They want her," he said, turned, and ran back up. He was still filthy, bruises on his face purpling.

Vanadei grimaced, wondering what Connar had been having Fish do, when mercy, or a sense of decency, would at least let him bathe.

He steered Lineas up to the royal suite, where Noddy and Connar sat on their mats, Connar wearing clean clothes, looking like his usual self except for the bulk of a bandage around his right arm, and above his left knee. Noddy was still in his dusty, blood-splashed clothes.

"Bring her in here," Connar said. "Otherwise we'll argue all night about whether or not she lost her mind."

Lineas stared at the wall, blinking slowly, her pupils enormous.

Vanadei said to Noddy with a pleading glance, "She needs to get to bed before the kinthus wears off. She won't complain. She never does, but she's got two fractures in that arm. The pain is going to be bad."

Noddy turned uncertainly to Connar, then said, "A couple of questions. So we can all rest."

Vanadei helped Lineas ease down onto a mat.

Connar leaned forward. "Lineas, what did you see when we arrived at the gate?"

"Evred's ghost," she said in a calm, detached voice. "The brightest one. I don't know the others. Many are just blobs of pale light. Though maybe they aren't ghosts. But some other life form?"

Noddy looked away, distraught. He was remembering the first time he'd noticed Lineas staring at nothing, like a cat. He didn't know what to believe.

Connar said evenly, "Have you ever seen it before?"

"Many times. I saw Evred the first day I came to the royal city." She spoke so low they had to bend forward to hear her. "Ghosts, I've seen them all my life."

Vana said slowly, "I think she's related to the Cassads. Somewhere in her family tree. You know they're famous for seeing . . . things."

"They're famous for being crazy," Connar stated. "I don't believe she's crazy. It has to be the fever she got in the sun, with the broken arm. She started hallucinating."

Noddy still looked worried, so Connar turned to Lineas. "Let's prove it. I know you're good at drawing. How about this, you draw a portrait of your ghost. And when we get back to the royal city, we can ask Da or Ma—anyone who actually knew Evred—if they recognize it."

Noddy's expression cleared, and he said soberly, "Can you do that, Lineas? Or does your arm hurt too much?"

She said in that dreamy voice, "If you put something down to anchor the paper, I can draw with either hand."

And she did. It wasn't her best work, but a face emerged from the chalk sketch. The two princes stared down at the young man sketched. It seemed eerily detailed for a creature of imagination, right down to the graceful arc of the dolphin embroidered across the sketched House tunic, and a chipped tooth.

Connar pinched the skin between his eyes. "My head hurts too much to think. We're done. Fish. See that she gets up to her bed."

By then Fish could scarcely move, and his various cuts stung mercilessly, but he'd not been granted time to see to them, much less bathe. He clamped his jaw tight and stuck his hands under Lineas's armpits to haul her up. As tired and stiff as he was, she was as light as a bird.

He steered her out of the door and down the hall—then spotted one of the house runners. Since Connar's order hadn't been to see to Lineas personally, he hailed the runner. "Can you get Lineas to her bed? Maybe get her out of those filthy clothes, too," he added.

First runners were ahead of house runners in the chain of command, making Fish's question an order. Besides, everyone liked Lineas, and it was clear that she hadn't long before she dropped.

"Leave her to me," the runner said, sliding an arm around Lineas's shoulders, careful to avoid the bandage.

Fish returned and found Connar alone, staring into space. At Fish's step he glanced up. "Rough day. You did well. Take the night off. And tomorrow."

He walked off to his room, leaving Fish staring in amazement. His eyes stung. Aware of it, he laughed at himself. Praise? Lineas wasn't the only one out of their mind, Fish thought, but still, he felt surprisingly buoyant in spite of aching muscles and the string of unwashed cuts rubbing against his grimy, sweaty clothing.

He hesitated, unwilling to leave a mess even if he had liberty—Connar was notoriously fastidious, and he might not wake to that expansive mood. So Fish tidied the room, and put away the chalk. Then he stared down at the drawing. What to do about that? His instinct was to get rid of it, but what if the princes remembered it when they all returned to the royal city? Best to be safe.

So he took it into his alcove and chucked it into his trunk, grabbed fresh clothes, and headed for baths, longing for clean water as hot as he could stand it.

Guilt gnawed at Connar.

He knew that Cabbage Gannan had deliberately planted himself and his damned company squarely on what should have been the road back so that he could kiss Noddy's heels in his "exercise." So Connar had gone to the map to find a way around it.

Yes, it was irresponsible not to ask if the way was safe, or really as fast as it looked on paper. As a result, Connar had blundered right into that trap. It didn't matter that no one had known those Bar Regren were there. Come to think of it, it was probably a Bar Regren scout shadowing him the previous night—and that was another deadly error, because someone had most likely been shadowing him for weeks, if they knew him by sight. But he hadn't been sending scouts ahead because he'd wanted so badly to lure that elusive Jendas Yenvir into attacking, because of course he'd win. Now, after his first real battle, he had to face his own ignorance. Very nearly lethal ignorance.

He did not know the final death count among their own men. It had to be far fewer than the wounded, and both numbers were quite a bit lower than that of the enemy, but that didn't hide the fact that anyone was dead at all because he'd blundered into a trap in order to avoid the very person who had rescued them so spectacularly.

And it *had* been spectacular.

Connar lay in bed staring at the ceiling. One shoulder throbbed, and a hundred small cuts stung—they were going to have to resume wearing helms, hot as they were, he knew that right now—but other than that, he was aware that that he'd killed more enemies than Noddy, more than anyone else.

There'd been more pleasure than terror.

But you couldn't say it when men on your side had died, and especially when it was your orders that led everyone straight into a trap.

He sighed. What was it Lineas said about justice that first night? If you rewarded people, it shut them up, or something similar. He'd been stupid and now he had to pay the price, which was to give Gannan the attention he wanted, and recommend him for promotion. Much as he loathed the idea. On the other hand, there were two advantages: first, promotion would give Gannan something to yap about besides figuring out Connar's blunder, and second, even if Gannan someday got promoted all the way up to being a company commander in the King's Army, he would come directly under Connar's chain of command. Once Connar took over the army.

If.

Yeah. If Connar was to get that command, no more sloppy mistakes. From now on, lancers and cavalry wore helms, at least carrying them at the saddle during high summer. They'd send scouts, even go back to scout dogs, though Connar didn't care for the messiness of dogs.

So resolved, he turned over and fell asleep.

Downstairs, at the healer's annex, Vana—given a night of liberty—had joined Healer's Assistant Inda, but he insisted on writing a report to Quill before retiring, so he sat at a little table as Inda kneaded the knotted muscles of his neck and shoulders. The healer could feel through Vana's tension how terrifying the day had been—how much he hated what he wrote—so every now and then he bent down to plant a reassuring kiss on the curve of Vana's neck.

In the princes' private bath alcove, Neit watched compassionately as Noddy scrubbed at his raw skin, scrubbed and scrubbed as if he'd never get clean, but she knew there was no scrubbing away the memory of your own hands covered in someone else's lifeblood.

And in Lindeth on the bay, Commander Nermand listened to the report by Gannan's just-arrived scout. Those two young fools had walked straight into the most obvious of traps—and yet none of his own people had known that Ovaka Red-Feather had managed to gather that many warriors and get so close. Nermand had to admit that he hadn't been lax so much as predictable, each year pulling all his command together to get the city through the festival. Of course they'd been watched from a distance. What he hadn't expected, and should have, was that once again, Red-Feather had found enough people to act.

But what had nearly been a disaster worse than the slaughter up the Pass twenty years ago was saved by a young riding captain and his first-year volunteers.

Nermand knew he'd get no sleep that night until he'd composed his report for the king. What to say when you nearly lost both royal sons, all unheeding, in spite of what you thought was careful preparation? "Start with the heroic defense by said sons," he muttered, squaring himself to his paper.

He finished halfway through the last nightwatch, and shuffled off to get what sleep he could.

Quill was still awake in the royal city at that late hour, reading Vana's report and pacing around his room in futile anger. Of all the people in the world who should never be in battle, he would first choose Lineas. Personality aside, she wasn't trained for battle. The Fox Drills were superlative, but they weren't a universal defense—they were at their weakest against mounted warriors. Fox had developed that fighting style for the close combat of shipboard, where there are no horses, and the royal runners had adapted the style to defense on foot, with weapons you otherwise kept hidden.

He knew Lineas. She had to be awake right now, castigating herself for not living up to some impossible standard, her version of the inevitable *what if I'd* and *I should have* that harrows one after action.

He circled his room a time or two more, then decided to break his rule.

Far to the north, Lineas was indeed awake, the pain-blanketing kinthus having worn off. The agony of her shoulder and arm, the aches in her body she could bear, as long as she lay still. It was the memories that cut, like the shards of one of the beautiful glassware cups they made here in the north, that she'd made the mistake of picking up the same way she'd pick up broken ceramic.

Shards of memory, for nothing was whole except her conviction that she'd been the most useless person in the entire cavalcade, which was why Neit had sent her instead of one of the scouts. And she hadn't even managed to find Gannan's volunteers—they'd found her. She recollected that much.

Why did it hurt so very badly? She tried to apply rational thinking to this bewildering sense of failure. It was easy to think she'd betrayed the others through weakness, but that wasn't right. She'd fought hard to keep the enemy from getting at the princes, but most of her desperate glances had been Connar's way, until the chaos broke up the circle—

Her mind shied away, ready to follow the familiar path of humiliation at her lack of physical prowess, but she forced it back. She knew she was very good at the Fox drills, with their emphasis not on strength so much as speed and balance. She was fast. Very fast. And she knew how to use her body to deflect blows from stronger arms than hers. But she'd seen at the outset that knife fighting aimed upward against a foe who would almost inevitably be taller was at a decided disadvantage when fighting on horse, against cudgels and spears. She'd managed to deflect the blows aimed at her, and the aches all down her indicated that she'd have the bruises to prove it.

Chaos—

Noddy's sword whistling overhead—

Another sharper shard. She shut her eyes against it, but the images pushed their way into the forefront of her mind: Noddy and Vanadei both trying to circle around her. Defending her. She endured the pulse of guilt that they'd found it necessary, and there was the old path to humiliation again.

No. She knew that she would do anything she could to defend her fellows. She had to grant them their choice to defend her. That was a side path, a familiar path, however much it hurt: her own shortcomings.

But there was a deeper shard.

And here was the image, of Connar surging into the thick of the enemy, sword whirling. Maybe he'd assumed she was good enough to hold her own.

She hoped so. That idea assuaged pride. But the truth? The truth was that he'd never thought to look back at her, though she'd turned his way every chance she could. She fought against the assumption that he didn't care for her the way she did for him. It was easy to choose hurt, when it was equally possible he didn't look her way because he assumed she was as good a fighter as Neit and Vana and Fish. Yes, that was the way to think. She spent some time trying to remember if he'd looked back for Neit, Fish, or even Noddy: no, she didn't remember seeing him looking back for anyone. He had charged straight into the enemy, confident that they all could defend themselves.

It was logical, and she sensed that there was truth to it. And yet there remained doubt. And below it, hurt.

Dismiss that, she told herself. Nothing had ever been said between them. He was a prince, and had different responsibilities. But Noddy, who had the same responsibilities, had looked out for her. Here was the shard of hurt again, because it was so easy, so very easy, to hate herself for not being good enough despite countless conversations about the balance of duty and desire.

Then she remembered Quill coming in one day when she was thirteen or so, and proclaiming to their work group that he'd discovered that Colend's butterflies in fans and clothing and even on ribbons weren't just decoration, they were a symbol for how crazy love was, how it didn't have any rules that made sense.

The memory dimmed on the outcry of disgust from the other thirteen-year-olds. She'd joined it, too. The last thing she wanted to think about in those days was adult stuff.

But she understood it now. She yanked the shard out by facing the truth: though Connar liked, enjoyed, even respected her skills, there was nothing he got from her that he didn't get from others.

Whereas she had never looked at anyone else because they were not Connar. She held onto that, as tears leaked out the corners of her eyes. Finally, because she was safely alone, she gave in and cried herself to sleep.

Of course that meant bad dreams. But morning comes anyway, and so she forced herself to sit up slowly, and with her good hand she automatically checked her golden notecase in its hiding place between the trunk at the foot of her bed and the bedframe.

It had been weeks since she'd received any letters, but there was one now. Moving with exquisite care, she clicked the box open and pulled out the folded paper, smiling when she recognized Quill's handwriting.

> *I miss the windharps. Did I ever tell you about the night I slept alone on the cliff below them? What do they sound like in this season?*

The windharps! How could she have managed not to hear them, instead miring herself in memories of blood and horror? The fight had happened. But it was not the entire world: the windharps were still there. Beauty still existed. She had only to reach for it. Again, she sustained one of those profound shifts of focus, but this one left her feeling a little lighter in heart.

She got up and went to the window. Though the air was gray, the sound a hiss of rain, she listened for any hint of windsong. Then sat down to write carefully with her good hand:

What happened on the cliff?

She folded and sent it, and at his end, Quill—who had kept the notecase in his pocket, though they were not supposed to do that—instantly found a secluded corner in order to take it out and read what turned out to be a single line in a different handwriting from her usual, evidence of her broken arm.

He pocketed note and case, continuing on his way to the king's interview chamber, where he was serving that day as runner-in-waiting. Of course Lineas wasn't going to confide in him. He'd thrown away the privilege when he ignored her for five years. But he could still try to buoy her spirits.

He ran up the stairs, mentally composing his letter about his night camping under the stars as the winds sang.

EIGHT

In Larkadhe, life resumed its accustomed rhythm. The ghost was forgotten, to Lineas's relief—she was horrified when she recollected that part of the nightmarish day. She began to suspect that the ghost episode was far overshadowed by their memory of the attack.

She vowed to lose the sling before the end of the second month, and to exercise her arm to get her strength back as soon as possible—and then to work harder to get stronger.

Connar was gone within a few days to resume his patrols, taking Ghost Fath as his captain, and a good portion of Ghost's men to replace those of Stick Tyavayir's too injured to ride.

That left Stick in charge of the garrison, where he could watch over his recovering men, three of whom were critically injured. He could also recover himself.

Connar and Ghost reorganized their company to include scouting forays ahead and behind. Their route now overlapped with Tanrid's Olavayir Riders' most northern reach, and Lindeth's northeastern territory; Ovaka Red-Feather, Connar learned, claimed to be king of the mountainous peninsula capped by the harbor called the Nob. Nobody assumed that the entirety of his followers had been on the road that day.

Back in Larkadhe, as Andahi Day and Victory Day came and went, bringing occasional bouts of cooler, rainy weather, Noddy kept putting off trial of the Bar Regren prisoners crowded in the garrison's detention wing.

It was partly because he did not want to deal with the prisoners, who he had discovered everyone expected to be executed. The thought of flogging to death, shooting, or even beheading (which was at least quicker) more than forty people—some of them no older than academy boys—made him sick to his stomach.

Then there was the fact that nobody could understand them, and they were apparently unable to understand Marlovan or Idegan or Iascan. With her other duties curtailed, Lineas set herself to the task of learning their tongue, which seemed to be an impossibility—a fact that Noddy was secretly grateful for, as it put off dealing with them, and he had plenty of other work to do now that harvest season was on them. Starting with overseeing all the conflicts that had to do with tax and tally gathering and accounting, the traditional dread of autumn up and down the kingdom.

No child of Danet's could have escaped basic lessons in keeping tallies, so vital to a kingdom's wellbeing. Poor Noddy had no head for numbers, though he did grasp what they meant if explained carefully: he could see the architecture of them, so to speak, though he could scarcely articulate how he saw that.

But Vanadei had been suggested for him partly for his ability to recollect columns of numbers, a side-benefit of having learned as a boy verses and verses of balladry. He only had to hear a column once, and he had nearly perfect recall. So it was Vanadei's turn to sit across from Noddy, handling the chalk and slate, as Lineas took on the chore of feeding the prisoners and seeing to it they had water, in hopes she could get some of their language.

The detention area had four empty cells, the rest used as storage, as punishment tended to be swiftly handed out by Marlovans. Having to feed people who sat around doing nothing seemed a pointless chore. When first herded in, the prisoners were arbitrarily shoved into each cell, roughly ten per.

When the weather took a sudden sharp turn toward winter, Lineas took it upon herself to wheel in a cart of blankets. There was no furniture whatsoever, only a blanket apiece. After two weeks, when those blankets weren't changed, Lineas collected them, hauled the filthy, smelling mess to the laundry cave adjacent to the hot springs the castle people used as baths as well as laundry, dunked them in the magic-purified vat, and hung them to dry in the windy corridor nearby.

After those two weeks of unsuccessful communication, Lineas went to Noddy and asked if they could separate out the young ones, and rearrange the others to balance out the numbers.

Noddy said, "Why? I thought they won't talk to anyone."

"No, but I see their faces every day. I think . . . I think if the older ones aren't there, some of the younger ones might talk to me," she said. "Might we try?"

Noddy gave permission, though he felt extremely ambivalent about any success, because that would bring the need for a trial closer.

The following morning Lineas discovered that three of the storage cells had been more or less swept out and the prisoners redistributed. The five teens were in a cell by themselves.

At night, when she returned to hand out the evening meal, she gave out more clean blankets, and also lugged in an ensorcelled bucket so that anyone who wanted to dip hands, or clothes, in, could.

So far the prisoners had refused to speak to her. They could all hear the armed guards waiting in the background as Lineas distributed food, water, blankets, so no one attacked the skinny girl with the arm in a sling. They knew what would happen. So they ignored her, though each day she tried a different language, rotating between Marlovan, Iascan, and Idegan, to no effect.

But the third day after the youths were separated out, and she brought breakfast, as usual she felt five gazes following her every movement. "Here is your breakfast," she said in Idegan, trying to improve her accent. "You'll notice that we're getting shirred egg as well as cheese in the biscuits. I found out the cook seems to think that adding egg somehow offsets cold weather."

She set out the last bowl—she always set them in a row inside the door, since there was no table—and turned away, when the skinniest boy snarled, his voice cracking, "You said we."

She turned back. "Yes, we."

"You're a prisoner too?"

"Shut up, Thiv."

"*You* shut up. They're going to kill us anyway, right? So why not talk to her? If they kill us for just *talking*, better than sitting here smelling your stink and being bored to death."

Since he'd spoken in Idegan, Lineas knew he wanted her to understand.

She said, "We as in all of us. We all eat the same thing." At the wary, skeptical looks she saw in their faces, she added, "Of course the garrison gets theirs hot, then everybody else, and you're last. I know it's cold by the time I bring it. Can't be helped. You get everything the rest didn't eat, which is why sometimes there's more and sometimes less."

One of the other boys muttered something in what Lineas suspected was their own tongue, and the one who told Thiv to shut up threw his hands out wide as he answered in the same tongue. Then, switching to Idegan as he eyed Lineas truculently, "No matter what we say, we're going to get killed, right?"

"I can't predict what is to happen," Lineas said carefully. "All I can tell you for certain is that the crown prince will hold a trial."

"A trial!"

Bitter laughter met this from the two who understood Idegan, after which the others clamored in their own tongue, asking (Lineas suspected) what was said. Then five mutinous faces glowered at Lineas. She saw the fear in tight bony shoulders and gritted jaws, and left, surprised at the flow of pity though memory of the attack still jolted her out of sleep, leaving her sweaty and gasping.

. . . they spoke fast, but I'm fairly certain I heard Idegan verbs—actually Sartoran verb roots—with different conjugation. And though they looked at me in anger, they did speak to me for the first time.

Lineas had been writing to Quill nightly ever since that first exchange about the windharps, a happy subject that lasted a week. Lineas reported each day's windsong, then woke up to comments about windharps elsewhere in the world, learned while Quill delved in the archives.

From there it seemed natural to talk about their day, and when Lineas took over the task of dealing with the prisoners, she shared her lack of success.

Quill responded with funny accounts of his disastrous first attempt at child-minding his willful little sister (involving bribing with jam, which caused him to wonder how a tiny pot of jam could not only get in Blossom's hair, but on every available surface), and like matters. They were all easy letters, undemanding, and Lineas began to look forward to them enough that she sewed a pocket on the inside of her winter singlet and carried the golden notecase there so she wouldn't miss the magical tap that announced the arrival of a note. Even if she couldn't get to it all day, just knowing it was there waiting cheered her through hard and increasingly cold days of labor.

After that first exchange with the teenage Bar Regren, Lineas wrote back what she'd observed linguistically, and together she and Quill worked on the language—Lineas unaware that Quill, during his limited free time, endured two long transfers in order to visit the stringers' guild at the Nob to obtain a list of basic Bar Regren words and their Iascan equivalents.

Once the wall of silence had been broken, the boys waited for Lineas to show up, bombarding her with insults and questions, truculent and anxious by turns. All she could say was, "The crown prince hasn't decided yet. It's his decision."

She found herself glad that it was his decision, a relief that sharpened as autumn closed in, bringing spectacular thunderstorms over the mountains as the west winds weakened with the sun moving northward again, and the icy winds off the eastern peaks strengthening.

One morning, as thunder rumbled beyond the peaks and the harps moaned a long, sustained series of low notes, Vana appeared in the kitchen looking for Lineas. She stood by the bake oven, warming up her hands. She loved her tower room, and she had plenty of warm bedding, but it was getting harder to get out of that bed into frigid air in the mornings.

"He wants you," Vana said, aiming his well-cut chin over his shoulder in the direction of Yvana Hall.

"What about?" Lineas asked as soon as they reached the hall.

Vana's bushy brows drew together in a line as he said in Old Sartoran, "Scout showed up from Prince Connar, asking when the execution was to be held."

Lineas's gut clenched as if an invisible fist had punched her.

They didn't speak again until they reached the hall, which was warmed by fire sticks burning brightly in both fireplaces, front and back.

Noddy said, "Do you know enough of their language to translate before the court?"

Lineas turned her gaze from Vana, who stared down impassively, to the scribe who sat with his pen poised, ink and paper ready.

"Yes," she said slowly.

Noddy eyed her. "You don't sound sure."

Lineas bit her lip. "I can. That's not the problem that I see."

"What is the problem?" Noddy's voice rose slightly.

"I don't believe the men will speak. They haven't. They won't. The boys . . ." She fought the impulse to twist her fingers together. "They talk. A lot. But I think you'll find that they don't know anything that would be useful in a trial."

"Isn't one of them the chieftain's son?"

"Grandson. Oba is the youngest. Big for his age, turned fourteen this spring. But I don't think he'll say anything before Yvana Hall."

Noddy's frown was more frustrated than angry, but Lineas's heart crowded her throat as Noddy said slowly, "We promised that all proceedings are held before witnesses."

Vana stirred, then stilled.

Noddy flicked a glance at him. "Vana?"

Vana turned his hand down. "Sorry."

Noddy slammed his fist on the table. "Nobody is talking to me. It's not just the prisoners. The guild chiefs talk around me when I mention the trial. The Idegans won't talk to me at all whenever the words 'Bar Regren' come up. Why won't *you* speak when I ask you to?"

Vanadei and Lineas turned to each other, then Vana said, "Our orders are never to interfere in royal matters."

Noddy was so rarely sarcastic that it was unsettling to see his lips twist sardonically as he commented, "And if I order you to?"

Another exchanged glance, Vana waiting for Lineas, as the court runner—and Lineas waiting for Vanadei, as Noddy's first runner—to speak.

The scribe murmured deferentially. "If you'll forgive my interjection, Nadran-Sierlaef, I have chanced to overhear references to the fact that many in the council feel that this is solely a military matter."

"Of course it's a military matter," Noddy said. "What . . ."

He frowned, thumbed his eyes, then said to the scribe, "Barend, where are the proceedings from the last military matter like this one?"

Barend's blue eyes narrowed, then widened. "There's nothing that I could say is *like* this situation, but . . .Would a similar situation be . . . the Slaughter at the Pass? I don't remember it. I was too young. But when in training, we had to study the debates . . ." He interrupted himself. "Those records are not here." He indicated the tightly packed shelves. "I'd have to go up to the storage."

"Bring them to me."

Barend laid down his pen and went out, casting a vaguely disgruntled glance Lineas's way. He clearly thought that a runner ought to be sent on what was obviously a runner's errand, but he'd been given a direct order.

As soon as he was out the door, Noddy got to his feet, crossed the room, and shut the door. "Barend's a good scribe, but he's a scribe. They all blab. Ma said once they can't help it. You two are royal runners. You're sworn to *us*, the royal family, and you don't blab. So tell me what I'm missing. Start with why a military matter sends them all scattering. When you'd think they'd be howling on their hind legs, if we held a trial without them."

Vana said, "I think in this situation, the Idegans want you to execute the prisoners without them having to witness. I think it's because everybody thinks the trial is a . . . mere play, that the verdict is foregone. This much I've overheard, the Idegans don't want the mountain Bar Regren hearing that they had anything to do with executions. And the guilds don't like anything to do with executions. They consider the subject *Marlovan*."

They all had gotten used to overhearing "Marlovan" said in that tone, meaning savage, bullying, uncivilized.

"But at the same time," Vana finished on a sour note, "they all hate the Bar Regren, who attack their own trade and towns repeatedly."

Noddy's voice deepened with his displeasure. "So they want us to get blood on our hands, and keep theirs clean."

Nobody denied it.

Lineas spoke softly, "The boys all believe they are to be executed, and they keep asking me when."

"Fourteen," Noddy whispered, pinching the skin between his brows. Then he glared at Vanadei. "If they really think we're holding a false trial, doesn't that mean they think *we're* false? Then everything we've been so careful with, it doesn't matter?"

Vana opened his hands. "When people are frightened, or angry, they'll say a lot of things."

Noddy thumbed his eyes again, then looked up at Lineas. "What was it you said? When we first came to Larkadhe. We talked about justice. You said, people will remember one injustice longer than all the proper justice. Something like that. Is that what they expect from us here, injustice?"

Lineas tried to feel her way among the mental thorns. "I suspect . . . they believe we Marlovans have the power to point at anything we want and call it justice. Including executions. And if they object, the finger might be pointed at them."

Vana added, "The subject here is that everybody, including the prisoners, seems to be convinced that no matter what we say or do, forty people, including boys of fourteen, are going to be marched out to the parade ground to their deaths."

"I *hate* that." Noddy slammed both fists on the table, making everything on it jump and clatter. "I need to talk to them. Should I go down there?"

Lineas said, "I think . . . I think if you go there, or they come here, they won't talk."

"How about if you talk, and I listen out of sight?"

"We could try that," Lineas said, trying to still her trepidation. She told herself that this was no different than serving as a translator occasionally when there was a language conflict. *Except for the outcome.* "But you must give me the questions you want answered."

By the time Barend-Scribe returned, looking dusty and put-upon, Noddy had recovered enough to address other issues. He took the closely written papers, laid them down and said, "I will read this later."

In injured silence, Barend settled onto his mat, took up his pen, and inked it with an affronted *pok!*

The watch change rang as the sun vanished behind the mountains, each day a little more northerly. Once the garrison ate and the day watch went off to recreation or to bed, the kitchen runner summoned Lineas, who waited with her cart. She divided the supper between forty-six bowls and headed down to detention, with Noddy and Vanadei following.

At the sight of the crown prince the night shift guards abruptly shut up and straightened to alertness. Vana, there to translate for Noddy, looked down so no one would see his amusement.

Lineas was too distraught to notice anything. She had been able to slice muscles and tendons when these boys were enemies—maybe one of those wounds on the bigger boy was from her—but the more they talked, the more they became people instead of enemies.

She served the men, who always fell silent the moment the key turned in the lock, then the duty guard opened the door to the boys' cell, and at a gesture from Lineas, left it wider than usual.

Vanadei stood behind it, ready to translate in Hand, as Lineas said in Bar Regren, "It's stewed pepper-fish tonight. You might recognize the spices. I'd never had them until I came to the north here. Where are you all from?"

"Nob," said Thiv, the skinny one with the prominent neck-knuckle, who gnawed his fingernails.

"Shut up," growled Ewt, the biggest one, with the bandage around his wrist.

"Why? We're dead anyway, you keep saying," Thiv snarled back.

"Bar Regren," Oba said. "We're all from Bar Regren, but I wasn't born on land." He added bitterly, with a wild look around the barren cell, whose only air came from tiny vents high up on the wall opposite the door, "I *hate* living on land."

"You were born on a boat?" Lineas asked as she stacked the bowls from breakfast and began to set out their dinners.

"Fisher," Oba said. "Ma's family owns two ships, trading in spice and coffee. After Pa died when Grandpa tried taking the Nob, he made me come off our fisher. Said it's my *duty.*"

"The Nob is *our* royal city, that's what the king said," Thiv added, scraping long front teeth over chapped lips. "Long ago, it was where the Red-Feathers were kings. He said if we killt the Marlovan princes and the rest of 'em, and leave behind Idegan weapons, and things, then the Idegans would get blamed, and the Marlovans would attack them, and they'd fight each other, and we'd get the Nob back."

"The king said it's our duty to fight. How do you think my brother died?" a hereto silent boy spoke up from the corner where he hunched.

"*And* my aunt," Thiv added, as he picked up one of the bowls.

"And my Pa," another put in. "Oba isn't the only one that lost his pa."

"Not that I cared," Oba muttered, under his breath, his shoulders hunched and his gaze turned away. "And my uncle ran and *left me* . . ."

Lineas saw in the lines of the boy's body that an unhappy story lay close to the surface, but he was not ready, or willing, to talk about it yet. She shifted the subject away. "Are any of you related to the other men?"

Five voices said, "Me."

Lineas had finished setting out the food. She scanned the wary, frightened, unhappy faces and decided enough questions had been asked for the day. She carried the dirty bowls out, the guard slammed and locked the door, and Lineas wheeled her cart toward the outer exit.

Nobody spoke until they got upstairs to the royal suite, which was empty.

Lineas said, "Was that all right? I didn't get to all your questions, but I thought a couple of them were answered in what they said. And the rest—"

"I heard enough," Noddy said. "I think . . . I think I know what I'm going to do. But, we always wait on judgments, right? Nothing sudden. No whims. Right? Tomorrow, if I'm still thinking the same, I'll go with you."

He was there, waiting, when Lineas went down to fetch her cart. Guards stood at attention, the silence thick with unspoken tension, emotion, question. In the distance, Stick Tyavayir watched, hard-faced. He was ready to order guards in with drawn swords at the slightest hint of trouble.

Lineas's shoulder blades crawled as she led the way, not to the end, but to the first cell, where five men sat with their backs to the walls, as usual. When Noddy walked in after Lineas, they stirred, two leaping to their feet before dropping down again at the sight of the enormous Marlovan in his war coat, knife through his sash, and guards at his back.

"Tell them you'll translate," he signed to Lineas.

She said in Bar Regren, "Nadran-Sierlaef will speak to you now."

One man made a spitting motion, to be kicked by another.

And Lineas translated as Noddy spoke, "Anyone who gives me his word he will go away to another life and never return, can have that life."

The men exchanged startled, skeptical, disbelieving glances, then one spoke for the first time. "If we don't?"

Lineas turned to Noddy, listened, then said unhappily, "Rules of war. But he promises, it will be quick. Also, if you break your word, and you return and are recognized, it's a death sentence."

"Then . . . we're free to go?" another asked with extreme skepticism.

"We will send you to the opposite shore of the strait as soon as a trader comes in that will take you. You will have your brains, and your hands, to begin a new life. You have the day to think it over. When we return this evening, you'll be taken out one by one and asked separately, so there is no coercion."

A younger man said sullenly, "What about my brother, Finger?"

Lineas said, "The boys will get the same offer."

She listened patiently to the often curse-punctuated discussion, translating everything for Noddy, who waited behind the door until he felt he had enough. He frowned heavily as he trod upstairs, and closeted himself in his room, writing.

When Neit returned late that night from her regular run to Lindeth, Noddy put down his pen. "I trust Vanadei and Lineas, but I think you're faster. Would you go to the king for me?"

What answer was there to be made to that? "First thing, soon's we have sun," she promised and tried to kiss the worry lines from his brow.

Neit was given an heir's pennon, which guaranteed the best of the horses at every outpost the moment she rode in, food and a bed. Though usually long riders took pride in how little they slept, resorting to the ground and even sleeping in the saddle in snatches.

Neit knew how anxious Noddy was—and she kept an experienced eye to wind and weather. If she could, she intended to get back to the north before the snow flurries flew in earnest. She loathed floundering through snow for any longer than a day.

The weather favored her as she galloped southward, past harvest gatherings. When she fetched up in the royal city, one of the young runners-in-training was sent to find the king and queen as soon as the sentries saw her pennon.

She soon stood before the king, who read Noddy's letter through twice, scowled, then sent one of his runners to fetch the queen.

When Danet came in, she, too, read the letter twice, then said to Neit, "I understand that you are not a royal runner, and so we should not expect a report in their style. But please, tell us everything that happened. Everything," she repeated.

Neit had planned out a succinct military report on the Chalk Hills Battle in case the king asked for extra details, knowing that he'd received the after-action report. But standing there under the queen's gaze, Neit found herself adding, "And when we returned to the castle, poor Lineas was delirious, seeing ghosts."

"Ghosts?" Danet repeated.

Arrow flat-handed he word away with a quick, impatient gesture. "I don't want to hear about ghosts. Obviously she had a fever." He leaned forward. "I read Nermand's report, of course, but he wasn't there. You were. Was the road the boys took a shortcut or not?"

"It looks like one on the map, but locals know not to use it," Neit said as neutrally as she could.

"You mean they blundered into bad territory without asking?" the king demanded.

Neit hesitated, then said, "I think they understand now."

Arrow sat back, his breath hissing out between his teeth. *Close. So very close.* Not that he was blaming them. He knew he was likely to have made the exact same sort of error. What was more important . . . "But you say they fought well?"

"Very well," Neit confirmed. "In fact, I think you could say they heartened everyone with their bravery. Noddy is slow, but strong. He's lance trained, and it showed. Connar was everywhere, smashing straight into the thick of them, Fish and a wedge of Captain Tyavayir's best Riders flanking him. They definitely held the line until Riding Captain Gannan and his volunteers turned up. Then it was a rout."

"Hah," Arrow said, relief flooding him. It didn't do to show how happy he was that his long gamble was paying off. The boys really were far better than he was at leading; if the kingdom could just get through a few more years, until they had some seasoning on them, he could confine himself to doing his part with reports and maps. That, he understood as much as anyone else around him. But if there as an invasion, there was that oath he made at Convocation every year, that he'd lead the defense, as Evred-Harvaldar did, with Inda-Harskialdna as his shield arm.

That was why 'Sieraec,' the old king-during-peace title, had been dropped when Iascan was dropped as the language of government. Marlovan kings promised to be ready to defend the kingdom . . . and Arrow knew he still couldn't do it. He watched the academy game every summer, and he was no better at following tactics than he ever was: it was still all dust and noise.

But his boys, exposed to it every day, were different.

He chuckled, and catching Neit's confused look and Danet's narrowed eye, realized he'd lost the thread of the talk. Damn! Early in the day, and already his mouth was dry. But his mood was good. "Let me get some paper, so I can write to Noddy and back up his decision. I'd execute 'em all, but if he wants to exile them, well, he's the man on the spot." He vanished in three steps.

"And I'm to tell you that there's a suitable trading vessel willing to carry your cargo for a fee," Connar said, the day after the first snow flurries landed softly on the steeply slanted slate rooftops below Lineas's north window. "What cargo?"

His company had just returned from the western edge of their patrol perimeter, having met Lindeth's East Company by arrangement between scouts. They'd ridden hard to reach Larkadhe before sundown, as snow threatened.

"The Bar Regren," Noddy said.

Connar tossed down his gloves, took off his cloak and slung it to Fish, then dropped onto his mat. "The what?"

"Bar Regren, what the prisoners call themselves. The runners learned their lang—"

"What?" Connar snapped. "Why would you need a cargo ship to execute them?" His eyebrows lifted. "You plan to send them out to sea and set fire to the ship?"

"No." Noddy looked revolted.

Barend dropped his pen, and Lineas, just entered after taking the prisoners their supper, stopped inside the door, her heart crowding her throat at the sight of Connar's furious blue gaze.

Noddy said, "We gave them a choice. Three chose death, and they went against the wall that day. The rest promised never to return once they're landed somewhere on the other side of the strait." He added, "Neit made a grass run down to the royal city, after I finished with them."

Grass run was leftover slang from the days over a century ago when the famous King's Runner Vedrid had crossed the kingdom in (legend had it) two weeks. Part of his legend was the saying *Don't let the grass grow under your ass.* In some stories it was said to him, and in some he said it to another, but a grass ass run, shortened eventually to grass run, was equivalent to a relay run, except that a single individual galloped from post to post, sleeping and eating in the saddle.

Noddy went on, "She got back yesterday. Here's what Da says—he agreed with me."

Noddy touched a paper sitting at the corner of his desk, Arrow's characteristic messy handwriting instantly recognizable. Connar, seeing that, did not read the words. "And you believe those shits down there?"

"They aren't in any shape to attack anyone, after being imprisoned since Midsummer," Noddy said.

"But that won't be true after they get a few meals into them," Connar retorted, and when Noddy began to speak, he lifted his hand, palm out, and turned around, catching sight of Lineas. "Do *you* agree with this? They nearly killed you."

She wanted to remind him that it wasn't her place to comment on the princes' judgments, but she sensed that that would only irritate Connar. "A lot of them didn't want to be there," she said softly.

"And yet I don't remember any of them hanging back when they were trying to kill us all."

"Some are very young—hardly more than children. And they had been taught to believe it was their duty to follow the man who claimed he was a king, and that he had the right to kill anyone in the way of his reclaiming his great grandfather's throne."

A muscle jumped in Connar's jaw on the word *throne.*

"But a lot of them don't seem to think it's true anymore, now that Ovaka Red-Feather is dead."

Connar walked out.

He remained silent until he reached the garrison, where he found Ghost Fath with Stick Tyavayir in the garrison command center. Ghost glowered, flushed with fury.

Stick, who had known about the judgment for months, looked on with bitter eyes and his mouth curled in mordant irony. He still suffered broken sleep full of nightmarish distortions of his first command lying broken and bleeding, by day watching the slow, painful recovery of the ones who'd survived. Two hadn't. He was haunted by midnight self-chastisement over his conviction that he should have known, given better commands, that he should have saved them—but solid and hardening by day was his conviction that Noddy's mercy was injustice.

Stick had never been very talkative, preferring action to words. In these days he became positively taciturn; his loyalty to Connar, already strong, intensified at Connar's fury.

Both Ghost and Stick waited for Connar to speak. Both knew that the king had sanctioned Nadran-Sierlaef's decision. Anything they said to the contrary was tantamount to insubordination in their own eyes.

"So you heard the news." Connar's lips curved in a humorless smile. He looked from one hard face to the other. "I have an idea," he said.

Their expressions altered to question.

The next morning, when the princes met for breakfast, Connar appeared to be restored to good humor. Noddy had passed a wretched night. As soon as he saw Connar, he poured out all the reasoning for his decision that he'd thought out so carefully.

Connar listened until he ran out of words, then said, "You were here. I wasn't. I didn't expect that, is all. What's done is done."

Noddy sat back in relief. "If you want me to continue the patrols, and you can take over presiding in Yvana Hall, I don't mind."

Connar lifted a hand. "It's nearly winter, and Captain Nermand said that there's rarely trouble once the snows come. For one thing, it's very difficult to run away when there are ice patches everywhere. So I can sit with you if you like. But we'll take one last patrol, because I want to go over the winter map with Nermand, before the snows close us in. So I suggest we combine errands, and we'll take your prisoners to Lindeth, and turn them over to your ship. How's that?"

Noddy hailed the suggestion with relief, knowing that he would have had to reduce his garrison considerably in order to send a proper escort, if Connar had taken his company out patrolling again; while he didn't believe the prisoners would raise any trouble, there was always a chance that some of Ovaka Red-Feather's bloodthirsty compatriots were lurking in the hills, waiting for the chance for another attack.

Chance? He knew they were. Lineas had learned a lot about the Red-Feather family after the boys began to realize they were not going to be put to death. Ovaka Red-Feather's second son, Oba's Uncle Mol, had fled the field, earning the bitter scorn of those he'd abandoned. Mol would have to either prove himself or vanish entirely. Though they knew better than to take the complaints of an angry fourteen-year-old as fact, a picture had emerged of a hard-talking man. He'd be back.

Connar and Stick hoped he'd be back. But there was no sign of the Bar Regren now. Connar and his two captains agreed that Stick and his company could ride with Connar, taking his recovered men with them.

Lineas had just gotten breakfast into the Bar Regren when a great clattering of boots and weaponry caused everyone to still.

"Time to go," announced a guard in Marlovan.

Lineas was about to translate but her voice collided with the clank of the doors being unlocked and thrown open. The Bar Regren were herded from the cells and taken out into the frigid air, still in the clothes they wore to the attack.

Many people lined up to watch the prisoners marched off toward Lindeth. Some were puzzled by the fact that the Bar Regren were really still alive, that it wasn't a rumor; a few were relieved on behalf of the boys. And some were disappointed. But overall, Noddy's reputation as a commander reflected that of Arrow in faraway Choreid Dhelerei: he might not be very inspiring, but if you had to have Olavayirs ruling you, well, it could be worse.

Connar and Stick Tyavayir rode side by side, the heir's eagle banners carried on lances behind them, the company bristling with arms as they rode at a sedate walk. There could not be more contrast between them in their sashed coats, their helms, the tear-shaped shields slung at the saddles with swords and bows, and the ragged prisoners shuffling along, many shivering. They clumped together for warmth, and because they did not like the grim looks cast their way by these stone-faced Marlovans who kept them moving.

Everything changed when they reached a bend in the river with a sheltered ledge curving around a broad beach dotted with pebbles. Here they halted, and at Stick's command, the scouts set up firesticks to build a fire. At first the prisoners made motions to draw close to the warmth, but swords ripped from sheaths, keeping them back.

And when some of them saw irons laid in the fire, whispers ran through them, and covert grumbling changed to apprehension.

Presently Stick said, "Ready." And hefted a glowing iron, his light gaze steady with cold anger under his expressive brows.

Connar crunched through the gravel to face the prisoners. He figured at least one might speak Marlovan, not that he cared if they translated or not. They'd soon figure it out.

"We'll honor my brother's decision, though I don't believe in your oaths. So I'm going to send you off with a mark that will alert anyone who sees you if you're ever seen on these shores again. This pain will be nothing to what we'll do then."

As he spoke, two of Stick's men—both of them nearly killed on that road that day—yanked a burly man to his feet and held his arms as Stick leveled the burning iron at the man's forehead.

NINE

Of course word got back to Larkadhe, after the stumbling, half-frozen prisoners were marched to the dock, each with a blistered red line on his face.

Nothing was said between the brothers. Noddy regretted having let Connar and Stick take them, but at least they were alive. Connar shrugged it off. What was there to say?

So the subject, not quite a question, lay between them, neither wishing to push it into being something else, as days flitted by and winter arrived early, with dramatic suddenness for those unused to the mountainous north.

Lineas was still writing to Quill every night, warming her fingers over her candles in her cold room that got dark so early. The sun now shone overhead for only a few hours in the middle of the day before vanishing behind the northwest mountains.

She couldn't bear to write about any of the turmoil in her heart.

'Justice.' She knew that Ghost Fath, a smiling, pleasant young man she saw often, agreed with what Connar and Stick Tyavayir had done. They considered their action justice, and she could understand some of their emotions, for she'd helped in the lazaretto in those early days.

She'd grieved over those broken young men, and she grieved now over Oba and his cousin, and the others, even the ones who had looked at her with resentment and fear. She would resent being locked in a barren cell for months, too, every day expecting to be taken out to a painful end.

Her days were empty now: there was no reason to rush to the kitchen from the baths, and after the day's labors in Yvana Hall, there was no reason to go to the garrison side of the mess hall.

She spent her evenings in her room, either reading or writing to Quill about customs, and harp songs, and anything she could think of to distract herself. And he always answered as fast as he could, sometimes writing on his thigh as his horse drank at a stream while he was running messages.

Therefore on Connar's return, he didn't see Lineas at all, for he spent those first few days either at the garrison, or riding restlessly around the city and its environs to learn the terrain. Restless days meant broken nights, and all the old turmoil.

He lay awake three nights running, staring upward in the darkness. Sport sex only gave him an hour or two of sleep; otherwise he glared restlessly at the hidden ceiling, hating that room, hating Larkadhe, and especially hating that horrible moaning sound coming down out of the mountains, with the wind whistling around the towers in an eerie counterpoint. He didn't believe in ghosts, but tell that to your mind when all is dark, your body is exhausted, but your mind will not let you sleep.

The next night, after supper, he climbed the stairs to the tower, and surprised Lineas reading an old scroll. She only had to see him standing there, the bones of his face sharply etched in the candlelight, sooty eyelashes framing ice blue eyes. "Why don't you have a fire?" he asked. "There's a fire place." He pointed.

Delighted that he would ask, she said, "No extra firesticks. And I was too bad at magic to make my own. It's all right. I don't mind—I'm used to it." As she spoke, sorrow harrowed her at the marks of tiredness under his eyes.

He didn't speak. Just held out his hand in appeal, and all the old feelings rushed into her heart.

Connar smiled to see the sudden, dawning smile on her face.

And with her by his side, warm and sweet-smelling, he slept.

So she went back to spending her nights in Connar's warm bedchamber, but she kept her golden notecase in her room, behind the trunk, as usual.

Quill knew something had happened to the Bar Regren prisoners when Lineas abruptly stopped writing about their language and customs, reverting to the windharp's winter song, and how people of the city seemed to spend more time in the underground caves. She seldom wrote about anything she was thinking, but now there was no sign of Lineas in her letters, only the world she found herself in.

Enlightenment arrived when Vana got his day of liberty, and could sit down and write it all out.

Quill was furious—all the more because he could do nothing. Back from his latest run, he went about his training duties with what he thought was his customary demeanor. He was too practiced to let his expression betray his thoughts, but his students, and peers, were aware that all the humor everyone thought an integral part of him had vanished, and there was a snap in his Fox drills that communicated itself to the fledges, resulting in more effort put in.

Three weeks passed as the fastest long riders relayed Noddy's latest report to Arrow. He brought it immediately to Danet. Neither dismissed their runners as they read and discussed it, so word spread among the royal runners.

Quill came upstairs from a long, hard scrap in the practice yard to find Mnar standing in the middle of the hall at the top of the landing, hands cupping her elbows tight against her body, head bent.

As he'd been expecting the news daily, he said in Old Sartoran, "So you heard about our new form of justice?"

Mnar's chin jerked up. "You knew? And said naught?" It had been years since she'd actually read Old Sartoran. This past decade or two she mostly used it in conversations such as these.

"What could be said?" And then his pent-up feelings sought escape, as he switched back to Marlovan. "Why don't you bring Lineas back? Why is she even *there?* They have trained staff in the north, surely!"

"She's there," a tart voice startled them both, "because I want her there."

Mnar and Quill jerked around as Danet mounted the last couple of steps.

Their hands slapped their chests in salute.

When she saw their distraught expressions, she relented. Of course they'd think of tender Lineas, who was so unfailingly kind, who shied away from violence. "I want her there," she repeated, more gently.

She could see Quill yearning to ask why, but that conversation she was not ready to hold. She might never be. So she turned, saying, "I'll come back later—I can see you're busy." She framed the words so they were not quite orders, but kept them on the other side of that invisible line that they did not cross.

Which was why she trusted them, she thought as she descended to the second floor again. But there were some thoughts she wasn't sharing with anyone.

When she got back to her suite, she found Arrow standing impatiently. "Not another report?" she asked. She needed time to think about what Noddy had written—not the facts, which were grim enough—but what he wasn't saying.

"Yes—no. That is, nothing new. Rat Noth just rode down from Ku Halir. He's downstairs yakking about horses with Bunny right this moment. His report corroborated what the runners say—all summer the east was the quiet again, third year running. Whoever they are, Adranis or not, they've given up."

"If that's true, I salute them for their wisdom," Danet said.

Arrow grinned. "Yeah, but I believe our boys are disappointed. They had so much fun four years ago, following those two companies of armed bravos around, wargaming and drilling where the foreigners couldn't fail to see 'em."

"Just as well," Danet said shortly.

Arrow spun around, coat skirts flaring. He knew better than to admit to Danet that his army was eager for action, after all that training. "Anyway. Young Noth's been promoted to captain, but he's still not got a wife, since Yvanavayir's girl gave him the back of the hand. There have to be some second daughters or cousins to jarl daughters or daughters to captains who didn't get matched at birth?"

Danet considered how to explain the difficulty, but he didn't leave her time. "I'll tell him to come up here so you can fix that." And he was off toward the state wing, his graying horsetail swinging.

He was as good as his word. A young runner appeared at the stable, where Bunny leaned her forearms on a stall, chin on her fingers as she and Rat Noth talked over the newest arrivals at the stable.

It was the same conversation they had every time he turned up at the royal castle. Nothing anyone couldn't overhear. But Bunny knew the language of the body, and had been aware of his shy, tentative interest for at least a year. She sensed that he was more Noth than most Noths, known for being loyal lifelong. She found the idea both intimidating and attractive, and she found his long, lean body very attractive—but she was betrothed to his step-brother, the heir to Feravayir, and word was, the stepbrothers hated each other. Would a dalliance cause political problems?

When the runner appeared with the summons, Bunny couldn't stop herself. "Come by when you have a chance, and see us work the colts."

She watched him go off.

Upstairs, Danet settled on her cushion to await Rat Noth and consider whether or not she ought to explain the situation to him. When she'd first worked out the betrothals, everyone was just a name on paper—most of them under two years old—her motivation to break up old Mathren alliances, and to avoid matching cousins of the first or even second degree. It was a kind of equality.

But now that she had begun to know personalities, there was a different set of considerations for all these loose ends. It wasn't just the Noth boy. Whose family would she disrupt with that spoiled Yvanavayir girl, whose sense of self-importance had deemed it a good idea to write her a long letter describing the type of heir she ought to be matched with? Not the Senelaecs. She could imagine how ill-suited in every way Pony would be for the dashing, laughing young man everyone now called Braids—who didn't have a prospective wife, but who wasn't the heir.

But that left her with two of Arrow's prized young future captains without wives, which raised the question of whether Rat's stepmother, the Jarlan of Feravayir, was going to ask for Bun. Danet still was reluctant to press. The jarlan's second son was living in Sartor (only her stepsons had been sent to the academy), which left Starliss Cassad also waiting. Another loose end. If Danet matched Starliss with Rat Noth, then that acknowledged the jarlan's total disregard for Danet's plans. . . but if she sent Starliss to match with Braids, that still left Rat.

Every decision you make matters. The entire subject gave her a headache.

The rap of heels outside her open door gave her a moment before Rat Noth appeared. He saluted respectfully, then stood there before her, tall, straight as a knife, steel glinting all about him as it hadn't occurred to him to stop and shed his weaponry, but Danet's women had passed him along without comment. They knew who he was, and Fnor and Sage were also well aware of his visits to Bunny whenever he was in the royal city, but said nothing.

Danet took him in. He was unprepossessing to look at, a lean brown figure (much like she was herself, she knew) with narrow eyes and nose and lips.

"The king wants me to find you a wife," she said. "Is there anyone you want to marry?" she asked.

Rat's eyes widened, then his gaze dropped to his hands, as if he'd find a way to explain what he wanted written there on his callused palms.

Danet, seeing his difficulty, attempted to ease the situation. "There are so many of you Noth boys. You're all good at what you do. But the king is interested in you in particular because you've earned his respect."

Rat looked furtively sideways, and shifted from foot to foot. Danet smothered the urge to laugh. He looked so tough, yet his posture reminded her forcibly of the time when Noddy was about four, and had stolen tarts from the kitchen for himself and Connar.

Rat, feeling the steel of the queen's gaze (rightly legendary, he was thinking as the back of his neck began to sweat), mumbled disjointedly, "Lots of us. Yeah. We don't seem to get…" He froze, his throat working.

"Get?" Danet prompted.

Rat turned purple, and Danet began to intuit at least some of the problem—the word 'get' was akin to suggesting sex. And the idea of talking about something that (at least in his mind) was so close to sex, in front of the queen, nearly slayed him with embarrassment.

"You Noths don't seem to have many girls among you," she offered, and his shoulders relaxed incrementally.

"Right," he said, with an apologetic swipe of a one of those sword and bow-hardened hands through the air.

"That's fine, because other families have plenty of girls. I think it all balances out," she said, suppressing the urge to laugh. "If you haven't anyone in mind, there's really no hurry. You're young. Though the Olavayirs tend to marry young, many families wait for years. Keep the thought in mind, and let me know, all right?"

He laid his hand to his heart, then exited with a speed that looked suspiciously like escape.

New Year's Week came and went.

Larkadhe had its own customs—such as plays—and competitions building snow and ice sculptures.

The underground caverns that housed the baths for the city became a social gathering place, complete with vendors selling spice-wine and hot snacks. The hot springs kept the caverns warm, so it wasn't surprising to see people spending a goodly part of their recreational time down there.

Lineas was fascinated by the board games that people brought out. Cards'n'Shards she recognized in three varieties, but others she had never seen before. City as well as castle people strolled about the caverns, not just entertaining each other but also doing business. A chatty older scribe, seeing Lineas looking around the vast space in wonder, told her stories about the past, pointing out the places high overhead where great rocks had scored the ceiling during the tremendous geyser a mysterious mage had raised during the Venn war.

There were few demands for Yvana Hall in this season, and once snow and ice closed the Pass to trade, those few halved. Connar sat in a few times, as he'd promised, but he never did master the intricacies of the ritual, and so, gradually, the brothers drifted back into their accustomed spheres.

Connar soon saw why Nermand said there were no company patrols during the heart of winter: overflow streams were common and wildly dangerous, the snow in places reached over horses' withers, and the blizzards were thick enough so that one couldn't even see the mountains looming overhead.

He loathed Larkadhe, dreading the long months till they could leave for home; by summer he knew he'd be counting the weeks. Every clear day saw him riding out, until word came during a thaw that Tanrid and Fala had had a daughter. Connar told Noddy that he'd ride down to Nevree to congratulate them and see the new addition to the family, as well as exchange news.

He took with him a mixture of experienced Riders and the new recruits sent as replacements for those who'd died at the Battle of Chalk Cliffs, the idea being to give them some seasoning.

It was a relief to have something to do, but Connar had a purpose, though he could not say what he expected to gain from hearing Tarvan's story of Evred and Mathren's death. They arrived at Nevree after floundering through fresh snowfall, and Connar smiled at the new baby, a fat little creature that looked, to him, exactly like every other baby he'd ever seen—but he listened to the fond parents praise each doughy little feature, comparing it to this or that relative. The only feature Connar recognized was the short upper lip that was characteristic in the eagle Olavayirs, though Baby Ranor's wasn't as pronounced as her grandfather's.

He also was taken to admire again the square little son they'd named Jarend, for his grandfather, but whom they called Cricket. This time the child took one look at Connar, and as he did with every new face, screamed. Fala petted and soothed him, and assured Connar that Cricket was truly very good-natured; as Tanrid led Connar away, he said apologetically under his breath that Cricket was good as long as nothing interrupted his routine.

Tanrid took him off to his own rooms, which was far more bearable than pretending an interest in brats. Tanrid asked for Connar's account of the Battle of Chalk Hills, which Connar described succinctly, leaving out his motivation for taking that route.

Tanrid listened all the way to the end, his expression mild as always, then he said, "Matches what Gannan told us. That was a good move, recommending him for promotion. He's very popular at Lindeth."

"He's always been enthusiastic," Connar said.

Tanrid grunted, then looked up. "Why were you so far north? I understand Neit was with you—didn't she tell you that was dangerous territory?"

"Everyone was half-asleep from the festival," Connar said. "It looked like a shorter route on the map." And, to get away from that subject, "Thanks for sending Neit up to Noddy, by the way."

Tanrid's face broke into a real smile, the first real smile of the day, Connar recognized. "I grew up with Neit," Tanrid said. "She's like a sister. Should have been born a boy, if you ask me. Can't you see her winning every competition?" Tanrid touched his sleeve, where the academy boys sewed their golds.

"Ma says girls are going to be in the army," Connar offered.

"Really? I thought that was rumor, because she started the queen's training again. Well, it's a good idea. Very good idea. We could use the likes of Neit up here, captain of a company. She used to captain our 'enemies' in our wargames when we were all young, and she won her share."

The talk then veered into local affairs, but it was clear that Tanrid had something on his mind. When the bell rang for the watch change, calling them to supper, he said, "Why did you brand those Bar Regren prisoners?"

"Because I don't believe they won't come back," Connar said. "I told them if they do, they'll be recognized immediately. We've given out orders they can be killed on sight, and get a dozen golds as a reward."

Tanrid whistled as he led the way out. "That's a sizable reward. You can support a family on that at Lindeth. I trust if anyone shows up to claim it, you'll want to see the body," he remarked as they crossed to the family dining room off the mess hall.

Connar frowned, hating to admit he hadn't thought ahead to enterprising people lying to get the gold. He'd have to demand evidence, if it ever happened.

There followed a dinner that included far too much talk about weddings and babies, as far as Connar was concerned, but Fala seemed to have such things on her mind. At least it was harmless.

Afterward, Connar was free to roam the castle as he liked.

Tarvan, he'd previously found out in casual conversation with Neit, was unsurprisingly Jarend's chamber runner. The jarl's suite was not far from the guest chambers. It was easy to watch for his moment, when Tarvan, a tall, slightly stooped man with a thin light brown queue, entered one of the side halls.

No one else was around, so Connar stepped out from the side hall, and smiled. "Tarvan?"

Tarvan halted, then laid two fingers to his breast. "Connar-Laef?"

"I don't want to keep you. I just have a couple questions. About the past. Maybe you can understand. I'm curious. Everybody gets curious about what happened before."

Tarvan's voice was surprisingly low, and clear, though his long, thin nose would have suggested something high and nasal. "You want to know what I witnessed that day."

"Yes."

Tarvan smoothed a hand over his thinning hair, his gaze up, then down. "There is little to tell. Mard was training me to be a chamber runner. Like I am now. The commander came in, and said a lot of things, angry things. I don't recollect any of it now. Most of it is a blur, except for the things I wish I could forget. Like the look on the commander's face when he killed Evred-Sierlaef, and half cut off his head. I . . . I was hiding behind the door. Looking in the crack, above the lower hinge. Then he killed old Mard, who was near blind. And then the jarl—he wasn't the jarl then, of course. Jarend-Jarl and Anred-Harvaldar came in, you understand, and Mathren said he'd kill them and the jarl punched him. Right here."

Tarvan touched the back of his head, behind his ear. "The commander went down, and the king—the king now, you understand—took up the sword, all bloody, and stabbed the commander. Then he sent me to get Chief Camerend. And he brought Captain Noth, and Chief Camerend kept me safe while everybody ran around. Then it was over. Except they hauled the old gunvaer down, and made me say what I'd seen before the entire castle." He blinked slowly, and waited with habitual patience.

"One punch, eh? That wasn't just a story."

"Just one." He drew a breath, then, "Is that all, Connar-Laef?"

"One more question. I take it you were not a royal runner in training?"

"Oh, no. Garrison. Those royal runner fledges, they had to learn a lot of languages and fast-writing, and the like. I was never good with my letters. But Chief Camerend was very kind to me, I remember that."

"He was kind to us boys, too."

Tarvan smiled briefly, his eyes crinkling.

"Thanks for telling me the story," Connar said, stepped aside, and when Tarvan had vanished around a corner, Connar backed away and ran back down the servants' stairs. Having gotten what he wanted, he intended to issue orders to his escort to be ready to ride out at first light.

He had done his best to cut out Tarvan without drawing attention. It wasn't necessary to hold a secret conversation. If that was even possible, short of locking up the man afterward. It was just that he hated the idea of having to discuss his reasons for delving into the past, a hatred the more violent because of a vague sense of unease, even guilt, for which he blamed Hauth. By forcing that summer conversation on Connar, Hauth had in effect made any thoughts Connar had about the past, or kings, or his birth family, seem like betrayal and treason.

And yet he hadn't told anyone.

Because when Hauth gets dealt with it will be by me, he thought as he reached the ground floor, turned left and right to orient himself, then remembered which way to the stable.

When he opened the back door, he halted at the sight of half a dozen figures standing motionless in the tiny court between the tack room door and the door to the castle proper. In the flickering torchlight he made out gray hair on the front figure. All of them sizable men, most, but not all, older than he was by many years.

Time seemed to suspend as the loyal remainder of Nighthawk Company faced their king, who stood there wary and still, outlined against the snowy courtyard. His height, the fine bones of his face, the easy strength in the contours of muscle shaped by the coat—he could be Mathren again, except for the black hair. A Mathren who had faced battle, who had charged straight into the enemy, killing at least a dozen, possibly more.

This was the king Lanrid should have been.

The foremost among them, tall, hard-boned, pale-haired, slowly raised his right hand, formed a fist, and struck it against his heart. The teenage boy at his side also struck fist to chest, his wide, unblinking gaze striking cold then heat to shock Connar's nerves with its intensity.

Thump, thump, the others followed suit. Then—before anyone could speak, the men melted away into the shadows in all directions, and were gone, leaving Connar stunned: that was the salute to a king.

He shook off his reaction, crossed into the tack room, and then ran upstairs to where guest Riders were housed. Though his mind was still stuck back in that doorway, he issued his orders, and then found his way back up to the guest suite.

And another sleepless night, all the more frustrating because what he'd heard that day was nothing new. Yet every time he tried to doze, he saw those men with their fists against their chests.

Of course they were old Nighthawk Company men, paid for in secret by Mathren robbing the very kingdom he was supposed to protect. Plans knocked down by one blow, because Mathren the Murderer was too arrogant to consider Uncle Jarend a threat.

The single clang of the hour before the morning watch finally reverberated through the stone. With relief, he gave up trying to sleep and went down to bathe and change.

When he reached the stable, Cousin Tanrid was there, waiting beside Fish, who held the reins to Connar's mount.

As Connar approached, Tanrid met him. "Did you get everything you wanted from Tarvan?" he asked.

Of course he knew about the conversation. "Yes."

"Good. He believes that the family has a right to hear his witness, but for his sake I wanted to tip you a hint that he really hates talking about that. So if Noddy needs to hear it as well, can you share what you heard with him?"

"If he asks, I will," Connar promised, and moved toward his horse.

Tanrid followed and glanced around the courtyard, his expression reflective. "There are a lot of people in the kingdom who think all of us Olavayirs are worthless, eagle or dolphin, no difference. But Uncle Anred has been a good king, all things considered. The more because he wasn't raised to it. That's one thing my da keeps repeating."

Connar shot him a glance, wondering if this blather was going to lead to that unnerving exhibition outside the stable. But surely those former Nighthawk men would have posted watch.

Tanrid went on, "Tarvan—the old days—some might remember the old treaty, but as far as Da is concerned, there's no need for it anymore."

The old treaty. *That* was on his mind?

" . . . as for Noddy, he won't be the type they sing ballads about, but he'll be good, too. You know him better than anyone. Know he's got a good heart, and he's conscientious. Tell him, when I'm jarl and he's king, nothing will change. No need for any more treaties. I'll always back him."

"I will." Connar swung himself into the saddle.

Tanrid stepped back and Connar clucked to the animal, who danced a little. *When I'm jarl and he's king.* Yeah, nothing ambiguous about that.

Connar raised his hand in salute and rode out.

TEN

Midnight, in Yvanavayir's great parade court.

Torchlight gleamed on the tears streaking Eaglebeak's face. He stepped forward to do the spell of Disappearance over the jarl, and began in a hoarse, grief-deep voice to sing the Hymn to the Fallen. Everyone joined in, full-throated and impassioned, for the old jarl had been well liked.

Then villagers, runners, and servants left in silence. As the family stood around the now empty bier, watching the Jarl's personal effects burn, Pony Yvanavayir was already thinking ahead.

She had to. She was very sorry Da was gone, but at least it had been peaceful—he just didn't wake up that morning. He was now beyond worry, leaving her facing a bleak future, all because of that *stupid* queen, Danet-Gunvaer.

It was she who had sicced Chelis Cassad onto them, and it was she who had ignored the letter that Pony had worked on for a couple of days, carefully explaining that, as a jarl's only daughter who had had to command the household in her mother's place from a young age, she was best suited to marry the heir to a jarlate.

But two months, three, five, a year had passed without even a return letter, much less notice of an appropriate betrothal. Then *years.* Maybe that stupid queen was spiteful enough to have listened to gossip. Manther and Eaglebeak had both pointed out how Pony had managed to make herself into a kingdom-wide jest after snatching her own brother's lover.

Pony stood between her brothers, staring into the flames as she thought over the past five years, which she'd spent riding the border as scout captain. When she wasn't riding Yvanavayir's borders, she worked on her archery, which kept her out of the castle and away from that swanking horseapple Chelis. It was funny, sort of, that she would probably win *all* the golds for shooting if she went to the royal city again, but she was too old for those stupid games.

Now it was winter of a new year, and Da was gone. Dry-eyed, she watched the last of Da's few belongings glow in embers, as Eaglebeak stood beside her, working Da's battered old shield in his hands. Da had never gained any kind of accolade, but he had been loved by everyone, and the boys wanted to put that old shield in the family's Hall of Ancestors. All very well—and watch Chelis's future brats take it down to make space for their stupid academy awards, or something equally inane, Pony thought sourly.

She swung her head, glaring in the direction of that needle-nosed snot, Chelis Cassad, now truly jarlan instead of merely acting.

Life, Pony knew, was going to be *horrible,* stuck in the castle all winter with that obnoxious Cassad interloper changing everything just because she could. It would be months before Pony could take off to ride Yvanavayir's borders, and not come back except to swap one set of clothes for another. She suspected Chelis would soon go on the attack, and Eaglebeak, though he was now jarl, would decamp rather than defend her against the enemy. Manther, home on leave for New Year's Week, wouldn't be any better.

The embers dulled to ash, and Da's old runners slowly began to sweep that up, to be carried to the kitchen garden. Those who'd chosen something of Da's went inside with their keepsake. Pony stood there empty handed. She didn't want any of his things. She wanted *him* back, already missing his gravelly voice, his fond smile.

When the parade court stones were swept bare, and her toes numbed in her boots, she went inside and to bed. Tired as she was, she couldn't sleep. When dawn blued the windows at last, she rose, bathed, and went to breakfast, where she discovered The Enemy lying in wait.

Chelis said, "Fareas, today we're shifting all the furnishings out of the jarl suite."

"Don't call me that," Pony snapped.

"Fareas is your name. Your brothers use it."

"I hate them for it," Pony snapped back.

"Pony is a nickname for a ten-year-old," Chelis said unwisely, but she, too, had had little sleep, with Eaglebeak sobbing and restless beside her all night—the cap to five years of keeping her lips tight while the jarl's daughter swanked about all winter under her father's fond eye, as the place got shabbier and shabbier.

"I don't care," Pony snapped, tossing her braids back in that habit of hers that made Chelis's teeth clench to the aching point. "Da gave it to me." To her horror, Pony felt tears constricting her throat, fought them back and let the anger loose. "You don't even understand grief."

"I—" Chelis looked away, then back. "I'm not going to talk about who I might have lost. I know everyone deals with grief in their own way. Grieve as you will . . ." *When you become jarlan you must start as you would carry on,* her aunt had instructed her.

Chelis stiffened her spine and firmed her voice. "But tomorrow at dawn, you're going to take charge of the household linens."

Pony stared, aghast. "Me? I hate needlework."

"Everybody hates needlework," Chelis retorted. "But it needs doing. Most of the household quilts are scarcely worth ripping apart for armor stuffing. Your father wouldn't touch them because your mother brought them from

Tlen, I know, but some of those were old when she came here forty-some years ago. Everything in this castle is threadbare, if not falling apart. That is going to change this winter, so it's done before the riding season begins."

"Our linens are fine," Pony said—though weakly. Her own winter quilt had thin spots that she had to cover with wool scarves now that winter had set in. But she was used to that. Moreover, she would set it aside when she chose, and not because the interloper decided to throw commands around.

"Yours could use some reinforcing," Chelis stated. "Before you say you don't know the stitches, I'll point out that anybody can learn, and by the way, why is it that a household this size is so short-staffed, without even a steward in charge of linens?"

She crossed her arms, and when Pony didn't answer—she'd gotten rid of that self-important old trouble-maker when she was sixteen, the first of a stream of impertinent and argumentative servants—Chelis said, "Exactly."

"She was a bonehead," Pony muttered.

"Once we finish the jarl suite, we're tackling rebuilding the bakehouse, which has been put off too many years. If you don't want to do the linens, then you can do stonework at the bakehouse. But starting tomorrow, everybody is going to work. Moping isn't going to bring the jarl back."

"I'll do what I want," Pony declared. "When I want. I ran this household *fine* from the time I was a child, until you stuck your nose in. And I say, we need a time for proper mourning."

Chelis said, "I warned you."

"And I warn *you*." Pony flipped her braids back. "See how stupid that sounds? Talk about ten-year-olds! What are you going to do, challenge me to a knife fight? Do it," she added, knowing she would win.

"No," Chelis said, eyes narrowed. "There's too much work, and no time for either of us to waste recovering from knife wounds." She got up and walked out.

Hah, coward, Pony thought, sitting back and reaching for another honey-biscuit—as usual hard as a rock on the outside and doughy inside. She bit into it defiantly.

The next morning, it was still dark when torchlight flared in Pony's bedroom, working into her dreams. She opened her eyes, heard the clang of the watch bell in the distance, then turned over to bury her head under her pillow.

A sudden crash and bang right overhead caused her to nearly catapult from the bed.

She jerked upright, to discover three of the house runners standing in a row banging biscuit pans together. A fourth, with a grim smile, scraped the edge of a knife on a piece of metal, bringing forth a hideous metallic screech that caused Pony to clap her hands over her ears.

Chelis appeared in the doorway. "Closer," she said.

The runners crowded around the bed, banging away within arm's reach of Pony's head.

Pony tried to lie back, but the runners knelt on her bed, banging away with increased vigor. "All right," she shouted. "Stop! I'll get up."

Chelis held out a sandglass. "You have this long to get bathed and dressed. If you're not down at linens by the time the last sand trickles through, Pan and Mlis will come into the baths and scrub you, then dress you." She indicated the two biggest women in Yvanavayir's castle.

Pony didn't have to look at those obdurate faces to know that they'd do it. She'd made no effort to hide how she despised them both—one a big, awkward stonemason's brat, the other a mouthy village hire—ever since they quit as her runners after the Ghost Fath fiasco. Though Pony knew she was strong—much stronger than Chelis—she wouldn't be able to stand against those two.

After a long, hideous day of sorting through piles and piles of tattered linens, she longed for escape. Manther would soon escape. He had orders to report to the new garrison at Ku Halir. Of course. The boys always got out of every kind of scut work, riding around looking tough in the stupid army.

Ku Halir.

On the same road as Tlen, where Ma had come from.

While she was turning over ideas in her mind, elsewhere in the castle, Eaglebeak confronted his wife. "I know Pony is hard to live with, but at least she's gone riding the borders most of the year."

"When she feels like it," Chelis said flatly.

"Well, yes . . ." Eaglebeak sighed.

"This place is a wreck," Chelis stated, arms crossed. "In respect to your father I've kept silent for *five years* while she swanks around like a queen, chasing off the servants, though the place is rotting about our ears. She's big and strong. Since we can't get help to stay, she can work like the rest of us while she's here. But I need your help to make her do it."

Eaglebeak knew that Chelis had the high ground there. Manther had said privately right after his arrival that each time he came home on leave, that the smell of mildew always made him sneeze, until he got accustomed. And it was getting worse.

So Eaglebeak tried maneuvering. "Fact is, there is nobody in the world who can bicker longer and harder until she gets her way than my sister. I've got enough to do. Far as I'm concerned, she's women's business."

He retreated to his own lair, and shut the door.

Husband and wife were not speaking when they all met at supper. Until Pony surprised them all by announcing, "I've decided to go visit my Tlen cousins. I can ride south with Manther." And glared from her brothers to Chelis, clearly squaring up for a fight.

Eaglebeak sighed, looking away.

Chelis said in a *good riddance* tone, "I'll help you pack."

When Manther came down to the stable a week later, prepared to ride to Ku Halir, Pony was ready.

Mather eyed her as he eased his gloves over hands scraped from shifting stones in the now-mostly rebuilt bakehouse. He said, "I want to get there fast. Before the next blizzard. If you slow me down, you're on your own."

She snorted with contempt. "You bumbling lancers with your big horses are more likely to slow *me* down."

He gave the sign to ride out. They and their escort—the Riders the Yvanavayirs owed the king for a season's rotation—exited the gates into air so cold the hairs in their noses chilled. The world had turned into a thousand shades of greyish white, under a low sky the color of milk.

As soon as they were through the village, Pony began complaining about Chelis, the outsider who was changing everything just because she could, haloo laloo.

Manther was quiet by nature. He'd gone through his trouble-making stage as a teen, but had outgrown it, preferring to avoid exactly the sort of argument Pony always seemed to get into. So in recent years he'd tended to avoid her, arranging his liberty for when he knew she'd be out riding the southern border. He'd asked for New Year's Week liberty only because Eaglebeak had sent a message along with a passing runner that Da was getting weaker.

Manther reflected on the long ride ahead, and cut into Pony's tirade, which showed no signs of flagging. "She's been here five, six *years*. And she's right."

"What?" Pony caught herself up. "Right about what?"

"Every time I come home on leave, the place looks shabbier. You at home never saw it because you don't leave."

"I leave for weeks at a time during the riding season," Pony retorted. "It's good to come home and find things exactly the same. Da said so, too."

"Da did like everything the way it was when he was young, but he's no longer here," Manther said, distracted by how his breath froze and began to fall before vanishing. Weird, how a person could make their own snow. But it didn't last. "You don't like improving things because you don't like *her*."

"No. I don't. And I don't see why I should have to put up with—"

He cut in once more. "Eaglebeak," he said, "does."

And Eaglebeak was the new jarl. He let that sink in, and when she opened her mouth to complain about Eaglebeak, he added, "I don't want to hear it."

She scowled between her horse's ears. This was going to be a dreary trip.

They traveled straight south, the sun always behind them. They made excellent time to Tlen, which Manther had stopped at often when he was under Sneeze Ventdor during the early days of the King's Army's patrol of the Nelkereth Plains.

Their aunt looked in surprise at Pony, who stared back equally surprised. Aunt Tdan looked so much like Ma! But her expression was unsettlingly different as she said, "Welcome. Your uncle is at the horse stud. You can meet him when he gets back. You'll find Owlet at the back barn, and Hibern inside."

Pony had two girl cousins her own age among the Tlens, Hibern and Chelis, the latter known as Owlet. Both earnest horse girls when young, and hardened by seasons of patrolling the east, these cousins were not much to look at, but they were first-rate archers and riders. They had competed hard against Pony at the Victory Day games; Pony thought them dull and homely.

But she forced a smile now, and said, "I'll go find them."

She had grown up in an enormous castle rebuilt almost two centuries ago to match the one in the royal city. To her eyes, Tlen looked like a paltry outpost, its four walls cluttered by a complication of scrub-wood and brick cottages thatched by sedge from the plains. These were built alongside the inner walls, crowding the center square, which could barely be called a stable yard much less a proper parade ground.

She walked into the main building, only two stories, and was greeted by the smell of boiled cabbage. It was very clear that the work rooms lay directly underneath the bedchambers, instead of in a different wing. Clearly all the smells and noise traveled up the stairs.

Goggle-eyed Owlet didn't seem any gladder to see Pony than Pony was to see her, but she spoke words of welcome in her stuffed-nose whine, adding, "The guest rooms have the Halivayirs in them, after Thistle's wedding to Garid. You can bunk in with either me or Hibern, or in the runner dorm out at West House, that is, the cottage directly adjacent the stable. There's three extra beds right now, with three out riding."

Pony hid a grimace, loathing the thought of sleeping in someone else's bed. Even on the ride she had her own bedroll. But the alternative was to slink back to Yvanavayir and Chelis Cassad's tyranny.

She forced a smile. "I can sleep anywhere," she said. "So Garid is married now! What about you two?"

"We both wanted to wait for twenty-five," Owlet said. With a sidelong look out of her big, round, watery blue eyes, "I don't relish going all the way to Jayad Hesea. I'll never get back for a visit, it's so far."

Already Owlet's whiny voice irritated Pony, but she forced another smile. "Well, at least you've got a couple years. But Hibern is almost twenty-five, right?"

"Yes, and the Marlovayirs want her to come to them this spring."

Owlet went on about how empty life would be without Hibern, they did everything together . . . Pony stopped listening, glad she had never been burdened with a sister.

That lasted for a month.

Owlet did everything Cousin Hibern told her, and chicken-brained Thistle, though she'd be jarlan someday, fell right in behind. It would have been fine—so Pony told herself as she went to sleep at night—if Cousin Hibern's orders had made sense. But when Pony ventured to give her hints about how they warmed up the horses at Yvanavayir, for example, Cousin Hibern looked at her with that heavy chin and those flat eyes as she said, "My mother likes it this way."

Cousin Hibern was also a snitch. Later that night, Aunt Tdan cut Pony out after dinner, and with that same flat look, said, "Hibern knows how we do things here."

"I just had a suggestion," Pony said sweetly.

Too sweetly. The jarlan's dark eyes narrowed. "Fareas, I've heard all about your antics. And I can imagine why you're really here. We never turn away family, but if you live with us, you follow orders. You don't give 'em. Hear me?"

Pony was forced to say, "Yes, Aunt Tdan," as if she were twelve years old.

"There's a reason we warm 'em slow. These here are problem horses. Either they had a strain, or they've come in with bad training. Something. The rest of you keep your animals over winter, but remember, most of our herds are wintering out on the plains. We won't go out to catch 'em until second thaw, and until then, we're slow and careful with these ones. Hear me?" she said again.

"Yes, Aunt Tdan," Pony said submissively, hating this proof that she was at the bottom of the chain of command—exactly as she would have been if she'd married that dullard Rat Noth. That meant she got the scut jobs no one else wanted.

Manther was long gone by then, of course. Riders had been to Ku Halir and back several times in that month, and Pony got the impression of a castle town full of young men looking for fun as they waited out the winter.

Men who weren't married.

As she exercised the young colts on the longe line one morning—the tedious, boring way—shivering in the bitter wind, she reflected on the fact that she was on her own as far as finding the right marriage was concerned. And it had to be marriage. Favorites could be found anywhere; most important was that as the daughter of a jarl, she should be marrying a future jarl. Right now she was the perfect age, but she needed to work fast, as all her peers were marrying.

And Ku Halir was full of young men.

While it was true that all the heirs were betrothed, and most her age and older were married, many of the younger ones weren't. If she couldn't seduce some silly youth of twenty or twenty-two into throwing off a betrothal to someone he hadn't even met, then she deserved to dwindle into an old runner for hire, which was her only alternative to marriage, other than learning some dull trade. And she did *not* deserve *that!*

The disadvantage of a younger heir was that he was likelier to have a younger father, which meant some tough jarlan like Aunt Tdan still reigning

—but that was a better future than having to hire herself out. It was ridiculous for a Yvanavayir to even consider such a fate, like some no-family drudge.

The next time the jarlan spoke of sending a runner to Ku Halir, Pony said sweetly, "I can run the message and save her a trip. I'd like to see my brother before spring riding."

No one complained.

Pony packed her gear up and left.

When she arrived in Ku Halir, she looked past the fine new castle built of the honey-colored stone from the nearby hills, and the colorful Iascan town curving along the lakeshore, to the promising sight of young men everywhere.

She rode to the castle with the jarlan's message, just to discover that there was nowhere here for her to bunk, except in the upper dormitory with the teenage stable prentices. Which would effectively make her a stable hand, unless she joined the bottom tier of runners.

She handed off the message at the scribe desk and left. Where to stay? She discounted Manther at the outset. He was a mere riding captain, which meant his quarters wouldn't be much better than those stable dorms.

She rode to the biggest inn. "Have you rooms? My own room, no dorms."

"Of course," the woman behind the counter said. "That'll cost ya three a day, including stabling for that big bay of yours. Five if you want meals, morning and evening watch bells."

Three what? Pony understood the concept of money—her Da had given her coins to spend in the royal city when she attended the Victory Day Games—but otherwise, she had never dealt with coinage. All she understood was trade in work and in kind.

But she had heard Manther talking once, and said with calm assurance, "I am the only Yvanavayir daughter. You can send to them to be paid."

The woman's pursed mouth eased at the mention of Yvanavayir. She said in a much lighter voice, "Very well."

Pony soon looked around a tiny chamber off the stair landing, not much bigger than the bed and trunk. But it had a window overlooking the frozen lake, and she had the room all to herself.

Best of all, Chelis would *hate* it when the inn people sent for the money—yet she'd feel honor bound to pay family debts. At least for a while. If Pony had to, she'd sell her bay, who was fast and beautifully trained. She hated the thought of that, and anyway, how long would that buy her?

"I just have to get what I want before that happens," Pony said aloud as she opened her gear bag and shook out her second robe before hanging it on the clothes peg.

And so she set out that very night to survey the field of campaign.

At first glimpse, everyone was about her age, mostly male faces above gray winter coats. But there were plenty of Iascans around, wearing bright colors even in cloaks, capes, and coats.

Pony walked a short way through the mushy snow, a frigid wind chilling her ears, then retreated to the inn's common room, which took up most of the ground floor.

A weed of a girl presented herself at the table. "I can help you. Everybody calls me Jam. Just ask for me." Her pale frizz bobbed about her head as she spoke, and she proudly tugged at the shoulder ties of her new apron, entrusted to her when she turned thirteen. "There are three dishes to choose from if you want dinner: fish, of course, fresh-caught at our hole in the lake, long-rice and hot bean-mash, or corn-chowder with preserved peppers."

Pony said, "I'll have the fish. Is this an old town, then?"

"Oh, yes! It's *old* Iascan," Jam said proudly. "We're a trade town on the crossroad, just as big as Hesea Spring. Some say bigger, because we get trade from over the mountain." She waved eastward. "Everybody likes to stop here summers, because it's nice and cool, and when it isn't, you can boat on the lake, and swim, and buy things." She said the last with a hopeful air. "Ever since they started building up the old post into that big castle, we've had *great* business."

Pony nodded, too ignorant of Iascan ways to realize she was supposed to offer a tinklet or two for the information. When Jam waited, looking expectantly, Pony made a little whisking motion with her fingers, figuring the girl was slow. "Run along," Pony said, pleasantly enough. "I've been in the saddle since sunup, and I'm hungry."

Jam went away to get her order, came back, and dumped it down without another word.

Pony shrugged off the girl's sudden rudeness. She was not here to chat with children. She ate, listening to the Iascan players on three instruments, two wind and one string. Occasionally people got up and danced, but she didn't recognize any of the dances. Tired from the long ride, she retired early.

The next morning she walked out. Though winter was beginning to wane, the inner curve of the lake was still was frozen, and there were all kinds of winter games.

The sun rimmed the distant mountains still, casting long shadows. Everywhere colored lanterns hung, reflecting in the icicles hanging from eaves.

She spotted a clothier that had ready-made robes hanging in the windows, Iascan style as well as Marlovan. She was tempted by the lovely Iascan colors, but she did not want to be taken for one. She found a silken robe in Yvanavayir sun-yellow, edged with silver, and ordered it to be remade in Marlovan style—open front, and the sleeves tubes instead of voluminous and tied up with ribbons. Then she took a long walk, determined to discover where the captains and above went during their liberty time.

Pony had never been beautiful, but she carried herself as if she were, and she had thick, glossy wheat-gold hair with braid loops that reached her shoulder blades.

She walked like a Marlovan as she examined every shop, eatery, and inn. The only places she skipped were the pleasure houses without entertainment, as any fellow who went to one would be looking for sport, not a wife. The houses with music spilling out meant people went there to talk, flirt, dance. She walked through the two from which drums rumbled in counterpoint, and male voices rose in the galloping rhythm of ballads. Both of these houses were filled with mere Riders, none of them with captains' flashes on their right sleeve, so she walked out again.

Her first day she considered a scouting foray. Her second day, she picked up her remade Yvanavayir robe, which she could wear at nights over her best linen shirt and riding trousers, with her good sash tied round her waist. When she spotted Jam, she said, "I want my bedding straightened. My travel robe is on the hook. Get it laundered."

And she walked out, leaving Jam staring after her, heart clanging, as she said later, like ten pails in a well.

Pony had already forgotten her as she began her hunt.

She was not the only hunter.

Long-time residents and travelers who noticed new arrivals and patterns of behavior spotted Pony. She made it easy—it never occurred to her to be anything but what she was, the only daughter of Yvanavayir House.

After about a week, during which she continued to issue orders to Jam whenever she saw her, thinking nothing of demanding extra services, word spread that Castle Inn was hosting a bonfire in celebration of the first real thaw of the year.

Jam's two older brothers filled the square with torches on poles. The neighboring shops, knowing that the bonfire would draw extra custom, kept their doors open late and hung lanterns from their eaves. Servants from all the houses united in sweeping the brickwork clean. Fire sticks were brought out of every house and laid in the center to lay in the bonfire lattice.

Musicians showed up, and of course hand drums. Iascan songs traded off with Marlovan, people getting up to dance around the fire. Pony wore her yellow silk, prowling around looking for newly arrived captains, who were likeliest to be related to jarls.

When she paused to get a spiced wine to drink, she was startled by a voice, "Will you dance with me?"

The man said it in accented Marlovan. But no Marlovan man would ask that. She turned her head to say no, and paused, because the man who addressed her was very, very good-looking, about her age or maybe a year or two older. Even his fine, well-spaced eyes smiled. She had a weakness for cheek dimples—that wretch Ghost Fath had those—and here, they were very fine specimens, under defined cheekbones above an equally fine jawline.

The mouth . . . her gaze was drawn to well-cut lips as he said, "My Marlovan is unintelligible?"

She said in Iascan, "All I know are Marlovan dances."

"Ah! And you do not dance together. What I think is the shame of a lifetime."

Her lip curled. "We dance to watch each other. And drum for each other, of course."

"Those drums, I can see the attraction. The beat gets in the blood. But Iascan dance, that can heat the blood as well. Come! Set that down. No one will disturb it. Permit me to show you."

It had been three years since her last lover. She didn't mind a dally, though she mustn't let it interfere with her search, as she knew that Chelis was very likely to send back a note with payment that there were to be no more coins sent.

She shrugged, intrigued. "All right."

He beckoned her to the edge of the group, and raised his hand. It was as well-shaped as his face, and his body in its high-collared long tunic slit up the sides, trousers tucked into boot tops. "Palm to palm," he said. "You must learn to sense the other's movement if you are not to stumble, or draw apart. It is very intimate," he added.

It was, once she got used to the awkwardness of attempting to match steps with someone else. But the steps were simple enough, once you caught onto the pattern, and it was a new, intriguing sensation to feel that warm palm against hers, and to look up at that fire-highlighted face smiling back at her. If he didn't speak, she was thinking, he could pass for Marlovan, with that long corn-silk hair (nearly as pretty as hers!) queued back in the manner of runners.

When that dance ended, it was the Marlovans' turn, of course a male dance, since most of the people gathered were male. She returned to her spice wine to find it had already cooled, the spices forming an unpleasant film on the top.

She looked at it in disgust, then turned to find Handsome at her shoulder, holding out a fresh cup. Well. This was pleasant!

They got over the boring questions. She said she was traveling, and had a brother in the garrison; he, traveling to see the world, was caught by a snowstorm and ended up staying, and trying to learn Marlovan while there. When he tried out his Marlovan in a heavily accented, stilted sentence or two, she corrected him with well-meaning condescension, which he accepted with gratifying thanks.

"It is a difficult language," he said.

"Difficult!" She laughed. "At least we no longer write in runes!"

"Runes!" he exclaimed.

"Well, that was centuries and centuries ago. None of us can read them now. They were mostly decorations on old tapestries, and after the war in the last century, when the Venn attacked, a lot of those were burned. We have one at Yvanavayir much too fine to burn, but it no longer hangs in the Hall of Ancestors. After the war, my great-great grandmother put it in the best guest chamber."

"Yvanavayir," he repeated, eyes wide. "You are from a distinguished family! There is much I could learn from you."

Who doesn't like being in the position of superior knowledge, especially when the other person is attractive?

She talked about the language for a while, dredging up what she could remember from lessons she'd yawned over. It was pleasant, but she still had her search to plan, and so she finally said, "It's getting late, and colder."

"Will I see you again?" he asked.

Well, that was gratifying, too. She wouldn't let him take up too much of her attention, but she could always find time for dalliance with a handsome man. "Call me Pony," she said. "My given name is only popular with old women. Pony Yvanavayir. And you?"

"Call me Lored."

"Larid?" she repeated, more used to Marloven naming patterns, Garid, Darid, Jarid.

"That will do. I would very much like to hear more about the famous Yvanavayirs. I've always wondered what is life like for your first families."

"I've things to do during the day. Meet me tomorrow evening," she said with a pleasant sense of anticipation, "and I can tell you as much as you want to hear." That would give her a full day for her search.

"I'll be here," he promised.

ELEVEN

In Larkadhe, winter had arrived early, and spring was late, at least for those used to less mountainous climes. Restless again, at first melt Connar rode down to Lindeth to meet Tanrid at Commander Nermand's garrison, in order to map out the patrols for the spring.

They hadn't even begun yet when someone bawled up the stairwell, "Grass!"

From front gate to inner chambers, runners and servants made way, passing the word "Grass."

Neit had made a grass run bringing back the king's corroboration of Noddy's judgment in the Bar Regren case, and here was another grass run scarcely months after.

Nermand, Connar, Tanrid and their attendants fell silent as the red-eyed, filthy royal runner stumbled in. Connar barely recognized Quill as the latter offered a small pouch of silk to Connar, saying, "Anred-Harvaldar charged me to deliver these words." And somehow he even sounded like Da as he recited, "Connar, you now speak with my Voice. You are to lay Jendas Yenvir by the heels, and secure Halivayir."

Stunned, Connar slid his fingers into the pouch, feeling the golden chevron, called an arrow, that only a commander could wear. It meant he could summon any captains to execute his orders. Only a garrison commander—with his two golden arrows on his shoulder—and the king or king's commander who rode to war with three golden arrows—could gainsay him.

Happiness ripped through Connar with all the force of a wildfire, to dim again when he remembered the rest of the message.

Halivayir? The smallest jarlate?

Quill now held out a sealed scroll. Everyone watched in silence as Connar unrolled it, thinking, *You kept your promise, Da.* He read the scrawled words written in Arrow's familiar hand. The urge to laugh for sheer joy doused before the reality before him. This was his first true command, and he had to be successful.

He looked up into faces who had witnessed that flash of joy. But the words that Connar spoke were a shock. "Yenvir and his brigands attacked Halivayir. Killed the jarl and most of his family. Stick, we're to take our entire company. Commander Nermand, Lindeth is to make a wider ring search covering the west, in case they try to slip this way." Connar handed the scroll to the commander, who glanced at it then handed it back.

"Halivayir?" Tanrid exclaimed. "What would they want there?"

That was a rhetorical exclamation, unanswerable. Everyone knew that Jendas Yenvir was a horse thief. And out of all the northern jarlates, Halivayir, with its hilly environment, was the least known for raising and training horses. Halivayir's main products were its stone quarries, and wool.

But why didn't matter. What did matter was that the prospective dull spring routine had suddenly changed. "Let's ride for Larkadhe," Connar said to Stick, and they clattered out, calling for their horses.

Commander Nermand said, "Royal runner, you know the rule: you get a week's liberty after a grass run. Tomorrow is Restday. Enjoy the town."

Quill blinked, forcing his attention back to the commander. "I'd like to take it at Larkadhe, if there's no objection," he said.

"None. Go catch some rest. I'll have a report ready for the king when you waken. That way you can ride straight south at the end of your week."

When Connar and Stick arrived back at Larkadhe, they left their sweating horses to the stable hands and ran into the garrison, fetching up in the map room. Ghost, alerted by the wall sentries, awaited them, with a pair of scouts in case they were needed.

Connar explained tersely, then added, "We don't know how long it's been. Let's assume they rode out hot after their attack. How far can they get from Halivayir? That's our target."

Easiest would be if the brigands ran west along the river, which would mean running straight into Tanrid's regular border patrol along the north bank, and Tyavayir's on the south. That would be fastest, but most dangerous. Most likely they'd gone north into ever higher mountains, until eventually they reached Idego and the north coast. East would take them through less daunting mountainous, wooded terrain, but straight into Yvanavayir's formidable Riders. South, toward ever-vigilant Tyavayir, Senelaec, and Ku Halir Garrison.

"We'll spread a net as we ride," Connar said. "But if we don't meet up with them, I think we're going to have to go into the mountains."

Stick grimaced. They hadn't trained for searching in heavily forested, hilly land, where brigands might know every tree and rock. Couldn't be helped.

When Stick turned up his hand in acceptance, Connar said to Ghost, "You'll run the outer perimeter of our net, in case they did venture into river land. You know that territory above Tyavayir, right?"

Ghost's palm flicked upward.

"We'll split once we reach the outpost here," Connar tapped the map, "and we'll go into the hills while you take your company to Halivayir. Clean up whatever you find, and hold it."

Ghost ran his hand through his nearly white hair, suppressing a sigh. He wished to be in on the chase, but he knew Halivayir.

Connar turned to the scouts. "Warn the posts we're running saddle to saddle, coming in hot. Have horses ready."

The scouts departed, grabbing always-ready gear bags on their way out. They departed on their own version of the grass ride to alert the outposts.

The next morning, under showery skies, Quill rode back to Larkadhe as the rain steadily increased. The previous day he'd stayed only long enough to discover Connar was at Lindeth, then rode straight there.

Now he walked slowly up the back stair of Larkadhe's castle, exhaustion weighing every limb as he took off his dripping hooded cloak. Though he'd gotten some sleep, it was not nearly enough.

He found the runners all waiting in the alcove off the landing where they congregated when not on duty. As a young runner in training silently held out a hand to take the wet cloak, Neit said, "We were hoping you'd stop back here. What can you tell us?"

He glanced around, repeated the king's orders, then said, "Where's Lineas?"

Vanadei glanced up from repairing a rip in Noddy's coat. "Probably in her room, since there's no Yvana Hall today. I'll take you there." He folded up the tunic, thinking, *And you can tell us both what's really going on.*

Lineas, as it happened, was writing a letter to Quill. At the sight of him at the door she dropped her pen, spattering ink across her paper, and leaped up with a happy cry.

No one came up that stairway unless looking for her, but Vana shut the door behind him, and since Lineas only had the little low table and its mat, the trunk, and the bed, she sat on the trunk and let them seat themselves. Vana dropped onto the neatly made bed with the complete unselfconsciousness of someone who has never given a thought to who slept there. Quill, consciously turning his attention away from that bed, opted for the mat.

"Week's liberty," Quill signed in Hand.

Lineas's smile was brief, her gaze steady and concerned. "So you were writing to me these past weeks on a grass run? Why didn't you tell me to wait until you arrived?"

Vanadei side-eyed him as Quill shrugged, his fingers expressive of flippancy. "I can read in the saddle."

"But you were writing, too! How could you have time?" And when he lifted a shoulder, smiling easily, she sensed something he would not say. She was puzzled, but too scrupulous to persist, certain it had something to do with secret orders. After all, wasn't he shortly to take Camerend's place as chief of the royal runners?

So she shifted the subject from personal to general. "Is there any other news?" She reached down beside the trunk in order to brandish her golden notecase.

Quill signed, "No. We don't have any royal runners at Halivayir. In fact, I don't remember any of us ever being sent there. We know nothing more than anyone else."

Vanadei rubbed his chin. "What does Camerend say?"

"He's in Darchelde, dealing with jarl affairs. He's as puzzled as anyone. Speaking of whereabouts. Nadran-Sierlaef?"

"He was invited to take Restday drum with the glaziers, and judge the mastery projects."

Quill's brows lifted. "He knows something about glass?"

Vana chortled as Lineas smothered a laugh. "He was assured that all he has to do is make an appearance and hand out a few compliments, because of course nothing short of perfection would be accepted as a master work, so there aren't any surprises by the time the project is complete."

"He loves glass," Lineas added, her long fingers expressive of her own pleasure. "Especially the colored kinds. They have so much of it here in the north. They not only makes it into cups and bowls, they put it into windows!"

Quill said, "It seems he's done well here."

"Yes," Vana and Lineas both signed, looked at one another, and smiled.

Vana added, "Larkadhe likes him. And at least half the household now talks in Hand on Restday, just because he does it."

"How long can you stay?" Lineas asked. "There are so many wonderful things to show you. I'll wager you never ventured beyond the baths in the caves."

"It's true, I didn't, except for visiting the windharps," Quill responded. "How about this? You show me some glass windows, and in my turn, as soon as we get a clear night, I'll make transfer tokens for us to go up to the old atan platform, so we can listen to the windharps under the stars."

He remembered that they weren't alone, and turned to Vana, forcing enthusiasm into his voice. "Sound good?"

Vana had been watching. He knew Quill, who'd even as teen never talked about his private feelings. But Vana saw the intensity of Quill's gaze, and heard a note in his voice that was unfamiliar. "Not me," he said easily. "Do you realize it's still winter up there?"

"We can bundle up." Lineas smiled his way, transparent as a spring in her friendliness and generosity. "It will be wonderful!"

Poor sod, Vana thought toward his bond-brother. I hope you get over her soon—this can go nowhere good.

He waved Lineas off with a careless gesture. "I don't find the windharps nearly as compelling as you do. You can keep your cold and your moaning stone."

Quill pitched in to help the other runners, though he was on liberty. The three went to see the colored glass, and attended the Larkadhe theater one snowy afternoon. Four days in, they got their clear night, and Quill and Lineas sat side by side on that high platform, drinking warm, foamy chocolate from the islands and singing old ballads as they watched the slow wheeling of the vast scattering of colored stars.

The wind sang in counterpoint, the rise and fall so eerie and beautiful that Lineas fell silent, her head tipped back, starlight reflecting tear tracks on her cheeks.

"Lineas?"

She knuckled her eyes. "Why is it," she exclaimed, "that something so beautiful can hit you right here." She tapped her heart. Then came the quick, anxious look.

Quill smiled her way. "Yes, it's normal," he said. "Do you want me to quote Old Sartoran poetry about the mercy of tears?"

She smiled back, knuckling her eyes again. "But you're not weeping."

"I . . . I feel it differently, is all. However, I can bang my elbow and bring up some tears if you want me to match you."

She uttered a soft laugh. "It's better, shared with another, isn't it? And this place! I can see the stars from my tower, and hear the harps, though in the distance, but this is so very much finer. Thank you."

His emotions were too intense—and too conflicted—for the easy release of tears, but he dared not say that. He dared not say anything of what he truly felt, because it was too easy to imagine her confusion, which would lead to self-consciousness, and he would hate to disturb her even more than he'd hate pity, or an earnest, painful explanation about how her heart was only loyal to one.

"Thank you for your company," he said, and meant it sincerely, but somehow those words brought the experience to its end.

Quill had worked a safe transfer Destination into his tokens, where they would not be seen. They walked from there to the gate just as Neit arrived from Larkadhe.

She glanced from one to the other then back again as they exchanged greetings, and she asked, "Where were you?"

"Out watching the stars and listening to the harps," Quill said.

"You're crazy," Neit commented bluntly.

Everyone laughed as they parted, the two to go inside to warm up, and Neit to relinquish her mount and report. She was uncharacteristically quiet as she helped unsaddle and rub down her horse. Usually she joked around with the stable hands, but her mind was preoccupied with what she'd seen on those two faces. Lineas's in particular. While reminding herself that it never did any good to interfere, she still resolved to watch the two.

Three days later Quill rode out, to start for the royal city with Commander Nermand's report, and a handful of other letters.

Lineas walked him to the stable yard. The three days had passed in a flash of good company and conversation. Somehow there wasn't enough conversation, and as he saddled up and rode out, she was aware of an ache behind her breastbone at the thought of all the things she could have said. That they might have done.

Then she remembered that she could write to him, and since this would be a normal ride for him, with time for stops along the way, she ran back inside to get started.

A day outside of Ku Halir, smoke drifted in a long, brown bank over the bare plains dotted here and there with emerging tufts of spring grass.

Braids Senelaec, newly promoted captain of the first flight of Queen's Riders, threw up his fist to halt. All three of his riding captains trotted up the line to him, no one speaking as they gaze northward.

"Could that be a summer fire?" one asked.

"Too early," a Fath cousin stated.

Braids shook his head. "I don't know the plains like my brother and da, but I've listened to them and ma talk. Spring is too wet for fires." He glanced down at a shallow pond peacefully reflecting the cloud-streaked sky.

He looked eastward, which was their assigned route, then north, then back at his flight. They'd broken column to gather around, something the army would never do. But when Rat Noth had taken Braids aside after his promotion, saying, *You're a compromise between the king and queen. Don't worry so much about the strict rules of chain of command,* to which Braids had said, *I grew up with girls. I grew up* as *a girl. Academy rules won't work with them, but I know what will.*

The women and girls chatted back and forth, something not encouraged in army column. Braids ignored the chatter, taking in the range of expressions from curiosity to Henad Tlennen's white-lipped gaze northward. Yes, she knew that was the general direction of Tlen, lying somewhat to the north and west, back in the direction they'd come.

"Let's go," he said. "We can always give 'em a good canter even if it's nothing."

The closer they got, the bigger the smoke cloud. When the westering sun faded below the orange glow beneath the cloud, no one had to say anything. They broke into a gallop, reining when they topped a gentle rise and peered between the trunks of a stand of red cedar toward the walls of Tlen. Flames flickered above the walls.

"What could burn like that?" asked a Marthdavan rider, used to stone castles.

"The village is inside the walls, thatch and a lot of old wood," Henad said tightly.

Braids gazed doubtfully ahead, his guts coiling with a sense of danger. He looked back at his command, only twenty-seven. Situations like this were best approached with a wing, or better, a company.

The youngest was sixteen-year-old Shen Sindan, another of the complicated tangle of clan alliances. Tears glittered in her eyes as she said, "Don't send me back. Don't. I won't go. I have to see. And if who did it is in there, I'll *kill* them," she added fiercely.

Braids sighed. He'd gotten used to the academy, where you never argued about orders. In Senelaec they'd always talked them over—sometimes argued, lengthily—and moved once consensus was agreed on. Maybe that was why nothing ever got done on time . . .

He reined the distracting thoughts, and forced his attention to the ring of waiting faces. One of the toughest things for the girls in the queen's training to learn had been to carry and use a shield. Braids knew that well because he'd had the same problem when he went to the academy as a senior. As border scouts, the girls traveled lightly. They had no remounts, and when they encountered trouble they were trained to shoot and run for reinforcements, a tactic that had served the alliance well for a generation.

So here they were, in a situation they'd only practiced in drill, the only patrol in sight, maybe for days, with no reinforcements.

"Let's take a look before we decide anything," he said. "Bows strung, arrows at hand, knives ready . . ." And he outlined a familiar academy approach—one riding to proceed, two spread out and covering them with nocked arrows—in case there were enemies hiding up on the walls.

He picked for the investigative riding the two women who had learned sword, both having had more experience with swords than Braids. Henad Tlennen had been trained by the jarl, having ridden as a girl on scouting forays that had clashed with horse raiders. She was as tall as Braids, rangy in build, pale of hair, with a strong, capable face. He'd picked her first as one of his three riding captains—which no one had argued with.

The other girl with a sword was a Sindan-related cousin, short, barrel-shaped, all muscle. She'd grown up with brothers, all Riders, and had been practicing with them since her first time at the Victory Day games.

The three of them formed the point of a wedge, three flanking them to each side, arrows nocked. Behind them, the others waited, with orders to shoot anything that popped up before it could shoot first.

Braids led the way . . . into silence, except for the buzzing of flies, and here and there the flapping of birds. Every one of the sprawled people was too still for breath.

Henad gasped. "That's Uncle Tuft," she said, pointing to a hacked-up man, hand outstretched toward his sword. He lay not far from the gate, with bodies all around him. Many were dressed in gaudy outlander clothes, with loose or short hair.

The jarl had died defending the gate, Braids thought, swallowing hard. "Spread out, in threes, no one alone," he ordered in an undervoice. "They could still be hiding."

Not likely, though. The stable was empty; the entire place resonated with an eerie emptiness. Nothing lived, except those flies. Acrid smoke billowed up from the still-burning cottages, the smoke drifting westward as they entered from the east gate.

They checked the few standing structures, to find only the dead, no one spared: at rough estimate there were as many dead enemies as Marlovans, if not more. But none of the obvious enemies were children or the elderly. Clearly the attackers had vastly outnumbered the Tlens, and took savage revenge for how hard the defenders had fought. The place had been looted, what remained hacked up, tumbled, and if flammable, set on fire.

Finally Braids and his riding stood in the court facing the main building. Heat poured off the fires, the flames shooting skyward to the roof. There was no use trying to get inside that building. Nobody could be alive in there, defender or enemy.

Braids wound his hand in a circle, and they retreated, coughing out smoke. The rest, seeing them trudge out, abandoned their positions and rode forward, clamoring questions.

Braids didn't hear them. He was trying to think past those terrible images. What now? He was not a commander. He followed orders. He preferred following orders. But there were no orders for this situation.

He looked back as Henad sobbed, turning swollen eyes toward Braids. "The gathering." Her voice cracked.

"What?" Then he had it: the rest of the Tlen household was out in the plains, gathering in the horses from their winter pasture.

"They don't know," Henad said through shut teeth. "They don't know."

Braids gazed around once more, then outward toward the plains as the enemy plan manifested: the enemy had struck when the Tlens were weakest, half holding the castle and the rest out in the plains rounding up the horses from their winter pasturage. "They're raiding for the horses," he said—knowing instinctively that he had it.

That meant he knew what to do. "We have to go after them."

"First we must lay Uncle Tuft and the others out properly for Disappearance," someone cried, choking on a sob.

"We have ride to warn the jarlan first," the oldest said urgently.

"We can't just leave Uncle there, and the others!"

Braids shouted, "Quiet!"

Silence and affronted looks for a heartbeat, then Henad said to her sobbing cousin, "What do you think Uncle would want us to do, spend the day gathering them for Disappearance, or warning Garid and Aunt?"

"But—"

"Wait, wait, wait," Braids said, this time without shouting. "There are no orders for this situation. Let's think it out. We're a third of a wing only. But that's better than nothing, considering those rounding up the horses don't know what's coming." He glanced at Henad. "Do you know where the winter pasture is?"

"Yes," she stated, her chin quivering slightly, her eyes betraying the fury she barely contained. "I rode with them every year after I turned ten, until I went to Queen's Training."

Braids turned to the rest. "I need a fast volunteer to get back to Ku Halir. Tell the commander. Roust out defenders. We'll go ahead."

Three volunteers came forward, eyeing each other.

"Who's fastest?" Braids asked, though he knew that already.

"Shen is," a half-dozen voices rose.

Shen's lips trembled, then tightened them into a line. "I'll go. Now that I know."

She clucked to her horse, wheeled, and was off without another word.

Braids said, "Henad, show us the way, but we're not going in column. We're going to spread out in a net, and look for the tracks of the enemy. If you see them, don't muddy them before we count how many, and . . ." He went on to outline a plan.

This time no one argued.

They rode out.

TWELVE

The sun had long set when Shen galloped into the garrison at Ku Halir. A stable hand took her shivering horse in hand as another tried to find out why she was crying.

His impatience vanished when he picked the words "Tlen" and "all dead" out of the disjointed stream. He led her straight to Arrow's cousin Sneeze, now Commander Ventdor, whose command until that moment had been a model of orderly ease.

Once Shen had told the assembled captains everything she knew (which wasn't much) and what she'd seen (that effectively silenced them all), a runner led her off as seam-faced, balding Ventdor faced his captains, which included Rat Noth, recently arrived from a very brief leave in Feravayir. In fact, the briefest yet; as a boy he'd never liked his stepmother, but as a young man, he'd come to loathe her as much as she despised him. So here he was, staring up at the map with the others at the drawing of Halivayir, which had only this in common with Tlen: it was small, the second smallest of the jarlates.

" . . . unrelated," Ventdor was saying. "Tlen's really just a horse stud. The big castles are at Sindan-An and Tlennen." He tapped the drawings at the southwest edge of the Nelkereth Plains lying to the east. Then he tapped Yvanavayir up north—

"Not unrelated," Rat said, as possible ideas sprouted in his mind. "Attack Halivayir, get everyone running north. Then go for the horses here in the south. It has to be Yenvir."

"But his gang's never numbered any more than twenty or thirty. That's what everyone says." Ventdor rapped Tlen's map image with a couple of knuckles. "From what young Shen said, there were at least that many dead at Tlen, so who took the remaining horses?"

Rat opened his hands. "Too many questions. But one thing for sure. Braids Senelaec will need backup."

Ventdor scowled at the map. "The princes are chasing around the hills up north—"

"Send somebody to Larkadhe as well as the royal city," his first captain suggested. "They'd better hear, whether this attack is related to the attack on Halivayir or not."

"Right. If the king wants to send us some fresh Riders, we can use 'em." Ventdor turned to Rat. "But right now, I think you'd better take your company to Braids Senelaec as reinforcement."

When Rat's three wings galloped out the gates, war banners snapping, followed shortly thereafter by runners bearing the royal pennons going in all directions, the denizens of the town stared, asking each other what was going on—and before the midnight bell clanged, word had spread about the destruction of Tlen, little more than half a day's ride from Ku Halir.

The sun came up on a sinister smoke pall smudging the eastern horizon.

Roughly the same time, far to the north, Connar stood under the sheltering branches of a fir, hands on hips, gazing into the rocky overhang that had obviously been a camp. Dry wood gathered and stacked inside for burning (few brigands had firesticks, which were very carefully rationed by the various guilds), and half a sack of moldy oats. Connar frowned, then—heedless of pouring rain—walked into the cave and kicked the firewood. It was all damp underneath.

"This is long abandoned."

"But we did see footprints, before the rain came," said one of the scouts. "Over that way. Half a dozen prints, man size, no horses. Now pretty mushy. I think there was a thin layer of ice that was slow to melt, on that slope."

"So within the last couple months, then," Connar said, and swung around, looking at the oats and the firewood.

Stick propped a booted foot on a rock and leaned his forearm on his leg. "Could be they left the oats because they were rotten. Took everything else."

Connar looked up. "Where'd the footprints go?"

"Downstream. Bending west, then vanished."

Nobody spoke the obvious—they could have gone in any direction from there.

A distant shout was followed by two brief, high notes on the bugle, announcing the arrival of a report. Connar waved a hand. "Send 'em up."

Stick nodded to his runner, who dashed down the trail, slipping in the mud.

A short time later the bushes thrashed as a pair of wet dogs appeared, tongues lolling. They sniffed all around, then sat to wait as a stocky, gray-haired scout in sodden tunic came toiling up the path, mud caked to his knees.

When he saw Connar, he stopped, slapped two fingers against his breast, then said, "Connar-Laef. There's something you better see."

"Where?"

The scout pointed northwards, into the hills. "Three, maybe four days' ride."

Connar felt the denial shaping his lips. He loathed the thought of blundering about in these hills any more than they already had—just to find another campsite that could have been used by anyone, at any time.

But this man had been hailed as a first-rate scout, brought down from Olavayir by Sneeze Ventdor around the time Connar was born, and well respected now.

"Lead the way," he said, hating it. He turned to Stick, issuing new orders, and then mounted up.

Three and a half days later, at least the weather had abruptly warmed to summery brightness. The scout took them up a narrow, rocky gorge with an ancient path running parallel to the river with its many falls, until they reached a plateau overlooked by snow-capped mountains.

Connar looked around the empty space, irritation spiking. He was about to snap out an order to leash the damn dogs racing and snuffling about, which were distracting in their noise, when their purpose struck him: they didn't get excited like that unless there were human scents. Fresh ones.

He looked around the flat space more slowly, wondering what about it looked vaguely familiar, though he knew he'd never set foot in these hills.

Then he had it: the very flatness. This was exactly what the two favorite academy campsites looked like, a week's ride from the royal city. They could always find them again because of the brush cleared out, all the big stones removed so that tent floors could be flat under bedrolls—

He looked again. This was a campsite, even bigger than the ones that accommodated the entire academy.

He turned to Stick. "An army was here."

Stick looked about, a frown between his mobile brows. "How can you tell? There's nothing save that stream over there, below the fall—"

"Stick, you've had rock duty on academy overnights. Look."

Stick's mobile brows shot upward. He stared around more slowly, then turned back. "This . . . is an army camp."

"And not all that old," the scout spoke up unasked, and began pointed out details of recent occupation.

Connar shut that out, his thoughts racing. If an army had been here, where was it now? He gazed upward at the northern mountains jutting up like teeth against the sky. Beyond those lay Lorgi Idego. There was no pass here, but that didn't mean the mountains were impassable. Assuming the Idegans had put an army here, why? And why attack Halivayir? What could they have possibly gotten there? Unless it was a feint of some kind.

He turned in a circle, wild to see, to understand, then caught himself up. He knew he was building what-ifs on top of what-ifs. Even Inda-Harskialdna would have made no sense of this, he thought as he gazed eastward. All right, unless they'd gone north again, after the most pointless attack in history, they had three other directions. West was out. Connar knew that no force could have gotten past his wide-spread net. That left east, into Yvanavayir, or south, toward Ku Halir . . .

What if Halivayir wasn't a feint, but practice?

South was Ku Halir, and then, straight south of that—

The royal city.

He turned to Stick, to meet his wide, light gaze, his brows slanting in question. "We need Noddy, right?" Stick asked.

"Yes. And Fath and his heavies, as soon as we can get them."

"I'll send Askan. He knows Noddy. He'll be able to explain . . ."

While Connar and Stick spread their net again and started southward as fast as the animals could run, in Ku Halir, Ventdor went about his duties, but every free moment snapped his mind back to the map as if he could somehow draw the truth out by glaring hard enough.

He was fighting frustration the next day as he tried to down a scanty meal, half-listening to his duty captains arguing what-ifs before the map, when noise out in hallway nearly drowned their voices.

Ventdor dropped the biscuit he'd been eating. "What is that racket out there?" He got up, thrust aside his aide, and yanked open the door himself, then stared at the gangling boy no older than fourteen in the process of dragging away a younger girl with frizzy hair.

"No, no, no, I *won't* go home!" she screamed. "I'm telling the *truth!*"

"What's this?" Ventdor snapped.

The two youngsters jumped as though stabbed, and turned distraught faces his way, the girl's tear-stained. "I know who did it," the girl shrilled, running toward him.

The boy flushed to the ears. "It's nothing," he said as he chased after her. "My sister just thinks she heard something because she hated somebody," he said miserably.

"I don't have time for this," Ventdor muttered, and the duty sentry turned to muscle the youngsters out.

But the girl grabbed the door frame, set her feet against it, and screeched, "I know who did it, I know who did it!"

Ventdor sighed. "Stop that noise. You have the count of twenty to tell me why you're howling down my castle. And if it turns out either of you are wasting my time, you'll regret it," he snapped.

It was an empty threat, but the youngsters didn't know that. They both paled, the boy looking sick, and the girl's jaw jutting. She kept a death-grip on the door frame and began shrilling a rapid stream of disjointed sentences.

Ventdor flung up his hand. "Stop."

"I told you," the boy muttered.

"You. Quiet," Ventdor said. "You're not helping."

Silence.

"Now. First, who are you."

"I'm Jam—Ndara Kiff—and he's my brother Retren," Jam said grittily. "From the Castle Inn. On Main Square."

"I know the place. Go on."

"I was serving that Yvanavayir woman and Lored from the Three Sails when I heard her, I *heard* her, every word, telling him *all about* Tlen Castle's defense!"

Retren said miserably, "Jam just didn't like her because she made extra demands and never offered vails." His dearest wish was to be accepted into the army once he turned sixteen, and he was terrified that Jam was about to get them all condemned, or worse.

Jam turned on him. "That's why I spied on her. Because I hated her." She swung around to face the commander. "But I'm telling the *truth*."

Ventdor's two daughters were both grown, one on the road somewhere as a runner, and the other a scribe in the royal city, but it wasn't all that long ago they'd been this age. He remembered what they were like when they were playing around, and he didn't get that sense from this child. He met Jam's earnest gaze, thinking that either she was the best liar in the kingdom, or she absolutely believed what she said.

"Slow down," he said. "Start at the beginning, and tell me everything."

Jam sent a sour look her brother's way, loosened her grip on the door, and began with Pony Yvanavayir's first appearance at the Castle Inn.

" . . . and then she started meeting that Lored, who all the big girls like because he's so *haaaaand*some," she declared with all the disgust of thirteen, "although he does leave good vails. I started spying to avoid her so she couldn't load more work on me, which she *never* tipped for. This one night, when they were together, she got up to go look out at the lake, and I was carrying some dishes, and I looked over to make sure I didn't go near them, and I saw him put some powder in her glass. And I thought, I hope it's itching powder, or something to make her barf. I'll laugh if she does. And I stayed around after she got back to see her drink it and barf and she said no she was right it's not raining anymore, not even a cloud, and she drank it right down."

Jam paused for a breath, noticed no one interrupting, and proceeded a little more slowly. "She didn't barf. All she did was blab and blab about how stupid the Tlens are. How they could run their horse training better, and when he asked if they defend their castle as badly as they train horses, she said no, they're good at that—wouldn't she know, she had to drill morning noon and night when she lived with them. And he asked all these questions about their holding, and how they defend it, and she talked on and on. I had to clear all the tables in the room and when I came back she was still blabbing, until she fell asleep, right there at the table, practically with her face in her plate, and I hoped she'd fall into the plate, which had some old corn chowder, but Lored left and Ma came along and helped her up to bed."

With a glare at her brother, "And we have *plenty* of customers who don't leave vails, and I hate them, too, but I don't *make things up—*"

Jam was so relieved that at last people were listening to her, she was about to embroider this theme when she saw that every man in that room was not only listening, but bent slightly toward her. With these terrible intent looks on their faces.

The commander said, "Jam, tell us again what happened that night. From when the foreigner Lored put the powder in Fareas Yvanavayir's drink. I want to hear the details of what he said, and what she said. Every detail you can remember. And if you don't remember, you tell us. Don't make anything up."

"I don't make things up." Jam's scrawny chest swelled as she took a deep breath, and out it all came again. In a different order, with a lot more side-comments, but the same in all essentials.

"That's . . . treason," one of the captains said on an interrogative note, when she was done.

"Isn't treason selling information to the enemy?"

"Treachery, definitely that," another said.

Ventdor cut through the talk and addressed one of his aides. "Find that man."

Retren spoke up in his adolescent honk. "Ah, Commander, if you mean Lored, or Larid, the way the Marlovans say it, he left the Three Sails."

"When did he leave?"

The siblings exchanged a look, both disturbed at the intensity in the commander's face. "Not sure. Maybe two weeks back, maybe three. I remember because Tolvik over there said he left all his clothes," Ret said, and Jam opened her hand in corroboration.

"Can you describe this man?" the commander asked. "I can get one of our sketch people in here, and—"

This time it was Jam's turn to interrupt. "Why not ask Var over at the weavers'?" And with the intolerance of thirteen, "She kept sneaking around drawing a million sketches of him, to put into a tapestry for her journeymaster work, and all the big girls always wanted to see them. Ugh!"

Ventdor said to a runner, "Find that journey-weaver and her sketches." And to another, "And take Fareas Yvanavayir into custody. I'll question her first, but prepare an escort to ride for the royal city. Questions about treason," he added, not without a sense of relief, "are a royal affair."

Two days of tracking later, though Henad Tlennen was certain she knew the route, Braids' company nearly missed the enemy. It was the leftmost rider who spotted the weather-smoothed pocks made by many horse hooves running at an angle almost perpendicular to their own, skirting the borderland of Sindan-An and heading straight into the Nelkereth.

She signaled wildly, and the rest broke formation and raced to see what she had found. "Rain's all but ruined them. Can't tell if those are our horse shoes or not," someone muttered.

Braids struggled against the urgency boiling in the pit of his stomach. Going off wrong would be terrible—as terrible as being too late.

"Let's follow 'em," he decided. "If they're ours, we can help 'em laugh at us. But let's not let them see us until we see them," he added, turning to his three captains.

A quick consultation between them and three experienced scouts were chosen to ride ahead.

Urgency gripped them all by the end of their third day, when the hoof prints had sharpened enough for everyone to recognize a mixture of Marlovan and foreign horse shoes, confusing for a sickening heartbeat or two until someone said practically, "This is no alliance party, riding in pairs. It's them riding Tlen horses, no order."

Braids felt stupid for missing the obvious. I'm no captain, he thought miserably. Out loud, "We're almost on them. Let's pick up our pace. Scouts, go ahead. In pairs, left and right of the prints. As far apart as you can get while still in line of sight." That much, at least, was usual practice.

The sky had begun to streak with gray clouds when one of the scouts came racing back. "Battle," she said. "It's too wet for dust—heard before we saw."

"If you weren't seen, then we can take 'em by surprise," Braids stated confidently, speaking from the experience of a solid three years of wargaming. "How many?"

She grimaced. "Lots. Lots and lots."

"More than us?" he asked, after a moment, when it was clear that estimation of numbers in the throes of fighting was not a skill she knew.

"Oh, yes."

Braids remembered the total confusion of all-academy wargames, and doubted he could make any better assessment. Regret gripped him. He was so very far out of his experience.

Well, when in doubt, try what you know. "We're not going to attack head on," he said. "There are only three of us with swords. So let's do what we do best. We'll run the edge, one shot, one enemy. At your fastest. Remember, they might be fighting the Tlens, so pick your target. Every arrow to an enemy—no wild shooting."

The horses tensed under them before the humans could hear the battle. That tension traveled through the animals' muscles to their riders, hearts thundering, breath coming fast, hands sweaty and maybe a little trembly, but they kept the mounts in a steady canter. They all knew that to gallop like thunder now would be to arrive with their horses blown.

They followed a slight ridge of land running adjacent to the battle they could hear, and when Braids saw his first scout, half-hidden in a copse of scrub oak, she pointed.

Braids looked back, kicked his mount into the gallop, and charged, screaming "Yip-yip-yip!"

The girls hesitated a beat, for that was the army's cry, but several of them felt it rise to their throats. Why not? They were now part of the army—riding to the defense of the kingdom.

They shrieked the fox yip on a high, shrill, angry note, and to the attackers, it seemed that Braids' company rose out of the ground and flew at them a hundred strong as they fought to both kill off the stubborn defenders and to corral the massive herd of horses.

Braids led his company in a long, tight line, twenty-six strong, nose to tail. In those first desperate breaths he couldn't tell who was foe and who friend, until he began picking out details: no Marlovan warrior wore his hair shorn, or loose, nor did they wear bright cloaks and flapping sleeves.

He started shooting, one enemy at a time.

At the sight of Braids' company riding to the attack, the exhausted remnants of the Tlen and Sindan roundup party took heart, and formed in a rough line to sandwich the enemy.

Fifteen of the brigands dropped nearly in as many heartbeats, then another twenty as his flight steadied their aim. Braids sought the leader. He glimpsed a huge man with long white hair flagging in the wind, with a black stripe down the top of his head. This man wheeled his horse, his red cloak swinging over his horse's foam-streaked flanks as he yanked up a horn, and blasted a hoarse, flat note.

The brigands wheeled as one and abandoned their attack. They galloped a fast retreat, their leader's laughter floating behind.

By then Braids had seen how many Tlens had fallen, many mere teens, hacked by swords, clubs, axes, and he knew what the survivors were going to go home to.

"Oh, no you don't," he breathed, and shrieked the fox yip with such fury the sound ripped from his throat as he leaped to the chase.

His flight was right on his heels, shooting as best they could at the retreating backs.

Braids was ready to chase them to the mountains until sanity returned abruptly when he reached down to discover he'd shot all his arrows. He looked belatedly to either side, to see that most of his women had also run out of arrows.

Hating the necessity as much as he'd ever regretted anything in his life, he flung up his hand as he slowed his blowing mount. The enemy (who outnumbered them by about half, and who all had swords) galloped over a ridge and vanished. He marked their direction, wondering bitterly if they would ride those stolen horses to death, then brought the company slowly to a walk so the animals could cool.

"Back," he said dully. "They might come around again for another try when they figure out we're not shooting. Retrieve every arrow you can," he added unnecessarily; the younger girls had already leaped from the saddle to fetch three spent arrows.

Splats of rain hit them, increasing steadily as they returned at a more sedate pace. They found the Sindans and Tlens trying to cope with the horses and wounded. Braids turned his company over to the command of the Jarlan of Tlen, who was trying to establish order.

The rain was beginning to lift when a scout shrilled, "Look!"

Everyone turned west to see a line of mounted warriors charging. Braids' body shocked cold—but that vanished when he recognized gray coats, and Rat in the lead.

Rat closed the distance, dispersing his company to right and left, as he said to Braids, "Report?"

"Twelve dead from the Tlens and Sindans. Nineteen bad wounds. Definitely Yenvir leading, unless there's two with the skunk hair in reverse. They retreated north. I'd say about fifty, fifty-five." He pointed in the direction Yenvir's bandits had gone, then swung his hand around to indicate the center of the muddy area, where a brigand lay surrounded by grim women, arrows sticking up from his shoulder and the opposite thigh. "One of 'em left alive."

A corner of Rat's mouth lifted in a mirthless smile. "Good," he said, in a tone that promise no comfort for the brigand.

He issued orders for the prisoner to be taken back to Ku Halir (whence he'd be dispatched straight to the royal city in a very hard ride), and then he and his company set out in pursuit of the brigands.

Braids turned to Henad, whose eyes gleamed with tears under her pale brows. "I'll tell her," she said softly, nicking her strong, square chin toward the Jarlan of Tlen. "It might come a little easier from me."

It wasn't going to come easy from anyone, Braids knew, but he turned his palm up, and watched her ride toward her aunt.

THIRTEEN

Quill rode south at a more sedate pace. Every night he found a letter from Lineas waiting, which he answered before sleeping.

This easy pace lasted until he reached the western edge of Tyavayir, when he received a tightly folded note on the back of a sketch from royal runner-trained Cama Stith, serving as Ventdor's scribe. Stith's note outlined the triple blow of Tlen's destruction, Pony Yvanavayir's conversations with the mysterious Larid, and then the near miss with the Tlen spring roundup.

Quill read while riding, then examined the drawing, which had been taken from a tapestry maker. It was quite clear—definitely distinctive enough for Quill to determine that he'd never met the handsome, smiling young man depicted there. But familiar? No . . . yes. No.

Damnation. Something nagged at him. He hated this sense that he'd left something undone, or had forgotten something important. Commander Ventdor and the King's Army were more than capable of taking care of even as infamous a brigand as Yenvir, he reasoned. There was nothing he could do when all he had was this cloudy sense of . . . what?

As night began to fall, he halted at an outpost on the river that divided Tyavayir from Senelaec—his first night sleeping in a clean bed since he'd left Larkadhe. His body sank gratefully into the soft bed as his mind drowsed about Larid, Lored, why did that sound familiar?

Midway through the night he jerked awake. He had it. *Lored* was too close to the Adrani *Alored.*

From there it was easy to leap to Mathias Alored Elsarion, younger brother to the Elsarion duchas. They were descendants of an Adrani duchas on one side, and the famous (some say infamous) Deis on the other.

He knew better than to take assumptions as truth. There were any number of young men named Alored living in Anaeran Adrani. And those half-familiar features belonged to several cousins—there might even be those who would recognize some of them in himself, especially about the eyes and eyebrows.

And even if this sketch was Mathias Alored Elsarion, and for some reason the wealthy young noble decided to go covert in Ku Halir, it was difficult to imagine a connection between him and a notorious horse thief like Yenvir the Skunk.

But the question would not let him sleep. He thought longingly of the days when Camerend was responsible for such problems, but Quill's father was in Darchelde now. Mnar Milnari was royal runner chief until Quill could take over; she had insisted that her duties remain with running education and royal commands, which was plenty. This situation was what Shendan had trained Camerend, and Quill himself, for: investigation for the good of the kingdom.

It was therefore Quill's responsibility.

And here he sat, in a private room. He loathed the thought of doing transfer magic while he was tired, but he knew he would not rest until he answered at least some of the questions buzzing through his head like an angry bee. So he wrote a letter to Lnand, one of the royal runners' best ferrets, half-hoping he'd get no answer. Or get a negative answer.

She responded almost immediately—clearly she slept with her notecase in reach as well as he did. She gave him a Destination pattern.

So he set two coins on the floor and chalked a letter between them to form an easy return Destination, then performed the spell. Magic ripped him out of the world and flung him back with shocking violence. He staggered as transfer reaction wrung through him, then looked about a moonlit chamber considerably colder than the Tyavayir posting house.

Lnand, who had been a senior when he was a fledge, pulled a night robe closer about her, and indicated a guest mat in her rented room above a boarding house. Quill sank down, aware of the day's long ride clinging to him with its various pungent aromas. "You might want to open the window," he said.

Lnand's facial planes shifted in the pale blue moonlight. "You sound exactly like your father. He always used to say the same when he'd been in the saddle all day, and morning baths were still a long way off. I'll live. To answer your question, yes, I remember quite well what Thias Elsarion looks like. He was a singularly beautiful boy—no, really I have to call him a young man, by now, your age. Popular along the southern pass."

Quill handed over Cama Stith's note, with a sketch enclosed. Lnand tipped it up to the window, saying, "That's Thias, all right. This artist even caught his expression, the one he wears when listening to music."

"All right, so we can assume we've identified the mysterious Larid. Next question, why." He looked up. "I was traveling when the king sent companies to chase those riders in the plains. Camerend said there was little result."

"Correct. The invaders retreated up the southern pass, where there are new castle outposts funded by the Elsarions. I visited them all, and heard the same thing: the outposts are guarding against brigands. No invaders came down for the next couple of seasons, so it was assumed that the brigandage had ended. The king recalled me. After which Camerend sent me here to Parayid Harbor, once he discovered that Demeos and Evred Nyidri were both back from Sartor." She glanced out the window at the path of liquid light on the quiet ocean waters of the bay.

Quill forced his mind away from the current problem to the older one surrounding the intentions of the Jarlan of Feravayir.

"So the Nyidri boys are back for good?"

"Oh yes," she said. "Full of Sartoran sayings, fashions, music, food. Rules for duels. Both are collecting admirers, especially Demeos, the eldest and heir. Everyone treats him as a prince, especially his mother. He acts like a prince—they both do, the younger one using his Sartoran name, Ryu, as he professes to despise Evred as a barbarian name. So Camerend has me here, watching from a distance."

Lnand handed the sketch back to Quill, who accepted that Camerend had placed Lnand in the best spot to observe the ambitious jarlan and her two sons. It was up to Quill to investigate the multiplying questions up north. "I think I'd better find the connection between Elsarion and what happened in Tlen. If there is one."

"Well, Ivandred is still up at the northern pass, as far as I know," Lnand said. "Still counting traders going back and forth, until the king decides to bring him home. Surely he would have spotted any companies of armed Adranis riding down."

"Yes," Quill said. "I'll begin with him, after I reach Ku Halir."

He braced himself for the transfer back to his outpost room.

Pony Yvanavayir enjoyed being the only woman surrounded by men for about as long as it took to ride from the new castle's stable yard down the main street along the lakeshore.

People on the street turned to stare. To *glare*. Her escort, instead of paying attention to her, treated her as if she were invisible. Except that they rode close enough so that she couldn't get past them, and if she tried, they scowled like she stank.

As they set out down the southern road, she considered forcing the issue, relying on her status as daughter, now the sister of a jarl. Then she caught a hateful look from a mere boy who couldn't be more than eighteen—like the beard spell was still a year off. Insolent puppy! And yet, young as he was, he topped her by at least a head, arms and chest shaped by muscle.

She was not about to risk a brawl unless she was sure of winning. And she didn't even have her knives. When they'd burst so suddenly into the inn to haul her off with no explanation, they'd searched her things without so much as a by-your-leave, and took away her mother's knives.

As they skirted the hills that marked Senelaec's eastern border, sometimes sleeping outside in the warm, aromatic breezes of ripening summer, and other times at posting houses (where she was locked into rooms—once a *closet!*) that impression never changed. When they had to look at her, or address her, it was coldly, or with averted glances. It was . . . insulting.

Then unsettling.

By the time they spotted the royal city on the horizon, the sense of insult was long past, and unsettling had congealed into disturbing. Equally disturbing was the way they left her in complete silence, until a contingent of royal guards surrounded her and took her to a part of the royal castle that she'd never been in: the garrison. Where she was led to a cell, and left with nothing but a jug of water, and a cot covered by a rough wool blanket that some apprentice weaver had obviously made while learning. It smelled of mildew, reminding her of home.

Her gear bag—without her knives—was tossed in with her, the door slammed and locked.

She crossed her arms. "This is ridiculous," she said to the stone walls. Her voice trembled.

Upstairs, Arrow stood in Danet's room, the door shut, the runners sent out.

"That Yvanavayir horseapple again," Danet said, pacing the room as she tried to shed irritation. "Do you know that I nearly had to intervene three times." She held up three fingers. "Three! Inspired by that snot and her stupid stunt abducting the Fath boy. Even though it didn't work, those two wild Sindan cousins snatched boys they wanted. And the younger Jevayir girl also ran a raid on her current lover of two. Whole. Weeks." This time Danet held up two condemnatory fingers.

Arrow had been scowling at the report, but he looked up at Danet, briefly distracted. "Sounds like the bride raids in the bad old days, except this time it's the brides doing the raiding. You didn't tell me about any blood feuds, duels, or the like."

"Because nothing came of any of them," Danet retorted. "The Marec boy went willingly—in fact I think he was in on it—and the family patched it over. They found a cousin to marry the Faral Noth girl in his place. The Sindans yanked the younger girl back and put her to work in the stable for a solid year, and the Toraca boy—too handsome for his own good—married Ndand Monadan, as he was supposed to, so I didn't have to intervene. And the Jevayirs solved theirs before my runner got there with my threats. Turned out the boy had moved on, and she hadn't, so she took 'Pony' as her model." Danet spat the word *Pony*. "I'd thought I'd never have to hear Fareas Yvanavayir's name again, but here she is, and this time they're talking treason."

"Treason," Arrow repeated, grimacing. "My da once said as soon as people hear the word, they pass judgment before hearing anything else."

"The answer is clear enough," Danet stated. "You listen to everything the witnesses have to say. Both of them, the child and Fareas Yvanavayir. Everyone else can be ignored."

"And then?" He threw his hands wide. "I know what they all expect. They want me to pin the slaughter at Tlen on her. As if that does the Tlens any good. And what a death!" He began stamping around the room. "I had to stand there while they flogged those shits who did in Kendred. Do you know long that took? The noises they made, before they finally died? I kept thinking I was going to puke. I swore I'd never sit through that again."

Danet said, "It sounds to me as if you've already passed judgment, too."

He swung around to glare at her. She stood there arms crossed, gazing back. His angry flush died down, and he passed a hand over his thinning hair. She did not like to see the puffiness around his eyes, but she wasn't going to say anything about how much he'd been drinking ever since the first report. He wasn't drunk. That was what was important.

"Listen to them both," Danet repeated. "Deciding, either way, comes after."

"Either way," he repeated, and then scowled. "I want you there. And don't say this is a military matter. You're in the military now whether you like it or not, sending those girls under Braids. And, from the sound of it, they were excellent. Rat Noth's report, I can show you it, says he couldn't have done better."

"Just as well," Danet muttered, hating the situation, but finding no argument to Arrow's words. So she vented an old complaint. "Just as well that Senelaec boy has turned out to be adequate. At least someone is in that family."

Arrow hissed out an irritated sigh. "Are you moaning about the seed again?"

"Four times out of six, the Senelaecs—alone out of everyone—need royal storage. It's as if they alone get famine and drought," she stated.

"That's what it's there for. It doesn't last forever," Arrow said with a wave of his hand. "Forget the seed. I need you listening with me."

Danet frowned. She'd been present for little Jam's testimony the day previous, so she couldn't pretend not to know what he knew about the entire sorry mess.

Arrow wiped his hand over his face, yanked open the door, and said to the waiting runners, "Bring Fareas Yvanavayir in."

Pony had had plenty of time to think. As soon as she faced the king and queen, she flung back her braids and put her hands on her hips. "When my father was jarl, he said that anyone accused had the right to face their accuser."

Arrow shot a glance Danet's way. Danet wore her steely face, and he knew she was reminding herself that the stakes were too high to let emotion run judgment.

"Very well." Danet glanced at the armed sentry. "Send for the child."

Word passed downstairs to the courtyard, where Jam strolled about with a pair of fledges who had been strictly ordered not to discuss the situation with Jam, but to remember anything she said about it on her own.

Jam was too intimidated to talk much. Her emotions swooped between wonder at actually being in the Marlovan royal city, which was bigger and scarier than she had imagined, and terror at having to actually be in the same room with the king and queen again. But Ma had said, *Tell the truth. Everything else is not your affair. Telling the truth is.*

Pony stared in surprise, then fury, when instead of some grim-faced warrior being escorted it, it was merely that brat who had been so snotty in Ku Halir. She glared at Jam, who glared back, then turned away—to meet the gaze of the Marlovan queen. Those eyes seemed to see right through her to the wall behind. Jam hunched a little, reminded herself of what Ma had said, and tried to straighten her back.

"Fareas Yvanavayir," said the king, "claims the right to hear her accuser. Go ahead and tell your story, what was your name? Ndara, that was it, right?"

Jam nodded—an Iascan gesture learned from her ma—then remembered that Da's folk, the Marlovans, didn't bob or wag their heads. "Yes," she said, and stated firmly, "She—Fareas Yvanavayir—told the foreigner everything about Tlen's defenses—"

"I did not!"

"—and everybody says he was an Adrani *spy!*"

Fareas stared in shock, as Danet snapped her fingers. "Never mind what everybody says. Tell your part of the story."

Pony's heart slammed against her ribs. "But she's lying! For one thing, the only person I talked to was a *merchant*, learning our language—"

The king scowled at Pony. "You listen. Then you'll get your turn."

Jam launched into the tale, which she'd told enough times by now she could get it out in more or less order.

Pony listened in growing affront and fury, mentally counting up the distortions and slanders as she argued mentally with each, but all the while bits of memory emerged among the vivid images of Larid's admiring smile, his sensitive hands, his drifting hair.

Her own voice repeated in her head in a strange way, as if someone else had spoken through her. But it *had* been her. She remembered the triumph she felt in describing Aunt Tdan's stupid drills, and how slow the Tlens were compared to Yvanavayir—

Jam's voice rose, overcoming her internal argument with the words, ". . . and then he put a powder in her cup."

Pony's nerves chilled as if snow fell after a fire.

Whatever had been in that cup, that was her way out.

She counted breaths until Jam's irritating voice halted, then she stated firmly, "There is nothing wrong with a flirtation with a tradesman from over the mountain. Nobody else ever said it was a crime. As for the rest, I don't remember any of it. I certainly don't remember drinking any powders." Her voice rang with conviction. "The idea is *disgusting.*"

And she saw that hit the king and queen.

The king said, "So you don't remember telling Larid about the Tlens' castle defense?"

"No." She resettled herself on her chair. "These are the subjects I recollect discussing with him: Marlovan ballads versus Iascan music played on strings. Dancing in Iascan style and Marlovan style. And I corrected a lot of his Marlovan, as he said he was learning it in order to have better success as a traveler. I assumed it was for his business, but as I know nothing about trade, I never asked what that was." She had completely regained her self-assurance.

Arrow turned to Danet, who said to the sentry, "Take them out."

Pony was on her way back to her cell, and Jam restored to her fledge companions, as Arrow and Danet faced one another. "What now?" Arrow asked. "She *says* doesn't remember."

Danet had seen the moment Pony's expression changed from angry fear to surprise, and then a semblance of composure.

Arrow said more slowly, "Did you see that, how she turned smug soon's little, what's her name again? As soon as the little inn girl mentioned that powder."

"So you saw it, too. But it doesn't prove anything."

"She was gloating when she said she didn't remember. I think she's lying."

Danet smacked her hand on the table. "Until we know, all we can say is we don't like her. That's not sufficient reason for execution, unless you want to gallop down Mathren's road. The powder was probably white kinthus. What rumor calls the truth herb, people talking against their will. I can't think of any other type of powder that makes people talk. Sleep-herb just makes people drowsy, and other herbs, the ones for headache and stomach upset, don't make people blab."

Arrow scowled. "I remember how Connar was when he took that kinthus stuff. He didn't blab, but he asked if the same would have happened to Noddy. He never said anything like that before, ever. It meant he was thinking about something . . . something important, or that bothered him, because he doesn't talk like that, not really."

"He was given the green stuff against pain," Danet stated. "Not the white. Why bring up that disgusting situation? It doesn't help with this disgusting situation."

"So what do we do?" Arrow slammed his hand against the wall. "If it was a warrior, I'd know how to get the truth."

"I'm sure Mathren said the same thing in his day," Danet commented sourly, and Arrow flushed. "I think we ought not to decide anything now.

Let Fareas Yvanavayir sit in your garrison detention for a couple days. Maybe her attitude will change when we talk to her again. Little Jam won't take any harm of spending time with the fledges, it seems to me. And perhaps there are other reports on their way in."

Arrow's brow cleared. "Right. Right! We'll give it some time. Who knows? Maybe Nermand has laid that Larid by the heels. *Then* we'll know something." He clapped his hands, rubbed them, and walked out.

No runners appeared the next day, which was full of early summer rain on and off, but the following day saw an armed flight gallop in, horses steaming. Two burly guards muscled a wounded prisoner straight to the detention cells.

A runner sought out Arrow over in the state wing, and reported the capture of one of the attackers on Tlen's horse roundup, finishing, "Captain Noth asked if we should try the truth herb on him."

"Do it," Arrow said.

A short time later, Commander Noth was summoned to the detention wing, along with the garrison healer's assistant.

"We tried to use the white kinthus we had in garrison storage, but the prisoner keeps retching," the grizzled captain he'd put in charge of the interrogation said.

The healer's assistant uncapped the tiny pot of white kinthus, then sneezed violently. "Tchah! How old *is* that stuff?" she asked, lips compressed at an irritated slant. "A century?"

The captain and his aide exchanged glances. "I don't know. Thirty years, maybe," one said, and as the healer assistant's black brows drew down, "we haven't been ordered to use it! In Mathren's day he wanted the truth beaten out of prisoners."

"That's as may be, but would you eat an egg that's been sitting around for thirty years? I didn't think so. What makes you think an herb, especially one that is very difficult to grind and to keep, wouldn't go bad? After two years, all we use it for is to harrow out the system when people eat badly. And the result is using the Waste Spell ten times in a day." She thumped her arms across her chest.

Commander Noth ventured a question. "Do you have some fresh?"

"You are aware, I trust, that white kinthus is dangerous? Two doses over an entire lifetime can kill someone—you've all surely heard about how Inda Harskialdna died . . ." She looked from one hard face to the next, saw the unspoken answer in their rigid expressions, then said in a stiff, borderline-affronted tone, "I'll fetch the healer chief. I think it best if he administers it."

As soon as the prisoner understood that they were giving him not the green kinthus that killed pain—both his wounds were infected, driving him mad with throbbing and itching—but the legendary white stuff, he fought as hard as he could. It took three big men to hold him down and attempt to pour the liquid down his throat.

He choked and gagged as the old healer watched, lips pinched, until at last he said, "I believe that's enough."

They waited as the prisoner, blood-crusted rags tied around arm and thigh, slowly blinked around the bare chamber, his expression smoothing to a vagueness that revealed his young age.

"Go ahead," the healer said. "Be precise in your questions. You are still going to get *everything*."

Commander Noth said, "What is your name?"

The prisoner looked up, confused. Noth tried again in coastal Iascan.

"My name is Barnut, son of Aiv Third Gardener. Your accent is hard to understand, sounds like mush in your mouth—"

"Did you attack the Jarl of Tlen?'

"I don't know that name," Barnut said dreamily.

Commander Noth exchanged glances with his two captains, who just stared back. He glanced at the healer, whose wooden expression was no help.

He said, "Why did you attack the castle?"

Barnut said, "Chief Jendas said the deal was, if we took the castle, then got the location of the rest of 'em, we'd come out with all their horses, every man a herd of his own."

"Deal?" Commander Noth repeated. "Was this deal between him and you?"

Barnut said equably, "No. With us he promised each man our own herd. I know where I can get a hundred six-sider gold for trained, fifty for—"

"He made the deal with who?"

"That foreigner."

"What foreigner?"

"Chief Jendas calls him Prettyboy."

"What does Prettyboy get in this deal?'

Barnut said dreamily, "Chief Jendas said he's running an attack once we make our feint. Chief Jendas said a feint that makes us rich isn't a feint but if the Prettyboy wanted to call it a feint—"

Noth turned to the captain nearest the door. "I think you'd better get the king."

The healer warned, "He'll only get wilder until he falls unconscious."

Barnut was already muttering disjointedly about his itchy wounds, how stupid they were, and how he would have spent his riches if only those winged riders hadn't come out of nowhere, curse, curse, curse.

The door shut behind the captain. Noth gripped Barnut by the chin. "Who is Prettyboy attacking?"

"Don't know. We weren't going to see them. We were to split three ways, drive our horses, me and Hound Crew head back to camp, and then we can go up the mountain."

"Where is your camp?"

"A day out of Three Fork, west o' Grunt Summit."

Noth glanced back, to meet equally puzzled looks. Nobody had ever heard of these locations. Obviously the brigands had their own names for landmarks.

"Can you make a map?"

"Map? You mean all that scribble-scrabble on paper? I ran so's I wouldn't have to sweat out letters, nothing worse . . ." Barnut yawned hugely, and began to drool.

Noth jerked Barnut's chin up. "How many did you kill?"

Barnut murmured sleepily, "At the castle? Only six, if you count the two't gave me no fight . . . Chief Jendas says they all count but I don't see counting grayheads or brats . . .And on the horse raid . . ." His head dropped to one side as he babbled fragments of sentences, then fragments of words, mixing two languages.

Arrow appeared then, breathing hard, the captain behind him. He gave an incredulous look at the drooling Barnut, then turned to Noth for an explanation. Which Noth gave in short, flat sentences, beginning with how hard Barnut fought once he heard that he was to be given the white kinthus.

Arrow listened all the way through. "An attack, but he doesn't know where, when, or how many? Send someone with that information to Ku Halir, and add that we'll pull reinforcements from East Garrison and run 'em north." He turned to the old healer. "Tell me more about this white kinthus. I thought the green and the white was the same plant."

The chief healer, who had lived through the tense years of Mathren and Kendred, had learned to speak very carefully whenever he was consulted outside of the area of mending physical damage. "Green is the stalk, white the bud, much harder to harvest—you have to get it right before it flowers, and then dried properly. White kinthus, erroneously called the truth herb, detaches the mind from the constraints that bind us to our bodies, a detachment that sometimes never rejoins the two. Persons who ingest it will enter that place where memories and dreams merge, usually talking freely of whatever they have seen, heard, or learned. Getting sense from people under the influence, especially at the usual dose, requires training in focused questions—"

"I get it," Arrow said. "I want you to give some to the Yvanavayir girl." He hesitated, glancing at the wet front of Barnut's clothes, where the fellow had obviously done his best to spit out the herb. "Put it in her food. Don't tell her what's coming. No, I can see you're about to protest, but that's an order. Whichever way this goes, I'm going to have to defend my decision to the jarls, who probably have runners on the road right now demanding a treason trial."

The healer took a step back on the word *treason.*

"And while I don't care if Noth beats the truth out of this turd here, after the way he bragged about killing people who couldn't fight back, until I'm certain Fareas Yvanavayir revealed Tlen's defenses with intent, she at least hasn't killed anyone."

The healer saluted stiffly.

"Noth, fetch Danet. I want her to hear whatever the Yvanavayir girl says."

By the time Danet had entered the garrison, which she hadn't set foot in for years, runners had been dispatched in all directions for the hardest rides of their lives.

Together the king and queen walked toward the cell where Pony was kept, as Arrow reported what he'd learned.

"I hate this," Danet said at the end.

"I hate knowing an attack is coming much worse," Arrow retorted. "And then there are the jarls, getting who knows what sort of garbled reports. We have to act *now*, with whatever tools we have. This kinthus is a tool."

As it happened, Pony had used up her water allotment in trying to wash her hair. She was so thirsty she drank down her tainted water without a hesitation. And so, when the king and queen entered her cell, they found Pony smiling gently, almost unrecognizable with all the anger gone.

What could have made her so angry, Danet wondered, then remembered her mother had been killed when Pony was small. With very mixed feelings she stood against the wall as Arrow gestured to Commander Noth, the expert in questioning people under normal circumstances, as there was no one expert in handling people under the influence of white kinthus.

"Fareas Yvanavayir," Noth said.

Pony looked up, blinking slowly. "I hate that name," she said conversationally. "Everybody calls me Pony, because when I was a girl—"

"Pony. I want you to think back to your conversations with Larid the tradesman. What did you tell him about Tlen Castle defenses?"

"I told him everything," she said with a slow, sly smile. "*Everything*."

"Why?"

"He was so interested in me, in us. He's impressed by Marlovans. I told him that Yvanavayir is so much better run, or was in my day but I'm sure that Chelis Cassad has ruined all our old drills just because she can. My Aunt Tdan Tlen is so proud, and of what? I told him how every drill and every alert was wrong, and how it could be better if only anyone would *listen* to me. But Cousin Hibern and that silly Owlet think just because they've always done it that way it's perfect. . ."

She began to launch into exhaustive detail, mixing disparaging remarks about the Tlens with Yvanavayir drills, interrupted by a jumble of excoriations against Chelis Cassad that had first Danet, then Arrow, exclaiming interruptions.

"She did *what?*" That was Danet.

"Ordered those two hateful slackers to bang hammers on metal over my bed, forcing me awake . . ."

"The new jarlan drove you out?" That was Arrow.

" . . . and she said, *I'll help you pack,* so the entire household heard, but Eaglebeak hid in his room all week. I never saw him except at supper and then he ignored me . . ."

"They kicked her out," Arrow said. "No wonder she ran down to Tlen!"

Danet scowled. "Correct. I thought better of the Cassads, especially Chelis, who was so quiet and—"

Noth looked at his king and queen, then interrupted with strained patience, "None of these questions touch on treason." And when the royal pair stepped back, Arrow red-faced and Danet icy, Noth said to Pony, "Did you ask why Larid, a foreigner, wanted to know about the Tlen defenses?"

"Yes, and he said he wants to learn from us. He wants to learn from *me.* At least he had the sense to ask my advice, unlike my own relations—"

"I've heard enough," Danet said, and walked out.

Arrow followed. When he caught up with her, Danet shot him a hard look. "She told him, all right. With intent to impress. But is that really treason? Isn't treason giving aid to an enemy?"

"That wasn't aid?"

"She did not know he was an enemy. Nobody did. She was trying to impress a flirt."

Arrow pressed his thumbs to his eyes. "With details of castle defense? Any bonehead knows not to talk about that sort of thing with a stranger!"

"It sounds like she got into detail from spite, that is, to prove how her Tlen relations were wrong, in the way jarls and the army and the academy *all* talk about defense."

"She knew it was wrong—she lied when she said she didn't remember."

"She lied after she found out he was an enemy. At the time, she was talking to a flirt."

"I see what you're saying. But this is for certain, the jarls are going to howl for her blood." He sighed. "I wonder if this is how the Great Evred felt when he had to put Mad Gallop Yvanavayir to death."

Danet said, "That particular Yvanavayir led an attack on this castle. He killed the king with his own hands, and sent his personal armsmen to kill the heir. Fareas Yvanavayir bragged to a man she wanted to bed."

"Not a man, a *foreigner.*"

Danet snapped, "She spent her entire life in Yvanavayir talking border defense and probably castle defense as well. The only time she left Yvanavayir before this was to come to the Victory Day games, where everyone talks defense. People in trade towns learn how to behave around foreigners. They know what to say and what not to say. But Fareas was like a yearling first seeing a saddle. The foreigner knew exactly what he was doing. She had no idea."

To which Arrow retorted, "Right. He did, since he used a very expensive herb on her. That sounds like a spy. If we find out he was a spy for the Adranis, it's going to be treason in everyone's eyes, come Convocation, when we have two empty benches that used to belong to the Jarls of Halivayir and Tlen. No son to take either of their places. The jarls are going to demand justice."

"You mean, they are going to demand blood," Danet said.

"Yes," he snapped. "I can even tell you who will be absolutely convinced it's treason."

She walked upstairs, where Noren was waiting. When Noddy's betrothed saw the glitter of moisture in Danet's eyes, she raised her hands in question.

Mindful of her own total ignorance of what was expected of a gunvaer when she found herself having to take on that duty, Danet had set herself to tell Noren everything. Well, mostly everything.

She did not hold back now.

FOURTEEN

From Haldren Arvandais, King of Lorgi Idego, to Nadran-Sierlaef of Marlovan Iasca:

My Farendavan cousins tell me you're called Noddy. They, and every rider our trade representatives in Larkadhe send to me, tell of your sense of justice, wisdom, and compassion, though you are little older than my own son. These reports from our own people, as well as the years of peace our two kingdoms have both enjoyed, give me hope for the future.

It is in regard to that future that I am writing to you. I have recently been apprised that there has been a large gathering in one of the valleys of the Ghildraith, on our extreme southeastern border. News was garbled for a time, for apparently they took care to avoid our regular trade routes.

A runner arrived today to say that this mass has begun moving south, and further they are well armed. Since they are moving in a southward direction, they will be no threat to us. With the above in mind, I thought it best to send a runner directly to you, to make use of this news as you will.

Lineas laid the Idegan king's letter down on the desk she had worked at for over a year. She raised her gaze to Noddy, who turned from her to Neit, then to Vanadei, who went to the door to leading to the Yvana Hall interview chamber, and shut it.

Noddy folded the letter up. Then he faced them.

"You three are the ones I trust most," he said, each word deliberate in the way they all recognized: when he was uncertain, he always began by repeating what they already knew.

Neit stepped up, kissed his cheek, and said in an equally slow voice, her tone mild, "It seems to me that we need a couple of long runners to take the news south."

"Grass run." Noddy rubbed his big hands slowly down his thighs. "Two." He held up two fingers. "Fast as fast can be, to Da and to my brother. Right?"

"Just what I was thinking," Neit said.

"As was I," Vanadei added. "Do you want to send runners to report to Captain Nermand, and to the Jarl of Olavayir?"

"Yes." Noddy ducked his head. "Them, too. Should we send reinforcements—no. I already did that." His brow cleared briefly. "I already sent Cabbage Gannan to back up Connar."

"That's right," Vanadei and Neit both said, Vanadei remembering that it had been Neit's idea.

Noddy said, "Connar will definitely need Gannan now."

The three runners agreed again, then Vanadei said, "Do you want us to settle out who goes while we copy this letter?"

"Yes." Noddy breathed out his relief, then looked around the empty chamber. "Yes. Do we have ink? I can fetch it."

"I made a fresh batch yesterday," Vanadei said. "It's in the storage room, with the new-pressed paper."

Noddy sloped off as if he were the runner. This was a specific task, one he could do, and the others knew how much having specific work reassured him when he perceived a problem for which he had no orders and no clear path.

Neit turned to the others. "You know I'm an expert at grass runs. Have either of you ever made one?"

"No, but we've both been instructed by Fannor, who was the fastest royal runner for twenty years," Vanadei said. "We both have," he added, and Lineas opened her hand.

"I can go," Lineas said, her tone a question. "Vana should stay and take care of the crown prince."

Neit pursed her lips. "Yes, but are you strong enough for a grass run? Have you drilled at all since your arm was broken?"

Lineas reddened. "Twice a day," she whispered, and the other two saw the remorse she would have hidden.

"Lineas, what is this guilt?" Neit clapped her on her good shoulder. "It would have taken an Inda to go into battle with a couple of little knives and no shield. And those shits wouldn't have gone after him the way they did you. Didn't you see it? They were trying to get through the smallest person there in order to reach one of the princes."

"I didn't," Lineas admitted, red with shame.

"That's because you didn't grow up having to run the enemy in your brother's and cousins' wargames, the way I did. Never mind that. If you've been drilling, then I think you're strong enough for a grass run. We'll ride together for the first portion, and I'll show you all the tricks."

Vanadei flicked a questioning look at Lineas, who flicked a finger in a brief signal: she would send a message by magic. Vanadei said to Neit, "Lineas and I will each make copies of King Hal's letter, if you want to choose the horses."

"Done."

Neit was gone in three long, hip-swinging strides, leaving the other two alone. "It seems so strange to trust her with so much, but not trust her about the golden notecases," Lineas said, with regret.

Vanadei opened his hands. "Whenever I think about such things, I tell myself it's orders made by people with much longer vision than I have. As long as I feel that our secrets are truly kept for the good of the kingdom, I can keep them."

Lineas brightened. "That seems a good rule—"

The door opened, and Noddy appeared, carrying paper and an inkwell.

Vanadei said to Lineas in the easy voice they always used before Noddy when he was anxious, "We'll copy out the Idegan king's letter, as we're fast. How about if you write whatever you want to say to Connar-Laef, and to the king?"

"Right, right," Noddy said, and they all sat down.

Shortly thereafter Lineas ran out, mentally composing her letter to Quill. She scrawled it out in her room, rolled her journal and notecase in the middle of a change of clothes, and ran down to the stable to find Neit waiting with a pair of horses.

Lineas's gaze went to the shields on both animals, and the sword sheaths.

Neit grinned. "Instead of the usual knife drill mornings, we're going to get into the basics of defense. If you're going to spend time around kings, you'd better pick up any skills you can."

Quill squashed down disappointment that his road would not lead him to the comfort of Hesea Springs, but he consoled himself by taking an easier pace as he rode through Tyavayir, listening to the farm laborers singing as they planted.

He forded a shallow area in the river that cut through a swathe of Senelaec's eastmost lands, noticing a significant difference within a day. Though plants and soil appeared to be similar to Tyavayir, there were many empty fields, making him wonder if the jarl had raised his entire family to go to the aid of the Eastern Alliance.

He decided against visiting the Senelaecs, as he carried no messages for them. Lightning Season was setting in as the east winds, strong all winter, died completely while the summer's west winds had yet to flow. That left the land baking under days of fierce sun in a brilliant blue sky.

Even the butterflies seemed lazy and dust-laden as he rode slowly along east-west road, until he felt the quiet tap of a note transferring to his notecase, which he carried in a pocket next to his skin.

Instantly worried, he pulled up. His heart rapped against his ribs when he recognized Lineas's hand. She always sent her letters at night.

He read it rapidly, then read it through again more slowly, aware of a mixture of reactions, the sharpest anticipation: he'd see Lineas again, after resigning himself to at least a year's separation. Hard on that was grim worry at the situation.

The sun had begun dropping westward when he reached the border road skirting wooded land, he caught sight of relatively fresh hoof prints, crisp in the dry dirt. The vast majority of the prints had been made by the distinctive style of horse shoes favored by Marlovans, so expected a sight he was about to ride on when he spotted a fresher set made by barefooted horses, crossing the first set.

He led his own mount to the grassy verge and dismounted to walk alongside the road until he was certain that a large Marlovan company was being shadowed by a small group.

Ordinarily he'd shrug the matter off. Any large body of Marlovans could be counted on to take care of themselves. But Lnand's observations, followed by the letter from the Idegan king, made him wary. The two things might not be related, but it would be negligent to ignore the timing, given all the unresolved questions.

So he decided to track the trackers.

After a day and most of a night of travel as long as the moon was up, he drew close enough to spot the pursuit—he could tell by now it was nothing less, the way the footprints led from sheltering bluff to screening hedgerows. These were not travelers following the middle of the road.

When the sun sank at last, releasing the heat of the day into the cloudless sky, he shrouded himself in his dark cloak and rode toward the village whose golden lights twinkled in a shallow valley. Below it lanterns winked like fireflies, outlining the tents of the Marlovan company. Unsurprisingly no one had lit fires—they would eat cold slabs of travel bread to avoid any more heat.

In the fading light he followed the shadowers, whose increasingly fresh prints had shifted to single file. When he passed the outlying houses of the village, he dismounted and began leading his drooping horse.

Curiosity and thirst: Lightning Season had set in hard, the two streams he'd crossed since morning dried up. He was wondering whether to find the Marlovans to report what he'd seen or seek water for the horse when the animal tensed, ears twitching.

Quill paused between an ancient, spreading oak in full leaf and an old round cottage built in the Iascan style, door on the opposite side from where he stood. He threw the reins over a branch and cut across the kitchen garden, leaping soundlessly from stepping stone to stepping stone until he reached the rough stone wall.

He peered out into a dusky yard—and stilled when he recognized Prince Connar strolling slowly toward an isolated cottage, with what looked like a bottle in hand. Quill was about to turn away—the prince was obviously seeking some kind of entertainment, none of his affair—but his ears caught the soft tick and rustle of stealthy movement, carried on the still air.

Quill glanced at his horse, who sidled and huffed. The animal didn't like stealth of any sort: rabbits, a bird taking flight from the grass. Quill slid his hands into his sleeves, closing his fingers around the hilts of his knives—and caught the movement of a shadow on the roof of the bakehouse adjacent to the cottage Connar moved toward, and a soft rustle in the shrub on the other side of the road. Then he saw a third shadow slipping alongside the neighboring cottage, the golden glow from a window glinting on naked steel.

Quill bolted across the ground, knives out—and the night exploded into shouts and the gleam of torchlight on swords as two attackers closed in from either side. Quill leaped, whirled, and took them both out, left hand strike, right hand back swing in The Falcon Turns, practiced thousands of times. He whirled toward the third.

From the shadows two men with curve-tipped Marlovan swords landed on Quill's target.

Quill wrenched himself to a halt, staring blankly at Connar, who stood a couple of paces away.

It was a trap. And the assassins Quill had just attacked had fallen into it.

The belated observation struck Quill's mind, leaving him feeling bewildered and not a little foolish.

Connar glanced down at the live prisoner pinned down by his two swordsman, a burly man dressed all in black, a black mask concealing his face. The prisoner struggled mightily in the gripping hands.

"Keep him alive," Connar said, and the two swordsmen stepped on the prone man's arms as they sheathed their swords.

Connar turned to Quill, the afterimage of that sudden lethal strike still vivid in his eye. "Where did you come from?"

Quill saluted, bloody knife pressed to his chest, as he said, "I've been shadowing them since I saw prints hunting a Marlovan party. Caught sight of you just now."

Connar said, "And came to the rescue." His teeth flashed in a sudden smile. "As it happens, the dog scouts discovered them shadowing us a week ago." He kicked the side of the still-writhing would-be assassin. "So we set up a little trap. I appreciate your stooping like a hawk out of the sky, but I'm glad you didn't reach this one, as we very much wanted at least one alive long enough to answer a few questions."

"Right," Quill said, thirst and the violent shift from urgency to bewilderment intensified the aftershock of awareness: he had just killed two living beings.

Connar was silent, still smiling. The rest of his men stood about in a half circle around their prisoner.

As Quill fought against the black spots swimming at the edges of his vision, he became aware that Connar's circle was not just standing there, they were waiting. For? *Me to leave so they can get on with their interrogation.*

Sure enough, Connar said, "Quill, why don't you go get some well-deserved liberty time?"

Though it was spoken as a suggestion, even a friendly one, it was an order, and Quill was relieved to go. His entire body shook with reaction as he retreated to where he'd left his horse. He knelt to clean his knives with handfuls of grass, fighting a violent surge of revulsion as his eyes, his hands, experienced the echo of those killing slashes. His mind fought back, offering justification—defense—what he'd been trained to do—but the two figures sprawled in death, one with wide eyes staring up at a night sky he would never again see remorselessly imprinted on his inner eye.

He fought back the nausea as he sheathed the knives, loosed the horse, and walked him into the village, which glowed with lamplight.

There wasn't far to go. The village did boast an inn. The horse was soon stabled and Quill sat in a tiny, stifling room directly over the noisy taproom where he could hear the roar of voices going on about the evening's excitement.

Tired as he was, he couldn't sleep. His thoughts bent toward Lineas, but he recoiled from seeking solace there, rather than risk throwing her back in memory to what she'd endured at Chalk Cliffs.

Perhaps he ought to find Connar and report what he knew, but again he hesitated. Connar had been waiting for him to leave. He clearly had either orders or an objective, neither of which Quill could, or should, interfere with without orders from the king. Which he didn't have. Likewise Quill was outside Connar's chain of command: the letter he carried was for the king. There were few actual facts to report, other than Thias Elsarion's name, the rest being conjecture. Maybe it would be better to try on his own to answer some of the questions before he reached the king, and could furnish a more useful report.

Yes, that was where duty lay.

Back in the clearing, Connar was still gripped by that vision of Quill leaping, robes flying, steel in either hand striking true. He recognized the visceral thrill of attraction driving the admiration, and snuffed it hard like a candle. Early on he'd decided against the royal runners as prey for play because they talked too much, and he saw no reason to change. Instinct said this one in particular was dangerous.

He blinked away the image, and breathed against the physical reaction, then gestured to a pair of Stick's scouts, who stretched the would-be assassin out on the ground, arms pinned wide. A third scout cut away the mask, his knife scoring the prisoner's face from jaw to temple.

Connar hunkered down at their prisoner's side, a knife held loosely in his fingers. Lantern light outlined his profile, gleaming in his eyes. "Talk or bleed," he invited.

The man gave a violent heave in a desperate attempt to free himself, for he knew what was coming next. He'd done it to prisoners himself, as excruciatingly as possible, to prolong the fun.

But Connar's men, every one of them still angry over the destruction of Halivayir, held firm: bootheels ground the prisoner's wrists into the dirt.

He sagged. "I'll talk," he said, fast and surly. "Yenvir says he owes us nothin' so I figure I owe him nothin'."

"Oh?" Connar said, sitting back on his heels. But he didn't sheathe the knife.

The captured man knew who Connar was, having shadowed him for weeks before Midsummer, and again—more prudently, due to the scouts and their dogs—more recently. He stared up at that handsome face, the slight smile and steady, merciless gaze, and decided his only hope of survival was to make himself indispensable to the Marlovans. "Yenvir's teamed up with Prettyboy over the mountain. We're the decoy, see."

"Decoy?"

"Yenvir wants you dead. Your scalp will net a man a thousand Sartoran golden wagonwheels. Your brother, two thousand."

Connar recoiled in disbelief. "The Skunk wants my *scalp*?"

The scouts muttered in disgust, and one spat noisily right next to the prisoner's ear. The man snarled, grunting in a muscle-popping effort to free himself, but the scouts stamped down with their heavy soled, high-heeled riding boots. A bone cracked in the prisoner's right hand, and the man howled.

Connar lifted his knife to stay the scouts. "Not yet," he said. "Let's give our friend here a chance to tell us what Yenvir wants with our scalps."

"Proof," the man's voice was high and husky, the lantern light shining on his sweaty forehead. "That you're really dead. So we collect our reward. And then he can send it on to the king, see, with a threat."

Connar leaned over, speaking in a low, intimate tone. "And yet you said you are a decoy. From what?"

"I don't know where Prettyboy is—"

"Does he have a name?"

"That's what we call him. Says he has his own men. Don't know nothin' more. Our job is to nail you." He saw in Connar's face that the truth had condemned him, and as Connar started to rise, he rushed his words. "I can help you! I'll show you where Yenvir camps, see—"

"We already know that." Connar glanced at the scout poised at the prisoner's head, lifted his chin, and the waiting scout cut the prisoner's throat.

A gasp and the hisses of whispers from the background recalled the villagers, who had crept out of their houses to goggle.

Connar looked down at the dead man, whose face had gone slack above the obscene black mark at his throat. No spell for Disappearance came to him, though the death was not by his hand. How could this magic possibly know that it was at his unspoken command? Uncertainty gripped him, a brief sense of visceral dread, which he shook off. "We're done here."

A stout bald man in the undyed linen of a healer stepped out of the crowd. "I will see to the fallen," he said flatly.

Connar flicked out his palm, handing the matter over. The assassin had come to kill him for gold. Connar did not regret ordering his death, and yet the magic of Disappearance not coming disturbed him. It was that implication that some unimaginable . . . something . . . might be watching, somehow. Some incompetent something, or why did assassins get away with their trade at all? The idea of being observed was so repellent that he gave in to instinct and moved away, gesturing to Stick, still holding back the rest of the gawkers with his sword.

"Let's go," Connar said. "New orders."

He needed the time to think. The assassin's words had brought back Cousin Tanrid's doubts about Connar's suggested reward for finding or killing any of those damned Bar-whatevers. That had been bothering him ever since.

He knew people lied. He'd been lied to. He lied when he felt he had to. Given how easy it was to lie, he couldn't be certain of any claim outside of dragging a rotting corpse along as proof. No one would do that anymore than he wanted to see it done. But hair—given the target was recognizable by their hair—that was practical.

As soon as he reached their camp, he motioned his captains around. "I want a wing to bring down Yenvir the Skunk. Bring back his scalp."

Some captains shifted from foot to foot, others side-eyed one another.

Stick's jaw dropped. "His *scalp?*"

Connar held up his hand "The assassin we just caught was ordered by Yenvir to bring my scalp, so that it could be brought before the king. Probably along with some sort of threat. Which do you think would have the most effect on him?"

He could see them considering that. Then one of his newer captains said, "Why does it have to be his scalp? Why not his hair?"

"I imagine it's because a scalp keeps it together." Stick grimaced. "Or you'd get hair all over before you even reached whoever you had to hand it off to."

Connar said, "Assuming we can find out who and where this Prettyboy is, how effective do you think it will be to offer him Yenvir's skunk-striped hair, with or without the scalp?"

A reflective silence met that.

"In fact," Connar said slowly. "What if that distinctive hair was hanging from, say, your helms as you rode against them, like a real horsetail?"

"Damn." Stick uttered a crack of laughter. "We should go back there and cut the hair off that big assassin before they ghost him."

Connar struck his hand away in negation. "No. We can take a lesson from Yenvir, who apparently wanted to brandish my scalp, and Noddy's if he could get it, before the throne. It'll be more effective if we employ their own ruse."

Stick uttered an angry laugh. "Especially recognizable."

This time everyone agreed, or kept silent if they didn't.

Connar smiled around at them. Stick laughed again, because the prince he followed was shaping up to be a great commander, because he had orders that he relished.

Connar grinned back. "Decide who's going, and ride out at sunup," handing off command to Stick. "The rest of us on to Ku Halir."

A single rider trained for speed is usually faster than a group. Quill reached Ku Halir first, knowing that Connar would soon arrive behind him. Driving himself to his limits bought him relative distance from the aftereffects of having killed two men. He had duty, and that required him to get as many questions answered as he could, so if the prince wanted a report he could have it before Quill rode down to the royal city.

He turned his horse over to the garrison stable, drank three dippers of water, then claimed one of the small rooms set aside by runners. The room was airless and stifling. It contained nothing but a narrow cot. Quill shut the door, sat down, and wrote to Ivandred, the older royal runner ferret who had been his father's favorite.

The answer came back before Quill could decide whether to get a meal or a bath first. Instead of a report, Ivandred responded with a makeshift Destination.

A spike of disappointment gave way to resignation. Ivandred was as little given to irrelevant gabbing as Lnand. If Ivandred felt he had more to say than could be written in a quick report, Quill had better endure the transfer to hear it.

He made certain he had the relevant papers tucked into the inner pocket of his robe, and did the magic.

Judging by the dramatic wrench out and back into the world, Ivandred was at some distance from Ku Halir. The man sat on a narrow bed in what appeared to be an attic room, judging by the slant in the ceiling at either side. He had shut the tiny window, rendering the room stifling; the weather this far north, closer to the belt of the world, was even hotter than Ku Halir, though not quite as dry.

Still fighting transfer reaction, Quill withdrew the papers and handed them over. As the transfer reaction wrung through Quill in diminishing pangs of nausea, Ivandred read rapidly through Lineas's summary of the Idegan king's warning, then he turned to the sketch. His bushy brows shot upward under his sweat-spangled dome forehead. Quill noticed distractedly that Ivandred, who had always seemed ageless, was balding, the rest of his frizzy hair gone gray.

"I know this young man," Ivandred said, tapping the backs of his fingers against the drawing. "He's a silk merchant, very new to the trade. Friendly, likes to chat. Through here every season, coming west with wagons full of silk bolts, well-guarded."

Quill said, "Nothing they said at Ku Halir indicated he dealt in silk." He summarized what had happened, before ending with, "Did he ever offer to unroll a length to sell in your presence?"

"No, and I never thought to ask. He didn't seem the least suspicious. No weapons or threat."

"Unless they were wrapped in the silk," Quill said—which was a useless guess.

Ivandred's thick gray caterpillar brows met over his nose as he reread Lineas's letter. Then he mopped his face with a handkerchief, and frowned into the middle distance, shifted on his stool, then said, "Listen, here's why I asked you to come. It's the news about the attack, which just reached me. Made me look again at my tally. I hadn't seen this pattern over the weeks and even months, but, well, most of the merchants, tinkers, and tradesmen have been going west and staying, many saying as they go through that word has gone out all along the coast that Idego is now prosperous and promising for trade. And . . . well, it just occurred to me now, but your silk merchant, or whoever he is, might be part of this pattern. At least, he always has different caravan guards around his carts each time."

Quill said, "When you say traders and caravan guards, are they men?" He hated asking, because he suspected he'd hate the answer. "So you're thinking that this stream of enterprising tinkers and so forth might be something besides traders and artisans?"

Ivandred reached behind the bed, and tapped a square in the rough wall. A tiny hinged door swung open. He pulled out a book, and leafed through the closely written pages, then pointed a long, bony finger at columns. "All going west. Few of them coming through going east again. See what you think."

Neat columns in Ancient Sartoran recorded the date, the profession, and a brief description of everyone passing down the narrow gorge beneath the cobbler's shop where Ivandred worked at weaving treated and dyed leddas into boots and shoes.

Quill paged back over the years since the king had withdrawn his new army from riding the Nelkereth further south. Ivandred counted up the men whose descriptions put them between eighteen and thirty. Each year the number had jumped exponentially, always in twos and threes, but arriving ever closer together—always going west, but not as many returning, and those who returned numbered women, older men, children with their families.

Even if a proportion of those moving westward were real traders, the number of young men far outstripped all other groups several times over. Most of these young men had driven wagons full of barrels and bolts and bales with non-military labels.

Quill met Ivandred's pained gaze. "I think we've been snowed."

There was no point in reminding each other that they had no authority to stop and search the wagons. Ivandred knew he should have spotted the pattern long ago, and figured out a way to check. Quill knew that he should have gone to Ivandred for a report earlier. But no one had suspected such a ruse—if it was a ruse. It would take not only planning over years, but a vast sum of money. Which a wealthy young noble next rank from a prince could compass, if he were as clever as he was ambitious.

"Damn." Quill chucked the journal back to Ivandred and said, "I'm afraid we've identified our enemy army. Now we'd better find it."

FIFTEEN

The first step was Ivandred having to unpick the binding on that meticulously kept journal so that the pages containing the previous month's numbers could be burned. There were enough earlier records to prove his point, and as time was pressing, they had to cover the fact that he would be transferring by magic, which meant the date of the latest entries couldn't be right before his arrival in Ku Halir after what was supposed to be weeks on the road. He stayed up all night restitching the journal.

Knowing that Ivandred would be arriving shortly, suitably covered in road dust as if he'd endured a weeks-long grass run, Quill endured the return transfer to his room in Ku Halir. He stood in the stuffy chamber as he fought down the ache and nausea of transfer reaction. It died too slowly, leaving him aware of his dirty, parched skin, and loose hairs sticking to his face. He clawed them back in tiny crackles of lightning and retreated to the baths, and while soaking his tired body, began to plan what to say in his report.

Lineas and Neit had traveled fast and hard, sleeping side by side under the stars on spongy turf as their animals—traded at every post—rested in their own way, either nibbling at the grasses or standing like silent sentinels as their minds drifted between dream and alertness.

Lineas enjoyed traveling with Neit, but regretted that she couldn't use her golden notecase without being seen. She hadn't heard from Quill since his brief note that he was on the trail of someone shadowing a large Marlovan party. But of course he could take care of himself.

As for Neit, she was well pleased with her companion. Though skinny, freckled Lineas was not much to look at, she was tougher than she seemed. Neit had liked Lineas from their first meeting, but had fallen into the habit of pitying her for the way she exerted herself to anticipate the oblivious Connar's every wish and comfort. He was shaping up to be a terrific war leader, but in Neit's opinion, a terrible match for someone like Lineas.

But no one was asking her opinion. No one ever thanked you for poking your nose into others' messes for their own good.

And yet, and yet. There was that day when Quill and Lineas had been star gazing, the looks in both their faces on their return!

She and Lineas made very fast time. When they arrived at the crossroads where Lineas would turn eastward toward Ku Halir and Neit would continue south, they discussed it, then decided it would be worth the extra half-day for Neit to ride into Ku Halir with Lineas, in case there was further news to be carried to the king.

As Neit and Lineas neared Ku Halir, the hot, dry wind had begun fretting their horses and sending dust twists twirling across the road and over straw-dry grasses. It was a relief to ride at last into the stable yard, which they discovered was full of horses, their shadows stretching impossibly long in the slanting late afternoon light.

"Big company just arrived," Neit said. "If it's Connar, then runners are going to be coming and going. Here's a hint for future travels: when the military turns up in big numbers, there's seldom room for us. So we go to the scribe houses."

"Oh! Yes, Fannor told us that once." Lineas wiped her forearm across her sweaty face, and looked away; it was true that the royal runners and the scribes worked together, and sometimes shared accommodations, but Mnar Milnari had warned them that scribes by nature tended to be nosy, thinking that all news ought to be shared back and forth.

Neit wheeled her horse and led the way to the smaller stable used by support staff, including scribes.

Indeed, it was somewhat less crowded, though no less busy. The scribe house was, like many of the lakeside buildings, stone from ground to the first floor windows, and wood above, going up only two stories, with wide windows under the roof open at either end to the breeze coming off the lake, which made the rooms cool off a little faster than similar chambers in the stone garrison.

Neit strode in with her usual insouciant confidence, scattering a gaggle of scribe students clustered around the door, watching the arrivals at the garrison.

"Royal runner here," Neit said, jerking her thumb at Lineas. "And me, running messages for the crown prince. Got beds?"

"Attic is the only free spot," an older scribe-apprentice said. "Is that one of the princes, just arrived? Do you know what's going on?"

"No idea! Attic it is," Neit said cheerfully, slinging her gear over her shoulder. "Better than dirt, which is all the bed we've had this week." She felt the eyes rolling behind her, and grinned.

Lineas cast the scribes a sympathetic glance and went after Neit. After the brilliant light of summer, she could barely see in the shadowy interior. She followed Neit's broad back up the stairs to the second floor. The stair to the attic was a ladder at the end of the long line of flimsy little rooms, all with doors standing open to catch any movement of air, hot as it was.

"Hey, I've seen you before, haven't I?" Neit said to a tall, handsome boy with dark brown eyes and pale hair.

His smirk changed to uncertainty as he opened a hand. It seemed to Lineas he wanted to speak, but Neit strode right past, toward the ladder. In the last room, near the top of a second stairway, Lineas caught sight of a young woman her own age sitting cross-legged at a low table, candles burning at her right and left hands as she carefully copied something out.

Lineas admired the beautiful script as Neit paused in the door. "Two candles are a bad idea in this season."

The scribe looked up, her mouth tight. "My script is perfect because there's no shadow cast. And I'm faster than anyone," she replied in a none-of-your-affair voice.

Lineas winced; though the scribe was rude, no one likes outsiders offering helpful comments unless asked. Of course she would be careful with her candles.

Neit shrugged and led the way upstairs, saying low-voiced, "I remembered Anderle, all right. Had a fun liberty with him, until he got bossy. Let him think I've forgotten. Be good for him."

She chuckled, then whooshed out a deep breath as they entered a murderously hot space under the slant of the roof, with four narrow beds in it, unoccupied from the looks of the smooth sheets and the blanket folded neatly at the foot of each. She slung her gear onto the nearest. "No use in unpacking. Likely I'll be riding out again, as soon as I can get anywhere near Ventdor. There's sure to be news, with Connar just arrived."

Lineas put her gear down, but from habit, slid her journal and notecase into her inner pocket, just in case there were curious roommates with sticky fingers. Everyone knew scribes were curious. She shook out her robe to obscure the pockets in folds before she followed Neit back down the ladder and out.

They headed toward the garrison to make their report. Lineas peered into the thickest group of gray-coated warriors for Connar's blue-black horsetail swinging between his shoulders.

Neit touched her arm. "Stay," she said, low-voiced. "I think I spotted royal runner blue going into the command wing. Let's catch up with whoever it is before we report, shall we? I don't know how it is, as you royal runners aren't any faster than the best of us long runners, but you always seem to have the news before anyone else. May's well know as much as we can in case the prince has questions," she added.

Lineas's heart rapped against her ribs at Neit's cheerfully careless *You always seem to have the news before anyone else*. Words of denial flitted through her mind, but she wouldn't lie. A quick glance at Neit relieved her. Neit wasn't questioning how that could be, as she peered over the crowd passing in and out of the building adjacent to the stable as they turned that way.

On the other side of the busy parade ground, Connar—always aware of his periphery—caught sight of runner blue. It was Quill, who stopped short, with a sudden smile that Connar could see from all the way across the parade ground. It was so intimate a smile, so revealing that Connar instinctively turned to see who among the mass of warriors could spark that kind of smile, and shock jolted him when he recognized Lineas's bright red hair.

At the same moment Lineas saw Quill, and her entire countenance bloomed with joy.

The world reeled, and Connar sucked in a breath, fighting a hot cloud of fury.

" . . .Connar-Laef?" There was Manther Yvanavayir, looking hollow-eyed. Connar hadn't seen Manther since he left the academy. He looked wretched. Old, even, though he only had two or three years on Connar.

"Royal runners," Connar said, fighting that sense of being off-balance. "Three of them. There has to be news." He started toward them, as the mass parted to let him through.

On the other side of broad stable yard, Quill got a grip on himself.

The four met, and Neit, taking them all in with a fast glance, spoke first. "Lineas and I made a grass run," she said. "She has the report. I'm just staying long enough to see if anyone wants to add to what Nadran-Sierlaef is sending to the king, then I'm off to the royal city."

"Let's hear it," Connar said to Lineas.

She regarded him through those wide eyes of hers, and silently held out a letter.

Connar took it, snapped it open, saw the word 'army' and ran his eyes down Noddy's careful handwriting. Too late to be useful. Connar already knew Skunk had a force, but it was clear from the painstaking words that Noddy had no more idea where this army was than anyone else.

Instead, Connar held the letter before him as if reading it closely, but considered Quill from the side of his vision, then shifted from one foot to the other, consciously reminding himself that he and Lineas had made no promises to be exclusive. It's just that he'd thought she was, for she was always there when he returned. For the first time, it hit him that she had a life when he wasn't there. And what would be more predictable than that she'd pillow-jig with the other royal runners?

Connar side-eyed Quill, who stood by impassively; Quill had ridden hard to bring the golden arrow Connar wore on his right sleeve. Equally vivid, Quill's leap, taking out two big brawlers in one smooth motion, fast as the blink of an eyelid.

Yes, he could see it himself. If you looked past the royal runner robe, Quill was tight. Good-looking, even. Certainly worth an idle mattress-dance. He shifted again, recollected himself, distracted right there in the parade ground with hundreds of eyes on him.

He crushed the letter in his hand and turned to Quill. "You don't have anything new, right? I just saw you—"

"Grass!" the wall sentry bawled, and another tooted the horn to clear the gateway.

Another surge in the sea of gray, and Ivandred rode in, dust-covered to his thin gray frizz. He spotted Connar standing with Neit and the two royal runners, rode up and saluted. "The king posted me up north. I've found a pattern that I thought had better be reported."

"Come into Ventdor's office," Connar said to them all.

They were so intent on hearing everyone's report that they were scarcely aware of the stunning heat.

To Connar the various reports felt like pieces of one of those paper chase games he'd always hated, fitting together to make a map leading to a basket of apple-tarts or a barrel of cellar-cold fizz. But this was real. The assassin appeared to have told the truth. There seemed now to be *two* forces, Yenvir's and Prettyboy's. Prettyboy was more than likely this Elsarion princeling, or whatever they called their rankers.

But they still had no idea of their locations.

In the way of people who had already given their information, they were repeating themselves as everyone bleated and barked obvious questions no one could answer. Connar ignored them as he stared down at the sketches of Elsarion. Now Connar understood Manther's haggard expression. It was guilt, shared family guilt on behalf of his blockhead of a sister—the same blockhead, he was fairly certain, who had run a snatch on Ghost Fath that damned summer, while he was lying on his stomach in the lazaretto.

He'd always liked Manther, who'd been a decent captain in academy games when he and Noddy were still in smocks. He tried to think of something to say, something a commander would say.

Then another runner stuck his head in the door to report that Rat Noth just riding in, horse steaming.

"Rat?" Commander Ventdor exclaimed. "He was chasing Yenvir!"

The captains squeezed up to make room for Rat Noth, who strode in, caked with dust to the eyebrows. Connar's gaze flicked to the two silver chevrons on Rat's right sleeve: one level away from a commander. The way everyone deferred made it clear how much they respected Rat, who had gained his promotions in the field. No family preference for him.

Rat saluted Connar before he saluted Ventdor. That sparked gratification. Though Ventdor held commander rank, Connar had been given orders by the king, and everyone seemed to know it. You were right about this much, Hauth, he thought. Rat never questions chain of command.

That inward reflection, brief as it was, caused him to miss the first few words of Rat's report. But Rat had always talked slowly and painstakingly, if he spoke at all. " . . . our animals were spent. They had remounts somewhere, probably the ones they took from Tlen. We lost them when they took to a river."

"Damn." Ventdor slammed his hand on the desk. "But that was days ago. You've searched, right?"

"That's why I'm back to report," Rat said. "Braids Senelaec and his scouts found 'em. Or found someone, even if it's not the same ones. I thought we had to cross country to chase. The Sindan-An girls, knowing that countryside, said to follow the rivers. They were right."

"Yenvir?" Ventdor asked.

"Don't know. They didn't get close enough to spot him."

Ventdor looked at Connar, who looked back, mind swimming with questions. But which one to ask without looking stupid? Ventdor's lips parted, and Connar opened his hand.

Ventdor said, "Was Braids Senelaec spotted?"

"No," Rat stated. "Saw plenty of prints, all the green cropped down by a lot of horses. The scouts went doggo till night. Crept to the edge of their perimeter. Heard chatter in some language they don't know. When I came up, saw for myself, no alarms raised, just a single perimeter line, with plenty of blind spots between the sentry posts. They think they're invisible to us. Waiting."

"For word," Connar exclaimed. "If it's Yenvir, from Elsarion. And the other way. We'll attack them first. Wait. What's the ground?"

He caught a slight uptick in Rat's jaw—approval. Gratification flushed through Connar, to vanish just as quickly. He didn't want Rat crowding his shoulder. Connar *had* to think first, think fast.

"They've got a perfect defensive spot," Rat said. "If we go in numbers, even those sloppy sentries are bound to see something coming uphill. Attacking uphill is already against us."

Nobody argued with that.

Rat went on, gazing at the map, "Approximately here." His bow-callused finger drew a circle west of Yvanavayir. "Somewhere in those woody hills. None of us know that territory. But if they come riding downstream, toward the river here, see, that's where we could come at 'em hard. There's a valley where I had my wing hiding out while I went to see what Braids' scouts found. They reach that, we ride down the banks, both sides." He clapped his hands.

It was a perfect plan—and just what Connar had feared would happen, offered before he could come up with it.

Since everyone was looking his way, he said, "While we're waiting. Rat, I want you to ride to the royal city and report to the king personally. I'm still under his orders. Ghost has Halivayir secured. Tell him our plan is to ride on this army before they can ride on us."

Connar watched narrowly, but Rat demonstrated no sign of resentment at being sent away as his fingers brushed his coat.

Connar forced a smile. "If you're fast, you'll be first in on one flank."

"I'm off," Rat said, and in a whirl of dusty coat skirts, he was.

Connar looked around. They were all waiting for him to speak. His headache had sharpened too much for clear thought. So he said, "Let's hear ideas."

"I've never been in actual battle," Sneeze Ventdor admitted. "But I've been wargaming with the King's Army ever since it was formed, and one thing I do know is logistics . . ."

He made sensible suggestions that Connar barely heard. Then others had to air their thoughts, round and round. They were beginning to repeat themselves for the second and third times when Ventdor reached for water, to find the jug empty. He blinked around the room, regarded the sweaty faces, and said, "I'm parched. Connar-Laef, my suggestion is to break for a meal."

Connar suppressed a wince against his headache, having an idea that a commander ought not to show any more discomfort than anyone else. He'd forgotten that he hadn't had anything to eat or drink since before dawn. "Lead the way."

Ventdor took him to the captains' mess. After downing four cups of water, then wolfing down a plate of cabbage rolls, Connar felt immeasurably better, enough to think beyond the war meeting . . . and there was the image of Lineas again. That joyful smile—for someone else.

The men had already been released until further orders came. Connar therefore had nothing to do. He recollected the three royal runners and Neit standing against the back wall, all silent but listening. When Ventdor suggested the mess hall, Connar had been too preoccupied with thirst and that headache to pay attention, but peripherally had been aware of Neit saying, "I'm off to the royal city," and Ivandred adding, "I'll ride with you."

That left Quill and Lineas.

Impulsively Connar set off to find Lineas, though he wasn't sure what he'd say. He wanted to see her face, that welcoming smile for *him,* to reassure him that everything was the way it had been.

On his way out he spotted a young runner in training hefting a stack of baskets. "Where are royal runners assigned?"

"They aren't," the boy said. "When we've got these many crowded in. They go wherever there's a bed. Either next to the stable, or over at the scribblers. They always have extra beds."

Connar successfully translated scribblers as scribes, and bent into the hot, dry wind to head across the parade ground. The merciless sun had dipped below the castle walls at last, throwing them into silhouette against a lurid western horizon.

At least his headache had all but subsided. Tomorrow early, he'd be back at drill, *hard* drill. First himself, with the best swordmaster Ventdor had, and then the rest of his command; they'd been perfunctory due to the need for speed, and these past three days they hadn't drilled at all, sleeping outside, and chewing stale travel bread and hard cheese as they rode in the merciless heat.

He reached the scribe house, and ducked out of the wind into a small chamber that retained the day's heat, where he surprised a couple of scribe students in the process of lighting lamps as they complained about the weather. At Connar's step they silenced, the younger ones with wide eyes going from his face to the gold chevron on his sleeve and back to his face.

One pointed toward the stairs and whispered—as though he'd attack if they spoke normally—"The royal runners are upstairs."

Connar suppressed the urge to laugh. "Thanks."

Sound carried up the stairs on that wild wind, to where Lineas and Quill stood perforce around the closest doorway, where the copyist with the two candles, who had introduced herself as Ndand, did her level best to attach Quill's notice.

Quill longed for water, food, and escape, but had set those needs aside the moment Lineas said as they exited Ventdor's office, "We can talk at the scribe house, where my things are."

Talk? About what? Probably she wanted merely a chance to exchange reports with no one listening, he'd cautioned himself, though all he could think about as Ndand nattered away was the flash of joy Lineas had expressed when she saw him.

Desperate to get away from this scribe who would not shut up, he became aware of the youngsters downstairs going silent. Then came that single word, *Thanks.* Quill recognized the voice as Connar's. He didn't know the younger prince at all; what he'd seen from a distance during their young days was that he was tight with his brother, though he was intensely competitive with everyone else.

Quill had been standing at Lineas's shoulder, doing his best with the angle of his body to indicate he was ready to leave. At the sound of Connar's voice, followed by the ring of bootheels on the stair, instinct prompted him to shift away from Lineas.

And so when Connar stepped onto the landing, he saw Lineas and Quill standing at either side of a door, looking in at a young woman in scribe robes.

At the sight of the prince, Ndand leaped to her feet. Or she tried to. After a long day of labor, she was tired, and a little light-headed: first this handsome royal runner appeared, followed by the black-haired, blue-eyed prince who, until then, she had only glimpsed at a tantalizing distance.

He was looking right at her as she rose—and her thighs caught painfully under the edge of her desk, which was no more than a writing board set on two storage boxes. And so her guttering candles, a waiting lamp, and all her day's work—plus a waiting stack of clean paper—tumbled together as the board upended, oil and hot wax, paper and flame mixing.

In less than a heartbeat, the wind, swirling in through that window not far away, scattered all those papers, ignited them in a hundred tongues of fire. In the same instant the burning papers fluttered madly along the floor and between Connar's and Lineas's feet as they stamped ineffectually.

Wind surged down the hall, lifting the burning bits of paper. Lineas batted at a flapping sheet that spun close to her head, throwing off sparks.

Ndand stood horrified, fists to her chin, screaming, "My work!"

At that moment the oil that had dripped down the upended table reached the floor. A sheet of flame whooshed up the tabletop, a wall of fire dividing her off from the doorway.

Sparks showered, and smoke began filling the air.

Connar gripped Lineas's shoulder. "Run," he said, turning to drag her after him.

But when she needed to be, she was strong. She twisted out of his grip, as Quill, light-headed from lack of food and water, looked around desperately for a way to quench the growing fire.

"We have to get Ndand out," Lineas cried.

Quill poked his head into the next room, then emerged again. "Mattress," he said.

"What?" Lineas, with no experience of dangerous fire, responded blankly as she began edging into the room to get to Ndand, who stood with fingers extended, keening in shock. Lineas recoiled hastily from the withering heat.

Connar, veteran of countless academy fire pits, yanked her out into the hall. Then he ripped off his coat and flung it onto the blue flames burning the oil spilled on the floor. "Get *back*," he said sharply.

The coat smothered the flames enough for him to venture a few steps, but immediately dark spots appeared in the cloth, little flames eating holes in the cotton-linen. Connar gazed down at the right sleeve, where fire already distorted his commander's arrow.

Then Lineas screamed, "Oh, Quill, thank you!"

Connar glanced over his shoulder at Quill, struggling to muscle a bulky mattress through the narrow doorway.

Connar gripped one end, and with a grunt of effort gave it a yank then flung it down onto the burning coat, sending sparks whirling furiously up. The mattress smothered the burning oil, creating a mattress-wide path.

He dashed over it, shouting at Ndand, "Move!"

But Ndand stared in shock. Connar coughed, then shouted, *"Get out!"*

Ndand's knees buckled and she swayed.

"Shit." Connar booted the half-burned plank-table out of the way in a shower of sparks, lunged the last few steps, and caught her under the armpits.

He hefted her up over his shoulder, and crossed the tiny room to where Lineas hopped about in the doorway, desperately stamping out patches of sparks. "Come on," he ordered.

Expecting her to follow, he bore Ndand to the landing, and thundered down the smoky stairwell stair, to where the scribe students stood about, frantically trying to cram papers and books into a basket.

"Leave it. *Move!*" Connar shouted, and carried Ndand out the door, trailed by the students.

"Go! Get someone to ring the alarm," Connar snapped at one of them, who blinked twice, then took off at a robe-flapping run.

Connar dropped Ndand down against a stone wall, then turned to ask Lineas if she was all right. But there was no Lineas.

Already dark was gathering fast, made worse by smoke pouring out of the open windows above, and now a thin, ghostly streamer from all the lower windows and the doorway. Connar stood uncertainly, trying to sort Lineas from the people dashing up from both directions, milling and shouting questions at one another.

Then the castle bell began ringing the fire alarm. By now the smoke was billowing upwards, carried on the wind. A couple of riding captains arrived at a run, and began organizing people into lines from the well to the scribe building, as stable hands and Riders arrived, buckets jiggling and clanking in their hands.

Ndand's shrill voice rose above all, "The prince saved me! The prince saved me!"

Connar found himself surrounded by grateful scribes yapping questions. He peered past, frustration mounting, until he spotted two familiar figures emerging from the doorway, one tall, one small, both covered with ash, and coughing hard: Quill and Lineas. He could not believe that pair of feckless *boneheads* had actually gone back into that dangerous building.

He tried to step past the circle around him but Lineas and Quill were too fast, running in the opposite direction—to the bucket brigades. Connar looked at the circle around him. Paying no attention to their yammering, he pointed and said, "They need more hands with the water!"

The scribes—including that witless Ndand, still pawing him and weeping *You saved me*—turned as one, looking at him expectantly.

Perforce Connar led the way. He and his trailing scribes were motioned to the third line, extending from the kitchen well, as the stable well was already crowded with people bringing up and passing along water.

The stars gleamed brilliantly overhead when the last embers were well doused. Tired, filthy, and parched, Quill and Lineas learned from the chatter around them that when the fire happened, most of the scribe staff had gone off to the castle to eat, except for the seniors, who were closeted with Ventdor, getting orders to be written out, copied, and dispersed as soon as possible.

Anxiety had gnawed at Quill, for he knew that his and Lineas's check from room to room had become increasingly perfunctory as the fire spread and the air filled with smoke. He and Lineas both feared they might have missed someone who'd fainted from the thick, poisonous air, the way that blabbermouth Ndand had almost done.

But one of the seniors made it clear that the upstairs had been empty except for Ndand, who always worked late. Spared the fear that they'd missed someone, Quill and Lineas wandered away from the scribes, light-headed with relief and exhaustion. Behind them, Ndand was still wailing about her work and declaiming that the prince had saved her by turns—and there was the evidence, Connar standing out amid all the smoke-stained grays and blues, wearing nothing more than a half-laced shirt over his riding trousers and boots.

Quill sank tiredly down onto the summer-dry grass at the edge of the kitchen garden beside the well. The wetness from the water he'd slopped down his front in his haste to pass buckets was cool against his skin. At least he'd managed to slurp a few swallows to kill the fiery thirst.

Lineas sank to her knees next to him, still coughing. She wiped a grimy hand across her equally grimy face, then turned his way. It was natural as breathing to turn to her, and he stilled as she leaned her forehead against his.

"I'm so tired," she whispered.

Not for all the crowns and thrones the world had to offer would he dare move, or even speak, as her slim fingers slid up his arms to rest on his shoulders. She used him as a support to push herself upright, and her lips parted—and then she looked into his face. Her own, so often studied as they grew up, first out of duty, then a brotherly concern, and finally in dawning love, was as familiar as his own hands. He knew—he thought he knew—her every subtle change of expression. This one was different as her eyes searched his, her pupils so large in the darkness that they swallowed the iris entirely. He could see the reflection of the torches along the sentry wall leaping and burning in them.

"Quill, I . . ." she whispered—then she leaned in again, her eyes half-closing, and softly, ever so softly, kissed him. She tasted of smoke—he was certain he did as well. "I missed you so much," she murmured against his lips. "I know it's stupid, but when you didn't write back I was so afraid . . ." Then she yanked herself away, her face ruddy in the torchlight. "Oh! I must stink terribly—"

Quill's whisper was husky with sincerity. "You could fall into midden waiting for a wand and I'd still want to kiss you."

She laughed, and then looked up as the most unwelcome footsteps in his life approached.

A young stable hand loomed over them, a big basket in both hands. "Anyone hungry? The cook sent around these leftover sticky-rice balls. Said to bring 'em to the fire fighters first."

"Thank you!" Lineas said, up on her knees again as she took a couple of rice balls. "Oh, I'm so filthy, I need a—oh, no! I just realized, my gear bag was in the attic!" she exclaimed in dismay, her hand going to her robe, whose dark blue—unlike her shirt and trousers, face and hands—hid the smoke smudges. For a heartbeat Quill made out a couple of square shapes beneath her fingers. That had to be her golden notecase and her journal, stashed inside the inner pocket.

Quill wanted to say she could stay with him—hesitated as he tried to figure out how to word it—and he was too late.

One of the scribes appeared at the stable hand's shoulder. "There you are! We're to thank you most heartily for helping. Ndand said that you two were there to aid the prince. I'm to say that the quartermaster is setting aside some extra clothing for anyone who lost theirs, if you'll go over to supply right away."

Lineas flickered a quick smile at Quill. "That would be me. I'd better go." She trudged tiredly off.

He sat back, determined not to move until she returned. He took three rice balls out of the basket, thanked the boy, then slowly began to eat as he watched the circle gathered around Connar, easily picked out by his ash-smudged white shirt. From the heady pungency carrying on the still, hot air, bristic had been brought out, bottles passing hand to hand. Drums rolled and rattled, and voices rose in victory songs, ragged at first, then strengthening, as they celebrated the prince as the hero of the day.

The fire already seemed unreal, except for the evidence in ash all over Quill, and the sharp stink rising from his clothes every time he moved.

He peered in the direction of the barracks wing, which he knew was next to supply, but there was no sign of Lineas. She was probably standing in a long line of scribes. He leaned back to rest his aching body, gazing up at the stars as the fretful wind, now somehow cool, played over him. He let his eyes drift closed . . .

Not far off, Connar was intensely restless. He moved among the talking, celebrating crowd, searching for that trick of glance and smile that promised a fast, hard tumble. Here was a square-chinned, brawny armorer giving him the hot-eye, and not two paces beyond him a willowy woman in Iascan colors, clearly having walked in through the gates to gawk. She smiled and drifted his way, saying something or other.

He let a couple of roistering Riders drift between them and moved away, knowing by now, after hundreds of encounters, that when he was in this mood, sex with some stranger would give him only the briefest release, leaving him to a restless night. His mind turned to Lineas, and he remembered her and Quill stumbling hand in hand out of that burning building.

He whirled around, swept the space, and spotted Quill sprawled on the grass, obviously asleep. Well, that answered that question. Connar looked away—and here was Lineas fifty paces off, carrying a bundle in her arms, and looking over her shoulder with a troubled air.

Instinct prompted him to lengthen his steps to intercept her, though surely that distraught face could not be on Connar's account. "Lineas. Why that look? No one was hurt in that fire, though I hope they forbid that witless Ndand from using candles on a board desk."

"It's not that," she said, blinking up at him; he could not tell if the circles under her eyes were tiredness or merely grime. "It's him." She glanced to the side, where Manther Yvanavayir stood in apparent reverie, sun-bleached head bowed, quite alone. "It's like everyone is afraid to talk to him. Surely they can't blame him for what happened with his sister," Lineas said softly.

Manther Yvanavayir. Connar knew Ghost was still close to him; were he here, Manther wouldn't be alone.

Connar turned back to Lineas when she sneezed, and he exclaimed, "You're covered in ash. What were you two doing in there, trying to get yourselves killed?"

Her brow furrowed with surprise. "Checking to see that no one else was there."

And that was Lineas, always worrying about other people, whether it was a gang of worthless Bar Regren or a blabbermouth scribe. "They'd have to be idiots not to run at the first smell of smoke," he retorted. "Of course they got out."

"Ndand almost didn't," she said soberly. "But you saved her. We had to make sure there wasn't anyone else trapped like that."

There was question in her tone, in her gaze, which made him look away. This was Lineas. Sympathy was part of her nature. She'd probably even find sympathy for Manther's shit of a sister. "Let's get out of here," he said, to get past a subject he already hated.

"I'm filthy," she protested, and held up her bundle. "All my things burned. I meant to go to the baths. Get myself decent."

He looked down at himself, then became aware of the stench of his own sweat, and the grit of ash on his skin. "I'll meet you outside the baths," he said, and walked away.

She glanced past him to where Quill lay, one hand loose, clearly asleep. She turned back in time to see Connar glance back at her. He was only some twenty paces away, his manner uncertain. It was that uncertainty that brought her toward the castle wing where the baths were located. The east wind had finally changed direction, chilling her skin before she got through the door to the women's side.

She paused at the door and glanced back once more. The foot patrol went about checking things, and shaking the sleepers awake. "Storm coming," the voices carried across the still night air.

She saw Quill get up, and stumble off toward the stable area. She was surprised at how sharp her disappointment that he didn't look her way, but she breathed it out. He was probably groggy.

There was time to finish their talk, she reminded herself.

She entered the bath, took off her smelly clothes, and wrapped her journal and golden notecase in them. Leaving them filthy was a sure way to protect the journal and the magic case; nobody would want to touch them. Then she dunked her robe in the barrel with the magic on it, and wrung it out. But when she held it up, she was shocked to discover tiny holes all over it from sparks. Fear serried through her, bringing afterimages from the fire; she dreaded dreaming about it.

She longed to leave the robe, but training forced her to take it, to be examined in the light for possible repair.

After a hasty bath in the crowded pool, she dressed in the borrowed clothes and walked tiredly up to the room they had set aside for Connar; garrisons were supposed to have dedicated space for command, especially the royal family. While no one dared sleep there even when it was crowded, the space had been used for storage, and had been hastily excavated. She passed barrels of flour, and baskets of coiled of leddas-strands waiting to be woven into belts, harnesses, boots.

Lineas found Connar sitting on the edge of the bed, wearing a fresh, unlaced shirt, trousers, and his boots. Fish had laid his winter coat on a trunk, and was probably seeking tailors to get a new summer coat made.

She could not see Connar's face in the weak light of a single candle, as his wet hair hung loose, long black curls hiding his profile. But she sensed tension in his shoulders, and in his hands as they rested on his thighs.

She set down her bundle and held up her robe between him and the candle. "I thought I felt sharp pinpricks. Look."

He glanced up, seeing the candlelight through the many tiny burn holes.

Nand at the Sword had told him when he first went with Noddy to the pleasure house, *There are two things I tell every first timer who comes through here—yes, I know it's strictly not your first time. You said you've romped with the boys at the academy. But you'll find that there are as many ways to have sex as there are to love. First: don't mix up the two. They can be blended, and it's wonderful when they are, but don't mistake attraction for love. There can also be love without attraction.*

Like a family? he'd asked.

That's one form of it, she'd replied. *Second, unlike the order in society, no one truly controls love. It can spark and die, whether you're a king or a cook. You can love someone passionately, and they won't love you back. It doesn't mean anything is amiss with you. Or with them. It just means love is like the weather. No one can command, or order away, a snowstorm. Remember both of these things, and you'll do.*

"No one truly controls love." He hadn't thought about love. He still wasn't certain what love really was, other than loyalty to his family. Lineas was . . . she had always been there when he looked for her.

She was here now. He understood that there were questions he could ask but he was not clear on whether or not he wanted to hear the answers.

She was here. For today, for right now, that was enough.

It was nearly dawn when the weather changed with a spectacular flare of lightning and a crash that reverberated through the stone. Lineas lay awake next to Connar, who slumbered on undisturbed. She slipped out of bed to close the shutters in case the rain was driven into the open slit windows, then crawled back in and shut her eyes.

On the surface, everything seemed to be the way it always was, but she sensed a shift in her heart, which she hadn't the experience to define. All she could think of was a memory from a time when she was very small, and her father had taken her down to the lake as winter waned. The entire world had gone white, from the ice on the lake to the smooth banks, where little humps dotted the expanse. Before she could ask what they were, a crack smote the air—the once-solid ice shot out spiderwebs of silver-blue—and those thousands of smooth white dots lifted into the air, stretching into birds in flight. They became a cloud of wings, lifting over the cracking ice, and then swooped down to settle on the far bank.

She turned her head to look at Connar's long lashes lying on his cheeks, a silky strand of blue-black hair tangled in them. Her heart warmed toward him, but it did not burn. The birds had lifted to the far bank.

SIXTEEN

It was Lineas's habit to rise early, and be gone before Fish arrived with Connar's breakfast. She stepped out into the narrow hall, her ruined robe, now dry, tucked tightly around her filthy clothes, with the journal and notecase wrapped inside.

She ran downstairs, then paused when she saw a long shadow cast by a single flickering torch. Cold air eddied around her feet, from the ground-level door around the corner. She slowed so she wouldn't bump into someone, then stopped when she recognized Quill.

He had been leaning against the wall. He straightened up at the sight of her, marks of tiredness in the fine skin under his eyes. His smile flickered, his brows lifting slightly in question.

"Quill," she breathed, her heart brimming with joy and tenderness and wonder so intense that her throat ached, and she had no idea how to go on.

He signed in Hand, "Come outside? Voices echo up that stairwell."

She assented with open palm. They slipped out into a world that had gone from simmering heat to the gray of a slow, steady rain, after the spectacular thunder a few hours ago.

Quill closed the outer door. They pressed up against the damp stone wall under the dripping eaves, and faced one another, barely an arm's distance between them. "Lineas, I would give anything to stay," Quill said. "But I'd better go before I'm given orders that I have to obey."

"Go?"

"You heard the report yesterday. We've been caught by surprise. None of us know how bad the danger is." He looked away, then down. "I'm as sorry as I can be that I managed to fall asleep while waiting for you to return. I didn't mean to."

"Quill." She reached to touch his lips. "Don't. I know how tired you were. I know how tired I was. It was as well. I . . ."

"I know you were with Connar," Quill said, his expression shuttering. "And if that's where you want to be—"

"I want," she said, "to be with you."

He stilled, his gaze rising to her face.

She sighed, hugging the acrid-smelling cloth to her. "But I think . . . I can't . . ." She struggled with inchoate emotions. Thoughts. Staring out at the gray sky, she said slowly, "A long rain ends, but it doesn't leave the world dry. There are the drips on the leaves, and the rushing streams. It's . . . it's like that, with Connar."

Quill had not even let himself expect that much.

She peered into his face, and what she saw encouraged her to go on. "He has this invasion to worry about, and I . . . I find the idea of saying no to him hurts, when he seems to need me."

Quill looked up, then down again. Though he'd spent that entire first year on his journey sporting with anyone who asked in his effort to forget Lineas, he hadn't been able to displace her from his heart.

This was new territory for them both. Better not to say anything about Connar. "I want to be with you," he said. "As soon as possible, as long as possible. If it can't happen now, then it can't happen now."

And he watched the tension ease in her face.

He went on, forcing a brisk, report tone, "I've been writing letters half the night. Vana is with Noddy-Sierlaef, riding down from Larkadhe. Ivandred went to the royal city. We have two royal runners here besides us, but both are under Ventdor's orders. There's no one else to find that army, and if necessary relay its movement by notecase. Camerend agrees—the danger is significant enough to risk revealing the secret of the notecases, if we can't hide their existence while relaying necessary information. The secret was going to come out sometime, and we've a more stable government now than in generations. And we dare not get caught by surprise anymore."

Lineas thought of Tlen and Halivayir, and pressed her fingers against her lips.

"So as soon as you and I finish speaking, I'll go to Ventdor and offer to get any messages to the royal city. I'll do the same with the scribe chief. And I'll send them to Mnar once I'm on the road, so she can release them when the time is right—and then I'll ride east instead of south."

Lineas said, "But Braids Senelaec and his company are there watching them—oh. Several days' ride away." Her throat hurt, but she forced out the word, "Yes, you're right to go. It's too important."

He smiled. "We can write to one another, can't we?"

Instead of answering, she pulled him into a tight hug. He pressed a kiss on the top of her bright, frizzy head, then let go, and stepped back. "Go first," he whispered. "Or I'll never get out of here."

She was shivering in the loose robe the quartermaster had loaned her. She opened the door, looked back once, memorizing his face, the raindrops dotting his robe, the strand of dark hair that had come loose from his queue, and lay on one shoulder. She stretched out a finger to caress it. He moved, pressing a kiss onto her hand.

She squeezed her eyes shut and ducked inside. Then she ran to the bath, keeping her head down lest she meet someone who would see the tears she could not prevent.

She cried herself out, for no reason she could define, keeping her face underwater as long as she could. When others arrived for their morning bathe, she rose and dressed.

Her old robe was impossible to save. She used it to wrap her journal and notecase, then reported back to the quartermaster to see what cloth they had, and was delighted to discover they had several lengths of what she recognized as Farendavan linen, dyed dark blue. Of course the queen would never forget the royal runners when going over the supply lists for the garrisons.

By the time she got outside, the sun was fully up behind the clouds, rain slanting silver. She could make a new robe later. She got a hunk of fresh bread, cut some cheese off the wheel, then headed for Commander Ventdor's office to see if there was any task she could do to keep herself busy.

She was passed by the outer guard. When she heard Connar's voice echoing from the commander's office, she paused, uncertain.

" . . . and I want you to send Quill to the royal city. He's the fastest of the royal runners."

"He's already gone," came Ventdor's voice. "He was here at dawn. Offered to take whatever we had, all right and proper. Rode out into the rain. He's as excellent as his da, that one."

"Already gone?" Connar said, and Lineas heard his smile. "Yes, that's what I'd expect from Quill. He's the best of the royal runners."

Rat Noth had been born with a slight stutter, which was during his earliest years a mild frustration. It was mitigated by his parents insisting it was a badge of honor, inherited from one of best of the kingdom's warrior princes, Jabber Montreivayir, second son of the Great Evred.

Then his mother died in a mysterious accident, and while he was trying to recover from that, his father married his stepmother, who already had two sons a couple years older than Rat and Mouse.

Rat had liked being called Rat, because that, too, was a well-respected nickname in the Noth family. But his Nyidri stepbrothers, Demeos and Ryu, started calling him 'Lamb' because he bleated, and laughed at him every time he tried to speak, which initially made the stutter worse. Then they'd pretended not to understand anything he said, and tormented him further by talking in Sartoran, telling him he was too stupid to understand it.

Rat learned to evade them. He then discovered that if he talked slowly, in very short sentences, the stutter could be tamed. By the time he turned ten and went off to the academy (his stepbrothers being sent to Sartor for schooling), he had nearly grown out of the stutter altogether, but the habit of speaking only when he had to, as short as possible, remained. He much preferred Hand, once he was introduced to it his first year at the academy.

The only situation where his silence worked against him was when he met girls.

Except, that is, for one.

An outsider looking in at Danet-Gunvaer with her daughter and soon to be daughters-by-marriage, might be amused by the range in expressions revealed by those three at their three-month meetings to discuss the kingdom's affairs.

Ranet was the most focused. In her earliest days at the royal castle, she had dreaded the allocation meetings, for she had not wanted to admit that she was mildly short-sighted, like many of her Senelaec relatives. Distance vision was fine. It was numbers and small writing she had trouble with. To get past her difficulties with reading, she had early on learned to memorize whatever others read out loud. She brought that skill to the allocation meetings, and had become so adept at committing the lists of numbers to memory that Danet more and more often turned to her to recover a stray number.

In contrast to her intense focus, there was Bun, whose mind wandered far afield. It was odd, Bunny thought sometimes, how long stretches of silence would let in the sounds outside the windows, while the circle sat inside talking away in Hand. Then someone would break it—usually Ma, who still got her fingers tangled in words—and then there'd be speech and Hand for a while, until they went silent again, usually when Noren signed, because her Hand was so much faster than speech.

The best was when the silence was broken by a sudden laugh. That was usually Noren. Her laugh was a kind of goose honk that Bunny found tremendously endearing, it was so real, unlike the titters of the girls in queen's training, many of whom giggled whenever their leader—whoever that might be—did. There was a falsity to those giggles, as well as a sameness that, when you thought about it, had to be learned, just like speech. It seemed sad to her that people had to learn a certain type of laugh.

In contrast to both Ranet and Bunny there was Noren, whose whole demeanor made it plain how much she relished these meetings four times a year: spring, when they looked at what they had left against needs across the kingdom; summer, they assessed what was beginning to come in against what needs had turned up since spring; autumn, they counted what was coming in from harvests. Last was the winter allocation, when they looked at the marriage treaties for the year, as reported either at Convocation or via messenger in the years Convocation wasn't held: who had been born, who had married, what they had worked out in their betrothal treaties.

Bunny was bored stiff by numbers, but Noren saw them as the warp and weft of the kingdom. Greatmother Tdor had called it a net, but Noren saw good cloth in all these things people made and grew, and then sent as promised. It was a cloth woven by faith that each would do their part to make the whole.

"That's it," Danet exclaimed suddenly, hands in motion. "We know what we have, but until Halivayir is settled, and we get a report on Tlen, we won't know what's needed. Let us hold ourselves in readiness."

She flashed her rare, thin smile as she leaned over and tapped a scroll. "Unless Andaun gets a sheaf of late letters, next spring is when we put our ten-year-olds in with the boys. I would not have minded waiting a year or so. But it's clear enough from what happened at Tlen. Braids' girls did well, and no one is going to object, especially given the attacks in the east and the fact that we've fewer nine-year-old boys for next year than we've had in fifteen years. That lack will be filled out nicely by these eighteen girls." She tapped the scroll again.

Noren kept back a grin: three of those girls were from Noth and Totha Rider families, and one from Marthdavan. Most of the rest were from the eastern alliance, save two from the Olavayir Riders, and one from the gunvaer's own birth holding, daughter of her brother.

Danet sat back on her cushion in satisfaction. Then she looked up. "I'm starved. Surely the midday watch change is about to ring. Go get a meal, girls."

Bunny jumped up with alacrity. Through the open windows had come the sound of a new arrival to the stable. She sped out to see who it was.

'Braids' girls,' she thought, laughing to herself. Girls! To the queen's training girls, Bunny and Noren were women with titles. How odd it was, to find yourself suddenly the oldest in group, after forever being the youngest. Maybe to Ma, she and Noren and Ranet would always be girls, even when they turned fifty—

She rounded the landing, and came face to face with Rat Noth. "Rat!" she exclaimed, every nerve thrilling in delight.

His reaction was even more intense. He turned a deep red, grinning down at his feet.

She exclaimed, "I thought you were up at Ku Halir, chasing after that Skunk and the rest of the murderers." She grabbed hold of his arm and began to tow him down the royal residence hall toward her suite, so she could get the full story, without the sort of interruptions that made Rat go silent. "What happened? I want to know everything! How are the horses?"

Rat hesitated, then laid a tentative hand on top of hers as he halted. "I have to report to the king," he said.

She smiled at his hand, squashing the urge to pull him close and hug him. Strange, how many lovers and crushes she'd had—all still friends—but the person she had begun to feel the most strongly about she had yet to even kiss. She wasn't even certain how it had happened so gradually over the years since that first time she and Rat spoke, when she was more interested in his horse than in just another senior academy boy.

She watched him go, hoping she could catch him before he was ordered off again; at the same time, he walked away, feeling the distance lengthen between them. He didn't understand how he could visit a pleasure house with his body afire, then as soon as it was over, he was done. Most of the time he and whoever he was with scarcely exchanged ten words. He'd always liked it that way—until he started talking to the princess.

As he crossed over to the state wing, his mind flashed back to a conversation that still made him angry. It was like picking at a scab, only worse, because at least a scab healed. But Rat couldn't forget his stepbrother Ryu smirking at him one morning. *Heyo, Lamb, you're always in and out of the barbarians' royal castle. Is my betrothed really as stupid as she is ugly?*

All Rat could say was, *Go look for yourself.* He still thought it was a boneheaded response, but everything Ryu did or said made him feel like a bonehead. At least neither stepbrother cared enough to see how much Rat liked her, or he would never hear the end of Ryu's cruel "jokes" at Bunny's expense.

He shook off the memory of Ryu the way he'd shake off a cobweb he'd walked into, then consciously rubbed his fingers over the place on his arm that she'd touched. It was worth it, riding hard during fierce Lightning Season heat followed by storms, just for that touch.

He reached the scribe chamber, where the runner downstairs had said the king was, and stopped long enough to get his thoughts in order.

Before he could reach for the door, it banged open, and the king himself took a step out, then fetched up in a halt. "There you are! Janold said you'd arrived. Come in, come in. Why are you here?"

Midway into Rat's report, Arrow, who'd dropped onto his cushion, one elbow on the table, sat upright. "Yenvir wanted *what?* He's going to do *what?"* He bounced up, strode to the door in two strides, yanked it open, and bellowed, "Ring the alarm! I want three companies out on a far perimeter. Now!"

He slammed the door, strode back and plopped down, scowling. "Go on."

Distracted, Rat looked about at the stacks of papers lay everywhere; and recognized one of his own reports lying on a table. "Connar-Laef told us that he dispatched the assassin once they got all that, and they rode for Ku Halir . . ."

At the end of the report, Rat swallowed, looking longingly at the jug at the other end of the table, beaded with moisture, then up as the king clapped his hands and rubbed them. "Go over to Noth. Tell him to come here. Then get something to eat. You'll be on the road before the sun dips a finger, leading a battalion picked by Noth. I want Elsarion and that shit Yenvir brought down. If they're not dead, put 'em in chains and we'll try all three of 'em."

"Three?" Rat repeated.

"That Yvanavayir blabbermouth, too," Arrow stated heavily. "You should see the letters coming in, demanding her blood. Tell Connar the entire kingdom is counting on you boys—you. Connar. Ghost Fath, and young Tyavayir, I forget what they call him—"

"Stick," Rat supplied.

"That's it." Arrow smacked his hands onto his knees. "Stick. Heh. Let's see what our training can do."

Stick Tyavayir and Ghost Fath's training first failed then saved them.

Stick's company had been riding northwards through the crackling-dry heat, stopping only long enough at every stream to let the horses drink. The men soaked their entire bodies as they refilled their flasks. It was a relief to gain the relative cover of trees once they crossed the great river, with hills at their right, hiding the sun until well into morning.

The day they reached Halivayir, which Ghost Fath had secured on Connar's orders, the hot, dry winds stilled and that night the weather broke in a spectacular storm. Stick kept his company overnight at the old castle, which was barely larger than an outpost.

"It's been quiet," Ghost said later that evening, as the rain roared outside the open windows. Stick and his captains heard *boring* in his tone—a completely wrong assessment, but he was not going to talk about how profoundly depressing it had been to ride into ruined Halivayir, the site of many happy childhood visits.

Ghost hadn't had any blood connections at Halivayir—only a great-aunt through marriage—but his intended wife Leaf Dorthad, daughter of the Rider captain, had been runner to the old jarlan. He and Leaf had been friends from childhood, and friendship would have been at the base of their marriage. According to one of the few survivors, Leaf had fought fiercely, shooting brigands from the top of the bell tower. And when her basket of arrows was empty, she had leaped head first to deny them the pleasure of killing her, and had been left for dead.

She still lay lifeless except for the shallowest breathing, in a cottage set near a waterfall that fed the stream running into the castle. The old nanny who had survived because the brigands didn't consider her worth killing had kept Leaf alive so far by patiently trickling nourishing soup into Leaf a drop at a time. But no one knew if she would ever waken.

The rest of the elderly, wounded survivors had managed to Disappear all the dead, but nothing in the way of reparation had been done until Ghost's arrival. That first week, after making certain the enemy was gone, they had spent cleaning and mending, every night singing the Hymn to the Fallen, and the Andahi Lament.

He hated being there, where he could do nothing to right the injustice, where grief overlay the old, good memories. And he'd tell Stick later—for he'd had a mother-side uncle who'd died on the wall.

But first, the general report. "Tanrid-Laef Olavayir sent me a wing of Olavayir Riders to patrol the border. I've also got some of our cousins from Tyavayir, as well as Riders sent from the freeholds, according to treaty. The queen's own family, the Farendavans, sent me a full riding."

"Sounds like you've got an army of your own here," Stick said, looking around—he, too, remembered a fond visit, and burned to catch those who'd slaughtered what amounted to a group of old people, guarded by a handful of women: Halivayir, small and peaceful for generations, had sent nearly all the Dorthad Riders to reinforce Sneeze Ventdor at Ku Halir.

Ghost looked around, though no one was in the room but the two of them, Stick's first runner, and three of Ghost's riding captains, all long known and trusted. Ghost leaned toward Stick. "If Connar didn't give you orders for me to stay, let me come with you."

Stick was silent as he gazed into the empty fireplace. He really wanted Ghost with him; he remembered quite well that Yenvir's campsite had looked like it could house three battalions or so. And he had only his wing of eighty-one.

"There were no orders about you," Stick said reluctantly. "The last orders were for you to secure Halivayir."

"And Halivayir is as secure as can be. I don't see why anyone would come at us again, not with *full flights* riding the border instead of merely a riding. They're carrying lances. The walls are bristling with my Fath cousins. Why would anyone attack here again? The worst of it is, the way old Goose Banth talked, this was only a ruse, or a test. Yenvir's shits robbed and ruined then rode right out again. There's nothing left to gain!" Ghost exclaimed, hands out wide, wispy strands of his fine, pale hair a nimbus around his face.

The three young riding captains in the background shifted their feet and exchanged glances at the suppressed violence in his voice.

Ghost sensed their reaction, and cleared his throat. "Look. We really ought to send a report anyway. They always hammered that in the academy."

Stick opened his hand. "True. We should send a report."

"So, how about we send someone fast, like Snake Wend, say, to report to Noddy-Sierlaef in Larkadhe. We ride north. He reports and then asks permission for me to join you. Snake then rides back from Larkadhe to meet us at that campsite we found, alongside the river below that long climb to Yenvir's lair. Snake is fast enough to get to Larkadhe and there about the same time we would. Of course I'll do whatever Noddy says: if he says I have to turn around and ride back to this castle, I'll come back. No harm done."

Stick wavered.

Ghost smacked the arms of the ancient wingback chair he sat in. "As for command, a first year in the lancers could hold this castle with all that reinforcement. They don't need me here."

Stick's mobile countenance eased. "Let's do that. Heyo, Keth, summon Snake! Tell him to saddle up."

Snake was seen off from the walls by a cheerful line of young captains, none of them over the age of twenty-five. Relieved to be going, to be *doing,* Ghost chose half of his eagerly volunteering company to ride with him, and while they readied themselves to rejoin Stick's company, Ghost walked up to the quiet cottage where the old nanny sat with Leaf, the open air in the window above the bed bringing in the chuckling sound of a small waterfall.

Ghost looked down sadly at Leaf lying there so still on the narrow bed, her hair clean and ordered on the pillow. She was so thin and pale and still she seemed dead, except for the slight movement of the light blanket pulled up to her collarbones.

Ghost knelt beside the bed, and held the limp hand lying on the blanket. "Leaf," he said. "I don't know if you can hear me. If you can, I'm riding out to get justice for what happened here." He looked around the plain, peaceful room, bees bumbling among the rows in the kitchen garden beyond the other window. He swallowed, then said, "If you can hear me, I want you to wake up. Get better. Help Nanny run Halivayir. I've left some of my company to watch the walls."

He tried to think of anything else to add. The still figure on the bed didn't so much as twitch, so he rose, dusted his knees, and walked out.

They departed before the watch change, and rode steadily north, until they reached the designated meetpoint, a rocky area at the base of a small waterfall feeding a shallow ribbon of a river, along whose bank ran the west-leading road. Above, knotted pines, and the hills that hid the brigands' hideout.

In spite of Ghost's confidence about Snake's speed, there was no sign of anyone on the west road. So they took a day to drill, from morning till night, with determined enthusiasm.

On the second day, still no Snake. They laid plans for besieging the enemy camp: proceed in single file, to hide their numbers, relying on the thick woods to keep them unseen, then when they reached the plateau, spread and charge.

Day three, no Snake. Stick was restive. He had specific orders, and his men were ready. More than ready. Ghost, anxious at the idea of being left out of the action yet again, pleaded with him to let him come along. "Look, you can't take the dog scouts. We know where we're going now, and we don't want the dogs responding to old scent all over those hills and running wild. The scouts can hold the camp, and send Snake up to us, right?"

Stick really wanted Ghost and his men with him. "Let's go," he said.

They did.

And here is where their training betrayed them.

Not that their plan wasn't excellent—for the terrain they had trained in for years. Stick even glanced upward from time to time, as did some others, but they were mostly checking for weather. They listened for the crack of twigs and branches, or the rustle of bushes that would indicate enemies, and didn't hear the song of unfamiliar birds, such as the distinctive whistle of the white-throated sparrow. Not even when these sparrows screeled from treetop to treetop.

And so they were taken utterly by surprise when they reached a steep turn in the trail, under great spreading cottonwood, poplar, and spruce, and enemies sprang from the branches overhead, howling with triumph as they dropped down onto the riders, bare steel in hand. The rest ran out from behind trees and bushes, roaring as they attacked.

The mountain warriors who scored a direct hit slit the Riders' throats. Horses squealed and plunged. Four of Stick's men died instantly. Two fought mightily, streaming with blood; one brawny brigand found his own sword turned on him. Before his curse of surprise had escaped his lips he stared down at his own throat spraying blood in a wide arc, then he fell after it, dead before he hit the ground.

Another struggled with a Marlovan slippery with his own blood from a wound that had gone into the back of his shoulder. They fought on the plunging horse, grappling madly until the Marlovan directly behind rode up and spitted the attacker with his sword.

Yenvir's warriors had the space of about twenty breaths to gloat over their surprise before they began to understand the difference between fighting on horseback and on foot as clumps of them fell before those deadly curve-tipped swords.

Surprise was gone, but they still had numbers: for every one that fell, another five emerged from the bushes to replace them, some trying to go to the horses' heads, for they were under strict orders to kill the Marlovans, but they must not to harm a hair of those precious animals that brought a king's ransom on the other side of the great mountains.

Stick and Ghost fought with desperate fury. No time to assess—to try to form a defensive plan. Strung out the way they were, there was no defensive strategy except to stay on the offensive, that is, ride the enemy down and try to gain the top, or die trying.

Stick flashed the hand signal to his banner bearer to wind the charge on his trumpet, which he did. The men kneed their horses into movement, in effect the dreaded charge uphill as they scanned the trees above as well as both sides.

The forest birds—and false birds—had gone silent, the woods ringing with the clash of steel, the roars and cries of fighting and dying men. Horses squealed and kicked out.

Back down the trail, Adzi, Yenvir's lookout who'd first spotted the enemy coming up the trail, cursed as he tried to climb higher in his tree in order to see the fun.

He'd joined Yenvir to shed blood, not roost in a tree all day. Though his lookout duty was punitive, he'd actually spotted enemies, to his amazement. He'd signaled on the whistle, so Yenvir couldn't be angry with him anymore, right? But Yenvir had said he'd personally flay Adzi if he came down before he was sent for. Yenvir never used figurative threats.

So Adzi figured he at least could climb higher so he could see the slaughter. Only the damn trees were in the way. He worked his way further upward. Surely there had to be some clear sight on the action. Of course there'd be no more Marlovans coming. Even they weren't stupid enough to send another batch after the first one, right?

Wrong.

This is where training paid off.

Snake was so eloquent that Noddy decided he ought to ride with Cabbage Gannan's company, who had been assigned to replace Stick and Ghost's companies at Larkadhe. When they reached the base camp, and discovered that Stick and Ghost had gone ahead just that morning, Cabbage —fired by ambition—urged Noddy to go after them.

They hadn't climbed long when they heard the sounds of fighting echoing down the valley. An exchanged look, and Cabbage sent two scouts ahead to scan.

Both these might have missed Adzi as Stick's company had, but for the wild thrashing of that cottonwood as the lookout worked his way around the top of the tree. They slowed underneath it, squinting up. Adzi heard the horse hooves and peered down, and for a heartbeat three astonished faces stared at each other. Then Adzi raised his whistle to his lips—

The older scout lifted his bow and shot him. They stood back as Adzi fell dead out of the tree: short hair, leggings, a vest over an embroidered shirt, a gold chain around his neck. Definitely not a Marlovan.

The elder scout nocked another arrow as he said to his junior partner, "Had to be their lookout. Go report. I'll scan ahead."

And so Gannan and Noddy heard the first scout's report a short time before they reached the first bodies. The trail was slick with blood as they made their way grimly upward, armed warriors working through either side of the trail in case of a secondary attack.

But Yenvir had shot his bolt with his tree defense. His working strategy had always been to overwhelm his enemies with numbers, rewarding those of his followers who could demonstrate the most kills. All his followers were either attacking Stick and Ghost's diminishing force, or else slipping back up the trail to the plateau, where they'd have a better chance at the enemy; when they saw the ratio of their own dead, many of them slunk away to hide until the enemy had been weakened by the others, their idea to turn up again in time for the kill.

Gradually the brigands withdrew in greater numbers, either falling back toward their plateau or crowding in at the back of the gruesome trail, keeping a wary distance. And so they progressed in three sections, the mountain warriors staying prudently out of range of Marlovan steel. Other lookouts, not under threat of death, abandoned their posts to reinforce their fellows. After all, who ever heard of two parties of attackers?

When Stick and Ghost reached the wide plateau, both wounded and out of arrows, they motioned the remainder of their force together, facing outward. They had swords, knives, and many also had double-sticks.

Yenvir himself strolled out of the main cave, examined the situation, and laughed heartily once he saw that his followers outnumbered the graycoats by a significant margin. However, that had been a far greater number before these enemies had dared his stronghold, which made him angry, and beneath that, a little afraid.

"Get 'em, boys," he ordered. "Disarm them! Keep 'em alive! And we'll have some fun."

Slowly, looking at each other as hands gripped weapons, Yenvir's followers began to tighten their circle, no one wanting to be first.

While that happened, down the trail, Cabbage Gannan was wild with fury after seeing the hacked-up corpse of his cousin Righty Poseid, who had been transferred to Stick Tyavayir after Chalk Hills. He and Noddy, angry and grief-stricken, passed one after another familiar face, bodies lying sprawled in death.

They caught up with the second scout. "They're at the campsite," he reported urgently. "Two bends up."

"Numbers," Cabbage snapped.

"Last I saw, maybe just under a flight left to Tyavayir," he said.

A flight: twenty-seven.

"And them, looked like close on two hundred, maybe a little less, now. It was closer to five."

Cabbage turned to Snake. "Give me the terrain."

Snake had led the way, having been with Stick Tyavayir when they first discovered the place. His report was succinct, after which Cabbage peered off into the trees, then said, "What worked once will work again. Lefty!" He beckoned to his cousin Lefty, now one of his riding captains. "We'll divide up, and . . ."

On the plateau, the enemy circle had advanced twice, then fallen back as the Marlovans sprang savagely to the attack. Every time they withdrew they were cursed more roundly by Yenvir, who stood on a boulder outside the circle. A dozen men lay in the empty space between the ring of enemies and the Marlovans.

"All at once!" Yenvir shouted. "I told you, all at once! Anyone hanging back, I'll flay him myself—"

Then, cutting through his furious roar, a high, eerie shriek, "Yip-yip-yip!"

And from the woods ringing the plateau at either side, horsemen changed, lances raised. The tired horses did not have to gallop more than twenty paces before the lances smashed into the tight ring around the Marlovans, to devastating effect.

Yenvir's men fell over each other in mad, frantic effort to escape, but the Marlovans wheeled expertly and rode them down, shooting and when they ran out of arrows swinging their curve-tipped swords, as Stick Tyavayir and his remaining company used their waning strength for a last, ferocious attack.

Yenvir tried to slip away but Stick had been watching, and brought him down with the willing aid of his personal runner and Lefty Poseid, the latter incandescent with rage over his dead twin.

Stick had specific orders from Connar. He shortened his arm to kill the man, who struggled in the grip of Lefty and the runner, the latter bleeding from multiple wounds.

Stick's lips drew back, exposing very white teeth. "Oh yes," he said, low-voiced. "It was you who wanted our prince's scalp. Great idea." To Lefty and the runner, "Hold him down."

They grinned, their grip brutal as Yenvir realized what was about to happen. He began yelping a stream of pleas and curses.

Tyavayir gripped the man's luxuriant mane of black and white hair, and Yenvir shrieked as Tyavayir sawed, then wrenched the bloody scalp away. On the backswing he cut the man's throat.

Yenvir dropped lifeless to the dirt, bone-white skull smeared with red looking oddly fragile. Or maybe it was that deadly anger dying with the man. Tyavayir stared at him, sweat dripping off his nose, then looked at the disgusting object in his hand. He dropped it to the ground, put his foot down and sawed away with his knife, cutting hanks of hair close to the flapping, drippy scalp. These he handed out to his cousins, saying, "Remember our orders. We'll bind these on our helms when we ride against the rest of them."

Lefty swallowed against nausea, the runner tight-mouthed as they wound the hair up and stuck it in pockets or pouches.

Then they turned to see that the rest of their company, who had witnessed Yenvir's defeat and death, had begun began taking prizes from the last brigands standing. They cut them down one by one, ignoring pleas and promises.

Cabbage Gannan saw what was going on, remembered what Snake had reported, and had his signal scout blow a summons. "Lancers," he shouted. "New orders."

Noddy sent his honor guard back down the trail to collect Marlovan wounded, then dismounted and handed the reins to Vanadei, who sheathed one of his knives to take the reins. As Vanadei scanned continually around Noddy, knife still at the ready, the crown prince examined the killing field, his expression furrowing at the sight of the carnage. The enemy was no threat now. They were all fled or dead, the domes of skulls bone-white in the ruddy, sinking light.

Noddy sat down on Yenvir's rock and stared down at his hands until Stick and Ghost limped up to him.

"Area secure," Stick said, coming up alongside Ghost. "Yenvir is dead."

Noddy turned his palm up. Those were his father's orders.

Ghost added, "It was Cabbage here who saved us."

At those words, Noddy looked around, his expression easing. He turned to Gannan, who, catching his eye, broke off talking to a couple of his riding captains and loped across the bloody field to join them.

Gannan said to Noddy, "We have all the wounded over there." He pointed. "I sent two ridings to go through the stash in the cave. Said to look first for bandages, then food and fodder. Their horses seem to have stampeded."

Stick said wearily, "Ghost. We should ride back down the trail. Maybe some of our people are still alive."

"Already seen to," Noddy said, and turned back to Gannan. "That charge was excellent. This is the second time you saved us—I wish I could give you a reward, one you deserve."

Stick and Ghost both agreed with heartfelt exclamations.

Gannan chewed his lip, weariness giving way to anxiety. Now that Yenvir was dead, there remained the old, still-burning goal, one he'd had since his academy days. Why not bring it out now? "If I had a wing of my own, they would be your First Lancers," he said fervently, his earnest gaze steady with conviction. "*Your* First Lancers. You always call us first, and we'll defend you with our lives."

Noddy gazed back just as earnestly. Stick and Ghost were excellent captains, but they were Connar's. Cabbage Gannan was *his* captain. "Right," he said. "My First Lancers. I'll talk to Da, first thing in my report."

Gannan smacked fingers to chest. "Whatever the king says, we'll obey. But riding as your First Lancers even for a week or two would be an honor."

Noddy brightened, then his smile faded as he looked around in the gathering dusk. "Before we do anything, let's lay the dead out proper, so the healers can Disappear them."

"All of them?" Ghost spoke the question in many minds.

"All of them," Noddy said, his deep voice a rumble as he gazed at mountaineers and Marlovans lying with limbs tangled, close as lovers. But beyond love, or light.

The pride and triumph vanished from the sweaty, dirt and blood-smeared faces around him. The runners, led by Vanadei, had already begun the grim task; the warriors still on their feet helped them. They laid out the Marlovans first, singing the Hymn to the Fallen, until all were gone. Then they dealt with the brigands in silence.

The sun had vanished, the area lit by flickering torches, turning the drying blood to black, when they finished. Someone brought out a drum, and another. They sang, and a voice rose in a raw threnody that shivered with grief.

One by one the battle laments rose, names of the dead added in verse after verse. As thunder rumbled in the distance and rain began to fall, they moved into the cave, where a couple of runners had found wine, and heated it over a fire, adding some hoarded spice.

That passed from hand to hand. When the victory songs began to replace those of grief—at first ragged, uncertain, then gathering strength as the bristic dulled pain—Vanadei slipped to an unnoticed corner with a candle, a quill, and a small bottle of ink. As one by one the exhausted warriors slipped into slumber, Vanadei wrote out a detailed report for Quill, and sent it.

SEVENTEEN

Connar drilled the entire garrison with a passionate conviction of impending victory that roused everyone, from Kendred and Mathren's fifty-year-old leftovers to the rawest newcomers sent by the jarls.

When he released them at the toll of the evening watch, they went off to roister or rest but he worked on, every night, with the best swordmasters in the garrison. He was frequently at it until the night watch, in an effort to fight the gut-churning anxieties about things he could not change, such as the weather, and things he might have done differently, such as going with Stick Tyavayir instead of sending him. Each day that dawned without a messenger had to be gotten through, and the only way he could get through them was by pushing himself to the limits of endurance.

Lineas, living as a castle runner, looked on with compassion and worry. Everyone knew trouble was coming—it was akin to a boulder rolling downhill, bringing all the smaller rocks with it.

She wrote every night to Quill, who rode eastward, careful to avoid leaving a trail, then north into the woods.

By nights he and Lineas exchanged letters, both avoiding the subject of Connar, each anxious not to pressure or distress the other. At first the conversation was tentative. Communication was actually easier by letter, for they couldn't anxiously watch one another for the slightest sign of hurt, mirroring concern into inarticulate helplessness. On paper (so she thought) one could be brave. He took immense pleasure in relating to her all the wonderful things he had cherished about her over the years, and she, in turn, tried to make him laugh by describing her childhood passion.

He revealed to her his heart, but not where he was.

The night before Vanadei sat in Yenvir's mountain lair, writing his grim report as the welcome rain poured down, Quill reached the outskirts of the hidden army.

The next day, Quill made his way up a rocky hill on hands and knees, careful to stay out of sight of the increasingly careless sentries—and Braids' vigilant scouts as well.

He lay under a prickly shrub on a rocky hill, peering down through his spyglass into the enemy camp as the sun dropped behind him, and then set.

He watched the fires lit, and the night watch change places with the day watch.

Since Yenvir was dead, this had to be Elsarion's camp.

Quill remained where he was until at last he saw what he was looking for: a tall, sauntering male with corn-silk hair lit bright gold in the firelight. Mathias Alored Elsarion was instantly recognizable, though dressed in sober colors, like his warriors. His only affectation was that long hair—as long as Marlovans', who never cut it. But, unlike Marlovans, whose horsetails were damaged by sun, wind, and weather, Thias Elsarion's hair flowed down his back in ribbon-smooth order, tied at the nape of his neck.

He joined a group at the main fire. His hands, fine and expressive even at the distance of the spyglass, gestured as he spoke, holding everyone's attention.

Quill's notecase gave the internal tap of magic. He rolled back out from under his shrub and worked his way down the hill. When he reached a little dell with a trickle of water, he brought out a tiny glowglobe, no bigger than a knuckle. Covering it with a piece of cloth except for a pinhole, he thumbed out the closely written piece of paper, recognized Vanadei's handwriting in the tiny light, and sat down to read that the camp had broken up, and Noddy had ordered them to ride south to join with his brother.

He read the ending again—*They know a few of Yenvir's hirelings escaped. At least one has to know where to find Elsarion, so they will be bringing the news. And Snake Wend is on his way to Connar on a grass run. They will probably get to their respective destinations at the same time, near as I can figure from the map, though I can't be certain exactly where we are.*

Quill sat as the night chill descended, deep in thought.

When rain began to tap at the canopy of leaves overhead, he withdrew to where he'd stashed his gear and his horse under a rocky outcropping. The horse grazed. Quill ate one of his now-stale biscuits and a drying hunk of cheese.

By the time he'd worked through this meal, and washed it down with cold water from the stream, he had a plan.

First, he wrote back to Vanadei, outlining his plan in case the worst happened. Then he wrote to Lineas, warning her that Yenvir was dead after a bloody rout, and that Wend was on his way to report. He kissed the paper then wrote below it, *Press your lips here. From me to you, with all my love.*

He sent it off, folded his notecase and weapons into his gear bag, and sent them to his trunk in Darchelde.

He was now alone.

He wrapped up in his robe to sleep, and when the first light of dawn began to lift the shadows, he walked the horse downstream until he was certain she would be well out of reach of the enemy. He watched her trot along the bank until she was hidden by the trees.

He took off his robe then turned it inside out, so that the light lining was on the outside, and the sun-faded dark blue on the inside. He checked that the plain wooden shank buttons at the edge were free, then walked back up the mountain, in full view of the enemy sentries.

His heart thudded against his chest the way hearts do when the mind is uncertain whether this is a good or bad idea, but is pushing the body ahead anyway.

The sentries stilled until he drew near, his empty hands held away from his sides, then they surrounded him, weapons out.

One snapped, "You want to die?" in very bad Marlovan, followed by the same demand in Adrani, and then in accented Iascan.

Quill replied in Adrani, which has Sartoran at its root, "No, I do not. I'm here to speak to my cousin, Thias Elsarion."

At the word *cousin,* the two spears and the sword wavering a finger's width from Quill's throat and heart withdrew a hand's width.

"Cousin?" one repeated.

"Tell him Cousin Senrid is here," Quill said. Whatever happened here, the name Senrid was so common over Halia that it would not identify him as a royal runner, but it ought to be recognizable to Elsarion.

"Search him," the leader said.

The steel withdrew. The search was thorough, and not especially gentle, then, "Nothing."

"What robe is that?" the leader demanded.

"Scribe," he said, and watched the sentries' stances ease further. Runners could be dangerous, but nobody ever looked at scribes when scanning for threat.

The leader sent the newest recruit to run into the camp with the news, and they waited there, as clouds drifted overhead, and a clean wind toyed with hair and clothes.

Presently the gangling youth returned, breathing hard. "Said to bring 'im."

The sentry leader stationed a guard on either side of Quill, and the rest of them returned to their patrol, as Quill and his two guards wound their way through the tent city in the process of waking to a new day.

Over at one side, a brawny captain barked orders, his breath clouding, as men formed up for warmups. Quill noticed their weapons were mainly straight swords, spears, and here and there big men with maces. All foot-warrior weapons, the spears short.

His gaze ran over the horse picket, which was not long in Marlovan terms: Quill guessed that the commanders rode mounted, and likely runners as well, but the army itself marched and fought on foot. Yes, there, resting against a tree stump, one of the huge, heavy shields used in shield walls.

Beyond that, mostly hidden by tents, lay a long set of wagons together, with an enormous spar resting on them. Quill's guide saw the direction of his gaze and snapped, "This way."

Quill obligingly turned his head, but he knew what he'd seen: a battering ram, with metal worked around it in bands. The end of the great tree had been clear-cut. Quill suspected that this was an artifact of hiding deep in the mountains, beyond the Wood Guild's reach, for that clear-cut end was not that of a fallen tree.

Another strike against you, Quill thought as they entered a clearing.

At the center lay a large tent, divided into two sections. Mathias Elsarion waited in the outer segment, the opening flaps pulled wide. He lounged in a folding camp chair. Quill noticed he wore knives in both boot tops, a long dagger at his belt, and a sword lay in reach on the top of a trunk. Four men at arms stood behind their leader, hands on the hilts of their weapons.

"You do look familiar," Thias said with a smile. "You have to be related to Camerend the Hostage."

"He's my father," Quill said in Sartoran.

"So you're the new uncrowned prince," Thias replied in the same language. "If you're still heeding that ridiculous treaty that keeps your family confined within your own territory? You are surely aware that the last of the Montreivayirs who forced that treaty onto your family after backstabbing your greatfather, what, ten or twelve generations ago, died out at the turn of the century?" In other words, *See, I know your Marlovan history.*

Quill's conviction was that anyone who felt they had to make an *Aren't I clever* speech usually wasn't as smart as they thought themselves.

But they could still be dangerous.

"I'm the eighth generation. The end of that treaty," Quill said, "will be my grandson's problem. If I have one."

Thias laughed, and waved his hand casually.

The men at arms bowed and withdrew from the tent.

"There. We're alone. You came here for a purpose, obviously."

Quill said, "Thias, it's true we are some sort of kin, if you go back far enough."

"A couple times over," Thias said appreciatively. "So you're here to beg for . . . titles? Land? It's a little early for that."

"I came to beg you to give it up. Go home. I don't know what your purpose is, but it can't be worth the cost in lives. Yenvir is dead, a day ago. His band as well. The Marlovans are riding for blood."

Thias sat back, the smile hardening on his lips, his eyes narrowed in question. "How do you know that? Oh, but then Camerend did have access to transfer magic, didn't he? Unlike the rest of your benighted Marlovans? I remember when he came to visit my sister a few years ago. They went on at length about family history, as I recollect, which is how I know we're related. Then he left by transfer. Convenient, for a hostage, isn't it? He can go anywhere he wants and your king thinks him locked up safely under his eye."

Quill didn't bother explaining that Camerend had ceased to be a hostage long before he himself was born. "Thias, why are you here? I don't understand why you're expending all this effort to become the richest horse thief in history. I don't believe you're laying claim to the Nelkereth, which dries up for half of every year. No humans can settle there."

Thias uttered a quiet laugh. "You seem to have given up your legitimate claim to your throne, as your father did. Well, if you like being a scribe, no fault to you. The world needs scribes to record the actions of those who do have ambition to make something of themselves. And I have ambition. More to the point, I'm not the only one. Your ignorant king has a bigger threat than I pointed straight at his heart from the south, in Demeos and Ryu Nyidri of Perideth. What I believe you Marlovans call Feravayir. See how long that name lasts!"

When Quill evinced no surprise, Elsarion leaned forward. "Throw in with me, Senrid. Ryu Nyidri has no family feeling whatever, except in acquisition. He and his elder brother want your Darchelde. Says it's the best holding in all Halia, and it ought to belong to the Dei descendants who can take it."

"I'm related to the Deis, too, if you look back far enough."

"Exactly, Cousin Senrid! Exactly! So am I. My mother was from the Sartoran branch, you know. That's why we're having this conversation! So throw in with me. When I go after the capital from the north, one or the other of the Nyidri brothers will come up from the south. Probably Ryu. I get the sense that Demeos is too lazy. Ryu wants to ride through your Darchelde to secure it first. If you join me, I can keep him from doing that. We can take this kingdom, and bring it into civilization."

"Why?" Quill asked, softly.

"I just told you, I have ambition to make something of myself. Every one of these," he waved his hand outward, toward the drilling field, "is here because he wants something, too."

"How is making war any part of civilization?" Quill said, knowing he'd lost his gamble.

"Civilization comes after." Thias's eyes widened. "First is the fun."

"War is fun?"

"Winning is fun," Thias retorted, and Quill thought, Oh, you're one of *those* Deis.

Thias went on, "And I'll win. If Yenvir really is dead, it would surprise me about as much as it would grieve me, which is to say, very little. He was nothing but a brigand, a suitable decoy. *He* was your horse thief. I've got two hardened commanders with me, one demoted due to a power play, the other cheated out of his inheritance by a cousin better liked at court. They want land, and titles, and are willing to do whatever it takes to win them."

"Cousin, the Marlovans know who you are."

"Old news." Thias shrugged.

Quill opened his hands out wide. "Do you really not understand what that means? If you persist in this scheme of yours, you'll make it a virtue to chase you all the way up the eastern pass to your Elsarion holdings."

"That would be my sister's problem, wouldn't it?" Thias laughed softly. "In any case, Yenvir proved twice that your Marlovans are not unbeatable."

"Surely you know that Halivayir was the smallest jarlate, the older generation outnumbering the young, and Tlen, equally small, was half deserted."

Thias smiled indulgently. "Boast of Marlovan prowess if it pleases you. As for coming up the Adrani pass, I'd love to see them try running a raid against castles atop thousand-stride cliffs."

"Then your outposts were never really intended to guard against brigands," Quill said.

Thias lifted his shoulders in a shrug. "Brigands, Marlovans, what's the difference, except maybe in the color of their garments? As for your information, I will do you the honor of believing your words about Yenvir. We shall prepare accordingly. But . . ." His eyes narrowed as he raised a lazy hand, signaling to the watching guards a short distance outside the tent. "I think you should probably stay with us, all things considered—"

"We're done," Quill said.

Thias lunged out of his chair. He was fast, but Quill was faster, touching one of his robe shanks as he spoke the transfer word. Magic wrenched him out of the world, leaving Thias clutching at empty air that tingled unpleasantly.

He turned away, wringing out his fingers and laughing, as far away in Darchelde, Quill fell onto his bedroom rug, and lay there until he'd recovered from the transfer.

Then he got up and shrugged out of his robe, turning it about again. He ran his fingers over the other buttons; it was a family tradition not to use the expensive golden coins as transfer tokens that most of the rest of the world used. The theory was fine—that much magic required the sort of object no one would want to lose. But the Montredavan-Ans kept their magic secret, and their tokens, by preference, were ordinary objects. Which incidentally helped when one was being searched by hostiles.

Quill walked down through familiar halls, until he reached the north wing, which was cooler in summer. There he found Camerend teaching two magic students who would eventually be sent to the royal city as royal runners in training.

At the sight of him, Camerend broke off what he'd been saying. "Go on, you know what to do." He indicated the door to the downstairs library, and the students scampered off, one with a backward glance. And to Quill, "Vanadei wrote to me last night. He was pretty frantic that I find and stop you. I take it you were not successful?"

"No." Then, wrung with a sense of failure, Quill told him everything.

Camerend listened in silence, expression sober. After the account of Quill's killing of the two assassins, he said, "If I could have saved you from that experience . . ." Here he turned his wrist, slashing his hand through the air in the Eagle Stoop two-handed knife strike. "I would. Being so close to those in power, you will have to come to terms with the tension between moral right and duty. But we've talked about that since you were small."

"Talking and doing . . ." Quill made the signs for night and day.

Camerend replied, "You know your next step."

Quill said reluctantly, "I'll be on the road to Feravayir by morning."

Camerend opened his hand, having expected this answer, then he met his son's gaze. "As for Lineas . . . I was glad to see you watch out for her like the brother she never had. I was close to her mother at one time, before I married yours. But now . . . ." He raised a hand, palm out. "My experience is irrelevant here, I believe. So I'll stop."

"Why?"

"Because what you're talking about is not merely a matter of the heart. You have ventured into different territory."

Quill sighed. "How can you say that? Neither Lineas nor I have made vows—I made certain of that."

"True." Camerend opened both hands. "And you can point out that Connar has lovers across the kingdom. Except as far as I understand the matter, there's only one he comes back to. And he descends from people not known for their ability to share."

Quill's eyes narrowed. He said warily, "But you've always said that children are not copies of their parents." He lifted his hand, pointing northeast in the direction of Anaeran-Adrani, and the kingdom-sized Elsarion holdings. "That the biggest mistake the Dei family made was in trying to shape their progeny into some ideal."

"All true. And yet . . . with age especially, many of us begin to look for ourselves, and especially those we've lost, in the young. You are very much your own person, neither a copy of your mother, or myself. Yet in the variety of your expressions, turns of your voice, even emotional patterns I sometimes catch glimpses of your mother. Shendan. My Dei cousin, whom you've never met. And also Mnar Milnari, who is so distantly related to you we might as well not count it, and yet you've some of her gestures. All of you do, not surprising as you've all been taught by her."

Quill opened his hand.

"And so, we come to Connar. Who is far smarter than either of his birth parents, both of whom I knew from my rides to Nevree, though I only met Fini sa Vaka once. Connar is a blend of them physically, but his nature is different, and in it I can see so much of Danet's fierce love of family. But every so often, I catch a quick glimpse of Mathren, especially when Connar is angry."

"I seldom saw Connar, but I don't recollect ever hearing of him throwing a tantrum."

"Mathren didn't throw tantrums, either. Garid joked and laughed his way out of trouble, Kendred whined and bellowed, but Mathren was quiet, except when he flirted, and of course when they loosed him on wargames. I also recollect that Jasirle-Harvaldar was savage in punishments, particularly if his son lost those wargames, because Mathren was intended to be a shield arm for Garid."

And so he had been, until he contrived his brother's death and made it look like bandits, Quill thought.

Camerend went on. "Mathren never raised his voice—ever. In fact, after Kendred took over the regency and Mathren the guards, it was when he whispered that sweat would break out on everyone's foreheads."

Quill grimaced.

Camerend temporized, "It would be ridiculous to say that Connar is a copy of Mathren, because it's not true. I can list a hundred differences, beginning with Mathren's passion for ballads, whereas I don't know if you ever noticed that both Connar and Noddy would stand there at festival singing staring off into space, clearly bored. As a child Mathren waged a continual, silent, and usually losing battle against his older brothers. He never shared. From the time they could walk, Connar and Noddy did everything together, a genuine bond. And so on."

Camerend leaned forward. "Given that, still. Every so often, especially since Connar got out of the academy, I catch glimpses of Mathren in him—and those are never the flirting Mathren, the singing Mathren, they are always the whispering Mathren. So to conclude, your relationship with Lineas might be scrupulously honest on both your parts, but it is unlikely to be private. Because of who Connar is, it's political."

EIGHTEEN

Quill to Lineas:

Who was it who said that love is the seeds of light? Somehow my memories of you are always in spring, even when we wore mittens and hats and our breath steamed as we laughed.

I just arrived here in Parayid, to investigate a remark made by Thias Elsarion about the Nyidri brothers riding north to attack the royal city.

It's possible that Ryu or his brother might be acting behind their mother's back. She's far too prudent to be reckless. Camerend believes her preference is to win by insinuation, and if she must strike, only against a supine target. If she knows about Elsarion's plan, I believe she would wait to move until she knows that the royal city lies in ruins.

More when I find out.

What the archivists on either side of the mountains don't know is that Thias Elsarion chose to attack the Marlovans after a short period of irritated brooding alone in his tent. Who would have thought the Montredavan-Ans would be sneaky enough to ward magic transfer onto wooden buttons?

Still, he believed 'Cousin' Senrid Montredavan-An had told the truth about Yenvir. His army, bored with sitting and waiting, was just as happy to carry the fight to the enemy without having to consider sharing the spoils with a gang of scoundrels they'd despised as much as they distrusted.

Braids' scouts, seeing the enemy begin breaking camp, withdrew, sending the fastest rider to Ku Halir. She arrived a day ahead of Snake Wend, who galloped into Ku Halir's stableyard, gabbled a nearly incoherent account of Yenvir's defeat to wide-eyed stable hands, then fell off the horse in a dead faint.

Connar—wound to the snapping point—was summoned to Ventdor's command center to hear the gist of Snake's report: Noddy, Gannan, and what remained of Stick and Fath's companies were riding southward down the edge of the wooded hills above the lake, toward Elsarion's encampment.

Connar knew he was now in an anomalous position: his orders had been fulfilled with the securing of Halivayir, and Yenvir's death. Ventdor, wearing two gold chevrons, had orders to defend the east. If Commander Ventdor wanted to command, he was entitled.

Connar went straight to the yard, drew his sword and picked up a second sword as if he were a front-line lancer and not a captain. He fought two-handed until he was crowing for breath—which did not prevent his mind from alternately arguing with Ventdor—his father—the world—about why he should be in command, and formulating the orders he would give.

Sneeze Ventdor, a father as well as an experienced organizer, watched from afar as Connar fought against three volunteers with sweat-dripping intensity, his internal debate scarcely less fervent: what was the right thing to do here? Could he command a battle when he never had before?

What could Cousin Arrow want?

That was the right question. He knew what Arrow would want.

When the night watch bell clanged and Connar put down his sword to get some water, Ventdor approached him. Though they were surrounded by people, no one was in earshot. "I know what your da's plans are for you," he said bluntly. "If he was here, I think he'd give you the chance to command if you want it. From what I hear of that business outside Lindeth, you proved you're ready." And he opened a hard, callused hand to reveal a gold chevron, pulled from his winter coat.

Connar looked from that longed-for symbol to Ventdor's face, and said on an exhaling breath, "I'm ready."

Ventdor handed off the chevron, and though his summer coat still sported two on the right arm, he understood what it meant, even if Connar was too caught up in the moment, as the young always were: he had not expected what in effect was retirement to happen so suddenly.

He looked down at his empty palm, feeling the world shifting away from him as the young took his place. He looked up. This was how the world worked. But he was nowhere near ready to hang up his sword and squat by the fireside until he was toothless. "Then I'm ready to carry out your orders."

Connar had craved hearing those words, but never expected to hear them for years and years. Disbelief vanished in the fire of elation.

That was truly Ventdor's perception, that the prince blazed with intensity. Ventdor wondered how Arrow's boy did that, seem so suddenly to be larger than life.

Connar turned to the nearest runner waiting over by the weapons rack, and opened his hand in summons. "At the hour before dawn, sound the general assembly. We'll ride out at sunup."

Under the deep blue sky of impending dawn, Connar—with that new chevron stitched onto his new coat by Fish's nimble fingers—faced the assembled warriors in the torchlit parade ground. Everyone saw the glint of gold on his right arm. They all respected field promotions, which were always (unless for dire reasons) confirmed.

Connar raised his voice. "We're riding against the enemy."

Lineas to Quill:

. . . and then Connar, with Ventdor at his back, and King's Army Captains Basna and Mundavan completing the diamond, did the sword dance. I have never seen Connar so happy.

All the warriors shrilled the fox yip. Cama the scribe, who was at that time over in the town fetching a fresh supply of paper, said that the sound rising so suddenly from beyond the garrison walls was so harrowing that the Iascan merchants, artisans, and idlers along the waterfront waiting for the inns to open for breakfast fell silent as the eerie shriek carried on the wind.

Everyone began to say, "The Marlovans are riding," and Cama was certain Elsarion's spies were probably among the traders galloping madly away. Not that word from the spies will be much help, for our Riders will be right on their heels.

My orders are to wait with the secondary horses, in case word to Ku Halir or the royal city must be sent. They are forming in column now, so I must go.

I kiss this paper, knowing that it will soon be in your hands.

Those familiar with the main events of Marlovan history have all heard about the Battle of Tlennen Plain.

As the ballads attest, Braids Senelaec raised the Sindan-An-Tlennen-Senelaec alliance, who were there waiting when Connar's and Elsarion's forces met half a day's ride outside Tlennen.

Despite this additional force, Elsarion had the numbers. But the Marlovans had the horses.

For the third time, the tide of battle turned when Gannan's lancers—this time charging across flat turf on fresh horses—drove across the plain in a line, smashing into Elsarion's hastily assembled shield wall with devastating effect. There are still extant tapestries depicting the distended eyes of the enemy as they took in Gannan, pale-haired Ghost Fath, and Stick Tyavayir with hanks of Yenvir's distinctive black and white mane flying behind their helms, as lightning crackled overhead.

Another fact the archivists didn't record after Gannan's First Lancers arrived so dramatically just as the storm broke: the First Lancers tried to ride down the scattering men, an aftereffect of charges that few brag about, especially when terrified enemies had already thrown away their arms and many fell to their knees, hands up. Lances spitted them and swords lopped off heads just the same, until Gannan—aware of Noddy somewhere behind, watching—rode with Lefty Poseid among them bawling curses, threats, and orders, forcing them back under control.

The two Adrani commanders had begun marshaling their forces as well when Rat Noth arrived from the south, and though he had fewer lancers, Elsarion's force had been badly shaken. One again, the Marlovan arrow drove right through the mass, this time shooting with inexorable speed and precision as the horses flew by.

Another fact the archivist don't know, but I've seen from the dangerously beguiling mirror in the Garden of the Twelve, is how Connar crossed the field on four horses in succession, until foam streaked their sides, in a desperate search for Elsarion.

Thias watched him from behind a broken supply wagon as Connar killed the toughest of his Adrani commanders with two strikes from a galloping horse, never looking back as he hunted onward.

Thias wound up his long hair with one hand, his thoughts a mixture of anger and challenge. He'd also seen those helms.

He pulled a woolen cap over his head, an old cloak over his mail shirt, and slipped away in the heavy rain.

Lineas to Quill:

We're back in Ku Halir, but only to eat and change horses, except for Captain Fath (the pale blond one they call Ghost), who has been ordered to stay to reinforce Ku Halir, since it seems that the enemy commander got away.

I was with the secondary horse picket, so I never saw any battle, just dust. We waited in a strained semblance of peace broken only when runners came for fresh remounts. They'd shout out what they'd seen, then gallop off again.

When at last the enemies were dead or scattered, and the orders went out to collect weapons and wounded, and to lay out the dead, Noddy rode back, then Connar. Noddy was unhappy. You know how much he hates battle. I saw him looking away from those helms with the hair on them. But said nothing to Captain Gannan, whose company was busy taking more of those dreadful hair trophies.

Noddy told us we wouldn't ride until the dead were properly Disappeared, then he said to Connar, "We missed Andahi Day."

Connar was drinking water. He looked very tired as he said, "There's always next year, right?"

I don't think Noddy heard him. He was looking westward, toward the setting sun all fiery red under the clouds, then he said, "If we ride hard, we can be home by Victory Day."

Connar laughed as he leaned over and clapped Noddy on the shoulder. "Excellent idea!"

I watched them smile at each other, but I don't think they understood the other at all—or at least their moods were so vastly different. Noddy so low, Connar so restless, happy and tense by turns: I know, because he told me, Connar thought Noddy's idea to ride through the gates on Victory Day would be a triumph, but I would wager anything Noddy just wanted to be home.

I rode with the team of oxen they found to pull the gigantic felled tree they called a battering ram, which had been found at the enemy camp. I assumed it would be turned over to the Wood Guild, or used to rebuild the scribe house, but orders got passed along to store it for now.

When we reached Ku Halir, Connar wanted me with him.

I don't know if what he feels is love. I'm not certain anymore that what I feel is love. It is certainly not what I felt at sixteen. I understand so little about love, except that it seems to be as changeable as the sky. When I was sixteen, my passion was the secret center of my day, and my happiness at night. I thought so strong an emotion must endure forever, but I wonder if I was simply in love with the idea of love.

Now my feelings are more complicated—fondness, with some worry and maybe even compassion, though he would hate that if he knew. Even when I was his nursemaid his last year at the academy, he loathed any word of compassion, which I think he found indistinguishable from pity. Any sign of pity made him so angry he would not talk about anything but immediate necessities for the longest time after he came out of his room. He still doesn't talk about what is inside his head, and he hates questions. It's silence he finds comforting.

Quill to Lineas:

I think in my last I told you I'd spend a few days scouting on my own, with no expectations, before I met with Lnand again.

That was last night. She was wary as she asked why I was there in Faravayir, and added, "I assure you, between my two venues and my two flirts at the palace, I hear everything there is to be heard."

I told her what Thias Elsarion had said. Lnand listened with her usual care, then said, "I see Demeos and his brother at least once a week, usually at the theater. All the gossip about them is who they are seeing, what fashions they have ordered from Sartor, and what entertainment they are planning for the festival they will be giving for the entire city of Parayid in spring. If either of those two was putting together an army, surely I would catch a hint of it. How much of Mathias Elsarion's claim do you believe?"

I said that Thias might have been bragging, but he had no reason to outright lie.

Lnand sat down. I was glad to see that her wariness was gone. "The only person who could lead a revolt would be Commander Noth. Who admittedly I seldom see."

She meant Ivandred Noth, married to Lavais Nyidri, the Jarlan of Feravayir. He commands the garrison, and comes to Convocation as the jarlan's representative when it's called. He's sometimes called a jarl, and given a jarl's fanfare. But he has not made a jarl's vows, whereas the jarlan has been very clear that the title, and responsibilities, are hers.

Lnand broke the silence first. "She governs. He stays out of it. His duties are defense, mostly of the harbor in recent years. When she speaks Sartoran to her followers, she calls herself a queen-in-waiting, assuming no Marlovan would ever speak a word of Sartoran. She grew up with her father's royal aspirations."

I asked: "I guess the question is, how much does she govern him? Would he rebel if she told him to? I think I need to get to know him."

To that she admitted: "A male royal runner can get into military areas that I can't. As for her revolting, I guess it's time to get closer to Demeos and his brother."

I could see her distaste. I expect no one outside of our circle would perceive the distinction between a musician passively listening to talk in venues and deliberately setting out to spy by courting an individual for information—the more since we heard about Elsarion's using Fareas Yvanavayir that way.

Lnand then said, "Two can play at that game," and I knew her thoughts ran parallel to mine.

So that's our next step.

When Noren was growing up at Tenthen Castle, she could only feel the bells when she was on the walls. She had learned to observe others, whose reactions to the bells gave her the watch changes, but the occasional rings announcing special circumstances took her by surprise.

When everyone in the girls' court started, looking skyward toward the bell towers, expressions altered from surprise to question, then mouths and hands flapped: "Connar and Noddy sighted!"

Noren turned to Holly, her personal runner, who seemed to know the gossip before it happened. "Find Ranet."

Holly grinned. "She's already here." Her fingers shaped the words, then whirled dramatically toward Ranet, who had jammed between a scribe and the potter's third assistant, peering upward at the sentries on the wall: when the heir's pennon rose, that would mean the riders were in sight.

If the princes were home, that meant the conflict with the easterners had to be truly over. And that meant hers and Ranet's weddings. Not in some dim future, but right away. Danet-Gunvaer had been clear about that.

Noren waited, watching the girls in her class talking. Here and there she caught the shapes of words, even phrases. When she was certain they'd gone from expressing joy to general gossip, she clapped her hands together hard enough to sting.

The girls closed their mouths and faced her, but eyes and hands betrayed scattered attention. She set them a difficult problem in calculating four types of trade and three of time, sure to steady them down for the remainder of the watch. Then she left the classroom, stopping when she saw Bunny at the other end of the hall, standing with her head averted, arms pressed close, hands gripping her shoulders.

Noren covered the distance in three strides.

Bunny looked up, her eyes unhappy. But then she smiled brightly—falsely—and signed, "Are you ready to get married? Ma and Da will insist on making a wedding out of the celebration. They want grandsons."

Victory fanfares pealed from tower to tower as the princes rode through the gate, banners at their backs. Everyone off-duty, and not a few who weren't, had crowded to the city walls. People banged on baking tins and pots, shrieking and singing war ballads—though, for the first time in many generations, "Yvana Ride Thunder" was not among them.

Standing on the castle gate, everyone at a respectful distance from them, Danet and Arrow looked down.

"Wedding first," Danet said firmly to Arrow, without using Hand, as Noren stood a short distance away. "Your treason trial has to wait."

"It's not 'my' trial. There's no getting around it," Arrow retorted. "Especially since Yenvir is dead, and it looks like we didn't manage to nab the other one, the Elsarion boy. I sure don't see anyone in chains down there. All the jarls' ire is going to fall on that damn girl. And if I don't do something by Convocation, then every one of them will be up on his hinds legs yapping and howling."

"They'll do that anyway," Danet said, and smiled because there, riding in honor behind Gannan's company, was Braids' company. Danet silently counted them. Two missing. That hurt, for she knew every one of them.

Then the princes rode beneath them, both looking up to smile at the king and queen, and it was time to go down to join Bunny and Ranet in the stable yard, to greet the boys on their triumphant return.

Noddy looked around happily, feeling light inside his chest for the first time in weeks. Connar smiled and laughed, his emotions in turmoil. Everyone hailed them for their victory, and that felt good, but he knew that it wasn't a true victory. Elsarion had slithered away, and Noddy had let the broken enemy lines throw down their weapons and run. To Connar, that was a stalemate.

But there were his parents, pride in their faces as they spoke of a banquet, which had been in preparation since word had been brought of their approach.

Connar trod up to his room, feeling odd—as if it had been ten years, not two, since he'd run downstairs to join Noddy in riding north. He caught sight of Fish at his heels, carrying his gear, and waved him off. "That can wait. Go on. Take the night. I'll call for castle people if I want anything."

Fish saluted in silence, carried the bag to the alcove where he collected laundry, then ran down the back stairs and cut through various courtyards to the supply wing. He knew that his father and Uncle Retren would be waiting.

So they were.

The academy's Victory Day games had been postponed a day in honor of the arrivals, so Retren Hauth had liberty as well. He sat there in the small outer chamber adjacent to the quartermaster's office, so intense he made the room seem smaller. His one eye hit Fish with its unwinking stare.

Fish was beyond exhausted. Emotions he couldn't name crowded his chest and he said with increasing heat, "Yes, he was heroic. I'm sure you've already heard from some of those old grayheads like Toast Basna and his like that Connar is just like Mathren on the battlefield, only better. He killed one of the enemy commanders at the canter. It took two of Gannan's lancers to finish off the other one. He loves it—everyone can see it."

"He's a natural-born commander." Hauth's voice was husky with emotion. "I knew it. I knew it." And, sharply, "Tell me everything. All the details."

Fish's mood turned vicious. He described the battle in increasingly bloody detail—for he'd seen it all, riding with a string of remounts behind Connar through the entire battle—until he saw that nothing revolted his uncle.

Hauth listened enthralled. If Connar had killed twice as many as he had—if he had slaughtered a hundred—Uncle Retren would probably have died in ecstasy.

As soon as he realized it, Fish summed up abruptly, "And that's the main of it. There was more of the same, but I was far too busy at his back, and seeing to the horses and weapons. You'll have to get the rest from someone else."

Hauth pushed himself up with a grunt. "So I shall. Captains and above will be in the royal hall, the rest in the garrison mess hall. That's where I'll get the details. I'll go now."

Fish waited until he was gone, then sank heavily onto the bench his uncle had just vacated.

"Well?" Quartermaster Pereth asked.

"Well, what?"

"What's the relations between the brothers?"

"Fine. It's the same as it's always been." Fish ran his hands through his filthy hair, then dropped them to his knees. "Da, I don't even know what to say to Uncle Retren. He only hears blood and glory, some distortion of the past, which I don't believe anymore was even real." He looked away, then back. "Uncle Retren wants Connar as king, just because he's descended from a man who connived against his family—who *murdered* them."

The quartermaster snapped his hand away, dismissing Fish's words. "Mathren understood duty above all. I saw him, after his wife died. And maybe he did kill her. But if so, he'd had a reason. He had a reason for everything he did. He loved this kingdom, and he'd loved her. I saw him sitting there grief-struck, up in his tower where nobody could see him, but I'd been sent to bring him new things because he'd burned his old clothes along with hers." Pereth gazed into the distance, then sighed. "Bad days, those."

"That's just it. They *were* bad. Mathren Olavayir loved an image of the kingdom that was about as real as a damn ballad, and as far as I understand it, he killed people right and left to make it real. We don't have bad days now, because nobody is killing each other in the royal family. Likely nobody will sing ballads about Arrow-Harvaldar, but as far as I'm concerned, that's good. It's great. He can hang on for the next fifty years, and I'll cheer."

"Son—"

"Oh, I won't blab about Uncle Retren, if that's what you're after. At least *he* hasn't killed off half the family, unlike your precious Mathren."

Fish stalked out and headed for the baths, after which he planned to get laid or drunk, whichever gave him oblivion the fastest.

NINETEEN

Danet and Arrow were as successful as they were because both understood the value of compromise. She got her wedding, but he let it be known that the trial would come hard on its heels.

Not a day had gone by without a discussion—or argument—about that trial.

Danet surprised Arrow by demanding they not wait for the somewhat traditional New Year's Week for the wedding, saying for his private ear, "You told the jarls in Year '80 they'd get five years before Convocation."

"I know. So?" Arrow exclaimed. "Why not marry 'em before the jarls? Get it all over at once."

"I would if it was all three of our children. But that horseapple Lavais Nyidri is still making excuses. Her boy isn't ready, he stayed too long at Sartor."

Arrow scowled. "That's right. I'm so used to seeing Bun with your girls out there with the horses, I never think about that."

"I suspect she does, though she never complains. I don't want her seeing her brothers marry and she's still left out. We'll set the boys' wedding the week after the postponed Victory Day games, still a traditional time. And when the jarls come, you can glare at them, especially Noth from Feravayir, and hand out all your war blabber as a hint. As well as tell them that come spring, girls will be in the academy. Not that it's real news, as the jarlans already know. But you're saying it at Firstday oaths will make it law."

Arrow chuckled and rubbed his hands. "Good thinking. That's what we'll do."

Danet, always with an eye to the budget, knew by that week the academy boys would be on their way home, the number of guests severely diminished. For which the tired castle staff would be grateful.

Hliss Farendavan had saved out the finest blue dyed cloth against this day. The boys went down the morning before the games to be sized by the stringers, then three days later, they were called down for the first fitting of their new House robes of blue, so that there would be time to affix the gold trim.

When they came out, one of their father's runners was waiting with a summons.

Earlier that morning, a pair of men had ridden in through the gates along with the market carts bringing in harvest produce. Both wore unmarked coats, and though one wore a horsetail and carried a sword, he looked to the sentries like a man-at-arms riding with a runner, and so of course there was no fanfare.

In the stable, the runner was sent to request an interview of the king, who was at that moment between tasks. Hearing the name of the arrival, he cleared his schedule with two short orders.

And so the boys, a couple hours later, arrived at the king's suite to see with him a vaguely familiar man half a dozen years their elder.

"This is Eaglebeak Yvanavayir, boys," Arrow said.

Manther's brother! No wonder he looked familiar. Noddy and Connar exchanged furtive looks. Manther had ripped off his chevron and fought as a Rider, a demotion entirely self-motivated. Ghost's company had taken him in, and he'd fought extremely well—some had said he was trying to get himself killed. He'd been wounded badly, taken by Ghost Fath into Ku Halir to be cared for.

"Tell 'em what you told me," Arrow said to Eaglebeak, his palm held out toward Noddy and Connar.

Eaglebeak swallowed twice, then said to Connar, "You didn't call for us to send our oath-numbers to reinforce you at Ku Halir. We would have."

"We thought it best for you to defend your borders," Connar said easily, as Noddy stared at the blue and gold eagle rug on the floor. "We did send messengers."

"I know why you really didn't call us." Eaglebeak sounded weary. "And I don't blame you. Manther won't come home, though Ku Halir is filled to the rooftops with wounded. My sister dishonored our name."

"After," the king interjected crisply, "you drove her out."

Eaglebeak held up his hands. "Don't you think we've been arguing about that ever since the news came in? I blamed Chelis. Said it was women's business."

"But Fareas is your *family*," Noddy mumbled, almost too low to hear.

Eaglebeak heard. He flushed, and struck his flattened hand away. "I know. Don't think I'm not aware of my own fault here. After Ma died, I learned to avoid her, as Da always took her part . . . Then he died." Eaglebeak looked upward with red-rimmed eyes, then sighed sharply. "I thought, Chelis can handle Fareas. She's so calm, so good, so smart. But, what we didn't see is, Chelis never got angry as a girl. Those Cassads are . . . are . . . like a herd of lambs—Colt is a boy when riding out, and a girl with her cousins, Barend won't even get on a horse to help his brother, but fools around with tapestries all day, an aunt talks to animals and insists they talk back. All things that might stir up any other family, but those Cassads don't even give a bleat. They all get along. So I guess making Chelis deal with my sister was like asking a weaver to pick up a lance and charge."

"The word you want," Arrow said, remembering one of his many tiring discussions with Danet, "is vindictive."

Eaglebeak flushed again. "Don't you see? Chelis never had a chance to learn how to handle someone who makes you angry half a breath after coming into a room."

Arrow said, "You married Chelis five, six years ago, right? You should have—"

"Da was alive. He *always* said, let Pony be." Eaglebeak sighed, then his head came up, and his voice dropped with suppressed violence, "I didn't ride here for should-have. There *is* no should-have with the threat of *treason* hanging over us."

Arrow said much more mildly, "All right. Get on with it."

"There's no getting *around* it, is what I'm saying," Eaglebeak replied. " And I do see it as my fault as jarl. I'm supposed to keep the peace at home as well as all the way to the borders. The truth is, I was glad when my sister rode out. And so, in short, she did what she did. I know what happens to traitors. I feel I'm honor-bound to offer myself in her stead."

Noddy looked up at that, his face lengthening in horror.

Connar turned to Arrow. "I don't think that's justice. Is it?"

Eaglebeak said, "I can't stand by and let her suffer that fate. I can't. I'd rather take it myself. I—we can't live down that dishonor. I'm glad I don't have any children. My Tlen cousins are all gone, and . . ." His eyes closed, and glimmers of unshed tears glimmered in his eyelashes as his throat worked.

Into the painful pause that was fast growing into an even more uncomfortable silence, Arrow said, "Go get something to eat and drink. You've had a long ride. Nothing is going to happen now. There's plenty of time to talk things out, all right?"

Eaglebeak struck his fist against his chest. The tears he couldn't suppress slid down his lean cheeks as he walked to the door, then out. Arrow jerked his chin at the waiting runner to go with him. They'd decide where to stash him later.

He shut the door himself, and put his shoulder blades to it. "Well, boys? What do you think? Better get some practice now. This is the kind of horseshit you have to face when you're in this chamber." He threw his arms wide. "The wand is in *your* hand."

Connar crossed his arms. "I don't see the problem. I can tell you exactly how many died because of her big mouth. She's the one who yapped, not her brother. She pays the price."

"No," Noddy said, sharply.

Connar tipped his head. "You'd put him up against the post, but not her?"

"I wouldn't do that to anybody." Noddy spoke slowly, painstakingly, as he always did when upset. "Unless it was someone who tried to kill Da. This is different."

"Have you talked to her?" Connar asked.

"No. But night before last, I read the testimonies. You know. I got in the habit up at Larkadhe, catching up on the judgment table, before I go to sleep."

Connar dismissed that. "What's unclear about the fact that it was her big mouth, describing, in detail, Tlen's defenses and weaknesses, that got them all killed?"

Noddy said, "Because she didn't *sell* it. She didn't know she was talking to an enemy. She was *swanking*. I thought treason is something you do on purpose."

"That's what your mother thinks," Arrow said. "Go talk to her. She'll explain better. Connar, I suggest you read the testimonies. Noddy, if you want to interview Fareas Yvanavayir, she's down there in the lockup. The little girl witness, what's her name, Jelly, no, Berry, well, something like that, anyway, the scribes have taken her in."

Noddy and Connar left. They walked in silence, then Connar said, "Look, you're the one who handled this shit in Larkadhe. Why don't you do that here. I'll go along with anything you say. My only thought is, we can't do nothing. The jarls—not to mention the entire army, every single garrison—won't stand for that."

"So you'd execute her?"

Connar was already sick of the subject. He saw no reason to read pages of details about what he already knew. And the last person he wanted to talk to was Pony Yvanavayir, who had been annoying ten years ago when he first met her. He couldn't imagine she was any more bearable now. The truth was, if making her dead ended the subject, he was fine with that. "The jarls, and the army, will want us to do something," he repeated.

Noddy walked in silence. They parted outside his suite, Connar going on to the garrison drill court.

Noddy opened his door. Vanadei wasn't there. He sat down on his mat, staring at the floor in silence. He was still sitting there when Noren passed by, on her way back from the baths. She hesitated, then remembered that she was about to marry him in a few days. Maybe it was time to start getting reacquainted.

She walked into his line of sight and asked in Hand, "Is something troubling you?"

He signed slowly, "I don't really understand what treason is."

Noren made the signs for Fareas Yvanavayir.

Noddy assented, then painstakingly signed the entire sorry affair. She already knew everything—for a time she and Danet had talked about little else—but she had learned that Noddy needed to state the obvious when unknotting problems.

So she waited patiently until he reached the end, then he added, "Is Lineas around? She always helped me when we had to sit in judgment at Larkadhe."

"I can sent Holly for her," Noren offered. And at the easing of his expression, did.

Within a day of her arrival, Lineas had been put to work by Mnar Milnari teaching up on the third floor. Lineas saw at once that the royal runners were extended in a way they never had been before—so many out running messages, instructing at the queen's training, and of course teaching the fledges who would be promoted into duty the moment they were ready.

Busy as they all were, it was understood by all that an order from the royal family took precedence. Lineas handed off her class to self-study, and a short time later, the four sat together, Vanadei having appeared with Noddy's midday meal, and been bidden by Noddy to join them.

Noren's expressive hands somehow conveyed Danet's dry tone as she signed, "I can tell you what the queen will say: she hates executions, and thinks them useless except entertaining the sort of people who love the sight of blood. She doesn't think Fareas Yvanavayir committed treason as she understands the word."

"What else is there?" Noddy signed unhappily. "Connar is right about the army. And the jarls. They won't accept letting her go. I don't think they'd accept restitution—how could they even make restitution, with two jarl families wiped out, and Tlen burned."

Lineas said slowly, "Who was it who said there are two ways of maintaining tradition . . . I can see the page it was written on, but not the text. Anyway, my point is, you exiled the Bar Regren," she said to Noddy, who looked up with a hopeful expression. "And the king approved. What if she were exiled?"

Noddy said, "I don't think they'll accept just sending her away. They'll say it's not traditional. The Bar Regren were enemies attacking us, not one of us letting an enemy . . ." He stopped, looking down at his hands.

When it was clear he was not going to say anything further, Vanadei shut his eyes and recited, "'We Marlovans regard tradition as secondary only to law. From our beginnings we've preserved our traditions from the effect of evil influence by exile and by death.'" He opened his eyes, then said, "Kethedrend Montreivayir, after the death of Anderle Montreivayir. He went on to say that the Convocation, in order to keep tradition strong, will have to define 'evil' each time, treason, cowardice, and disobeying orders at the head of the list."

Noren studied each face, then signed, "Put the idea to the king and queen. What can it hurt?"

Noddy spent the rest of the day mulling the problem, then at dinner with the family, he brought it up.

"Exile?" Arrow flattened his palm down. "Too easy."

"Does someone really need to die in that disgusting way?" Danet demanded. "What's so easy about putting her on a ship the way Noddy and Connar did those mountain brigands up north?"

Arrow sighed. "You don't understand what a treason trial means."

"Then use another tradition! Exile her on her own land. Ironic, considering in the ordinary way she would never have left Yvanavayir if she had stayed single, or married a Rider captain. And we are agreed that Eaglebeak and Chelis Cassad are also at fault. So you exile all of them on their own land, the way the first Anderle did the Montredavan-Ans. Not for ten generations—ridiculous—but for ten years, say."

"Isolate the Yvanavayirs on their own land?" Arrow asked. "Then we're back having to guard them, an expense that's useless. Yvanavayir is so large that it would take half the army to watch their border. And don't bring up volunteers. I'd have old Gannan slavering to lead the pack in order to slip in to execute justice his own way."

Noddy's head bowed. Connar frowned. Memory flickered, standing in the Ku Halir stableyard, Lineas covered with ash. He said, "Manther doesn't deserve any of this. He was on duty at Ku Halir garrison the entire time she was yapping Tlen's defenses."

Noddy's head came up. "True. He fought hard at Tlennen Field."

Connar went on, "Since Eaglebeak claims responsibility in some way, let him. But that can't be said for Manther."

"Technically it can," Arrow said heavily. "If you're going by Eaglebeak's reasoning, tying everything up in family honor. Manther's the one who escorted Fareas to Tlen, on his way to his duty at Ku Halir. Here's the truth. As soon as anyone drags in the word honor, wits fly out the window. It's not as if Eaglebeak or his brother knew what was in her head when she left. *She* didn't know, until Elsarion gave her the hot-eye in Ku Halir."

Noddy said carefully, "I choose exile. Like we did the Bar Regren. For Eaglebeak, too, if he says he has to share in her judgment."

Arrow said, "You mean exile the entire family?" He whistled as the ramifications set in. "Oh, that would hurt. Much as I loathe executions, I've read the reasoning behind 'em. The watchers are supposed to think, that could be me if I did something similar."

"If a quarter of them get that message I'd be surprised," Danet snapped, then raised serious eyes. "Exile means giving up their land. Really, giving up their name. That is, they can take it elsewhere, but it won't *mean* anything. I'll wager nobody beyond our border has ever heard Yvana Ride Thunder, though we've sung it for generations."

Connar gazed into the distance, vivid memories of Hauth's ranting about the dolphin clan crowding his mind. Images of Hije, sitting with her hands shaking as she talked over her porcelain cup. Names meant something. He knew the pain of discovering that he'd nearly never had a name.

He looked up. "Exile from the kingdom, losing everything but their lives, that should impress the jarls. Except, I think you should give Yvanavayir to Manther. He doesn't have jarl responsibilities, and he fought hard for us. That's fair."

Danet turned Arrow's way, her expression shuttered. She had never been all that expressive, and had become less so over the years, but Arrow was tolerably good at reading her. He slapped his knees. "I'll ride it from here."

The younger generation took that as their signal to leave.

As soon as they were alone, Arrow turned to Danet. "Is it the exile plan you don't like, or . . ."

"There is nothing," she said with a snap to her words, "here to like. What pleased me is Connar thinking of Manther Yvanavayir, who isn't part of his favored circle of young captains. But that suggestion to give Yvanavayir to him, well, he's young, and it's meant well."

"Right." Arrow opened his hands. "Manther's young, too. He might see it as generous, rather than profiting by his brother's downfall. Which some brothers might even relish. Though those two sound like our two. Never mind guessing. We'll send an experienced runner to sound him out. Quietly. As for Connar thinking of him, he's shaping up to be an excellent shield-arm to Noddy."

Danet accepted that. She crossed the corridor to her room, where she knew Jarid Noth was waiting.

"You look pensive," Noth said when she walked into his arms.

"I'm thinking about Connar," she said against his chest. Generosity, Arrow had said. She wanted that to be it. Out loud, she said, "How much he's improved." Then in a rush, the thought she'd meant never to share, "It has galled me for years, what you said about him not having a conscience."

"Me? I never said that!"

"Yes you did. Surely you haven't forgotten that hateful business over the academy game."

"I've haven't forgotten that. I just don't remember anything I said. But that was years ago. They were boys. Better to make your stupid mistakes when you're young."

Danet lifted her face. "*I* remember what you said. And saw, or thought I saw, certain other signs . . . I forced Mnar Milnari to send that little redheaded runner Connar likes so much to Larkadhe with the boys, in hopes she would be his conscience. I think it's working."

Noth smiled back at her. He doubted very much that a hot young stallion with Connar's reputation for burning through lovers would listen to lectures from a runner, lover or not. "Or he grew up, the way boys do," he said indulgently.

The double wedding, everyone agreed, fit their idea of splendid, from the brisk, sunny day to the banquet that had been in preparation for weeks.

The princes and the two new princesses wore their new House tunics of deep royal blue, with golden eagles worked in beautiful stitching across the chest for the princes, and twined gracefully down either arm for the princesses, as their robes were usually worn open over snowy white linen shirts and riding trousers. On the front panels, Ranet had chosen small, highly stylized hunting cats, the Senelaec symbol, and Noren had small owls on hers, aware that this would be the last Algaravayir formal garment ever.

The only one propelled to the giddy heights of happiness was Ranet. At last she stood beside the handsome prince she'd adored since she first laid eyes on him. He was even more devastating close up, the blue of his tunic no more intense than the blue of his eyes. She knew he was not in love with her, but she had hopes he would be some day. It was enough that she could stand beside him, and share the wedding cup, and when he smiled at her, her breath stuttered in her chest.

That night, when all was over, he asked if she would like him to come to her bed. Sex with her handsome prince was everything she had wished for. He seemed to like her being on top, which she actually preferred; by then she had enough experience to see to it that they both reached ecstasy together.

But when their passion was spent, he wished her a good sleep and went back to his own suite. And the second night, as she loitered in the hallway, she glimpsed him with Lineas before they vanished into his room, and she went to bed alone.

She had told herself all along that it would be that way. The next morning she went about her work at the queen's training as if there was nothing on her mind but shooting well, and horse training, but she chatted and smiled, rode and drilled with an invisible boulder behind her ribs.

At the end of the day, before the girls clattered off to their mess hall as the last reverberations of the bells echoed along the stone walls, she spotted Lineas alone in the tack room, without any idea that Lineas had been expecting her.

Ranet came up to her, glanced behind, then in Hand, so their voices wouldn't carry (and hers wouldn't tremble) she asked abruptly, "Is it a love match with you and Connar?"

"No. It's more habit, I think," Lineas signed back, her glance lowered. "He has other lovers—many—but he's comfortable with me. I'm the oldest."

Ranet had made it her business to know that there were many, but Lineas was the only one he came back to. "*How* are you the oldest? What can I do?"

Since Lineas had no idea what it was that drew Connar to her, she made some suggestions, which Ranet could see were honest and sincere. Then they parted, each thoughtful: Lineas hoping that Connar would see what he had waiting for him right here in the royal castle, and Ranet sensing that something was missing, though she could not define what it might be.

Arrow and Danet waited to hold the trial, ostensibly for the jarls to arrive, but in reality until the royal runner Ivandred made it to Ku Halir then Yvanavayir and back.

"Manther Yvanavayir refused," Ivandred said.

"He did?" Arrow repeated. "What did he say?"

Ivandred hesitated, thrown back to that overheated room under the roof that smelled of sweat and despair. *If my brother has to give up title, land, and name, then I will too. Send me into exile,* he'd cried, starting up, one of his bandages tearing.

As blood welled up, dyeing the linen with horrible crimson, he'd fumbled at the side of the bed for a knife, yelling, *Better dead, better dead,* until Ghost Fath grabbed his wrists and pressed him flat onto the bed. Then held him as Manther lay tight-lipped, tears leaking from his eyes, their gazes locked in a fierce communication that everyone watching could feel.

Ventdor had stood by looking sick. He'd drawn Ivandred out, shutting the door before saying, *I know Arrow means well. None better. But can't you see that boy takes that offer as a complete betrayal? Fath's been sitting with him day and night, just got him to start eating. I'm afraid it's . . .* He flat-handed the subject away. *Better ride back to Arrow. Get this trial over with as quick as you can, or I'm afraid he will cut his own throat.*

Ivandred blinked away the memory. "He was delirious," Ivandred said heavily. "But it's definite. Commander Ventdor recommended you make it quick."

Arrow grimaced and dismissed Ivandred, who trod heavily upstairs, pausing halfway to lean against the wall as he tried to shake that memory.

Alone in his chamber, Arrow was thinking that he was too old for this. It was time to retire. Only kings didn't get to retire, did they?

The days slipped by, falling back into their usual patterns. But it wasn't the same after all. Noddy, of his own accord, spent his free time over at the state wing when his father held interviews. He never spoke, but sat like an enormous statue, only his eyes moving as he listened.

Connar was everywhere at the garrison, leading the drills of a handpicked elite, and at night studying the detailed maps that Arrow had ordered made. Lnand had drawn detailed renditions of every castle in the southern pass, which led directly to Elsarion on the other side of the mountains.

The trial loomed, then the day dawned. Pony Yvanavayir had not believed anything could happen to her until the days turned into weeks. After that, Pony couldn't eat, and slept badly. It didn't matter how right she believed she was, because nobody else did, and unless a miracle happened, she was going to experience the worst of deaths.

The trial was held in the throne room, with three jarls and the Jarlan of Tlen, who had lost her entire family, present besides Eaglebeak Yvanavayir, other jarls represented by trusted Rider captains or commanders.

Poor little Jam had finally found out what might happen because of her words. The scribes had kept quiet, as ordered, but no one had thought to warn off the garrison children, a couple of whom gleefully described in bloodthirsty detail what happened to traitors. Jam came when summoned, but she got sick to her stomach outside the hall, too fast for the Waste Spell.

But she stuck to her testimony.

Danet watched with her fingernails dug into her palms as Pony, gaunt from not eating, tried to justify herself, but her voice seemed lost in that vast room, with the straight swords taken from the enemy commanders at Tlennen Plain crossed over the ruined banners of Tlen and Halivayir on the walls. She glanced up once or twice; that smoke-stained Tlen banner was a silent accusation she could not argue with, and her voice faded to a monotone that even she heard as unconvincing.

Danet and Arrow let the jarls argue back and forth. The division was roughly half and half between traitor and criminal, but the heat had gone out of the voices. By then everyone at least understood one thing, even if it remained unspoken, that the woman standing before them had been guilty of no more than cupidity that had turned lethal without her knowledge. Mathias Elsarion, who should be on trial, had escaped.

But the Jarl of Gannan led those who demanded that someone had to pay.

Finally Danet, noting that they were getting into repeating themselves, flicked a look Arrow's way.

He stood up. "I've listened to the testimony and your arguments. Not everyone is in accord with the definition of treason, or whether Fareas Yvanavayir's actions constitute treason. There is also the plea entered by Aldren, Jarl of Yvanavayir, known as Eaglebeak, who feels honor-bound to substitute himself for his sister. I have taken all this into consideration. The final judgment is exile. Yvanavayir Jarlate is forfeit, the name Yvanavayir to be struck from the roll of jarls."

A gasp and a rustle and hiss echoed through the vast, cold chamber.

Arrow went on in a grim voice, "The former Jarl of Yvanavayir and his sister Fareas have until New Year's Firstday to cross the Marlovan border, on pain of death. Chelis Cassad as jarlan shares the exile. Manther Yvanavayir, wounded in service to the kingdom, may choose whether to remain in the king's service, or to follow his family into exile. But he and his heirs, if any, will not inherit the jarlate."

That shocked the jarls into silence. In a way, many thought privately, it was worse than a bloody execution, which at least would be over. To lose your lands, your name! That was *forever*.

The Jarl of Zheirban stood up. "Who's to succeed?"

Arrow saw the anticipation the jarl couldn't quite hide, and scowled. "That is to be determined."

Thus it was.

Arrow permitted Eaglebeak, who had been made as comfortable as possible in the lockup, to slip out with his sister through the back gate of the academy. It was empty until spring, so no one saw him other than the wall sentries, who had been visited personally by Arrow, and informed that the two riding out were invisible.

Eaglebeak did not have to endure the shame of riding out with no banner, and no fanfare. The great yellow banner with the blue eagle flying the opposite direction of the crimson Montreivayir eagle would fold up as its rival had, and be seen no more.

Pony rode with him, a silent wraith compared to her former days. Eaglebeak had no idea what to say to her, so they rode in silence, aware of the patrol that was no honor guard riding in sight behind them.

They avoided all towns, including Ku Halir. Pony had begun to speak now and then as they turned north at last, but when they passed the eastern edge of Tlen, she fell silent, and stayed that way until they crossed into what had been Yvanavayir.

No longer home.

Chelis had already begun to organize things, after Ivandred's visit to warn her what was likely to come. She intended to leave the castle clean and swept. Honor required no less.

Eaglebeak and Pony arrived after harvest was in. Chelis was there waiting. She said, "I've already sent two carts of our household belongings, but Eaglebeak, you must talk to the Riders. The Veneth clan is split, the Basnas and the Iascans wanting to stay for whoever comes after—the Iascans all seem to believe it will be Manther—and the rest want to come with us, except for the Hamads, who have already ridden north to see if their kin in Idego will take them."

"Right, I'll go out to the garrison now."

Chelis's voice softened. "And when you're done, you must decide about the things in the Hall of Ancestors,

"Leave them," he said flatly. "Except for Hawkeye's shield. Like the banner. That's *ours*."

Chelis opened her hand, then said, "Then all that's left is to pack your personal things. I spent the last three days going into the village to take formal leave."

He turned up his hand, and walked out, leaving Pony and Chelis facing one another.

Chelis had imagined many conversations, including taking the blame for handling the situation badly, made worse by the recent death of the old jarl. Though not if Pony had strutted in the way she used to. But the Pony standing before her was gaunt, her arms thin in her flapping sleeves, her whole demeanor defeated. "I want to blame you," she said dully.

Chelis held her breath.

"But I can't," Pony said, almost too soft to hear. "I can't."

"I can't blame you either." Chelis worked to keep her voice neutral. "When we reach Lindeth Harbor, you can take ship on your own, or you can come with us. I expect that my Dei relations in Sartor will take us in, at least until we can get up the language and find out how we might make a living."

Pony walked to her room, where she sank onto her weapons trunk, bowed her head, and for the first time since she lost her mother all those years ago, wept.

TWENTY

During his seven years as Connar's first runner, Fish Pereth had always done exactly what he was told, and never asked questions unless they were to clarify an order. Connar believed Fish was still reporting to Hauth, so he told Fish nothing of what he thought. He didn't tell anyone.

It wasn't until he overheard Vanadei and Noddy arguing over something inconsequential—and it wasn't heated argument, just talk, talk, talk—that it occurred to him how perfect was the silence Fish gave him. He obeyed orders, he was as tidy as Connar himself, he was quiet. If Fish decided to marry that new favorite of his over in the city, Connar would have to find another first runner. He might even be stuck with a royal runner, who blabbered in Old Sartoran with the others, saying who knew what.

So he said one morning, "If I'm promoted, you'll need your own staff. You choose who you want." Then he walked out so he wouldn't have to hear the answer.

Not that there would have been one. Fish knew better than that. He was left to stand there, fingers to chest in salute, reflecting sourly how much more it meant to him to hear that than effusive praise from anyone else. The weirdest aspect was, he didn't even like Connar as a person.

But he was shaping up to be a great commander.

Two mornings a week, Arrow refused to make any appointment except for breakfasting with the princes. Arrow tried to pick some ruling topic to go over, and sometimes they went over old battles. Connar turned out to be expert on the details of Inda-Harskialdna's battles (still remembered from his countless readings of Hauth's papers), which pleased Arrow.

Noddy sat silently, listening to the battle talk because it was part of his future duty; when they talked about guild matters, he joined in. It was Connar who remained silent, often letting his mind wander back to what he privately considered his personal failure; victory meant Elsarion lying dead at his feet, cut down by his own hand.

The only interest Noddy took in martial training, other than morning drill, was lance practice. One morning, Cabbage Gannan sent a message over that he was holding a competition to replace the Riders who'd died at Tlennen Plain, and did Noddy want to watch?

Noddy so seldom showed more than perfunctory interest in defense that Arrow gladly gave him permission to skip their morning meeting.

When Connar heard where Noddy was, he said, "I wanted to talk to you anyway about the Adrani passes, specifically the southern. May I fetch my map?"

"Let's look on the big map," Arrow said, instantly jettisoning his planned topic.

They unrolled the big canvas map on the floor. This map was an improvement over the old one, with more details of individual mountains, rivers, and especially the two Adrani passes, painted by Lnand herself.

"I know everyone calls Tlennen Plain a victory." Connar rapped his knuckles on the map. "But it was a battle victory. Not a war victory, because Elsarion is still up there, and though everybody whooped it up because we drove them off, I won't call it a real victory until Elsarion is dead at my feet."

"Damn!" Arrow sat back on his heels as he glared at those painted mountains. "I've been thinking the same thing, late nights. What's to keep him from ordering up a fresh batch and coming down again? That's been galling me under the saddle for years, ever since Camerend warned us about those outposts up the southern pass. The Adranis swore they're there to guard against brigands, but they're stuffed with Adranis. Of course they'd whistle and look up at the birds if an army comes riding down from the east."

They bent over the map, Arrow scowling. Elsarion had used the northern pass to send warriors disguised as traders, but that wouldn't work anymore. Arrow had a regular rotation up there now, searching every wagon coming west.

"If Elsarion really does maintain an army in those outposts, it has to cost the Adranis a king's ransom to supply them." Arrow tapped the little squares that represented outposts at either end of the southern pass.

Connar said, "We need to know. My idea is to send a scout up there to sketch out the defenses of those castles." He tented his fingers over the stylized representations of the four outposts along the bow-shaped pass.

A quick triple rap at the door brought Arrow's head up. His runners knew there was a very short list of people he'd take interruptions from during his talks with the princes. "What?" he shouted.

The stable runner poked his head in. "Quill is back."

"Quill!" Arrow beckoned. "Send him in."

Connar rose. "You want to hear this privately?"

"You should definitely hear it, especially if you're going to take command. And I was going to talk to you about that. Never mind, we'll go into it later. Here's what matters. Quill is as good a ferret as Camerend. He heard someone yapping about Feravayir attacking this city if Elsarion took Ku Halir, and rode down there to track down the source of the rumor."

Connar sat back, intensely interested, and gratified to be included. One of Arrow's chamber runners rapped next, and opened the door.

Quill entered, his hair damp from the weather, the hem of his robe sodden. He'd clearly come straight from the stable, bringing the stink of horse.

He saluted the king and the prince, and took up a reporting stance, but first Arrow waved him toward a mat. "Sit! Want something hot to drink?"

"Thank you. It can wait," Quill said, looked down at himself. "I can stand. I'm muddy. Lnand and I both investigated the rumor I reported at the end of summer, I going among Parayid Harbor city and its outposts, and Lnand using her own methods. First of all, there is no sign that Commander Ivandred Noth is part of any secret plans. That is not true of Demeos or Evred Nyidri, who now uses his Sartoran name, Ryu."

Arrow snapped, "Don't give a spit what he calls himself. What happened?"

"Lnand and I separately discovered that the Nyidri brothers, Ryu in particular, have been using their wealthier friends to recruit men of their holdings, calling them defense groups. Practice for competitions. Challenges against other villages. As far as I could tell some of them knew they were being recruited and others genuinely thought there was some festival being planned. They've been training mostly under outlander swordmasters, brought in and paid for by the Nyidris and four of their friends, all with significant holdings in Feravayir, except for Artolei, whose land lies over the border into Jayad Hesea. He's a third-cousin of the Nyidri family."

Here Quill paused, frowned into space, then continued. "I have a list of testimonies."

"Just one for now," Arrow said.

"As you wish. The most substantive was by an angry shopkeeper whose husband was recruited to be the village commander, one of three under the Nyidris' mother-cousin Artolei. According to what this shopkeeper overheard, the plan was for these groups to be assembled as soon as word reached Feravayir that Thias Elsarion had breached this city," Quill said.

Arrow stirred, then raised a hand to Quill to continue.

"Then news arrived of the defeat at Tlennen Plain. There followed a hasty retreat. Several of Ryu's would-be captains sailed to Sartor. It was after that I interviewed the shopkeeper, whose name I promised not to reveal to either the jarlan or to you. She was quite bitter that her husband, husband's father, and his brother had gone off to, as she put it, play warrior, leaving the finishing shop entirely to her to run. When they returned after word went out about the defeat at Tlennen Plain, it was empty-handed. Rumor had it, pay was to be in plunder."

"Rumor. That's not evidence."

"There's *no* evidence outside of second-hand stories like hers," Quill stated. "Ivandred Noth himself told me the jarlan was planning a spring festival, and he allocated outposts for competitors to gather. He was furious when we presented the testimonies."

"Shit," Arrow exclaimed. "Shit, shit, shit! Of course Lavais Nyidri was in on it. If not behind it." He remembered that he and Danet had expected to marry Bunny down in that pit of vipers.

Quill said in his trained neutral voice, "According to the jarlan, her devoted, wonderful son Demeos has been organizing this festival for the benefit of Feravayir, full of art and music. But her equally wonderful son Ryu was organizing a wargame *in the Marlovan tradition*—they emphasized that—as chief entertainment. The outposts were to house the competitors."

"In the Marl—what d'you think they meant by that?" Arrow asked suspiciously, then sighed. "Never mind, I hear the dig at our past troubles, though they're too snaky to come out and say it."

Quill didn't deny it. "Ivandred Noth promises to send his own report after he investigates at the command level, but he admitted that he was unlikely to find any concrete proof if we hadn't. He was thoroughly duped. Lnand remains there as ferret."

Quill handed the report over, and backed up to exit, but Arrow flung up a hand. "Wait. I'll read this right away, but first, Connar was just telling me we need to send a scout up the Adrani pass to spy out the castles. Lnand was there, what, six, eight years ago? I remember she made this map right here." A rap of the knuckles on the vast canvas. "Maybe we ought to recall her from Parayid, and send someone else down there."

Connar said to Arrow, "I don't see the need to recall her. I was planning to send our two best scouts up the southern pass, the ones who found Yenvir's lair—"

Arrow was eyeing Quill. "Is there a problem?"

Quill debated sharply within himself, suspecting he was not going to get his hard-earned liberty after all. But he'd sworn an oath. "It's that our scouts look like Marlovan military. Even if you dress them like farmers or shepherds, they move like Marlovan military, and sound like them. If Elsarion really has taken over the pass, at best Marlovan scouts will be lied to, at worse scragged. You need someone who actually practices another trade, doesn't just pretend to. Who can think like civilians, who won't make them think of Marlovan Riders."

"Right," Arrow exclaimed. "Camerend said the same thing, years ago! We sent Lnand, who's also a musician. She could sketch maps, but she wasn't trained to assess military capabilities." Arrow peered intently at Quill. "Are you trained in that?"

Quill looked at the king, but he was aware of Connar at the periphery of his vision. "Not in the way you train at the academy," he said, wondering why the second prince had gone so still. "We're trained to observe, listen, count, and map, but none of us can plan a campaign."

Arrow grunted as he glared at the painted twists and turns of the southern pass on either side of Mt. Skytalon, the highest point. "Do you think they might recognize Lnand up there—think her suspicious?"

"Bards wander," Quill said, allowing himself to hope. "She was careful never to raise any suspicions."

Arrow sighed. "But another fact is, she didn't dig out what those Nyidris were plotting until you got there. I want *you* to go up the southern pass. You're the best of the best."

"That's true," Connar said, and Quill turned his way at last, to see him smiling under that watchful blue gaze. "I've seen the proof myself. Quill, no one else would be as good as you. I'm going to be planning an entire campaign on what you give us."

Quill could not confess the true danger, that Elsarion—if he was there—would recognize him in a heartbeat, whatever guise he wore. Every instinct in him warned against admitting how he'd confronted the enemy and escaped by magic transfer, when he was understood by Commander Ventdor and the rest to have ridden south to the royal city.

"As you wish." He was committed.

"Excellent." The king turned to Connar. "What do you want Quill to look at?"

Connar tapped the four little painted outposts with long, sword-callused fingers. "I need everything you can get on these: guard routine, how many and what type of training, defenses. Alternate routes. While he gets that. . ." Connar turned to Arrow. "I can take a company of volunteers each from Ghost and Stick. We'll spend a season at Halivayir, running attacks from the outside, then go up into the mountains and run wargames, until we figure out some strategies."

"Excellent plan. Ah, ha, ha!" Arrow chortled, rubbing his hands. "Excellent! Quill, I want you on the road as soon as you can, as fast as you can." He relented slightly. "If you need a night of rec time, take it, seeing as you just got off the road. No more than a night, mind."

Quill walked out, and headed straight to the baths, encountering Vanadei, who gazed at him in surprise.

"You're back? I didn't know that."

"I'll be out again before anyone knows I was here," Quill said tightly, and gave him a one-sentence report.

Vanadei watched the tense set of Quill's shoulders as he ran down the steps toward the baths. Vanadei was duty-bound to tell Mnar Milnari, and so he retreated upstairs to the lair to do so.

"He was here and he's going again?" Mnar asked incredulously, then set aside a pile of reports and was about to sail down the hall when Vanadei stepped out and for the first time, blocked her path. "Let him come to you," he said.

Mnar stopped, her graying brows lifted. "Why?"

Vanadei had grown up knowing that Mnar was impatient with any emotional attachments getting in the way of duty, so he said, "He just got back from a long, cold, wet ride. Let him soak in the baths for a time before he has to get back on his horse. You know he'll come to you before he leaves."

Mnar's eyes narrowed as she sorted his words. Every one was true, though Vana's tone, the way he'd blocked the door, indicated something unspoken.

Well, if it was dire, he'd speak, and it wasn't as if she hadn't plenty to do.

"Very well." She sat back down and picked up her reports.

Vanadei slipped down the hall to where Lineas was supervising a class of fledges in handwriting. He paused in the doorway, caught her eye, and made the 'feather' sign, which was Quill's name in Hand. Her eyes widened, and he backed away.

While that was going on, Quill hastened through a fast bath, wrenching his mind determinedly to ordering duties in priority. It didn't matter what he wanted, which was enough time to see Lineas face to face. Bitterness soured his gut, and he consciously fought it back. Duty. First, change out his gear for winter, including a couple of firesticks. Report to Mnar . . .

When Lineas appeared in his open door, he was sitting on the edge of his bed in an unlaced shirt and brown riding trousers, wet hair hanging about his shoulders as he pulled on one brownweave riding boot. The other sat on the floor beside him; two knives and a sword lay beside him on the bed.

He glanced up and froze. Gaze met wondering gaze, and the next thing she knew he'd crossed the room as she leaped to meet him.

She locked her arms around him, he pulled her close, rocking them both as all their pent-up yearning flashed to desire. Dizzy before the ferocity of their heat, she longed for all the fabric between them to vanish, leaving them skin to skin. Closer.

He groaned into the top of her head, and when she lifted herself up onto her tiptoes to fit herself against the evidence of his desire so that she could hug him even tighter, he groaned again, a different tone that made her chuckle into his chest.

She lifted her face. They kissed, and kissed again, desperate as the sun-parched finding water at last. He barely had the presence of mind to whirl them about and kick the door shut behind him before they fell on the bed, bouncing the weapons to the floor.

"There's so much to . . ." he murmured into her lips.

"Not now," was all she said. "Not now."

He had never let himself get this far in his imagination. "The king. Said I could have till tomorrow morning. I was going to be good and leave today . . ."

She grabbed him by the back of the head, and showed him how little she thought of his being good.

Outside, in the hall, Vanadei heard the door slam, and smiled to himself. And for the rest of the watch, he lurked here and there, always in sight, and anyone who showed an inclination to look for either of them, he unapologetically sent off to distant parts of the castle, sure that they could be found there.

As soon as Quill left, Arrow turned to Connar. "I always meant to wait until you reached thirty, or got some experience, whichever came first, to put you in command. After what you did up north—what you just said—I think you're ready now."

The ferocity of Connar's joy burned through him. He lost the words, nearly lost the world, but a correspondingly fierce effort focused him again as Arrow finished, " . . . and we'll call all the garrison captains in at next Convocation to witness you getting your three gold arrows. Let 'em all see it, everything orderly, no more about Olavayirs at each other's throats. You'll be right behind me in chain of command."

Arrow swung to his feet with a grunt. Now he could have that drink! Grinning at the happiness in Connar's face, he said, "What was it, yesterday? When we went over to see Hliss, Noddy told me you should be promoted over him. He likes it over there at the state wing, and he hates the idea of running battles. I find all that astounding. I heard from everyone after that Chalk Hills business that you both were brave as well as skilled, and I remember what he looked like at the Victory Day Games, smashing lances."

He shook his head. "But that's what he said. Even stranger, he really does read every word of those damn reports. He must have inherited Danet's eye for lists and numbers. Better them than me . . Hah! Go get Noth. Let's tell him."

Connar dashed out, scattering waiting runners, then stopped at his room and poked his head in. "Fish! Prepare to ride to Halivayir. All my winter clothes."

And he was gone again, leaving Fish to reflect on how fast the news would travel in the prince's wake with him running about so exultantly.

Fish knew what would come next: a summons to his father, where Uncle Retren was sure to be lurking around asking questions Fish couldn't, or wouldn't, answer, and handing out orders about how Fish was to influence the future king.

Fish longed to ignore him, but he knew if he did his father would harrow him, then his mother would summon him into the city to hear a long lecture about The Importance of Never Forgetting His Dolphin-Clan Birth, and far worse, his brother would land on him like a pile of bricks—with a couple of his husky sentry friends along, in case Fish fought him off, as he had a few times. (Not that his brother cared a whit about who was king, as long as he got paid. He resented being lectured by their elders about Fish's perceived shortcomings.)

Wishing he were an orphan would not solve the problem. So the thing to do would be to first, delay until right before the watch change, after which he could plea orders, and second, to go with some kind of diversion in hopes of warding the usual harangue-and-harass about reporting Connar's every word, thought, and deed. He couldn't make something up, because between his brother the sentry, his father the quartermaster, and his uncle the academy master, they heard all the gossip as fast as it happened—so if they hadn't heard it, they'd be certain to query. And land on him collectively and separately for lying.

So . . . what? He looked around in despair. He also had to get things organized. Fish and the tailors had provided Connar with all new clothes, from the House tunic on down to two replacement summer coats, so once the carts from up north had finally caught up with them, they'd sat in Fish's alcove untouched.

The trunks contained all their winter clothes from those stiff winters at Larkadhe. He'd better get busy sorting those now, and get as much done as possible before the inevitable summons.

Mentally considering and rejecting diversionary ideas, he prepared Connar's saddlebags first, storing secondary clothes back in the trunks for the carts that would be sent off come morning.

Then it was time for his own gear. He unlatched his trunk, threw the lid back, and pulled out his neatly folded heavy-linen winter shirts, trousers, drawers, and stockings, and set them aside. Then he grabbed his old runner's coat, and paused as something crackled.

Startled, he dropped the coat and reached in more carefully, and pulled out a somewhat crumpled drawing. When he recognized the sketched face, the aftermath of the Battle of Chalk Hills flooded his memory, including Lineas going on and on about ghosts.

This would be perfect as a diversion, Fish decided. He didn't believe in ghosts. Whether or not the drawing depicted Evred Olavayir, it was certain to get his father and Uncle Retren sidetracked into slandering Evred, or Lineas for pretending she saw ghosts, or any other subject that would (Fish hoped) use up the time he'd otherwise be interrogated and then harangued about Connar, until the watch bell released him.

When the expected under-assistant showed up from the quartermaster's, Fish said, "I'll be there as soon as I carry out my immediate orders."

Then, smiling, he took his time to finish sorting his belongings, packing his gear bag with winter things and reorganizing his trunk with secondary winter clothes and spring and summer things.

When he had calculated to a nicety how long he could dally before they'd start to get angry, he rolled up the drawing and headed for the quartermaster's.

Before his uncle could open his mouth, Fish said, "We've orders to ride north. I had to sort both our trunks. And I found something I'd nearly forgotten. Remember I told you about the Bar Regren attack at Chalk Hills?"

His father opened his hand, and Uncle Retren said, "Connar's first command, the success of which is almost exactly what Mathren—"

Fish cut in before his uncle could gallop down the old familiar road. "I told you that Lineas claimed she saw Evred's ghost. I don't believe it, of course. But I saved this drawing she made of this ghost, because I wanted to ask you two, as you knew Evred better than I ever did. I was what, half a year old when he died?"

He began unrolling the paper. "Anyway, I thought I'd ask. So if she makes any other such claims, I can counter with eyewitness accounts that, no, it's nothing like Evred."

He snapped the paper open, and watched his father shrug. "That could be anybody. But it's not Evred."

Hauth blanched, his lower face sagging.

Fish had begun to say, "I thought so. She might have been hallucinating. She was running a fever after riding all afternoon with a shattered . . ." He stuttered to a stop at Hauth's shock. "Uncle Ret?"

The quartermaster slewed around, staring at his brother-by-marriage. "Ret? What's wrong?"

"That's not Evred," Hauth said hoarsely. "That's *Lanrid.* To the li—"

Such was the collective astonishment that no one laughed when Hauth choked off the word *life.*

"That's impossible," the quartermaster exclaimed, all the more forcefully in an unconscious effort to make it undeniably true. "That girl is too young to have met him. She copied a drawing."

"She drew it right in front of us," Fish admitted reluctantly. "No drawings of any kind in that room."

His father shrugged sharply. "She saw a drawing of Lanrid somewhere else. Remembered it. I'm told art-makers do that all the time."

Without hearing either of them, Hauth snatched the paper out of Fish's fingers and stared at it as if he could devour it. His eyes gleamed with tears, the sight of which made Fish's guts lurch. Impossible. It was just impossible. There was some perfectly ordinary explanation, some cheat on Lineas's part, though he remembered that she'd been in terrible shape.

"Why?" Hauth whispered. "Larkadhe . . . Lanrid was only there the once, before we rode up the Andahi Pass." A deep breath. "But Connar was there."

"Ret," the quartermaster began, though he wasn't sure what ought to come after.

Hauth looked up. "Didn't you tell us she sees the ghost . . . here?" He extended trembling fingers at the file-and-supply crowded office, as if a ghost somehow lurked in the dusty, crowded corners.

"That's what she claimed," Fish muttered, wishing he'd burned the damn drawing. Even a rant about The Future Great Connar-Harvaldar would be better than this weird talk of ghosts. What was worse, it was *still* going to lead right back to Connar.

"Lanrid . . . is here," Hauth repeated, his eyes still glittering with unshed tears. "Then went north, with Connar. Is he trying to watch over him? Or tell us something? Why?"

"Ret," the quartermaster cautioned. "Even people who believe in ghosts don't talk to them, from anything I've ever heard. Ghosts *can't* talk. They don't breathe, or have a body in order to make a sound."

Again, Hauth didn't seem to hear. "He's in this castle. . . . but why can't I see him?"

The quartermaster rolled his eyes at Fish, who sighed. "You know it has to be fake," he said as he reached for it.

Hauth struck his fingers away so hard and fast that pain shot up Fish's wrist. "Touch it and I'll cut off your hand," Hauth uttered in a guttural whisper, veins standing out in his forehead. Then he sighed, wiped shaking fingers over his face, and muttered, "I have to think about this."

He rolled the paper with heartrending care, grabbed his cane, and walked out, shoulder-bowed.

The quartermaster heaved a sigh. "Son, you shouldn't have—"

Fish slammed the door on his words.

Lineas accompanied Quill to the stable very early the next morning, well before the single ring of the hour before dawn. Neither spoke; they had exchanged their farewells in his room, after he reported to Mnar Milnari.

He rode off, ostensibly to the north, but as soon as he was out of sight of the sentries, he cut westward to a well-known path then veered southward toward Darchelde.

During their precious night, neither she nor Quill had mentioned Connar, but his presence had been there, a potent if silent reminder. Neither had admitted even that. He understood the complexity of her situation. He was still euphoric, having not let himself even hope for her to turn to him; he had to let her decide how to proceed.

All day Lineas's emotions swooped from the pinnacle of elation to the depths of dread that she'd be ordered to accompany Connar. She worried even more about meeting up with Connar himself; she tried scolding herself for being unable to go from one lover to the next, the way Bun did, and many others. It was perfectly acceptable if one hadn't made promises. She knew that, but all day, as she went from task to task with a tremble in her fingers and no appetite, she felt as if she were being ripped into two, right through the heart. The larger part going with Quill.

Quill hadn't said anything, which was such a profound relief. She'd even caught his reflective gaze on her, and sympathy in his smile; this situation was *hers* to solve. To clarify. But she wasn't certain how to clarify it to herself.

Meanwhile, rumors flew about the castle that the king was sending Connar to the north to begin winter training exercises, with a chosen company of elites. Each mention rubbed Lineas's spirits raw as she worked hard to go about her tasks as usual.

She counted the hours, shutting off what-ifs with the mental reminder that as long as no summons came, she would get a respite.

But it would be just a respite. Connar would return for Convocation. At least, she thought, that would give her long enough to understand her own mind and heart.

The sun crawled across the sky without anyone being sent to fetch her from classes or drill, until midafternoon when pealing trumpets heralded their departure.

Lineas had been busying herself in the queen's training tack room. On hearing the fanfares, she ran up to the wall to peer into the stableyard from the south tower. She saw Connar and Stick mounting up, spirits clearly as high as their snapping flags in the wintry breeze scouring across the plains.

Connar rode with three golden chevrons gleaming on his coat, and behind, the cherished king's banner, signaling to all that he was the royal shield arm, under direct orders from the king—and so could commandeer both men and supplies as needed in order to carry those orders out.

Still nearly delirious with happiness, Connar insisted that Stick ride next to him. The entire castle turned up on the walls to watch them, the girls of queen's training thinking the two young commanders impossibly dashing. Experiences of the past two years had planed most of the humor from Stick Tyavayir's sharp-boned face, but many of those girls only found him the more attractive, and there were plenty who resolved to return to their drills with renewed effort in order to be chosen to join Braids Senelaec's company, which everyone knew was to be expanded.

"We'll be rid of Elsarion sooner than later," Arrow said when the last of the Riders vanished on the horizon. "See if we don't."

Danet said nothing to that. Her mind went straight to what she now thought of as her girls, those who had come to the summer games and then queen's training. Who she kept track of by letter.

She had roamed her room, raging uselessly when word arrived of the deaths at Halivayir, and then of the Tlen girls, including the new bride; Stick Tyavayir's future wife had died out there in the Nelkereth, trying to protect the Tlen horses. Evidence that women could, and did, die even if they weren't part of the army.

When she got back to the far side of the castle, where the girls were returning to their court, she caught Noren's eye, and signed, "I talked Arrow into keeping Noddy home. I want grandchildren."

Noren's heart lurched in her chest as smiled and opened her hand. It could mean anything, but she knew that the queen assumed assent, so in effect she was lying.

She had always respected Danet-Gunvaer, and had come to love her.

I did my best to explain to the gunvaer when she came to visit us that our blood is tainted, her mother had said before Noren left for the last time, *but I knew the king would not listen. The day will come when the gunvaer will ask you to take gerda-herb in order to conceive a child. And you might be tempted, but if you are—*

I will remember my promise, Noren had responded.

No, her mother chided gently. *Don't remember your promise. Remember your twin sister, terrified of thunder, strangers, and anything that draws her from her paths counted out by precise steps that nobody else can see. And remember my own brother, your Uncle Indevan, whose sensitivities we will never understand because he hadn't the words, but their weight is so terrible the only place he can bear is a dusty archive in Sartor, where he must live his life behind a wall of ancient text. I thought when I had you girls that you at least would be safe, that we had a generation or two before we had to fear the waterfall again. But I was wrong. It's now striking every generation. The Algaravayir line is too burdened. It must end with you.*

Noren dug into her trunk and pulled out the herb that carried a similar scent to gerda. The only effect it had, the healer had promised, was a tendency toward dry skin on hands and feet, and it left one somewhat thirsty.

Then she called Pan Totha and Holly to her, and gave the precious herb-pouch into their hands. Even gossipy, cheerful Holly was silent as the three stood in shared conspiracy, understanding the lie that they must now live.

TWENTY-ONE

When Quill reached Darchelde, he went around to greet everyone, then, as was their habit, he and Camerend went up to the highest tower to look out over the rolling hills to watch the sun come down.

Quill explained his orders, ending with, "I thought I'd put an illusion over myself before I go up the pass."

"Up from which end?" Camerend asked, hands clasped loosely, his gaze patient.

Quill was about to say from the west—of course—then understood. He rubbed his jaw, aware that he should have thought his plan through. "They'll scrutinize anyone coming up from our side, won't they."

"Count on it. Listen, Senrid. My suggestion is, start from the east end. As for illusion, that can be broken so easily, and then you not only become suspect, every scribe is suspect as word spreads. Don't use magic unless you're desperate. The most effective disguise doesn't require magic, is simple, and most of all, forgettable."

Royal runners were taught to be observant and unobtrusive, but Quill understood that now he was consciously going to use those skills to be a spy.

Camerend said, "First, let your jaw hang down while keeping your lips almost closed. Like this." He turned away from the sunset, the lurid colors reflecting off his face as it lengthened and took on a bovine aspect. "Don't look at your auditor, but past them." His gaze went slack-lidded and unfocused. "Second, add either a stutter or else a dawdle phrase in each sentence—whichever one comes easier for you."

"Dawdle phrase?"

"Each sentence prefaced, or punctuated, maybe both, with phrases such as *you might say,* or *so to speak,* or *to put in in a word,* and then add ten words. If you can get two or more dawdle-phrases into a sentence, speaking slowly and mildly, repeat yourself frequently, I guarantee they'll bustle you to a desk, and then ignore you as if you were not there. Copyists are already considered the lowest and most boring of all scribes."

"Jaw hanging. Dawdle phrase," Quill said. "Repeat." He looked up.

Camerend added, "And resist the urge to embellish. You don't want to be memorable. Vanda, my former partner now living up in Idego, on an assignment to the Nob during our young years couldn't resist adding clumsiness. For fun. It resulted in our being kicked out of not only the garrison but the town, the two sides united in cursing the stupid Marlovan stable hand who broke crockery and footstools. Disruptive habits are remembered. Slumped shoulders aren't."

"Got it."

"Practice, while you copy out the testimonial papers I used, so the handwritings will match. I'm afraid these were all chosen for their tediousness, so you're in for some boredom. It'll take you a couple of weeks to build a convincing portfolio, but you can practice your dawdle and your cow face while you copy." He smiled up at the emerging stars. "Do you know, I never get tired of being here to watch the sun rise," he indicated the eastern plains, "or set." A tip of the chin toward the rolling hills and the forest, now dark, to the south, before he turned to lead the way down the long staircase.

Following his father, Quill wondered if that was a result of Camerend having spent his young years as a hostage longing for home.

The copy task was as wearisome as Camerend had warned, but it was time well spent; Quill figured he had the month or six weeks it would have taken to ride to the southern pass to ready himself.

After those two weeks, he transferred by magic to Anaeran-Adrani, well outside Elsarion, to the scribe guild in a town Camerend had spent time in. There he bought the correct fabric for scribes on this side of the border, and made himself a robe. During the three days it took to finish it, each day he took a walk from his inn to the guild house, listening to people talking in the streets, and conversation in eateries.

There was plenty to hear.

On this side of the mountains, with news traveling with the speed of magic rather than of horse, everyone had heard of Mathias Elsarion's defeat —rumor accelerating as survivors of the attack emerged from the southern pass, spreading their horror stories. Trade caravans halted! Merchants cancelled planned journeys! Trade disrupted everywhere! People stranded without jobs!

By the time Quill was ready to try the local guild house, he understood the turmoil of this otherwise quiet town. It was at least a week's ride from the road to the southern pass, yet many people were packing up to go elsewhere in case the horse barbarians boiled up the pass in a frenzy of vengeance.

Not everyone was leaving. At the guild house, Quill found a cluster of newly-made scribes hoping to slide into a job vacated by alarmists. A sour-faced woman about his own age was in the middle of disparaging young men bored with apprenticeships, who downed tools and streamed toward Elsarion to volunteer for their lord's army. "My brother being one," she said. "Thinks fighting will be much more fun than drudging at a trade the family pushed him into."

A young man cracked his knuckles, then said, "I've got a cousin yelping at everyone that if you go, they pay, and you could become a duchas over the mountain—it being even bigger than our kingdom."

"Yes," drawled a tall, bony scribe, slouched on his bench. "So Lord Mathias sends a bigger army over there, and this time he wins, and what then? You can set yourself up as a duchas in a land where everyone says they eat and sleep on the stone floors of Iascan castles, wearing hemp and straw, and you have to have fifty guards around your bed every night, because otherwise every man, woman, and child will be coming at you with a knife. I've heard all about those Marlovans!"

"Let them stay on their side of the mountains." A short, round scribe made a spitting motion to the side. "But nooooo," she cooed. "Lord Mathias just had to go poking at the hornets' nest with a stick."

"Which will bring all the hornets back to sting *us*," a third stated grimly, crossing her arms with a thump. "Who didn't do anything to them. My ma says we're crazy to stay in town, but everywhere clear to Shiovhan, they say they're full up—only hiring those they trained."

"I heard the same," the second scribe said, flicking her fingers like shooing insects. "Lasva Pree told me last night that half the staff here is also running, all the plum jobs open. I wouldn't be surprised if we don't all get hired." She included the room with a wave of her hand.

She was right.

Quill was asked little more than his age, his guild status, and where he'd been trained. He provided the answers that Camerend had recommended, and was promptly hired by the overworked seniors, for with the town in flux everybody was writing letters or making copies of their accounts before they decamped a prudent distance to await events.

The rest of his month he spent working on his accent, acquiring another Adrani scribe robe, then pounding the hem with rocks and scrubbing the color out of the shoulders and seams to make it look worn—the people at the main guild house had been too desperate to notice a very new robe, but he wouldn't count on that being true at the pass, if the Adranis were really as jumpy as rumor claimed.

The first flurries of snow had crowned the mountaintops when he set out. He discovered that though trade had nearly halted, the outposts in the pass still needed supplies, and the infrequent supply caravans that had been promised double pay.

The chief drawback of beginning at the Adrani end of the pass was its proximity to Elsarion. The chance of running into Thias Elsarion was higher, but Quill gambled on Thias, raised to aristocratic comfort, being reluctant to flail around the pass at the start of winter unless given a reason.

Quill was determined not to provide that reason.

The weeks flew by.

Four days before New Year's Week, Connar galloped back into the royal city at the head of an honor guard, banners snapping as snowflakes whirled around them, stippling horses and gray coats and helms.

Word sped through the castle, and Noddy ran down to the stable yard, kicking up fresh powder as he greeted Connar.

Lineas joined those along the sentry wall. She rejoiced to see Connar's happiness, visible from the distance, as below, he and Noddy greeted each other.

"What news?" Connar and Noddy asked at the same time, then laughed. Ranet and Noren reached them, and gloved hands flickered in Hand as the four crossed the slushy yard, the cold wet wind kicking up around them.

Connar had gotten into the habit of doing a sweeping inspection of defenses: where sentries were placed, what weapons they bore, how alert they were. He was aware that many of the male heads turned to watch Ranet walking at his side, the wind pressing her robe against her form. A quick glance: her attention wasn't on them, but on him, a smile that brightened more when he grinned at her.

"Ranet." He kept forgetting that she was no longer a scrawny teen.

"Good ride?" she signed.

He turned his hand up and rolled his eyes toward the sky, his mouth awry, and she laughed softly, her breath clouding.

Unaware of this quick exchange behind him, Noddy finished listing who among the jarls had arrived.

"What about Ivandred Noth?" Connar asked.

"First arrival. He was up there with Da first thing. Da hasn't said much."

"So there's no proof of any conspiracy down there?"

"None, but Noth was really angry about it. Both his stepsons went off to Sartor on some excuse or other, and the jarlan stuck to the festival story. So Noth's increased the patrols, but Da says that's like sitting in the barn after all the horses stampeded out. As for everyone else, no real news."

Connar's mind shot eastward, as had become habit: Quill, riding his fastest, had probably just reached the western mouth of the southern pass. If he hadn't been stranded in a snowstorm somewhere around Lake Wened.

Connar was content to wait. No one was attacking anywhere with the brunt of winter still coming. And *nothing* was going to ruin the prospect of his official promotion before the jarls. He was at last where he'd always wanted to be, commander of the entire King's Army. It remained only to stand before the throne and lay his sword before Da's feet.

But his exhilaration dissipated as the day waned. Until now, he and Noddy had avoided the jarls at Convocation, except at the banquet, which they'd decamped from as quickly as possible. But the jarls had listened to every scrap of gossip culled from sons, nephews, and various Riders about the princes who would one day be expected to lead them. If they didn't turn on each other the way Olavayirs had in past generations.

Abruptly Connar found himself cornered by jarls at every turn, congratulating him on his victories, then almost in the same breath, offering him long-winded advice on how to defeat that Elsarion shit once and for all —usually by listening to, or promoting, their own sons or Riders' sons or cousins.

The most obnoxious of these, by far, was the huge, loud Jarl of Gannan, who interspersed his bad advice ("You run our boys straight up the mountain and watch those Adranis piss themselves in fear, ha ha!") with loud hints for praise of his second son, "You named him Cabbage. I have to admit I didn't much like that, until I found out that 'cabbage' is now your academy slang for smashing the enemy, har har har!" It was a loud, crashing, utterly humorless laugh that irritated Connar to the back teeth.

Connar was saved only by the watch change summoning him upstairs to meet the family for dinner, and he had yet to make it to the garrison.

When he reached the king's suite, Danet took one look and said, "What's amiss?"

Connar opened his hand, but she waited for an actual answer. He tried for lightness. "I'm beginning to see why Da hates Convocation."

Danet snorted.

Noddy glanced over. "I promised two jarls I would recommend their sons to you. Oh yes, and the Jarl of Gannan asked me to tell you that he will help you plan the attack on Elsarion, and he has a list to put forward as replacements for Halivayir and Yvanavayir." Noddy added slowly, "They all seem to have someone to suggest for Yvanavayir."

Arrow entered on those last words, trailing bristic fumes. But his eyes were clear. "Welcome to my life, these past years. Ho, ha! Grin and bear it, but don't agree with anything, unless we've already planned it."

Connar flipped up the back of his hand in the direction of the state chambers. Arrow gave another crack of laughter, and dinner progressed happily.

Before they all parted, Danet caught Connar by the arm. "I told the others, and now I'm telling you: I want grandchildren, the sooner the better. Let the rest of the kingdom see prospective order for the future as well as now."

Connar sent a panicked look at Noddy, who'd paused just outside the door, looking both sympathetic and unsurprised, and Connar understood that he'd already been hearing a lot about grandchildren.

Danet went on, "I told Ranet to get her girls to brew up gerda-herb as soon as you rode into the stableyard."

"Ma," Connar said on an exasperated note.

"That's all I have to say." Danet patted his shoulder—and said more anyway. "You know families are my domain. You boys have done well securing our present day. It's our responsibility to look to the future."

"Right, Ma," Connar said, and made his escape, his head already panging.

As Lineas was no longer assigned to the royal family, she could only go to the residence floor if summoned, which meant she saw none of the royal family after Connar's arrival. She discovered as the day progressed that she was now part of those hearing castle gossip second and third hand.

She worked an extra watch at the roost message desk, for the royal runners were hard put to keep up with all the errands with so many of them out on the road. Between logging messages, passing them along, and copying those needing copying, she imagined Connar's happiness blazing through the day as he celebrated his impending promotion. Surely he wouldn't think of her anymore. Or if he did, if she said something, he'd shrug and . . .

What *would* she say? Her imagination always foundered on the exact words. She just wanted him to be quit of her without her having to say anything at all; it was then, as she tidied away her writing utensils, she realized that he had always been the one to reach for her when he wanted her. She had never dared to reach for him. Nor had he encouraged her to.

And that had suited her, as whenever he was home he was never far from her thoughts. At sixteen, all the romance had been in her head. He had provided the handsome face and body.

When she was sixteen, that had been enough. But she wasn't sixteen anymore. Round and round her thoughts went.

When at last the night watch rang, she walked tiredly down the back stairs toward her room at the far at the end of the royal residence floor, up against the old harskialdna tower, where the royal runners assigned to the royal family had their rooms; though she was no longer Bun's runner, nobody had reassigned her living space in the two years she was away. She yawned tiredly as she reached to light a candle, then paused when she heard the ring of bootheels echoing down the stone hall outside her room.

She knew that walk. Quick as instinct she dashed to the side of her door and stood by the hinge as Connar rapped twice. Lineas pressed her forearms against her belly, holding her breath. She was a coward—hiding was stupid—but she didn't move, viscerally aware of him an arm's length away on the other side of the ancient wood of the door.

He rapped again, then unlatched the door, which had no lock. The door pressed against her arm as he glanced in; she turned her head and saw what he saw: the neatly made bed, the plain table, the window slit which she never put stuffing into, preferring the flow of air even in winter cold.

The door closed with a click and his steps moved away down the hall. She let out a long, shaky breath, and discovered that her forehead and palms were damp, her heart banging frantically against her throat. Why had she hidden like that? It could have been so humiliating! She stood there staring at the dim blue sky through the window slit, partially blocked by the bulk of the harskialdna tower, which sheltered her from the cold east winds.

She had, for the first time, avoided him. It felt like a new road taken, though she knew it really wasn't. It was only avoidance. But she was tired, her heart sore; he hated talk, but she would either have to explain or go back with him, which no longer felt right.

So think! First, he would probably come back, or send Fish. So she had to find somewhere else to sleep. Somewhere no one would discover her, so she wouldn't have to lie. Her thoughts automatically turned to Quill, whom she longed to ask—and then it struck her, there was his empty room up in the lair.

She dashed to her trunk to fetch clean clothes for the morrow, then slipped out, down to the far stairs above the baths, and up to the third floor.

She darted across the empty hall, unlatched Quill's door, slipped in and shut the door noiselessly behind her. She stood there in Quill's bedroom, which was only marginally larger than hers, but like all the rooms on the third floor, had a fireplace—empty now, of course.

She undressed quickly and climbed shivering under his covers, which smelled of him. She pressed her face to his pillow, sniffing the slight scent until it was gone; as her own warmth pooled around her and she began to slide down into the realm of dreams, it came to her that never, in all these years, had she ever even thought of sleeping in Connar's splendid chamber when he was gone on duty.

But here, she felt safe.

Connar had gone back toward his own room, restless and annoyed, then halted when Ranet opened the door to her suite across from his. "Come to my bed," she invited, as Lineas had advised her when they had talked what seemed so long ago.

Those words about grandchildren echoed in his ears, and he looked at her leaning in the doorway, the enticing curve inward at her waist and out over the flare of her hip. Definitely not that twig of a teen anymore. They were married. So why not?

Ranet rejoiced as he followed her into the warm room, clean and orderly, except for the scent of a cedar spray she'd tossed onto the fire stick in the fireplace when she heard his footsteps through the crack in the door, for she'd watched him go down the hall, then heard him come back empty-handed. So far, she was thinking, it was just as Lineas had said: *He comes to me out of long habit, I think. If the rumors are true that he gets asked by all these others, then he's not used to asking, right? So you should invite him, the way women did in the old days.*

So far, Lineas was right.

But that didn't last.

When Connar joined Ranet in the bed, she reached for his shoulder, remembering what Lineas had said about him liking her to work the knots out of his muscles. "Do you want me to rub your back?"

He stiffened, turning so fast his arm smacked her hand away. "No." And though they'd blown out the candle, the moonlight in the windows was strong enough to show her shock at his reaction, his flat voice.

He stilled, reining himself hard. "Why would you—" All desire vanished, his mounting irritation flaring to anger as a new idea occurred to him. "You've been yapping about me with Lineas?" Because she was the only person in life he permitted to see his back.

Ranet said softly, "I only asked her what you like."

"You can ask *me* that," he snapped, then reined himself again, thinking fast.

Ranet and he were new together. She was younger. She was only doing what he'd done when he first went to Nand at the Shield. Of course she'd ask Lineas. Who, in all the years Connar had known her—even when she'd been Bunny's freckled shadow—had never been a blabbermouth. But when asked, she always took the other's view, even when it was annoying, like she'd done with those Bar Regren prisoners, though they'd half killed her first.

Ranet sat, breath held, during the protracted silence until he said in a milder voice, "What I like is quiet. I'm a bad sleeper."

Ranet's ardency hadn't abated a whit. She traced slow fingers from the hard edge of his collarbones over the sparse, soft hairs on his breastbone, ran her thumb appreciatively over the ridges of his abdominal muscles, then down to his hip as she said, "You can have, and be, whatever you want in my room."

That, he liked to hear.

In a flash the heat was back.

After an interval thoroughly satisfying for both, he crossed over to his room to sleep.

The next night, after another frustrating day of stupid conversations and clumsy insinuations about whom to promote and what to do against Elsarion—the Nob—even the Idegans, which he'd thought a dead subject, again he went to Lineas's room, to find it empty. And Ranet waiting on his return.

It had to be a conspiracy made among the women. It was just like Lineas to do such a thing. Maybe Ma had even said something to her about those damned grandchildren.

The third night, he sent Fish to find Lineas as soon as the watch bell rang.

Fish was back after a protracted wait to say, "I never saw her. Vanadei didn't know where she was, but one of the students said she'd seen Lineas up on the third floor."

Where Connar had never been. Until now, he hadn't given the place a second thought. He was going to send Fish, but suspected he'd be intercepted at the top of the stairs, where he'd heard all his life a runner was always on duty. He loathed the inevitable yammer that would cause.

Ranet tapped on his door, attractive, willing, but, "I know you much prefer silence. That's all right with me . . ." And she went on talking about how she wasn't going to talk if he was happier that way, which irritated him the more because it *wasn't* quiet. He was still obliged to find the right thing to say, or behave like a horse-apple to the person he was now married to, who would be living across from him for the rest of their lives.

On the last day of the year, Connar evaded the jarls as much as he could, while hunting through the castle to find Lineas. The only glimpse he got was when she was surrounded by other royal runners lined up in the hall outside the banquet room.

Frustrated and irritated, he joined his family, aware of watching eyes.

The banquet seemed to drag on forever, until at last the family walked back together, Arrow tipsy and drumming with one hand against his leg as he swayed down the hall.

Ranet paced beside Connar—and followed him to his room. He'd drunk too much, to kill time, and she was there, and willing . . .

But, as always, when the heat was gone, there was the old restlessness, the crowded sense of someone else in his bed he had to listen to, and keep his back away from to avoid questions or comments he didn't want to hear. He gritted his teeth, waiting until she dropped at last into sleep, then rose, dressed, and ran down to the garrison, where there were always night guards to scrap with.

Ranet woke abruptly at the single bell clang an hour before the dawn watch change. In the dim, wintry light she saw from the shapes and shadows of the tumbled bedding that she was alone in Connar's bed. Why was an empty bed in his room so much more awkward than her own? She lit a candle, rose, and threw her robe over herself before slipping out and across the hall to her suite.

Never again, she vowed as she crouched down on the hearth. She hugged her knees tightly against herself, staring into the flames sheeting upward from the firestick. Everyone said Connar was as volatile as fire. He'd never been volatile with her—distant, when she first came, and polite since their marriage. These past few days he still hadn't said much, but he'd proved to be skilled in bed, everything she could wish. Except for staying to cuddle.

He was more difficult to get to know than any of the other lovers she'd had, whom she'd regarded as practice.

Well, another day, another try.

New Year's Firstday dawned blue and dim with impending snow. She got up to get ready for Convocation.

At the same time, across the hall, Connar returned from the baths to his room to get ready. He braced for more conversation, but to his relief he found his suite empty other than Fish laying out his House tunic. He met Ranet outside their respective suites. She smiled. He smiled, and they walked down to the throne room with the rest of the royal family, all dressed resplendently in their blue and gold.

Ranet didn't speak, but took his hand in hers, hoping to convey that she understood what he needed, and that it was all right with her.

He clasped her warm fingers dutifully, suppressing a sigh of impatience. He didn't like holding hands with anyone—he preferred his hands free. But Ma had said many times that a marriage worked with give and take, and he'd come out much better than some. It could easily have been that Yvanavayir wretch—might have been if Da hadn't made friends with the Senelaec jarl.

Connar reminded himself that he wasn't about to be attacked. He wasn't even armed; a runner had the swords for the sword dance stashed in the throne room. Ranet was beautiful, she was enthusiastic in bed, liked being on top, and enjoyed any other position he suggested, which kept her eyes and fingers away from his back. If she wanted to hold hands, he could hold hands.

From the rear of the vast chamber, Lineas saw him holding hands with Ranet, and relief sighed through her, almost assuaging the gut-churn of guilt for her cowardice in avoiding her room and hiding in Quill's.

Danet, from closer by, hid a smile as the princesses joined her to the left of the throne. Everything was good, she thought gratefully. If you could ignore the border troubles, but at least there was peace right here in the royal city.

And so, Arrow sat on the throne with his sons beside him. As he began his Convocation state-of-the-kingdom speech, Lineas watched the three ghosts drifting in through the far wall.

A step at her side. She started, then looked up at Fish, who muttered softly, "Are you still seeing it?"

"It?" she whispered back, though afraid she knew what he meant.

Sure enough: "The ghost. The one you called Evred."

"Why?" she asked, as she did not want to admit the truth, but could not bring herself to lie.

"Because it's not Evred," he said, with a grim look. "It's Lanrid Olavayir. Who died in the Andahi Pass the summer before the Night of Four Kings."

Arrow had two items on his agenda, the first of which was Connar's promotion. The jarls looked at that tall, splendid young man, and even the most jaded among them (such as the Jarl of Gannan) were impressed. They'd all heard about his prowess.

Arrow raised his voice. "From now, Connar-Laef is Commander of the King's Army, second only to me."

He laid his sword in Connar's outstretched hands.

Connar flashed a smile, looking and sounding splendid as he swore to protect and defend the kingdom. He laid the sword at Arrow's feet, then took a stance at Arrow's side in shield arm position as Arrow promised the jarls that Connar would pursue Elsarion's army until they were defeated, which raised a shout of approval.

As soon as that died away, Arrow got to what interested them most, beside who would command the army: who was to replace the exiled Jarl of Yvanavayir, whose territory was one of the largest in the kingdom?

"I've placed interim commanders in Tlen, Halivayir, and what used to be Yvanavayir," Arrow said. "Backed by our best border scouts. For now these jarlates are all crown-protected, but I promise by next Convocation you'll be welcoming new jarls among you," Arrow said, and then, to forestall questions and demands, he signaled the drummers.

Connar picked up the sword before the throne, then he and Noddy moved out to perform the sword dance, Connar at the forward point of the diamond as new commander, Noddy behind him, Tanrid Olavayir to one side, and Jarid Noth at the other. Drums thundered from the gallery as the four danced—Noddy every bit as enthusiastic as Connar, so much so that when he swung his sword with those powerful shoulders, the blade cracked against the steel wielded by the others, sending up blue-gold sparks.

The jarls roared their approval, then Arrow got up and moved out—as usual, keeping it short. He hated being in that freezing room.

They paraded across to the great hall, where the Firstday banquet was being readied. Most of the jarls found a way to talk to Connar, once again asking for details of his battles, then bringing forth all their advice all over again.

Connar endured it with teeth-gritted determination, but as soon as the meal was done and the spiced wine and bristic began circulating, along with the jarls and their captains, Connar slipped away.

Once the serving line had brought in the covered dishes, Lineas withdrew with the rest of the royal runners not on duty. They trooped happily up to the roost, where Mnar Milnari had their own Firstday banquet awaiting them in the warm library, before a three-stick fire. Voices clamored as hot, pungent spiced wine passed from hand to hand, Lineas relieved that at least up here, she had, so far, never seen a single ghost.

Lineas held her cup in her fingers, breathing in the heady scent as she listened to the hum of voices. To avoid thinking about that Lanrid Olavayir ghost, she was trying to determine what note it was that laughter added to such different voices when the tenor abruptly changed, first to question, then to silence as people turned toward the door.

Connar stood there. Shock chilled her nerves. He seemed to loom over them in his splendid blue House tunic with the great eagle in gold spread across his chest.

Mnar said, "May I remind you that this area is protected by royal decree, Connar-Laef?"

Connar was aware that he'd drunk too much at dinner, but right now he was too irritated to care. "I'm here to talk to someone. I'll be gone as soon as I do."

Mnar was furious that Connar had shoved his way in too fast for the celebrating runners to institute their much-drilled safety protocol, though it was clear he was here for a person, not for a purpose. She kept her lips clipped; better to let the gunvaer handle her sons. She flicked her eyes toward the door, and the entire party filed out and into the workroom two doors down, old Ivandred thoughtfully picking up the jug of spiced wine on the way, leaving Connar standing there facing Lineas, whose feet had rooted themselves to the floor.

Connar glanced back, saw the hall empty, and looked in at Lineas's pale face, her freckles standing out around her enormous eyes, the cup gripped in her thin fingers. She stood there, a slight, freckled and thoroughly unprepossessing figure, but his chest ached as he said, "Did my mother tell you to stay away from me?"

Lineas struggled against the impulse to justify her hiding, and spoke the truth: "Ranet wants to be with you."

No, it was *a* truth. Not the whole truth, and he knew it as much as she did. She could see it in the way his eyes narrowed.

He said, "You know that wasn't a ring match."

She made a convulsive movement to sign *I know*, but forgot the wine cup, and wine slopped down her front.

"Then what?" he persisted.

She set the cup carefully on the edge of a table, where it promptly crashed to the floor as she mopped uselessly at her robe with her sleeve. It looked in the firelight like blood.

"I'm with someone else. " She looked up unhappily, sensing that she was making a mess of what everyone else around her seemed to manage amicably.

But then none of them had had this conversation with Connar.

"Fine." He turned up his palm. "So is the rest of the world." He looked around, remembering the courtyard in Ku Halir the night of the fire. "If it's Quill, he isn't even here. He's been gone for weeks—might be gone a year. Or more."

I write him every night. The words almost came out. She looked at Connar in horror, her mind blanking. She sucked in a breath, emotions spiraling, intensified by that sickening sense that she was not normal after all, that she was the same failure she'd been as a twelve-year old mage student unable to perform the most basic magic. Her eyes burned as she groped mentally for the right words. But there didn't seem to be any right words.

Connar studied her miserable face, bewildered by the sudden change in her, by how painful it felt. He knew he wasn't in love—whatever that meant. Those ballads that mooed on intolerably made it clear what "in love" was; she was not central to his existence, nor would he sacrifice himself for her smile, or any of the rest of that midden. Nor did he expect the same from her. It's just that she had always been there when . . .

His thoughts shied from that path in the same heartbeat that she tried again. "Connar, you have everything you want, now. You also got a beautiful wife who is kind and good and adores you. You don't need me."

Need. That was the word he hated.

A spurt of anger replaced the ache. "Need?" he repeated contemptuously, all the more because he'd thought it himself. But they could not possibly mean the same thing. Could they?

He eyed her, the person he'd let get closest to him. "So all these years, you saw me as an object of pity?"

"No!"

But he didn't stay to listen to whatever assuaging words she'd spin out. The truth was plain. For whatever reason she wanted to justify, she'd bunked him out, and meanwhile he was standing in a doorway with every damn one of the royal runners no doubt listening avidly from down the hall.

Three steps and he reached the stairs, and disappeared down them. Lineas listened to the rap of his heels diminish to silence, then drew a sobbing breath. She couldn't bear to face the others.

She fled to Quill's room.

The royal castle woke up the next day to a world of white—and the news that the new Commander of the King's Army had departed at dawn, to return to his command; at breakfast Danet and Noren asked Ranet if he'd said anything.

"Only that he needed to get back to Halivayir," she said. There was no hiding her disappointment, but she knew he'd be back.

Up in Quill's room, after a restless night of sleep, Lineas climbed out of bed and crouched on the cold floor, her toes curled. Shivering, she took out her notecase and a tiny scrap of paper and wrote:

Connar and I parted. It was horrible.

And sent it to Quill before she could change her mind.

TWENTY-TWO

Arrow should have known that his speech and his sons doing the sword dance was not going to stop the jarls from pestering him for private conversations, during which they hinted with all the delicacy of a lance charge that they had trusty and wonderful candidates in third sons, nephews, cousins, and cousins' boys, all loyal, talented and true, who'd be perfect for Yvanavayir, that oldest and most prestigious of the jarlates missing a jarl.

Arrow hadn't told any of them that, before the trial, while he waited for his runner to return with Manther Yvanavayir's answer, Noddy had suggested his favorite, Cabbage Gannan, in case Manther refused—which Arrow and Noddy had both expected would happen. Arrow was not about to reject Noddy's first appointment, and he was certainly impressed by Cabbage Gannan's spectacular performance in the field . . . but he also loathed the Jarl of Gannan, and his eldest son even more. Of course they would meddle if the second son was suddenly promoted to a jarlate superior to his father's.

This appointment is only for a year, mind, the king had said to Cabbage, before sending him off. *Then you'll be replaced by someone who won't be riding with my son. You'll be back here picking the lancers before we send them for their two years of seasoning. Ride out,* the king had added. *Best to get up there before winter sets in hard. Of course we don't expect to see you, Holdan, or Fath at Convocation, being interim appointments.*

Cabbage had finished scouting this year's lancers then departed immediately, without telling anyone his real reason for reaching Gannan fast: to get there, and away, ahead of possible rumors. He knew very well what would happen once his elder brother Blue heard about the appointment. Blue would get the worst of their Stalgrid cousins to scrag Cabbage to remind him of his place, since Blue couldn't beat him bloody anymore. And their da would shrug it off, saying Gannans had to be tough to get ahead.

Ride fast he did, until he reached the small, square, cheerless castle he'd grown up in. Old habits made him enter quietly, his orders to Kendred, his first runner, having been issued before they even spotted the walls. A question to the tight-lipped stable chief elicited the welcome information that Maddar Sindan-An, Cabbage's bride, was out in the paddock.

He made his way there. The women were surprised at his sudden appearance, his mother with that quick, worried frown he'd grown up seeing. Any change made her tense, because it might ignite his father's temper. "I'm home only to get Maddar," Cabbage said. "Not even a home leave. We have to ride out at once."

A turn of the hand and Ma went back to watching the yearlings, Lnand Sindan—Blue's wife of two years—sending a sympathetic glance after Maddar. The only one who grinned was short, curvy, irrepressible Snow.

Maddar followed Cabbage out, and he hid his heart-lift of pride at the sight of her curving smile, and the even better curves below. Though he knew he could take no credit for it, he still relished the fact that the queen's training girls had, in the mysterious ways of girls, chosen Maddar as second prettiest of their particular group before they'd all dispersed to their future lives.

"We've got a new post," he muttered. "Yvanavayir. For a year. I want to get out of here before Blue hears."

Maddar completely understood, but she had her own stipulation. "Snow's coming with me," she stated, glancing back to where Snow trailed them out of earshot.

Cabbage turned up his hand, having expected as much. They'd been married during his two weeks' liberty, in a wedding that Da had only permitted to take an hour out of a regular work day—"good enough for a second son," he'd said.

That liberty had been filled each day with chores, so though they'd slept together a few times, Maddar had been frank about the fact that she was tight with Snow ("I was nicknamed Snowball when I was born, being small and round with near white hair, but now I'm large and dark so Snow will do!"), a scribe turned baker.

Da had accepted Snow once he found out that she was a full scribe, and willing to carry out any scribe chores at Gannan without being paid—and when he discovered that she also helped in the bakehouse, also unpaid, he wouldn't have cared if she was a Venn.

Maddar saw Cabbage's acceptance, no less than expected but it was always good to get things clear. "We can be ready in an hour."

They rode out in less time, once Cabbage had told his father it was the king's orders to leave immediately.

The jarl didn't argue. He didn't like losing the women's labor, but with the three of them and their runners gone, there were far fewer mouths to feed, and anyway he was readying for his ride to the royal city for Convocation.

By the time Cabbage, Maddar, and Snow rounded the lake, Cabbage understood that there would never be any chance with Snow, though she had exactly the kind of figure he liked most. She liked women only, but she was easy to get along with. When they camped out, the three of them shared a tent, but Maddar laid out the bedrolls, each with their own, and she slept in the middle.

The closer they got to Yvanavayir, the more intimidated he felt at the idea of running a jarlate, even for a year. Growing up, he'd paid little attention to what his father did as jarl, and would have been beaten for his temerity by both his father and his brother if he had. Instead, he'd made it his business to be as far away from Da as possible, which meant he'd pretty much lived in the stable, or out practicing in the field.

They made it to Yvanavayir two weeks before the end of the year, and Convocation.

Yvanavayir turned out to be far more intimidating than he'd expected.

The first flurries of snow were falling when they rode through the high, iron-reinforced gates of a castle every bit as large as the royal castle. In fact, they were told by a quiet, somber man left by the Yvanavayirs as interim steward, Yvanavayir Castle had been rebuilt by Mad Gallop Yvanavayir on the same plan as the royal castle, except it didn't have a huge garrison wing beyond the actual building, as the number of Riders in those days was fixed. So half the castle housed the Riders and stable hands and staff, but it was still enormous.

And shabby, though someone had begun reparations here and there. "There's a new bakehouse," Snow exclaimed on their walk-through. "It's like they knew I was coming!" And she remained behind to ask questions of the kitchen staff.

Cabbage and Maddar toiled on. When the steward indicated the tour was finished by a morose mumble that he'd await orders, the interim jarl and jarlan were left completely alone.

Cabbage's habits had changed a lot in his years away from Gannan, but admitting to things was still difficult. Still, as Maddar gazed around the vaulted ceiling of the otherwise bare room they stood in, he mumbled, "I have no idea what to do first."

Maddar turned, bright blue eyes mild as she shoved her thick blond braids behind her shoulders. "I do. I've been helping my mother ever since I was small. Sindan-An's castle isn't nearly as pretentious as this," she waved a hand outward, "but the jarlate is as big, and much the same in terrain to be ridden."

Snow caught up with them then, her dark eyes mirthful. "The Riders seem to regard Cabbage here as extra tight. It's not just this command, it's they think he's got a handsome wife *and* a handsome lover." She swung her hips suggestively.

Maddar laughed. "Don't let 'em think otherwise. Cabbage here will need all the rep he can get when he starts handing out orders."

Which he did, after Maddar told him what to say.

And so, when New Year's Week began, Cabbage, Maddar, and Snow sat in the south tower, which had been brightened with two Iascan flower tapestries. Two weeks of hard labor by everyone, from the three of them on down to the ten-year-old stable wander, had rendered the castle livable, if sparsely furnished as yet.

Maddar's unshakeable calm and Snow's jokes had eased the Riders into laborers for that time. Now the three sat on new mats, sharing a jug of New Year's Week spiced wine as they looked up at the tapestry that Maddar had bought from one of the village craft guilds days ago.

"There's no battle in it," Cabbage said. "No story. Just those flower and bird things in that wiggly line, with all the old-fashioned letters."

"The letters are part of the art," Snow said. "And it does tell a story. In a way. The brightness of the flowers out of the shadows of winter, with the Sartoran symbols to make it clear."

"Clear only if you already know what they mean," Cabbage said, taking a swig of the spiced wine.

"That symbol there in each corner means influence—Sartoran influence. The letter itself has an interesting history, the marks meaning shadow-sound or sounds out of the shadows, which grab your attention. That sense of peripheral awareness could have come to mean influence," Snow said, leaning over to refill her cup.

She saw that Cabbage was getting restless. "Well, you get the idea. Iascan, which comes from Sartoran, is full of those, is all I'm saying. The letters all have little stories in them."

"That only scribes can read." At the look Maddar cut him sidewise, he heard his own voice sounding more sullen than he'd meant it to. It was a boring subject, but they'd worked hard, and he liked the warm room and the wine, and maybe if Maddar ended the evening in a good mood, she'd sleep with him, because he hadn't found any likely favorites yet. Too busy. "Scribing seems like hard work. Is that why you went back to baking?"

Snow grinned. "Opposite. Too many scribes, too little work. I'm from generations of bakers. I know the trade, and people always need food, even if they don't need my pen. It was different a century ago, our teachers said, when scribes were in demand everywhere," she added. "When they were busy translating Iascan records to Marlovan."

"I thought Marlovan had its own records." Cabbage reached past Snow for the jug.

"No-o-o-o," Snow drew out the word. "In those old days, they made this big fuss about how Marlovan was the language of war, hoola loo, but what it actually meant was, Marlovans didn't have any writing, much less records."

"Of course we did," he protested. "It was that Venn runes stuff. You see it in some of our older tapestries."

"But we didn't *use* it." Maddar held out the basket of crisped cabbage rolls, and Snow speared one with her knife. "Even I know that. Back in the

Venn days, only certain people could learn runes, and our ancestors, who weren't elite, that is, the leaders, didn't. Maybe that's why they left the Land of the Venn."

"Because they couldn't write?" Cabbage hooted. "Try another one."

Snow put her feet up on the table next to the pile of dirty dishes left from supper. "Why do you think the really old ballads have so many verses?"

"Grandma told me that they used to memorize all their lessons," Maddar said.

"Right. Everybody spoke two languages a couple centuries ago, Iascan and Marlovan, not just folks up here, where there are lots of Iascans still, or in Marthdavan, along the coast—though their dialect is so thick I barely understood them when I visited my grandmother once."

Cabbage grabbed another biscuit. "Well, all I can say is, the bakehouse sure turns out good eats. These are way better than ours at Gannan."

Snow grinned. "I could go on about stinginess with ingredients, but none of that is new to you. Bringing me back to the bakehouse here. Excellent bakehouse. Which is why I think you two should do what you can to be promoted to jarl and jarlan."

At Cabbage's startled look, Maddar and Snow exchanged glances.

Cabbage might not be imaginative outside of his own interests, but he wasn't stupid. "The king gave *orders,*" he said, raising his voice to hide how uneasy that glance of understanding made him. "Someone will show up here next New Year's, by *the king's command.*"

"Yes, yes, we all know that," Maddar said in a soothing voice. "You needn't bellow. We're all right here, and nobody is listening to us."

At that moment the crash and tinkle of crockery echoed up the stones from the courtyard below, followed by the roar of drunken voices.

Snow cocked her head. "They're already trying to do the sword dance with cups on their heads?" she asked rhetorically. "Anyway, as I was just about to say, I'd love to be the household steward. And neither of you wants to go back to Gannan any more than I do."

This was so true it was entirely unanswerable.

Cabbage mumbled, "I wish we could get Lnand out, too." Lnand Sindan was not merely a quiet presence; Cabbage had overheard her saying to Blue within days after her arrival, "I can see that there's a lot going on in this castle that is not what I'm used to. Just so we start out understanding each other, if you touch me with one of those fists, you won't live out the week."

Cabbage had admired her with unspoken intensity from that moment.

Snow chuckled. "Don't worry about Lnand."

Maddar's smile glinted with the edges of her teeth. "Lnand is biding her time. You'll see. Once the jarl drops dead of an apoplexy—by rights it should be soon—things will be different. And when she has a child, she'll rein Blue hard by saying if he once lays a hand on him, she and the child, even if it's a boy, will be smoke. Blue knows the entire Eastern Alliance will back her. If the queen doesn't get at him first."

Cabbage knew he should protest the slurs against his father and brother. It was disloyal to the family not to. Except they weren't really slurs if it was true, was it? He'd loathed both his father and his brother since he was small. He muttered, "My mother probably thought things would be different, too. Maybe that's why she's so sour."

"That's because she had no cousins to back her. Or a tough gunvaer." Snow clacked her mug against Maddar's. "We've ridden with Lnand. I'd back her against your father any time. She's quiet because he's jarl, and the Riders all follow him. But see if she doesn't rein Blue before then. Give her five years once she's jarlan. Gannan will be a different place."

Maddar sensed Cabbage's conflict, and took an oblique approach, elbowing him in the side. "Wouldn't you like New Year's Week to be this fun every year? If we improve this place, surely Noddy will want to reward you? Just mention it to him, is all I'm saying. He likes you. And you earned it."

Snow leaned over. "See, what you do is, invite Nadran-Sierlaef to Yvanavayir—"

"Don't say Yvanavayir," Cabbage muttered. "They're gone."

"About that." Maddar put her fists on her chin. "Nobody seems to know what to call this jarlate, and you didn't get orders, right, about a new name?"

"Right," Cabbage said cautiously.

Maddar saw his wariness and flicked her fingers out. "Don't worry, I'm not suggesting you use your name. Far from it! It's just, when I went around to the local villages to meet the guild chiefs, what I heard most often was that this was Stalgoreth in the local language before we Marlovans turned up. Nobody is squawking about getting rid of us, so why not give them a small salute by using the old name? Only until the king appoints someone, of course."

When Cabbage hesitated, Snow said, "Mad can write to the gunvaer about it. How's that? After all, we have to call it *something,* and everybody is so awkward every time the Yvanavayir name accidentally comes out."

"Write to the gunvaer," Cabbage said, glad to pass the decision on.

"And your part," Maddar went on, walking her fingers up his broad chest, "is to invite the crown prince here for next year's New Year's Week, since there won't be any Convocation. Inspection, call it. Give him an excellent time, and show him what we've done." She poked a finger into the cleft in his chin.

Cabbage Gannan was not imaginative, but even he could easily picture never having to see his brother again, except at Convocation once Da was gone, if they were both jarls. He'd even have precedence over Blue, wouldn't he, as Yvanavayir—Stalgoreth—was so much bigger and older? All his life he'd dreaded what would happen once Blue was jarl, and he'd have to live under his brother's heel . . .

On the other side, if the rumor was true and Connar was being promoted again . . . Cabbage grimaced into his cup. Connar had been the one to suggest his first promotion after being stupid enough to nearly run both himself and Noddy straight into the Bar Regren, when anyone could have told them to stay well away from Chalk Hills unless they had a full battalion at their backs. Connar had written to Nermand to recommend promotion, but he still looked at Cabbage as if he had shit on his shoes.

Cabbage hated him for it, but that didn't matter nearly as much as the fact that Connar hated *him*. And now Connar was at the top of the chain of command. Cabbage remembered seeing Connar fighting his way through the Bar Regren—and again at Tlennen Plain. He fought like lightning.

If Noddy was promoted to run the army, life would be great. But Cabbage wasn't so sure about Connar. Maybe being a jarl would be better than Commander of First Lancers, if Connar became Commander of the King's Army.

He looked up, to see Maddar and Snow waiting for him to answer.

So he answered. "I'll write to Noddy come spring. How's that?"

Maddar whooped, grabbed him by the shirt laces and gave him a smacking kiss. He kissed her back, laughing, then the three of them clacked their cups together.

As for Connar, officially Commander in Chief of the King's Army, about the time that Cabbage, Maddar, and Snow were charting what needed doing and who was to do it to improve Stalgoreth-used-to-be-Yvanavayir-used-to-be-Stalgoreth, Connar and his company rode for Ku Halir.

Two nights running he scarcely slept at all, but sat in his tent poring over the kingdom map as he formed plans that always ran up against what he didn't know, what he couldn't predict.

At the point at which the north road diverged, he sent Ghost to Halivayir to prepare it for winter games, and also—as Leaf Dorthad had recovered from her coma—to get married.

By the time Connar and Stick galloped into Ku Halir ahead of a blizzard, Connar's mood was bleak. Sometimes he hated Inda-Harskialdna, who (it was said) never experienced the slightest doubts. He just went out and won every battle.

Light, warmth, good food, and leftover spiced wine, all offered by a cheerful Ventdor, helped to smooth the surface of Connar's turmoil. Everywhere he looked was order, ready salutes to him as Commander in Chief. He and Stick gave their company general liberty to make up for the week of fun they'd missed by riding out of the royal city on New Year's Secondday.

That left Connar and Stick to Ventdor and his captains. Ventdor asked about everyone at the royal city, and then said, "Tomorrow is enough time to get to waiting affairs."

The good mood soured. "What waiting affairs?" Connar asked.

He understood his voice was too sharp when Ventdor looked startled, nicked his chin at a waiting runner—who vanished through the door—then he raised his hands, palms out. "No, no, nothing dire. Would have sent someone, of course." He glanced aside, then back, and forced a hearty tone. "Young Tanrid, that is, the Jarl of Olavayir—Cousin Jarend having handed off the title, you know. Well, quite rightly, has sent along his treaty requirement before the king could even call for volunteers for dealing with the Adranis."

Connar wondered why Ventdor sounded so disjointed, his gaze going to either side, up, down; he didn't know Ventdor enough to recognize the signs of an inward struggle.

Sneeze Ventdor was trying hard to hide his prejudice against the son of a one of the most fervent of the Nighthawk survivors after Mathren's death: Halrid Jethren.

Ventdor knew that kindly Jarend-Jarl, who hated violence, had done his best to integrate those men into the Olavayir Riders—and apparently they had been models of order and proper behavior ever since. Their skills in the field unmatched. Maybe Nighthawk had died out, as Jarend had hoped. One thing for certain, these boys certainly came with high praise for their skills.

Aware he'd let a silence build, Ventdor cleared his throat. "Kethedrend Jethren comes with the former jarl's recommendation, as being the best of the younger generation. Young as he is, Keth Jethren's been promoted to lance captain over the three ridings he brought, along with scouts and runners."

Ventdor paused at the clatter of arrivals echoing down the hall through the open door. Connar forgot Ventdor's flat tone and oblique gaze when he saw the four who came in behind the runner. All four seemed familiar, though he didn't recognize any of them by name, and he wasn't certain of place. They were led by a pale-haired fellow Connar's own age, tall and broad-shouldered.

This was obviously the leader. He raised his arm, and—stepping behind Barend Ventdor so that only Connar could see him, he laid his fist against his chest in the secret salute in the stable annex at the Nevree castle.

Cold shock rang along Connar's nerves.

He knew them now. This young captain was the tall boy with the unblinking stare who had been part of that silent salute to a king in the Olavayir castle's back stable.

Connar's mouth tightened, but the fist was only there the briefest moment as Jethren's hand flattened into the proper salute.

It could almost have been a mistake.

Ventdor was saying, " . . . sent a runner to the royal city. While we waited, they've been taking watches alongside our men, and going out for drill. I'd hoped to hear from your da . . ."

Not your da, whispered Hauth's voice, followed by the usual acid spurt of hatred. *Yes, my da,* Connar argued back, unaware of the thin line of his mouth, the flatness of his intense blue gaze. *My da, who chose me, raised me, and gave me this command.*

" . . . but here you are. I figure, you can always use trained lancers." Ventdor faltered to a stop.

Connar barely heard. He and Kethedrend Jethren took in the other, each recognizing that Connar remembered that day—and that he obviously hadn't spoken about it.

Connar recovered first. Trained lancers. They always needed them. Still. Connar opened his hand in a gesture of acceptance, thinking: *One word, one sign, you're taking orders from Hauth, and you'll be sent to the Nob to wand shit.*

Jethren was thinking, *The king at last.*

TWENTY-THREE

Quill to Lineas:

First, I want to thank you for your letters every night, though I had to read them in stolen moments. Thank you also for your understanding my infrequent answers. Is it strange for me to find it comforting to think of you sleeping in my bed? Though I wish I was there beside you.

The trouble with caravan living, especially at the bottom of the hierarchy, is the lack of privacy. I shared a tent with three others, one a wagoneer whose snores shook the wagon we all had to sleep in with the tent pitched over us until we reached the outpost. The ground (and the air, and everything we wore or carried) was too wet for sleeping on.

At last, as you can see, I have a little time to myself, now that I've warmed my hands enough to write.

I wonder if it's human nature that the slower a person speaks and moves, the faster everyone else's patience runs out.

I successfully inserted myself into the last supply train before winter, having bribed the scribe in charge of the lading bill to quit the day before departure in favor of spending New Year's Week at home. I showed up in time to be hired for a job no one else wanted, and so we wound our way up the mountain slope until today we reached the fortress, no longer a mere outpost. On the map, it's just east of Threefold Falls. That landmark really is three waterfalls, quite spectacular, especially the lower level, as long as the upper two put together.

As for this "outpost," I now know why our Marlovan traders and runners the past five years were housed so splendidly at the better inn near the old gates: so they wouldn't see the very extensive fortifications being built behind the second set of gates.

Being loyal Adranis, we have been invited to spend New Year's Lastday here, to make up for the weather having made us miss the rest of the festival week. All the more welcome as the commander has quite heartlessly scolded all outland travelers—after searching everything they carry and wear to the seams—to keep moving. Tomorrow we must push on as the wagon chief is worried about clearing Skytalon Peak before winter sets in hard. Apparently from there on the supplies will be sledded down to the lower outpost.

I've managed to secure to myself a tiny space about the size of a broom closet for the night, but I share it with no one, so I can sit here with my candle and reread your notes while I wait for the mess bell—

And there it rings. I would so much rather try your patience by writing out everything I thought to share with you over the days of bumping along the bad road, but I suppose I had better go out there and be dutiful. . . .

In Marlovan Iasca's royal city, The new year began with a hard frost that the royal family welcomed with relief, for it sent the jarls hustling to start their trips homeward under the hard blue sky and white, heatless northern sun.

Lineas remained in Quill's room until the morning she arose, early as always—but Mnar was earlier, waiting outside in the dim hall still lit by torchlight.

Lineas stopped guiltily, though there was no reason for guilt. It was her old habit of worry about breaking invisible rules she hadn't known about.

Mnar said, "I'll accept my part of the blame for leaving you in that tiny closet of a room with no fire nook, but really, Lineas, why didn't you speak up? You needn't be creeping up here to empty rooms for warmth."

Lineas's lips opened but no sound came out; if Mnar noticed the cold fireplace there next to Quill's bed, she said nothing, only, "That tiny room was appropriate when you had to be in call of the princess, and because you were rarely in it except to sleep. But now your schedule is more regular. You ought to be up here with the masters. Ivandred has moved into the city now that he's officially retired, and has relinquished his room."

Lineas glanced at the door directly across from Quill's, and flushed, not knowing what to say.

Mnar said, "I'll send someone down to fetch your trunk, if you'll have it packed by the morning watch bell." She walked away, leaving Lineas staring after her, wondering if Mnar knew about her and Quill. So far, no one had said a word to Lineas about Connar's surprising appearance in the roost, for which she was grateful.

She hastened down to the baths, then to her room—her old room—to pull the few clothes off the peg, sweep pen and ink off the little desk, and fold everything into her trunk. A brief glance out the slit window that she would never watch the light change through again, and away to her class.

That night, when she turned habitually toward the second floor, she forced herself to keep going. No more would she walk the royal floor unless summoned. How odd it felt, such changes.

She reached her new room across from Quill's closed door. It was warm with a firestick glowing on the tiny hearth. The bed was freshly made, her trunk adjacent. Someone had thoughtfully left a lamp lit on the desk, which was not only twice as big as her old desk, it had a bookcase up above it. And on the other wall, a long deep-set window—wide enough to sit in and read during summer, after the winter shutters came down.

She opened her trunk and dug down to take out her notecase. No note from Quill. He must be with another caravan. She cut a small strip of paper, jotted down the day's small news, kissed it, sent it, and burrowed under the quilts in her new bed.

Quill to Lineas:

It was so cheering to open my notecase on the sly and find more little notes covered in your handwriting. My happiness is marred only by the awareness that I can so rarely reciprocate, but you know that when I can, I shall.

We were mired twice in snowstorms, but the caravan chief was determined to get us to Mt. Skytalon, and so at last we did.

East Tower is an outpost on a cliff so high only the top of the tower is visible, if you know where to look. I wonder if that's even visible during summer melt, the stone being indistinguishable from the stone around it.

The road up is guarded by traps watched by hidden guards, also invisible from the road below.

We were taken up with the supplies. The outpost is a single tower packed with guards, with a view of the entire eastern end of the pass, down into Anaeran-Adrani. I discovered when our carts pulled in at last, and we were allowed to walk around, that the castle has been built over an Ancient Sartoran atan, a sky-viewing platform. I recognized the beautiful tiles, worn down by wind and weather over the centuries, even if no one else did . . .

Quill paused, gazing out into the weak, wintry blue light of the grotto he crouched in as he stuffed his fingers under his scarf to warm against his neck.

It was absurd, this instinct to shield Lineas from what he thought of as close calls, when he considered that she'd survived the Chalk Hills attack, and had been sent as auxiliary to Tlennen Plain.

There was already one subject he hadn't raised lest she choose to raise it: Connar. She hadn't mentioned him since that single line reporting that they'd parted.

"Let's not make that two voids of silence between us," he muttered, his breath clouding.

And so he dipped the pen in the congealing ink and wrote quickly:

When we had all stamped the worst of the snow off our feet and exclaimed about the cold, one of the guards said that before we embarked on the sled for the downward slope, there were orders being passed on.

"We'll send a guide to get you past the traps leading to West Tower. Once you begin your descent, you're to be on the watch for suspicious individuals from the Marlovan side, not just disguised warriors. Here's the list of specific individuals to report if seen . . .

Among those listed: ". . . anyone claiming to be a Marlovan scribe: tall, dark hair, brown eyes, pale blue robe with wooden shank buttons, talks fast, his Adrani Iascan-accented. This is a Marlovan spy. When you secure him, be sure to take the robe, as the shank buttons are bespelled for magic transfer, and who knows what else."

"Brown hair? Everyone has brown hair," the caravan chief declared, sounding disappointed.

"I thought all those horse boys had yellow hair," our cook commented.

"We got us a brown-haired scribe," Old Snorer put in, jabbing my way a thumb the size of a potato. "But he speaks regular words, no foreign gabble, and he's in proper green. No buttons."

At this they all swung around and stared at me in my stained blue-green Adrani scribe robe, no wooden shank buttons in sight, as my transfer token is worn against my skin.

"And besides, he's slow, if you know what I mean," the caravan chief added, rolling her eyes and poking her chin a few times in case the guard didn't catch her drift.

The guard looked at me with my cow-jaw hanging, looked back, then said sourly, "Did he come from the west?"

"No," they all said, wagging their heads the way Adranis do. I wagged my head, too.

"Well, then, he pretty much doesn't fit any of the description, does he?"

"Brown hair," the cook grumbled. "If you ask me, more scribes will have some shade of brown than yellow or black or red. That description is useless, if you ask me."

We were let into the mess hall, which smelled of pepper soup. I crowded in among the carters, ate as much as I could hold, and then blundered about, taking note of not only the defenses, but the fact that there was not only a dispatch desk with a tray revealing the glow of magic, for the sending and receiving of important reports, but in the back of the command office someone had worked a transfer Destination into the floor.

When I finished my soup, I caught a mutter somewhere behind me, ". . . didn't come from the Marlovan side, but he does have brown eyes and dark hair. With that large of a reward offered, doesn't it make sense to at least make sure?"

I decided not to wait to hear the end of the discussion. In the general shuffle to find a place to bed down in the crowded tower, I grabbed my gear and slipped out into the cold. Here is where our studies came to my aid. You are probably thinking, as I was, where there is an ancient atan platform there are surely morvende trails.

I found one that led upward, certain that any search party venturing into the frigid air would instinctively head downward toward the pass. The upward trail was battered by enough wind to erase my footsteps in the powdery snow.

I climbed up and up, always thinking that surely I'd reached the summit, until the trail bent in a promising manner—which led to my current quarters, a grotto filled with rock formations. It is cold, but I have my firesticks, and am out of the wind as well as dry.

I believe it's time to shift away from the pass and look for those alternate routes. Yes, it's very cold—and so my ink might freeze up—but I have my transfer token if I get too desperate. In the meantime, if a few days pass without my writing, it will because there is little to report beside rock, cold, and snow.

I close this thinking of you warm and secure, which in turn warms me.

The one thing he didn't tell Lineas was how difficult it was to breathe. He'd thought he was acclimated to the thinner air while riding ever upward, but when he began to climb, he discovered how wrong he was. He had to halt every fifty paces, then every thirty, and finally every ten, breathing carefully through his scarf. Too sudden a breath and his throat and lungs burned with cold fire.

Cold.

Winter cold on the top of the highest mountain in the eastern range required another word besides 'cold.' Winters on the plains ranged from sleety cold to frozen cold, with windswept ice for variety. This was a type of cold so severe it burned with merciless cruelty.

The second discovery besides the difficulty in getting enough air was that his woolen coat, mittens, and scarf were not enough. After a terrible night sitting close enough to his firesticks to singe the wool of his coat, he shuffled out to explore the bleak gray world outside the grotto, clouds so low it seemed that if he reached up he could touch them.

The third discovery was how very difficult mountain climbing was on the feet.

He edged near a cliff. Alarm jolted through him when he spotted a bulked-up group of armed warriors laboring single file along the southern slope, moving toward another tower, visible at a distance, built at unimaginable cost. That had to be West Tower, overlooking the west end of the pass. This meant that those holding the towers could see anyone coming from either end. And there had to be similar traps and treacherous footing on the that tower's road leading down to the floor of the pass.

He watched the patrol, who confined themselves to their established road, until they vanished down the icy trail to their tower. He took care to keep himself hidden, but none of them ever looked up; whether they were a regular patrol or searchers for him, clearly none of them believed anyone would be mad enough to go higher.

When they vanished into West Tower ahead of a storm sweeping in, sending ice as sharp as arrows flying horizontally, Quill withdrew to the grotto, gasping and crowing for breath. He collapsed, black clouds boiling across his vision. For a long time all he could do was fight for breath. When a sense of lassitude nearly overwhelmed him, he forced himself to sit. Shaking almost uncontrollably, he fumbled for his firesticks.

He crawled painfully back and back until no wind reached him, then brought both fires to full capacity, though that used the magic faster. Gradually the warmth thawed him, and also warmed the air so that breathing became marginally less of a battle.

He got up, scouted out rocks among the windblown rubble, and carefully made a Destination pattern on the ground smoothed millennia ago by unimaginable cataracts. He braced against his dwindling strength, and used magic to transfer back to Darchelde.

The wrench knocked him out. He came to lying on the floor of his bedchamber, fighting nausea as his body thrummed with pain. He crawled to the trunk beside the cold fireplace and dug out firesticks, snapped the fire to life, and crouched there until he recovered from the transfer reaction.

When he could bear to move, he took his grimy self down to bathe for the first time since he joined the caravan.

When he came out, Camerend was there, having been alerted by a servant. Camerend eyed his son, then said, "Come to the kitchen. I asked them to heat water for listerblossom steep, and there's half a chicken pie, just put back in the oven to warm."

Quill discovered he was ravenous. After eating and drinking, he recovered enough to tell Camerend everything he'd found. "Thias Elsarion has spent a princely sum building those outposts in the Pass. And now he's spending more to build up defenses. Against us."

Camerend sighed. "I'm told that not a month ago, the king stood there at Convocation and promised justice to the jarls. Connar was so eager to get started he rode off in the teeth of a storm the very next morning in order to run winter exercises. It doesn't take much effort to guess toward what end."

"You're saying war is going to happen no matter what?" Quill said flatly.

"I'm saying," Camerend leaned forward, "gather all the evidence you can. It seems that Thias Elsarion is planning an invasion, but that invasion has not happened, and further, the final decision is not yours."

"Right." Quill expelled his breath.

"Arrow is not a stupid man. You've just begun your scouting trip, and already you've learned a lot. There's far more to be discovered. And by the time you return, tempers might have cooled, and various alternatives considered."

"I'm not going to survive winter up there if I don't take a yeath coat," Quill said. "Wool is nothing against that cold. The thin air seems to worsen it."

"Then take a yeath coat. Take plenty of travel bread—and write everything down." Camerend leaned in, eyeing his son, who looked drawn, gaunt even. "Senrid. You are in a very rare position, one you've been trained for. The king will listen to what you say. You have to write down every detail to back up your observations and conclusions."

"I know." Quill shut his eyes. "What do you think has been occupying my mind most while I was up there struggling to breathe, and to avoid losing limbs to frostfire?"

"Never forget that," Camerend said earnestly. "Right now you are the most important person in the kingdom. You are in the pivotal position."

Quill sat back. "That's right, close another vise around my head. I don't feel nearly enough pressure."

Camerend got to his feet, a rueful smile flickering. "Come upstairs."

Yeath fur—long, soft as feathers, beautiful white and silver—is far more costly than cloth of gold, for yeath are only found in mountains at the extremity of the tree line. When spring comes, they scrape off their winter fur on brambles, which has to be carefully picked lest one's fingers get cut up. Then it must be brought down and woven in various ways, but for warmth nothing is better, and it lasts longer than good linen, if cared for.

Camerend went up to the old storage trunks, and brought out a black coat, tight to the waist to keep the warmth in, and long in the skirt, to below the boot tops. He held it out to Quill.

"It's heavy!" Quill rubbed his fingers over the thick, soft weave. "Yeath! Black?"

"I don't know if it's dyed, or if the animals vary in fur colors in other lands. That coat is said to belong to our great-father Fox, left behind when he sailed for the last time. He bought it somewhere on his sea journeys, as I guess winter is fierce on board ships. You may as well use it."

"Will it fit?"

"It doesn't button—that would let cold air in the gaps. It folds right over left." He indicated a sash to keep it close.

Quill slipped on the coat. The sleeves were quite long, down to his second knuckles, and the hem came down to his ankles. Either Great-father Fox had been a full hand taller than Quill, or he'd liked the extra length for warmth.

Quill took the coat, extra scarves, and more socks, which he picked over with the care of one who had endured blistered feet and still had to keep walking. While he slept in a comfortable bed for the first time in weeks, the kitchen prepared journey bread for him, thick with honey, nuts, currants, raisins. Quill had traveled with it before, and knew that a steady diet of the stuff (which lasted longer than any other food) got wearing—but this, too, would be evidence. He would note down exactly when it became difficult to choke it down.

The next morning, he transferred back to the cave now marginally less frigid from the steadily burning firesticks, and discovered a howling blizzard outside the grotto. He staggered against the wind to the opening to peer out. His lungs struggled for air. Simply breathing set his chest on fire unless he breathed slowly, through the thickness of three scarves. The cold was so deep it felt more like a slow, torturous burn straight to the bone.

He peered out, his head reverberating. Even the light was different, objects so sharply delineated that every shift of his eyes seemed to cut like glass shards. The starry sky, wheeling slowly overhead, had altered to bits of diamond, colder than ice, unlike the soft-edged stars seen through the warm, humid air of summer.

He stood there until his eyelashes rimed, and his toes and fingers began to numb, watching as tumbling clouds formed overhead, and a howling wind rose, even more impossibly frigid: nothing human could exist in that maelstrom.

So he retreated into the grotto, aware of anticipation—even enjoyment. He had time now to explore this ancient complex that had nothing to do with war or vengeance.

As days and weeks slipped by, he detailed each new wonder he discovered, sometimes sketching the salient features for Lineas.

He lingered longest over the ancient paintings on cavern walls. Some depicted stars in no recognizable pattern, a faded mural seemed to be flying people, who were rumored to still live on the higher mountains to the north. Intricate patterns marked one set of caves, where the echoes crisped the air, and he knew that morvende had once lived there, singing their echo music.

When he emerged at last, it was to find a white world. Below, it was the beginning of spring.

Time to get back to his orders.

He ate a chunk of travel bread, crouched down between his two fires, and wrote:

While there is no sign of spring here, the lack of storm clouds and wind is probably the equivalent. It might be a few days till I can write again.

He kissed and sent it, doused the fires, stowed the rapidly cooling sticks in his pack, and ventured out, his footsteps squeaking on the fresh snow.

In the royal city, the time was a little earlier in the morning; Lineas had just wakened, and was lying in bed enjoying the warmth, when her hand tucked under her pillow next to her notecase felt the magical alert of a letter.

She sat up to read it, then carefully folded it and tucked it into her little carved treasure box, hating that he was venturing out into danger again. At least, if she couldn't share his danger by his side, she could from a distance.

That night she wrote:

I think of you still trudging through snow while here spring has definitely arrived. You asked me to tell you how the girls' first day at the academy went.

The king and queen decided to restart the shearing tradition, which is why I was there. They felt that for this first time, especially with girls among the first year scrubs as they call them (our fuzz), it would be better for the queen's training staff to oversee the shearing. As Ranet is still feeling queasy in the mornings, Noren asked me to choose some of the more responsible senior girls, and Bunny said it sounded like such fun she refused to be left out.

And it <u>was</u> fun! We made up two lines. The little boys and girls were blindfolded and sent running down the middle as we encouraged *them along with pretended, outrageous threats, guiding them with little pushes and picking up the ones who fell.*

Most of the children were laughing by the time they reached the end. A couple of enterprising ones charged like cavalry, one through the line in the wrong direction, and had to be towed back.

I was at the end, my job to remove hair clips and braid ties. Bunny and Noren took charge of the actual cutting, using their wrist knives to saw off braids and tails right behind the ears, which made the first-years all look alike, their faces so round with short hair framing them.

There had been more debate about whether or not the girls ought to go back to braids once their hair grew out, until the gunvaer thought to ask Henad Tlennen, who has been promoted to captain of her own company. Bunny told me Henad said that braids are awkward to stuff up under helms unless you start the braid at the top of the head, and that ended the debate. These girls will put their hair up in horsetails same as the boys when the time comes.

After the shearing was over, off they went to their first inspection, as we all returned to duty. I overheard a conversation among some of the staff who had turned up to watch.

Vnat from the kitchens asked, "What about bathing?" She sounded scandalized in that false, coy way she uses.

Sage, walking in front of me, said shortly, "They'll bathe together, half an hour before the rest of the academy."

Vnat looked mock horrified, but even she dares not argue with a queen's personal runner, then Halrid from the masonry said, "Give them a week of staring and they won't care anymore."

"That's what the queen thinks. She found records going back to the days of Inda-Harskialdna that say the same," Sage put in, still in that squelching voice.

Liet from the buttery (as opposed to Liet-Runner) cut past Vnat to say, "If they start that way they'll grow up to it."

Vnat started flouncing. I suspect it was at Halrid, who wasn't looking at her. She said, "If that were true, why haven't we been bathing together all along?"

Then Old Chelis from the potters said, "My gran once told me that it was because women wanted a place of their own for a space. Everything else in our lives has men tramping through. But go ahead to the men's side, Vnat, if you've a mind. There'd be a lot less foolishness of a morning on our side if you did." And what a look she sent, every bit as fierce as the queen's gaze.

Quill endured four months of tramping about Mt. Skytalon, mapping both animal and morvende trails in a world of white marked only by stone. He pushed northward, down the back side of the mountain, the terrain changing to lush woods; bits of green excited him, as a thousand streams trickled downward.

He took off the black coat and carried it folded over his gear bag. Going down was so much easier than climbing, now that his feet and legs had been conditioned to mountaineering. But he was aware that behind him he still had the second half of the pass to go, easily the most dangerous.

He stopped long enough to make himself a Destination beside a likely-looking stream, bound a transfer to it, then started the long trip back up the mountain.

At least it was summer—though the higher he reached, the cooler, then colder, the air. When he passed the tree line again, and had to resume the deep, careful breathing he'd learned during the long winter atop Skytalon, snow still lay in shaded crevasses and folds. The landscape without snow seemed so very different, he had to stop and sketch landmarks.

At last he reached the top and looked down once more on the pass. By now, he hoped enough time had passed to diminish any interest in pursuit of the bovine scribe who had disappeared at the East Tower. His description might still be on the 'lookout' list, but the stream of faces coming down the southern pass since the snows melted surely had dulled the most fervent of scrutiny.

Even so, he'd better change his appearance.

Marlovan plains riders didn't cut their hair because their ancestors hadn't. That was about as far as a sense of fashion existed in Marlovan Iasca. The rest of the continent sported a variety of fashions in hair, from close-clipped to elaborate long-hair styles with color and decoration.

He worked his way over the mountaintop past West Tower, and then along narrow animal trails parallel to the pass; by now they were second nature.

At last he spotted the fortress called West Outpost lying at the extreme west end of the pass. West Outpost was as large as the fortress at the other end of the pass. He lay on the edge of a cliff, mapping the traps visible from above the massive new castle. Most of these traps he suspected were invisible from below. They were lethal, masses of rock held by iron-reinforced ramps that could be loosed by the cut of an axe on the ropes holding them.

Now all he had left was get inside to finish his survey. Just as well—the summer sun this low had dried up the smaller streams, and his two flasks had little more than a drop or two left in them.

As he contemplated the best way to get inside the castle, his gaze caught on a party of boisterous young lords wearing layers of robes over flowing pants divided for riding, their long hair braided elaborately with jewels, and jewels at their ears. Whatever their reason for coming down the pass, they would serve as camouflage. Worn open, Fox's long black winter coat looked suitably dashing. Quill could cast an illusion over his grimy clothes, conveying the impression of layers of silk. He divided up his filthy hair into a multitude of braids and tied it back with a string given the illusion of a jeweled silk clip, then made his way down an animal trail, avoiding the traps he'd spotted above.

Casting an illusion about himself to drive the eye elsewhere, he moved from rock to rock down the difficult slope to the floor of the pass. There was nothing he could do about the stale smell of sweat in his clothes, but he counted on the lack of bathing facilities in the pass to render all the travelers much the same.

At the floor of the pass, he calculated his moment, dropped the stone illusion and slipped among the stream of summer traffic, then worked his way up the line until he was trailing the unheeding party of young lords. As they shuffled through the east gate, he assumed a vacuous expression as he made up a story about being a prospective horse-trader from Brenn on the Elgaer Strait.

His story was unneeded. Traffic coming down from the east got little more than the most cursory of glances. All the muscle was clearly gathered at the western gate, the castle walls, and the two towers overlooking the western plains that formed the eastern limit of Marlovan Iasca.

Quill followed the crowd into the east entrance courtyard, listening to the hubbub of voices as stewards bawled directions. The old inn was still operating, but it was clear that the Adranis had taken it over. As Quill moved quietly from one group to another, he surveyed his surroundings, mentally compiling a list of the overlapping defenses, all focused westward toward Marlovan Iasca.

Quill noted the general layout of the ground level, and headed for the nearest stairway, his plan to feign being lost. He'd bumble his way upward in order to count the sentries and estimate the number of defenders. Two posted guards at the foot of the stair waved off travelers heading that way. Quill hung back and waited, shifting behind this or that group until he saw a gangling teen wearing a close-fitting black jacket similar to the guards: a runner.

This young runner ducked between the travelers as he headed for the stair. Here he paused, holding out something on the palm of his hand. Both guards bent to examine it, then one of the guards even gave a cursory glance at the chalk tablet the runner carried in his other hand before letting him pass.

Very tight security.

Quill faded back, contemplating this challenge. Nearly ten months all told. He was very nearly done with everything the king had required of him—except the west end of this castle, facing the plains of Halia. He had to get up there, then out to survey the defense outside the gates, but he hadn't seen what sort of badge or tally the runner had carried.

He considered an illusory copy of a guard, then just as quickly dismissed it. Illusion was so flimsy. A single searching look, a blink, and the magic vanished.

A bell clanged. Watch change. Shouts and a surge of motion as guards shouldered their way through the travelers. A couple of younger guards had clearly been detailed to keep the travelers moving toward the old inn. So far, Quill had managed to shift from one group of arrivals to another, but it was only a matter of time before someone noticed him lurking about.

Then a pack of guards thundered down the stairway and streamed off to the right toward what had to be a mess hall, judging by the savory scents mixing with the general smells of horse, wool, and people. Another troop queued up, waiting to pass up the steps.

It was late in the afternoon, getting later. Shadows thickening in corners. Quill backed to the gloom under the stair, glanced out at the chattering guards gathering to go upstairs, and quickly drew illusory shadows around himself. Again, as long as no one peered at the shadowy blur, he should go unnoticed.

It was not a great solution, especially as he had to fight instinct and not gaze into anyone's face. Sight and instinct are so fast. One can be subliminally aware of being watched, prompting a searching scan that would notice the blur of illusion. And break it.

Quill waited until the stream thinned, then the night watch waiting to go to duty began swarming upward. Now was the most dangerous part: Quill chose a gap between a pair talking about some wager and a threesome complaining about an expected rainstorm and, matching step, slid among them.

His heart hammered. The two at the bottom of the stair looked at the flashed badges of the first pair—and both pairs of eyes blinked past him to the three behind him. Quill suppressed a sigh of relief. He still had to get upstairs without anyone bumping into him.

Up and around . . . a landing. He slipped to the side as the rest passed upward. No one checking badges on this level—it was warriors only. Quill worked his way down the hall, checking doors: locked, locked, locked, open . . . empty, except for barrels and stacks, stashed around . . . a transfer Destination.

He stared at the tiled pattern on the floor, his heart beating hard. Every one of these towers had a Destination, presumably so that their commander could come and go by magic transfer.

Quill backed out and drifted down the hall until he reached the second landing. Here he paused in the shadow between the doorway and the curve of the stair reaching upward, when among the general noise of voices echoing down a familiar note reached him and he froze.

A laugh—familiar—

Another, deeper voice, " . . . and we've been careful never to call them prisoners, as you ordered, but they're clamoring for justice all the same."

"By all means!" *Thias Elsarion.* "Let us get them sorted and on their way."

"Very well, my lord. We've been keeping them in the south tower, down the hall the other way . . .

Quill backed into the storage room with the transfer tiles, his fingers tightening on the transfer token he carried.

Footsteps approached—and passed on by, as Deep Voice embarked on what sounded like a list of the prisoners and their claimed identities. Quill slipped out and up the stairs, which gave onto a smaller landing with supplies loaded between the archways.

A pair of sentries approached, and Quill ducked behind a basket of lanterns, watching sideways as the sentries turned and started back.

Quill peered out after them, a splat of cold rain catching him in the face as he hastily estimated the number of sentries. He tried glancing below, but the rain and the sinking sun vanishing into clouds obscured the courtyard. If anyone looked his way they might see the rain blurring.

He wedged himself in between two stacks of baskets. Here, he fished out one flask, and emptied the last of the water into his mouth, less than a sip. All it did was fire his thirst the more.

He thrust the flask back inside his coat pocket, then, keeping his transfer token tightly gripped in his fingers, resigned himself to a long, thirsty wait until well into the late watch, when eyes were weariest.

Hours trickled slowly by, then the midnight watch clanged once, startling Quill out of an uncomfortable half-sleep; his neck shot pangs down his back as he forced himself upright. He stilled as the late watch marched out, replacing the tired, shuffling sentries. Now he had another wait to endure, until these fresh sentries began to tire.

Quill balanced on one foot then the other to fight against sleep, thirst, and waves of exhaustion. When he couldn't trust himself any longer, he slid out, noting the position of the sliver of moon in a hazy sky. Good. Dawn was three hours off, the weariest part of night.

He renewed the illusion around himself and eased out from his cramped position, wincing at the pins and needles shooting up from his feet. He made his way along, counting stationary as well as moving sentries, then mentally multiplying by three, for three watches. Add staff . . . that was an army in itself.

He worked his way toward the western wall to figure out how to get down. A glance over the wall revealed a broad courtyard between the castle wall and the outer gate. Perfectly flat, but too uniform in color to be stone tiles.

Well, he had to get down there anyway, and get to the outer wall to complete his mission. Slowly, carefully, he made his way past sentries, ducking into shadows and forcing his attention away as they paced within arm's reach.

One flight. Two, down the back stair apparently forbidden to travelers, as no sentries were posted. He eased through the archway, and there was that court. He checked himself. The glimmering blur reassured him that the illusion was still strong.

He put his foot out to take a careful step—and knew as soon as the worn sole of his boot touched down that he was about to step on raked gravel. At this time of night, in still air, the crunch would reach the sentries above.

He jerked back into the archway. No noise, except the cadenced steps of the sentries on the wall.

Quill crouched down, eyeing the open space, so innocent-looking from above. From this vantage, he made out the fact that the gravel was not evenly spread after all. It humped subtly in neat rows.

He frowned at those, then pivoted on his toes, and peered at the base of the wall, discerning a long, dark bar too defined to be shadow. With painstaking care he crawled along the base of the wall—the gravel painful under knees and hands—and felt the iron bar, with a chain welded into it, stretching perpendicular to the bar.

He worked his way back, and surveyed again. His nerves chilled when he made out the dull gleam of starlight on steel at regular intervals about halfway out into the court.

Now he knew was he was seeing. The gravel covered a series of chains to which sharpened spears had been attached. These could winched up to chest height: horse killers. He thought of those sentries above with crossbows, and knew that this was a carefully planned killing field.

Sickened, he surveyed the rest of the court, which might cover other lethal surprises. He lifted his gaze to the outer wall with the massive iron-reinforced gate. He counted the sentries.

I'm not getting out that way, he thought.

He was done.

He straightened up wearily, and clenched his fingers over his transfer token. The visceral wrench of magic to that Destination beside the stream on the other side of the mountain flung him to the grassy ground. He dropped down unconscious.

TWENTY-FOUR

When Noddy rode into Ku Halir and saw the King's Army banner flying, he grinned with relief and anticipation.

He was still grinning when he dashed impetuously into command headquarters and spotted Connar and Ventdor on either side of the table, reports and a big map spread between them.

"Connar!" Noddy exclaimed. "I hoped I'd catch you here before you rode off again."

In two strides Connar closed the distance between them, and he and Noddy each pounded the other on the back. "This is a surprise!"

"Cabbage Gannan invited me to inspect Yvanavayir—Stalgoreth," Noddy conscientiously corrected himself. "I can't quite get used to Stalgoreth, such an odd word."

"The old Iascan name, before we turned up," Connar said, laughing.

"I know. Da said going back to the old name is a compromise, that the people up there like it. He said to keep it for now, at least until he decides on the new jarl. Which I'm going to suggest for Cabbage. All year there's been nothing but good reports, and Da said, if it's as good as the reports say, he may as well remain there another year, as you've got everyone else readying for the Adranis." At the word 'Cabbage' he saw Connar's expression shutter, and old habit caused him to turn the subject. "I hoped I might catch you here," he said, starting again. "It's good that I did."

"Come! You must be thirsty." Connar flicked a glance at Fish, who turned to one of the waiting runners and sent him with a brief gesture.

As the runner vanished down the hall, Noddy said, "I know you've been inspecting at East and Hesea Garrisons. Da and Ma were hoping you might stop into the royal city on your way north again."

Connar raised a hand. "Too much to do. I set out to make my inspection somewhat late last spring. I was hoping for a report on the Pass. Unrealistic, I know. I didn't even make it down to Old Faral, much less all the way to Parayid garrisons, nor will I make it to the Nob this year. I'm leaving those until after we deal with the Adranis. And I still have Lindeth and Larkadhe to inspect before winter hits us. We were going to ride out a few days ago, but . . ."

He paused, thinking over the past week, during which Commander Ventdor had been reminiscing about the struggle to form the King's Army out of the remains of Mathren's force, and inside gossip about various commanders since—all the sort of thing the adults had kept to themselves, but which now, Ventdor had said over his third cup of bristic, Connar ought to know.

Connar considered what to say, realized that Noddy likely didn't know any of it, and promised himself to share it with him later. Meanwhile here were all these watching eyes. He finished quickly, "I had to stop for some matters having to do with Tlen and the Eastern Alliance. I sent a detailed report down to Da, which you can read when you get back, if you want. It looks like *you* have news."

Noddy unslung his gear back and reached into it, pulling out a carefully rolled scroll, tied with a fine linen strip, then slung the bag again so he could sign in Hand as he spoke, habit by now. "I told the runners that I'd bring word, in case I was able to catch you. You have a daughter! She was very nearly born on my Name Day. Ranet wanted to name her Danet, but then thought that Noren might want to name a daughter that, when . . . if," he amended, his smile wavering.

Connar pitched his voice in an attempt to cheer. "It'll happen. We're young. We have years yet."

"I know," Noddy said quickly, lest it seem he might be complaining. Noren was an excellent, loyal wife, hard-working and *kind.* It seemed a betrayal to even hint how much it hurt that in a year of trying he had yet to get her pregnant, and he worked hard not to feel anything but happiness that Connar and Ranet had managed to successfully conceive a child in the week Connar had been in the royal city the previous winter.

His gaze dropped as he held out the scroll. "I remembered that Lineas was so good at drawing, so I asked her to make a sketch of little Fareas. That's what Ranet decided on. For her mother, and also Noren's ma, though already everybody is calling the baby Iris, on account of her blue eyes. They chose a flower name because of Blossom. Who thinks the baby is her toy."

He paused and unrolled the drawing, then held it out so everyone could see the sketch of a round infant face indistinguishable (most thought) from any other infant, except for the thatch of black hair. The room full of men said everything that was appropriate, the fathers among them demonstrating real, if brief, interest.

Noddy was still holding out the drawing. Connar took it and laid it on the desk, as the runner reappeared with a loaded tray. "Go ahead. Help yourself."

Noddy pulled his knife, speared three cabbage rolls, plopped them into a shallow dish, and passed them to Vanadei standing behind him. He speared one for himself, gobbled it in two bites, then said, thickly, "That's all the news I have. I hoped you had more."

"I expect my scout report at any time," Connar said. "As soon as I finish the inspections at Larkadhe and Lindeth we'll be back to preparing." He paused as the watch bell clanged. "I expect those are what we're having for dinner. Come join us."

Noddy wolfed down the last two rolls as Ventdor led the way out.

Connar lingered behind, tidying the desk. When he was alone in the room, he looked down at the drawing lying beside the map, then laid his hand over the careful sketch Lineas had made, his fingers spread. Gift, apology, appeal?

Pity?

A spurt of anger and he crushed Lineas's drawing, turned to one of the candles a runner had brought in, and held the paper to it until the flame caught. He watched it burn nearly to the end, then pitched it into the fireplace and walked out.

Quill woke with a throbbing headache and blinding thirst. The stream had diminished to little more than a trickle this late in the season, but it was enough.

He crawled over on hands and knees and slurped water in his cupped hands until he was breathless, then turned and lay on his back as the sky wheeled gently overhead. The cool water worked its way through him, and the worst of the headache receded, leaving him in a stupor of hunger and lightheadedness.

The sun had nearly gone. It was far warmer here than on the heights, so the old urgency to find shelter had receded. But he needed to get moving. Urgency gripped him again, much stronger: if he was gone too long his absence might be misinterpreted, causing the king to launch a war.

First, Lineas and Camerend.

Camerend had twice sent resupplies of ink, paper, and traveler's bread. Quill fetched out his nearly ruined pen, a scrap of paper, and scrawled on it, *I'm out,* at the top and on the bottom. He tore the paper in half, stuck one in his notecase and tapped Lineas's sigil, then sent the second to Camerend.

Then he forced himself to pull out the half-loaf of traveler's bread still remaining in his bag. The sight of the bread made Quill's stomach lurch, after months of eating nothing but. He forced himself to gnaw a few bites, washed them down with more water, filled both his flasks in case the stream beds had gone entirely dry further out, then got wearily to his feet.

All he had to do now was walk, on flat ground, until he was spotted by the right perimeter riders. He started out slowly, working his way downhill before finding a sheltered spot under autumn-yellow leaves. He sat, decided he was done for the day, and stretched out on the grass, and dropped into sleep.

The soft air, after months of wintry frost-burn, was benevolent. He slept hard, woke, drank, ate, walked; when the sun rose behind him, he oriented himself and proceeded in the direction of Lake Wened, fumbling his notecase out to read as he walked.

Both Camerend and Lineas had immediately written back. Lineas was in Darchelde, having been given home leave after the Victory Day departures, and had visited his mother in her seclusion. Camerend reported on that as well, and both conveyed his mother's good wishes, which he scarcely needed; he had grown up knowing that though proximity was sometimes more than she could bear, she somehow kept track of him through his dreams, a benevolent presence.

The rest of the news was small details that added up to the kingdom being quiet: the first year of boys and girls in the academy had finished with only the loss of one girl and one boy being sent home; the birth of Connar and Ranet's little Iris.

Quiet, but not peaceful: everywhere, the talk of war.

Quill hadn't the strength to respond, though he mulled words as he walked, and dreamed them when he slept. Most of his mental strength went to the wording of his report.

His mind drifted on a tide of deep exhaustion, his thoughts remote from the world. Perhaps it was the gift of his mother, but he could not entirely shut out physical awareness: the warmth of the sun on his cheek, the buzzing of insects, the sough of breezes over the yellowing grasses that smelled of sun and wind, the passage overhead of birds going north to avoid the coming winter; the stately parade of clouds driven by the weakening summer winds from the west.

He lost count of the days before he finally heard hoof beats. He'd drunk all his water by then, and the crackling grasses underfoot made it clear he'd find no more. He didn't care who the riders were. He could probably survive the transportation spell if he was snapped up by Elsarion's scouts.

These were Marlovans. He was scarcely aware of their suspicion at his Adrani clothing turning rapidly to concern after his murmured, in Marlovan, "Royal runner, returning from scouting the pass."

"Oh, you're that one?" a cracking teenage voice exclaimed as they all exchanged looks. "We've got orders about you."

The riding captain, a hawk-nosed young woman who looked like the Tlennens, turned to a weedy teenage boy. "Report to Captain Sindan. Tell her we've got the royal runner, and are going straight to HQ."

The boy took off, and at a gesture from the riding captain, the smallest female extended a hand down to Quill. He used the last of his strength to vault up behind her, and they rode on.

They camped out on a clear, moonless night, then resumed riding at sunup. He nodded and swayed, half-dozing, until the clack of hooves on cobblestones roused him sufficiently enough to slide down from the horse.

His knees nearly buckled; someone took his arm and guided him into a small stone building, where he gazed incuriously into a weather-beaten Senelaec face under a sun-lightened horsetail.

"Wait—I've seen you before. Royal runner? *Quill?*" Braids exclaimed. "I've got orders about you. What happened! You're nothing but bones!"

"May I requisition a horse, and riding supplies?" Quill winced, his husky thread of a voice taking on a semblance of life. "No travel bread, please."

Braids grimaced in instant understanding. "I used to ride the borders every summer, and by autumn I couldn't stand the sight or smell of honey. How long have you been eating it? How long have you been gone?"

"King sent me about this time last year."

Braids whistled, then his mobile face lengthened in concern. "I've got orders, as I said, but I really think you should rest for at least a week before riding out."

"Can you guarantee the king hasn't launched the army yet?" Quill asked.

"The king?" Braids said slowly, "You do know that Connar-Laef is now Commander in Chief? And he issued specific orders to both Henad Tlennen and me to send you straight to him if we saw you."

Quill rubbed his eyes. "Where is he?"

"I don't know, but Commander Ventdor will, and Ku Halir is definitely close, straight west." Braids smacked his hands on the desk. "At least get a meal into you—no honey or raisins, I promise—and a night of rest."

Quill passed a hand over his face. He longed for just that, but he had to stop a war that would lose more than it would win—if won at all. "I have to write my report anyway," he murmured, mostly to himself. "Show it to Connar, take it to the king."

Braids rolled his eyes at a waiting runner, who guided Quill out.

A hot meal, some lister-steep, and a much-needed bath restored a semblance of focus, enough for him to establish that he'd been brought to Wened Lakeside, which was currently Braids' headquarters as his company watched and guarded the mouth of the pass. Anyone who came down the pass was surrounded and interrogated before being sent on, weapons confiscated.

Quill thought of the young lordlings, though perhaps they'd been recruits for West Outpost, and hadn't attempted to travel into Halia despite their claims of being in search of horses to buy. "Do they cooperate?"

"They have to," Braids said, with a brief, grim smile and a flash of his palms. "Those trying to buy or get our horses, we send 'em straight back to the pass, like it or not, and watch to see that they go. Anyone we think might be a spy gets muscled straight to Ku Halir. When the traders complain, we tell them to blame Mathias Elsarion. They don't like hearing that," he finished with satisfaction. And then a puzzled look, "You say you were scouting the pass? How far up did you get?"

Tired as he was, Quill understood he was on the verge of a blunder: he must avoid mention of transfer magic. "Climbed up over the mountain. I managed to see the east end of West Outpost, but couldn't get through it to scout the west end."

"We've been watching nothing but," Braids said. "Taking it won't be easy. What's beyond the gate?"

Quill told him. Braids grimaced at the mention of horse killers, but reverted to his former train of thought. "So . . . if you went over the mountain, that explains how you ended up so far north. The patrol that found you thought you got lost. I didn't think royal runners ever got lost."

"I knew where I was, but I got back so late in the season I was out of water. Please tell Henad Tlennen thanks."

Braids flashed a grin. "Just following orders." He watched Quill inhale a last bite of fresh-water fish cooked in pepper sauce, then said, "If you don't mind some advice, I think you should rack up now. Sleep as late as you like. We'll have a meal ready when you waken."

Reluctantly Quill turned his hand flat. "I'm already late. What I need is paper and ink so I can compose my report as I ride."

"Ink, paper, horse, anything you want."

Quill had enough strength left to thank him, and follow a runner to the attic over the stable where runners were usually housed. Someone had hastily excavated the usual tiny chamber at the end with a door, meant for people not sick enough for the lazaretto, but who were coughing or sneezing enough to disturb everyone else in the dormitory-style space.

The next day Quill woke and felt immeasurably stronger—or so he told himself. It was mostly an absence of hunger, thirst, and ache. He bathed again, grimacing as he put back on his dirty clothes. Laundry could wait until he safely delivered his report; after all these months, what was another week.

In spite of many earnest wishes that he would stay, urgency pressed him to depart.

Over the next week he rode west to Ku Halir, thinking out his report by day and carefully writing each night when he camped. When he reached Ku Halir, Ventdor ordered the quartermaster to furnish him with proper royal runner's clothes, and Quill to get a meal and rest, in that order.

Quill gladly rid himself of the Adrani clothes as well as his old stockings, which he had walked holes into. He kept only Fox's black coat. Clean, fed, and dressed properly, he reported back to Ventdor.

Now that Quill didn't "look so much like an Adrani brigand," Ventdor told him where Connar could be found.

It was a two-day ride. Quill used that night, camping alone, to finish writing his report by firelight, then read it through, and rewrote a page until he was satisfied he had explained everything clearly. A report must state eyewitness facts, without opinions, but he strove to make it clear just how expensive in lives as well as materials attempting to take all four castles in the pass would be.

A long line of gray clouds tumbled against the north in the fading light as Quill rode toward Connar's camp. He was handed from outer perimeter scouts to inner perimeter to guards, all young, formidably armed, alert.

The smoldering red sliver of sun sank below the western hills as he dismounted at the picket line, where he recognized tall, pale-eyed Fish leaning against a supply wagon, one heel propped on a wheel spoke. As runners took charge of Quill's horse, Fish straightened up, his face entirely in shadow. "He's waiting."

Quill knew that word would have gone ahead, but he'd expected to be shunted off somewhere until Connar had time for him. He hefted his gear bag over his shoulder and followed Fish through an orderly tent city. The clammy late-autumn air carried the cadenced clash of blades and shouted orders from somewhere out of sight as they approached a clearing surrounded by tents, in which a circle of men sat around a fire talking as they shared a meal.

Connar sat cross-legged among them, eating from one of the shallow wooden bowls Marlovans had carried for generations while in the field. Runners came and went, bringing more food and drink.

At Quill's approach, Connar looked up, and the rest fell quiet. Quill was peripherally aware of sharp, eager glances, as if they were all waiting. Connar took in Quill's thin, even gaunt figure, not without a spurt of contempt. *This* was what he'd once found attractive? Done in after wandering around a mountain, then a ride across the plain?

"Quill, here at last," Connar said, on a suppressed laugh.

It always surprised Quill how warm, even musical Connar's voice was, though he could not recollect ever hearing him sing. "You must be thirsty." Connar flicked a glance at Fish, who walked away into the fast-gathering darkness. "Your report?"

Quill took up a recitation stance before him, feet planted, hands clasped behind his back. Remembering his near blunder with Braids Senelaec, he had thought out how to begin his report. "The Adranis were so watchful that I figured it was better to get over the pass by trails and start down it from the east end." Sure enough, no one evinced any interest in how he got to the eastern end of the pass. Connar waited, his expression intent as firelight beat over his face.

Quill went on to what they wanted to hear. "I discovered that the Adranis search every person coming up from the west. Anyone the least suspicious gets clapped into prison. Elsarion is understood to interview them personally."

Someone spat, and Connar gave a soft laugh. "Exactly what we do with anyone coming down from the east at our end. Henad Tlennen and Braids

Senelaec have been sorting through them, and sending the suspicious ones to the lockup at Ku Halir."

"I was swept up by one of Braids' patrols on my return." Quill resettled his stance, aware that he still hadn't completely recovered; he wished he could sit down. "I had to spend the entire winter hiding in a cave at the top Mt. Skytalon. Nothing living survives caught out in those storms. But once winter abated I was able to map the two higher outposts—towers, really, built on platforms—from which the Adranis can see the entirety of the pass in either direction. Eventually I got down to the fortress at our end. I was able to get an approximate head count of the guards. I also scouted most of the defenses, except I could not get past the outer wall facing the western plains."

"Never mind the outer wall." Connar waved a hand. "We've had steady reports from Braids and Henad on what's there. What I want is what lies beyond that wall."

"The first thing you'll encounter," Quill said, "are horse killers that can be winched up in an instant."

He paused at mutters and curses around them. Connar said, "Go on."

Quill did. At length, starting with the fortified castle at the eastern end of the Pass leading into Anaeran-Adrani, to the daunting height of the platform-towers at either end of Mt. Skytalon. He enumerated the traps and troops that guarded the narrow access roads, also under view from the towers, then moved to the western outpost castle and its formidable defenses aimed westward.

The men listened in silence, until he finished up, "I've written out a report, as ordered." He moved at last, to slip his bag off his shoulder. "I made a map, marking all the traps and defenses that I found. I mapped everything, in fact. I cannot promise I got all the traps—and they might be building more as we speak." He paused, sweeping his gaze around the firelit faces. "In summary, they expect to be attacked from the west."

"Of course they do," Connar sat, sitting back on his mat, hands on his knees, elbows out. His teeth showed in a broad smile. "We won't disappoint them."

Quill stared back, clenching his jaw against exclaiming *Didn't you hear what I just said?*

But even years of training couldn't suppress the flash of incredulity widening his eyes. Not everyone saw it, but most of them were not watching him as closely as was Connar, whose eyes narrowed.

Quill wasn't sure how, but he knew he'd blundered. His expression smoothed into royal runner neutrality. He passed his hand over his face, and then tried again, from a different angle. "I'm not trained to think in terms of military strategy, but I have been taught to evaluate cost. I believe it would cost us least, and be most practical, to stiffen our defense of the west end of that pass. There is no chance Thias Elsarion can ever bring an army down either pass to surprise us again. The cost, right now, is entirely on the Adranis. Building, and maintaining, and supplying those castles in the southern pass would drain even a king's treasury. He has four castles to maintain, in terrain impossible to cultivate for growing food. We can defeat them just by waiting."

He stopped before uttering the words *Whereas there is nothing to be gained by riding over the pass into Adrani territory—unless you plan to hold it.* That might be construed as strategic advice, and while the king might, no, would, ask about that, as had been his habit according to Camerend, there was no indication in Connar's ready posture or his bright, cold, anticipatory gaze, that he desired to hear advice.

As if reading Quill's mind—or rather his unhidden dismay—Connar said, mildly enough, "I swore before the jarls at Convocation that I'd get justice for Tlen and Halivayir, and Yvanavayir, all the way to Elsarion. They hailed it, to a man."

Quill opened his hands, and tried a third angle. "If we take the southern pass, we can't even hold that. And then the cost becomes ours. *Elsarion* can't hold it indefinitely, unless he's richer than kings. Every bite has to be dragged from a distance. Winter, especially at the top, is nearly unendurable, and the summers at least at the western end have no water."

Connar said gently, "But you endured it, am I right?"

Their gazes met, Connar's bland, but there was nothing bland in the tightness through his shoulders, the fists resting on his knees. His smile.

The pause lengthened into a silence. He expected an answer.

"Yes. I did," Quill said.

Connar replied, in that warm, light voice, "If you can, so can we." He glanced around at the waiting faces as he said more strongly, "We don't have to hold it." His voice rose, challenging, compelling. "We just take the battle right back to Elsarion, until he's dead at my feet. Problem solved."

"Yip-yip-yip!" a man shrieked, joined by everyone there, an eerie sound rising to the sky.

Quill's thoughts stuttered to a standstill before a profound sense of failure. A quiet step at his side. Fish silently held out a flask filled with spring water.

Quill drank it down, then Connar said, "Come. Let's see that report. There's a map, you said?"

"Yes." Quill's voice was barely above a whisper. Again he passed a hand over his face. He was too tired. He should have taken Braids' advice and holed up another week. After more than a year, what was another week? But he'd felt the pressure to . . .

A mental shake. All right, he'd failed here. But Connar was not the king. As Quill handed the map and report to the prince, he reflected that once Connar had read it, it was right and proper to ride to the royal city and report to the king—who had backed down from dealing with the pass some ten years ago, when it wasn't nearly as reinforced, for much the same practical reasons, once Camerend had laid them out. The queen would be also there. She, more than anyone, understood costs. Together, the royal couple would be as prudent as they'd been since Quill was a boy.

"Fish is bringing you something to eat," Connar said. "Help yourself, while I read this." A lift of his hand, releasing Quill.

Fish appeared at Quill's shoulder with a plate of rice balls with grilled trout and snap peas. Quill took it with a word of thanks, sank down onto a boulder outside the circle, and began to eat mechanically as Connar's gaze rapidly took in the report, shifted to the map, then back to the report.

Quill had finished the meal and surrendered the plate to Fish again when Connar finally glanced up. "This is far better than what we'd had previously. Far better than I'd hoped. Talk to me about these traps."

Was he changing his mind? "Most of them are shored up rock fall that can be loosed with the release of a chain or a rope. There are covered holes, sharpened sticks, and the like. These two outposts here don't need such defenses as they are both built on high cliffs, with complete views of the pass in both directions."

"Yet they must have an approach."

"Yes. Both have a narrow approach, well-guarded, infested with traps, and completely under the sight of the towers."

"And yet you got around them in order to make these maps."

"Yes. There are what might be called goat trails up there, possibly what the morvende used, or use, as the histories insist there are morvende geliaths in those mountains."

"Geliaths?" Connar repeated.

"It's what they call their cavern cities. I found a grotto, which is how I survived the winter. It gives out onto a trail higher up the mountain than either of these towers."

"Ahhhhh." Connar's smile widened.

This was not changing his mind. Quill wiped his hand over his face, schooling his voice. "You can't imagine how cold it is up there. How perilous. Even in summer there are snowstorms. Two could rarely walk abreast. Horses would never survive up there. The mountain ponies don't go above the tree line."

"But you walked it."

"I—yes. To prove to myself that there is no access for an army."

"Armies," Connar said, still with that little smile of anticipation, "move one man at a time. We learned that up north, when Elsarion first began slipping that army over here. So there is a way into the mountains besides the pass. And access to the two highest outposts. Now, about this big one here at the western end—our end—of the pass."

"Guarded with at least a thousand trained warriors, not counting staff. Who can all be coopted to fight," Quill stated. "Judging by complaining I overheard, they have to drill on top of their regular work."

"If," Connar said, "the eastern side were to be blocked at the top of the pass—those two high outposts taken—West Outpost could be besieged, right? As you just pointed out, those castles have to be maintained and supplied. If we cut off the supplies from the east end, the west end would starve, correct?"

"Well, they do have magic transport Destinations," Quill said. "So some stuff could be brought in. But not enough for a thousand."

"That's right." Connar sat back, arms crossed. "You're one of the ones who goes around putting the magic on our bridges and barrels and baths. But we don't have these, what do you call them, Destinations?"

"No. Those of us taught the renewal spells are taught about the concept," Quill said picking each word carefully. He was on dangerous ground here—and already he had blundered. "But historically Marlovan kings never trusted magic, or mages, which is why they didn't want a mage school for more advanced magic."

"I remember being told that," Connar said. "Go on."

"Magic transfer is painful, dangerous, and you can only go one at a time. Two doubles the pain and danger. You can't transfer a horse, for example. The larger the object, living or non, the more the air, or whatever it is that exists between the two transfer Destinations . . . oh, say it burns up, for lack of a better expression. There are very few places in the world, we are taught, where it is safe to send goods, especially a string of them. These are well known, well-guarded, and none of them are anywhere near the mountain passes here. These outpost transfer Destinations will burn up if overused. So, to get back to your question, a siege is possible if you cut off supplies from the east."

Connar leaned forward. "You didn't mention what other magic they teach you. Can you use it for war?"

Quill flattened his hand, palm down, in negation. "Purifying magic buckets and barrels has never been effective for fighting."

Connar's smile flashed to a grin, then he said, "I need to read this report again, more closely. Fish, find somewhere for Quill to rest."

"Thanks, but I'd rather get started on my journey back to the royal city. I've been gone a year. I'd as soon not keep the king waiting any longer."

"I'll send your report along with mine," Connar said. "You can ride with us, in case there are further questions."

Quill tried to find words to insist, to object, as his gaze shifted away—but not before catching on the three gold chevrons glinting on Connar's sleeve below his shoulder pauldrons. Reminders that, next to the king, he held absolute command. And though his words had been spoken in that mild voice, with a semblance of suggestion, they were, in fact an order.

Another brief pause that began to lengthen as Connar watched Quill process that, then Quill rose and followed Fish's long back.

Connar watched that gaunt, hollow-cheeked face turn away, his thin form shuffling in those shabby boots. Pity, measured with scorn, washed through him: the royal runners were good at what they did, but they obviously had not been tempered the way warriors were.

He summoned another runner with a glance. "Summon Braids Senelaec, and Henad Tlennen. Yes, and Gannan up at Stalgoreth. They're to meet me at Ku Halir . . . no. Somewhere we can control every person in and out. We'll meet at Tlen by New Year's Firstday."

The runner saluted and ran off, as Connar beckoned to Stick Tyavayir. "Send someone fast to fetch Ghost from Ku Halir. He'll want to be in on the fun," he said.

Stick laughed with anticipation.

Quill woke to the clash of steel. Alarm shot through him for a few frantic heartbeats until he registered that the clangs and clashes were too cadenced for battle.

He lay back and closed his eyes . . . and when he woke next, Fish thrust aside the tent flap, letting in humid air as he said, "Breakfast by the command tent. We're riding out directly after."

Quill jerked upright. "My report." His voice was hoarse. He coughed, and said, "I need to take it to the royal city."

Fish's expression didn't change. "Cheese Fath rode out with it at sunrise." He let the flap fall and his footsteps crunched away before Quill could speak.

Not that he needed to. Relief breathed through Quill. He remembered Cheese Fath as a military runner. They prided themselves on their speed. They and the royal runners were always comparing grass run times with one another. Surely commander in chief to king would be another grass run, and the royal city was not that far off. Any orders from the king to Connar would rate another grass run, and winter was coming on. Nothing would happen over winter. There was still plenty of time to halt a useless war before it began.

Though physically Quill still felt as if his body were encased in rock, his spirits lifted as he perched on a rock, a single figure in blue amid a sea of busy gray coats as the camp began breaking up, horses saddled, gear loaded. Weapons strapped on.

The crimson and gold eagle banner rose, limp in the still-humid air, and they began the southward ride. Quill found himself in the center of the formation; with a faint gleam of bleak humor he wondered why Fish rode behind instead of beside him, perhaps in case he fell off his horse.

Up in front, Connar—having sat up nearly until dawn writing—blinked as the sun glanced shards of light off rain pools before shattering into thousands of glints as the outriders' horses splashed through. He had to have a plan within a month, and to put it into effect before spring. It was clear from Quill's report that Elsarion was definitely coming, and the longer they gave him to prepare, the harder it would be to defeat him in rough territory like mountains.

Elation sang in his blood.

Two brief storms swept overhead as they skirted the lake, the sky and the water mirror images of gray, with shifting sheets of rain obscuring the hills above Ku Halir. Quill was nodding in the saddle by the end of that first day's ride. He slept as soon as he ate. They rode at the first lift of dawn's light, establishing a pattern.

Connar never spoke to Quill on that ride. He was an occasionally glimpsed figure, riding at the front before the banners, or surrounded by his captains at the campfire, or at the center of the fighting drills that they stopped for at noon so that the runners could fix a meal and water the animals. The knife drills, Quill noted with that weird detachment, were the old Marlovan single knife drills, mainly there to work the arm not carrying a sword. But the double-stick drills were Great-father Fox's improvements.

By the time they reached Tlen, after riding through a series of spectacular late-autumn storms as winter began to conquer the last currents of warm air out of the west, Quill's mind was shifting in and out of that feverish borderland of reverie and dream.

When they reached Tlen, Quill went to the lazaretto, chose a bunk, and slept straight through a night and a day, rousing long enough to drink water from the jug he found by his bedside.

He woke to noise in the courtyard below. He sat up, coughing; there was a faint but persistent stink of burned wood in the ambient air, though when he looked around he perceived the other simple beds were all new wood. Smoke must have permeated the stone when Yenvir's rabble put the place to the torch.

Quill pulled on his grimy travel clothes, shoved his stockinged feet into his ruined boots, and got up, sitting down again as his head spun. That, he knew, would vanish as soon as he ate.

When he emerged into the rain-swept courtyard, his eye caught on an unexpected sight, Marlovans with drawn steel ringing a man leading a horse and cart, with a pair of sturdy children huddling fearfully close to him. All three had hair cropped behind their ears, making them look round-headed, their clothes short jackets, trousers, leggings, low shoes.

Quill heard snatches of conversation, one of the Riders speaking in the overly loud voice that the monolingual often use to those who don't speak their language, as if volume somehow replaced vocabulary. The carter responded in a very thick, nearly garbled Iascan accent.

Quill turned away, sniffing for the location of the mess hall in hopes of what would obviously be a very late breakfast, when Stick Tyavayir called, "Royal runner!"

Quill turned back, his stomach grumbling in protest. He actually had an appetite. He was definitely recovering. Suppressing a sigh, he joined the group.

Stick, who was trying to remember Quill's name, said, "This man speaks some sort of Iascan, I think. But it's a kind I don't understand. He was picked up as a spy. What's he saying about where he comes from, and where he was going?"

Spy? Quill glanced again at the two frightened children, the man's arm curved protectively around them, and approached, breakfast forgotten for now.

The ring of armed guards parted, and Quill stepped up to the cart. "Where are you from?" he asked in Iascan, doing his best to sound non-threatening.

"I go to take cheeldress . . . prentess . . ." The accent really was garbled, in what seemed to veer between two dialects as the man described heading for the river to pick more leddas, which he pronounced *leedah*.

"Leddas," Quill exclaimed, and most of the ring of watchers inadvertently glanced down at their blackweave boots. "You were going to pick leddas at the river?"

A violent bobbing of the head. "Besst leedah, besst leedah." The man stabbed a finger into the air, then added more garble out of which Quill picked something about one of the children being apprenticed out.

But the changing nature of the man's accent bothered Quill. On impulse, he said in Bar Regren, "Which of the children?"

The man's eyes flickered, his jaw tightened, then his face blanked in assumed confusion.

Quill turned to the nearest child, and said in Bar Regren, "Are you prentice?" He knew his accent was bad, his grammar probably wrong as he was drawing on Iascan for that. He'd only studied the language for a couple of months in order to help Lineas and had not used it since.

But he could see terror in the little face before him. The child turned its head—with that short hair and the similar clothing, there was no telling if these were boys, girls, or one of each—and Quill opened his hand as he said to Stick, "He seems to be a shoemaker, heading to pick a fresh supply of leddas, but he took a side trip to apprentice out one of these children."

Stick said, mildly enough, "That might be why we found him heading south, toward us, and not north toward the river."

Quill remained silent. So far he hadn't seen any sign that Connar or his captains welcomed unsought opinions. At an open-handed gesture from Stick, releasing him, he resumed his quest for a meal, to be stopped again as

Connar stepped out of a doorway. "What was that you said at the end?" So he'd been listening from a distance.

"I asked him a question in Bar Regren. The child, too."

"They didn't answer." Connar's words were not quite a question, more observation.

"No. But I think they understood me." Quill heard his own voice, and wondered if saying that would cause a summary end to what might be innocent individuals. "They might be afraid to be understood for any number of reasons," he added in haste.

"I know that." Connar flicked up a hand, amused. "Go get something to eat. You're no use to anyone looking like a walking corpse." He laughed and passed on by.

Quill continued on inside, reflecting that at least he should be able to leave soon. Connar didn't seem to need him anymore. With a hard ride he could get to the royal city in time to speak to the king, and for the king to send someone to Connar with new orders before winter set in.

The mess hall was empty, as this was mid-watch, but the kitchen had a bowl of leftover biscuits, and plenty of cheese and greens. Quill stuffed bread with both, wolfed it down gratefully, and then washed that down with coffee from freshly crushed and scalded beans—a luxury he suspected followed Connar around, though it didn't seem the prince allowed himself many others.

On his way out to locate the bath, Quill encountered tall, pale-eyed Fish Pereth pushing a weapons rack. They'd had nothing to do with one another beyond the passing of orders back and forth since the days Fish was dismissed from royal runner training, but in recent years Fish's antagonism seemed to have dissipated to indifference. Testing that, Quill asked, "What did they do with the carter and his children?"

Fish paused, his expression difficult to read. "Let 'em go." After a slight hesitation, he added, "There was old leddas caught between the boards in the cart." Then he leaned into the rack and trundled by.

Quill sensed he was missing hidden meaning, then it struck him that the leddas in the cart boards might have bought the man his life.

Quill exerted himself to avoid building assumptions on that guess, and continued on, locating the bath, as usual in a basement where someone had diverted an underground stream. He stripped out of his clothes, palming his golden notecase from next to his skin and wrapping it in his old shirt. After a fast bath, he dressed in the second set of royal runner clothes that Ventdor's quartermaster had issued him, restashed the notecase inside his clean shirt, and dunked his clothes in the cleaning barrel, wrung them out, and hung them in the airing room to dry.

Next, to find someplace out of the way in which to write to Lineas. But when he stepped outside the bath, there was Fish leaning against a horse post, where he could watch the entire court.

"He's waiting," Fish said laconically, with a tip of his head toward the door on the other side of the court.

Quill was waved past an army sentry and several waiting runners into a newly furbished room with little more than a desk covered with papers, and a few stools. In the middle of the desk lay the map he'd labored over so arduously—water-stained, blotched, wrinkled. The handwriting he'd had to thaw his fingers repeatedly to make as shaky as if he'd downed a jug of bristic before writing. Clearly Connar had not sent it on with his report, but maybe he'd had someone make a better copy to send to the king.

Connar stood behind the table, the map before him. Flanking him to either side were Rooster Holdan, currently holding Tlen, Stick Tyavayir, Ghost Fath newly arrived, and a tall, husky pale-haired young man Quill didn't recognize, who wore a single chevron on his sleeve. Not academy-trained, whoever he was.

Connar looked up. "Quill. Talk to us about these traps."

"I told you everything I saw."

"You told us that there were traps cinched up by chains as well as ropes, with rocks piled on. I want to know more all the details you can remember. Including if you ever saw one tested."

"I didn't, though I did see one being loaded." Seeing their interest, Quill recollected lying on a boulder and peering down under a sky full of racing clouds as wind tore down the canyon below.

The men had struggled with the rocks, as raptors wheeled above, watching. A strong buffet knocked someone into someone else, who dropped the boulder he'd toiled up the steep incline with. He danced out of the way before it could smash his feet, and everyone had stilled to watch the boulder bounce crazily down the hill, gathering smaller rocks in a general tumble until they crashed into a huge rock no one could have moved; it teetered, then fell, slamming into the hillside with a thump Quill felt under him, as the men shouted and whooped. Then someone cursed at them to get back to work before the coming storm.

Connar and the others listened intently to this anecdote. Then Connar turned to the big blond captain. "Jethren."

The man Quill didn't recognize saluted and walked out without saying a word; a few heartbeats later his voice echoed off the stone walls, yelling orders.

Connar asked a few more questions, until Quill began repeating himself. When he was done, he hesitated, aware of some current of tension he could sense but not define. Then he decided to speak—he certainly had the right. "I'd like to request leave."

Connar's smile curled at the corners. "Do you need more R and R? We've tried not to load you with any duties."

Quill sensed he'd made a misstep. When in doubt, be plain. "Usually after grass runs we get a day or two of leave before new orders. My last day of liberty was over a year ago, and it was a single day after several months down south." He heard himself shading from explaining to complaining, and shut up.

Stick's chin came down, and Ghost shifted his stance as he sent a questioning look at Connar. It was clear that they found his words reasonable.

Connar, still smiling, said, "Take what you time need right here at Tlen. You're excused from duty. You still look as if a good wind would blow you off your mount."

When the captains turned back to the map, Quill understood he'd been dismissed. But not released.

He walked out, counting the days mentally since he'd first ridden into Connar's camp. He moved unseeing as he calculated again. Even given his state, he was fairly certain of the number. Moreover, short of a blizzard, Connar's runner ought to have reached the royal city within that number. Once the king sent new orders—surely he would—then Quill could ask again.

He took the time to explore the castle complex. It was small, much of the wood so new it still smelled freshly sawed and oiled. Their company pretty much filled every space.

Quill stationed himself in sight of both a door and a window in order to spot any comers, and wrote to Lineas, catching her up with a few words, then asking what she'd heard of the king's reaction to his report.

He sent it, forced himself through a Fox drill, then joined the others for the midday meal. No answer; by afternoon, still no answer. He tried to nap again, then rose and explored once more, using up time as the day wore on.

South and west, in the royal city, Lineas had woken each day wondering if this one would bring Quill riding through the gates. Each night, her last thought was a hope for the morrow.

At her release from duty that evening, she returned first thing to her room to check her notecase, and to her delight, found that Quill had written at last. Supper forgotten, she sat down at once to write back.

A couple hours later, it was Quill's turn for the leap of joy. He ran down to the airing room to fetch his clothing, knowing that no one would be there. The castle people usually retrieved freshly dried clothes on the way to the baths in the morning, then dunked the previous day's and hung them up to be dry by the next morning.

He shut the door and stood with his back against it, unfolded Lineas's closely written note and held it directly under the lantern hanging on the hook.

He tried to master everything at once, so strong was his yearning to know everything in her heart, to be there, to share his thoughts and hers. Words leaped out—king—baby Iris—jarls—queen.

Forcing himself to slow down and read each word in the flickering light, he learned that Lineas no longer had instant access to the royal family. She mostly got her news from Vanadei, to whom she recommended he write for firsthand royal news. What she could report was that Connar's runner had arrived sometime the week previous, and the news had made its way to the royal runners' roost that Quill had indeed made it back, and had reported to Prince Connar. The king had been going around very pleased, having issued orders that any runners from Connar be passed to him instantly, no matter what he was doing, including the middle of the night.

Quill looked up at the candle, stunned. Had he truly failed? Useless question. He'd write to Vanadei, who, as Noddy's first runner, would surely have heard what the king said about his report, if Noddy didn't share it directly.

He read Lineas's note through a third time, slowly, to take in the little things. She was well, the royal castle peaceful. Reluctantly Quill destroyed the note, dashed off a quick query to Vanadei, then a longer reply to Lineas.

He was halfway through that when he received a short reply from Vanadei:

This has to be brief. We're on the road to East Garrison. There was no report written in your hand, only the one that Connar wrote out, detailing what you found in the pass, and promising a plan by the turn of the year.

Quill leaned back against the door, sick with fury.

Connar had not sent his carefully written report.

Of course he hadn't.

Quill tried to breathe out the rage, recognizing it was all the stronger because he'd been thoroughly outmaneuvered. He'd been taught to take the long view, and here he'd thought he had. But he hadn't, or rather he had, but Connar had taken a much wider view. As he looked back, he could see it so clearly, beginning with Connar's *We won't disappoint them.* His smile of anticipation.

Maybe he believed that tearing up the pass and killing everyone in the way until he reached Elsarion had to be done before Elsarion chose the time as well as the terrain. And Quill was equally certain the jarls had made a lot of martial noise at Convocation. But surely Elsarion could be choked off at the western end of the pass more efficiently than forcing an army up the pass from this end?

Whatever the motivation, Connar wanted this war. He'd been planning for it. Who'd know better how the king would waver, presented with those carefully noted details?

So Connar had spread a net to bring Quill in, to make certain he heard the report first. He probably spent that night rewriting it, using only the parts that he felt would support his strategic thinking.

Quill breathed out again, pinching his fingers between his brows. All right, he'd made a serious error. There might still be time to rectify it somehow. Meanwhile, though Connar was the representative of the king, he was still a single person. Stick Tyavayir, Ghost Fath, and the rest of them were united behind the idea of carrying war up the pass. Quill would find no help there. Maybe he could get Vanadei to share the report with Noddy, and convince him to take it to the king and queen. Only how to get it to them without revealing the magic notecases?

He would put it to Camerend—and begin with sending him a copy, as near as he could reproduce it.

It wasn't a great plan, but it was something.

As soon as Jethren and his three ridings, scouts, and runners were safely out of sight of the castle walls, Jethren called for a halt.

"We're being sent away *again*," the youngest of the runner protested, his freckled face crimson with fury.

Jethren silenced him with a look. "I told you we'd be tested. And we were. But we proved to Gannan and the First Lancers that our training, our *real* training, is as good as theirs. Better."

No one argued with that. They'd spent their lives since earliest boyhood enduring two kinds of training—that which everyone at Olavayir got, and then the much tougher secret training mandated by Mathren, the true king's grandfather, who had been trained by the great Anderle Vaskad.

"Now we're going to prove it to the true king. Prove it by action, not by bragging. Here's the orders. This is not being sent away, this is a task. When the true king first told me, I sent Sleip and Punch to scout. They found us a white-stone ruin three days' ride south, in the higher hills west of Sindan-An. We're going to work on the top of those hills until we learn how to bring down the side of a mountain. Smash that ruin out of existence, a big enough landslide to be seen from the next valley."

At that news, everyone except pale-haired Moonbeam, Jethren's first runner, sent up a cheer. Moonbeam grinned, a toothy, savage rictus in his scarred face that caused several to look away.

TWENTY-FIVE

Quill only had the lazaretto to himself for one more night. The next day he was joined by a Rider with a spectacular cold, then by a runner who caught that cold, following which the irascible old medic—by far the oldest person in Tlen—forced everyone to drink a vile concoction whose main flavor was lemon peel. This included Connar.

A week of that, and the colds vanished. Or if people hid their symptoms, at least there were no more rattling coughs.

By the end of that week, Quill had been shifted over the stable with the other runners. He'd begun exercising with them, and when he could find a secluded space, doing his Fox drills. When he could find time and a sufficiently private place, Quill began sending Camerend as close a reproduction of his report as he could remember, bit by bit.

He tried not to think, because his thoughts chased around in circles of frustration at his failures. So he worked as hard as he could, then harder, ostensibly to recover his strength. The real goal was to work so hard he fell into bed each night and slept until morning.

Every other night he still lay awake, his mind wheeling round and round: what he'd done wrong, what he'd said wrong, how he should have expressed himself. How might he still change things.

At the beginning of the next week, he wrote to Lineas:

. . . I've been thinking about command, specifically obedience to command, being an act of will on the part of those who choose to follow orders. My own actions force me to consider that I'm no different than anyone else.

I told you I've been given regular runner tasks around the castle, which helps pass the days. But this morning when I saddled a horse to take a ride to clear my head, two of Connar's runners turned up to ride with me. No explanation, no threats either.

Perforce I welcomed them on the ride, thinking that at least I might learn something useful from them once we were well out of earshot of the castle population. But the frigid wind whistling in our ears, the threat of clouds over the mountains—for the wind has finally changed east—drove us back early. They might not have spoken to me anyway. Connar's runners are singular for their silence. As for their commander, Connar has not spoken to me since asking about the traps in the pass.

So I contemplate my anomalous position, not quite a prisoner. Of course I could escape any time I want to. I also carry a transfer token, but wouldn't need to put myself through that. I've consoled myself by spotting fields of retreat, brief as they are. But what would be the consequences? I've been shortsighted once. Twice would be inexcusable, especially as—

"—I sense Connar watching me." Quill hesitated over writing that for such a long time the drop of ink on his pen had begun to dry out, and he heard footsteps in the hall beyond. In haste he folded the note, sent it, and chucked his writing supplies back into his bag.

The subject of Connar was still a sea of silence between him and Lineas, experiential instead of emotional. *We parted. It was horrible.* Horrible how? What were the consequences? Quill waited for her to choose when to break that silence, as far away in the royal city, she kept herself so busy she wouldn't have to think about her wretched parting with Connar, or about what Quill said about how eager the prince was for this war.

A rapid series of sleet storms and one snow flurry crossed the kingdom, east to west.

In Tlen, when it abated, the cessation of bad weather brought the captains Connar had summoned. Each only arrived with a riding, their escorts left to ride the outer perimeter and arrest any random people poking around, no matter what their excuses.

"Quill!" Braids Senelaec hallooed across the busy courtyard, still sun-browned though the sun had been playing hide-and-seek for weeks. "You're back up here again?"

"I never left—"

Quill's voice was drowned by the clatter of new arrivals pushing in, this one bearing a huge crimson and gold eagle banner with pairs of silver chevrons in each corner: the First Lancers. And riding beneath it, Cabbage Gannan.

Quill looked away from those helms with the hair-trophy horsetails.

At the other side of the court, Connar watched with gut-churning disgust. He'd given specific orders not to be flying company banners as he didn't want any Adrani spies putting the signs together of a captains' war council. Of course they knew he was going to come for them, but let 'em sweat wondering when, and how.

Cabbage Gannan had just finished a year of success in Stalgoreth, bolstered by Noddy's enthusiasm. Not surprising, he very much liked being a jarl, even an interim one. In spite of that success, he found himself scanning the busy courtyard until he found Connar, standing there with Jethren.

Connar stood there with arms crossed and curled lip.

Cabbage's confidence faltered into the old, gnawing doubt, which sparked the old resentment. At least Jethren would speak up for him, he reasoned—he and his three ridings from Olavayir had ridden with Cabbage's First Lancers until late summer, in order to catch up with how the academy trained captains to do things. Keth Jethren was a hard rider, hard everything, but Cabbage had been justifiably confident about his own people. Ever since Lefty Poseid lost his brother to Yenvir the Skunk's rabble, he'd made certain their training was tough.

So why would Connar give him that stink-eye? Oh. The banner. He'd forgotten to have it rolled up after he'd met up with Braids' company, a reminder who was senior.

As Cabbage dismounted, he hurried into speech, "We rode down Stalgoreth, and people like seeing the banner. Knowing that it's us and not Adranis, and we can't just leave it lying about, right?"

Too loud, too exculpatory, followed by the guffaw that had grated on Connar since they were teens. But Cabbage Gannan was Noddy's pet commander, and anyway, Connar reminded himself as the runners began efficiently dividing everyone off and showing them to quarters, Cabbage had a place in his plans.

"Come inside," was all he said.

They were all there, looking at him expectantly.

Connar had hammered out his plan with Stick and Ghost. It was an old plan—based on his first academy success, though he hadn't told anyone that, even Stick and Ghost. If they'd remembered, fine; that they hadn't mentioned it underscored the fact that Connar had, unlike the two of them, had so few wins during his academy years that he still recollected every detail of both. No, make that three, really. Despite those stupid rules that no longer *mattered,* just as he'd foreseen.

But one thing he'd learned in countless wargames since was that there were actually very few actual plans that differed from the basics: you wanted to flank your enemy, and surprise him if you could. From there you just got infinite variations depending on terrain, numbers, skills, the limitations of captains, and so on, right down to the weather.

So it was with confidence that Connar waited until the two runners he'd appointed to handle the maps unrolled the big one. Then he said, "When the last snowstorm clears out, I want the Adranis to look off the walls of West Outpost . . ." He tapped the castle drawing at the Marlovan side of the southern pass. "And see our First Lancers lined up across the horizon."

Cabbage exclaimed doubtfully, "What good can lances do against gates?"

"None," Stick said, easily enough, and Connar tightened his jaw against the sarcastic rejoinder he'd wanted to speak. It wouldn't do to sound like they were back in the academy digs. He'd let Stick handle Gannan.

Stick described the formidable castle and its defenses, accurately repeating everything Quill and Braids had observed, then said, "Gannan, you ran this ruse back in the academy. You and your lancers can charge any Adranis who try coming out the gates, otherwise ride back and forth making as much noise as possible. Threats. Taunts. Try a couple feints. Send fire arrows over, and the like. We want all their attention on you, thinking that you are our big attack."

Gannan's big mouth will be perfect for that, Connar had said to Stick and Ghost in private, and Ghost had wondered why that old grudge still lingered. In his experience, Gannan hadn't been what he considered mouthy for years.

Stick flashed a mirthless grin. "Let the Adranis get a good look at those helmet trophies, so they know what's coming. Lots of night noise. Don't let them sleep."

Connar then spoke. "Braids, Henad," he addressed the skirmisher commanders standing against the side wall. "Hold the east until I return. Any strays wandering around, lock 'em up until I come back. Any. Just last month we scooped up a Bar Regren cobbler. While I don't think those Bar Regren are in the pay of the Adranis, I don't trust them not to be. Let's kill the question entirely by grabbing anyone even slightly suspicious. If my plan works, we'll have the pass cleared, and Elsarion dead, by summer's end."

Cabbage Gannan—of course it would be he—said, "Where will you be?"

"Flanking 'em. Once we hit them from the east side, you'll actually come at the gate, so figure out a way to do that."

Cabbage rubbed his big hand over his blond brows and up his high forehead as he said, "How are you *getting* there? Braids said on the ride in, that castle blocks this end of the pass from cliff to cliff. You can't get up those cliffs unless you can fly. And even if you could, wouldn't they pick you off with their arrows?"

"This is not to be shared beyond this room," Connar said in a flat voice. "We're going up over the mountains and coming down the back way."

The effect on Cabbage, Braids, and Henad, was almost funny. Going over snow-covered mountains? Was that even possible?

Then Cabbage said, "How will we know when you're there, if that castle is as large as you say? Will whirtler arrows even be heard above the noise?"

Stick laughed. "Oh, you'll know."

Connar smiled grimly. "I'm using Inda-Harskialdna's first strike against the Venn: we'll bring down the towers from the top of Skytalon. The old records claim that Inda-Harskialdna's avalanche was felt halfway up the pass, and the dust visible in the air cloud-high. We figure, what's possible in Andahi, which is much longer than the eastern pass, will be possible here."

At the back of the room with the rest of the runners, Quill listened, appalled. That avalanche, started by the Marlovan defenders desperate to block the Andahi Pass from the Venn invasion, had taken place while Inda-Harskialdna was far to the south. He'd known nothing about it at the time.

Quill wondered where Connar had managed to cull that piece of misinformation. Of course he hadn't read the Fox record, and ever since Lorgi Idego had broken away from Marlovan Iasca, a lot of the old ballads in praise of those on the north shore were no longer sung, which argued that parts of century-old history were being forgotten, or elided into other events. But then, as Quill took in the reactions, he understood that it didn't matter what the truth really was. The name Inda-Harskialdna had a powerful effect.

"Isn't that impossible?" Braids asked doubtfully. "I mean, the whole reason why the pass is the only way over is because the mountains are impassable, right?"

"Im*pass*able in winter. Difficult in spring. But not im*poss*ible. Our own royal runner scout did it, alone." Connar opened his hand toward Quill, standing against the wall at the back. "Carrying his own supplies. If he can do it, we certainly can," Connar said as the entirety of the room gazed at Quill and then back. "And Quill will be leading the way."

Quill stared back, heart and mind flash-frozen to ice.

Connar went on to explain how he had shifted up reinforcements from East and Hesea Garrisons to stiffen Lindeth and Larkadhe against trouble from Idego, the Nob, or the mountains in between while the main of the Marlovan army was known to be in the east. Nobody had forgotten the Chalk Hills attack.

"So like I said, patrol the east." Connar gestured to Braids and Henad, then swept his hand down the map from Stalgoreth to Nelkereth. "My cousin Tanrid will cover the west, with Lindeth and Larkadhe. I've sent a runner to assign Rat Noth to protect Ku Halir and the middle ground. Everyone's orders are the same: any trouble, contain it. I'll deal with them all when I get back."

To Cabbage, "It's up to you to figure out how to break past the horse killers and the rest of their outer defense. You have half the winter to work up some tactics. I'll also have Ventdor ready his lancers to reinforce you; they can bring the battering ram."

"So that's why you saved it," Cabbage exclaimed.

"I knew I'd find a use for it," Connar said in that flat, goading voice Cabbage hated. That's aimed at me, he thought, imagining Connar breaking down the gate at Stalgoreth.

Connar went on, "Remember. First thaw, I want you there on the horizon."

Cabbage thought it best not to respond except with a salute.

The only problem with regaining his strength was waking up in the mornings with saddle-wood, and an acute longing for Lineas. He worked the harder, but as he did, he let his mind range back through memories in an effort to bring her by his side: when he did handstands, there she was as she'd been as a skinny teen learning handstands, making the other fledglings laugh as she rambled on about how she was pretending her feet pressed the sky, and all the world around her hung from invisible strings.

Traveling at night during the latter part of a wet, messy winter resulted in the Winter Company arriving at their rendezvous without having been seen by anyone on either side. It was a slow, nasty toil through slush and mud, bringing them a month after the rendezvous date.

Quill was assigned to Stick and Ghost, to be sent into small towns for news and fresh supplies, as nobody questioned the presence of itinerant royal runners. They were the last to arrive at the rendezvous, with their collection of laden horses and carts, sent away again once unloaded. They found the rest of the Winter Company in the valley adjacent a thundering waterfall full of snowmelt, drilling under Connar's watchful eye, a string of mountain ponies peacefully cropping new grass.

At the sight of Stick and Ghost's company riding up, Connar raised his fist and the combatants stepped back, weapon-hands dropping.

"You're here. Excellent. Get the supplies distributed and loaded. Food and extra supplies on the ponies. We've been warned about overloading them. Each man carries his own personal gear. We have a target, to reach Skytalon and destroy the towers before the first resupply can get down the pass from the east. I'm certain their spring thaw began in their lowlands at the same time as ours. Stick, Ghost, over here."

Stick and Ghost sloshed through the mud to report as Quill made his way to the runners, who absorbed him into unloading the carts and distributing the packs among the sturdy ponies.

A sense of urgency gripped them, radiating from their commander. Very soon the Winter Company started up the trail, Connar at the front setting a brisk pace and the runners leading the ponies.

At first many of the company looked about, especially up at the slow, milk-white waterfall far overhead to the left, water laden with pulverized rock crashing down, to be filtered by the land before emerging again as the sweet, slow rivers they had grown up with. It was odd not to be riding, but they were young and strong, eager to prove that a stroll up a mountain was easier than a charge across the plains.

The trail ran with trickles where it wasn't deep mud. Shoots of ferns thrust up on both sides, and the nubs that would be wildflowers poked up from the soil on the sunny sides of the mountain slopes. Slowly it became a relief to plunge downhill into still-sheltered gorges and ravines, where snow still extended in long white fingers toward the rushing water below.

Gradually the climb became toilsome, their packs heavier. Connar forced himself to keep a brisk pace, until the westering sun hiding behind the bluffs deepened the shadows to danger on an already slippery path.

No one said much when at last the signal to halt was passed down, but Quill was aware of the easing shoulders and long breaths of relief as they emerged onto a clearing shaded by enfolding crags. Connar climbed a little ways up farther, satisfied himself that any fire they made couldn't be seen from the plans below, and gave permission.

Many, with furtive looks, pulled off boots and rubbed tender feet.

Quill unslung his pack onto a rock and helped to set up a picket for the ponies, aware of the warmth of muscles he'd spent an entire year strengthening on his previous climb. He was not the least tired, but said nothing as mutters and whispers here and there indicated what he'd experienced, painfully, and would have warned them if they'd listened: they were unused to walking long distances. A Rider could be as strong as a tree —except for the bottoms of his feet, which were primarily used to lock down in stirrups.

They enjoyed a balmy night, rising in the pale blue of impending dawn. Men swung their arms and tried to stamp the stiffness out, calves cramping. Some wore the inward looks of suppressed discomfort, gazes cast downward as their captains—after a low-voiced conference at the far end of the clearing —roused them for drill. Blisters, Quill suspected, would only worsen.

The eddies of cooking food mitigated the discomfort. Ghost, used to those winter games in Halivayir, had seen to it they brought baskets of eggs. These wouldn't last, but they would get them off to a good start; after a heartening breakfast of shirred eggs and pan biscuits, they set out once more at a brisk pace.

This day was more grueling. The sun was merciless where it shone, baking them in their heavy layers. Many stripped off their coats and threw those over the ponies' backs—catching sour looks from the runners in charge of the animals, who had carefully worked out how much each animal would carry without slowing its pace.

Several men who had grown up along riversides, going barefoot for long seasons, took off boots and stockings entirely to walk barefoot in the mud. More joined them as they made their way up a north-facing slope, until the sun began to hide behind a stately sailing of patchy clouds that, as they accumulated, darkened to a heavy gray.

When the long line rounded the slope and entered shadow, quite suddenly the air chilled. Snow appeared again in crevasses and sheltered gorges below which unseen water rushed and thundered. When they encountered rocks and ice, back on came the boots, their owners running hastily to catch up, breathing like bellows as they resumed their place in the line.

They had slowed that hard pace by the time Connar, invisible to Quill at the front of the long snaking line, at last called a halt. A slanting storm battered them with sleet. They crowded against a hillside under overhangs of rock and twisted trees. That night it was a cold meal, and what sleep they could get sitting back to back on boulders as water rushed down the trail. Quill fell asleep, aware of the soft sound of a whetstone as Jethren's first runner honed a thin-bladed knife.

Nobody changed their clothes. When the light lifted the next morning, they could see their breath. More than one reflective gaze was cast up the trail to where the mountain vanished under low clouds.

Quill knew they had yet to see the worst.

The only relief from mud was an occasional scattering of bright yellow aspen leaves that had somehow survived through the months of winter, and lay on the trail in a dappling of brightness over the unending mud, slush, and snow.

The steady tread of foot and hoof was broken now and then by the stamp of feet to shake loose thick cakings of muddy snow. Colonies of aspen stretched upward, broken by ancient, wind-gnarled willows and poplars, the orange leaves of the latter scattered here and there among those yellow aspen leaves, a trail of bright gold obscured by the melt.

That first week, they drilled once a day, either on rising or if they'd had to shelter in miserable conditions as they had their second night, somewhere along the trail. Connar led each drill with a grim determination that silenced outward complaint, though Quill—who had endured a year in these mountains—observed the lowered gazes and set mouths of ferocious moods.

Jethren's men stood apart, in precise rows. At first they finished drill with sparring; Quill was distracted by Jethren's first runner, a thin pale-haired figure who displayed brutal strength, grinning in a rictus as he slammed his opponent down and wrenched limbs.

Quill helped repack the gear each day as they consumed their supplies, distributing the weight evenly among the ponies.

Eight days in, Quill overheard that young runner of Jethren's muttering to a companion, "When we halt next I'm going to rip the darn-knots out of these shit socks."

"And have your blisters rubbing right on the soles of your boots?" his companion retorted with no sympathy. "Turn 'em over, and wear the heel side up top, that's my advice."

Quill, from ahead, turned back to say, "Don't do that. They'll slip down under your heel and torment you more."

The redheaded runner cast him an ugly look, as if everything were his fault, and at their brief halt for a meal, Quill glimpsed him pulling off his boots, wincing at the bloody blisters over his toes and the sides of his feet, and turning one sock so the heel bunched over his instep.

Quill knew how that was going to go—and as they started again, he spotted the young man muttering increasing curses under his breath as he had to stop every twenty paces or so, insert his fingers into his boot and yank the sock up again.

When they stopped that night, as usual, Jethren's men watched Stick's and Ghost's men for signs of weakness, and the other way about. When Stick Tyavayir walked up to their gray-haired medic, who had kept pace, more than half the rest joined in twos and threes until there was quite a line.

While dispensing salve and bandages, the medic warned each of them, from the young, sullen runner to the captains, to dip their socks in the purified bucket.

"Will they dry?" Stick Tyavayir asked doubtfully.

Everyone was listening. Quill, sitting apart from the rest with his freshly grilled fish, wondered if it took their captains admitting to normal human pain before the rest would dare.

The medic put his fists on his hips, and glared at Quill. "You're the only one with experience. Will they?" His voice rasped with unhidden exasperation.

Quill understood in that moment that the medic had seen what Quill had—but was misinterpreting his silence.

"Not unless you have a firestick to dry them over," Quill said, and all eyes turned his way. "I didn't, so I hooked 'em through my belt when I walked. Changed my socks every night."

"I'm already wearing all mine," someone protested.

That cause a brief, bitter spurt of laughter, as those who had firesticks looked appreciatively at their fires, which they had been building into a circle in order to share and magnify the heat.

The medic warned, "It's only going to get colder. So preserve those sticks, and use the salve I passed out."

"*How* cold?" Stick asked, turning to Quill as Connar watched from the other side of the clearing.

Quill said, "I don't know how to measure, except by externals. The sound of the snow squeaking underfoot changes. At its coldest the sky is so intense a cobalt you feel you're falling into it. The shadows on the snow change from the color of slate to a blue close to violet. The cold is so much colder than any cold you've ever felt that it burns."

"Burns?" someone repeated, eyebrow cocked skeptically.

"Any skin you leave exposed frostburns, not over time as happens if you're not careful in our winters. It's fast. Almost instant. Then there's snow blindness, unless you wrap your face to let in as little glare as possible. Also, your nose hair and eyelashes freeze from your own breath. And you have to breathe slowly, or your lungs feel like they're on fire."

A man muttered, "*That's* what's coming ahead?"

Quill said, "I hope not. That was winter on Skytalon. Spring, even summer at times, were more like winters at home. But every so often there was a day like that. You can't predict them."

A brooding silence met that, then the rest broke into muttered conversations.

Connar said nothing. He'd already revised his assumption that royal runners—or this royal runner, who had endured long rides, and who had swooped out of nowhere and dropped those assassins with only a couple of little knives—could not endure what his warriors could. A stupid assumption, which he knew arose out of that old sense of competition, to prove he was good enough. Better.

"We have a target," he reminded them.

His mood lightened at the unthinking obedience as everyone picked up their gear and formed into lines. The competition was over. He was where he wanted to be, that was what truly mattered.

From then on, especially as the climbing got slower, and only Quill seemed to finish the day much as he'd begun it, there were no more remarks about the cossetted royal runners.

They walked into fog a week later. The icy vapors seeped into everything, rendering them damp and miserable. Four and a half days they spent enduring the thick, swirling mists, sometimes unable to see the man in front of them except as a silhouette. Only the ponies seemed undisturbed, though they moved much slower. Finally the line emerged at last above the clouds into pale sunlight, which glared brightly on the soft blanket extending westward to the horizon.

Everything around them had changed. Gone were the occasional antlered beasts peering at them from crags, and leaping up and down the rocks. Gone also were the familiar trees, replaced by conifers stretching to the intensely blue sky.

Three days into their climb above the fog, the ponies had slowed to a stop, snorting and finally balking altogether.

"They can't breathe under these loads," the runner in charge stated to Connar. "Time to let them go."

They'd all known that this time was coming, but hearing the words and experiencing what they meant was profoundly different.

Silently the runners helped unload the animals; at last all were free but one, and began to nose their way back down the ice-crusted trail, some traveling in a herd, and others seeking a new herd. They didn't give a thought to the humans they left behind, who stood staring at the gear piled on the slushy ground.

Quill watched from the side, resigning himself to what was to come. The company was really two companies, Jethren's men competing against the others, each side trying to prove, without actually saying it, that they were tougher.

As they eyed one another, no one moving, the medic slowly unloaded the last pony, set the medical supplies on a rock, then replaced them with his bedroll and personal gear.

Then he led the pony up to Connar. "I told you I didn't think I could make it. This is as high as I can go, so I might as walk back down with Twitchears here. I've enough travel bread to make it, I think, and I have my own firestick. Your runners all know how to set a limb, how to bandage. You all know to use the salve. I suggest you stop as often as you can to breathe."

When Connar didn't speak, the medic turned his scrawny shoulder and started down the trail, leading the small pony.

Connar flicked his hard gaze to the three captains. "Divide up the rest of our stores."

Quill bent down to heft one of the packs of medical supplies. He slung it around his shoulder as others began to move.

When everything had been shouldered, Connar turned toward the trail, blinking up at Mt. Skytalon's peak, which didn't look much closer than it ever had. "Let's move," he said.

TWENTY-SIX

From the open door leading to Halivayir Castle's stableyard, Leaf Dorthad heard the approach of a quick heel-to-toe step. A familiar step, but not one she heard every day. The breathing was quick, higher in tone, a female, tall—

"Neit?" she asked, wondering.

"Leaf!" The footsteps stopped. "They told me you woke up blind. You got your eyes back?"

Leaf's hand flattened in negation. "Only a little on the extreme right. Mostly shifting lights. And of course if I try to look that way, it shifts with me. I was turning around in circles until I figured it out." Leaf snorted a laugh.

Neit looked at her fondly. Leaf had never been what anyone called tight—those goggly-round eyes protruding from a round head, and round cheeks, stuck atop a body that never seemed to get any shape no matter how much she ate. But she'd always been a fine rider, and nobody their age shot better: Neit was glad to see the wink of gold on Leaf's robe, from her wins that first year girls were allowed at the royal city Victory Day games.

Neit grabbed Leaf's skinny form in a massive hug, suspecting that Leaf didn't even know the medals were on her robe, if she couldn't see 'em. What it meant was, the Halivayir people were taking good care of her.

As they should. Leaf had always taken good care of them, from the time she left the border Riders at age fourteen to take care of that crusty old grand jarlan, a job nobody else had been willing to undertake.

"When I heard you woke out of that coma, I wanted to come right away," Neit said, setting Leaf down again. "But I've been riding my ass off, so much has happened, and of course the rankers all have to write a lot of letters about it. Well, better than being cooped up, I always say. Except in a blizzard."

"What brings you here now?" Leaf asked, leading her to the side chamber where the old jarlan had received guests. Leaf knew the room by the smell of hemp. It had become their basket-making center, but it still had good cushions, and the firestick in the fireplace kept it warm.

"Riding straight down the river on my way to Ku Halir, then either the royal city or back to Nevree. I was in Larkadhe. Took the east road. Stopped in Farendavan. You know the gunvaer always awards a thumping bonus to anyone bringing letters from her nephew to the Chief Weaver."

"I met Andas a couple years ago," Leaf said, her gaze vague in a way that Neit found disturbing only because it was so unlike Leaf, whose gaze had been quick and bright. She'd been able to correctly name a bird on the horizon, part of why she'd been such an excellent shot.

But this was Leaf now, Neit reminded herself, as Leaf went on, "Brother Farendavan asked his Fath connections to take Andas on a perimeter ride that one summer, before the trouble. They stopped here before turning west." Leaf's chin lifted, and she said, "Oh, good, Lnand is bringing fresh biscuits."

Neit glanced around the empty room, startled. Was this another of those weird ghost things, like Lineas after the Chalk Hills disaster? But then she heard the approach of footsteps, bringing the warm aroma of rye biscuits just out of the oven.

A maidservant almost as tall as Neit, and as muscular, hefted a tray full of good things to eat and drink. She set this down on the scarred table at Leaf's right. "Cook says, you're to make a good showing, or she won't get up apple-layer tarts anymore. Steep on the right, fizz on the left."

"You've got berry-fizz?" Neit asked, reaching.

Lnand smacked her hand away. "Jarlan first," she scolded. "She needs to put some flesh back on."

"I'm not a jarlan," Leaf sighed. "I *wish* you wouldn't keep saying that. If they do appoint someone, they won't like hearing that."

"You will be the next jarlan," Lnand stated, flinging up the back of her hand to the idea of anyone else. "That gunvaer hasn't forgotten what you did. She won't stab you in the back, putting some woman over you, leaving you in that nasty cottage. You'll see."

"I *like* my cottage. It's *quiet*," Leaf said—but under her breath after Lnand had marched virtuously out.

Neit watched Leaf's hands drift over the tray, checking where everything was, then efficiently fill her plate. After that she poured out two cups of the deep purple fizz, not spilling a drop.

"Help yourself," Leaf said. "Tell me how Andas is doing. Such a sunny boy."

"He's gonna be a looker, like his ma," Neit stated judiciously. "Too early to tell if he'll run for boys or girls or both, but one thing for sure, they'll all be after him. And yes, he's still sunny. No strut, though you'd expect some of anybody with four, no *six*, parents, if you count his ma in the royal city, and the king, who they told me writes once a week, always begging him to come visit. But that tough old Ma Farendavan won't let him a step past the river bend. Anyway, all six of 'em in their various ways all slathering him with butter, you'd think it would spoil him rotten."

Leaf smiled. "Ma Farendavan is too strict for that, all the Faths say. I expect Uncle Brother would spoil him if he could. Tialan Fath, too. I used to ride with her. She's got a good heart, and I hear she's a good ma for that pack of brats. So's Hanred," she finished, naming Brother Farendavan's favorite of ten years.

"Add in Young Miller, Tialan's pillow-jig, and you have it," Neit said with satisfaction. "The gunvaer's reward is good—it buys me a prime weekend at the Shield whenever I hit the royal city—but truth is, I like stopping there. There's always something fun going on, and even that old crabapple Ma Farendavan cracks a smile once a year."

Leaf gave her old whoop of a laugh, then cut it short, wincing.

Neit put down her third biscuit. "Leaf?"

"Nothing, nothing." Leaf waved a hand. "Just, sounds are somehow sharper, including inside my head, since I woke up out of that coma."

"What did the healer say?"

"About that? I didn't tell her about how sharp noises are. Sounds too much like complaining, and I did enough of that about whatever it was got shaken loose inside my eyes."

"I take it they can't fix it? Or might it heal on its own, like a broken bone?"

"She said they don't have any way now. Not even in Sartor, though in the ancient days they could."

Neit snorted her disbelief. "In the ancient days, if you believe all the songs, you could change yourself into a horse in the blink of an eye, and wish food out of the air as well as kill with a thought."

Leaf gave a soundless laugh, then leaned forward. "Neit, about sounds. Would you do something for me?"

"Do what?" Neit said cautiously. She'd stopped to see Leaf, hopefully get a good meal, and let her horse do likewise before pushing on. She was happy with small errands, but anything that would keep her cooling her heels for days . . .

Leaf sat back. "It's all right."

Neit saw the frustration it didn't occur to Leaf to hide, and she felt like a horse apple. "It's just, I did want to get to the Riverbend at Tyavayir border by nightfall, but if there's something important, I can always . . ."

"Not important," Leaf said, her brow contracting as her gaze read over the ceiling. "That is, I don't know." She drank the last of her cup, then stood. "Tell you what. Let me show you my cottage. I'll explain as we go."

She led the way, her right hand out for orienting as she said, "The servants think it odd that I still sleep out there, and I let them think it's because I got attached to the place because I woke up there. Because I don't want to tell them their noise bothers my ears now. They make *normal* noise. I know that. But somehow everything is so sharp, like sound is when it gets so cold you can't touch anything metal outside. Clear and windless nights, I can hear the farmers on the other side of the apple orchard beyond the south wall."

Leaf kept her voice low as they walked along a side-corridor away from the main rooms, then cut toward the back of the castle, to the kitchen yard. They emerged into cold air, and splashed through rain puddles, past the hen coop, and then a bit farther—an area Neit had never seen before.

She had perforce played wargames for so long (always as an enemy, finally as enemy commander before she was able to escape them entirely into being a long runner) she couldn't help but assess defenses. There was no back wall, she saw. Instead the east end of the castle was a long, solid stone ridge at roof height, with thick forest visible above, the trees budding with hints of green.

Tucked up against the stone was an old cottage, its tiled roof so mossy that at first glance the entire thing looked like part of the cliff. A few paces away a waterfall trickled into the stream that ran through the kitchen yard.

Leaf hummed softly under her breath, hands out. She stopped a pace or two before the door, then stepped up inside. Neit cast a glance around. Someone kept the stone floor swept. A bed sat under the window overlooking the waterfall, neatly made up. The space was small, but cozy.

"I can see why you like it here," she said.

Leaf smiled. "The water mutes hard noises. But I can hear everything . . . ." She turned toward the back wall, chiseled out of the ridge stone. "Up there. It's been intermittent. At first I thought it was rain falling up on the hill, but no rain falling here. It happens—I'm sure you've ridden on dry road with rain falling a few paces away, or the reverse."

"Many times. You usually get a rainbow."

Leaf smiled in memory. "If Ghost were still here, I could tell him and he wouldn't fuss at me, but he got called away the day after our wedding—"

"Nobody told me you two finally married!"

"Yup. He had to ride out almost as soon as he got here, as I said, so it wasn't much of a celebration, but it did straighten out the chain of command here, Ghost being interim jarl, which makes me *interim* jarlan."

"Did you at least get a good wedding night out of it?" Neit asked—then remembered that Leaf had never chased boys *or* girls when they were younger.

Leaf's "Eh," made it plain she still felt the same. "Ghost offered, everything proper, but you know me. Besides, Manther is riding with him, and he's still . . . you can hear the grief in his voice. I told them to take the big bed, and I came out here. *Much* quieter, with all those men whooping it up with the spiced wine . . . Oh, that doesn't matter. You're in a hurry, but this noise. It's sporadic, see, these rustling sounds I thought might be rain. But too steady, so I thought of animals, but what animals go in numbers? And I said recurrent, right? Two days ago, morning then night, and this morning again, I heard a branch snap and it woke me up."

Neit wondered how much of that 'sharp noise' was left from the horror of the attack, but she wasn't going to bring that up if Leaf didn't. So she just said, "You're talking about up on the ridge somewhere? You want me to go up there and take a quick poke around?"

"Would you?" Leaf's anxious expression eased. "I don't want Lnand worrying at me anymore than she does, and I got up too late to ask Captain Venad. They were heading to the river for some exercise with the Tyavayir Riders today."

Neit hadn't done rock climbing since she was a girl running with Floss, her brother, up into the hills at Nevree to play. At least the weather wasn't hot, she thought as she walked out and eyed the mossy stones alongside the waterfall.

A few were loose, and she was wearing her heavy riding boots for warmth. Not great for climbing. So she took her time, scrambling only when she neared the top.

Instead of an easy walk she found herself confronted by a thick tangle of willow and cottonwood uniting to battle an army of aspen shoots, and winding among them all, fierce berry shrubs of at least three varieties—all thorny.

She thought longingly of the metal armor warriors were reputed to wear someplace overseas as she toiled a difficult ten paces without being able to see much ahead. Then she placed her foot on a muddy something and nearly tumbled into a totally hidden shrub-choked crevasse, carved by the stream that fed the waterfall.

She caught herself against a low willow branch before taking a nasty tumble, looked around, cursed under her breath, then swung herself upward into the willow.

Three broad branches up and suddenly the navigation became easier. She clambered her way along the branches woven together, willow, ash, oak, oak again as she moved away from the running water.

It was only after she had worked her way from tree to tree to tree, then paused to orient herself that she discovered she had cleared what amounted to a hedgerow along the cliff, some twenty or thirty paces deep. If you didn't know that Halivayir Castle lay directly to her right—west—you wouldn't catch a glimpse of it.

She lowered herself hand over hand and dropped to the moist ground. Then she froze, aware of anomalies in the confusion of growing things in the dappled sunlight.

The area was still. Too still. No birds or small animals. Ahead—eastward—the pale wood of broken small branches here and there. She edged along a mighty root, reluctant to make prints, though she had no reason beyond instinct as yet. As she passed the mossy remains of a gnarled oak that had probably fallen in her grandmother's time, she saw a trail winding among the trees, the mud churned up with footprints. Many footprints. Fresh ones—as fresh as morning, at least made since the previous day's rain.

Rider patrol? But Riders rode. She joined the multitude of prints, her own lost among them as she looked for the expected perimeter trail. But there was no sign of any such thing winding back toward the Halivayir castle. Neit followed the trail for a ways, noting it bending gradually eastward, away from the castle, which was still completely invisible. When she came to another, wider stream, she followed the western turn downstream, stooping often.

She had to crouch down to ease through the brambles and berry bushes, until she came out in a rocky area south of the castle walls, barely visible through the twisted branches of a very old apple orchard.

It was marked off by a bramble hedgerow. Sighing, she paced alongside it until it gave onto someone's farmland.

Crossing field and stream, she found the road at last, then ran up it until she reached the front gates. Here, she surprised the gate sentries as she walked through, muddy to the knees, her robe torn in several places. She peered up, question on the tip of her tongue, then decided to talk to Leaf first.

She found Leaf in the kitchen with her steward, discussing the shifting of ale barrels. Before the steward could react, Leaf's head turned in Neit's direction, and she exclaimed, "Neit! I was beginning to wonder if you'd been lost!"

"Just took a stroll," Neit said with as much cheer as she could muster, though her mood was vile. "Hoping for early berries."

A couple of kitchen servants laughed at that.

"Come see me out. I'd better ride, if I want to reach Riverbend by nightfall."

Leaf readily assented, question in her face. Neit paced beside her until they reached the courtyard. Making sure they couldn't be overheard, Neit lowered her voice to a whisper. "Do your people patrol up there in the woods?"

"Of course not," Leaf said. "Even when we were small, we couldn't get up there, not without the brambles shredding us, and for what? The kitchen staff is probably making all kinds of jokes about bellyaches and berries right now."

"Well someone is patrolling. If it's a patrol."

Leaf's brow furrowed. "What do you mean?"

"I mean that a whole lot of people have been moving down what looks like an old trail, which seems to bend eastward, away from Halivayir." Neit scowled down at the stones. "Ghost and the rest of his company scored out the brigands, right?"

"Oh, yes. Last summer. They and Fath Riders and we even had some Riders all the way from Lindeth come help, though they didn't find any lairs down this way. There aren't any caves this far south. All those were up north, west of Lake Arrowhead. They cleared them all out, even the deserted ones."

"And then they stopped patrolling, right?"

"I don't know that they ever patrolled. It was a dedicated search," Leaf said. "I was still recovering, but . . . why do you ask?"

Of course they don't patrol because Marlovans think of mountains as barriers. "Never mind. Leaf, don't say anything to anybody. If there's something sneaky going on, then whoever it is counting on surprise. But they're passing you by, and even if they can't see it, they have to know Halivayir Castle is right there. My thought is this, you get your captain here to start the spring with battle-alert games."

All the humor had drained from Leaf's face, along with most of her color. "Yes," she whispered.

Neit clapped her thin shoulder. "Remember, it might be nothing but a bunch of traders heading to market somewhere. Just because we never pay much attention to trees and woods doesn't mean Iascans and the like don't. I'm going to make a grass run to Ku Halir and report it. If they laugh at me, say it's some training mission, or a bunch of the wood guild doing a sweep for winter branches that fell, or however they collect their wood, it won't be the first time I've been laughed at. But I want someone to know."

They reached the stable. Neit was on horseback and trotting out the gate shortly after, leaving Leaf listening to the hoofbeat rhythm shift to a canter as she made her way back inside, her mind churning.

While Neit rode, Quill and the Winter Company climbed.

Quill recognized his surroundings now. As if the labor to breathe fully were not enough, the equipoise of elements had altered, water found only in fallen snow, or icy vapors. Climbing at the rear of the line, he noticed when items began to be discarded by the wayside as men tried to lighten their packs, almost always after a nearly vertical climb forcing them to crawl from rock to rock. An extra pair of boots. Another. Clothing. And one day, a spear; that night, Jethren marched two of his men up the trail, and angry voices echoed down, one rising, "I can't. I'm coughing up pink, and getting black things in my eyes."

Someone else went back down and returned with the spear.

The day after that, they lost a man. Quill didn't see it happen. He was bent forward, working on breathing as he climbed a very steep patch slick with runny mud when he heard a sudden scrabbling, a muffled voice, then a shriek that died away.

Quill, at the back, saw three of Jethren's men glance around warily, then up front toward someone out of sight. It was a deliberate yet furtive scan. Did they think that man was pushed? His blood chilled.

Stick Tyavayir snapped hoarsely, "Keep moving!"

The wind began rising, a merciless onslaught of ice-needles. Quill was not the only one hugging the rocky wall to the left, and avoiding looking down the edge of the cliff. When the path at last opened onto a slope covered by a thin layer of fresh snow, he breathed somewhat easier.

Connar stopped them at the other end of the slope, where long ago water had hollowed out an overhang marked with layers of ancient sediment. The sky overhead had begun to cloud up with dark gray towering clouds, greenish light glowing at the defined edges: thunder imminent.

They set firesticks at either end, but the wind blew the flames sideways and so they put them out to conserve the magic in the firesticks, which they had been using heavily. No one actually spoke, but there was a shared sense of dread of losing the magic entirely before their climb was finished.

As they passed chunks of travel bread to gnaw on, Quill was aware of some kind of argument going on among Jethren's men. Over the spears? There were sharp looks sent at the teenaged runner with the red hair, and Quill thought he heard someone mutter in coastal Iascan, "It wasn't Moonbeam. *You* pushed him, you little soul-sucker."

"I didn't!"

"Get away from me."

Quill didn't know any of them. They kept to themselves, so he avoided them when he could. He pulled on the Fox coat, which he'd only been wearing at night to sleep in, pressed his back into the stone, drawing his knees up to his chest, and watched the others through the thin space between his woolen hat and the two scarves he'd wrapped around his neck and lower face.

The red-haired youth's sullen voice cracked as he argued, until Jethren shot a look his way, and tipped his head toward his scar-faced first runner. "You need some time with Moonbeam?"

"Sorry. Sorry," the redhead muttered.

Quill turned his attention away, tucked his hands in around his gear bag, which was pressed between his thighs and his stomach, and laid his forehead on his knees.

He slept fitfully, waking to a startled, "Shit! He's *dead!*"

Quill looked up, his neck sending a pang down his spine; the redhaired youth sat at the extreme edge of the shallow overhang, where the wind had hit the hardest. He was very still: frozen to death.

Connar walked over, held his fingers to the boy's nose, then said tightly to Jethren, "That's two of yours." He walked out, clearly displeased.

Voices carried on the frigid air, a whisper, "Was it Moonbeam?"

"Naw. There wasn't a mark on him. You know Moonbeam always cuts them up."

Moonbeam sat on the other side of the overhang, a faint skritching sound rising as he methodically honed another knife, this one long, with a thin, wicked blade, his gaze a light, flat stare. At a gesture from Jethren, one of his other personal runners cut slices of half-frozen travel bread, which were passed out to be gnawed with grim determination.

When this brief, bleak breakfast ended, Jethren motioned his entire company out into the snow. The wind had stilled, revealing that aching blue sky, so pure, so merciless.

Jethren's company huddled together, vapor freezing and falling as they spoke, then they came back in a body. Nobody said anything about drill. The boy was laid out properly, his weapon in his frozen hands. Jethren did the Disappearance spell; Quill reflected that it would not have come to him if he'd been responsible for the boy's death. It seemed more like the redhead had separated from the others in a sulk, paying no heed to the icy wind.

His load was divided out. As they began to shoulder their burdens, Quill walked a little ways away, to where the snow was fresh with no footprints, and bent to stuff snow into both his flasks.

"What are you doing?"

Quill turned his head to see Stick Tyavayir standing warily nearby.

"Filling these with snow. Streams are going to be much rarer up here. I found that the headaches weren't as bad if I kept drinking, so I fill these with snow, then put them here." He opened his coat to indicate the side pocket at either hip. "The snow melts. Every time I drink, I try to refill it."

Stick walked away, shouting to his men, who obediently began to fill their flasks. Ghost's company did as well; Jethren's all looked toward him for orders. When he saw Connar bend down and pick up a handful of powdery white, he jerked his chin down, and his men began to stuff their flasks with snow.

They resettled their packs and started out.

Quill waited, then rounded the rock toward the curve that of the slope, halting suddenly when he came face to face with Connar, who stood waiting.

For?

Quill recollected that they were not men sharing a dangerous journey, but commander and runner, and brought his fist to his chest.

Nothing was visible of Connar's face except his eyes, the same blue as that overhead as he spoke, "Do you recognize this terrain?"

Quill looked out past Connar to a mighty slope stretching away westward. "I know where we are right now. But the upper slope can get confusing, especially if there's a storm. Also, streams are much rarer up here."

"Then you guide us." Connar handed Quill his much-folded map, then walked to the rear of the company. Quill silently paced past the line of scarved and hatted faces that had halted to watch.

At the front he paused to draw a deep breath, and he began to walk at the steady pace he'd developed at such pains the previous year. From behind Jethren glared at his company to match that pace, and so they proceeded.

At the same time, down in Ku Halir, Commander Sneeze Ventdor at Ku faced Neit across his desk.

He knew the Olavayir runner Neit as a young relation—her mother was his second cousin—though she'd been born around the time he left Nevree for good. When she brought dispatches from Olavayir, she was always willing to catch him up on news of his kin and old friends among the Riders.

Other than that they'd had little interaction, so he was surprised when she came into his command post, dripping rain from her cloak, and said, "I have a report to make. Firsthand. And I think . . ." She glanced around at the staff coming and going.

Ventdor set down the folded letter in Tanrid Olavayir's neat, square hand, and looked a question.

Neit said stolidly, "It's personal. Family news."

Ventdor's brows shot up. "Family? Everyone out." His hand took in everyone but his grizzled cousin Barend, now one of his most trusted captains. Everyone filed out and Barend put his back to the door.

Neit cast a sharp sigh. "When I stopped at Halivayir . . ."

Out came what she witnessed, in admirable scout-report style. If he wanted to hear what she surmised, he'd have to ask.

At the end, he frowned at her. "You didn't see anyone."

"No."

"Hoof prints?"

"None as far as I walked. I don't think you could get a horse in there. Branches too low, too many brambles."

Ventdor said, "That's much what I heard when we sent patrols through there after Tlennen Plains. Could it be villager traders? There are a few villages up there. Stick Tyavayir said they'd been preyed on by Yenvir's rats, but maybe they turn brigand by night?"

Neit turned up her palms. "All I can tell you is what I saw, and what Leaf Dorthad heard. She's never been one for fearful fancies," she added.

"No, not from what I hear." Ventdor remembered the tale of Leaf's defense, and her deliberate dive off the tower to what she'd intended to be her death. "Meaning no insult here, but could it be her brains got addled along with her eyes?"

Neit pressed her lips together, then acknowledged it was a fair question. Ventdor hadn't seen her. And what Leaf had said did sound odd. But. "I talked to her a while. She's no Cassad, talking to ghosts, if that's what you're thinking. As sane as they come."

"Damnation," Ventdor muttered, kicking over an unoffending stool. "I'm stretched as it is, holding all my lancers to reinforce Gannan at the pass soon's I get word. And every patroller I've got has been on duty, no leave, for

. . ." His gaze went distant, then he said, "Rat Noth. He rode out not a day ago. I'm surprised you didn't see him."

Neit had spotted Riders on the other side of a river, going the other way. "I think I did. I was riding too fast to stop."

"His orders are to cover everything west of us, right?" Barend Ventdor spoke for the first time, turning to the map covered with colored bits of clay.

Ventdor hummed under his breath, then said, "But surely he could spare one patrol to go over to Halivayir, which is right across from the river. I don't like not knowing what's there, right at our back. Yes. Tell Rat to see to it."

Neit clapped her hands onto her thighs. "Me? But I do have this letter for the Weaver Chief—"

Ventdor snorted. "Everybody knows those letters net a stiff reward from the gunvaer. My runners will be falling all over each other to take it to the royal city. Leave it here, I'll see to it."

Neit hated foregoing said reward—and the weekend of fun it would buy—but she knew Rat Noth would have questions only she could answer, and laid the letter on the desk.

"You'd better talk to Rat directly." Ventdor paralleled her thoughts. "Let's do everything right, thin as we're spread."

Neit exited in three swift strides.

Ventdor gazed at the map, murmuring to himself, "I wonder if they've reached Skytalon Peak yet . . . " He shut his eyes and counted up the weeks since Connar had departed, then turned to his cousin. "I think it's time to get that damn ram on its way to Wened, where it'll be just a couple days away when they need it."

"Ah, during the daylight? I remember it was brought in during the night." Barend said.

Ventdor waved a tired hand. "That was young Gannan, as I recall. Thinking the Adranis wouldn't notice. But we know there are spies all over the damn town. What's more, they know we know there are spies all over the damn town. We can't completely hide our movements, not something like that, anyway, but we don't have to make it easy on 'em. Take it out whenever you want. But anyone poking around, treat 'em as a spy," he finished on a grim note, then muttered, "Let's hope Rat Noth isn't out of reach."

Rat Noth was not. He had no reason to expect trouble. If he'd resented being ordered to patrol the quietest portion of the kingdom, there in the middle, he gave no sign of it. He made certain his patrols overlapped, and appointed rendezvous places so that he could always be found, riding in a huge circle that intersected the smaller circles of his patrols.

Neit found him two days outside of Ku Halir, camping alongside the river, where he had appointed a rendezvous with Pepper Marlovayir and his riding. Neit galloped into their camp just as the sun was sinking beyond the horizon. The Riders had gathered around a cook fire. Rat and Pepper

Marlovayir sat a few paces distant, playing a game of cards'n'shards on a flat rock as their first runners grilled fresh-caught fish.

Neit leaped off her horse, breathed in deeply, and exclaimed, "Heyo, that smells good!"

Pepper exclaimed, "Neit?"

Neit turned his way. The Marlovayir twins looked identical, tall, strong, hair (like hers) much the color and consistency of straw. "Salt? No." She remembered that Salt had a crooked tooth. "Pepper?"

"That's *Flight Captain* Pepper to you, runner." Pepper puffed out his chest.

Neit made a business of peering around. "I take it your command is invisible?"

"Ha. Ha. How's Floss?"

Before Neit could report that her brother was fine the last time she saw him, Rat cut in. "You're coming from the direction of Ku Halir. Is that accidental?"

"No." Neit's grin vanished, and she began giving a report as she rubbed her horse down.

Rat and Pepper pitched in to help, and when the mare was chomping peacefully at the picket line, Neit joined them around the campfire as the runners brought wooden camp bowls.

Neit finished describing what she'd seen behind Halivayir Castle, then pulled a knife from her sleeve and speared her fast-cooling fish.

Rat and Pepper were mulling her words. Rat said, "This is exactly the kind of thing I'm supposed to be looking for. Though on the other side of the river."

Neit said, "I thought about that as I was riding. Ventdor by rights should be investigating."

Rat stretched out his booted feet toward the fire. "I can think of two reasons he isn't. One, he's stretched thin." Nobody argued with that. "Two, he knows that Ku Halir is infested with spies. If there's something to be found, the less blabbing about it the better. Which is why I think I ought to go with you, Neit. Though I don't know the area at all."

Pepper set aside his plate. "But I know who does." His swift steps receded to the other camp, where the Riders sat chatting over their meal. He came back with a youth with jug-handle ears and rusty red hair. "This here is Wim. He grew up in Ku Halir—"

"Actually, in Alreth," Wim said in an apologetic tone. "It's a fishing village at the north end of the lake. I came down to Ku Halir to prentice when I was fifteen, but I didn't like trading in fish, so I volunteered at the garrison stable—well, what I mean is, I learned to ride, up and down the east side of the Spine."

"Spine?" The Marlovans said.

"It's what we call the hills north 'o the lake."

Rat, Pepper, and Neit considered that; they hadn't had a name for that wooded line of rocky hills, as to them it was a merely a border. Spines were in the middle of something.

Rat shook away the thought and gave Wim a speculative glance. "You know the area?"

"Favorite place to play around when I was a cub."

Rat turned to Pepper. "You stick with this area. Spread out." To Neit and Wim, "You, you, and me. We'll ride come sunup."

TWENTY-SEVEN

The Winter Company slowed as they neared the peak.

One evening one of Ghost Fath's men muttered something about going out to check the perimeter, though they were not posting guards. He got turned around, lost his way back, sat down on a boulder to rest his eyes, and that's where they found him the next morning, frozen stiff.

A day later, Stick Tyavayir's first runner, who had been coughing up pink froth, wandered out seeking clean snow with which to pack his flasks, but nothing looked clean enough with all those dark spots he was seeing . . . he vanished, never to be heard of again.

At the other end of a sudden, brutal storm that began with horizontal needles of ice and ended as a thick blizzard, as quickly gone, a third man slipped on ice and cracked his skull, possibly his neck; he was unconscious, breathing halfway through the night before that ceased.

The first, they sang over, breathless and hoarse, but after that with each the less was said, and the more warm clothing, never more to be needed, was claimed by those who did. Sometimes with shamed glances, for tradition was strong in how the dead were to be respected. Everyone knew the next could be themselves. But the determination to survive was stronger.

They reached the north end of the morvende geliath just ahead of a powerful storm that boiled up out of the west as the warm air currents from the far seas clashed with the cold of the mountains. Lightning struck the ground twice, to the left of them and nearer on the right, before Quill pointed at a slanting crevasse like a gash in the striated rock and shouted, "Here it is!"

There was no pretense at toughness as the exhausted Winter Company crowded in after him, nearly running one another over.

They shuffled a short distance and then almost as one dropped their packs and slumped to the stone floor, breathing hard.

Connar sat back against a stone wall as thunder reverberated through the stone with such power that tiny stones sifted from the rock curving overhead. They'd made it. Barely.

Then—he couldn't help himself—he swung his gaze at Quill, at the other end of the lines of slumped, weary men, straight and tall in that long, piratical black coat of his. Ghost had asked where he'd gotten it, and Quill had said, *Handed down in the family. For very cold weather.* Connar wondered, from whom?

Bitter laughter welled in Connar. At least the shit wasn't aware of the violent conflict inside Connar; anytime he looked at Quill he was aware of equal desires to slam him against the rough rock and kiss him until his lips bled—and to smash his fist into those teeth.

No doubt, if competition there was, Quill had won this one. Even Jethren looked destroyed.

Connar braced up, and raised his voice. "Let's move on."

Quill swung to his feet with no apparent effort, reached into his bag, and fetched out a firestick. As soon as the company had dragged themselves to their feet, the first runners, new and old, lit firesticks so that their commanders could see to walk over the uneven stone.

Quill led the way. It was so good to be back in this beautiful geliath again, especially without the pain of winter breathing. He hoped he might get a chance to sketch the rooms that in winter were too cold for his hand to hold chalk, even with gloves on.

The long walk sloped downward for the first time, then along reasonably flat tunnels and caves. They camped early, and—safe from weather—set up warm fires.

The runners in charge of cooking toasted the travel bread that was the only thing left of their food stores, except for a third of a wheel of cheese, which was doled out in such small slivers it was only there for taste. Though everyone was tired of travel bread, they were grateful not to be gnawing it half-frozen.

Connar let them sleep after the meal.

Quill was the first one awake. He looked around at the oblivious lumps burrowed into coats and scarves, and took his firestick to do a little exploring. When he returned, the company had roused, the air filled with the dank smell of wet wool, soon replaced by the odor of honey-laced travel bread being toasted. Socks and gloves lay drying over every stone as bare feet, covered with blisters in various states of healing, stretched toward the fire, and bleeding hands were rewrapped with fresh bandages.

The division between the men was apparent in the buckets. Most of the non-essentials had been tossed away along the trail. Fath's and Tyavayir's men shared one ensorcelled bucket for dipping those socks. Jethren's silent first runner had charge of their own bucket, which he never offered to share, nor did his captain insist. Even Jethren's men kept a respectful distance from Moonbeam.

Such small things, Quill thought as he walked softly among the groups. Refusing to talk, to share, could mean so very much in extreme situations.

"Eat as we proceed," Connar said once the last of the bread had been distributed.

Jethren snapped his fist to his chest, gave his men a hard glance, and they leaped up as one, hastily packing and dressing, their bread gripped between their teeth.

Stick and Ghost's men ignored them, except for a few mutters and rolled eyes as they put themselves together.

They formed in column by two, and Connar extended his hand outward, giving Quill a wry look.

Quill started walking.

Though breathing was still problematic, it was so much easier to walk in the more or less level stone corridors. Survival was no longer the entire focus; Stick's youngest runner caught up with Quill, and said, "These tunnels look carved in places."

"They are. We'll soon reach the actual geliath."

"What's that?"

"It's where the morvende live during different seasons. Or lived. It's difficult, at least for me, who knows so little, to tell whether they were here last year or a century or a millennia ago. They never leave anything when they move, except their art. Past these formations, you'll see one of their gathering chambers."

They entered a vast cavern, the entire ceiling painted a cobalt blue with tiny stars that still glittered with magical illumination.

"Why this cave and not that one back there?" someone down the line whispered.

"Don't you hear it?" Quill said. "How sound carries in here? The chambers they value most are those with echo qualities. They write music around those echoes." Quill readied himself to share his pleasure in the morvende and their amazing music and art—but his gaze caught on Manther Yvanavayir, pacing beside Ghost Fath, that chevron-shaped dark smudge still below his right shoulder pauldron.

Quill had feared that Manther would be the first to fall—that he might unconsciously or consciously throw away a life that seemed to have become meaningless—but Manther paced by Ghost's side, enduring with a silent, grim resolve. What's more, Stick's and Ghost's men still saluted him as a captain, unacknowledged by Manther, the tight lines in his profile revealing deep, smoldering anger.

Manther wasn't enduring, he was driven. To? The answer was obvious: vengeance against the man who had seduced his sister into unconscious betrayal, which in turn had destroyed his family, one of the oldest and proudest in the kingdom.

Quill looked around, evaluating the others, and saw no interest, no appreciation. Except for the curiosity of the young runner, their thoughts were about as far from music and art as possible. He swallowed the words he'd been preparing, and mentally revised their path. He'd intended to lead them through the cavern with the hanging rocks that looked like lace, and the nearly spherical chamber made entirely of blue and violet crystal, as well as a couple of the better painted caves.

Instead took them in as straight a line as he could. They ate when hungry and slept when needed. Since he dared not keep track of the passing of days by writing to Lineas, he counted meals. So it was eight suppers later when they proceeded up a rise, toward great shafts of light.

They emerged into a morning as pure as if the world were new-made. The sun shone, warm and benevolent as Quill said, "Down toward that way you can easily spot East Tower. Go along this path to the right here, and you'll see West Tower below the next slope. I suggest keeping low. I don't know if the tower sentries look this way with field glasses. I always assumed they did."

Connar lifted a hand. "Jethren. Over to you."

Keth Jethren flashed a grin of ferocious joy. "I'm going out to reconnoiter." And to his men, "Today is liberty. Tonight we move."

He slipped out, then bent over, making certain not to create a silhouette that could be seen from below, and vanished among the rocks.

Connar jerked his head, and everyone withdrew back down the tunnel, the two groups separating off to rest or poke around. No one was calling for hard drill; breathing was still a matter of conscious thought.

Connar's attention was on the crevasse leading to the pass overlook, and no one else was paying Quill any attention.

He slipped away to locate one of the morvende chambers and check his notecase. The upper reaches of morvende caverns were chosen for the angle of the sun at certain times of the year, suffusing the glittering, striated rock with radiance. He'd been trying to guess which season this geliath had been used for, and remembered a chamber above a mighty waterfall, with an unimpeded view westward over the land below.

It wasn't that far off. He glanced at the map, oriented himself, then found his way to a cavern with the archway carved in trefoil out of a great slab of rock fallen from some impossible height no long extant. Words had been carved across the arch's peak in Ancient Sartoran. The archway opened to the air overlooking the west, now caparisoned in the verdure of ripening spring, the distant sky wreathed in wisps of white vapor. Seen from so vast an elevation, the beauty was both detached and exalting.

If the top portion of the trefoil framed the summer sunset, this would argue for a summer geliath. It was too early to test his theory, and anyway the season was not summer. Still, Quill stood in this peaceful place, taking his notecase out as he wondered if on a clear day one could gaze all the way to the sea.

He found three notes, covered with tiny writing: one from Lineas, one from Camerend, and one from Vanadei.

From Lineas:

Darling Senrid—Quill—you must tell me which you prefer. I confess that hearing the warmth and color in the voices of both your parents when they say 'Senrid' so matches what lies in my heart that I have gone back to thinking of you by the name that first enchanted me when I was twelve. But your wishes are of course foremost.

Here I am, rambling down a side trail even though time presses. I wanted this moment for you and me (because I write these seeing you with me) before I must bring in the world.

There is news, and I must carry it: Jarend-Jarl of Olavayir, the king's brother, died in his sleep. The king and queen are both grieving, for they loved this jarl most of the rest of us never met, but about whom no one else said anything that wasn't praise for his kindness and his love of peace.

Because the news must go out, along with all else, though the academy and the queen's training are to begin next week, it is my turn to ride. Mnar is sending me to Commander Ventdor. Ku Halir is not that far, and anyway me the queen was specific in requesting me. The gunvaer said that the Commander and his cousin, Captain Ventdor, will want the news spoken and in a compassionate way, and she trusts me to carry that out.

So as soon as I write to you, I will be riding out. Seeing the gunvaer's grief causes me to cherish you the—

The crunch of gravel from the stone corridor on the other side of the chamber caused Quill to crush notes and notecase inside his robe. He clasped his hands behind his back, gazing through the archway to the distant plains as the steps entered, slowed, and then:

"What does that say?"

Quill had expected Fish Pereth. At the sound of Connar's voice he turned sharply, gravel skittering under his boots, and suppressed the urge to check that the notecase was safely hidden.

Connar sauntered in from the back entrance, his attention apparently on the words carved in Ancient Sartoran. Quill made an effort to still the hammering of his heartbeat as he became aware that Connar was alone for once, without his mantle of captains and runners trailing behind him.

Quill cleared his throat. "It says *And yet the greatest gifts are those from the world that is invisible.*"

Connar turned slowly, scanning the chamber. "Strut." He gave a snort of contempt, breath clouding. "As expected."

"Strut?" Quill asked, more curious to see if Connar would answer than in anything he might say.

Connar flung a derisive look back. "What else would you call it? Pomposity? Superiority?"

"I see an invitation, but I know the context. I once had to write it out fifty times as a correction. It's from what they used to call the pursuit of the dichotomies, among which was the interplay between the physical world and that of the spirit."

When Connar made no answer to that, Quill put his hands behind his back and took up recitation stance. "*Love is the only passion that requires another. At its most powerful, rapture obliterates past and future, creating that pinnacle at which time ceases to exist, and the self is erased. The lover of beauty sees it everywhere; the lover of civilization overlooks the petty and timorous to cultivate the virtues that each might possess.* There's more."

When Connar did not ask to hear it, Quill raised a hand toward the archway. "Whoever designed it probably wanted to invite one to think about these things while looking out. I suspect," he added, "this chamber was a chamber of reflection. Or what we'd call a lockup."

Connar uttered a crack of laughter. "So they weren't perfect."

"They never claimed to be."

Connar had moved to the other end, where the stone had been smoothed, as if once furnishings had been placed there; he wondered if it was a weapons rack. He glanced over his shoulder. "Much more surprising, royal runners got into trouble! What did you do, drop a book? Forget to cap the ink?"

Quill knew he was being baited, but not why. There was no chance Connar had seen the notecase. The prince's moods were difficult to discern, but suspicion was not present. Quill had seen Connar suspicious. This mood, whatever the case, was not that. "I ruined a batch of paper—at the mould and deckle stage—because I wanted to get down to the mess hall before the fizz gave out."

"What's mould and deckle?"

"The frame for making the sheets of paper. Before that a lot of work goes into it. A lot of work," Quill added under his breath, remembering having to clean up the mess and prepare it again on his own. After the writing assignment, which was intended to give his ten-year-old mind something to work on besides resentment.

"So that's the sort of thing they teach you up on the third floor." Connar dropped onto a boulder, one foot propped on a smaller rock, the other stretched out before him, the knife hilts at the top of his high black boots winking coldly in the pale light. He leaned his forearm on his knee, assuming a posture of one ready to be entertained.

Connar had only spoken to Quill once during the entire journey to the summit; now, here he was, alone, and talking.

"We make our own paper, yes." And Quill thought that if he was to serve as today's entertainment, he might as well get some use out of it and make one more try to talk Connar out of his bloody intent.

But Connar forestalled him. "Have you ever considered that, if you go back far enough, you're the heir to the throne?"

Quill snorted a surprised laugh, remembering that Thias Elsarion had brought up the same subject. But Quill wasn't willing to draw any conclusion from that except that Connar knew his Marlovan history. "No."

"No?" Connar's brows lifted in disbelief.

"Well, I learned early that people in Darchelde cannot go beyond our borders, and they told us why, though the events seemed impossibly distant to us when small. I do recollect seeing our name for the first time when I was reading a history of our early days. I've a vague memory of being glad of my escape, considering the bloody ends of so many subsequent princes, or those who claimed to be princes, or those who wanted to make princes out of descendants of kings."

"So you're content to make paper." Still in that tone of disbelief.

Camerend had taught Quill to figure out the assumptions behind a question or statement, and to address those if possible, as a way of reaching understanding the quicker—or at least circumventing an argument. The danger was, of course, acting on the wrong assumptions.

Let's go back to what I want to talk about. "Well, that's a very small part of what I do. In any case, I haven't the temperament for thrones. I would far rather be mashing pulp than leading a war that will bring a lot of destruction but very little gain."

Connar sat back, hands propped on his knees, a pose of ease belied by the tension in his shoulders. For a heartbeat Quill missed his knives, sitting at the bottom of his gear bag, an instinctive response that, once his reached consciousness, startled him. There was no reason for Connar to attack him. Nor was he threatening as he sat there, consciously breathing deeply, as they all had to do at this altitude.

Then Connar tapped his forehead. "The gain is here." His hand dropped to his knee. "You didn't stand before the jarls and promise justice for two families completely wiped out."

"True. I did not."

"Justice, not revenge," Connar said, even more softly. "You know Elsarion walked away from Tlennen Field. He'll be back as soon as he can."

"Perhaps," Quill responded, just as calmly. "But if he does, he can't win."

Connar's lip curled. "So you are a military expert, then?"

"No. But you are." Quill opened his hands. "You will never be caught by surprise again."

"Let me give you your first lesson in military strategy. You take the war to the enemy if you possibly can."

Before Quill could say *Then you wait at the mouth of the pass and catch him if he's mad enough to try,* Connar swung to his feet and sauntered out, leaving Quill looking after him in disgust. There are few things more unshakable than self-righteousness, he was thinking—and then he had to laugh, because he knew he had the same tendency. He had certainly written enough self-reflection essays, growing up under Camerend's eye.

Connar made his way back to the others, veering between amusement and irritation. Talking to Quill was like sliding over ice. Impossible to see the below the surface.

Stick Tyavayir broke off what he was saying to one of the scouts and looked his way. "What?"

"Nothing. Nothing at all."

Three mud-splashed figures trotted into Ku Halir from different directions. Pepper Marlovayir went to the mess hall to see what he could scrounge, while saying cheerfully to anyone who asked, "Nah, no news that I've heard. What's new here?"

Rat Noth, aware that he was recognized, trusted to his slow approach to cover the fact that he had urgent news both vital and bad.

Neit was the third, riding in behind a pair of young women driving a cart full of pottery. They chattered in Iascan, she asking how business was, and what kind of paint gave that effect like a rainbow on those drinking dishes, and when they asked what it was like to be a runner, she said it was fun, especially if people got good news and tipped her. "And if they aren't in any hurry to send me back," she said with a grin. "Which hothouse do you recommend?"

They parted amicably, and she led her horse into the castle stable, suppressing the urge to run. Spies everywhere, she reminded herself, a weird thought that intensified a crazy impulse to laugh. She was too tired, that was it, and worried, and shocked, but at the same time, aware of a deep . . . call it appreciation for Rat Noth. In whom, after days of crawling through mud, sleeping, and eating side by side, she sensed a similar . . . appreciation. But no intent. She knew when a man was about to ask, or wanted to be asked, and he never did: she suspected he was loyal to someone else. And so she let herself enjoy the appreciation, a shaft of sunlight in an otherwise vile, filthy midden of a situation.

She made her way toward the command center—and was intercepted by Captain Barend Ventdor, looking haggard.

"His own quarters," the captain stated, and immediately turned away.

Neit took the servants' passageway to the wing where the officers were housed. The commander's quarters weren't much larger than any other room, but he didn't have to share.

She found Rat, Pepper Marlovayir, the young, jug-eared scout Wim, and Braids sitting with the commander, who looked tired. He looked *old.* "They've attacked already?" she asked quickly.

Ventdor looked up sharply at that. "What?"

Rat turned to the commander. "We'll get there. Let me finish briefing Senelaec here."

Braids's characteristic grin was gone, rendering him almost unrecognizable, as Neit had the odd experience of hearing her own words about Halivayir succinctly repeated.

Then Rat opened his palm toward the commander, who was staring down at his empty hands. "Commander Ventdor sent Neit straight to us." He turned his thumb between himself and Pepper. "Wim here is part of Marlovayir's riding. He knows this area, as I said before." He paused, wondering how much he should describe of the arduous, sometimes painful search through brambles and rocky, slippery hillsides down to the lowland marsh north of the lake.

None of it. He told himself to get to what mattered. "Commander, here's where you come in. We found an army gathered north of the lake. They're squatting in the marshland. Waiting."

Commander Ventdor's head jerked up at that, and Neit's nerves chilled when she recognized grief only as it changed to intent. "How many, and who are they?"

"Bar Regren," Neit said. "One night we got close. I recognized Bar Regren words."

"And I estimated three battalions, maybe more." Rat turned to Braids. "That's when I sent Baudan to summon you in secret."

"Shit." Braids' blue eyes rounded. "What are they doing all the way down here? Aren't Bar Regren what they call the mountain people up around the Nob?"

" . . . trade city," Wim said, low-voiced.

Braids eyed him. "What?"

Ventdor stated flatly, "You live closest, you should know that Ku Halir is the richest trade town in the north besides Lindeth."

Braids reddened. "Never thought much about it."

Neit sent a worried look at the commander. "But the traders and merchants do. Everybody coming from the east stops here before going west, and everybody from Larkadhe clear down to the royal city, and even more south, comes this way before heading for the pass to Anaeran Adrani."

"Bar Regren used to try to take it every generation or so. They were coming at the Iascans once again right around the time the Marlovans came galloping down from the north," Wim spoke up; though intimidated by all the chevrons around him, this was his territory. "Marlovans drove them off once and for all and built the first castle here. That's what my da said. Uh, it was an outpost then."

The others knew that much of Ku Halir's history, as they all had been alive when the king gave the orders to turn Ku Halir's old outpost into a garrison. Everyone knew someone who had come to Ku Halir to work.

Rat leaned forward. "So we decided we'd better come in soft. Separate. We know there are spies all over town, and maybe even in this castle. Elsarion's, who knows what else."

"Running in and out of my office, sure as horses shit," Ventdor said, still in that flat voice, with a tremor beneath it. "Short of dosing every living one of 'em with kinthus, which is impossible, we have to meet like this until the king decides what, if anything, to do."

Braids sent a suspicious look Wim's way.

"Rein up, Braids," Rat said sharply. "If he was running both sides he could've betrayed me'n Neit to them any time, and no one would have known. He's the one found 'em squatting out there, where we probably would have wandered around lost until they jumped us. Soon's this is done, I'll recommend him for promotion." He said this last to Ventdor, who turned up his palm in approval.

Braids turned to Wim and said contritely, "Sorry. It's just, hearing this, I don't know what to think. Or whom to trust. So they're waiting for what?"

Neit leaned forward. "Let's go back to the spies. Everybody knows the army is taking the war back to the pass."

Ventdor said, "Right. The entire town seems to know the lancers will be riding out as reinforcements as soon as we get word. The boys have reported questions from hothouse girls and inn workers like, *When are you riding?* And *What's the news from the pass?*"

Rat made a spitting motion to the side. "If it was me, and I wanted to bag me a castle town, I'd wait until the lancers rode out, and the defense was spread thinnest. Connar's got all the western plains patrolled within a day's sight of each other. And the east. I didn't think about it until Wim took me and Neit back that way, but none of us patrol what the locals call the Spine the way we do the plains. We've ignored those hills and marshes since routing out the brigands."

"Not horse country," Neit said.

Ventdor pressed his fingers against his temples, his eyes closed. "I have orders about the lancers. There's no getting around that. There's also no getting around the fact that we'll be on watch-and-watch here after they ride out, we're spread so thin."

"Then it's up to us, is that what you're saying?" Braids looked appalled. "My orders were clear, to hold . . ." He gazed into the distance, brow wrinkled.

"Hold the east to Ku Halir," Rat said to Braids. "We all got similar orders, I'm holding the midlands, including Ku Halir, and Olavayir and Lindeth west. Watch and hold. Capture spies, limit movement. Any trouble, bottle it for when Connar brings everyone back. Except this army out there in the marsh, when they come out, they won't be bottled because they outnumber everybody I've got as well as those you've got—and mine are spread from the upper river to Hesea Spring."

"Mine are just as spread." Braids looked grim. "I can send someone home to Senelaec, and raise everybody there. Though we aren't *near* three battalions." He sidled a glance Pepper Marlovayir's way, as if expecting some sort of insult.

Pepper intercepted that hairy eyeball, noted the commander's tight mouth, and swallowed the crack he'd been about to air. "It's too far to send someone to Marlovayir. What about over at Tlen? How many have you got there, Senelaec?"

"*I* don't have anyone! They're all riding the east. Henad Tlennen's company is divided between running as skirmishers for Cabbage Gannan and scouting the environs of the pass. I'm not about to ask her for anyone, as they're first line. Rooster commands at Tlen, and we've all been stealing so many from him he's down to watch-and-watch." Braids scowled, rapping his knuckles gently on the table in one of the galloping drum beats.

Rat put fists on his knees. "Commander. You sent us to investigate, and we've come back with a completely different strategic situation than was here when Connar left."

Neit's gaze shifted between these tough commanders stating the obvious, and wondered what was not being said.

"Three times," Braids said slowly, "I was told to hold Ku Halir. Connar would deal with problems on his return. If I report what's going on to Amble Sindan and he convinces the jarls of the Eastern Alliance to rise, that's not holding, that's taking action."

Neit's neck gripped. The context was Connar. They weren't planning the defense yet. They were more worried about what would happen if they broke orders.

Ventdor sighed. "Sorry. Sorry. Too much too soon . . . look, boys. Defending Ku Halir *is* holding it. There's not much I can do, except remind you that I'm above you all in the chain of command. I know you all want to honor your orders, especially those given by a new and eager commander in chief. And we have to remember that he put you two—both proved captains—here to a purpose. I think it likely he foresaw some kind of attack once his back was turned."

Rat's brows shot up, and Braids whistled. "Oh. I didn't think of that."

"Right," said Rat. "Right, right, right. That's why we're not in that pass right now. He knows if he tells us to hold something, we'll hold it."

Neit watched the relief in Rat's and Braids' faces harden to determination.

Pepper Marlovayir spoke up. "I know exactly where the rest of my flight is. I can have everyone back here by the end of the week, if we ride hard. Ten days outside. But that's less than thirty. Senelaec, can you get to old Amble

Sindan and back in time, and how many do you think the Eastern Alliance can raise?"

"I've already got most of them patrolling." Braids frowned into the air. "Connar counted on that when he gave me the entire east. But we can pull in whatever we find in, say, a four days' ride . . .Three? Two? How long do we have?"

Rat opened his sword-callused hand. "Wim, how long do you think it'll take them to march around the lake, especially if they want to take us by surprise?"

"Going at night, especially coming into waning moon nights, seven, maybe ten days," Wim said. "It'll be slow going, all those inlets. The marsh."

Rat turned up his palm. "If we can get that, I'll be able to pull together a wing to stiffen what we get from Senelaec. The rest of my command will stay west of the river, as ordered. Altogether that isn't three battalions, but it's the best we can do."

"Do you want me to make a run to Olavayir?" Neit offered, knowing it was a long reach.

"Nobody can get there and back in time," Pepper stated. "Marlovayir is closer. I can send someone home, in case anyone's near the eastern border of our land."

Rat turned to Neit. "You stick with Wim here. Help watch those shits squatting in the marsh. When they rise, we have to know."

Neit said, "I can do that. But heyo, I do wish Lineas were here."

Ventdor's head jerked up. "Lineas? The freckled redhead of Connar's?"

Neit said, "Royal runner Lineas. While I was attached to Nadran-Sierlaef at Larkadhe, it was Lineas who learned Bar Regren so she could talk to the prisoners when he had to sit in judgment."

"But she's here." Ventdor jerked his thumb toward the stable, and the runner chambers over it. "Probably asleep. She rode hard to bring news . . ." His voice trembled as he met Neit's gaze. "Cousin-niece, she came to say that Jarend-Jarl is dead."

Neit gasped as if an invisible fist had punched her in the heart.

Rat, Braids, and Wim, none of whom knew the former jarl except by reputation, looked uncomfortable in the way people do before vast and sudden grief they don't really share.

Rat said, "How about I find this Lineas, and pull her up here?"

"Do that." Ventdor's voice was a husky whisper as Neit turned away, her shoulders shaking in silent sobs.

TWENTY-EIGHT

Skytalon Peak vanished in a roiling fog that flashed violently with green light followed by thunder so loud it brought powdery stone sifting from the dark reaches of the caverns overhead.

Captain Jethren's men had gone out, to come running back when lightning exploded near them, killing one and burning the other down one side. They managed to get him inside, but he sank down, stiff and unseeing, unhearing.

Jethren left him there and rapped out orders to the rest until they were lined up, spears and gear in hand, ready to go out the moment the storm passed. Jethren waited a pace or two inside the crevasse that opened onto the slope overlooking the pass, his silhouette lit with flickering blue-green.

Ghost and Stick exchanged glances, each understanding the other: Jethren had orders, and this lightning-struck man couldn't carry them out. For whatever reason the Olavayir captain was not going to ask for help.

Stick's new first runner hovered uncertainly, but Ghost's, after a glance at him, bent down, and they covered the man with his own bedroll, and tried to get some listersteep down his throat. He stirred, then opened his eyes, looking bewildered, pushing their hands away.

Ghost's first runner offered him the salve they'd been using. Seeing him taken care of, Quill withdrew farther inside, away from the noise, and settled down to sleep.

He woke abruptly, aware of quiet. He rose, drank some water, and got to his feet. Firesticks had been set along the tunnel at intervals, burning low enough to preserve their magic, but to permit them to see where they were going. None had been lit anywhere near the crevasse, lest even that faint light somehow be made out from the towers below.

Quill felt his way along, until he saw a figure silhouetted against the starlight outside the crevasse. Jethren and his men were gone; Connar stood there at the entrance, gazing out.

Quill knew he would not be watching the sky. He turned away, but before he could take a step, Connar said, "Orders."

Quill halted. Did Connar think he was one of his captains?

Connar said in that amused voice, "I recognized your step. First, is there a faster way down to West Outpost than the pass?"

"No," Quill said. "The three paths I found are too treacherous. They'd take at least twice as long."

"Figured as much. Once we descend, stay to the rear."

"As you wish."

Connar didn't move, or even turn his head, so Quill retreated.

He forced down a few bites of travel bread, then paced off to one of the inner chambers, one he was fairly certain none of the others would find, at least without him hearing their approach. Here he set up a tiny flame, just enough to write by, opened his notecase—and there was nothing from Lineas.

He sat back, breathing against the sharpness of disappointment. Of course she was still riding, perhaps in company with someone other than royal runners. He remembered the long silences she'd had to endure from him the year before, and let remorse chase out the disappointment.

He took out a slip of paper and wrote:

Lineas: We're above the pass. Whatever is going to happen will commence at sunrise, I suspect.

He hesitated. There was so very much more to say. But in person. So he finished, *I long to see your face, and hold you in my arms.*

And sent it.

He wrote Camerend a hasty report, replaced his notecase inside his shirt, and began to make his way back.

He hadn't gone twenty paces when Fish Pereth appeared around one of the natural columns, breathing hard. "There you are." The words were not quite a question, but carried a tone of accusation.

"I was doing some last exploring." Quill lifted a hand toward the carvings of twined leaves overhead, and spoke only truth, "We studied geliaths, but we rarely get a chance to see them. They'll be asking me all kinds of questions when we get back to the royal city."

"That's what I thought," Fish said with resignation, and Quill wondered if Fish had been detailed to watch him. But Fish said nothing, as always, and they returned to the others.

Connar was nowhere in sight; Jethren and his company were also gone. Quill turned toward his gear. He might as well catch some rest before whatever was to happen next.

A hand caught his arm.

He turned to find Stick Tyavayir there, Ghost at his shoulder. The flickering light from the firesticks played over their faces, emphasizing the sharpness of their bones, the contours planed by the arduous journey.

"Thank you for bringing us here alive." Ghost brushed his fingers over his chest in a salute, his pale hair dangling unkempt over his shoulder.

Quill saluted back, and the two walked away.

Quill tried to find a less awkward position on the ungiving stone, shut his eyes—and slid into slumber.

He woke at a shout, "Come see! Come on!"

Quill followed the others as they streamed out of the great crack opening above the pass, no one paying the least heed to being seen, though the air was clear, the sun resting above the eastern peaks. It was too late for those below to do anything about it.

One of Ghost's younger runners whooped in amazement, pointing up the slope behind the crevasse. Quill turned his head, shading his eyes from the glare of the sun, to see Jethren's men working with levers under massive boulders. These were those long spears that Jethren's men had brought up the trail, now held together by metal bands to strengthen them.

Quill could see that Jethren's men had excavated three massive boulders, each roughly the size of a cottage. As the company crowded around the ledge outside the crevasse, the first rock teetered, sending small stones tumbling down the slope maybe sixty paces to the east.

A man howled wordlessly, at the pitch of exhilaration.

Thud! Kadump. The boulder hit the ground, jarring the watchers to the teeth.

Cr-r-rack!

The boulder struck a pillar of rock, and stopped. Many of the watchers let out disappointed howls, then shouted as black lines spidered through the pillar.

It exploded beneath the weight of the boulder, force shooting shards everywhere as the boulder teetered and began once more to tumble.

CRASH! Each time the rock hit the ground, it shook rubble into following it as it picked up speed. It leaped up and spun in the air, then smashed down again in a mad clatter of stone chips. Then it plunged past the tower, sending a spray of rocks racketing off the stone wall, as the boulder plummeted down the sheer cliff, cleared the narrow access road—upturned pale faces could be made out as it flew overhead—and then crashed into the pass. A second boulder even larger followed, from some thirty paces farther off, and a third.

A shout from the other direction caused everyone to whirl around. Jethren had divided his men into teams, half to each tower. Those above the western tower loosed their avalanche. The ground trembled beneath the watchers' feet as mighty rock splintered, causing a crag to break apart, rumbling downward. The ground cracked and an entire cliff shifted, at first slowly, slowly. It began to break apart, picking up speed, a brown and gray river of massive stone thundering straight for the west tower.

Tiny figures froze on the top. Quill turned away, hoping they had transfer tokens, but unable to look; he could take his part in a fight, but watching someone helpless in the path of disaster sickened him. A scream of laughter an arm's length from his left barely reached his ear, as distant as a gull's cry. He shifted his gaze as rockfall led by a vast slate monolith struck the east tower, smashing it in an explosion shards a heartbeat before the avalanche swept it all away.

Quill shut his eyes as the landslide roared on and on, shaking the ground. The tumult reached an ear-shattering pitch and the company stared, or screamed, or danced about in a frenzy as the two towers were swept entirely away. The landslides met in one great cataclysm, quaking the entire mountain, and sending a geyser of dust shooting skyward.

What goes up must come down.

"Get back, get back," Quill shouted, but no one heard him, or they were too shocked to listen. He ducked into the crevasse moments before a rain of sharp stones descended.

Shouts. Curses. Ghost's and Stick's men crowded back inside the tunnel to escape, but some were already bleeding from nicks and cuts. Jethren's men had thrown themselves flat onto the ground on the slope above.

Quill looked toward the entrance, to see Connar with his hands braced at either side on the stone of the crevasse as he laughed.

Connar had read over and over in the Inda papers Hauth had given him a second-generation account of the dust cloud over Andahi at the start of the Venn invasion. He had chosen Jethren to figure out a way to accomplish a landslide big enough to signal Cabbage Gannan to commence his attack, and to unnerve West Outpost because so far, Jethren had obeyed orders without a word. And without repeating that fist to the heart, salute to a king. But Connar still remembered it, vividly. And so he pushed Jethren as hard as he could, not certain if he wanted him to prove trustworthy, or to retreat to Olavayir in a sulk.

The second would be so much easier.

Their great gouge into the southern face of Mt. Skytalon succeeded beyond their expectations. The dust pall hung in the sky, golden against the sere blue. Elated by their success, Jethren was determined to be the first to the floor of the pass.

Though it was insanely dangerous, he drove his company down the unstable landslide, as far to the west, at the mouth of the pass, those in West Outpost and their besiegers watched the light brown cloud high in the air. Some later swore they had been woken by a deep abyssal *boom* that had reverberated through the castle foundations.

The castle defenders had no idea what that cloud portended—other than trouble—but Cabbage Gannan and Henad Tlennen knew this had to be the promised sign. Henad turned to her fastest scout. "Get to Wened and alert the relay."

Three hard days of riding later, the last person in the relay reached Ku Halir, her horse in a lather.

And so, at noon on a summery day, the horns blared from the garrison walls, the great eagle banner rose, and two by two the lancers rode out, weapons held at the correct slant, swords and shields glittering in the strong light.

Ventdor watched from the courtyard until the last Rider was through the gate, then his eye caught on a jug-eared stable hand standing nearby with a saddled horse. Ventdor's chin came down minutely, and Wim climbed into the saddle.

He rode out the opposite gate at a slow walk; when he had cleared the west end of town, out of sight of the last inn, he whistled to the horse, bent low, and rode like the wind to report to Braids.

That same morning, Connar and the rest of the Winter Company made it down to the pass to discover a tumble of pale stone and old dirt piled up in a fifty-pace high berm smashed up against the thousand-pace sheer cliffs on the other side of the pass. Atop the rubble Jethren stood balanced on the shattered remains of a cart, one boot propped on a wheel, the morning sun making a nimbus of his tousled blond hair.

Baskets, boxes, and sacks had been lined neatly beside him. He slid, catching himself, and sent a fresh pile of pebbles bouncing down the berm. He fetched up before Connar and struck his fist smartly against his chest.

"What's this?" Connar asked as he worked his way over the loose soil.

"We caught ourselves a caravan." Jethren grinned. "They escaped the avalanche, just to meet *us*."

One of his younger Riders gave a crow of laughter.

"Did anyone see you? Get away to warn them below?"

"No. Made sure of that. We let the two oxen go—they're useless—but we've three horses." Jethren tipped his head over his shoulder, to where his silent, pale-haired, silent first runner held the horses by their reins.

"Where are the traders?"

"Dead." It was no brag. Killing a gaggle of carters who hadn't offered even a vestige of a fight was merely a matter of report. Certainly no triumph, but the careless indifference in the man's voice and face spiked a jolt of hatred through Quill, who stood a few paces behind Fish. Quill wondered if he knew the carters.

Sick with disgust, he tried to breathe out his reaction as Connar looked over the booty, fists on his hips. "What's this stuff? Not the supply train."

"Shian says these colored rolls are silk."

Connar remembered seeing silk, a shiny fabric, at Lindeth. "No use to us," Connar said, peering westward. The landslide seemed to have filled the pass, but he glimpsed what had to be the old road beyond it. It was still difficult to breathe, though less so, and from now on it was all downhill.

From here on in they would drill again, he decided. But after they ate.

Jethren spoke up. "Silk might be no use, but their stores are." Jethren pointed to the baskets. "There's greens. Oats. Jugs of various sorts. Eggs, even."

Better and better. Connar swept his gaze around the waiting men as they stood at attention, waiting for him to speak. It seemed Jethren had lost two more on his descent, but he saw no regret in the man's face—he was waiting for praise. And from the twin looks of reserve in Stick's and Ghost's faces, they were as aware as Connar that Jethren was shouldering his way into the inner circle.

Connar didn't quite trust Jethren yet, but he could use him. And letting them all compete for his attention meant everyone would work harder. "Well done," he said. "You did everything I asked."

Jethren flushed, but before he could speak, Connar turned to Ghost. "Call everyone together. Quill!"

"Here." The royal runner appeared behind the lightning-burned man, who was leaning on a stick.

"How far to the castle from here?"

Quill's eyes narrowed. "This is the easiest and fastest part of the southern pass. If the weather doesn't hold us up, we could be there in a week. But we'll need to watch out for traps. I can't be sure I got them all marked on the map."

Connar smiled at the remains of Winter Company. Fewer than a hundred men, and three untrained horses. Cabbage Gannan had better have kept his end of the plan. "Jethren, send scouts ahead to find and spring the traps. The rest of us will get a meal, and then move out. We have West Outpost to surprise."

The defenders of West Outpost had felt all the shock Connar could have wished, early in spring when dawn revealed that long line of silhouettes sitting astride their horses just out of reach of their arrows.

The Marlovans galloped up, shields high against defensive arrows and shot every wall sentry who didn't have a shield up. The Adranis' own sharpshooters had practiced against the butts at considerable distances, but couldn't get a draw on galloping enemies, and wasted a great many of their own arrows—with no new wood to be had.

Their commanders bawled and cursed everyone too slow to figure out that making targets of themselves was deadly, and after that, the swooping runs resulted in fewer deaths atop the walls and the lookout towers. The Marlovans were still out there watching, shooting the moment they saw something to shoot at—and every so often loosing a lethal rain of arrows over the wall into the courts.

The defenders kept shields lined against the walls inside the courts; orders were passed down to hold one overhead when passing to and fro. The number of dead and wounded dropped to one a day, then none.

Terror had turned to derision. There were those who liked to stand below the castellations and shout insults in what they were told was Marlovan. But scorn didn't quite settle into complacency: three times they tried sending people out in the worst hours of the night, under the cover of terrible weather, to gather those spent arrows. Nobody returned.

Then there was the steady diminishing of their stores. At least, they reassured one another day after day, night after night, as the hours were broken by the sinister drumbeat of those galloping hooves, the Marlovan horses couldn't really fly. There was no way for them to get into the pass. They hadn't even attempted the gate.

Warm days arrived, then the occasional hot day under the cloudless sky, heralding the dry heat of summer soon to come. There was still plenty of water running down from the heights, captured in barrels against the dry months, but the supply caravan had yet to appear.

Moods lightened when a rider came down the pass to report that the snows had melted off the heights at last, and travelers should start coming through. The supply caravan was always first let through at the other end, though oxen being much slower than horses, it was never the first down to the west end. Still, the news that the pass was clear meant supplies were on the way.

Then came the day they felt more than heard the shivering of the fortress, and the rock beneath them. And the next morning, the eastern sun was obscured by a weird golden cloud.

Three days after that cloud formed above distant Skytalon, two more riders arrived, both with stories of quakes and rocks raining down, but they didn't know any more than that. The top of the pass had been fine, if muddy, when they rode through, and yes, they both passed the supply train—twelve wagons in all.

A few days after the weird cloud dissipated, morning light revealed the sight the captains had feared: a roofed caravan bringing their own battering ram, cut illegally out of timber from the northern mountains and reinforced by iron.

So much for the claim that the Marlovan barbarians were too stupid to know what to do with one. Covered with overlapping shields, the ram was safe from both arrows and fire.

The first thud happened late the next night. The defenders' own lanterns and torches kept them from seeing the figures down below. When they tried dropping oil-wrapped brands, those were immediately extinguished by furtive figures. The best shooters nailed two of the shadowy enemies, but missed the rest, as the ram began its rhythmic BOOM, swinging back and forth in its cradle of chains.

"I alerted West Tower when the ram was first sighted," the commander admitted to his captains as they met in his quarters. I've received nothing back. This morning I wrote—"

BOOM.

"—to East Tower. No answer so far, and say what you like about old Tharvitre, he always got right back to you, if only to curse you for being incompetent, and how in his day they fought pirates off the coast with their —"

BOOM.

"—bare hands." The small joke fell flat as the stones of the walls ground minutely around them. He looked around, mouth pursed, then said flatly, "I think it's time to alert Lord Elsarion."

No one disagreed.

It took three drafts before the commander was satisfied with his note, which had to be factual and not look cowardly, but at the same time convey the seriousness of their situation.

A gratifyingly short time later, Thias Elsarion transferred to the Destination. He had clearly been at some sort of entertainment, for the torchlight played over his flowing silks and caught in the diamonds in his hair, on his fingers, and at one ear as he strode out, his sword with its jewel-chased, elegant hilt clasped in one hand.

He entered the command center, brows lifted. "What is it? You pulled me from hosting a ball for the Duchas of Marsael—"

BOOM.

Elsarion stilled, then glanced around. "I see. Well, let's take a look, shall we? And you can give me a report, beginning with how many of them."

"Right now they have fewer than half our number, but that's what we can see," the commander said as they ran up the stairs to the southwest tower. "We can't get anyone out to scout beyond the ridge—ah, please halt here, my lord—"

BOOM.

"—they shoot soon as they see something to shoot at. So far, out of everyone catching an arrow, only six survived."

Elsarion peered through the slit window, seeing nothing but a confusion of shadows below the glare of the torches lighting the sentry walk. "Douse the lights," he ordered. "Use the moon. As they are."

BOOM.

"Yes," Elsarion said a few heartbeats later, still drawling. "I was at the moment your communication arrived endeavoring to negotiate an agreement with Marsael. He has a small army of his own. Let me see what I can do. The pass is clear, right?"

"Yes, we know that much. Snows melted off some time ago."

"Odd. No one is answering at the towers, nor do the Destinations seem to be functioning. Magic," he said under his breath, like a curse. "So useful until suddenly it isn't. Never mind. As long as the pass is clear, I can send reinforcements if you think you can't hold the castle with merely twice their number—"

BOOM.

Elsarion's sardonic tone flattened. "Put everyone you have at this west gate, and hold it until I can get more people down here."

He flipped a transfer token on his palm, closed his eyes, braced—and vanished.

A day passed, and he did not reappear.

Two days. Three.

The shocks kept up the entire time, making sleep difficult as it was impossible to get away from the noise. Those off watch tried to rest with their weapons lying next to them.

In the staff wing, a different set of worries confronted the cooks and servants as they studied the remaining stores. "Three weeks left, the way these brutes eat," the head cook said, his brawny arms crossed. "Six if we go to half-rations now."

BOOM.

"Better tell the commander," said his assistant.

"Why bother, and get cursed for your pains? They'll know when they see half of everything in their dishes come morning."

BOOM.

Out in the field, the reverberations could still be heard, as Cabbage Gannan faced his captains. "Tevaca thinks the gate will break by tomorrow late, maybe the next day. Remember, they expect to see a charge, so we're giving them a charge." He addressed Henad Tlennen. "Make it slow and splashy as you can. Singing, whatever you can to get their attention on you, and stay there, while my boys slip inside through the ram house to destroy the horse killers."

Henad opened her hand. "We're not shooting, then? None of us can handle a lance and shoot while on the canter."

"Right," Cabbage said, mentally readjusting. "Then don't use all our lances. It's a fake charge, a decoy. Put your best shots on the wings, arrow to a target, as always."

To his cousin Lefty and his other captains, he said, "From the looks of things, they're stiffening the wall defense. Surprise will help us, but it'll only last a heartbeat."

Connar's Winter Company could hear the *boom* echoing up the canyon as they approached the last turn in the pass.

His blood fired with anticipation. He waved his divided company forward, toward the eastern wall of West Outpost bulking against the moonlit night.

Connar flashed a grin. *His plan had worked.* "We'll wait for nightfall," he said.

When the shadows had lengthened and melded, he signaled Ghost with a raised hand. Ghost's picked archers shot the two wall sentries, one falling outside, the other inside.

The Winter Company stilled, waiting for someone to ring the alarm.

Nothing.

"Unless they're crouching behind that wall, waiting to jump us as soon as we breach, my guess is, they're all at the west end," Stick said.

Connar turned his palm toward Jethren, whose men moved covertly to the wall. The huge east gate was shut, of course, but Jethren's men had lashed spears together to make ladders.

At the rear of the Winter Company, Quill strapped his knives to his wrists, but he was determined not to use them unless in self-defense. The slaughter of the supply carters, the two couriers coming down behind it, and the single rider who'd ridden up the pass in search of the supply caravan had sickened him to the soul. He and the younger runners under Ghost and Stick had laid out the dead and Disappeared them, but there was no sense of virtue in that, only grief and disgust. It was all so useless.

His mood was the bleakest it had ever been in his life as he watched the three ladders tap against the castle wall, and Jethren's men go up in twos. He and the runners were last, tasked to pull up the ladders after them, descend last, and undo the bindings to free the weapons, after which they coiled the bindings around their arms and divided the spears between them.

The rest of the Winter Company swarmed over the wall and down to spread out, encountering bodies sprawled, black blood splattered and pooled, marking the trail of Jethren's company.

Quill had reached the ground level and began dismantling the ladders when the cry went up at last, "To the wall! To the wall! They're attacking from—"

That voice cut off, but shouts, curses and shrieks swiftly followed as the defenders discovered the stealth attack from the unguarded east wall.

Quill picked up his share of the spears, then followed his fellow runners. They emerged into a court, and nearly tripped over a man lying across the threshold, open eyes staring sightlessly at the sky. Somewhere in the fitful, confusing torchlight through an archway steel clanged and clattered on stone. Voices rose in Adrani, "We surrender! I give up!"

Jethren shouted, "No prisoners!"

Quill caught sight of a pair of terrified children, probably kitchen servants from their clothing, and dropped the spears. He said in Adrani, "Over here!"

Two fearful faces turned toward him. He threw an illusion of shadow around them, then motioned them to follow him along the walls. One whimpered, the other muttering "Hurry, hurry, hurry," jerking like a stringed puppet, until he got them to the destroyed west gate, and said, "Run."

Two floors up the commander dropped his sword, breathing heavily.

Ignoring his dripping wounds, he grabbed a piece of paper with one bloody hand, dipped a pen, and wrote to Thias Elsarion:

My lord, I must report that I failed in my task.

The Marlovans attacked a short time ago from the east wall, which we left unguarded according to orders. We also lost the west wall when the gate came down. The fighting has reached the inner court. I can hear my men trying to surrender.

Geraint just reported now that they are killing everyone, including those on their knees, weapons down.

I expect this will be my last communication.

TWENTY-NINE

A week to the west, Lineas crouched among the leddas and pricklestickle, head low as she watched the ghostly figures through the slanting rain. She had lain there since morning, when Neit had vanished with the dawn, exhorting her to stay put or they would never find one another in the murky marsh under a hard spring rain.

Lineas's heart jolted as a figure appeared abruptly above her, then she recognized Neit's outline despite the fact that she was covered with mud, including her hair.

"They're definitely on the move," Neit whispered as she dropped down beside Lineas.

"Let's get to our relay."

Neit's hand came down on her wrist. "Wait."

Lineas stilled, absently wiping a questing insect off her neck. It seemed she'd been crawling around this noisome swamp for uncounted ages, though she knew objectively it had been a matter of days. But the continuous fogs, the dank smell of the tangle of growth humming with life, broken intermittently by the sharp alarm of movement among the hiding Bar Regren, had stretched into a nightmare of little sleep and anxious striving.

All she had accomplished during her days of hiding and spying was to identify those gathering in the marsh as mostly Bar Regren, others speaking Iascan in an accent similar to what she'd heard in Larkadhe as they complained about the lack of food being passed out—the wait—sodden shoes—and above all, curses aimed at the Marlovans.

Presently Lineas whispered, "What are we waiting for?"

Neit's muddy face turned her way, her teeth the only visible thing in the dim light as she flashed a grin. "Explain later."

Another group of Bar Regren emerged as shadows in the rain. As soon as they'd passed west, Neit smacked Lineas's shoulder and jerked her thumb sideways.

And so began yet another horrible hands-and-knees crawl among the cattails and leddas, but at least they had left the pricklestickle. Lineas had given up making sense of Neit's movements. She knew there was a logic to them, and that Neit would explain when there was less chance of the sound of their voices carrying over the pools and streams.

At least the rain was beginning to wash some of the mud off her face and out of her hair. The grit in her soggy clothing was hopeless—but, she chanted to herself as she had over the past days, all things come to an end. Including living in wet clothes and itching in every fold of her body.

For Neit, the grim watch was over. The fun of the hunt was on. She glanced back, to find Lineas sticking grimly to her heels. She waved toward the south. Lineas's anxious face eased: retreat, at last.

They crawled, slid, and splashed until they slipped down a bank slimy with mud and drowned grass after the latest rain, and into a stream. They dropped into the water and wiggled arms and legs to rid themselves of the worst of the nasty-smelling marsh mud. Then they rose, water surging off them, and climbed up the bank to head for their patiently waiting relay, who lurked in a dell with waiting horses.

Their clothes were nearly dry (and stiff with residual dirt) when the relay brought them before Braids Senelaec, camped alongside a stream in a sheltered vale outside of Ku Halir.

Braids had been sitting on a fallen log. He shot to his feet as Neit advanced on him, saying, "They're massing on the river."

"Then we can nail them before they reach Ku Halir's gates." Braids smacked his hands together. "Let's ride."

"No." Neit caught his arm. "That's just what they want you to do."

"What?" Braids turned to her, anger borne of extreme tension tightening his mouth.

Neit spoke quickly. "Look, I spent my entire young life being the Venn so Olavayir Riders could defeat us. I've seen that kind of feint—I've *run* that kind of feint. That's not the main group. I spent all yesterday and this morning making sure. I think these ones counted on being seen. They *want* you to chase them."

"Why?"

"Because they'll lead you right into the marsh. Me and Lineas just spent a thousand years crouching in that marsh, being buzzed by every bug in the kingdom. We've been all over the east side of that terrain. You get these horses into that marsh and they can kill you, and the horses, any time they like."

"But I was told they attack in mass," Braids said.

"Oh, they will. Ovaka Mol, second son of Ovaka Red-Feather, will have to lead them if he really expects to take over as new Red-Feather. He ran at Chalk Hills, so now he has to prove himself."

Here Neit glanced at Lineas, who opened her hand in confirmation. "All the gossip I listened to mentioned him," Lineas stated. "Even if you allow for how rumor changes facts, it sounded like he's been making all kinds of promises in order to get all these villages—including some North Iascans—to join together with him. The North Iascans want Ku Halir because it sits directly on the northern trade route. The Bar Regren want their kingdom back."

"They'll get their kingdom back by taking Ku Halir?" Braids repeated, incredulous. "Even I know that their kingdom used to be all those mountains west of the Andahi Pass, up to the Nob!" He pinched his fingers to the bridge of his nose. "Never mind. Where is this Ovaka Mol?"

Neit said, "Don't know. My guess is, they'll attack from the west while this marsh feint draws us to the east. I tracked a mass of them yesterday moving west along the lakeshore. It's treacherous. All black rock and thick woods. Their territory."

Braids' head ached. "That's where Noth will come from." That's where his own Senelaec people would come—but he didn't say that out loud, lest it seem like they were the only ones he cared about. "Did you see any drill? Overhear battle plans?"

Neit flicked her hand away. "Bar Regren are all captains with only servants as followers. They attack in a mass, trampling all those they don't kill outright. The ones closest to the edges are considered the bravest."

"And so . . ." Braids said.

Neit sighed. "My guess is, they'll hit the road from the north side when they see a column. Then storm the west gate. They might even try to do both at the same time, if there's enough of them."

Braids frowned, wondering how long it would take the runners he'd sent to find out what was keeping Noth. Right now, all he knew for certain was that he was outnumbered.

"Shit," he said under his breath. In the background, runners grimly began packing up the camp, everyone aware that their gamble with Rat Noth bringing extra forces might very well be lost.

Braids glared at Neit. "Did you really command in Olavayir wargames?"

Neit saw the anxiety in that glare, and met it straight on. "Small games, for years. Only a couple of the big games, when the captains were elsewhere. I was always the attacker. And if I didn't command, the jarlan always put me in as second runner to Tanrid or Cousin Hal. Ah, he's—"

"I don't care who he is, unless he's here," Braids cut in rudely, flinging his arms out wide as if he could shake off the mounting tension. Everywhere he turned, or looked, there was no escaping the grim reality: he was about to break orders to run a defense that looked more impossible with every heartbeat.

He stepped up to Neit. "Look. I never really learned command. I was only at the academy a short time, and—oh, never mind that. What I know is running the flanks, weak left, strong right. I'm really good at that. I'd intended to run that now, along the river. But I've never put together a defense outside of a couple small ones at the academy, and this isn't small. You know the territory. You've run big games. I think you should take command."

"Me?" Neit's voice squeaked. "Right. You're joking. Ha. Ha."

But nobody laughed.

"Field promotion," Braids said grittily. "At least, until Rat shows up. I don't believe he'd bail on us. But he's late, and if you're right, he's going to get jumped before he can get to us."

Neit did not want command. She wanted to protest, deny. She was a runner. But while she consciously argued, she was seeing the map. She knew Ku Halir's terrain at least as well as any of the rest of them. Maybe better.

It was her turn to sigh sharply. "If I were to command, I'd want runners going right now, running off-road to avoid the spyeyes, to find Rat."

"I sent runners," Braids protested.

Neit was silent—everyone was silent, knowing what that probably meant.

Braids turned to his captains, and to Pepper Marlovayir, who stood a few paces away, arms crossed. "Everybody here is a witness. This is a field promotion, Neit to Commander. After this order, I'm stepping down to second in chain of command—until we catch up with Rat Noth." Because he hadn't spent years in the academy, he forgot to salute, but even Pepper Marlovayir didn't want to say anything about irregularities.

Braids faced Neit. "You want me taking the marsh?"

Lineas had been watching silently, hurting for both Braids and Neit, both such good-humored people, their faces made for smiling. Both with the sun-bleached hair of people who lived most of their lives outdoors. Both clearly aware that whatever they did next would spend lives. Not just enemy lives, but their own people.

Neit's head jerked up, her clean-lined jaw jutted. "No. Lineas? I know you can make a grass run. Did you royal runners train in running doggo?"

"By which you mean, remaining undiscovered?" Lineas asked, her heart pounding. "We did."

"Good. You're already covered in mud. Good camouflage. Get the fastest horse here, run west off-road and find Noth, or whoever is forward, and warn 'em what's coming at 'em. Pepper, you take your flight to the marsh. Don't let 'em reach the east gate."

She turned to the rest. "Braids, we're going west. You and your fastest are going to have to be the hammer. The rest of us are the anvil."

She clapped Lineas on the shoulder, Braids gave her a lopsided smile, and the two began issuing orders.

Lineas backed away, thinking hard. Notecases could be replaced. But secrets, once out, could not be unlearned. To make a run knowing that enemies are actively hunting you means you have to consider the fact that you might be stopped and searched. Her journal had three levels of code, the top one substituting farming terms for other words. The real danger was the notecase.

Should she write to Quill before she hid her notecase? She wished she had more experience with relationships! Would it be more of a burden then a relief for him to know she was heading into danger while he was already in danger?

Lineas mulled these questions as she crossed the camp to the picket line, where runners were already saddling the fastest of the available mounts. Braids' first runner handed her a stale bun stuffed with crumbling cheese and slightly withered greens, which she accepted gratefully. She began to eat as she rode out, doing her best to ignore the occasional bite of grit from her less than clean hands.

When she reached the place where the path diverged, she halted. No one was around. She slid off the horse, holding her arms tightly across her front as she sifted her way to a decision: Quill was on a dangerous mission, therefore it seemed right not to distract him with her current orders.

She unwrapped her notecase, pen stub, and ink, and wrote a brief report to Mnar Milnari, ending with the promise to bury her notecase as soon as she sent the note.

That done, she aimed the horse between the paths, oriented herself on the sun, and began her run.

That night, Pepper's flight reached the marsh to the east of Ku Halir roughly about the time the Winter Company searched through the silent West Outpost at the mouth of the southern pass, taking scalp trophies and looking for any hiding survivors to kill.

Already the flies were gathering about the dead.

Quill slipped back in among Ghost's company, who he suspected had been selectively blind toward obvious noncombatants making their desperate way toward the ruined gate.

Pale light filled the V of the pass behind them, dawn imminent. The ferocious spike of battle lust had ebbed, leaving Connar's combined force filthy, stinking of sweat and blood, exhausted. Tempers ranged from exultant (Connar, and at the other end of the castle, Cabbage Gannan), to vile.

Jethren could not be read by anyone. He seemed tireless, striding everywhere to check that no enemy survived and that his company was diligently searching. Quill, watching in order to keep at a distance, noticed how often Jethren turned toward Connar. Expecting what?

Connar seemed unaware of him. Unaware of anything, including the piles of dead, until at last the captains converged on him, Gannan prudently keeping himself behind Connar's favorites.

"Outpost secure," Stick said, after a glance from Ghost.

Connar's exaltation at how his plan had worked was already diminishing: not surprising, Elsarion had not been among those in the command center. But enough of his good mood remained for him to turn Cabbage's way, and say, "*Excellent* attack. You'll take command here, with your people. Hold it until our return. Where's Henad Tlennen?"

"Here," she said, coming forward, avoiding Quill's gaze; he suspect she had also colluded in pretending not to see the castle children and their minders or guardians fleeing.

Connar pointed toward the west gate and beyond. "Keep patrolling. Orders still stand, anyone suspicious, kill them. If there's a question, lock them up until we return."

He lifted his voice to include the lancers Commander Ventdor had sent. "The rest of us will make the run up the pass, all the way to Elsarion."

Jethren roared, "Victory!"

His company responded with as much force as they could muster, raggedly joined by most of the rest. Many were silent, shocked by what they saw, which only worsened as the darkness began, inexorably, to lift.

When the shouts died away, Connar beckoned to his three captains. "Withdraw to the supply wagons. There should be a meal prepared. Half a day of rest, then a hard push. We've cleared the traps, so there's nothing left to slow us. The less time we give them to dig in at the other end, the better."

Connar caught sight of Quill. "Prepare to ride with us. I expect we'll need translation when we dictate terms." He turned away.

In a sharp, hortatory voice that to Ghost Fath and Stick Tyavayir managed to sound sycophantic, Jethren marshaled his diminished company into strict order. His intent was to demonstrate their instant obedience as well as their superior discipline, but the effect was to divide them off even more thoroughly from the rest of the Winter Company, many of whom looked on in weary, not-so-covert disgust at such unnecessary swagger.

Quill had hoped to be sent to the royal city with a report. That clearly was not going to happen, but at least he had half a day.

He waited until the last of the Winter Company and the lancers had departed through the east gate, then forced himself back inside the castle hecatomb, where he spotted Cabbage's company healer and his aides already laying out and Disappearing the dead.

Quill slipped through the smashed gates that were being dismantled by a party of carpenters. He walked far enough away to breathe air not tainted by blood, and then a little farther to be certain he was unseen.

He took out his notecase and pen, noting wearily that he had very little ink left. He wrote Lineas:

I'm free. Where are you?

He waited—surely he'd caught her between bathing and breakfast? But no answer. He put his head on his knees to rest his eyes . . . and woke with a snore, drool pooling at the corner of his mouth, his neck stiff.

He squinted upward. The sun had not even moved a finger. He must have slept no more than the small sandglass's quarter-hour.

He opened his notecase, in case he'd slept through the signal. Nothing. Dipping the pen carefully, he wrote:

Vanadei: West Outpost taken. I've orders to ride up the pass. Is Lineas on duty?

An answer came back almost immediately:

She was sent to Ku Halir a month back. We're stretched thin here. She might have been sent anywhere. I've not heard from her.

Quill's ink was nearly empty. He got to his feet and went back inside to commandeer a horse in order to rejoin the Winter Company, leaving Connar's victory at his back.

At first it was just the Bar Regren gathered about Ovaka Mol, whose prestige had taken a drubbing after he abandoned his nephew and two other clan boys to the enemy at Chalk Hills. It took some weeks of fast talking and judicious use of fists to shift the blame to where it properly belonged: on the Marlovans.

During that time, Ovaka Mol had discovered what many did before, that there are few things more exhilarating than binding together a divisive group in righteous hatred.

When word passed up into the mountains that the Marlovans were going east to chase after the Adrani lordling who had teamed up with Yenvir, Ovaka said, "This is our time."

He almost lost them in the argument about how to use their time—specifically, where. But greed won: Ku Halir was so much richer than any of the northern cities. The Bar Regren had long wanted Ku Halir, down there at the southernmost reach of their particular curve of mountains. To them it made a perfect match to the Nob, at the far end of the peninsula, which they had twice failed to retake. Ovaka Mol's new plan was to trade Ku Halir for the Nob, once they'd looted it to the seams.

So they drifted along the mountain-tops in what they called hill-walking. At first it was just scouts, to make certain that yes, the Marlovans really were all going to the east. And when the scouts returned without having been seen, the Bar Regren began gathering in small groups, which got larger and larger.

It was true! The Marlovans were completely blind to anyplace they couldn't take their horses, useless beasts in mountains. The bracing news that the Marlovans were, in fact, stupid, absolutely begged for boldness.

As winter gave way to spring, and more and more in the tiny mountain villages saw Bar Regren hill-walking south, they were joined by others:

revenge, bloodlust, greed, gave way to larger parties, mainly of youth who were more than willing to down tools (especially with spring planting nigh) and walk off to the promise of a short adventure and plenty of loot.

Everybody was enjoined to walk in silence, which added to the excitement. And finally, you could only join if you brought a month's worth of food, for there was no supplying so many. The last of winter stores got dumped into packs and bags, reinforced by discovery of gleanings along the way; toward the end, bolstered by sheer numbers, the venture took on a festival atmosphere.

Not for all. A few got tired of waiting in mud and bugs, and left for home. Others said warily the plan sounded too easy—and were scorned for their cowardly croakings. As the spring rains came on, turning the marsh into soup, the festival atmosphere gave way to grim determination: the Marlovans had made them suffer. They would pay for it.

People clumped closer to their own groups, until at last someone came around, saying that the time had come, and divided them up, promising that everyone would get an equal share of loot as long as they all acted together.

It was time to attack!

Lineas was fast, but no human on horseback would have been fast enough.

She realized it when she encountered her first riderless horse running wild-eyed through the trees past her.

Until then she had been fighting weariness. The sight of that horse, shortly followed by another, acted like hot needles to her nerves. She broke cover and headed north to where she knew the road lay—and so was first witness to arrive at the bend in the road where Wolf and Mardran Senelaec, leading the vanguard of Rat Noth's hastily assembled company, was taken by surprise.

Her shocked gaze swept a sea of attackers waving hoes, scythes, bludgeons and here and there rusty blades besieging mounted Riders who stuck up like islands in a furious ocean.

"I'm too late," she cried, and then whispered, "I'm too late, I'm too late."

Horses kicked and plunged, Riders fought with sword and knife. Her horse sidled under her, ears flat; Lineas knew with profound, sick certainty that she would be useless riding to their aid.

She looked desperately—no familiar faces among those mounted Riders.

Rat Noth is not here.

He had to be still coming. She clucked at the horse, backing up behind a hedgerow, and skirted the area, heading west as soon as she dared lest she miss Rat Noth . . . who was in a grim mood, after being mired by three hard storms in a row, the middle one of which caused two of his summoned companies to ride completely past one another. When he saw the foam-flecked horse galloping toward him, a figure so dirty swaying on the animal's back that he couldn't tell the age or gender of the rider, he held up his fist to halt the company.

Lineas caught up, her mouth working before she could get words out. "They—it's bad," she cried hoarsely.

Rat looked at those dark-ringed, bloodshot eyes and knew that if he wanted a coherent report he had to get it a piece at a time. "What's bad?"

"They attacked—I think it must be Senelaec? Braids said his family would come first," Lineas said numbly.

"Where?"

"Bend in the road, just past the west end of the lake—"

"Who is where? Tell me exactly where Braids put everyone."

"Neit put them," Lineas said in that same distant voice, trained to be exact.

Neit? Rat made a motion as if to swat away the questions in his mind: get to what mattered. "Where did Neit put everyone?"

Lineas could do that. Relieved, she recited, word for word, what Neit had ordered.

Halfway through it, Rat had the picture. By then his riding captains had all crowded up to hear. He brought them in with a fist, issued a stream of orders . . .

And you know the rest, if you've heard "Noth's Arrow" and the middle seven verses of "The Ballad of Braids Senelaec." Once again, iron discipline, delivered at the gallop, smashed into what had become a mob completely out of control.

Senelaec and his company had been utterly taken by surprise by a host more than five times the size of his own, but Rat Noth was not. And, like often happens with mobs, the mood changed with lightning speed from bloodlust to fear.

Those not shot, stabbed, beheaded, or ridden down, turned and ran, scrambling over one another—then fighting one another—to escape the scything swords and the lethal rain of arrows.

Panic scattered those left alive, swarms running back to the lake in the darkness, where the press of their own numbers forced many into the water to drown. Others decamped for the woods.

Patrols of very angry Marlovans galloped through in waves until the roads were quiet, deserted except for the dead.

At dawn Ku Halir's gates finally opened to the weary defenders.

THIRTY

When not riding with weapons ready, the Winter Company drilled at every stop, and when they camped, they worked on shaping more arrows from materials scavenged from West Outpost and the settling rubble that used to be West and East Towers.

Jethren's men were always the first to volunteer if Connar asked for anything, and the first to set up his tent when they camped, before their own. They irritated Fish to no end with their encroachments on his duties, but of course he said nothing. If Connar didn't want a king's honor guard, which is what Jethren was striving to give him, he could say so.

They all found the emptiness in the pass eerie, heightened by the moaning, soughing wind around the spires and down the sheer cliffs. By night, they camped with a triple perimeter, swapped out every four hours.

On the eastward descent they still saw no one, only fresh prints. Someone was riding ahead of them, watching from a distance. Quill suspected that whoever paced them had a notecase for magical transfer.

At last they approached the east end of the pass, carrying bows loosely slung, arrows in reach, swords ready in saddle sheaths, knives at belt, boots, wrists. Helms crowned with long locks of hair gently bobbing.

Finally, between two slopes, they caught sight of a glimpse of the plains of Anaeran Adrani.

That night, Connar paced out of the center of the camp to where the off-duty runners camped beside the horse picket.

The runners, whose hands were busy with sewing, arrow-fletching, and other repairs, looked up and saluted, echoed by Quill. When they saw Connar's gaze go to the single royal runner, then flick at the others dismissively, they rose as one and carried their work away from their fire, leaving royal runner and commander alone.

Quill had stood with the rest, holding the harness he was repairing. Connar waved at him to sit back down. Quill did, but held the harness on his knee as Connar hunkered down next to him. He glanced away, the fire outlining his profile, then back. "My guess is, we're two days out. You know they've been watching us."

"Yes."

"I think it's time to see exactly what lies ahead. I want you to scout. You're the only one who understands the language."

"You mean, if I get captured."

"Don't get captured," Connar said, amused.

Unsaid—but thought by both—was the equal chance Quill would be shot, which would be its own sort of information. Quill said nothing because there was nothing to say. He'd been given an order.

Connar rose and walked back to the center of camp, and sat down again with his captains. The runners returned to their fire and resettled around Quill like an ungainly flock of birds.

Ghost's youngest runner said, "What was that?"

"I'm to scout ahead."

"Shit!" the runner exclaimed—softly. "I wanted to scout. I offered."

"I speak Adrani." Quill was peripherally aware of Fish sitting impassively nearby with some mending. Quill had discovered during the journey up the pass that it wasn't just him Fish avoided speaking to. He was silent with everyone, except for immediacies like "We're camping now," and "Where's the flour bag?"

The others glanced his way, and the subject dropped—before Fish, anyway.

Quill rode out as soon as the light began to lift. He did not expect to be shot off his horse. If the Adranis picked him off, they gained absolutely nothing, whereas if they captured him, they had to have a book's length of questions about what was coming, what Connar wanted. What the Marlovan king wanted.

What worried him was the possibility that Elsarion would be among whatever force waited at the other end, and that he would instantly recognize Quill.

Half a day ahead of the rest of the Winter Company, he stopped to water his horse at the stream running alongside the road. He perched on a rock and took out his notecase, pen, and ink. He caught up some water to add to the ink, which he knew would write a paler and paler gray.

He sent off one line to Lineas, waited, and . . . . nothing.

He rode on, over the next two days evolving various plans contingent on seeing Elsarion, mages, whether the Adranis shot on sight, called threats, or even a truce.

It all went out of his head when he rounded the great headland that was the start of the pass from the east side, overlooking East Outpost, and behind it the plains of Elsarion.

His horse picked up his tension and turned in a circle, ears flicking and flattening. Though he knew himself out of range of arrows, he felt exposed. Of course there were countless field glasses trained on him from the uncounted sentries atop the towers and castle walls, helms gleaming in the sun.

If they wanted to be nasty, they could have put Destinations all about, to which they could transfer warriors with crossbows. Of course these warriors would have to recover from the transfer, during which he could vanish . . .

He shrugged off useless thoughts, scanned more slowly, then clucked to the horse and rode back as fast as he could.

The Winter Company and Ku Halir lancers were a day behind him. It was late afternoon when they met up.

Connar called a halt.

Quill rode to him and saluted.

"Your report?" Connar said.

"The castle has roughly twice what we saw at West Outpost. They line every surface—they wanted to be seen. Camped beyond it, covering the entire slope into the plain, is the royal Adrani army."

Stick whistled; Jethren let out a guffaw. Ghost said nothing, just leaned his forearm on his knee as his horse nosed the ground for promising rootlets. Next to him, Manther Yvanavayir watched, pale eyes unblinking, and on his other side, Stick Tyavayir squinted skyward, watching a raptor riding an air current as sun struck ruddy highlights in his dark red tangle of hair.

"How many?" Connar said to Quill.

"I would estimate between five and seven thousand. At that distance, numbers are difficult to guess. Last, there was a white flag at the tallest tower."

Connar raised his brows, turning to his captains. "Five thousand! Quite an honor, eh?"

The captains took this as permission to speak.

"We can take them," Jethren stated. "Five hundred against five thousand? I like those odds."

"I don't," Stick said flatly, not looking his way.

"More to the point. The king never ordered us to invade Enaeran Adrani." Ghost spat road dust to the side. "Our orders, before Convocation, were to get justice from Elsarion." He also didn't glance Jethren's way.

Connar's lips parted. Quill's gut churned at the avidness he saw in those blue eyes. But he regarded Stick with a meditative air, then said, mildly enough, "We may or may not be able to take them, but we couldn't hold whatever we took. And as you say, Fath, we don't have orders." His smile widened and he addressed Quill. "Let's see what this white flag is about. You lead. This time as interpreter. We'll camp at Threefold Falls." He tapped the waterfall on the much-folded, grimy map.

When they rode down to the headland the next morning, there was, if anything, twice again the number that Quill had reported, though most of the additions were spectators who had climbed the hills below the bluff, and perched—many with blankets and baskets of provisions—prudently out of arrowshot, but with a grand view of any prospective bloody spectacles.

The evening before, Quill had pulled his dark blue royal runner's robe from the bottom of his gear bag, stale-smelling and wrinkled, letting it air all night. The Marlovans had polished helms and boots, brushed and dusted their coats, and rode in strict formation, Connar at the front with two great banners behind him, the long yellow swallow-tails hanging from the blue cloth fluttering in the breeze.

Adranis stood shoulder to shoulder along the walls and towers, each with bows, arrows aimed at them.

Connar lifted a hand, and Quill rode out from behind the banners, holding a white pennon that had been stitched from three linen shirts whose seams had been unpicked and then resewn together for the purpose.

Someone on the wall of the castle lifted a hand, and the archers lifted their arrows, keeping them notched.

Quill sighed inwardly as he began to walk his horse down the middle of the rutted road. He sighed again when he got close enough to be fairly certain that that slim, narrow-shouldered figure in black and gold at the center of the wall directly over the gate was the Duchas of Elsarion, Thias's sister.

If he could see her features, she could see his, and he knew he resembled his father. But if she recognized him, she gave utterly no sign.

Behind Quill, Connar halted his army at the very edge of arrowshot—expertly calculated. A silent challenge.

Quill rode forward alone, carrying the limp, wrinkled white flag on one of Jethren's spears. It smelled of stale sweat in the heavy summer air.

A herald with a booming voice called sonorously in Adrani, and then Sartoran, "Elsarion is currently held by Prince Valdon-Rassael Shagal, while the Elsarion family is under sanction. I am to convey the orders from the king that entry into Elsarion will be considered an act of war." He paused. "Do you understand, or shall I find a translator who speaks one of your tongues?"

Ah, an insult. Quill answered in Court Sartoran, "The King of Marlovan Iasca demands justice. He sent us to bring Lord Mathias Alored Elsarion back to face trial for capital crimes against the kingdom. I can provide a list of said crimes as well as witness names."

A whisper and rustle went through the nobles at the top of the wall over the gate, noticeable by the gilt on their armor and the plumes in their helms. The only one who remained still was the single figure in black and gold.

Then she spoke herself, her fluting voice carrying. "Your accusations come too late. The Wood Guild in four kingdoms led the names in a petition against my brother. Justice has already been carried out by our king's will. Thias Alored Elsarion sits in the Garden of Time."

Connar had given Quill answers to various demands or threats, but no one had foreseen this twist.

Quill turned his horse and trotted up the raked gravel path to where Connar sat in the middle of his captains, the banners flanking him.

Connar said, "What was that long speech?"

"The herald said it all in their language and in Sartoran. It comes down to their king having sent a prince to occupy the Elsarion territory. They say that the Wood Guild brought accusations against Thias Elsarion. The king passed sentence by placing him in a Garden of Time."

"What's that?"

"It's also known as a Garden of Shame." And when Connar made no reaction, Quill explained. "A Garden of Shame is for lesser criminals than nobles, usually located in the middle of cities as a reminder to obey the law. Sartoran mages put a stone spell on the judged person, which wears off after the stipulated time. People might get a couple years, five, ten. Nobles, especially those who run afoul of the monarch, are kept in the more secluded Gardens of Time. I'm told that a hundred years is usual when nobles have put together armies but aimed them elsewhere than at the home government, then got themselves into trouble. It's a diplomatic move to halt a war. Nobles who run against the king are usually executed."

"No doubt if Elsarion had won against us, this same king would have showered him with gold?"

"History is full of examples of kings turning a blind eye to their troublemakers taking their troubles elsewhere. Thias Elsarion is related to the Adrani king, and he kept his depredations against us, the handy barbarians, rather than riding against his own country, so the king clearly didn't think it necessary to put him to death."

Connar's eyes narrowed. "Assuming it's true. Can we demand they undo whatever it is they did?"

"It can't be undone."

Connar glanced to the side, as if thousands of eyes were not fixed on him, hands tight on weapons. "The Wood Guild here has that much power?" he commented.

"When it's convenient, I expect. Kings find ways around them when it's convenient—such as paying them off, whereupon the Wood Guild brings seedlings to replace whatever was cut down to make warships, or the like."

Connar slewed around, shoulders tight, his expression one of superficial amusement. "How do you know all this? Ah. While we were running wargames in the field, you were reading books about the Wood Guild."

"Yes," Quill said.

Connar uttered a short laugh, then kneed his horse, and rode down toward the gate. Quill quickly followed.

It was a risky move, but not a mad one. They had to know who he was. But then, they would also know that the Marlovan king would certainly send the entire kingdom over the mountains if someone shot his son under a truce flag.

"How do I know you're telling the truth?" Connar shouted up to the Duchas, and Quill translated it into Sartoran.

The Duchas looked down expressionlessly. "I thought you might wish to corroborate the truth of the king's justice." She turned her head, beckoning to someone.

A woman in a white and silver robe stepped up, the military people backing to either side.

"Who's that?" Connar muttered without turning his head.

"The white and silver usually means a high-ranking mage from Sartor," Quill answered in an undervoice.

The woman's lips moved, and she tossed something metallic down to the ground before their horses' forehooves.

The animals' ears flicked, but they were too well trained to do anything more than twitch.

The woman made a gesture, and an image appeared in the air.

"This is a captured image from the Garden of Time in Nente, our royal capital."

Beautifully kept trees showed the green of full spring, bordered around by flowers. It was a secluded garden, in which what looked like stone statues could dimly be made out—except for one in the foreground.

It showed a tall, handsome young man with long hair flowing over a simple robe. His head was bent, his hands hanging at his sides, his expression turned inward. Everything in shades of gray.

"That looks like the drawing of Elsarion," Connar observed. "Is that a carving?"

"No, it's he. A stone spell is just that, it turns you into stone. Or nearly into stone. I'm told you're still alive, taking a breath a year, or some such." Quill suppressed a grimace.

Connar's gaze went from that solitary image to the Duchas on the wall. "That's not our justice."

Quill translated.

"War," she said, "is never justice. What my brother failed to learn is that every war sets back civilization."

After Quill translated that, Connar turned his head and finally looked at him. "They think we're stupid."

Quill said softly, "No, they think we're barbarians. There's a difference," and at the disbelief in Connar's curled lip and raised brows, Quill said, "Five thousand differences. They're not certain they can intimidate us militarily with ten times our number—and no doubt more crossing country as fast as they can—so they're trying by other means. I'm very certain at least half those up there know some Marlovan, if not Iascan."

"Then why didn't that loudmouth up there use . . ." His mouth thinned. "Right."

He stared back up at the Duchas, who seemed sufficiently moved to add, "Tell your king that Elsarion is required by royal command to pay penalties for a generation. We are also required to fund a guild-appointed council to restore the travelers' rests on this side of the pass, before the guilds send representatives over to negotiate with the guilds in your kingdom, that we might reestablish disrupted trade."

Her voice was ice-cold and controlled, but Quill could see what Thias's exploits had cost her. That huge army out there, no doubt quartered at Elsarion's expense—local businesses disrupted as people had probably fled in expectation of a barbarian incursion—the Elsarions would likely be beggared for the foreseeable.

Connar shifted slightly. About to give a command? No one person ought to be able to drive so many to death—and yet the argument ought to be with the followers who chose to obey that command. Impulse drove Quill to speak. "Elsarion played the game of kings and lost. This is their version of what happens to losers."

Connar shot him a slack-lidded, speculative glance. Quill shut up.

As the mage's illusion faded into nothing, Connar peered up under his hand toward the figures now silhouetted against the rising sun.

Quill held his breath, intensely aware of every sound—the shift and clop of his horse's hoof, a snort from one of the banner carriers' mounts—and a quiet conversation among the row of captains behind the banners, a row that included Manther, still wearing that invisible chevron.

" . . . feel like I can breathe," Manther was saying. "That turd is as good as dead. Not running around free."

"King will sing us," Ghost Fath said.

King. Quill saw the word impact Connar in the tightening of his hand on the rein, and in the nervous shift of his mount.

Thank you, Fath, Quill thought.

Connar blinked. Turned his horse. Raised his hand and opened his palm toward the pass.

The banner bearers turned their horses. The captains as well. The column waited, and as the captains rode to either side of them, they fell in, right and left in perfect order. Quill fell in behind them.

As they passed under the bluff, the picnickers cheated of the horror of ghastly sights leaned out to wring the last entertainment by staring, many commenting loudly.

One in a cook's apron relished each sign of barbarity, counting them like trophies to her friend. "They really do have hair on those helms! So disgusting!"

Her friend sent pebbles skittering down the slope as she peered out. "If I wore knives like that I'd cut up my ankles."

"Those flags—"

"The metal links—d'ya think they wear 'em next to the skin?"

"I hate to think of the chafing, which would be a crime with those pretty thighs. Mmm! Myself, I wouldn't toss that black-haired piece of work out of my hammock for eating with his fingers."

"Nah, I'll take the big blonde with the shoulders and the jaw. Might be as stupid as a rock but I bet he'd be fun in the hammock." Her voice was amplified by the stone on the other side of the bluff.

Quill's gaze shifted from Connar to Jethren, both unaware of their physical attributes being discussed loudly right overhead, and smothered the flutter of hilarity behind his ribs.

As the castle slid out of sight behind the bluff, and they started up the first dogleg of the pass, Ghost and Manther talked softly, using Hand intermittently. Stick, riding behind them, cracked jokes at Thias Elsarion's expense. The two captains burst into laughter, and Manther briefly smiled at the image of him crowned by a hundred years of bird shit.

Connar listened without turning his head.

They, and their riding captains, as well as the lancers, clearly regarded the whole as a victory. *There's a difference.* He gnawed inwardly at the inescapable fact that so much of what was termed truth was not. The victory Connar craved was Elsarion's bleeding body at his feet, his blood dripping off Connar's steel.

He didn't care what Jethren thought; he was very likely Hauth's mouthpiece as well as a bootlicker, though useful. Ghost and Stick didn't give a spit for dolphin clan claims. They were loyal to the king, to the kingdom, to *Connar.* And no one could ever say that either of them was weak. If they called this travesty a victory, then others would say the same. Call it a victory, and it's a victory.

There's a difference. What did Quill Montredavan-An call it? Fury surged in Connar once more and he told himself savagely that it didn't matter what Quill thought. His reason for existence was to carry out orders. Not to give them.

But he couldn't stop brooding as they rode westward up the pass, until he reached a conclusion he didn't like. It was that report Quill had written, carefully setting out the cost of a war against what might happen. He'd foreseen pretty much everything.

In fact, though those royal runners might call it something different, Quill Montredavan-An was no stranger to strategic thinking. That and his easy familiarity with the Sartoran language were all state matters.

He could also fight.

Connar shot one glance back, and caught sight of Quill riding modestly at the back, chatting with a couple of the younger runners. Seeing a look of question in Ghost Fath, he straightened around again, gesturing *It's nothing.*

When the company reached Threefold Falls, where they had camped the previous night, Connar signaled for a halt. As the runners began taking the animals to drink, and to refill theirs and the captains' flasks, Connar sent Fish to summon Quill.

The royal runner appeared out of the swarm of runners' purposeful movement, still wearing his dark blue robe that somehow looked less squalid than the rest of them did, after weeks away from proper cleaning.

Quill approached, made his salute, and waited, breath held.

"Game of kings?" Connar said, looking up at the ribbons of the falls. "I take it that means war?" A quick, sardonic glance.

"You see the expression a lot when reading and translating Sartoran texts. It's not an expression of approbation," Quill added, and saw a tightening of irritation around Connar's mouth.

"And yet," Connar said, "they have wars."

"They do."

Connar tipped his head back, squinting toward the topmost fall. "Would you say Inda-Harskialdna played the game of kings?"

"Inda-Harskialdna," Quill repeated, wondering how Connar could have made the leap to the man who'd died more than a century ago. "No. Not at all. He was if anything a piece on kings' and would-be kings' game board. That includes pirate kings."

"Pirate kings," Connar repeated with a breath of a laugh, as water thundered, and behind them, a horse nickered. "I suppose those Sartoran records go on about us being barbarians?"

"They might." Quill sifted his words, distrusting this conversation, Connar's mood. Distrusting *Connar.* "Of course we only see a small sampling. The ones we read mostly detail the after-effects of war. Which last a lot longer than people realize."

Connar eyed Quill, who waited with an appearance of tranquility. There was no guessing what went on inside that head. But one thing for certain: Connar had spent entirely too much time thinking about him.

He looked away. What Quill thought didn't matter. He was a tool, there to obey. "Get a fresh horse. Report our victory to the king. Make it fast."

Connar glanced back, to discover no reaction—certainly no sign of disappointment at being turfed summarily from the Winter Company.

Quill saluted, turned away, and fairly soon they saw his straight back as he rode up toward the avalanche-clogged middle of the pass on his way home.

No one could see his smile of profound relief.

PART TWO

ONE

In the royal city, summer had ripened when Rat Noth and his fellow commanders rode in to make their report.

They were brought straight to the king's suite, where the royal family had gathered as soon as Rat's company was sighted by the sentries.

On their ride they'd worked out how to report, but when they found themselves under the royal eye and the king said, "Well, Senelaec?" Braids—still reeling from losing his brother, and forced to leave before he could be sure his father would recover—forgot everything they'd discussed so painstakingly, sweat breaking out as he fumbled between Hand and speech.

Rat stood at attention, keeping his gaze diffuse after sneaking a glance at Bun, who'd met his eyes straight on. He didn't dare look again until the king released them, but he felt her presence the way he felt the summer sun on his back on a morning ride.

Neit stood behind the two, in the proper place of a runner, biting down the impulse to roll her eyes at how badly Braids was fumbling. Pepper Marlovayir listened narrowly, habit making him expect at least one crack aimed his way, though the feud had long since been little more than verbal stings ever since their academy days.

" . . . and we promoted Marlovayir there to wing commander, but that's all he had, eighty-one, to hold the east gate. We heard the signal for 'no more arrows' and Basna came to try to tell us they were right up against the gate, with Ventdor's wall sentries almost down to throwing rocks before Noth came . . . ."

Braids shook his head, his gaze distant.

Neit coughed.

Braids' attention snapped back, his neck and ears reddening. "Here's the truth, I'm good at running the line, but I'm no good at seeing . . . ." He tapped his eyes then opened his rough, callused palms. "Neit kept tooting the flank attack. She'd said, *Don't let them surround you,* and of course that's what they were trying to do. Every time I heard that we'd reverse our run right there, and sure enough, find another crowd of 'em coming at us."

He sighed. "Well, there were so *many* of them. We'd charge, but it was like hitting a block of ice. They pressed in and we got hemmed, the west gate was over there, but we couldn't get near. They were separating us, sheer numbers . . . and then Noth turned up."

He stepped back, opening his hand toward Rat then Neit. "They can tell it better than I can."

Rat sent Neit a look that she interpreted correctly: *You were in command. This is your report.*

Neit took a moment to settle herself in the runner's report stance, feet braced apart, hands behind her back. She had the words, but first came the images, still raw and painfully vivid: that first night after the battle, when Ventdor had sent her to find Braids to deal with trouble among the Iascans. She'd gone looking for him in the castle, and through every hothouse in town, until someone had directed her to ride up to the road where the Senelaec vanguard had taken the brunt of the Bar Regren attack.

There, lit by torchlight, she'd found so many Senelaec dead neatly laid out, runners and Riders moving among them with careful hands, twitching hair and clothes straight before Disappearance. At the far end, she'd found Braids rocking back and forth, sobbing beside the viciously hacked remains of a young man she could scarcely bear to look at—someone said it was his brother Cub, and that Wolf, the jarl, was in the lazaretto suspended between life and death.

The next morning Braids had been back on duty. And had been ever since.

Yeah, she could see why he'd mangled their report.

Rat was still staring into the middle distance; she became aware that her pause had become a silence. She cleared her throat. *You ordered it, now you ride it, Neit.* "After Lineas and I finished scouting the marsh, we met up with Braids here to report on the enemy movement. He said I knew the territory, and so he asked me to take command this once."

She went on to deliver a precise report of her orders: how they'd reorganized their company; ridden through the night; camped through the next day to rest and ready themselves; and when the moon finally came up, attacked the Bar Regren mass where she'd expected them to be.

"Cloud cover was thinning, and we had enough moon by then to see each other, but the light was not good for either side. They had the numbers, but no command once they were let loose, so no signaling. I told Braids to get between them and the west gate and scythe at them to drive them back. The rest of us punched up from the south, trying to push them back to the lake."

"How many were there?" Arrow asked.

"Too many to count. A mix. Not just Bar Regren. There were Iascans, mostly northern Iascan, a mix of brawlers and youngsters prentice age. A lot of them didn't even have weapons. A few had put rocks in the lap of their tunics, but once they tossed those, they mostly got in everyone's way." She sighed. "Lineas had taught me a few Bar Regren words. I charged anyone with a sword, but a lot of those brats, I whacked them with my sword and yelled at 'em to run. Some ran. Some didn't." Her voice roughened. "They had crowd-madness on 'em. You could see it. It's worse at night, I think."

She wiped a hand over her forehead. "Like Braids said, it was back and forth, back and forth, even when the sun came up. We worked not to let them surround us, but twice they did. I think it was spillover, there were just so many of them and they had nowhere to go. So when we got circled, I had Tevaca blow the retreat, then attack, retreat, then attack, the idea being—"

Arrow leaned forward. "Turn outward and charge, right?"

"That's it. I saw my uncle use it in a game once, and well, it worked twice, drove them back to give us breathing room, but we were still surrounded. Then Noth came at the charge to relieve us."

Royal attention shifted to Rat Noth.

Rat said flatly, "Royal Runner Lineas caught up with me. Reported Neit's orders, and that Senelaec vanguard was taken by surprise. When we saw what they did to the Senelaecs, we used a double-wing wedge to break down the middle, and then flight wedges to break 'em further, until they began melting."

"And?" Arrow prompted.

"Soon's they broke and ran, I sent Basna to reinforce Marlovayir at the east gate while the rest of us dealt with the rest. Basna reported that he arrived there to find that somehow the enemy seemed to know that they'd lost. They were already running. He and Marlovayir chased them right back into the marsh. Then it was a matter of cleanup."

He chewed the inside of his lip, noticed the queen's unblinking gaze, and said, "The worst of it was not our people. Reined 'em tight fairly fast. They all know what happens if we catch 'em looting. Trouble was mostly Iascans in town going at each other, saying this or that person was a collaborator. Looting. Set a few places afire."

"Shit," Arrow exclaimed. "They didn't think to bring that to Ventdor earlier? Of course they didn't," he added sarcastically. "They were waiting to see who won."

"Mostly that seems to be it. When we left to come here to report, Garrison Commander Ventdor was sifting through all the accusations. He told us that it might take time, but the one thing he heard consistently was that Elsarion had apparently stopped paying most of his spies at the end of winter."

"Once he knew the boys were coming for him," Arrow stated, and smacked his hands on his knees. "Well done, all of you." He paused, and eyed Neit. "So . . . what are you now?"

Rat Noth, Pepper Marlovayir, and Braids Senelaec turned to Neit, who had insisted on going back to being a runner as soon as the battle was over.

"Runner, to the Senior Jarlan of Olavayir—"

Danet's voice cracked. "No."

Everybody turned Danet's way.

Danet crossed her arms and fixed a fiery gaze on Arrow. "Field promotions hold, don't they? Especially after a victory?"

Neit looked down, then up. "I'm a runner," she said, her voice rising. "I've had no training for command—"

"What," Danet said trenchantly, "would you call all those years of wargames at Olavayir?"

Neit shot a betrayed look at Noddy, leaning on the back of Arrow's chair. He looked away.

Neit braced her shoulders. "I love being a runner. I'm best outdoors. The only time I have to deal with papers is carrying them to hand off, and I'm good at *speaking* reports. It would take me days to write one."

Danet said, "That's logistics. *My* realm. I have people trained for that. This isn't the time to talk about why I need you, and where, but you'd be out in the field, training. You and Henad Tlennen. We'll address it later." Danet sat back.

Arrow rubbed his hands. "The Battle of Ku Halir! Oh, I can hardly wait to hear it sung. Rat. All of you," he added, with a fast glance at Danet, "promotions all around. I've sent for young Gannan, what's his name again?"

"Cabbage," Noddy said, smiling briefly from his place behind Arrow's wing chair.

"I knew it was a vegetable." Arrow snapped his fingers. "Why? No, don't tell me. It won't make any sense. It never does. We'll put your Cabbage in as jarl until next Convocation, and if he keeps doing as well as he has, the jarls will shut up about Yvana—Stalgoreth." Arrow frowned, then smacked his hands against his thighs again. "Yes. Stalgoreth. Young Gannan is going to have to change his name. Start a new line. That'll divide him off from that horseapple of a father, and as for that shit Blue—"

Danet cleared her throat. Arrow's head jerked up, and he became aware he was rambling on about affairs best kept to themselves. Dull red mottled his cheeks. His nose was already red, the effects of the long siege of heavy drinking ever since the news arrived about his brother.

Arrow mumbled, "Never mind that. It can wait. This is what I wanted to say. Rat, this is twice you've been here after a victory, and I've asked what I can give you as a reward. You turned me down flat. Not this time. There has to be something."

These words, so generous, knotted Rat's heart, and anxiety cramped his middle, worse than charging from the front line into battle. Why was it that, though he'd mastered his childhood stutter years ago, when he needed words the most, that was when he was unable to speak them?

In despair he lifted his head, turning toward Bunny—

And saw her smile as her fingers flickered, *Ask.*

He stilled. Did it mean—no. How could she possibly—

"Ask," she signed again.

It took more courage than mere battle to turn to the king, and to say, "I—I'd like to marry. Your daughter."

Arrow's jaw dropped. He gazed back blankly, never having given the possibility a thought. Then he pivoted in his chair and threw a helpless look at Danet.

Whose thin smile curled. Oh, this was perfect, she was thinking. That damned Jarlan of Feravayir had been avoiding Bunny for all this time, well, the decision was now out of her hands. It was her own stepson who had triumphed in war, now asking for Bunny's hand. No honor denied, except maybe to the older brother, but he'd had *years* to come forward.

Danet turned to her daughter, about to ask what she thought—and caught such a bright-eyed grin that she wondered if she'd been blind. Never mind.

"So asked, so it is done," she said formally, echoed in a slightly dazed mumble by Arrow.

On her way out, Bun whispered to her first runner, "Go get a good helping of that gerda-leaf from the big cannister Noren's Holly keeps in your runner annex. I know Noren won't mind."

The streams running down the pass had dried to a trickle by the time Connar and his company reached West Outpost. They found it orderly, restored except for the gate, which was gone, the wood no doubt claimed by the wood guild. Same with the battering ram.

A young man with a single chevron came running downstairs and fetched up to salute. Connar didn't recognize him at all.

"Where's Gannan?" Connar demanded. "I told him to hold this outpost."

"King summoned him to the royal city." Tevac quailed at the irritation he saw in Connar's tight mouth, and though he hadn't thought of that disaster with the Headmaster's office and the prince in ages, residual guilt prompted him to stick strictly to his own orders. If Connar-Laef wanted to know about anything else he could ask. Yes, that was safest.

"Who are you?"

"Tevac. Riding Captain, and Temporary Outpost Commander's Aide, left in charge while Temporary Outpost Commander Gannan is in the royal city."

Tevac . . . then Connar had it: the scrub who'd ratted him out that last year in the academy. His back twitched. He eyed Tevac, a weedy young man, long-nosed, blond, indistinguishable from many. If he said *anything* . . .

But Tevac stared straight in front of him, and Connar fought down the urge to gut the little shit. He glanced around, making an effort to sound indifferent. "Anything to report?"

Like . . . Ku Halir? No, better to stick strictly to his own orders. "No one has come down from the east since the royal runner. The only people from the west are our supplies. We've had to set up daily deliveries of water barrels from the lake this past month, as everything's dried up." Tevac's voice died to a mumble under Connar's flat blue stare.

Connar was remembering Quill's *If we take the southern pass, we cannot hold it.* Irritation surged again, and he turned away, saying, "We'll need water for the ride west. But as soon as we reach Wened, I'll see that you get replacement."

"Thank you, Commander." Tevac saluted.

Connar walked away, as behind him Tevac flicked a glance at his two fellow riding captains, giving them tacit permission to vanish.

Connar had forgotten them already. He desperately needed a bath, which he was not going to get unless at least his captains could do so as well, but there was not enough water. Or food. Also, they were on summer rations.

For the sake of the horses needing to drink well before starting the hot ride to Lake Wened, they spent the night. They rode out before dawn to get a good start before the heat.

When they reached Wened, Connar inspired a festival atmosphere when he hired every available carter and barrel to carry water and as much food as possible to West Outpost. It was satisfying to say, "The crown will pay for it"—though he was annoyed by an echo of that voice about the cost of war.

We'll see that the Adranis pay it, Connar promised himself, and turned his mind to the prospect of a bath, clean clothes, and something, or someone, to distract the gallop of his thoughts since he couldn't outrun them.

The word went out that the crown was paying for the prince's company's liberty, which turned the entire town into festival cheer.

A night of liberty did a great deal to restore good spirits to the company. Connar was not quite halfway through his first cup of cold ale in months when he caught a pair of hot eyes.

Down went the cup.

Four times all told, two men, two women, before he retired for a few hours of sleep in the room summarily cleared for him.

He woke at dawn, his body more relaxed that it had been for months, but his mind still galloped ahead, to Ku Halir—victory?—what had happened during the months he was away, specifically how his orders were carried out. He should have asked more of that horseapple Tevac. He should have . . .

He slammed off to bathe again.

They rode out directly after the morning meal, orderly as always, but those who paid attention to the distances between people, and who spoke to whom, were aware that the Riders returning from the Adrani pass were three distinct groups: the Ku Halir lancers, eager to get back, and a further more subtle division between Jethren's men and Stick's and Ghost's.

At last, Ku Halir rose on the horizon.

Connar expected salutes and cheers when they were sighted. They got them, but it wasn't the frenzy he'd anticipated, and deserved, now that Elsarion was effectively dead. Maybe Quill had gone straight to the royal city without stopping to report.

Ventdor came out to the stable yard, looking older and more careworn than Connar remembered. He spoke the words officially releasing the lancers to their commander, who immediately gave them all liberty. Then Connar said, "The rest of you, liberty as well. We'll have orders at morning muster."

He waited, catching Stick's and Ghost's glances, and they acknowledged with the Hand sign for *got it.* Manther Yvanavayir went with the two captains.

Jethren, watching obliquely, saw all this unspoken communication and walked away, strictly controlling his temper. After everything he'd done . . . but, he reminded himself, Ghost and Stick had been with the true king all his life. They were together at Chalk Hills, and Tlennen Plain. Of course it would take more than a year to prove himself, much less to replace them.

Unless something happened.

Connar turned his back on Jethren: out of sight, out of mind. With Stick, Ghost, and Manther at his back, he proceeded to Ventdor's office, where Uncle Barend was holding the desk.

Commander Ventdor waved all the runners out and shut the door.

Connar said, "We cleaned the southern pass all the way to Elsarion, and he himself is effectively dead."

Ventdor opened his hand. "Young Quill stopped to change horses, and gave us the gist of the report he's carrying to Arrow. They turned him into a statue! Should have turned him over to *us,* but . . ." He shrugged. "They're Adranis." He said *Adranis* in the same tone as one would say *boneheads.*

Ventdor seemed to regard the subject as closed. Connar felt impelled to say, "Did Quill report on the battle at West Outpost?"

"Yes," Ventdor replied. "Said it was fairly hot. He didn't say a lot, but I heard enough to recognize that you cut it tight, scrambling over some mountain in order to come at the Adranis from the back end. Very well planned. Your father is going to enjoy that."

'Scrambling over some mountain.' Connar did not know what to say to such profound understatement. Just as well, because Ventdor went on, "I guess no runners got to you while you were running up and down the pass, so you probably want the details of our battle."

"Battle?" Connar repeated, expecting—wanting—Ventdor to correct himself and say skirmish, scuffle, dust-up.

Ventdor opened his hands. "I didn't think it could get much worse than Tlennen Hills. I was wrong."

And he told Connar, in excruciatingly vivid detail. Halfway through this account, Connar began to perceive that this was the battle he should have commanded. *Of course* the Bar Regren, or the Iascans, or even the Idegans, would try something as soon as they discovered that he'd taken the best of the northern garrisons east. He should have sent Rat Noth over that damn mountain, but he'd wanted the pleasure of killing Elsarion himself, and so he'd assigned Rat Noth a patrol area as far from any possible battleground as he could.

Inda-Harskialdna had never made this kind of mistake.

Ventdor, unaware that he'd all but lost his audience, went on at length about Rat Noth's excellence, once more coming to the rescue. The Senelaecs' heroism. Neit—Neit!—in command! Lineas running a heroic race to bring Rat Noth just in time.

Ventdor finally paused to draw breath, and glanced at the prince, expecting to see his own emotions shared. He didn't recognize the expression on Connar's face, but instinct prompted him to add, "Of course the credit overall goes to you for putting the right people in the right places, so whatever happened, we had the entire north covered. That was excellent foresight," Ventdor finished. "Not a bad start for your first two years of command."

Connar stared back as he struggled to assimilate the fact that the torment of Skytalon, and the triumph of West Outpost, had been entirely overshadowed by the Battle of Ku Halir.

But everyone seemed to think he'd foreseen it.

Danet listened to Quill's report with growing horror, and then a rising fury. It was even worse than she'd dreaded. She looked at the faces gathered around Arrow, then away: one of the worst things you could say after hearing how many lives had been lost was how utterly useless it had been.

She glared at Arrow, who coughed, then used the back of his hand to wipe his eyes. Was that a tremor in his fingers? Her anger shifted to resentment at how old he looked. She could blame the bristic, but she knew that grief caused him to drink more heavily than he ever had. Jarend was dead, not from an assassin's knife, or from leading a battle. He'd died in bed, from a malady that struck the old. But they *weren't* that old! She was just short of fifty. Jarend hadn't been even sixty!

Arrow peered at Quill, whose bones had sharpened considerably since the last time he'd reported. He counted up, shocked that two years had passed so quickly. "Good work," Arrow said, and recollecting that he'd sent Quill away on the heels of that business down south, "Take the day off."

Danet shot him a glower. "Quill. Tell Mnar Milnari that you should have at least a week before taking up your duties again. She and the others can handle one more week."

Quill saluted, hand to heart. The only emotion he betrayed was a flush along those blade-sharp cheekbones; he'd done his best to report what happened, not what he thought, but he'd seen the queen's reaction.

As soon as he was gone, Danet considered what to say. Too late for *Connar was far too young for that kind of responsibility.* Arrow was no longer able to ride like thunder across the plains. He said himself he'd never be able to direct a battle.

So avoid battles, Danet longed to say. Except the Bar Regren hadn't permitted them that luxury. But would that have been true if Connar hadn't gone chasing up the pass?

When Arrow shot her a wary glance—he knew her well, and had sensed her bristling—she said only, "When Connar gets back, perhaps it's time for him to complete the long-deferred tour of the south. I think he needs to get a good sense of the entire kingdom, don't you?"

Arrow's brow lifted. "Yes. Good idea. Very good idea. And when he gets back, he can start taking some of the load off Andaun, who keeps making noises about retirement. He's been running the academy coming up on thirty years, and he wasn't that young when we corralled him into it. Seems to me it's time Connar takes a hand over there."

Danet bit back a tart response that with the second year of girls joining the academy, Noren or Bunny could as easily help Andaun, couldn't they?

One thing at a time.

"Agreed," was all she said, and then glanced at Noddy, who stared down at his hands, his big, bony face long, his mouth unhappy, and a pang stabbed deep in her chest at how much he reminded her of Jarend. He had looked exactly like that that terrible day when he became king for an hour.

She flicked a glance at Noren, who caught Noddy's attention with some easy questions.

Upstairs, Quill finished summarizing his report to Mnar.

"We've missed you," Mnar said bluntly. "Seems to me there's a lot you didn't say, but I can't imagine any of it was easy."

He opened his hands, a gesture that reminded her so strongly of Shendan that her throat hurt. She said gruffly, "Go get something to eat. You're too skinny."

But he had other things on his mind.

He walked through the castle, breathing the familiar air, and listening to the sounds of normalcy. Sanity. Safety. Oh, how good it was to be back in the roost! He took a long bath, and returned to his room, where he found his clothes neatly laid aside. Nothing of Lineas's was there—she was too scrupulous for that—but her scent was there, very faint, but there, on his pillow. He breathed deeply of it, feeling iron bands loosen from around his heart, bands he had not known were there until their merciless grip eased.

Still two hours in the day watch; he didn't trust himself to seek Lineas out. It was beyond him to maintain proper decorum if he saw her face. So he obeyed orders after all, retreating to the baths, where he dealt with all his clothing. He went off to the boot-maker to order more boots, and last to the mess hall, where familiar faces hailed him after his time away. A meal of just-baked hot pie, rolls, and fresh berry compote filled him up.

When the night watch bell rang, he went up to the roost, his heart beating in his ears.

She was there. Standing in the middle of his room. Everything he felt he saw in Lineas's face. One moment for each to see that the other was truly there, and then they were together, mouths frantic, hands ripping impatiently at clothing as they tried to touch everywhere at once.

Later—much later—Lineas curved against him, and tenderness shivered through her at the minute shifts he made while drowsy and half-asleep in order to fit her more tightly against him, one hand coming up to brush over her cheek, and trace down to rest on her hip.

"It's the details that can betray us," he murmured into her soft cloud of hair. "I couldn't transfer. A loose horse coming down the pass would have raised questions. I had to run the entire pass alone, and at West Outpost Gannan pressed his own favorite mount on me, which meant I must ride it myself to Ku Halir. At least I could get out West Outpost after only an hour, though by the time of my arrival it was mostly cleaned up, all except the ghosts."

Lineas's muscles tightened, and Quill's drowsiness vanished. He cupped his hand around her chin and gently turned her head so he could see her face. "You know that's just an expression. Truth to tell, if I could have the memory of that slaughter cut out of my skull I'd thank the person wielding the knife."

She laid her head against his chest, listening to the timbre of his voice through the fremitus. The grief she could feel, and hear, chilled her.

"Lineas?" he asked.

She shivered again. "Just a foolish reaction."

He said, "Lineas, I don't believe you're capable of foolishness."

"Oh, if only you knew."

"If I don't, then tell me." He kissed her. "I remember when you were small you worried so much about being perceived as normal. Whatever that is. Sometimes I think there is no such thing. There is only an agreed-on fiction that we all pretend to. But I've always treasured you for being you. Always. Far before I woke up to all the possibilities of love."

"It's . . ." She rolled away, and propped herself on her elbow so that she could see his face, and the sincerity there.

He loved the subtle changes in her expression, the twitch of her eyebrows, the way her eyes narrowed with hidden laughter. The deep dimples beside her mouth, enhanced by the freckles.

"That is, I do," she whispered. "Tell you everything."

"Almost everything," he said. "There are two subjects you've avoided, Connar and ghosts."

She chuckled, surprised, her expressive brows lifting then furrowing. "I . . . have learned to avoid the subject of ghosts. And there really isn't much to say." Her gaze shifted. "Connar . . . I never wanted him to be a, a thing between you and me."

"He isn't," Quill said. "He's an important part of our lives, for a variety of reasons, but if you were thinking of resentment or jealousy on my part, I don't resent your relationships present or past. We can talk about the future."

"Oh, I'm so glad," she murmured. "It's very hard—I feel I somehow failed, because everyone else can part with ease, but I . . . didn't. He walked away, and I knew he was very angry with me. Though neither of us had ever made any promises."

Quill was silent, thinking over his few encounters with Connar. There'd been some kind of tension there. "It couldn't be jealousy," he murmured, more to himself.

"Jealousy?" she repeated, her brow furrowed. "Impossible. He has numberless lovers. And we never made promises, as I said."

"It's a guess only, and I'm probably wrong," Quill admitted. "I hope I am. Camerend told me when I was small that jealousy is one of those emotions that gives you absolutely nothing but pain. Even anger can be useful. But not jealousy. Maybe Connar doesn't trust me."

"Why?" Lineas rose on an elbow, looking worried. "But he sent you on such vital missions!"

Quill was sorry to see alarm widening her eyes. "Mistrust might be the wrong idea. Or maybe it's a personal distrust. Eh," he added, as the alarm in Lineas's face did not abate. "People do get sudden antipathies, same as sudden attraction. I've seen so little of him over the years, I don't know him at all. I'll exert myself now to keep it that way. It's a big castle, a big kingdom. Lineas, my point is, if you want to talk about him—about why your parting was terrible, or what's happened since—you can."

"I'm going to try to stay away also," she said softly. "As for ghosts . . . I see them." Her whisper was so low he almost didn't hear her.

"You . . ."

"See them." She let out a soft hiss of decision. "The day the king and queen took over the throne, the old gunvaer saw Evred's ghost. Everyone talked of that. So I assumed that he was the one I saw my very first day here, right before I met you, and frequently since. Well, I thought it was Evred Olavayir. But the one I see is actually Lanrid Olavayir. The son of Mathren Olavayir."

Quill sat up, all vestiges of sleep gone. This conversation was straying into territory he was only used to hearing from his mother. "How did you find out? Where have you seen him?"

Relieved at his lack of the usual annihilating disbelief or contemptuous skepticism, she told him what had happened at Larkadhe, and then Fish's surprising comment. "I guess that drawing I made got saved, and shown to someone who knew Lanrid," she finished.

He said slowly, "But Lanrid Olavayir was never here, was he?"

"As a small child, he was. Then he and his little brother were sent to Olavayir after their mother died. This is not a child ghost. He's a young man. But then how ghosts appear, where, and why, I have *never* understood."

Quill lifted a strand of curly hair off her forehead, where it had tangled with her eyelashes. "What does it mean when a ghost hangs around like that?"

"I don't know. No one does. Maybe the Cassads can talk to ghosts, or at least make sense of them, but I can't. It's the most useless . . . thing . . . in life."

"Really?" he asked, laughing under his breath. "I thought the most useless thing in life was male nipples."

She clapped her hand over her mouth but could not hold the laughter in. It wasn't that the comment was so very funny, it was mostly relief—and a heart overflowing with tenderness. She really could tell him anything! Why was it so much better to have a living, breathing person hearing one than the silent neutrality of the journal?

TWO

A month later, Lineas woke alone to the sky clouding up.

Lineas's morning class had been assigned to the barns. She stood before her window, hands cupping her elbows as she gazed out into the rain.

It was the first cold rain of the season, a harbinger of winter to come. Ordinarily she loved the changing of the seasons, but somehow the chill rain hissing against the castle walls, turning them from warm dusty gold to dull brown, matched her mood.

The happiness of this month together had been almost too much to bear, because each night when she sank into Quill's arms to sleep, she knew that one of these mornings she would be alone again in that bed. Connar was due back at any time, and might very well summon Quill to another long, dangerous duty, whatever his motivation.

A knock at her half-open door, and a fledge leaned in. "Lineas, you're wanted."

Lineas turned away from the window. "Who is it?"

"The tall captain. Wears a runner robe when she's not garrison-side," the boy replied.

"Neit?"

"That's the one!"

"Bring her up."

He slapped an awkward, big-knuckled hand against his scrawny chest, and with a flick of ragged sash-ends and equally ragged hair, he was gone.

The rules were strict: no one upstairs unless escorted. He reappeared soon, bringing Neit, who overtopped him by a head. To Lineas, she looked even taller and more imposing wearing a Rider's gray coat, the skirts swinging as she strode in. You couldn't say she had a man's stride—there was a natural swing to those magnificent hips that was not even remotely masculine—but that stride seemed more suited to a parade ground. Neit seemed too big for the room.

"Neit? Is something amiss?"

Neit snorted. "I was going to invite you over to get something to drink, and ease my way around to it."

Lineas's smile widened at the notion of Neit attempting to ease her way around to anything. "You know I don't like to drink."

"I remember it. But I never *believed* it, until you started in about ghosts, after Chalk Hills. Damn, that was scary. I know that was sick-Lineas. Is that also drunk-Lineas?"

"Drunk-Lineas falls asleep with her head on the table, and wakes up covered with drool, and a hammering headache," Lineas retorted. "Which is why I don't drink. Come in. There's my chair. Tell me."

"I need to talk to you about the gunvaer."

Lineas was about to sit on the bed, but at this, she whirled around. "Neit! What makes you think I know *anything* about the gunvaer?"

"Because you ran for her daughter for years, then for the boys. Because you were down there on the second floor at least as much as anyone outside her own runners. Because I know you." Neit crossed her arms over her chest, her cleft chin raised. "I need advice, not argument or fart noise about duty, or just-wait-everything's-fine." She tipped her head. "Speaking of the royal family, there's also Noddy—nah, that can wait."

Lineas sank down onto the bed. "I'll help if I can."

"I need a way to convince the gunvaer to get me out of this command," Neit said seriously.

Lineas stared. "You've only been doing it for a month. Are the men giving you trouble, is that it?"

Neit snorted. "As if I didn't learn how to handle *that* when I was at Olavayir. Oh, I've had a couple dust-ups, but it's only with snotty eighteen-year-olds fresh out of the academy, who seem to think I got promoted over them on a whim. No problem." Her mocking grin vanished. "It's the rules. The saluting. I never can remember who gets what, and when."

Lineas said seriously, "It's a reminder of the chain of command, and of order."

"I *know* that. Here." Neit tapped the top of her sun-bleached head, then snapped her fingers wide. "Not here. I grew up only saluting when carrying a formal report, jarlan's or jarl's voice. And even then, in Olavayir, we seldom salute—everyone knows one another."

She looked away, and sighed. "I know the gunvaer is trying to get women fitted into the King's Army, but seems to me Henad Tlennen and her two cousins are the best at that. They were in the queen's training, so they know all the protocol. They're just on the young side."

"What do *you* want?" Lineas asked.

Neit pursed her lips. "Besides out? Hadn't thought that far, other than go back to normal."

"I'm the gunvaer." Lineas stood up, bent her head and tried to glare under her brows at Neit. "Now tell me what you want."

Neit had to compress her lips against the impulse to laugh—skinny, redheaded little Lineas with all those freckles was as unlike the tall, brown gunvaer with the steely stare as it was possible to be.

Neit shut her eyes. Then she said slowly, "I'll help run battles if I know the territory. And wargames, too. But I'm just no good at daily drill and the rest of it. In fact I hate it." She sighed. "And if you say 'go tell her just that' I'll have to punch you."

Lineas flattened her hand in negation. "If you do go back to Olavayir, who will you be?"

"Runner to the . . ." Neit began in an impatient you-know-that voice, then faltered.

Neit had been runner for Ranor-Jarlan until the latter's sight began to fail. As Tdor Fath slipped into the jarlan role, using her own runners, Neit had been given long runner duties, which she welcomed. But even those got taken over by Tanrid's and Fala's runners, which was what made it possible for her to serve at Larkadhe for nearly two years, and then put her in a position to help at Ku Halir.

But now Jarend-Jarl as well as his mother were dead, and Tanrid was completely responsible for Olavayir. He had his own command tree, and he, like his father, liked order. *His* order. His wife had her own command tree, including a lot of her connections from Lindeth, which brought good relations between the harbor city and Olavayir.

Neit could go back to Olavayir, and they'd take her in, but she'd have to find someplace to fit.

Lineas had been watching Neit's strong face, and the gradual sobering of her expression. "I think you should talk to Noren, rather than the gunvaer. If you tell her what you just told me, I imagine it would be easy for her to make you some kind of attached captain, to be called on if there's trouble. But in the meantime, there's always a need for runners."

Neit slapped her hands on her knees. "I'll do it. I don't really know her, and my Hand never was all that good even in our Larkadhe days, worse since I haven't had to use it. But I can get by. Same as I do in North Iascan." She got to her feet. "Maybe I can find out what's with Noddy, at the same time."

"Noddy?" Lineas asked.

"He's been . . . hovering. I can't explain it better than that. Like he's got something on his mind, but he won't say it. And so he looks at me in that way he has when he wants you to know what it is he's thinking. At first I thought he was getting upset when I forgot saluting and rules—you know how he likes everything to be just so, same as his uncle did."

"Maybe he's the one to take out for the drink?" Lineas asked.

Neit laughed. "I'll do that. Noren first."

She walked out, then decided that there was no time like the present. It was midday, between watches as many caught their noon meal, which meant she was likelier to catch Noren between duties.

She ran down to the next floor, and found the expected pair of duty sentries. "I need to talk to Noren-Haranviar."

"Go on," said the senior sentry.

Neit made her way down the hall to the royal suites. She'd been to Noddy's countless times. It seemed odd to knock at the opposite door.

A cheerful-faced runner opened the door. Neit walked in, noticing a conversation going on, though all she heard was the swish of fabric, the muted snap and pop of joints as fingers danced and fluttered.

Noren was central. She looked up, a solid figure a head and a half shorter than Neit. Smart, observant gaze.

Calling up all her knowledge of Hand, Neit explained that she'd been talking to Lineas, who suggested she come to Noren. Somewhat surprisingly, Noren glanced consideringly around at the busy runners, then in a quick series of gestures, cleared the room.

Neit grimaced, wishing her Hand was better. But Noren was patient as Neit worked through her explanation.

At the end, Noren said in Hand, "Lineas's idea is excellent. I think we could use you as one of our Queen's Training runners, especially as our girls are being fitted to the garrisons. We have fewer runners who know both the military and how to make grass runs. Just remember, the gunvaer wants more women in command. If we need you, we'll summon you."

Neit pressed her palms together in thanks, feeling stress drain off her shoulders. She prepared to leave, but Noren flicked up her fingers to halt her. She looked uneasy, then finally asked in Hand, "Has Noddy spoken to you?"

Neit opened her hands, unsure how to word the odd way Noddy had been sidling around her this past week or two. It couldn't be a simple question for a night of fun—he knew he could ask for that any time, as he and Noren hadn't made a ring marriage.

Then Noren signed, "Would you carry a child for him?"

Neit stared, unsure she'd understood the signs.

Noren slowed down, making each sign distinct, then patted her stomach in emphasis.

Blank-minded shock gave way to horror, which Neit struggled to hide, as Noren went on, "It's important to him. To the gunvaer. For him to have an heir. We have had no success. He really likes you. If you don't want to be a consort or favorite and live with us, we'd be happy to adopt the baby—whatever you choose, he'd be the next heir, if a boy."

Neit rubbed her suddenly sweaty palms down her coat skirt. She had never wanted to be tangled up in a permanent relationship, much less deal with babies. Leave that to Floss! But if she were to have a child, she knew she couldn't just hand it off. She'd feel in some wise responsible, and the idea of a child of hers raised as a prince and caught in the steel blades of royal politics . . .

This royal family was good people. At least, she liked what she'd seen of the gunvaer—though she was intimidating—and Noddy was a dear. The king was little more than a distant figure, much missed by Ranor-Jarlan and

Jarend-Jarl when alive. Connar . . . she didn't really *like* him, but he was shaping up to be a good commander. She had no complaints about any of them, but she'd also grown up with stories about generations of bloody conflict between princes, and whispered anecdotes about the Nighthawk Company in the wake of some of those grim old Olavayir Riders.

Neit forced herself to think ahead. When Connar had sons, would they be friends with any son she had? A girl would be less of a problem, but there were just too many ballads about princes riding to death in the name of glory —against each other.

And yet Noren had just been really decent about her situation. Feeling like a snake, she sighed, "May I think about it?"

"Do," Noren signed back. "You can always talk to either of us whenever you're ready—"

The bells tanged three times: royal arrival. Through the open windows, over the sound of the rain, a distant echo of trumpets carried to Neit. She signed to Noren, "Connar's back."

Noren opened her hand in acceptance. Neit thanked her with a formal salute, and decamped with what she knew very well was craven haste, leaving Noren sitting alone.

Noren had seen the horror that Neit had tried so hard to hide. She'd have to warn Noddy off before he got the resolve to put his question to Neit, and they both got hurt. It was going to wound him enough as it was. *Oh Mother. You did tell me that my false pose would be hard on me. But I don't think you had any idea how much pain it would cause to the innocent.*

She knew she had to join the rest of the family to welcome Connar back from his long campaign. She forced herself to her feet, and reached for the little bell that let her runners know she was through being alone. She shook it hard enough to feel the vibration in her fingers, and the runners swarmed in, hands flicking *Connar-Laef.*

Close behind them was Ranet, blue eyes wide with joy, carrying little Iris on her hip. Danet arrived behind her, flanked by Noddy and his father.

They started downstairs, Danet leaving orders for a feast in her suite.

Connar's company splashed up the street toward the royal castle, sodden banners limp and streaming. By the time they rode into the courtyard, the entire royal family was there to welcome them, plus a crowd of anxious family members standing behind to see who arrived with him.

Connar saw that the though the castle walls had castle denizens cheering and banging drums, and the people on the streets all shouted, the entire city had not turned out. If he'd left the Elsarion land behind in smoking ruin, and dragged Elsarion back over the pass covered in chains, that would have been the Inda-Harskialdna victory, a *real* victory, which would have brought the entire city out on the walls even in a thunderstorm with lightning striking all around, and sleet like steel arrows.

But, he reminded himself, at least he had returned with *a* victory. And it was his first action as Commander of the King's Army.

They rode into the courtyard of the royal castle, and there was Noddy's happy smile, and sincerity in his, "You're back! What a triumph!"

Ma was next, looking thin and careworn, but the shock was Da, who'd somehow in the last year gone to white hair, his horsetail thin and bedraggled as it dripped rain. But he walked with his old swagger as he came forward to pound Connar on the back.

"Excellent, excellent," he said. "Everyone's agreed, no one could have done better. You put the right people in the right places . . . hey, get something to eat, and meet your little crawler. Hard to believe you've never even seen her!"

He stepped back and there was Ranet carrying a child, and looking beautiful even in the rain. Connar smiled from Ranet to the child, who stared back incuriously; he didn't hear one word in ten, or watch her hands. He was aware on the surface that the Winter Company had dropped the habit of talking in Hand because Jethren and his company only knew a few signs.

Maybe it was recovering the old habit of talking in Hand, but he felt a sense of constraint tightening around him as Ranet pressed up against him, expecting a kiss. As was her right.

Still, he was aware of a spurt of impatience as he kissed her. Ranet was a perfect wife in all the possible ways anyone could ask, and yet he could not shake this sense that she was another duty.

Impulse prompted a scan of the busy courtyard, then the walls for a familiar red head, before he realized he was looking for Lineas. Who was not there.

Everything was good, he thought consciously as everyone pressed around with questions. But the knot of disappointment in his gut was proof that it could have been better.

A few buildings back of the main castle, the sound of the prince's arrival fanfare had risen above the diminishing rain, carried through Chief Weaver Hliss's open windows, where she sat with Quill as Blossom laboriously worked on a lesson.

Hliss had been considering pros and cons of imminent departure for what had become her customary winter-over in Darchelde with Camerend.

She sensed a slight movement and glanced over to see Quill had stilled, his profile shuttered in a way that reminded her of Camerend when faced with unpleasant duty.

Quill bent to correct Blossom's grip, and as he praised her letters, his shoulder hid his face. Hliss waited for him to say something, but he didn't.

Presently a runner appeared, inviting Hliss and Blossom to the queen's suite for Connar's welcome home meal. "I'll get back to the roost," Quill said.

Mother and daughter walked hand in hand, Blossom skipping as she caroled, "Do I get to play with Baby Iris?"

"Oh, certainly, if she's not with her minder."

Blossom clapped her hands.

Upstairs, any thought Connar had had of shaking free ended abruptly when Danet turned in the hall, her gaze lingering on Iris babbling away as she said to Ranet and Connar, "I'll send a runner when the meal's ready. Take some time together."

After which Ranet smiled up at Connar and whispered, "I started drinking gerda-root as soon as the runner arrived saying you were on the way." She held out the baby to him. "Iris, this is your Da! Can you say 'Da'? . . ."

She kept up a stream of talk about how brilliant the baby was, and news about the queen's training and how many volunteers were staying for their ten years of service instead of going home again.

She talked, happily sharing the two years of news she believed he wanted to hear until he found himself swept into Ma's outer chamber with the family, including Aunt Hliss and her brat, busy making noise over there with small Iris.

Connar sat down between his father and Noddy, his longing to get down to the garrison having to be squashed. It looked like he wouldn't get there until after he gave his report. That was fine. He just wished he could do that now.

But his da looked around at them all, his grin a match to Ma's obvious pleasure in having him back again. Connar met Hliss's cool gaze and then slid away in disinterest; he knew he should be happy to be back, but he wished he was sitting around a campfire with Ghost and Stick, planning a campaign.

Hliss sat beside Danet, taking in her sister's happy profile. Danet was never chatty, but the way her gaze strayed from one to another young face showed how greedy she was for family gathered close. Numbers, Hliss had said once to Camerend, were Danet's greatest comfort, and here was family in number. Danet smiled at Ranet and Connar, sitting across from one another. Hliss knew that smile. Danet wanted more children, to insure order.

Hliss's gaze strayed back to Connar as his father asked for details about the battle at the pass. "Later, maybe?" Connar said, in that warm voice that so rarely used warm words. "When I make my report? Then I don't have to go through it twice."

"Good enough," Arrow said. "Soon's we eat, we can go into the map room."

Connar opened his hand, then bent toward Danet, who started talking about Henad Tlennen, " . . . she's only nineteen or twenty, which is probably too young yet for battalion command—what do you think?"

As Connar answered his mother, Hliss was thinking that Connar was so very beautiful, even startlingly so. He had come back, if anything, more beautiful than when he'd left, as if whatever experiences he'd had had planed him the way an artist slowly planed wood to create raptor claws, or the pattern of wings.

Hliss tried to see Connar as a person, and not as the nephew she had secretly disliked ever since that day in the court with Andas. She knew she ought not to blame the boys for her having lost her son all these years. That had been her own decision, but the heart has its own logic.

Or maybe it was that Noddy had shown real remorse that day, and had asked about Andas ever since, in contrast to Connar, who'd just shrugged and then had run off, towing his older brother. And had never, once, asked about Andas afterward. It was as if Andas had ceased to exist.

It might not be true that he thought that way—she knew that Connar and Noddy shared everything, including news. And it certainly wasn't fair to judge boys by the same standards as one would an adult, so she kept her feelings to herself, all the more before Danet's and Arrow's obvious pride.

But as the meal wound toward its end, and Arrow and Connar rose to go across to the king's chamber, she remembered that stillness in Quill when he heard the fanfare. She knew he had spent a year in Connar's company.

In a pause after an idle conversation about new sashes for Connar's coats, she said to Danet, "I think I'll leave for Darchelde tomorrow, now that the rain has lifted."

"Already?" Danet asked, brows up. "Isn't it early for that?"

Hliss opened her hands. "The flax is bedded until spring planting. And Blossom misses her father."

Danet sighed. "Connar will probably be off again, too. I wish I could keep everybody bottled up. Certainly. Go whenever you feel best, and give my regards to Camerend."

"I will." Hliss hugged Danet's familiar bony form to her, and suffered a quiver of sorrow when she noticed gray threading Danet's brown braids. "I intend to take Quill as my escort," she added as she stepped back. "And might I take Lineas as well? I'd like her to tutor Blossom in Hand."

"Of course," Danet said, her mind clearly already moving on. "Now that things are quiet, we can spare two royal runners. Take whoever you want."

It was a relief when Connar and Arrow were alone in the king's suite, with the huge map spread out on the floor between them, and Connar at last could release the words that had been tangling in his head for weeks.

It gratified him to see how closely Arrow paid attention to everything he said, whistling long and low when Connar described the avalanche that took down the two towers at the top of the pass.

"That was good thinking," Arrow exclaimed. "And damn tight timing."

"The plan came from what happened at Andahi, when Inda-Harskialdna fought off the Venn."

Arrow whistled again. "Do we teach that in the academy? Another salute to Andaun. Who, by the way, really wants to retire. But we'll talk about that later. Tell me again, with all the details. So you had Gannan still out here at the front gates of West Outpost, right? And Sindan's skirmishers here and here . . . ."

Arrow bent over the map, fingers tapping. Connar glanced away from the pinkish scalp under the white strands of hair at the top of his head. But there was nothing old in Arrow's narrow gaze as he listened intently to Connar's description of the battle at West Outpost. " . . . made sure none of them were left to backstab us," Connar finished. "Then we ran back up the pass . . ."

And so to the end, then, the part that had kept him arguing in his head ever since, especially late at night: "I know I should have stayed at Ku Halir. But I wanted to be the one to take Elsarion down."

"And so you should," Arrow declared, sitting back on his heels, hands out wide. "And so you should. You would have finished him off right and proper, if the Adrani king hadn't had the same guild and merchant groups howling at his door as I did on this side. What you want to wager there's a band of stiff-necked guild chiefs on their way here, on your heels? Your mother and I talked about that, soon's your runner showed up with the report. We can shut 'em up by turning West Outpost over to 'em. Let 'em work out who pays for what. The guilds are stiff with gold. Let *them* run it!"

Connar stared, shocked. Hand over West Outpost, after all he'd done to take it? "I'd thought I'd put Cabbage Gannan there permanently," Connar said.

Arrow flicked the words away. "I see your idea there. Good organization, heavy lancers if needed. But the same thinking goes for putting him up there at Yvan—that is, Stalgoreth. Turns out, his wife trained up with her mother—one of the best of the jarlans, everybody says so—and young Gannan learns fast. He can also quarter the First Lancers there, so they're in position to ride hard anywhere in the northern part of the kingdom. And Stalgoreth can support 'em. Whereas, putting them at West Outpost would mean a long supply line for half the year, which would have to be guarded."

Connar shrugged away the logistics, his mind on Cabbage Gannan. A jarl? He wanted Gannan right where he'd put him, to be wielded as a sword when needed, because he was an excellent commander of the heavies, but kept firmly subordinate. Making him a jarl put him independent of army command, that is, under the king . . . Connar bit back irritation and said as casually as he could, "You're going to make Cabbage Gannan a jarl?"

Arrow said in a confidential tone, "He's not nearly the horseapple his father is. Or that brother, who's worse. And we're going to make him change his name. Start a new family. That should cut old Gannan right out of assuming he can run Stalgoreth as well as Gannan. That boy is loyal to Noddy, who likes him. And his wife is a jarlan's daughter from the Eastern Alliance, so I feel certain the jarls won't howl too loud at my decision."

As the sound of cadenced yells echoed in the window from the court below, where the castle guard was drilling, Connar made one last try. "I'd thought to suggest Stick Tyavayir—that is . . ." He faltered, realizing he'd forgotten Stick's given name, and had to resort to "Tyavayir Tvei." Though he hated making any reference to the academy.

"I know who you mean." Arrow snapped his fingers. "This is also good thinking, but not broad enough. As it happens, I was down at the garrison while you were with Ranet and little Iris. Spoke to them both. Once Gannan is settled at Stalgoreth, the next one I want to settle is young Fath at Halivayir. The people there don't want anyone else, but I've still got the jarls elbowing each other to get their sons and nephews put there. So, soft and easy. Fath to command there. In a few years, when everyone is used to the changes, make him jarl. Change the name to Fath, no more 'vayir' tacked on the end. That's the old Montreivayir custom. None of the Eastern Alliance or Senelaec got it tacked on by any of our Olavayir kings, and no one's squawked."

He paused expectantly and Connar perforce agreed, for the first time finding himself impatient with one of Da's decisions.

Arrow gave him a fond grin, and went on. "As a jarl, he can make Manther Yvanavayir Captain of Riders—not my business—and that finishes the last of the Yvanavayir mess. As for the Tyavayir redhead, Sneeze keeps talking to me about retiring. He wants to go home to Olavayir, and I don't blame him. I would if I could."

Arrow sighed, his gaze sliding away. "Though without my brother . . . well. Never mind that. I'm stuck here till I'm dead, it's just the way of things. Anyway, for Ku Halir, between one thing and another it seems to be the garrison seeing the most trouble. We need a fighting captain there. Who better than your boy, young Tyavayir? I asked him, and you should have seen him light up. He'd be relatively close to his homeland. Your mother is trying to find him a good wife, as I'm sure you remember his was killed."

Connar had completely forgotten. He still didn't know what Stick thought about that. He'd been silent on the subject, though Connar knew they'd been friends. All he'd talked about was taking down Elsarion.

Arrow went on, "At Ku Halir he'll be good. Happy. And that keeps us strong in the north."

Connar agreed with the reasoning for all these decisions. Leaving him nothing to say.

Arrow squinted at him. "Don't like it?"

Connar turned his palm flat. "It's . . . I guess I thought . . . no, I see it."

"You have to think in terms of the entire map," Arrow said, hands widespread as he tried to read Connar's face. But he couldn't. He said on a coaxing note, "I know these boys are your riding mates. And if there's a big war, which I hope there won't be, they'll be riding under your banner. But until then, we need to put them where they're needed. Where we've got old commanders who've given us good years. Deserve to go home again, or if they want to stay, lighter duty."

He looked away, somber. His voice roughened with grief. "Cub Senelaec . . . I remember when he was a fuzzball, black hair and all, like your Iris. Feels like it was yesterday. They say his horse stumbled over the corpses of those damned Bar Regren he was fighting off—he had a hundred of 'em pressing in around him—and they tore him apart when he fell. Wolf crippled for life. Shit. *So* glad Rat Noth hammered them flat for that."

He went on about the battle of Ku Halir, as Connar listened, aware that the reaction to Ku Halir far outstripped that to his arduous and deadly climb. No one seemed to realize how terrible that had been, but they had no reference. There were no ballads about surviving a grueling hike over a deadly mountain. Connar himself had thought it would be easy, even after Quill explained how difficult it was. Connar remembered how he'd scoffed. And why.

" . . .but that's enough of a sore subject. It's going to take a while to forget that." Arrow sighed. "Bad. Very bad. So!"

He clapped his hands to his knees in the old way. "We try to look ahead, and that brings us to the south. While all this trouble's been going on, we pulled a lot from our southern garrisons to reinforce us here at the royal city, and to send to Ku Halir. Though I've never liked leaving those Nyidri horseapples loose down there in Feravayir. Time for you to ride the south on inspection. See first-hand."

"I thought you trusted Ivandred Noth," Connar hedged.

"I do. But speaking of retiring, he's got ten years on me, at least. As far as I can tell, he does his best, but those Nyidri snakes get around him. We learned that before your southern pass campaign, remember?"

Connar had utterly forgotten that false festival, but Quill's report emerged in memory, bringing back the righteous fury he'd felt then. "There's been no word of conspiracy since, right?"

"Right. The two Nyidri boys slithered off to Sartor. Ivandred had patrols regularly watching all the would-be captains we were able to discover. Though he didn't learn all of them. The jarlan interfered with any investigation of her precious 'nobles.'" He sighed again. "Meanwhile that jarlan is squawking and squalling about something she calls the Tax Gang."

Connar leaned forward. "*Tax Gang*?"

"That's what I heard. They're attacking here and there in the south. Carrying off loot. Though they're not like Yenvir, slaughtering left and right.

That horseapple of a jarlan's had the frost to send sent runners demanding I do something about them. But here's the thing. Ivandred Noth is silent. Like the subject doesn't exist. So I want to know what's really going on down there. If this so-called Tax Gang is a rumor the jarlan started, as a deflection. Or what. But I'm more interested in what they're up to. If there's any evidence of the Nyidris running another plot, then maybe it's time for Noth to become the jarl in fact. Him, I trust. What's more, the jarls do, too, and that's a consideration, what with three jarlates in effect vanishing in as many years. None of it's my fault, but it's my rule it happened under."

Connar's spirits soared. "We can ride by week's end."

"Hold hard." Arrow put up his hand. "I salute your eagerness, but there's no 'we.' Not if you mean your captains. Fath is going home. I told him he can leave any time. And Tyavayir is going up to help Sneeze."

Connar grimaced. "Well, I'll put together a new command."

"Do that. Start with Rat Noth. He's good. I trust him. And he knows the south."

"Right," Connar said. He could ride with Rat, who did what he was told, and did it well. Rat still seemed to think that Connar had put him west of Ku Halir because he expected an attack.

"Stay through New Year's Week at least. You should be here for your sister's wedding. Be with your wife. She's as good a girl as you can get. Everyone likes her. And . . ."

Arrow looked away, then back. "I know it's early days yet, but both your mother and I will feel more settled when either you or Noddy get a boy. Or even Bunny and Rat Noth. Everyone says the Noths always turn out boys. Well, look how many of 'em we have either down there at the academy, or spread over the garrisons. Not to mention the Riders. We can adopt Rat in. Your ma's already talking about it. Between the six of you, we should be able to get us a couple of boys, and start training them up. Then everyone knows what to expect for the next generation."

Connar suppressed a grimace. Rat Noth was like a bolt of lightning leading a charge on the battlefield, but the rest of the time he was nothing to look at, awkward in speech. Silly Bun was even worse. Connar rarely thought about the future generation—his interest was all in the now—but the idea of a jug-eared, cross-eyed, stuttering or silly future Sierlaef was repellent almost past bearing.

"Right," he said again, determination subsuming his resentment at his evening having been planned for him by his mother. The resentment spiked the expectation he'd tried to ignore: he'd avoided Lineas for two years, but riding in, he'd known he was going to find her, if she was here. And . . . what? He just wanted everything to go back exactly to the way it was—but what *was* it? Had she really been with him out of *pity?*

He gritted his teeth against the irritation, and left to do his duty.

After their arrival in the main castle courtyard, as Connar went off with his family, Ghost and Stick Tyavayir were towed along to the garrison side by old academy mates, to be pumped for details.

Kethedrend Jethren hadn't expected anyone to greet him, as he'd grown up in Olavayir, so when he came face to face with his father along with Uncle Tigger, he gaped in surprise. "What are you doing here?"

Halrid Jethren, once Lance Captain of the Nighthawk Company, whipped up his hand. Jethren tensed as his father clapped his son on the shoulder. "Young Tanrid changed everything back at Nevree. Tigger and me—" His thumb turned toward his silent brother, who'd earned his name from how hard he'd tigged lances back when they were fighting for position under Mathren. "We decided we might as well come home."

"Home?" Keth Jethren repeated, then recollected that his father had once mentioned being born in some mining village not far from East Garrison.

"But we're staying with Hauth for now," said his father. "Do you have liberty?"

"For today," Jethren muttered, Ghost's pale head vanishing through the archway ahead. Nothing had been spoken, which meant they'd get orders at morning muster.

His father grunted. "We can talk at Pereth's quarters, while your runners get your company into digs. Hauth and Pereth want to hear your report."

Jethren's expression cleared at that. "He's great," he whispered. "He's *great.* You should have seen him at West Outpost . . ."

"Save it," his father whispered. "For when we're all there to hear it."

And so, while the royal family gathered in the queen's suite, down in the quartermaster's room, the Nighthawk men squeezed into Quartermaster Pereth's office. Fish was there as well. He'd tried to avoid it by getting started on going over all Connar's gear, but his father sent a young runner up to fetch him.

Halrid Jethren, as senior captain in the Nighthawk Company, took charge of what he called a war council.

"My boy has the most to report," he said, ignoring Fish as a mere runner. "Let's hear the rest of you first. Get that out of the way."

Quartermaster Pereth turned over his hand, and gazes shifted to Retren Hauth. Who said, "I haven't spoken to the true king for a few years. He's been on the ride, as is right. But something . . . strange came up while he was at Larkadhe."

Here he laid down, with careful fingers, the paper that Lineas had drawn on.

The three blond Jethren heads bent over the paper. Keth Jethren looked back up again in indifference, followed by his Uncle Tigger, but his father whistled, eyes wide. "That's *Lanrid.*"

The name jolted them into silence.

Halrid said, "Who made this drawing?"

Hauth put his fists on his thighs. "It was made when Connar was at Larkadhe. Like I said."

"Impossible. Connar wasn't even born yet when Lanrid died in Andahi. Somebody made this before Lanrid rode north. Preserved it."

Hauth glared at the Jethrens. "It was made by a runner who saw Lanrid as a ghost. Fish Pereth there watched her sketch it."

Halrid Jethren gave a derisive snort. Tigger chuckled.

Hauth flushed with annoyance, his one eye narrowing. "Then explain how that girl could have drawn it otherwise. It's exact." He slammed his hand on the table, making the dishes jump. "And Fish was *there*. Provided the paper."

Halrid had been about to ask if Hauth had been at the bristic again. But when he looked down at the paper, he had to admit it was Lanrid to the life—the long dimples beside his mouth, even the slightly chipped front tooth. The eyes, staring right at you.

He turned it over. "I don't know what it means. Except if it's a real ghost, he has to be . . ." His harsh, derisive tone rose to question. " . . . watching his boy?"

"That's what I think, too," Retren Hauth stated. He fixed Fish with a one-eyed glare of absolute conviction. "I think he won't rest, or do whatever ghosts do, until his boy is king. The way he was supposed to be." He slapped the back of his fingers on the paper. "Lanrid grew up knowing that he was the real heir. He was about to ride to the royal city to take his rightful place!"

No one argued with that.

Hauth turned to Fish. "Now that you're back, I want you to ask that runner if she's still seeing Lanrid's ghost. Before we approach Connar about it."

Fish was thinking that he'd rather eat rocks, but kept a prudent silence as Halrid, clearly disconcerted by the subject, turned to his son. "Now. Your report, Keth."

Kethedrend Jethren had been trained to give reports. He described his time with Cabbage Gannan's First Lancers, his winter preparation for the avalanche, and then the journey over the mountain and its results.

Though Fish was there, it never occurred to Keth Jethren to turn to him for corroboration, or even to acknowledge him. To Keth, Fish was only a runner. More to the point, his family were mere connections to Hauth. The Pereths had never been part of Mathren Olavayir's selected and trained elite, the Nighthawk men.

Fish sat silently through the long report, as if he had not also walked every step of the way over Skytalon, fought at West Outpost, and followed behind Connar every step during his battles.

When Keth Jethren finished, his father grunted in approval. "Good beginning, my boy. Good beginning."

Keth Jethren lifted a powerful shoulder. "I lost four men on that mountain and he still doesn't trust me."

"That will come. That will come. You have to prove yourself first. He might say he hates Mathren Olavayir—it's to be expected, growing up hearing the eagle clan's lies—but from what you say, he's Mathren to the life. You prove your loyalty with your sword, and he'll make you his right hand. Just as Mathren did. With us." Halrid Jethren slapped his hand to his chest, his blue eyes wide and bright with conviction. "And when he's ready to become king, it's you who will make it happen."

The next morning, by the time Connar left his room, bathed, and dealt with orders, he discovered through Fish that Lineas had departed at dawn.

THREE

The Tax Gang.

It's time to catch up with Colt Cassad, who we left disgusted at the Olavayir king's typical short-sightedness about the academy. As if Colt couldn't have handled a bunch of randy boys!

But nobody argues with kings, so Colt continued to ride as Colt, a male Rider, out in the field, but at home in Cassad, Colt was Carleas to her female cousins. Colt felt exactly the same way inside. It was others whose traditions set up how people were to be regarded. The idea of sweating down to Sartor and enduring tortuous pain in order to change body parts that nobody saw anyway seemed crazy. He was who he was.

Once those girl cousins married off, there was nothing keeping Colt at Cassad—meanwhile, all his connections southward talked of Nyidri lies and rapacity. The Feravayir tax guild turned out to be all jarlan appointees, getting their cut of the extra taxes. The Olavayirs, typically, were either blind, ignorant, or indifferent, busy with their northern wars . . . and so Colt had a Cause.

Gathering like-minded riding mates, he set out to sting the Nyidris where it would hurt most: in the money chests.

Though the weather was miserable all the way to Darchelde, the many pages in Lineas's journal devoted to that journey scarcely mention it. A reader could be forgiven for assuming it was summer; later she'd remember it as a halcyon time, for she and Quill not only shared a tent—as runners often did—they shared a sleeping roll. His face was the first thing she saw each morning, disarming in sleep, entrancing when she watched the soft, veined skin of his eyelids lift and their gazes blended, igniting mutual heat.

One bleak morning a week into their journey, Hliss warmed Blossom's mittens over the fire while watching Lineas set out breakfast. Hliss said with a rueful glance, "Why are you smiling, Lineas? Nobody else is. There's nothing to smile about in rivers of mud and the threat of yet more sleet. I'm beginning to believe you aren't quite human."

Lineas blushed a deep red, clashing with the brightness of her hair, then she saw the humor in Hliss's gaze, and understood that conversation would be a welcome distraction. And, being Lineas, either she was silent, or (if she trusted the person she spoke with) she talked about what was on her mind. She had never mastered social chatter.

"It's the middle part of love," she said. "I think I like it best."

"How much longer?" Blossom said fretfully, digging her wooden spoon into the jam-laced porridge.

"Days," her mother said, as she had each of the previous five mornings. Blossom would learn to endure just as fast without being scolded. "Lay aside your spoon a moment and put these mittens on. They're nice and warm. Bring your bowl here so I can braid your hair." And with the child sitting cross-legged before her, Hliss looked up at Lineas. "What is the middle part of love?"

"Maybe there's a better word?" Lineas said. "There's the fire of admiration and desire, when you simply see the person. At the other end there's the fire when the one you desire reaches for you. But in the middle there's looking at the person's clothes, and liking to touch them when you fold them. And hearing his voice outside, talking to others. There's watching how he holds a biscuit, how he runs his hand over the saddle's belly band and the halter. All those things are . . . precious."

She cupped her thin hands and held them close to her chest. "And then seeing that the other feels the same about you. Is that so ordinary no one else thinks of it? I've only had two relationships. The first, the admiration is there still, though the third has gone away. But the middle . . . was never there."

Hliss's brows twitched upward. "Sounds like the whole range of love. Though I suspect we all define it differently. I gather Connar was careless with his things? That doesn't sound like him."

Lineas wasn't certain that mentioning Connar's name was somehow disloyal, or inappropriate, but Hliss's matter-of-fact tone reassured her. "Oh, he's not careless with his things—very much the opposite—he likes things just so. But he has Fish to oversee it all. And . . ." Lineas looked out the open tent flap at the bleak threat of clouds, and the uniform brown of the muddy landscape. "On Restday a couple days ago I dropped the cloak I was mending and ran out when Blossom called for me. When I got back, Quill had not only finished mending my cloak, he had folded it. I apologized for leaving it that way, and he told me he enjoyed matching my stitches. And folding it brought me closer. With Connar . . . there was never any of that. With me," she amended quickly. "Of course he might feel differently about others he's closer to."

Hliss was fairly certain that Connar had been closer to Lineas than to anyone else, and for longer. But Connar was a subject she tended to avoid discussing with anyone besides Camerend.

Hliss said, "In my experience—which might not match anyone else's—what you call the middle is real love. The other two ends are more akin to lust, which are fun, as long as they last."

Lineas cocked her head. "So you're saying lust doesn't last even when one has the middle part?"

"I think everybody is different," Hliss stated, and correctly interpreted the anxious pucker in Lineas's usually tranquil brow. "Some mate with one person for life, and neither love nor lust ever fade to indifference."

Lineas let out her breath in a sigh. "That is so, *so* my hope."

It was Quill's hope as well. He had inherited both his parents' inclinations toward monogamy, and even while he'd taken his father's advice to get as much experience as he could during his years of travel, his thoughts had always come back to Lineas.

And so, one morning not far from Darchelde's border, as rain thudded against their tent, Lineas woke to find Quill watching her. There was no mistaking the tenderness in his eyes. He said, "Marry me."

"Yes," she whispered, thrilling in every nerve. "When?"

"As soon as we reach Darchelde. No, let's wait for New Year's. It's traditional, and since I don't plan ever to marry again, and I'm the only Montredavan-An child, they'll want to make a festival of it. As long as we don't get orders between our arrival and then, New Year's Week?"

With Quill, she had ceased to worry about sneaking out to be bathed and in fresh clothes whenever he turned her way. Though it was morning, and she'd had nothing to eat or drink since the night before, she kissed him in answer—and he kissed her back with a hunger to match hers.

New Year's Firstday was Oath Day everywhere in the Sartoran-influenced part of the world. When Convocation was not held in Marlovan Iasca, this and MidSummer Day were frequent days for weddings.

In the eight festival days between the close of the year 4086 and Firstday 4087, there were six weddings held in the kingdom's castles.

Two of them are my focus here, the first taking place in the magnificent castle in Darchelde, home of the Montredavan-Ans, as Camerend's only son, Senrid (known as Quill), married Lineas Noth, a descendent of Whipstick's eldest boy.

Lineas was intensely aware, even at the sublime heights of happiness after exchanging rings and vows with Quill, how conditional such happiness was. She had feared a summons every day as soon as they had crossed the border. As she drank the wedding cup and then led the women in the first dance, she dreaded the appearance of the inevitable summons to duty, pulling them away from the glow of happiness and throwing them back into the churn of danger and politics. With another long separation, of course.

Both her parents attended the wedding, with their current partners, old and comfortable friends all. Isa Eris, Quill's mother, had even come out of hiding, her beloved Frin always at her side, and for the sake of her son endured the emotional barrage of many people in a small space. Those who noticed she never touched anything, including the food, looked away again, familiar with her oddities.

Though few understood her, that was not true for Isa, who secluded herself against seeing far more than she might have wished both of the living and the dead. But what she saw of Lineas, whom she'd glimpsed over the years since the early days when she had attempted to teach the girl magic, she approved. Her son had chosen well.

She also saw below the superficial elation, and caught Lineas between dances, to say, "I will withdraw presently, but I wished first to offer an observation."

Lineas wiped her brow, having just finished an exhilarating dance with the other women. Her smile faded as her eyes widened with concern.

Isa touched her cheek, a gesture very rare indeed—and one that Lineas appreciated. "You have a good soul," she said. "And the makings of a good life. You've been taught to be watchful, and it is well. But I can see in your eyes, in your silences between speakings, that dread shadows the sun of your joy."

Lineas reddened.

"This is not a scold, darling child. Let me invite you to consider my words. *All* things become memory. You know this to be true. So revel in bliss with a whole heart while it lasts, so that you do not look back in later years and see only its shadow amid a long chain of worries that no longer matter."

Lineas flushed. "Thank you," she said, hand flat to her breast in salute. "I know it's a fault of mine. I need that reminder."

"There are worse faults," Isa said softly. "I am sure you've discovered that Senrid is quick. Quicker, perhaps, than he lets the world know. I believe you would not wish him to shoulder those dreads on your behalf when he, too, reads them in your eyes."

"Yes," Lineas whispered, and Isa passed on by.

Frin lingered, a tall woman with a direct gaze. Lineas forced a smile, though Isa's words had chilled her. "Aunt Frin, thank you for coming."

Frin stepped closer. "Do you have a wedding gift for young Senrid?"

Quill had said they could take their time with such things, as neither of them had come to Darchelde with anything but their travel packs. One of the many things she loved about him was how he avoided reminding her that one day all Darchelde would be his, and effectively he could command anything he wanted there, while she had nothing but the clothes she made for herself, and her journals.

She raised her gaze to Frin's. "We agreed to forego that tradition for now."

"If you should change your mind, I know what he would like, and you could compass it, if you will."

"What's that?"

"You still like embroidery, do you not? I know you did as a girl."

"I *love* it. I loved it." Lineas had to laugh. "It's not practical for us. Mending and sewing must come first, whether on a run or at the royal city, where there are always stockings to darn until the fledges learn to do their own."

Frin said, "You know that the fox banner belongs to the heir. But there's so much political, ah, weight attached to it he has been warned since boyhood never to even mention it. However, I know it has always meant something to him. So if you were to embroider a small thing, like a robe purse." As she spoke, Frin pulled out a folded piece of paper from inside her own robe pocket. "I know he would treasure it far beyond mere land, gold, or titles. If you agree, here is a sketch of the banner, from the archive."

Lineas's lips parted. "Thank you," she whispered, taking the sketch with both hands.

Frin hugged her, and then followed Isa, both vanishing back to their cottage.

Blossom danced up, chattering for attention. Lineas slid the sketch inside her new robe of pure white trimmed with black and embroidered in gold with the family's screaming eagle. A robe that she would never wear outside of Darchelde, for gold was a royal color.

She caught sight of Quill smiling a question her way. Remembering what Isa had said about him, she returned a bright smile, and so she allowed herself to be drawn back into the celebration.

The second wedding was held in the royal castle, as Hadand-Edli (Bunny) was married at last, to the popular hero Ganred (Rat) Noth, descended from the legendary Whipstick Noth.

Fragrant boughs of cedar and pine decorated both castles, one the main hall, the other the throne room. In both settings the best candles were brought out, casting a warm glow over smiling faces, the gilt edging on House robes, and the evergreen boughs. Hot spiced wine was not only poured for guests, but also into mugs carried to the wall sentries.

Another characteristic shared between the four was happiness. In Darchelde that found expression in ring vows.

Rat Noth and Bunny didn't make ring vows. In her enthusiasm, Bunny had at first insisted, but Rat knew his soon-to-be wife had a roving eye. He preferred the thought that Bun would always welcome him with her sun-bright smile if she wasn't tied to a vow the rest of the year, when he might be gone for months on duty. She'd agreed a little wistfully, and they decided to revisit the question in ten years.

Rat Noth stood along the wall in his new blue robe, trying to get used to the idea of being—at least legally—an Olavayir. He suspected he'd never get used to it, and it was likely whoever he commanded would also have trouble with it, but what it really meant was that any children he had would be Olavayirs.

Truth to be told, he wasn't certain how he liked that idea, but he refused to let it interfere with how happy he was that he and Bunny were together at last.

As the drummers began another women's dance, Connar joined him. "Take liberty this week, if you like," Connar said with a smile. "We'll ride out on the new year's Firstday unless we're under blizzard."

Rat was the happiest he'd ever been in his life, but he still had a strong sense of duty. "We've got orders?"

Connar explained briefly. At the first mention of Rat's stepbrothers, his face hardened, and there was a glimpse of the enemy-smashing captain instead of the awkward lovestruck fumbler who'd been underfoot for all these weeks on the second floor.

Connar's tone warmed with approval as he finished, "We'll split south of the royal city, me to make my inspection of East Garrison, and you to proceed down to Hesea, where I'll meet you. We'll ride south from there."

Connar was in excellent spirits. Earlier that day, before they parted to bathe and dress for the wedding, Ranet had met him in the hallway and confessed that she had now missed her second monthly. "And I've got other signs that I recognize. Such as, I'm beginning to feel slightly queasy, but it usually goes right away as soon as I eat some bread crust." She looked up at him in appeal, adding, "I don't want to say anything to Noren or Bunny, since it seems I'm the only one, so far."

The other signs were breast tenderness and a longing for extra sleep—and in telling him, she'd hoped for a quiet night in each other's arms. Or even a quiet hour, if he had a restless night. Sex with Connar was wonderful, of course. Loving him was what she'd always wanted. But of late the sex every night had begun to feel . . . maybe a bit like habit? Each night he came to her room, they went at it at least once, then he always went away again, leaving her to fall into deep sleep. It was great—it was marvelous—but these past few nights, especially as the mild discomforts manifested, she wished he would just hold her. How she longed to sleep the night away with him in her arms!

That night he didn't come at all.

She told herself that it made sense. His mind was already on the road, and all that had to be done to get there. And she knew that comparisons were evil. But . . . Rat Noth continued to sleep with Bunny all night.

Well, of course, she told herself as she dressed on the sixth day. That's what newlyweds who'd chosen each other *should* do.

And so, the eight days of New Year's Week passed. On Firstday of the new year, Connar and Rat were to ride out side by side, with Jethren commanding Connar's new honor guard.

The company gathered in the courtyard, many in high spirits, some with a doubtful eye turned up toward the weather. The three princesses stood in a row next to Noddy and the king and queen, Noren serene, Bun disconsolate but resigned, Ranet with one hand pressed covertly against her flat stomach under her robe, the other holding to Iris's little fingers, as she watched Connar's shining blue-black tail of hair.

Her feelings swooped like a bird diving and soaring. She consciously reminded herself that she was in one of the most enviable positions in the kingdom, married to its most handsome and dashing prince, living among married relations she liked, her days filled with work she enjoyed. It would be wrong to even think a complaint, much less utter it.

But her eyes stung as Rat Noth gripped Bunny in both hands and gave her a long, desperate kiss. His men hooted and cheered, then he and Connar mounted up.

You could say that they were a love match instead of a betrothal. But standing next to Noren at Ranet's other side was Noddy, his arm slung around Noren's shoulder as he blocked her from the bitter wind. Theirs was no love match, yet love had happened, even if it wasn't a great heat on one side or the other.

Give Connar time, Ranet told herself as she watched Connar smile and lift his hand to them all. Then he closed that hand into a fist and the company thundered out the gates.

We are not quite done with the subject of weddings.

Far to the south, Lavais Nyidri, ignoring a fine concert of musicians brought at great expense from Sartor, was wishing that she'd succeeded in crowning the changing year with a wedding.

But (she reminded herself) she was a patient woman.

She schooled her expression to one of enjoyment as her gaze rested on the unprepossessing figure of Seonrei Landis—easily forty if not more, goggle-eyed, who no amount of gossamer silk robing could make look less like a ball of wool on legs, the mirror image of her father, Third Prince Nanlyu.

But frog-like as she was, that diamond-studded gold band bound round her brow attracted every eye because no one but the Sartoran royal family wore them.

Seonrei was a Sartoran princess, and one of her sons marrying her would make him a Sartoran prince.

As Lavais waited for the lugubrious ballad to end, she couldn't help reflecting that Seonrei was even uglier than that cross-eyed princess up in Choreid Dhelerei, whose willowy frame at least looked very good on horseback. But a Marlovan barbarian princess smelling of horse sweat could not compare to a Sartoran princess in any useful way, in particular with regard to the prospect of power.

Whichever son Seonrei's royal eye favored would get to wear gold around his brow, and everyone in Sartor's court, from duchas to baras, would defer to him.

Demeos, of course, was more handsome than Ryu—but she thought complacently that the latter had a better sense of style. Sartorans valued style. Either way, Lavais could accomplish much once one of her sons married into the royal Landis family.

The piece ended, and everyone turned to Seonrei to discover what they were to think of it. Seonrei wondered if she was alone of all in that room was actually listening to the tight counterpoint and ravishing shifts in chords as the tiranthe finished the piece in a cascade of harmonic intricacy. All right, she wasn't entirely alone. Bronze-skinned, handsome, languid Demeos also seemed to be enjoying the music.

But when the last of that chord died away, his eyes as well as those of the rest of the company turned her way. She snapped her fan open with a practiced flick of thumb and wrist, holding the gilt side up, the highest sign of approbation.

Snick! The boys' fans opened, almost fast enough to seem genuine. Was she supposed to be flattered? Probably. How depressing. No, better to be amused.

Anyway, approbation accomplished. But that opened a new problem. Seonrei wondered if Lavais Nyidri would force those poor musicians to play until their fingers bled and their tongues dried to sticks. They had come with their company on the ship from Sartor. Was it possible that the Nyidris knew nothing of etiquette concerning hired musicians, especially those who had won accolade at the Music Festival?

With the speed of a lifetime of practice, Seonrei assessed the room from behind her fan just as Lavais shot a significant glance toward Demeos lounging nearby, as if to remind him to do his duty—and Seonrei knew that flattering was coming next. Her stomach tightened in disgust, the stronger because she had let herself think, for a while there back in Sartor, that his smiles were really for her and not for what he wanted from her. The disgust was self-directed at how stupid she'd been.

She could not bear another fake semblance of courtship. She rose. "Superlative music," she said toward the musicians, fan sweeping in the *art knows no rank* arc. Then she turned to Lavais. "I do hope we shall hear more. But tonight, I find myself fatigued. The dry air before a freeze always has that effect." She touched her head.

The company perforce rose, bowed, and she withdrew to the guest suite, where she found Iaeth waiting. It was still a shock seeing her second-cousin wearing the cream and gray of a body servant. "How is Donais?" Seonrei asked.

Iaeth, forty-two to Seonrei's thirty-nine, small and vivid, flashed a grin that took Seonrei back to their childhood. "He makes a very imposing herald-scribe. And they have him simply *surrounded* with spies."

Seonrei laughed. "I trust he will not be bored?"

"I can't promise anything for the future, but I believe he's enjoying himself now, ordering around people who would have sent him scurrying without a thought, if they knew he was a tailor."

"Good. The more the better, and that includes going about. I want them worrying about where he is going and what he might be seeing, which will grant you freedom. But I trust he can maintain the guise."

Iaeth's smile vanished, her small mouth tightening. "Oh, have no fear. I don't think you know how clever Donais is. It's just that he has no ambition outside of style, fabric, and what they say through symbol. He told me that he intends to create an entirely new fashion to present in Sartor on his return, once he is able to see real Marlovans, how they move, how they live."

Seonrei had been a fool to believe that the beautiful young Demeos could be interested in her, but the queen had said to be hospitable as she was curious about the mysterious Marlovans, who were one of those rare kingdoms that showed no interest in diplomatic exchange with Sartor.

Seonrei had her own reasons for accepting Lavais's invitation to visit her kingdom.

Kingdom. Heh.

Seonrei turned to Iaeth. "I've heard enough about this kingdom within a kingdom from Lavais Nyidri. She's told me what she wishes me to believe. I want you to discover how the people view it."

Iaeth perched on the arm of an imposing wingchair. It was huge, with a spreading back carved to resemble actual wings, the arms and legs fashioned into a stylized semblance of raptor claws. It was impossibly barbaric, but caught the eye. "Why?" she asked. "Even if you were to marry one of those spoilt sons, that woman would never let you do anything but preside over wine in your diamonds."

Seonrei dropped her fan onto a side table. "If I could bring the Marlovans into diplomatic accord with us, would it not be a crown merit?"

Iaeth regarded her cousin fondly. Seonrei had always been a fascinating combination of shrewd and idealistic. Which was why the Sartoran queen trusted her so much. She considered telling Seonrei what the highest level heralds knew: that the queen was considering a return to the old rules from the Days of Austerity a century previous, when no one carried royal titles except the immediate offspring of a monarch. During that time, four generations of Landises either having had only one child, and one, none, had diminished the family line so badly that when the fourth generation had produced three children, and those three had children, the royal titles had carried in order to strengthen the line.

But now the royal children of the previous generation had produced a clutch of lively cousins. Iaeth was more aware than most of what it meant to have royal relatives all down one side, but to be one step away from that rank oneself.

She liked being a herald. She had more freedom than courtiers, and more chance of real influence. Witness the fact that she knew this aspect of the queen's thinking, whereas Cousin Seonrei, much valued by the queen, didn't.

And yet Seonrei no doubt knew things the queen had not vouchsafed to anyone else. No, the queen had kept silent on the subject for a reason. Iaeth would do what she had been ordered, by both Seonrei and the queen, and see how events unfolded.

FOUR

A day or so later, up north, Connar and Rat Noth reached Hesea Garrison. Connar bade Rat Noth farewell, and turned east.

Rat and his company started south. A few days into their journey, they encountered a split in the road, and to everyone's surprise, Rat indicated for the outriders to take the west branch.

His chosen captains, knowing that they had the freedom to speak when not under orders before impending action, looked surprised, and lanky Plum, one of Rat's distant cousins from the Cassad jarlate, spoke up. "Doesn't that road go into Darchelde?"

"So it does," Rat said. "I've a purpose. And the king doesn't care."

They knew that. It was habit that kept them on the road skirting Darchelde, though it took them a week, or even two in winter, out of their way. Habit and stories about history, containing dire warnings about Darchelde's inhabitants coming out, or anyone going in.

They turned their horses aside and began cutting through the once-forbidden jarlate, so old it had its own name, rather than sharing its name with the family governing it. Only the even more legendary Choreid Elgaer shared that distinction, though it had been cut into pieces over the last century, the name now mere memory.

Everyone looked around with interest.

After a time, Plum, who carried the banner directly behind Rat, said, "I don't know if it's weirder that nobody is stopping us or that it looks the same as what we see on the border road. I guess I half-expected Darchelde to look different."

"Different like what, covered in spider webs and ruins?"

"Something like that," Plum said unrepentantly.

Rat shrugged, squinting against the glare off the snow, which was fierce even under a thin layer of cloud. "Runners have been cutting through Darchelde ever since the king lifted the border patrol. I guess you reached the academy after me n' Mouse left, but we always rode through here on our way to the academy. Stayed with Cousin Flax in the guardhouse."

Plum gazed out at the white-crowned hills, the woody areas of winter-bare trees, the frozen streams, and snickered. "You know what's really weird."

Rat glanced back at Plum, whose nose was dull red in the cold, his generous mouth twisted in his I know-a-joke grin. Unasked, he went on, "Really funny, if you think about it, we all learned that the Darchelde people got confined inside because of dirty doings by one of the earliest kings. Meant to keep Montredavan-Ans in, but the only ones who go out are the Montredavan-Ans."

"I don't know what's funny about that," Rat said. "They were forced out of Darchelde to train as royal runners a few kings ago. That king wanted 'em right under his eye."

Plum squinted against the glare, wiped his eyes with a mittened hand, and gave out a voiceless laugh, his breath clouding. " Just think it's funny that they're supposed to be tucked up tight, but they actually live right on top of the king."

Rat snorted. "Because the royal family doesn't want to sweat up three flights of stairs. They could if they wanted it. The Montredavan-Ans still don't go to the academy, or command in the army, or marry out their sons."

"D'you think all that will change?"

"Dunno. Don't care. Leave that kind of thing to the kings. No good ever comes of anyone else blabbing about royal doings," Rat stated.

Plum shrugged, and the talk turned to other matters.

A week of bad weather later, Rat remembered his thoughts when he saw the intent looks on the faces of his column as they rode upward from the river valley, catching glimpses of the Montredavan-An castle between the trees at bends in the road.

Then the forest cleared, revealing a magnificent castle, built of the familiar sand-colored stone—but in a very old style, with columned archways that none of them recognized as Sartoran in influence. They saw only that these arches, and the way the buildings connected, drew the eye upward in a way that the familiar square castles didn't. Built across the broadest hill, the Montredavan-An castle conveyed the impression of wide-spread wings swooping over the river valley below.

That had to be deliberate, Rat thought. This had once been the royal castle, under that black and gold screaming eagle banner, waving high at all eight towers. A banner never seen anywhere in the kingdom but here.

The sentries, women and men mixed, looked out at them expectantly. Of course Rat's company had been spotted by scouts when they'd crossed the border, though the Darchelde scouts hadn't revealed themselves. But neither had they challenged Rat; he expected that one of his kin rode with them.

So they crossed the bridge toward the open main gate, as inside, Camerend sent a runner to fetch Quill to greet the visitors. Camerend had been surprised when the border scouts sent word of Rat's arrival, not alone as he'd done during his academy days, but with a company. He and Quill were there at the stable door to welcome them when they dismounted.

As greetings were exchanged, he became aware that Rat Noth—whom he found to be an honest, uncomplicated sort of person—had something on his mind. Rat, in his turn, took in father and son, seen so rarely together. They looked a lot alike. Both with marriage rings glinting on their hands

Rat's gaze caught on that, and he wondered who Quill could possibly have married as Quill said, "Rat, this is a surprise! Come in and drink something warm."

Quill led Rat inside. Camerend stepped aside to say to his chief steward, "I think we'll eat in the alcove."

Quill turned his head, his brows lifting. Then he veered away from the sunny mess hall shared by stable and castle denizens alike during the winter months, with its back wall against the baking ovens.

Rat barely got a glimpse of that broad, warm space before he was taken deeper into a part of the castle he'd never seen before. He'd always stayed in the guardhouse with his Noth relatives.

Quill led him to a small, warm room. Camerend and Quill sat side by side at a beautifully carved table, and Camerend said, "Are there private orders from the king or queen?"

"No." Rat quickly outlined the general orders, then said, "Connar-Laef is in command, of course. But Quill, I keep remembering that you were the one to uncover the conspiracy that blindsided my father."

Quill held up a hand. "Only because Elsarion was overheard bragging about an expected attack from the south. Lnand gets her full share of credit for helping me sift for clues down in Feravayir. We never would have known to look but for that piece of information."

"My father is still very angry about that. Not at you," Rat added hastily, the tremor of his stutter threatening to return. He drew a breath and worked his jaw before continuing more slowly, "I wanted to ask you, if you aren't under orders, to come as my runner. Someone said Lineas is down here as well. I want her, too."

"I'll go fetch her while you eat." Quill rose from his mat as servants came in with spiced cabbage, hot coffee, and rice rolls with fish braised in wine. Rat was about to demur when the aromas reached him, and his stomach growled noisily.

"Right," he said, and picked up a biscuit.

Quill found Lineas where he expected to find her at this time of day, in the big barn where the chickens lived during winter. He paused a moment to watch Lineas, the weak wintry light from between the slats in the upper walls turning her hair to a dark rust.

She stood by as Blossom tossed withered scraps of greens and laughed as the chickens darted about, pecking at them. Lineas looked up, saw him coming, and her heartbeat sped up. He wouldn't be here without cause. Fearing that the arrivals had brought bad news, she said, "You know what to do now?"

Blossom bridled, and said self-importantly, "Strew the feed. Then collect the eggs. I can do that *myself.*"

"All right, then the job is now yours," Lineas said.

Blossom looked gratified, and reached for the feed bucket as Lineas met Quill, her anxiety plain in her eyes.

"It's Rat Noth. He wants us for something." Quill took her hands, and felt some of her tension ease at the mention of Rat.

They walked together up into the castle, dropping their hands outside the alcove. Both adopted the royal runner impassive countenance, too well-drilled to be conscious, as they entered. But there was that ring on her finger, which Rat noted. He was glad to see it. He'd always liked Lineas, the few, brief times he'd spoken to her, but he'd come to respect her after her hard run at Ku Halir.

"Connar and I are going south," he said. "The king's orders are for inspection, but he knows my stepbrothers are probably back at plotting. You two know the language, and I trust you both—what?" This last was addressed to Lineas, whose head dropped, her fingers tight.

Lineas looked up at that. "I—it's just that I failed the Senelaecs at Ku Halir."

"What?" Rat exclaimed in astonishment. "No!" he said forcefully. "I spent an entire week doing nothing but reading the reports, talking to Braids and Neit, and looking at the map. *Nobody* could have come in hotter than you did. You got to *me* in time."

"We've all tried to tell her that," Quill said, reaching for her hand.

Lineas's eyes gleamed with unshed tears. She looked away, then back, holding tightly to Quill's fingers as she confessed, "But the truth is, I was too late. Senelaec rode straight into ambush, and I will never not have nightmares about what I saw." Her voice trembled.

And Rat understood. "Look, why do you think I spent a week with the maps, after the cleanup? Every death I could have prevented, or saved, they all get at me in the night." He scowled at a last bite of rice roll on his plate. "Only way I can see to live with it is to learn from it. Next time, maybe we'll be better. That's why I'm here now."

"What can we do?" Quill asked.

Rat hunched toward them, big, scarred fists on his knees. "Well, it's like this. Two days before I rode out, Jugears, my second runner, came back from the south. I'd given him leave to go home with the news of his cousin dying at Ku Halir with Cub Senelaec. Jugears came back saying my stepmother and stepbrothers were expected to arrive in Feravayir by New Year's Week. If they're back, I know they'll be up to trouble."

"We heard that as well," Quill said. "Lnand has been on the watch, and she and I still communicate. They brought back a princess from Sartor, and the rumor is, she's choosing between one of the brothers."

One of Rat's knees bounced under his hand. "Maybe that's good news. If Ryu is busy trying to flatter some princess into marrying him, he won't be back to his 'festival,' right?"

Camerend, silent all this while, exchanged glances with Quill. "If," Camerend said, "he isn't promising her a kingdom."

"Shit," Rat breathed. "You're right. That's *just* what he'd do. We'd better ride out come morning."

Which is what he did, carrying fresh supplies from Darchelde's castle steward, and with Quill and Lineas added to the column.

When Rat called for a halt as the light began to fade behind the low clouds, Quill edged his horse over. "Where are Lineas and I in your chain of command?"

Rat understood immediately. He beckoned to lanky Digger, his first runner, and said, "The two royal runners are attached directly to me."

Digger tapped his chest and went about dividing the camp chores among the other runners. As royal runners always took care of themselves, there his responsibility ended—though not his curiosity.

When the runners had pitched Rat's tent, Digger said, "Better put two extra mats in. My guess is, captain wants a planning huddle."

Sure enough. After everyone had eaten hot, pan-fried biscuits and rice-and-cheese rolled in crisped cabbage, Rat called for Quill and Lineas. The cook had ground and singed coffee beans, pouring boiling water through his cloth filter. Quill and Lineas each carried a thick clay mug, Lineas more grateful for the heat than for the bitter liquid, which she forced down only to warm herself from within.

Rat waved the two to mats. "I've been thinking all day about what you said yesterday. What exactly did you tell the king in that report about the festival conspiracy two years ago?"

Despite all that had happened between that report and this day, Quill recollected it accurately. His report was even shorter because invariably Rat would wave off explanations of who this or that person was in relation to the Nyidris.

At the end, Rat said, "Pretty much what I learned. Areth, Korskei, Lemekith, Jaya Vinn—They're all Demeos and Ryu's riding mates, except for that old Holder Nireid. Her family were duchas when Feravayir was the Kingdom of Perideth. Their rank dropped to the regular 'holder' when we Marlovans came in, but they still live like the duchas rankers over the mountains." He sighed, fists propped on his knees. "My idea was to send the two of you ahead to get the latest word from my father. I'll give you a note to take with him," he added. "He'll know where to put you. My stepmother and stepbrothers don't know either of you, am I right?"

Quill looked at Lineas, then at the tent wall.

"What?" Rat asked. "Something wrong with that?"

Quill said after a lengthy pause, "Are these Connar-Laef's orders?"

Rat pursed his lips. No one spoke, and Lineas was aware of the easy murmur of chatter around the campfire some fifty paces off. The snort of a horse. The sough of wind in trees.

Rat's brow furrowed. He spoke slowly, "You're saying without saying that Connar doesn't like anyone acting without his orders. I know that. He was the same in the academy. I was going to tell him, of course, when we meet up at Old Faral. Thought I'd save him time. He'd be sending scouts, sure."

Quill sat back. If Rat put it just like that, everything should be fine.

Rat saw the easing of his expression, and though he didn't say anything, he was considering that the next morning, as the two departed.

He said nothing outside of the flow of orders as the camp broke and they began riding. After a time, he waved the "ride east" command, and the column broke into twos and threes.

He trusted all his company. They were people he'd chosen. But some subjects were by their nature a burden. Definitely anything to do with kings and upper command. When he was satisfied that everyone's attention was on their pass-the-boring-ride chatter, he let his horse slow until he was riding next to Plum.

A glance, and when Rat tightened his thighs to signal the animal to pick up the pace, Plum rode beside him.

Rat had learned long ago how much space was needed to avoid being overheard.

"Plum, here's what happened in the tent last night." He gave a fairly exact account, then said, "Quill traveled with Connar for two years. Those royal runners are more tight-lipped than anybody else. He was definitely warning me."

"About?" Plum widened his eyes. Long and lanky, with a strong jaw, Plum was a lot like Rat in temperament as well as outlook. "Seems to me, those orders are good. Anybody would give 'em. You'll report 'em. Everything the way it's supposed to be."

"Right." Rat idly ran his gloved thumb along the ridge of the horse's neck. The mount's head came up as Rat said, "Here's the thing. I was thinking ahead, see. I know there's going to be trouble. It's a matter of when, and if Demeos and Ryu brought back some princess from Sartor, it can only mean they have, or are trying to get, backing from Sartor to run their rebellion."

Plum jerked a shoulder up. "Jarlan's been on about that since we lost the north, right?"

"Right."

"Well, no surprises there. So what's the problem?"

"It's timing. I was thinking, if they do something soon, well, why not have the garrisons on alert and ready to ride. Maybe even on maneuvers close by, see, so if word comes, then it's days and not weeks of hard riding, just to arrive maybe too late, like we did for the Senelaecs."

"Right." Plum breathed the word.

"The thing is, it takes *time* to for even the fastest runners. Then more time to assemble men and supplies. I learned that hard when coming to defend Ku Halir. So I was going to send someone to alert them to be ready. Maybe even be wargaming near enough where they can drop everything and come in hot, saddle to saddle, if needed. Now . . . it seems a bad idea."

Plum said doubtfully, "But that's what Connar would order, right? He's a good commander, everybody says so."

"That he is," Rat agreed, stroking the horse's neck as he worked his way through the thicket of doubt. Connar was an excellent commander and an excellent warrior. But even back in their academy days . . . .

He scowled at the snowy ground. "That year in the academy, before I became a senior . . ."

"You mean when he cheated? You told me he wasn't completely wrong."

"I still think so. Not completely. If I'd had any way to weasel information ahead of those damned Bar Regren coming down out of their damn mountains, Cub Senelaec would be at home drinking wine punch today. It was . . . it was . . . *how* he had to win—and how he didn't talk to anyone. Not even Noddy."

"Well, the Sierlaef wasn't any good at command. Everybody said so," Plum interjected reasonably.

"But Connar didn't talk to Stick or Ghost either. And nobody ever said they weren't good at command."

"No argument there," Plum said, patiently waiting for Rat to work through things they both knew in order to get to what bothered him.

Rat prowled through memory, and caught up with Connar's sudden, scathing blue glare. "That's it. He doesn't talk it out with anyone. Well, he's good enough that I guess he doesn't need to, like the rest of us. But he also hates it when someone acts outside of orders. Really hates it."

"Maybe that's the way you get, being born a prince."

Though Rat didn't think that was quite it, he said, "Maybe. What I'm getting at is, even sending an alert on a grass run takes time." Rat pounded his thigh with a fist as he tried to articulate what was mostly instinct.

At least one thing was inescapable: maps and distances. "Waiting until we meet up at the old Faral castle. . . And remember he's never been south, so it's conceivable he could get slowed up coming through the woods. Then waiting for him to send that order to the garrisons . . . well, it might be too late. But I've got no orders to send a runner to order the garrisons to ready for a ride. That's command privilege."

Plum squinted at the snow lying smoothly to his right, tiny tips of hardy grasses sticking up. "So it seems to me you might send the alert to *us*."

"Us?" Rat slewed in his saddle. "You mean, the Noths?"

"Sure. Most of us are in the army, so they can be trusted to keep tight. But we're also Riders for half the families up the coast, and inland besides. If the jarls don't squawk, seems to me it would be easier to arrange border games for defense practice, and the like. And those of us in the army can be blabbing at mess, and the like, and if their captains overhear and think, well, we might just do some southern maneuvers, then nobody's done anything outside of orders, right?"

"That's good," Rat said cautiously.

"If nothing happens, then everybody goes home again and toasts a fun game. If it does, well, they're in reach."

"That's it," Rat said, relieved. He examined the idea from every angle. The sun had moved two fingers in the sky before he turned up his palm decisively. "Let's do it. I'll send Cousin Itch back to Hesea, then around Toraca, Algaravayir, and over to your Noths with the Cassads. He can be trusted to keep tight. Say the right things. And he's fast."

Plum turned up his palm, the two slowed until the loose column rejoined them, and when they stopped to water the animals and eat the midday meal, Itch Noth was sent back up the trail; anyone who noticed him assumed he was riding a report back to one of the garrisons.

That same midday, at East Garrison, Connar reveled in walking on inspection as commander in chief. Everything was perfect in the way that meant utmost respect—he'd experienced enough inspections from the other side to recognize the signs of unspoken doubt, indifference, even resentment.

There was none of that, but the gratification was alloyed once it was over, and the signal blown for a watch of liberty, as customary after a successful inspection.

At once captains surrounded him to ask questions. The first was about the West Outpost battle, but hard on that came a sea of questions about Ku Halir. Everyone seemed to assume that he'd not only foreseen that battle, but somehow predicted how it would go. While no one cared a whit about how Connar managed to cross mountains and close the pass before getting to West Outpost.

He hid his reaction, of course, but instinctively shot a glance at Jethren, who kept his hand-picked riding of honor guards in strict formation at all times. Jethren's tight lips and narrowed eyes reflected Connar's feelings exactly.

Connar said nothing. He still didn't completely trust Jethren, though he used him. But that shared expression went a ways toward reconciling Connar with Jethren—surprising the latter when he said in a far easier tone than ever before, "We'll ride for Old Faral tomorrow."

Princess Seonrei turned her fan up in the gesture of Appeal to Enlightenment. "So tell me about the court rituals among the Marlovans."

Ryu uttered a crack of laughter. "Rituals?" He covered his lower face with his fan in the angle of amusement, his pale eyes peering over the gilt edge. "My barbarian so-called cousins don't have rituals. They have duels, and even those . . ."

"So what happens when you go north at New Year's, then?"

Demeos lifted a shoulder, his beautiful dark eyes languid. "I've never been. I prefer Sartor, to tell the truth. And civilization."

Ryu leaned over his brother's shoulder. His long hair, dyed the pale blue of eggshells, matched his robe of peach silk over blue and cream, embroidered with cranes in flight amid kingsblossom. Loud hint, Seonrei thought. As if anyone didn't know what the Colendi meant when they talked about "the crane dance." And the kingsblossom was, at the least, in dubious taste.

"Mother," Ryu drawled. "Tell her."

Lavais's drawl matched her son's. "The Marlovans have no ritual that deserves the word. The throne does face southward, as is common enough in kingdoms outside of the quintessence of Sartor's Star Chamber circular tree, but that is only because they took the royal city from the Iascans, who knew how to build a proper throne room. After their defeat the Iascans took away all the trappings when they abandoned their castles. The Marlovans were too ignorant to notice. Those have never been replaced. The throne room is all bare stone, save for war trophies and banners."

Ryu affected a shudder. "And you ask why we have not gone?"

Seonrei wondered what the real reason was, but kept her attention on Lavais, who was very ready to disparage further. "There are no left and right orders of ranks. There is no proper hierarchy. There are benches facing the throne, on which the jarls sit with their captains, and their sons when old enough. Behind them sit the garrison commanders. And behind them, the guild chiefs. These last two are not permitted to speak. That is, unless there is time of war, then the garrison commanders may speak."

"No women?"

"Only once. As it happens, in this reign. The first time in history."

"So the women are isolated, then?"

"No, they write letters back and forth," Lavais said. "And of course the current queen has been putting them into their army training. Most of them are already trained in barbarian ways. They ride the borders, shooting anyone who ventures over, I'm told."

Seonrei very much wanted to meet one of these women, but kept that to herself. By now she was fairly certain that if she were to ask Lavais to arrange a meeting, a suitably vulgar woman would be presented to her, coached in what to say.

With that thought came the reflection that though Iaeth was investigating, Seonrei herself was sitting where Lavais wanted her, in a bejeweled prison, seeing only those Lavais wished her to see.

That, at least, she could alter. "This land is quite beautiful even in winter," she said. "I would very much like to see more. I'll send my herald to trouble your steward about suitable conveyance."

"No trouble at all!" Lavais didn't quite hide her surprise, but then she smiled, perceiving a way to turn the princess's whim to advantage. "However, unnecessary. My sons would like nothing better than to show you their land."

It was a daring venture to use the words *their land* instead of *the land*—implying rule—but Seonrei made no demur, from which Lavais pleased herself to believe that the princess might look with favor on her taking back the kingdom that was rightly hers.

Next step, to get that favor in material form.

FIVE

A hard frost set in over the south, days of intense blue sky overhead, brilliant as a polished bowl, the ground like iron. It was bitterly cold, but Lineas and Quill—traveling together for the first time in their lives—were transcendently happy.

Being under orders from Rat Noth, they were given fresh mounts at every outpost, which sped them along. They worked on the southern dialect as they made a game of their grass run. Though they had the farthest to travel of either Rat Noth's or Connar's companies, they arrived in Parayid only two days after Rat (having been mired by three storms in a row) reached Old Faral, now the northern outpost for the Cassads of Telyer Hesea.

Lineas was thrilled to see the famous harbor. She'd loved her single glimpse of Lindeth way up north. There, the sea in summer had been deep blue, but now it was steel gray, reflecting the low bands of clouds overhead.

Cold, wet wind whipped straight off the sea. "Snow coming," Quill commented as they rode down out of the gentle hills toward the city, which was dominated by the fortress on the palisades, fine homes to either side at a respectful distance, and all along the lower cliffs below.

"How old is that castle?" Lineas asked.

"A century," Quill said. "The great Evred put it in. He wanted it raised on the heights, where pirates could see it from the horizon, and think twice about attacking. There were a lot of pirates raids in those days."

Lineas burrowed more deeply into her woolen scarf, remembering reading that the Venn had supported the pirates, an unimaginably wicked thing to do. She hated the parts of history that included such malice.

Chilled, she burrowed more deeply into her scarf as they rode down the path.

Ivandred Noth had standing orders about royal runners. He was to be alerted as soon as they rode through the gates. He was standing on the tower overlooking the harbor when his first runner reported their arrival, adding, "One of them is Camerend's boy."

Ivandred Noth did not take his eye away from his spyglass, though he had two other lookouts also watching the harbor. "Send them up."

Lineas and Quill soon mounted the top steps of the tower. Snowflakes were already fluttering sideways on the rising wind as they spotted the tall, lean figure. Lineas reflected at least they hadn't bothered beating the ice crust from the hems of their robes.

"Senrid," Commander Noth exclaimed when they joined him. "Orders from the king?"

"No. Your son sent me," Quill said, and proffered the note that Rat had given him.

Noth smacked the spyglass to, and set it on the stone wall before him. He took the crumpled, damp paper as his gray brows met over his nose. "Where is he?"

"I suspect he's reached Old Faral by now, to be joined by Connar-Laef," Quill said.

Noth unrolled the paper, noting that his son had not sealed it. That meant Camerend's son was in his confidence with respect to these orders. He slid the paper into his tunic, then snapped the spyglass open again.

Lineas peered out at the gray sea. To her it seemed the clouds were so low she could reach up and touch them. A ship moved very slowly on the gray seas.

Noth said, "What do either of you know about ships?"

"Little," Quill said. "I sailed once, when I returned home from Sartor."

"Less," Lineas said softly.

Noth grunted. "I've never been on one. But I can tell you a lot about them. That is, I might not know the terms used by sailors, but I've come to know a great deal about sails, rigging, and how sailors use wind and tide when maneuvering in the harbor. How they position themselves when masking an attack. The tricks of a pirate disguised as a merchant."

Quill and Lineas stared with interest at the ship rocking gently on the sea as it approached under what appeared to be half of a big sail and a small one on another mast.

"That ship there might be any number of things. A sea-going yacht, built for speed, carrying passengers. A merchant with small but precious cargo. Or. . . a pirate who wishes us to think it might be those first two. Ah." He turned his head. "Mareca! Signal to anchor in the harbor and prepare for inspection. They'll dawdle and misread the signals, is my guess. Have the harbor watch go covert. Excellent practice."

He snapped the glass to, and said, "What orders did Connar-Laef ride under?"

As they started down the tower steps, Quill said, "This is what Rat told me." He repeated them, then added, "May I ask how you know this ship is a pirate in disguise? The coming snow blurred the ship a little, but I didn't see much beyond fifteen or twenty sailors tending their sails."

"Ah, but how many are crouched belowdecks, weapons at hand? I don't know either, and it's entirely possible I'm wrong, and Jened down at the harbor will be running a drill instead of a defense. It was the appearance of four ships out at sea, similar rigging. They could be any number of innocent ships, but why would they sail in what we call a charge line, instead of in column, like traders? I think this one here is to keep us busy while these others slink up."

They turned down a corridor overlooking a courtyard from which shouts and clashes of steel echoed up the walls. Both Lineas and Quill recognized the sounds of sparring.

Noth turned into a room, his gray horsetail swinging. "Shut the door. Take a seat." He indicated a waiting bench, then sat behind a desk. To one side was a tall cupboard with stacks of paper neatly stored, and on the other wall, a map of Feravayir.

Noth scowled down at his hands, fisted on his knees, causing Lineas to think of Rat. Finally he looked up. "First of all, you need to understand that one of the reasons I couldn't find anything is that the people, in general, hate us."

"Us?"

"Me. My men."

Quill glanced toward the wall, beyond which lay the sea. "For fighting pirates?"

"Not so much here in Parayid, for many reasons. That being one. But in the rest of Feravayir. Most of that is because of the raised tax."

"But everybody paid it," Quill said. "the King's Tenth, the war tax. That's *old.*"

Noth looked grim. "You have to remember that we garrison commanders stay strictly out of politics. If we're summoned to the royal city for Convocation, we can only speak on subjects pertaining to defense. So I cannot demand to see tax tables. All I can do is detail companies to guard the caravans taking what's owed to the royal city. My people can't touch what's in the wagons. The guilds don't have to talk to us."

Quill and Lineas stared. They knew all that.

"So I can't prove it, but I think Lavais doubled that tax. At the least."

"Jarls can do that," Lineas said tentatively.

"Except that the common people all seem to have this idea that Feravayir, and the Jayad, but mostly Feravayir, bears the burden of paying for the northern wars. As the taxes keep rising."

"But the king didn't raise the taxes after the jarls agreed at Convocation," Quill said.

"You know that. I know that, because I was there. I think the people are being lied to by Lavais's tax guild. But even if I could prove it, that'd still be seen as interfering. So that's the terrain. Now, to the Tax Gang. Lavais demands I do something, and I've sent some carefully chosen Riders, but they have private orders from me to never catch up with the Tax Gang. Because the Tax Gang is striking at the most corrupt of my former wife's followers. The ones adding yet another burden of taxation on top of what's already there."

"Former wife?" Lineas spoke.

Noth looked grim. "She lied to my face about that conspiracy. We both knew she was lying to my face, though she denied it. Still denies it. But I saw the truth when she read the summary page written by young Senrid here after he exposed Demeos's *festival*." He spat the word. "Claiming that report as strictly defense matters, I refused to let her see the rest, detailing who discovered what where. She would have seen to it they vanished." The lines in his face deepened.

"About the Tax Gang. Connar will be obliged to go after them," Quill said.

"I know." Noth got up, went to the window to overlook the courtyard, then walked back. "I can't tell you what to do. I'm oath-sworn to the kingdom. And though I don't believe Cassad's gang is any threat to the kingdom, there is still the chain of command."

"Cassad?" Lineas asked.

Noth blinked, his gaze diffuse in the way of people mentally reviewing what they'd just said.

Then he dropped back onto his chair. "I may as well tell you everything. You'd find it out fast enough, I expect. The Tax Gang is run by Colt Cassad, and a host of hand-picked unsworn Riders."

"*Colt* Cassad?" Quill repeated. "I thought I knew all the Cassads. I've never heard of a Colt."

"Colt was born to the jarlan's sister, though I'm told he dropped the family name when he left the family a few years ago. The Tax Gang started running right around the time Demeos and Ryu were planning their conspiracy," Noth stated with grim pleasure. "Hits all the holdings where corrupt tax collectors have been plundering on their own, unpunished. Rumor has it, Ryu takes part of the corrupt tax gatherers' loot."

Noth turned his palm down and struck the air, pushing it away. "Back to the first matter. My son sent you to scout. My suggestion is for one of you to be placed directly inside the Nyidri stronghold." Noth glanced Lineas's way. "A female is easier than a male, but neither in royal runner robes."

Lineas's nerves flashed cold: she was to be a spy again, only this time moving among the enemy instead of listening from the marshy reeds and grasses. "Very well," she said, and Quill saluted, hand flat to his heart.

Someone rapped at the door.

"Take a night of liberty, while I make arrangements," Noth said, and, "Enter!"

Lineas and Quill passed a waiting crowd of runners with reports. They ran downstairs, and when they were out of earshot Lineas whispered, "Did he forget to give you orders, or are you supposed to stay here?"

Quill flashed a grin. "Might be he'll have orders come morning."

"*Might* be?" She looked a question, then the meaning struck her: unspoken orders. "Then that wasn't accidental? The mention of 'Cassad,' I mean."

"First thing, let's get something to eat. My feet are like a pair of half-numb icicles. Second, I think I'd better write to Camerend."

Though the castle was busy with activity, the evening watch was much livened by a celebration for the harbor day watch, who apparently had successfully put down a short, bloody attack by pirates (the accompanying ships having veered off, hopefully to be chased down by a navy patrol).

Lineas was summoned by one of Noth's runners to meet someone. On the way, she asked what the whooping and singing were about, and on being told of the celebration, she asked, "Were the pirates carrying pirate loot or coming to get some in the town?"

The runner grinned. "Both. Whichever watch fights 'em gets a part of any take. Half if there's blood. Word is, they were bringing in expensive trade goods direct from Sartor, and a lot of extra men."

"Where does the other half go?" Lineas asked.

"Horses, usually. Armor. Arms. Here you go."

Lineas was turned over to a silver-haired older woman, who introduced herself as Plix, a kitchen steward from the Nyidri household. Plix asked a series of questions, and on learning that Lineas was a royal runner—trained not just for courier duty, but to serve as first runner to any member of the royal family who might be in need, which meant she could perform any servant task—she favored Lineas with a grim smile. "Scribe training?"

"Yes. Also, I'm fluent in Hand. My mother is deaf, and I've been teaching with the Haranviar."

Plix's eyes widened. "Now that," she said with satisfaction, "is *perfect.* I'll send someone to get you in the morning. She'll tell you everything you need to know. You'll have to be smuggled out of here, down to the harbor, and onto a boat, so you can be seen arriving. She'll explain a story, once we concoct it."

She exited, leaving Lineas aware that once again she'd been assigned to the strange realm of spies. Only this time she wouldn't be hidden, as she'd been when she listened to the Bar Regren outside of Ku Halir. This time she expected to be living, under false guise, among people who in most respects must be regarded as enemies.

Quill was waiting for her. "I grabbed us some spice-wine. This closet is cold as the courtyard. At least it feels that way. Quick, before it turns cold."

She needed no urging. They undressed fast, and climbed into the bed, legs tangled as they shared warmth.

"You're tense," he said. "Bad interview?"

"No. Plix was brisk, but I sensed good will. It's the thought of falsity. The Nyidris', and my own."

"You don't want to spy."

"Doesn't matter what I want," she said, sipping wine. "What did you learn?"

He sat back against the stone wall, his loose hair covering his bare shoulders. She admired the curves of muscle in his arms, painted with warm color in the light of the single candle. His eyes looked black in the light. "I learned that my father can still take me by surprise. Though I guess I ought to have expected him to be familiar with this Colt Cassad and his gang, many of whom are apparently outlaws. The rest don't belong to any one jarl or Rider family. Some are from farm or artisan families, picked for their skills, and their allegiance to their leader."

He leaned over her to set his empty cup on the trunk beside the bed, and she pressed a kiss to his shoulder.

His grin flared, and he put his arms around her as he said, "Camerend says that Colt trained himself fighting those brigands that came over from the Adranis on the southern route. Cleaned 'em out of the northern Jayad, which is why, I expect, the jarl over there has only managed to send Riders to where Cassad's gang has already left. He has no liking for that snake Artolei, Demeos's cousin, whose holding lies over the border into the Jayad."

Lineas sorted all this information, then said, "So . . . outlaws in what sense?"

"What do you mean?" His fingers stroked gently along her arm.

"Outlaws as in, have done terrible things, or outlaws to the corrupt, who set bad laws?"

"I don't know. Probably not so easy to define." He smiled. "You want clear heroes and reprehensible villains. Not that I blame you."

"I want . . . everyone to live well, harming no one else." She stared down into the rapidly cooling wine, then set it next to his cup. "Pretense . . . hurts." And then, swiftly, so that he would not make the connection to spying, "Why are you surprised that Camerend-Jarl knows about Colt Cassad?"

"It's not that specifically. It's his reach. Though I've always known it, I never really considered what it meant until we were able to spend those weeks with him at Darchelde. He knows at least as much of what is going on in the kingdom as the king. Maybe more. And his plans are longer."

He felt Lineas's breath hitch, and turned to look into her steady gaze. He uttered a laugh. "No, my darling, you are not hearing the kernel of a royal conspiracy. Even if he, or I, were mad enough to want to challenge for the throne, who would follow us, outside of Darchelde? In effectively dividing us off from the rest of the kingdom, Anderle Montreivayir all those years ago knew what he was doing. It's habit to be wary of Darchelde. No one in the rest of Marlovan Iasca would follow us. They don't know us, except as runners."

She let out a small sigh of relief.

"But my great-great grandfather Indevan knew what he was doing when he set up the royal runners. With the full knowledge and support of Hastred, who I think at least as great a king as Evred. Maybe greater, because he managed to hold the kingdom without any wars. Nobody seems to make ballads about good years, but you can bet people enjoy peace and prosperity."

"We all read Indevan Montredavan-An's royal runner archive," Lineas reminded him. "One of the first assignments I was set, when I came at age twelve. And I discuss what he wrote about our purpose with my first and second year classes."

Quill hummed in agreement, and she enjoyed the vibration in his chest, on which her head lay. He said, "We turn our focus toward service, and non-interference, but it wasn't until Camerend told me to reread Indevan's records that I understood what Indevan really intended."

"I refuse to believe we've been wrong," she stated, rubbing her cheek over the patch of soft hair that grew over his breastbone.

"And so do I." She felt his tremor of laughter more than heard it, before he said, "We don't interfere. That is, we don't carry swords. We don't lead companies. And we don't give out orders. But we can, and do, have quite a bit of influence on events in this kingdom. It was a way for us to be a part of the kingdom's affairs. And Hasta knew it. He and Indevan worked it up between them."

Lineas said, "I haven't read that."

"You can. It's in the family archive. Which now you have access to, if you like."

Lineas knew that many records were only kept at Darchelde, a few of them in a room guarded by magic.

Quill went on. "We don't give the orders to make things happen, but we are everywhere. Listening. Recording. Communicating." His fingers drifted up her side to cup her face as he leaned on an elbow and looked earnestly at her.

Her gaze traveled lovingly over the contours of his cheekbone and jaw to his clever, fine-cut mouth as he said, "I like this life. I wouldn't want to be fighting the princes, for what? To keep fighting to hold what I won so bloodily? Assuming, of course, I didn't get my throat cut at the outset."

Lineas wasn't certain how to evaluate his mood shift.

He saw it, and laughed silently, sinking down under the quilt and pulling her with him. "Whew, why didn't you say your arms were getting cold? I'm done maundering. Blow out the candle, will you?"

To the outside world all the Landis children excelled as ornaments to ancient Sartor. Within the family there was an ever-changing hierarchy, all the more intense for the silence in which the competition was conducted.

Princess Seonrei and her siblings as well as her cousins outside the direct line knew they hadn't a hope of sitting in the great tree-shaped throne set in the circular Star Chamber. That prospect belonged solely to one of the queen's three children, who were all smart, educated, and ambitious. The most ambitious among the cousins courted the favor of the royal three, some because of natural liking, and others in hopes their candidate would be chosen heir, which would bring the obvious benefits.

So powerful was the Landis mystique that when Seonrei began to suspect that Lavais Nyidri might be entertaining the idea of keeping Seonrei as a hostage until she chose one of her boys, the sense of gentle coercion vanished like fog on a summer day after she dropped a mention of her daily reports to the queen. The Nyidris all knew she had a golden notecase. They had them as well, highly prized and (Seonrei discovered subsequently) rare in Marlovan Iasca.

Landis prestige protected her more thoroughly than any number of highly trained herald-guards, covert or overt.

Iaeth has reported back to me. She has seen for herself dilapidated villages so poor that winter cannot be kept out of the holes in roofs and open windows. Everywhere the people are angry over the burden of taxation so that the king can conduct his northern wars. Iaeth spoke to one guild master who said that taxes increased four-fold so that the king could build a new fortress up north somewhere.

Moreover, she reported that every person she spoke to, or overheard, begins a confession with some version of, You didn't get it from me, *or even more chilling,* Please, no names—my family is entirely innocent.

It was not until I came here that I began to truly understand what we've been taught all our lives, that each monarch must redefine what governing means. My travels so far have been in Sartor, and to its neighbors, who model their forms of government upon ours. Here—I cannot speak for this faraway king whose crushing taxes are forcing people to starvation in order to conduct wars—no, as I write that, I remember that pretty, soulless Elsarion scion who came to court my cousin that one summer. It was said after he sailed home without having attached himself to a princess, he started some war over the mountains, and I believe those mountains were actually the border into this kingdom I now travel across. In which case said war was probably a real event and not just rumor. I expect you would know the truth of that.

From my limited perspective, this much is clear: to arrive at summary judgment would be an error. I believe Iaeth's unnamed witnesses' testimony more than I do Lavais Nyidri's smiling assertions, but I did test her, when she dropped a very obvious hint about how, with aid, she would wrest her benighted kingdom away from the Marlovan conquerors if she could. I asked, what then?

She replied with the usual butter: better lives for all, peace and contentment, but I looked at her sitting there in a new gown, the cost of whose labors might elsewhere repair an entire house, and I wondered how much more civilized than her barbarian Marlovans she truly is. I understand that prestige depends upon appearance, but we were raised to be ashamed if people in our territory lived in houses without roofs, for that was testament to poor guardianship. Perhaps it's merely a leftover from the Years of Austerity, but in all my years at court, I don't remember anyone reluctant to go about in old silks until regional prosperity was reestablished; the word famine-fashion has been understood for generations to mean wearing old fashions until the effect of famine has been eradicated in one's governance. . . .

After Seonrei sent her letter, Iaeth came close, and as she began to twitch at the ribbons on Seonrei's over-robe, she breathed, "There's talk that the prince who now commands the entire army has been spotted at some castle directly north. Officially he's riding on inspection of all the garrisons. But there have been messengers riding off in all directions, mostly from Ryu."

Seonrei picked up her fan, and spread it, inspecting the painting of firebirds chasing across it. "I want to meet this prince."

Around the same time, that prince was dismounting into mushy brown snow at Old Faral, but his mood was sanguine because he knew by the time he reached whatever room was set aside for commanders, he'd find his second set of boots dry and waiting, a change of clothes, and hot, freshly ground and scalded coffee.

Connar peered under his hand at the garrison lined up to receive him, as behind him, his honor guard went about unloading horses, and running his banner to the tower.

He liked having an honor guard. At least, this honor guard. If he didn't want to speak to anyone, he could get through an entire day in silence. He'd tested it. All he had to do was look at something, and Jethren would make a brief gesture to one or another of his men, and the thing was done. And Jethren kept his mouth shut. He'd learned that much from Fish.

As Old Faral's commander came forward to salute, Connar gloated inwardly. He outranked Hauth now, by a wide margin—and he'd earned those three gold chevrons on either arm. He'd *earned* his command in *spite* of that dolphin-clan fart noise. He hoped the old turd stewed every time he saw the eagle banner.

So in spite of the horrible weather, and the sodden cloak trying to trip him up by clinging to his snow-crusted boots, Connar's mood was high as he glanced at Rat Noth and his company drawn up in straight lines, ignoring the white fluff gathering on shoulders and heads. Every eye in the place on him.

Connar enjoyed giving Jethren the barest glance instead of a spoken command. Jethren turned to the waiting runner who trumpeted the dismissal. Connar tipped his head at Rat Noth, who promptly fell in step beside him, Jethren at their heels.

"Any news?" Connar said, surprised at how relieved he was to see Rat's unprepossessing face. Rat knew the south. After his mountain journey, and then the rough ride of the past few weeks, Connar had gained a visceral understanding of the importance of knowing the territory ahead. And this was Rat's territory.

Rat turned up his gloved hand. "I expect the same news you got. Those two shits I no longer have to pretend are my stepbrothers are back."

Connar said, "So Ivandred Noth and Lavais Nyidri parted?"

"Yes. Right after Demeos's conspiracy."

"Why'd he marry her in the first place?"

Rat huffed out a sharp sigh, sending a cloud of vapor outward. "My brother'n me used to wonder. Asked Da, finally. Said she lured him into it after the jarl died. He thinks she wanted to get him to go her way. You know, sheer off the south, so she could be queen of Perideth. Shit, how I hate that word, Perideth. When Demeos and Ryu—he was still going by Evred back then—when they sicced their toadies onto Mouse and me, they were always on about how they were princes of Perideth, and we were nothing but a couple of Marlovan horseapples, not fit to wand out the stables."

Connar had never heard so long a speech from Rat in his life.

Rat snapped his hand out. "Anyway. Da said, he figured out she was a lying liar, but he decided to stay close to watch what she was doing. Ended it when she nearly outmaneuvered him. And still lied." He sighed again, then added, "We all know the jarlan has spies in the royal city, though I was never able to find out who they are. Don't really know how to *find* spies. Though I tried. My point here is, the Nyidris surely know we're on the way."

Connar paused, and looked at him with brows raised. "You think they'll give us trouble?"

"If they think they can win," Rat stated without hesitation. "So I was thinking about that after you and I parted, and I thought maybe I ought to send someone ahead. Found a couple of royal runners at liberty. I also sent one of my runners—a cousin—to carry word to the local Noths. Said, if they want, they might run some wargames in the south, or find some other excuse to roam the Feravayir border. They could turn into backup fairly fast."

Connar laughed inwardly at the idea of a bunch of Rat's cousins riding up —but then, they would be well trained, and certainly useful. And he'd never turn down reinforcements, especially riding into unfamiliar and potentially hostile territory. "What's your da say to this news?"

"Don't know. Latest dispatch is waiting for you up in the tower here."

"Excellent," Connar said, and smiled with anticipation as he led the way inside the tower stair. They both stamped snow from their boots and whacked at clothes and hair as they started up the stairs. Then Connar paused halfway up to flick a look behind him. "Where did you collect royal runners? Which ones?"

"I rode through Darchelde, where I found Quill. And Lineas, who made the grass run at Ku Halir. I don't think even my cousin Flax is faster," Rat said.

Connar straightened around, annoyed by the shock along the nerves at hearing Lineas's name. "You rode to Darchelde?" he repeated, to cover his reaction.

Jethren, following a step behind Rat Noth, flicked his gaze from one to the other and back as Rat shrugged.

"The king lifted the border patrol years ago," Rat stated what they both knew—to him it was reasonable. "My brother and I were going through Darchelde soon's we started riding to the academy on our own. Saved us at least couple of weeks each way, and who's going to sleep in mud and sleet if they don't have to?"

"True." Connar laughed. "I expect I'd have done the same. Though why did you send two royal runners?"

"Because Da always likes to send one to sniff around, and keep the other to run hot with his report. Figured he'd want the same."

"Makes sense," Connar said as they reached the landing below the watchtower, and headed into the alcove where the command desk was kept. The space was crowded, but warm from the fireplace directly behind the desk. Connar picked up the sealed note, and the others waited as he read it.

"The Nyidris are making a progress with a Sartoran princess they brought back." He looked up. "What's a progress?"

"I can answer that," Rat said grimly. "It being something royals do. Or those claiming to be royals. It's halfway between an inspection and a visit to a jarl. Same purpose as a king riding to a jarl—who has to host all the king's company for as long as the king wishes to stay. Only in this situation, I suspect she and my two former brothers are trying to impress this princess, as part of courtship."

"Ah. Their route has to be west to east, doesn't it? As Parayid is as far west as one can get in all of Marlovan Iasca." Connar squinted, trying to recollect the southern end of the map. All in all, he was very glad Rat was with them.

"Yes."

"In that case, let's run our inspection east to west." He grinned broadly. "And meet them on the way."

As Lineas walked behind a runner to the stable, she felt naked in a horrible way that had little to do with clothing. The Nyidris dressed their servants in unfamiliar garb: undyed, lesser-quality linen undertunic and long winter knickers not meant to be seen, and over it all a long garment of linsey-woolsey dyed a soft gray-green, belted at the waist. It was narrow, but slit to the knees on the sides. Both males and females wore them.

The nakedness had to do with the absence of not only her journal, but her notecase. Before they parted, Quill had said, "We'll both send our personal things to my desk in Darchelde. Each of us is heading somewhere we'll no doubt be searched to the skin. There will be no communicating, except through Commander Noth's runners."

Her throat was still tight, not so much from surrendering her things. It was remembering the unsmiling tension in Quill's eyes. But he hadn't said anything. She knew how much he hated her going into danger. She felt exactly the same way about him.

However she was the only one who could pretend to be that much-valued item, a deaf scribe also trained to serve. It was not merely a matter of knowing Hand as well as speech, or pretending not to hear. There would of course be tests.

And there were.

Only Quill knew about her first few years, how she had first lived as a deaf person, though she could hear. Now she found it necessary to recover that view of the world, in which sound became irrelevant. So even if someone tried to sneak up and bang a sword against a shield directly behind her head, she reacted only to the vibration.

And so she was on her way—not riding on a horse in the fresh air, but riding backwards in a stuffy carriage for the first time in her life—to the royal household to replace a servant Lavais Nyidri had begun to suspect might be her ex-husband's spy, and who thus had come to a short, sharp end.

She caught up at the next stop, at the castle of one of Lavais Nyidri's supporters. She was attacked by noise twice, once by a vicious whisper to which she remained oblivious, and then by being sent out to fetch something from the pottery at the back, where servants leaped out at her, hammering various metal objects and screaming.

She signed, "Is this a cleaning process, like beating rugs? Should I be doing it, too?"

Her mild bewilderment was duly reported to Lavais Nyidri by her chief maid, "She can't hear a thing. And she's stupid as well. But she writes an excellent hand."

"She'll do."

And so Lineas joined the long train of servants brought along to see to the comfort of four people.

SIX

Quill left his royal runner's robe in Parayid Garrison. He rode for the Jayad as an anonymous man. He had studied Ivandred Noth's map to see where the Tax Gang had struck recently, and worked out the area to ride from that.

He didn't think he'd be able to find them. He was certain that they would find him, if he asked about them in enough places.

He was right.

He crossed the east-west river late one afternoon, a bank of clouds bringing the darkness before he quite reached the promised village where two main roads crossed. Gentle flakes of snow drifted down when the road rounded a hill, revealing the golden lights of the small town.

The road branched. He remained on the main road, bisected by wagon tracks. As his borrowed horse ambled toward the promising smells of barns and other horses, Quill's relief shifted to heightened awareness. Even in winter, it was odd, to be completely alone so early. The sun had barely set. People should be closing up shops, walking to the local gathering places, feeding animals.

As he rode past a couple of houses on the outskirts, quiet and shut up save for golden light in windows, the back of his neck gripped, and his mind was thrown back to that summer's day when he entered a northern town under similar circumstances, to discover assassins converging on Connar—

And here they were.

His leg had slipped over the saddle and he slid to the ground before his mind shifted from memory to the present. His ears twitched as he assessed the approach: four, from different directions. Not hiding their footfalls.

He slipped his knives from his sleeves, aware of every tiny sound. Such as the slight check between one step and another at his left, when he pulled his knives. He shifted his grip, holding them up his forearm, blades out, and waited, balancing; he nudged the horse sharply with his shoulder, and it ambled away.

And they struck.

He knew immediately within two blocked blows that they weren't aiming to kill him. Yet. He shifted his grip again, and used the backs of the blades to score across the first attacker's neck as he blocked, whirled between a pair, and stabbed right and left in The Tree Falls. But he pulled at the last moment, using the knife handles to punch low on one assailant and higher on the second.

"Halt."

The silent attackers backed off instantly. Quill's hands dropped to his sides. But he still held his knives as he tried to quiet his breathing.

For a terrible moment it seemed one of Lineas's ghosts emerged from the darkness—except she'd always said that they were actually luminous, as if made of moonstone, lit from within. The brightest still with hair and clothing colors.

This slender figure separated from the darkness only at his approach. Thin and narrow-shouldered, he wore unrelieved black, his face equally muffled by scarves except for the eyes. Same with the others.

"You sought us. You found us." The voice was much younger than he expected, tenor.

"Colt Cassad?" he asked.

"Who wants to know?" another, deeper, voice asked.

Quill had intended to be entirely anonymous. That had sufficed to get him across Feravayir, but the heightened suspicion around him caused him to change his mind. "My name is Senrid Montredavan-An of Darchelde." There was a certain amount of satisfaction in admitting that, he discovered. "Everyone calls me Quill."

"Well, Quill, get ready to ride."

A horse, already saddled, was brought forward.

"What about my mount?" he began.

"Get your gear. The horse will be well taken care of. You're half a day's ride from one of the best of the Jayad horse studs."

Quill did as told, slung his saddlebag over the fresh mount, and swung up onto the animal's back.

"You can talk as we ride. Begin with what caused you to seek us so brashly across Feravayir?"

"I knew I couldn't find you," Quill said, trying to evaluate the air of challenge that still surrounded him. "So I hoped you'd find me."

"Because?"

"Connar-Laef is riding south to Feravayir, and the jarlan demands that he eradicate you and your group. But there are many who don't want that to happen."

Silence prevailed, as the snow began to fall more rapidly.

Finally, Cassad said, "Ride. We'll talk later."

Quill rode. The darkness and snowfall made it impossible for him to see much, but his escort seemed to know where they were going. Even so, they reached a point at which they stopped, and someone nudged a horse alongside Quill's. "You'll ride the rest of the way blindfolded."

It wasn't a question.

Quill submitted to having the cloth tied around his head. He considered the manner in which it was done, the person tying it running a finger inside the knot, and then around, to make certain it was not too tight, and yet still snug. Quill could see nothing.

And so a long ride, with a change of horses. He'd had little to do but think of what to say and how to say it, but he reassessed all that, based on his experiences so far.

Eventually they halted, and the blindfold was removed. He found himself in a barn. Dawn had begun to turn the world blue-gray, snow falling fast. The barn was only slightly less cold than the air outside, warmed by the sweet, humid breath of cows.

Cassad's company and their horses had crowded in, and someone built a fire with two firesticks. Quill brushed clumps of snow off his clothes and his woolen cap, then sat on a milking stool that someone placed near the fire.

"So you are saying someone knows my identity, and yet you will not tell me who they are?"

"Correct."

"Why not?"

"Because even though that person feels that your efforts are in some measure justified, you're still running outside the law. My message is to warn you that Connar-Laef will probably be exhorted to send a company after you. He'll probably be obliged to do so." And he might even take pleasure in it, was the unspoken thought.

Cassad sat a little ways away, forearms on knees, head slightly bowed. Though his gloves looked sodden, he had not removed them, though most of the rest had, including Quill.

Cassad glanced over. "Darchelde," he said. "Good enough. We'll talk it over."

"What about Darchelde makes my words good enough?"

Cassad turned his gloved palm flat. And when Quill's expression reflected his incredulity, Cassad flashed a mirthless smile. "I won't answer that because you are running inside the law."

With that he moved away, and was swallowed in the gloom beyond the circle of the fire.

Suddenly Quill was awake. He remembered where he was, and with whom, and lay still, eyes still closed, as he listened for whatever had brought him so abruptly out of sleep.

" . . . do with him?"

He slitted one eye, and made out silhouettes hunched around the campfire. They were discussing him. Must have been mention of his name that woke him.

"Make him come with us? I'm not saying he's lying. But it could be a setup."

Two grunts of assent, and one, "Nah, I don't believe it."

Cassad spoke, a soft tenor. "I confess I'd like to see more of that fighting style."

"Me, too," a lower voice spoke. "I'm not saying we wouldn't have taken him if that fight had gone red, but he would have done for at least one of us, maybe even more."

No one disagreed, then a high, female voice put in, "It's not the Odni."

"No," several agreed.

An older voice spoke up for the first time. "I think what we saw was whatever is left of the shipboard fighting style his ancestor taught, the Fox of the Fox Banner. With Inda the Harskialdna."

"You're right!"

"Yes—let's keep him. He can train us."

Cassad said, "He won't. You heard that, about us being outlaws."

"Laws," someone spoke derisively, and there came the sound of a juicy spit, and the sudden hiss of the fire.

Who can say how different history might have been had not Lineas been utterly ignorant of the intricacies of Sartoran custom?

Her introduction into the complexities of the Nyidri household was an exercise in humiliation.

She did not know how to wash silk.

She could not repair a fan.

She knew nothing of coach etiquette, or how to tie a ribbon.

Because they believed she couldn't hear instructions, some of those tasked to teach her took out their frustrations by pushing her roughly, yanking her back, and of course there was the continuous commentary on her lack of brains, her ugly freckles, and so on.

As a child, she'd been briefly bullied, an endless period while she was living it. She withdrew into her still-remembered defensive habit, turning a stolid face to tormentor and would-be friend alike, remaining as isolated as if she truly were unhearing in a mostly hearing world. Only when she was dismissed at the end of very long days did she let herself weep soundlessly into her pillow.

But each morning she rose determined to master each new task, while resuming her old skills at effacing herself. Awful as it was to have gained a reputation for stupidity—deemed useless except for her excellent writing, her ability to sew and to clean—she worked to preserve that, knowing that it might give her more freedom in that atmosphere of sharply delineated social boundaries, gossip, and innuendo.

Assuming she was not just deaf but a dolt, the household stewards assigned her most often to serve in the various chambers their careless superiors spent most of their time while in company. Servants in Nyidri households were the equivalent of furniture. If the family ever noticed you, it was never a good thing. So it meant a lot of standing around in silence, until given an order.

Lineas soon became effectively invisible: the freckles, frizzy red hair, pale skin, and thin body could not catch the idle eyes of Lavais's sons, who only bestowed their attentions on beauty; as far as they and their mother were concerned, the fans, shoes, ribbons, lace, books, hair ornaments, and other items dropped carelessly on every surface or on the floor magically vanished into their proper places, each miraculously cleaned and mended.

Seonrei, whom Lineas saw rarely and only in company (there was no use in placing a deaf servant among the Sartorans), paid her no heed as well, assuming that all Nyidri servants were ordered to report everything she did or said, if they weren't outright spies in the guise of servants.

Like Iaeth.

And so the dreary days passed, some in motion as the progress progressed, others endured hour after hour as hosts and guests dueled with word and gesture. The horrible, stuffy coaches, desperately overcrowded (servants were crammed in, their laps piled with impedimenta) were in their way as tedious as the long days of picking up after silk-dressed nobles. The one bright spot was Plix, the kitchen steward. They could not speak together in front of the other servants, but the older woman's smiles of approval bolstered Lineas's flagging spirits.

When they did briefly encounter one another, Plix whispered quick words of praise, and exhorted Lineas to find her first if she thought she heard anything that should be passed along. Lineas didn't even know who the courier was, for safety.

The only sure relief was sleep—and the days when certain items could not be trusted on the baggage wagons because of the threat of sleet, and so the bottom rung of servants were forced to sit in the wagons instead, allowing the precious items to ride in the servant coach. Lineas and the boot boy and the kitchen sweep sat shoulder to shoulder, shivering, but at least the air was pure.

And so, it was tediously same . . . until it wasn't.

Lineas firmly believed her mission was a waste of time. She'd discovered within a day or so of her arrival that the Nyidris all possessed golden notecases, and they had personal runners for messages to those they didn't, or couldn't, communicate with by magic. She was never going to see any of those messages.

At least she was warm while serving in the plastered and painted rooms exclusive to the nobles. Each piece of furniture was a work of art, and she liked dusting and polishing them so she could admire the details, but the entire effect chilled her. All these still, artfully posed statues, those wrought so cleverly in gold, seemed to replace the living, breathing company that might look less perfect but would bring warmth and love to those otherwise empty rooms. One reward she could furtively enjoy was music, though she had to make certain her face reflected indifference: though nothing was said, Lineas wondered if she would be forbidden the room if Lavais Nyidri didn't believe she was deaf, for she became certain that the jarlan would believe that servant ears would pollute the music through pleasure in hearing it.

But music was rare. Only when the Sartoran princess was present. The talk was invariably about people and places she did not know. She learned to shut out the idle, often cruel, gossip as if she were deaf, and retreat into memory.

But one evening Lavais's sharp voice changed, and Lineas knew the woman was looking her way. "She's deaf. But if you're worried, speak in Sartoran. Alef said she comes from the north coast, where the Iascan is even more barbarous than Marlovan, and they're too ignorant to know what Sartoran is."

Demeos said, "The only use we could possibly get out of Connar Olavayir is to sic him on the Tax Gang. But they have to have listening ears in every tavern and stable between here and the mountains. They surely know he's coming. And they won't come anywhere near."

"They're *thieves*." Ryu laughed scornfully. "You put out a tempting enough prize, thieves will come out from behind every barn and bush." He draped himself over a beautiful chair carved with intertwined lotus leaves. Tapping one knee with his fan, he mused, "What would happen if we were to, oh, put out the word that we're shifting the king's tax from somewhere to somewhere."

Demeos flicked his fan at his brother. "Yes, and what then?"

"They come for it, of course. And we sic the Olavayirs on them."

"And?" Demeos drawled. "And then Connar Olavayir offers to escort the rescued treasure north to the royal city."

Ryu prowled around the perimeter of the room, then turned suddenly, and leaned against another chair. Demeos held up his arm to admire the light running along the gold embroidery down the length of his sleeves.

Lineas had always been sensitive to beauty of all kinds. Demeos was also, she'd noted. Ryu affected the accoutrements of beauty, but his gaze always stayed on people. He carried himself as if he were beautiful. Demeos was as handsome as Connar, his ruddy-black hair braided with gems, contrasting the light silks he wore; unlike his brother he never colored his hair.

She watched them to make certain they did not notice her. If their posture indicated a turn her way, she focused on the table of refreshments she was there to refill whenever a tray, plate, or bowl was empty.

"But what if he doesn't go back?" Ryu smiled, and asked dulcetly, "Because he's dead?"

"What?" Demeos looked up.

"You saw that report." Ryu waved his fan to and fro. "He's not riding down here with the entire army. It's barely as many as our former and tiresome stepfather's garrison holds."

Demeos turned the colored side of his fan flat, his upper lip crimping slightly. "Surely you do not wish to turn our people, who've only their pitchforks and sawblades, loose on them? It would be a slaughter."

Ryu licked his lips. "I read the description of Ku Halir that you ignored."

"It was disgusting."

Ryu lifted a shoulder. "It was enlightening in its detailed proof that Marlovans die just as well by a pitchfork as a blade. Slower."

Lavais spoke up mildly. "Ryu. We do not need the details."

Ryu flung his long hair back, and reached for a goblet. "My point is, the ratio of Marlovans was too high, and so the northerners lost. But it was a very near thing. If we contrive it, Connar Olavayir will not have that advantage." He drained the goblet, then held it out sideways. Lineas picked up the spice-wine decanter and filled the goblet.

His muscles tightened, which was all the notice she would get that he was about to pull the goblet away: servants had been thrashed for spilling a drop. She lifted the lip of the decanter a heartbeat before he brought the goblet to his lips to drink, and she faded back.

Demeos sighed. "According to what I keep hearing, half the countryside is secretly in sympathy with the Tax gang—"

"Something," Lavais interjected in her quiet voice, "we ought to address, if that's true."

"Anon, Mother," Demeos drawled. "But my point remains, the rumors insist they give away what they take, and the greedy commons could never resist that. Thedren insists most of the boys apprentice age would join them if they could find them."

"All the more reason to see them dead. Soon. Set it up at the right place, Connar rides in, wipes out the Tax Gang, and then our people rise and bottle him." Ryu set down goblet and fan to clap his hands lightly. "And we do what the north shore Idegans did, declare independence. What are the Marlovans going to do? The king is too old and too drunk to fight, everyone says. The heir too stupid. The worst of the young commanders is that shit Rat, and he's with Connar. We make certain he dies first. In fact, I reserve that privilege for myself."

Demeos sighed again. "It sounds vile."

"You don't," Lavais leveled a cold gaze at her son, "seem to be achieving any kind of success with your music and courtship."

Demeos lifted a shoulder. "I tried. Speaking of. Where does Seonrei fit in your hypothetical plan?"

Ryu's lip curled. "Since Seonrei is writing to the queen every day, we'll make certain that what she writes is alarm. She's being attacked by the barbarian Olavayirs. If she dies," he added in an undervoice, for he'd come to loathe her for her total rejection of his advances, "then the Olavayirs get blamed. We win either way."

Demeos rose at last, and stopped before his mother. "My only worry is Noth."

"My only worry," Lavais interposed smoothly, "is, what if it fails. You must be certain to protect your names. Your previous plan left you safe because there was no proof leading to you. Which, I will attest to Ivandred Noth's credit, if in no other wise, he insists on obtaining. As well the king is a lazy sot, too; if this had happened in Mathren Olavayir's day, we all would have died in our beds one night."

Demeos sighed more quietly, and Ryu flicked away the words with his fan. "But this isn't the past, which is the whole point. We *do* have a lazy sot as king. As for the rest, Demeos and I can be champions of the people without claiming our right rank. Yet."

"So who leads, then?" Demeos asked, hiding his growing ambivalence. This entire plot threatened to be even messier than the last one.

"Who else, but Cousin Artolei? You know he'd love it. But . . . Mother, you're right about Ivandred Noth. He's neither lazy, nor a sot, and he's much too close."

Lavais had been thinking rapidly. "Ivandred won't ride against commons."

"Even if Rat is the first to die?" Ryu took a bite of a pastry, curled his lip, then threw it aside so that it skittered off the porcelain dish and landed on the floor.

"Not if it's all over by the time he arrives. Which means whatever you do must be at the far end of the kingdom," the jarlan said, as Lineas noiselessly picked up the pastry and with the cloth tucked in her sash began to wipe up the fine tiles of the floor.

Lavais tapped her diamond-studded nails on the gilt-edged porcelain plate before her. "He won't ride against common people if they throw down their arms—"

Lavais's eye was caught by the red-haired servant cleaning the floor. Deaf, right? Still, they were breaking their rule about private discussions. "Get out!" she snapped.

Both her sons startled.

Lineas nearly did. Shock jolted her nerves, cold as ice down her back. She hadn't reacted, had she? She kept scrubbing at the smear of apple-pastry on the marble, until Lavais tossed a fan and hit her back.

Lineas jolted, hands trembling.

Lavais pointed at the door.

Lineas picked up porcelain, cloth, and mess. She closed the door noiselessly, her heart thundering.

Back in the room, Demeos said patiently, "She's *deaf.*"

Lavais retorted, "Whenever you talk war, make sure *nobody* else is in the room."

Her sons sighed, exchanging a long-suffering look. They said obediently, "Yes, Mother," hoping to stave off another lecture about carelessness.

Lavais tapped her fingernails on the porcelain, tink, tink, tink, not hearing her sons debate what locale would be best. She moved to the door, opened, it, and saw her maid waiting in the hallway.

"Follow the deaf girl. See where she goes," Lavais ordered shortly, then resumed her seat as Demeos rolled his eyes. As if she had seen that, Lavais snapped, "It doesn't do to be careless. Ever."

Demeos hastily smoothed his expression, as outside the door, Lineas walked softly down the hall, still carrying the ruined pastry, the broken dish, and the cleaning cloth. Every nerve felt unsheathed; invisible, inimical eyes watched her, or so instinct clamored.

So she moved with deliberate care, going to the back of the kitchen where the crockery was stored. She laid the broken dish on the table, for someone to decide if, and how, it was to be repaired: if it was Sartoran, it might be mended with gold in the cracks.

Next, the ruined apple tart went into the pig pen, and the cloth to the laundry. When she came out, she was certain she felt soft footfalls behind her, always one turn away.

She had to get word to Plix—who was on duty supervising the kitchen until the jarl family retired for the night. Lineas's neck prickled as she made her way to the kitchen. One glance at Plix, whose mouth tightened, and Lineas wondered what showed in her face.

She recollected what Quill had taught her about cow-face, and let her jaw hang as she signed that the jarlan has dismissed her.

Plix awkwardly signed back that she could retire.

Lineas left. She could hear Plix going about her business, readying all the bread pans and flouring them, for the bakers who would be coming in soon to start the morning's bread.

She heard the footsteps all the way to the attic, where Lineas had the last bed in a long dormitory.

The maid returned and reported to the jarlan that the deaf girl was dismissed to bed, and interacted with no one on the way.

Lineas's dreams were full of shocks and starts. It was a relief to rise, and a bigger relief when a dour servant cut her out of the scrum the next morning, all jostling to get to the baths first, and said that she'd been assigned to take the scraps tor the chickens, and to bring back whatever eggs there were.

Lineas bundled up and trudged across the slushy yard to the roost, where the hens had all congregated together on one of their long shelves above the row of nests. It smelled musty even in the cold. Lineas bent to fill the shallow bowls with the withered greens set aside the day before—and shock ran down her nerves when the roost door creaked open behind her. But she kept moving without a hitch.

"It's I," Plix said. "The jarlan's personal maid was shadowing you last night. What did you hear?"

Lineas cleared her throat—she hadn't used her voice for weeks—and told her.

At the end, Plix stared at the chickens murmuring fretfully in their roost. "It might just be talk . . . but that's not for us to decide. I'll send someone to Noth. Do and say nothing."

Orders, Lineas reflected as she searched for eggs, she would gladly obey.

Plix left her to it, and withdrew in another direction. The timing could not have been worse. Both of her trusted contacts had been sent in opposite directions. She'd have to send her brother, who would complain bitterly. But his hatred of the Nyidris ensured he'd go.

It was a couple of days before she could arrange a pretext enabling him to get away, under cover of a fast-approaching storm as the sun sank behind the clouds.

The only other movement at that late hour was the cousin Demeos and Ryu had been expecting to return: Khael Artolei, whose mother had grown up with Lavais Nyidri. Nearly ten generations previously, the Artoleis had finally schemed and married their way into the elite of what became the Jayad—but as their honed strategy was to divide and play factions against one another, within the six years of their rule, they had managed to cause general unrest that threatened to erupt into civil war.

That was when the Marlovans came. And after a disorganized resistance best called token (the ruling Artoleis ran off), the Jaya family proved to be orderly, generous, straightforward, and best of all, gave short shrift to the brigands constantly coming around from the sea to the east.

The remaining Artoleis were permitted to retain their old lands, and the next generations lived peaceably, until Khael's grandfather's time. He had ambitions to regain that lofty royal rank, and raised his daughter to share those ambitions. She and Lavais were sent to Sartor together to learn the language, and subsequently their sons were sent to do the same.

Khael Artolei inherited early, when his mother resigned the Holding to him after snagging a prince in one of the little countries along the Sartoran Sea.

He was in a foul mood because of the weather. His company were all seasoned flatterers because he didn't tolerate anyone around him who contradicted him. He, like his cousin Ryu, also plumed himself on his martial abilities.

He was nearing the end of a cold, boring ride, and his mood was vile until he spotted a lone rider coming from the opposite direction, who spotted his livery and then immediately pulled his horse into some trees to avoid an encounter.

"Assassin," Artolei declared as he pulled his bow, slapped an arrow to, and twang!

The figure, half in shadow, tumbled from his horse. The animal panicked and ran off.

"Look at that," Artolei crowed. "Dead. Single shot!"

The uttered the expected praise as they all rode forward to inspect the dead assassin.

"Oh," said the first toady. "Isn't that what the Nyidri servants wear?"

The toadies exchanged looks, not daring to glance at their lord.

Who said, "If you don't say anything, they won't know. You. Drag him off somewhere. If they find him, we'll blame those Tax Gang shits."

No one voiced the obvious, "What if he was coming to give you a message?" But Artolei was thinking it as he finished out the ride. He was aware of himself as a hanger-on to the Nyidris, and hated it. He had just as much right to a royal title as they did—but there was no taking on the Jevayirs, everyone knew that.

He was still thinking up various excuses as a servant took him to meet Demeos and Ryo . . . but when the three were alone, what Ryu had to say made him forget all about the stupid messenger, who shouldn't have been hiding in the first place. If he'd dismounted and bowed, as was only proper, he'd still be riding, wouldn't he?

Ryu outlined his plan. Artolei listened with growing delight.

Demeos noticed his enthusiasm, and suppressed his own lack, very aware that if Ryu continued to take the lead, Mother might decide he was the more kingly after all.

SEVEN

The royal progress, as Lavais called that winter journey (ostensibly in honor of Princess Seonrei) changed its route again, this time to fetch up against the border with the Jayad, at a sight promised to be truly splendid: Frozen Falls.

And it was.

The Artolei family had built a winter palace on a bend in the river, from which could be viewed the semicircle of falls in a vast panorama, below which the great river rushed over rocks before dividing into two. When winter was coldest and the water was low, the falls sometimes froze, as they had this year, and on certain mornings, the gradually strengthening northern sun would catch the ice at an angle that struck an icy luminance.

To the delight of those who enjoyed such spectacles, the weather cleared for three days, during which sleds were driven out to a point that granted an unimpeded view.

For Seonrei, these three mornings proved to be the highlight of what had been a strange journey so far. She gazed on the shifting colors glimmering in the ice as the sun moved incrementally, and enjoyed a chance to talk with Iaeth, who came along as maid in charge of the basket of hot foods carefully packed.

"And the Marlovan prince is expected by week's end," Iaeth finished reporting, as she poured chili-chocolate from the cloth-wrapped heated jug into two tiny cups, and added cream. "Which brings me to another question. I gathered that they don't expect more than a hundred or maybe two hundred Marlovans at most, and yet there are these wagons."

The point, on a cliff, overlooked the lower north shore, from which they could see a long train of covered wagons worming slowly toward the gleaming spires of the Artolei palace.

"Well, considering the number they've already gathered, plus servants, it isn't surprising," Seonrei said comfortably, sipping her chocolate, which was perfect: hot, spicy, creamy.

"Yet there are wagons every day. Further, it's all men—husky men—tending them."

"They probably hired men to dig out the wagon wheels as well as to carry barrels and baskets and trunks."

"Except," Iaeth said, "none of them are leaving."

Seonrei shifted her gaze away from the wagon train, and back to the falls, the lights already fading blue and green. "Something is going on," she said slowly. "Ryu is full of glee, like a child with a secret. And I notice that Lavais has ceased disparaging the Marlovans, and is full of anticipation for the delights they are going to show them. They might be putting together a theatrical in the old style."

"Except who does that anymore? All the records make it clear that few in the court liked being forced to sit for two, even three days—sometimes all night—watching some prince or princess prance around while musicians played their fingers bloody, and teams of choristers praised them in fifty verses."

Seonrei laughed, though it was her ancestors who had set that fashion. "At least Tivonais was reputed to be a very good dancer."

"In and out of the bedroom," Iaeth commented sourly. "It could very well be. And I have to admit, this frozen fall makes a dramatic background for a drama of any type."

"Yes," Seonrei said, working the little cup back and forth between her palms. "Yes." She turned a sudden, serious gaze to Iaeth. "Perhaps these wagons require further investigation."

Iaeth had already resolved to do exactly that.

At the same moment, a week away, Connar, Rat, and Jethren sat around a fire, contemplating the personal message they'd received from the Nyidri brothers the evening before.

> *We look forward to your arrival, and trust you will enjoy the entertainment we have planned for your benefit. But we also rely on your strength to protect the kingdom. As previous messages have indicated, we have had no success in eradicating the bandits called the Tax Gang. Just recently we have been made aware of rumors that they are going to attack River's Point, the small town where two roads meet—enclosed is a map—where we are told there is a caravan of goods for the king's tax stranded by the snow.*
>
> *It is not completely out of your way. If you are able to rid the kingdom of these outlaws, there will be that much more to celebrate.*

"I don't like this," Rat said.

Jethren said caustically, "Afraid we're outnumbered?"

Rat sent a flat glance over his shoulder at him.

Jethren remembered Ku Halir, and flushed. "That was a joke," he offered.

Rat tugged at one of his long-lobed ears, and sucked the inside of his cheek, the way he had when he and Connar were boys in the academy—usually right before he led the wedge that invariably smashed his opponents. Then he flicked a squinty glance at Connar. "I think it's a ruse."

"To trap the Tax Gang."

"No. Us." Rat's big, scarred hand tapped his chest.

Connar's brows lifted. "Us? How do you get that?"

"Because, if they have this neat trap all ready, then why don't *they* spring it?"

"According to the message, that's our job, as defenders of the kingdom. I have no argument with that."

Rat tugged at the other ear, shuffled his feet, then said, "Maybe. Maybe. If it was anywhere but in Artolei."

"What?" Connar said, and Jethren crossed his arms, but remained silent.

"Artolei is the holding we'll reach in two days, maybe three. It's divided by the border between the Jayad and Feravayir, though most of it lies this side of the border. Which is why they get away with running the holding the way they do. The Nyidris look the other way, so long as they get Artolei's support. From the look of this map, this town the Tax Gang is going to raid is roughly midway between Artolei's stronghold, and their winter palace at Frozen Falls."

"So?"

"I guess you have to know about the Artoleis. The holder, Khael Artolei, is somewhere around our age. Though Artolei is a holding, it's run like a duchas, especially since Khael Artolei's grandfather's time."

"What is the difference between a duchas and a holding?"

"A duchas is like a jarl, put it that way," Rat said. "The jarlan used to go on and on about how civilized Sartor's chain of command is, because it's all about birth and how well-bred you are, and nothing to do with defense. Anyway," he said hastily seeing the impatience in Connar's tight brow, "my point here is, he can rule however he wants to. Such as, all the servants in his castle are hostages, as well as his private army."

"Hostages?" Connar repeated.

Rat flattened his hand, palm down. "They call it service. They keep careful records, and every guild chief and artisan and farmer above a certain level has to send a child to serve the family. And if Artolei doesn't like what they do or say, those children suffer accidents. Nobody gives him trouble—ever. You didn't know that, but the Tax Gang, who are supposed to have ears in every inn and barn for weeks' ride, have to know it. No one would dare lift a hand to help them, so by rights this trap the Nyidris have set up has to be the easiest in history to spring. So why isn't Artolei springing it with all his fine guards in livery?"

"They're really civs," Connar said. "We've got the training."

"Not in Ryu's eyes. Growing up, all I heard about is how he was tougher than me'n Mouse as well as more *civilized*." Rat's upper lip lifted briefly on that last word. "He and his followers dropped on me every chance they could get, until I finally got enough size on me to flatten him. Thinks himself a natural commander and a great warrior. By rights he should be crowing about taking this Tax Gang down, not setting it up for us."

Connar's mood shifted from indifference to a wary anticipation. "Ryu Nyidri is another Thias Elsarion, then?"

"Don't know about that. Ryu likes bloodshed. He likes seeing other people in pain, is what I'm saying. Much more than Demeos, at least when we were small. Haven't seen either of them for a few years." Rat made a spitting motion to one side.

Connar said, "How about this. We'll send a runner to reply to this message, promising our help, as that's orders from the king . . . No. Two runners, one running doggo."

Rat accepted that with a flick of his fingers.

"Ideally we get reports from both runners when we catch up." Connar slapped the backs of his fingers to the message. "We'll ride hard, and fast. They might plot against us, but I doubt they can outride us."

Rat said, "True."

While the runners began riding, and the three captains discussed contingencies, their ostensible target sat with his captains in an attic room over a pottery. The ovens provided a welcome heat, which nobody noticed as they sat in silence, digesting the news their own scouts had just brought in.

"I say we kill that royal runner."

Colt Cassad regarded the sixteen year old girl who had broken the silence, then sighed at that unthinking teenage bloody-mindedness. *I was much the same at that age*, he reminded himself. "But we don't know that he's part of this rather obvious trap."

"Moving trunks of the king's tax goods in the middle of winter?" the youngest burst out in a tone of insult. "Do they think we're *stupid?*"

"Peace." Cassad held up a palm. "My point is, live prisoners can be made dead if justice requires it. But if we've judged wrongly, dead prisoners cannot be brought to life again."

A scowl was the only response, but Colt didn't seem to expect anything more. He said, "There's something else we might do."

The others looked up expectantly at his sudden grin. "Let's use this as an opportunity to rid ourselves of all our spies. The royal runner with them: we'll send them into this trap, and offer them the chance to do what they like with the bait."

"And us?"

Cassad sat back. "If it's a trap then someone has to be springing it, right? Who wants to wager against me that Artolei is behind it?"

No one would take that bet. The proximity to Frozen Falls was too obvious.

Colt's grin showed teeth. "And no one can be in two places at once . . ."

Quill, asleep in an adjacent room stuffed with seconds in pots and plates, woke up to the sound of muffled laughter.

As sometimes happens, Connar and his captains spent a lot longer discussing contingency plans, and practicing for them, than the actual situation required.

They rode through the quiet, snow-covered countryside, as Ryu's guard and the huskiest of Ryu's resistance army huddled in farmhouses and villages, eating the denizens' winter staples as they waited for the signal to attack. The snow hid their traces, and any runners but those identified by Ryu had been summarily killed. The only person who saw them was Iaeth, whose skills in covert movement far outstripped those of the locals.

Iaeth duly reported this massing of a potential army to Seonrei, who said after careful thought, "We are not here to interfere with internal affairs."

Iaeth accepted that, though they both knew Seonrei wanted very much to interfere—but for peaceful purposes.

So Iaeth watched from the treetops as Connar's columns rode through the snow-blanketed land under a milk-colored sky. Armed for battle, they headed for the trade town at the crossroads that would lead to Frozen Falls to meet the Nyidris and the Sartoran princess.

Before they reached the town named so helpfully by Ryu's note, Connar and Jethren formed up, ready to outflank the expected attack.

Rat and his company rode ahead as bait for the baiters. He found the small town shut up tight, scarcely a gleam of light escaping the shutters of the buildings, and not so much as a cat to be seen roaming. His company rode slowly, weapons out, bows strung. The only sound was their own horses' muffled foot falls. Nothing, nothing, nothing . . . and there at the crossroads sat wagons mired in drifts of slow. A lone figure sat huddled on a wagon, awaiting them.

At the sound of their approach, the person's face lifted, a pale blob in the moonlight.

Rat gestured for a lantern. Then, *"Quill?"*

"Ah, Rat," Quill said genially, hopping off the wagon.

"Where are the rest of the ambush?"

"We were actually bait, I believe. Anyway, I decided to wait it out, unlike my former companions, who I expect were Nyidri spies." He twiddled his fingers in the air like insects running off in two directions.

Rat gestured for his company to spread out to search, just to be thorough, but he didn't expect to find anything, what with Quill sitting there.

Quill noted the hand signal, and the silent movement of the warriors, swords out, bows at shoulders, arrows in reach. "The rest of the bait is busy scattering across the countryside," he reported. "As for the wagons, the trunks and boxes have a thin layer of silver at the top, with spoiled seed and suchlike beneath. I image the locals can use it for the soil, once we've cleared out."

Rat grunted. "Who'd fall for such a stupid trap?"

Quill turned his palms up. "There's something else going on, but what it is, I can't tell you. Cassad's gang nearly gutted me over it."

Rat sighed. "Then let's get out of here. Salt! Report to the Commander. We'll rejoin soon as the search is done."

Salt's footsteps diminished in the slush.

Rat stepped up close to Quill. "This whole thing stinks."

Quill said, "Where are you headed?"

"We're supposed to meet up at Frozen Falls, Artolei's winter palace. Meet some Sartoran princess. Where were you?"

Quill said, "Your father sent me to warn the Tax Gang of your coming. Which I did—and why I'm here. What's the latest from Parayid?"

"Nothing," Rat said. "Which also stinks. Last runner we got was weeks ago. Said they were in winter quarters. Looking forward to us reaching them by early spring, we'd have some war games. Look, Quill. Everybody in the south knows we're riding on this tour of inspection, but we've had no runners since that one. We even got a runner from the Nyidris, sending us here." He opened his hand toward the wagons. "I might be jumping at shadows, but I wouldn't put it past Ryu at the least to put out orders to kill every runner going west, if he's got some plot going."

Quill's expression tightened—of course he thought immediately of Lineas. But she'd know to go covert, which most garrison-trained runners might not necessarily think of, unless given orders. They were so used to crossing the kingdom back and forth. Though the only way to be sure would be to make the cross-country run to Parayid himself.

Rat was thinking along parallel lines. He looked up to find Quill silent. Listening. Then he caught on. Quill was waiting for orders.

Only that was Connar's privilege.

Connar had accepted Rat's sending the runners from Darchelde, and with the message to the Noths as potential reinforcement, but Rat was certain that a second trespass might not be accepted as readily.

He'd been gazing at the slush around his battered boot tops. He blinked, and found Quill still waiting. It would take no more than a day to reach the rest of the command, at which time Connar could send Quill to Parayid. Would a day's wait make any difference?

Quill, watching closely, saw the uncertainty in Rat's demeanor, and said, "I could make a grass run, if I had a horse to start out with."

In other words, he was volunteering.

That changed everything, as far as Rat saw it. With a profound sense of relief, Rat summoned lanky, laconic Digger, his first runner. And before the search was finished, Quill had a fresh horse and a half-loaf of travel bread. He vanished up the road to the west, and Rat watched with satisfaction as he was swallowed in the night.

A short distance away, silence lay over the snow in all directions; Connar and Jethren led their companies in a line, horses walking, weapons ready, as they waited for the trap to close around Rat and his small company up ahead.

No one spoke until the sound of galloping hooves caused Connar to signal a halt.

The scout rode up to him. "Fresh tracks, looks like maybe a wing, two at most, and so many footprints mushed together we couldn't count them. They headed off northeast, away from the crossroads village. From the way some of the horseapples were still steaming, a few hours ago."

"Investigate. Don't engage. Catch up with us," Connar said, and the scout rode off in the dim light of a half-moon.

While the scout rode on their trail, Khael Artolei, Ryu Nyidri, and their two hundred strong, armed with Iascan steel, followed the terrified servant who had come to report an attack.

They galloped ahead of the foot army until they arrived at Artolei Castle to find every window glowing with light, and servants running to and fro putting out fires in the state rooms.

"No!" Artolei shrieked, and kicked his sweaty horse back into a gallop.

What had happened was clear: while he and Ryu were forming their trap for the Marlovans at the crossroads, the Tax Gang had arrived just after sunset.

Since Artolei had taken every able-bodied warrior with him, the outlaws had spent the night stripping the entire castle of every trace of silver and gold, every gem and jewel, leaving behind a bonfire of the Artoleis' records in the center of the Hall of Justice.

EIGHT

Frozen Falls really was a frozen waterfall, the Marlovans discovered as they rode in column up the low hills toward the first palace many had ever seen. It was built of red stone, white marble, and the more familiar sandstone they were used to, topped by decorative spires with arched windows for viewing. The palace itself wasn't defensible, but the massive walls curving around the jut of land the palace was built on, and the long drop below to the rushing river, were.

From the hills, Connar's company could see for a considerable distance, the snow undisturbed except for the muddy road between chest-high walls of snow to either side. Though there was no sign of anything amiss for days' ride in any direction, they still rode weapons-ready, spearheads affixed on the poles carrying the banners.

Below the palace, people lined the road on either side to watch them approach.

Connar was thrown back to the ride down the eastern end of the pass, below the cliffs as hostile Adranis had stared and yakked incomprehensibly. But these Feravayir spectators lined the road in complete silence.

The Marlovans approached the massive gates, which had been thrown open, blue and gold banners alternating with the brown-and-white stag of Feravayir.

No sign, of course, of the three crowned stars of Perideth against a sky blue background.

At the gate Lavais Nyidri stood, her two sons at her right and Khael Artolei at her left—an arrangement she had made mostly so that her dear Ryu would not be overshadowed by the other two, so much handsomer. Who would have thought that pale rabbit of a grandmother would turn up in her son, hair the color of dirty water beneath the flattering magical color, too much nose and too little chin. But he made up for it in style, she thought fondly as the double-fanfare for a prince in riding echoed down the icy road.

She and Ryu bitterly resented that fanfare, she with the hatred of a life of disappointment. She had never dared claim her birthright while Mathren Olavayir was alive, and on his death, she had fully expected to seduce Ivandred Noth into riding against the Olavayirs. For twenty years she had tried.

Ryu's hatred was jealousy, heated by anticipation; he knew the Marlovans had nothing to do with the Tax Gang stripping the Artolei ancestral stronghold, but that had been *his* plan. And the Marlovans were going to pay for its failure. He snorted out harsh breaths as those brassy notes reverberated on the icy air.

Demeos was indifferent to the fanfare. To him, horns tooting was merely evidence of a lack of civilization, so very different from the chimes and tuneful fluting of the Sartoran Progress, when nobles moved formally between palaces.

And here came the much-talked of, much-hated Marlovans, riding in perfect formation two by two, great swallow-tailed banners rippling, deep blue and gold.

Four sets of eyes snapped to that figure at the front.

Alone of the four, Lavais had seen Connar previously, but she had since talked herself into believing that such an uncouth background would have coarsened the pretty boy she'd glimpsed across the throne room at the Convocation in '77, ten years ago.

If anything, he was more beautiful, his straight limbs having hardened to a splendid form. He rode easily, impossibly masculine—broad shoulders and narrow waist set off by that gray coat unadorned except for the glint of gold below the shoulder pauldrons, his sash gray. Beneath the long, glossy blue-black hair, the cut of his cheekbones and jaw were no sharper than the cut of his mouth, all dominated by eyes of such a blue the color seemed to gather lucence from those banners piercing the sky behind him.

Ryu's jaw dropped.

Lavais looked askance at her son, and she watched the heads turn as Connar Olavayir rode by, her thoughts churned rapidly. Maybe having that pretty young animal as the target of all eyes would work in their favor.

Connar reined up before the gate. Lavais stepped forward three paces and bowed as she spoke words of welcome and introduction. That signaled the rest of the gathered company in making bows, Sartoran-style—her intent to demonstrate civilized manners going right past the intended targets.

Rat rolled his eyes (which was seen by Ryu, whose ears reddened under his golden hair); one of his captains muffled a snicker when Jugears, Rat's second runner, commented under his breath that the servants at the back must be impressed by all those butts sticking out.

"And wouldn't I like to be the one to deliver a good kick," was the whispered response through unmoving lips.

"If you care to dismount, your host, Holder Artolei, will personally conduct you to Princess Seonrei," Lavais said in her clearest voice to Connar.

Artolei, still mortified by the looting of his ancestral home, and the loss of the records detailing the commons and their service, stepped forward, forcing a semblance of a smile.

No one paid him any attention.

Connar leaped down from his horse. As Fish supervised the handling of the animals and the gear on the saddlebags, Connar said to Demeos and Ryu, "Your Tax Gang wasn't anywhere near the village. Someone must have warned 'em off."

Though his scout had reported a fire and a great to-do at the Artolei castle, Connar wasn't going to let on he knew. He wanted to find out, if he could, what lay under the surface of things. "I can send out a company to search."

Artolei flushed with fury.

Demeos said hastily, "No need, no need. It's winter—bad weather—they've surely gone to ground. It's a matter for spring. Our information was entirely remiss."

Connar and Rat remained stolidly blank in demeanor, their lack of surprise watched suspiciously by Artolei as they were led inside the warmth and color of a splendid palace furnished in all the latest Sartoran styles—lyre-backed chairs everywhere, low tables with curved legs, and a profusion of refreshments awaiting the guests.

Here they were introduced to the Sartoran princess. Rat had told them that the dialect of Iascan used in the south had a lot of Sartoran words—enough for them to fumble through a brief conversation.

Lavais gave Seonrei six painful, stumbling exchanges to see how awkward the Marlovans were, then signaled for everyone to move to the dining room for a meal. Connar and his two captains were separated off from the rest of their men, who were led to a series of cottages that had been cleared of their residents—along with most of their furnishings.

Demeos, Ryu, and Artolei had invited a carefully curated list of young nobles, mostly from the Feravayir side of the border, except for some friends and a hanger-on cousin or two from the Jayad side whom Artolei trusted to do exactly what he said.

Lineas watched from among the servants.

Until she saw from an upper window that they had actually arrived, she expected every day to hear that the Marlovans had turned toward Parayid—had ridden away—anything but what actually happened.

When she was summoned downstairs to join the long line of servants carrying the food to the banquet hall, she met Plix's shocked eyes, and remembered that it was the steward's brother who had been sent to Parayid so that Noth could send runners to warn off Connar.

That night, Lineas and the rest of the servants were kept up half the night dealing with a flurry of orders, everything to be done at once. Many of the orders conflicting.

The Nyidris had spared no expense in luring entertainers. As Lineas hauled away dirty dishes by the cartload, she heard musicians in four separate locations. Laughter and the giddy smells of spiced wine floated through the beautiful chambers whose carved and decorated walls boasted hangings painted delicate colors to offset embroidered cushions and matching tapestries.

They scarce had three hours of snatched rest before the orders flowed in again, sending them scurrying, and so passed another exhausting day, followed by a third.

For Connar, those days passed in a haze of sensory delights. After a miserable ride, it was good to be clean again. And warm. And met with inviting gazes on every side.

Jethren, too, got his share of flattering attention. The only captain who stayed sober and went to bed alone was Rat. He hated the situation, hated the false smiles, and especially hated the smirk he glimpsed on Ryu's smug face whenever their eyes met. But Ryu didn't say a word to him—in fact, he went out of the way to pretend Rat didn't exist. All his teeth-scrapingly false flattery was aimed at Connar.

Human nature being what it is, many of those who protested the loudest about barbarians went back two or three times to really make certain just how loutish they were in intimacy—that is, those Connar obliged. Those to whom he turned an indifferent eye were sharp in their criticism, but whoever wished to note whom the barbarian prince rejected smirked behind fans held up to hide one eyebrow.

Lineas kept away, in an agony lest Connar spot her lugging dirty dishes away, and react in some way that would call attention to her. And yet she had to speak to them—warn them. She could no longer be certain Plix's brother had been able to. But the Marlovans were always surrounded by the nobles, not just during the day, but the gossip going around the kitchen was that they had plenty of company over the nights as well.

She didn't even know where they were kept, except it was over on the nobles' side, where she was forbidden to go: useless (the Nyidris believed) as a spy, she had been demoted to the army of kitchen slubs, fetching endless stacks of dirty cups, goblets, and dishes, and dunking them in the ensorcelled barrel, drying them, and lugging them out to be filled again.

After the third night, enough of a rhythm had been established for the servants to be caught up. By midnight most were sent to bed, to be called the hour before dawn, as usual. As she made her way along the servants' routes, she poked her head in at the entertainment rooms, hoping she might catch sight of Rat, or Fish, or someone she knew, who wasn't the center of attention.

There seemed to be a lot fewer guests. Or maybe it was just the smoother routine that made it seem that way.

She dismissed that thought as irrelevant; speculation was useless. She had to get to Rat, to tell him what she'd overheard those weeks ago. Even though she'd never again heard anything but the dullest talk, there was too much in the present circumstances that matched that plan the brothers had been hatching. Rat should know, even if he scoffed.

But if she asked through gesture where the Marlovan captains were, someone would be sure to ask why she wanted to know. So she stopped in the supply room to fetch a cleaning bucket and cloth, which implements effectively made her invisible, and set out to find them.

By venturing into halls she'd never had time to explore, and listening to snatches of talk, she finally discovered that the captains were housed in separate cottages in the side garden, Connar in the biggest and closest. Judging by the snickering about his staying power, Lineas assumed he was not alone. But Fish would be.

She made her way to a side exit to the garden, stashed her bucket and cloth behind an ornamental shrub coated with snow, and began to slip along the close-growing junipers—

Until something hard hit her in the back, and she took a header, knocking the breath from her lungs.

Furious at herself for her inattention, she rolled as a figure tried to pin her down. Lineas fought off her attacker, and in grappling discovered that though the person was smaller than she, it seemed to be made of whipcord.

But it was not yelling for the guards—

At the same moment she changed her intent from breaking a limb to blocking, the assailant also backed off. "No assassin goes unarmed," a voice whispered in the purest Sartoran Lineas had heard since she left Shendan in Darchelde. Then the voice—it was female—began a question in heavily accented Iascan.

Lineas whispered back, "I speak Sartoran. And I am no assassin. Who are you?"

"Let us leave that question for a time," the woman responded. "Your purpose?"

"What is yours?"

A shift, and a thin face looked up into Lineas's, dark pits for eyes. A small gasp. "Aren't you—the deaf maid?"

Lineas opened her hands.

"Ah, so you have your own purpose, it seems. As do I: I am entrusted with my princess's safety. And you?"

It was Lineas's turn to gasp. "You're one of the Sartorans?"

"As you see." Two pale hands gestured gracefully, in a manner no Marlovan would ever use.

Lineas dithered for a heartbeat, then decided to speak, for this Sartoran had not called for the guards—who would certainly have come a-running to protect that royal guest. "I must get to the prince's quarters. There is something I need to tell him."

"Has it to do with the sly departure of the lower rank of guests, then?"

"What?" Lineas asked.

Her assailant was Iaeth, who was a far better spy than Lineas ever would be. Iaeth had tackled Lineas before she moved too close to silent watchers planted in the garden, all of whom Iaeth had located.

Iaeth said, "From the first morning, the Nyidris have been sending some of the guests out the servants' back way, in a style I can only term furtive. You did not know?"

"I *thought* we were doing fewer dishes." Lineas gave a soft sigh. "What does it mean?"

"I endeavor to discover that myself," Iaeth said with mordant humor. "I sense danger all around."

Lineas rubbed her aching neck. "This is what I want to tell Prince Connar's . . ." Lineas realized that she did not know terms for first runners in Sartoran. "His principal servant." And, rapidly, she described what she had overheard that day in the guest parlor.

At the end, Iaeth exclaimed, "Life! This is much worse than . . . come. I will take you to the one who sleeps alone. But you must in your turn permit me to hear the conversation."

Lineas agreed. And when she then learned that there were Artolei watchers posted throughout the garden to report on any movement by anybody, whom she most certainly would have stumbled into, she was very glad that she had.

Iaeth took her by a circuitous route to Rat's chamber. By then Lineas's feet were numb in her silent servant slippers, her hands icy. But she shivered more with excitement than cold.

When they reached the cottage, Lineas tapped at the door. Though the windows were dark, the door opened at once. She made out a familiar long head—"Jugears?" she whispered, naming Rat's second runner.

"Who's that?"

"Lineas Noth, royal runner, and a Sartoran runner to the princess."

Jugears held the door open and shut it behind them. Still in the dark, he said, "Are you doggo?"

"What's he saying?" Iaeth whispered.

Lineas said to Jugears, "Yes. We need to speak to Rat." And to Iaeth, in Sartoran, "He wants to know if we're trying to avoid discovery. Rat knows the Iascan of the south, if you can speak that."

"I have learned this," Iaeth said in the Iascan she had worked hard to master. "If you can comprehend this, my accent."

"It's very good," Lineas assured her. "Much better than my Sartoran, I am sure."

Iaeth gave a faint chuckle, scarcely more than a breath. "Your accent is charming. I met one once before with this accent, some years ago."

By then Jugears had fetched Rat, who said, "Come into the bedroom."

They did. It was lit by a candle. Rat stood before them in unlaced shirt and pants, barefoot, his hair hanging down his back. Digger, his tall, lanky first runner, was also there.

Lineas swiftly repeated what she'd just told Iaeth—and Plix, weeks ago.

Rat listened in grim silence.

At the end, Iaeth said, "Here is what I have seen: twenty caravans of supplies, one a day, sometimes two. The men bringing the carts took them to the village half a day away, over the east hill. There they remain, these men."

Rat's eyes narrowed. "So what it sounds like is, Artolei and the Nyidris are ridding themselves of the civs here a little at a time. And there's an army out there."

Iaeth was going to protest the word army, which meant something specific to her. But then she remembered the numbers she'd seen—and how she had kept silent about them. Regret pulsed through her, and she said, "Effectively, so."

Rat gritted his teeth. "I sent a runner to report to my father that we've arrived here. What do you want to bet he's lying frozen dead on the other side of the river."

Neither woman answered that.

Rat muttered, "How much time do we have? No, you wouldn't know. But my guess is, if this is still their plan, nothing will happen until the Nyidris leave. They'll hide behind Artolei. Pretend they know nothing about it."

He fell silent, brooding. Then glanced up. "And my best two long runners are . . . ." He shifted his gaze to Lineas. "You're the fastest one left. Can you get out?"

"I—I think so," Lineas said, but cast a doubtful glance at Iaeth.

Iaeth spoke up. "I can get her out."

Rat's lips had pressed into a white line. "Then do it. Grass run to the Cassads—it's closer, straight north." He briefly outlined the message he'd passed to his Noth relations before the ride south. "Seems to me we're going to need them to come in force, saddle-to-saddle, hot ride."

Lineas had tucked her hands into her armpits. "If you can get me some gloves and boots and a coat, I'll go straight from here."

"Not Marlovan coats," Iaeth put in. "If Ryu Nyidri is killing your messengers, then that coat makes you an easy target. Here. Take this one I'm wearing. I swapped my Sartoran coat for it, from a chatty glazier I met a month ago."

Lineas was going to point out that its sleeves would be too short, but Rat produced a long pair of riding gauntlets that she could stuff into the sleeves. Between Rat, Iaeth, Digger, and Jugears, she was soon kitted out in ill-fitting clothing. At least she would not get frostburn.

"There." Iaeth stood back, regarding Lineas critically. "You look anonymous enough, but I still wouldn't trust any locals for aid, not with that Marlovan accent."

"Why not?" Lineas asked.

Iaeth's eyes widened. "Tempers are quite hot due to your king's extra demands."

Lineas and Rat spoke almost together, "What extra demands?" and, "The *king*?"

"Where do you think all the food you people are swilling and gulping came from? Winter stores from every family for weeks' ride was required at swordpoint—it was said, by royal order."

Lineas and Rat exchanged startled looks. "But that wasn't the king. I left the king at New Year's, and he knew nothing about this gathering, only that we were leaving for inspection. And I've never heard of him demanding anything from civs at swordpoint."

Iaeth regarded him narrowly. "The food demands are on top of quadruple taxes."

This time Lineas and Rat's voices blended perfectly, "The *what?"*

"There is no quadruple tax," Rat said slowly. "The guilds wouldn't stand for it. We've had the king's tenth since the jarls agreed to war at Convocation. The Adrani war is over, so I expect that we'll go back to the usual half-tenth at the next Convocation."

Lineas opened her palms in assent.

Iaeth scraped her teeth over her bottom lip, then asked gently, "Is it possible your king and queen tell you one thing and do another?"

Lineas uttered a gasping laugh as she turned wide eyes to Rat, who said, "If you'd ever met them, you'd know how impossible that is. Or, at least, the queen, as I haven't had much to do with the king. Everybody says Danet-Gunvaer can smell a lie at a hundred paces. Her eyes are like swords. I don't know anybody who doesn't sweat through their clothes talking to her, even when telling the truth. As for her, I think if she ever told a lie she'd drop down dead."

Lineas had been thinking rapidly. She should leave now, while the palace was quiet, but instinct kept her. This conversation seemed important in ways she couldn't yet define.

So she said, "I've listened to much over these past weeks. Things people didn't realize I understood. While I never heard the Nyidris actually accuse Anred-Harvaldar of quadrupling taxes, I have heard things that . . . put blame away from the cause." She scowled. Even that was too imprecise to be useful. So she tried again. "As I traveled cross Feravayir, I saw villages with houses needing repair. People in ragged clothes. I thought a war had happened, a long one, that we did not know about in the north."

Honest Rat said, bewildered, "No wars. And what has that to do with anything?"

Lineas put her palm up, her attention on Iaeth. "Further, this I can attest to, the king and the queen eat exactly what the household eats."

Iaeth let out a long, "Ah-h-h-h."

Rat gazed with furrowed brow from one to the other. "I don't get it."

Iaeth smiled at him. "What she is saying is, the Nyidris are lying."

Rat rolled up his eyes. "That, I could have told you at the outset. I had to live with them for years. They lie to everyone, and to each other, so much that if any of 'em said the sun was out at midday, I'd think it was time to ring the nightwatch."

Iaeth said, "Ah. You are *that* Rat, the former stepson! The cowardly, bullying, untrustworthy, grasping stepson."

Rat's lips twisted. "That's me. Though I think that damn well fits Ryu." He jerked his chin at Lineas. "I've got some travel bread left over from our trip south. Digger, fetch it."

The first runner reached into a saddle bag and pulled out a tightly wrapped cloth. Lineas took it gladly, though she could feel even through the wrapping how dried and stale the bread was. She'd have to saw pieces off. But at least it would be filling.

Iaeth turned to Rat. "You and I will exchange information, yes?"

"You know where I am." He held out his hands to either side.

With that, Iaeth and Lineas slipped out into the frigid night under stars as bright and cold as ice.

Rat could not go back to sleep.

Remembering what the Sartoran woman had said about watchers roaming the ground at night, he snuffed his candle, then sat in the dark, fighting the urge to go find Ryu and choke the plan out of him. If it had been only Ryu, it would be worth it.

But he'd learned early that all three Nyidris had a way of drawing people after them. Ryu in particular liked violence, as long as he dealt it, and he had violent friends.

Demeos was harder to describe. That is, he was still a shit, but like Rat's father had said once, he'd been made into one. When they were all boys, Rat remembered distinctly how eagerly Demeos had asked about the academy—he'd liked riding hard, playing hard, dancing hard. Until the jarlan said firmly that he was to go to Sartor for his education.

Looking back, Rat wondered if Demeos might have been different if he'd gone to the academy. At his age, he would have been in that group with Manther Yvanavayir and the rest—hard riders all, excellent shots, but decent people. They dealt with violence because you did in the army, but they didn't go looking for it the way Ryu did.

As the sun blued the curtains, he shifted away from useless might-have-beens to the present. What to do?

Connar had to be briefed, that was first. And . . . in a way that didn't draw attention.

"Jugears."

His second runner came from the tiny room adjacent.

"Get me a crock of beer."

Jugears' eyes widened. "Beer?"

"It's a ruse," Rat said, and when Jugears grinned, he added, "One our lives depend on."

The smile vanished. Jugears remembered the conversation, and tapped his chest before going out. Rat said, "Digger, go loiter outside Connar-Laef's quarters. As soon as you see lights, come get me. And Digger, unbutton your coat. Take out your horsetail. Look like you just got out of bed."

Digger pulled out his hair clasp as he walked out, brown hair straggling nastily down over his shoulders.

Jugears appeared a short time later, saying, "Digger's right on my heels."

"Good." Rat took the crock and splashed the beer over himself. He'd already loosened his hair and coat. Then he walked out sashless, feeling weirdly naked, though he wore shirt and trousers under his coat. It was all in what you were used to, he thought.

Connar was just coming out of his cottage, probably heading for the baths they'd been assigned—which Rat expected was ordinarily for the servants. That was fine. Water was water. He knew from his earliest memories all the little covert insults of Perideth hierarchy, and didn't care about any of them.

He took up the crock by one of its handles, and started out. At first he put in a couple of good sways and stumbles, but he saw Connar begin to move fast. This was going to be the hardest part.

He increased his step to a stumbling run. When Connar saw him, he stopped, brows rising, then his mouth tightened into a line. Rat remembered that today was supposed to be the first day they'd return to discipline and routine.

Before Connar could speak, Rat flung his arm around Connar's neck, which caused beer to splash over them both, and muttered into Connar's ear, "Go with it."

Connar stiffened, but didn't resist as Rat propelled him back inside his cottage and kicked the door shut. Fish gazed in astonishment, his arms filled with laundry.

Rat said, "Keep the shutters closed. We need to talk, and without listening ears."

He launched straight into an account of the night's interview. Connar resented the sharp pang behind his ribs on hearing Lineas' name. He hadn't even known she was here.

Unaware of Connar's falter in attention, Rat spoke on. " . . . so I can see them wanting to humiliate us before they run an assassination."

"Wait." Connar's reverie broke on the word *assassination.* "If this is really a plot to get rid of us, why the festival with the princess and all? Why didn't we meet an ambush?"

"We almost did," Rat reminded him. "At the crossroads village. But I'll wager anything that this is a backup plan. Cooked up between Ryu and Artolei. It's the sort of thing they would think up. Ryu likes to kneecap you if he can. Make you helpless so he can play longer, especially in front of others. Lavais always went in for long plans, ones that she could deny plausibly. And having all these other nobles around, so it really seems like a festival gathering, would give her an excuse to count herself among 'em, even though she knows exactly what's happening. Especially if they're still trying to win over this princess."

Connar's eyes narrowed, his lips a white line.

Rat went on, "All these nobles they invited, they've been seeing us swilling and swiving—for us it's liberty. I'm sure they were told this is us all the time. And if they're being sent off with that in mind, they'll believe whatever they're told after we're dead."

"But what's the use of it, if we're supposed to be dead anyway?"

"Because all those nobles, and the people they govern, will believe the worst that the Nyidris say of us. If they believe we're bloodthirsty corrupt villains, they'll rise against the king when the Nyidris tell them to, and when Lavais declares herself the new queen, well, her double taxes will be a relief after the four-times tenth that apparently the Nyidris have been forcing people to pay in the king's name."

"But the king has to . . ." Connar paused. "*Wouldn't* he know?"

Rat turned up his palms. "Not sure. Especially if the tax guild down here is in Lavais's pocket. But here's what worries me. The king, if he thinks all the people rose, he won't want to send the army in to slaughter civs in their own homes. It's different if an army attacks Marlovans. Like at Ku Halir. Right?"

Connar said slowly, "Right. Right. All those years ago, Da couldn't go to war against the north to bring them back, because he had no army and no treasury. But afterwards, he had both, and he still let it go. Noddy and I saw that much when we were up at Larkadhe, trade back and forth over the Andahi Pass. But two separate kingdoms." His eyes narrowed. "So what you and this Sartoran spy think is that Lavais Nyidri is going for that, at the price of our lives?"

"Oh, I think our lives are Ryu's idea of fun. If she gets the populace roused up, whether we're here or not, she can try to break away from the kingdom. But it's a lot easier, is my guess, if there's an enemy that they can all hate together."

Connar considered that. "And so we're back to people being robbed of their winter stores, and the Nyidris blaming us." He hit his chest.

"That seems to be it. But it's all guesses on top of what Lineas and this Sartoran spy have overheard. And of course what we're seeing here."

"Lineas. Where is she?"

"Didn't I say? I figured you'd want someone who could get past Ryu's killers making a grass run for my Noth relations at Cassad. Whatever happens, I figure, seeing them coming up the road might balance things out a little."

Lineas on a grass run? Connar wanted to laugh, to scoff. To regret. He said somewhat more forcefully than needed, "That would have been my first order. Good idea sending her out under cover of night." And when Rat acknowledged with a flip of his fingers and a slightly questioning glance, "When do you think they'll act? When they've sent the rest of the nobles out, so it's just us, their personal guards, and this army of carters waiting in some village somewhere?"

Rat said, "What I think is, as soon as the Nyidris leave, we better expect action. They won't want their hands dirty in the eyes of their nobles. Artolei thinks he's in command, but I'll wager my best war horse he's being set up to take the blame if it fails."

"And some sort of outland title if he wins. Right." Connar turned his head. "Fish!"

The first runner appeared silently. "Fetch Jethren. No. Find out where he is—while getting breakfast. I'll go to him. Rat has the right idea. We're going to ride along with the swilling and swiving. I don't want us going back to drill under their eyes while they assess our strengths."

Rat grunted in agreement.

"Let them think we're drunk day and night. But I want the word spread, you to captains, captains to riding captains, and from man to man: roust and whoop all you want, but no one is to get drunk, not any more. Spill it if you have to, when no one is around. We're going to establish our own watches, while running our own ruse while we learn the terrain. I don't even know how many buildings are here, much less how to defend ourselves among them. Until we have our own plan, everyone weapons-ready. But doggo."

Rat smacked his fist to his chest and walked out, coat skirts flapping, leaving behind the smell of stale beer.

When Seonrei woke, Iaeth was waiting for her, the marks under her eyes indicating a sleepless night.

"Oh, good," Seonrei said. "Maybe you can explain why the sled journey to the frozen falls was cancelled? Are the locals really concerned about a blizzard? Something is amiss, I sense it, though our hosts just keep smiling and pressing the spiced wine on us at every turn."

"I made a very interesting acquaintance last night," Iaeth said.

"That gorgeous prince?"

"No. But I met one of the other captains . . ." And Iaeth delivered a summary of the encounter with Lineas, then with Rat Noth, followed by her journey with Lineas through the servants' area at the back of the walled manor—the opposite side of the manor from where the Marlovans had been housed.

"I stayed and watched her make her way down the hundreds of steps to the bottom of the cliffs," Iaeth added. "Which is the only way to keep out of sight, though it's icy and dangerous."

Seonrei listened with surprise, then horror. "And so . . . the Marlovans are housed directly against the cliffs?"

"Yes. That whole area back of the garden, where the artisans used to live. The Marlovans are effectively cornered, unless they really do have flying horses. Which, by the way, are all at the stables at the other end. So they have to go through the main house, and past all the Nyidris' people, to get to them."

Seonrei brooded as she stared at her rapidly cooling breakfast tray.

"Lavais made them sound not just uncouth, but criminal," she finally said. "It was easy enough to assume that, much as I have come to dislike her, I figured they must be far worse. The wars, the taxes. No art. No music. No refinement . . ." Her lips twisted. "When I laid eyes on that Prince Connar . . . ah, my only excuse—and I know well it is a weak one—is that beauty has a power of its own, altering everything around it. Lavais had made him sound scarcely human. When I saw him I wondered if they had lied about everything, but that very first night he sat there in the next chair to me without a thing to say. That could be excused, but more difficult is how very bored he looked during the concert."

Iaeth snorted. "Not everyone indifferent to music is wicked. And not everyone who loves it can be exalted over others."

"Do I not know it well? Demeos, I have seen, does love it, and yet he still looks at me to see how to respond."

"That is arguably courtship."

"Which is another road paved with falsity, but it is far off my current path."

Iaeth put her hands together and bowed her apology—not without a hint of mockery.

Seonrei ignored both. "The worst was, I could smell human and horse sweat from those three or four paces away. Prince Connar didn't even think to bathe, much less change to garments suitable for such a gathering."

"He wasn't offered the chance," Iaeth reminded her. "Brought straight off the road to the banquet, and then to the listening hall."

"I perceive now that it was calculated, but the Marlovans themselves certainly haven't helped improve their reputation any." She picked up a porcelain cup, then set it down again. "My mind keeps snagging on all these irrelevant details, but what it all really means is, we're about to see a revolution, are we not?"

Iaeth said seriously, "Yes."

Seonrei pursed her lips. "If we insist on leaving, will that precipitate bloody events?"

"I don't know. It's all guesswork right now," Iaeth reminded her. "But I'm going to find out."

Seonrei sighed. "If it comes to it, we all have transfer tokens. But to return by magic would be a failure on my part . . . it wouldn't speak well to my desire to work for peace through diplomacy, would it?"

Iaeth stated neutrally, "I promised the queen your safety would be my first concern."

"I know that. Why do you think I keep wearing this thing?" She tapped the graceful golden coronet around her brow. "Besides as a reminder to Lavais Nyidri of our respective ranks," she added sourly. "Magic transfer is two words away, so permit me to remind you that my safety can be left to me to judge, for now. I desire you to make information your first concern."

"It shall be done," Iaeth said, and at the sound of someone approaching, she exited through another door.

Seonrei moved through next few days with heightened awareness. The urge to single out the Marlovans for her questions had to be resisted; she was aware more than ever of living in the quiet eye of a storm not of her own making. When she moved, the storm moved around her, tightening as more Nyidri servants pressed in, asking what she needed, warning her of the threat of weather. She couldn't fault them. They were doing what they were told, and maybe even believed it was right, given the astounding fabric of lies Lavais Nyidri apparently had been weaving for years.

Instead, Seonrei pretended nothing was amiss as she obsessively counted guests, something she had never troubled with before, and—definitely finding fewer—ruminated on mad plans and governing.

She was not the only one feeling isolated. Fish had listened while Rat related Lineas's report. He'd caught at a brief reference to a bucket and wash rag, which enabled Lineas to become effectively invisible to the upper levels of society, if not to the other servants.

Fish armed himself with a bucket and sponge, then did his best to map the complicated manor, having to keep everything in his head until he returned to Connar's quarters to sketch it out. Struggling with that threw him back to his earliest days as a young runner in training among the royal runners. His resentment had long since faded when he saw how very hard they worked. Sometimes he even admitted to himself (though he never would to them) that it was a relief he'd been booted out. But one likes to make those decisions oneself, he thought as he roamed the building, sloshing bucket in hand. And in any case, their relentless training making maps would certainly have been useful now.

Connar burned with anticipation. He had a righteous cause. His nerves were entirely bound up in worrying about when to strike. Every pair of waiting eyes that turned to him in mute question was a reminder that the wrong decision could be disaster.

Keth Jethren also burned with anticipation; the violence that had shaped him had become the tool he loved most, making him strong and skilled enough to take his rightful place at the true king's side.

Iaeth continued to listen, to count, and to watch, aware that she was seeing only the surface.

They all existed in isolation, ostensibly royally entertained (or serving those being royally entertained) while the days moved at the pace of melting ice . . . until the frozen cataract broke.

NINE

Ryu's tension had wound up so tight he couldn't sleep, and when alone with his family, he paced back and forth, obsessively reviewing every aspect of his plan. It was working! He had the enemy right there under his control, deliciously oblivious, while outside the gates his army waited impatiently, desperate to get at them.

The last element of his plan was still unresolved, which frustrated him extremely: to detach the Marlovans from their weapons. He'd detached them from their horses right at the outset, though he couldn't remove the horses completely—they balked, kicked, whinnied and made so much commotion when his servants had tried to take them that he and Artolei had had to abandon that plan. They didn't dare raise the Marlovan servants' suspicions.

Besides, the horses would be useless to the Marlovans now that they were locked in behind the gates.

The weapons were the main problem. He'd assumed he could send servants around to collect them in covered carts while their owners were drunk and elsewhere, but he reckoned without the runners, who guarded their masters' weapons with the care they guarded their own lives. Ryu had issued various orders to try to separate one from the other, to meet with a stone wall of silence. He was afraid to push too hard, lest that soulsucking Rat figure out what was going on. It was a miracle that he hadn't, but then from the smell of him, he'd been drinking day and night since their arrival.

"We'll have to bring in more supplies for our rabble," Artolei reported to Ryu late one night. "They've just about run out."

"Then start taking the food from here," Ryu snapped. "Do I have to think of everything?"

Well, yes.

Artolei gazed at him in question, and a little affront. Descendant of a grandmother picked for beauty and lack of brain, and a grandfather who had believed himself far cleverer than he actually was, Artolei was a handsome, strong, well-trained dolt. And further, Ryu knew it. He wouldn't have trusted Artolei if he'd been smarter.

So he relented, and said in a less truculent manner, "Slowly. So the Marlovans don't notice. Just leave the liquor."

On a day of snow flurries whirled by a fretful wind, his mother and Demeos quietly followed the last of the local nobles out—watched from a rooftop by Iaeth, who passed the news on to Jugears, detailed to shadow her.

He reported to Rat—Rat reported to Connar—and from Connar came the order to stay armed.

"We can wear our knives, but if we all start carrying swords, they'll get suspicious," Rat warned. "We haven't been drilling. If we start now, they'll know we know."

Connar frowned, then flashed an unpleasant grin. After days of music being inflicted on them, what could be better? "When we go into that hall again, let's give them the sword dance. Rat, you set up the drummers."

Rat uttered a husky bark of a laugh.

Connar's tension communicated itself through the captains as the word spread. The drunk ruse had already become a wild near-riot. This promised to be even more fun.

In the main hall, as Artolei's servants struggled to keep the food and drink flowing—Ryu having slipped the Nyidri servants out a handful at a time, to make certain that his new quarters, though humble, would not lack for comfort—the drums rumbled. "It's time for us to entertain you," Connar said, hands on hips, coat-skirts whirling.

Artolei had been waiting for the princess to object to the swords, for weapons were never worn in the presence of the court in Sartor, but she seemed oblivious, so he dared say nothing. The galloping beat thrummed in blood and bone, an intoxicating experience for Seonrei, used to interleaved Sartoran subtleties; dread and excitement thrilled through her nerves, heightening the sense of unreality.

Crash!

Swords crossed on the marble floor. Heels rapped and rang and coat skirts snapped, sending the candles streaming wildly then guttering. Those were not the play swords of the theater, or the jeweled and gold-chased rapiers of the nobility, with their strict rules of dueling.

Seonrei's mother, as blunt in private as she was subtle in court, had said once, *The rules for duels are supposed to keep men this side of civility. Always men, you'll find—women don't often want blood when they duel, though they might crave utter humiliation of the adversary. Something happens to men after the age of interest. Nothing will satisfy some but letting some other man's blood. One could wish they would find a bed somewhere instead.*

Duels had seemed so very alien an idea. Barbaric, even. Though the single duel Seonrei had witnessed had not been *barbaric.* Instead it had been deeply disturbing as the duelists sat across from one another in the most formal of the salons, both dressed for court. One played an ancient silver flute, the other an equally old stringed tiranthe. The music had gripped the listeners with its passion until one duelist stumbled, just two notes, recovered into an eerie flight which resolved into the same passage over and over—ever since, she heard that four-note passage as *I surrender*—until the other at last lifted fingers from the tiranthe. The loser rose, bowed, retired from court, yet to return all these years later.

At least they had each walked away. Seonrei became increasingly aware that if she had one of those rapiers at hand, she would dearly love to poke Lavais Nyidri hard enough to see her yelp, she was so disgusted not just by the woman abandoning them on the pretense of a trip to see the falls. It was the assumption that Seonrei was too stupid to notice the diminishing of the company to those the Nyidris disliked, or outright wanted to be rid of, along with Artolei's hangers-on.

The drumbeat increased, a second drum thrumming a wicked counterpoint that shot sensation deep inside her, and prickled over her flesh in what was so very close to heat. The two young men, fair and black-haired, were both so very striking, displaying strength and grace with effortless ease, the flash of their coat skirts revealing and concealing the clean lines and muscular curves of their bodies. This cadenced drumming was music—of a kind. The sword ritual was dance—of a kind. The message was simple, not at all subtle, but perhaps the more compelling for all that.

At the end, she dropped her fan to clap her hands together, the guests marveled and commented, and a few—male and female—rose, mimicking drunkenly.

At a glance from Connar, Rat obligingly played the drums for them, but the swords had vanished as Connar and Jethren faded into the shadows. So out came various poles and sticks as people attempted to learn—then adapt—this new style.

Sadly, it was the first evening of real hilarity, and it didn't last. Iaeth turned up, slipping through servants to kneel at Seonrei's chair as she watched. "They're attacking," she whispered harshly, the pupils in her eyes huge and black.

Seonrei stared, her heart thumping its own drum. Think about that later, she told herself as she breathed, "Better tell the Marlovans."

But Rat's and Jethren's scouts had already spotted the would-be assassins spreading in groups to each place Marlovans stayed. Word reached Connar, who said, "Go."

A short, savage shock awaited the assassins as their drunken targets sobered in a heartbeat and came at them in lethally trained teams, fighting with pent-up fury.

Those left alive stampeded for the gate, which had already swung shut, once the signal went out that the Marlovans were fighting back. And winning.

Seonrei knew something had happened when all the gray vanished from the colorful, silken company. When Iaeth brought back the news, Seonrei returned to her room in a fury. She knew she should take time to consider her response, but she was tired, and furious. She had not trusted Lavais Nyidri for weeks, but this wasn't mere abandonment, it was outright betrayal.

She settled herself, pulled out a strip of her most formal paper, and when she knew she had command over her fingers, wrote in her finest formal script:

Lavais Nyidri, Jarlan of Feravayir:

We Sartorans have no part of this trouble of yours. I wish to depart before it progresses further.

Then she sat by her desk, staring down at her notecase.

Weak blue light glowed in the arched windows when an answer came back:

To Princess Seonrei Landis of Sartor:

We dare not move against the Marlovans who hold you hostage.

Seonrei wanted to kick something. No, she wanted to kick someone, and wondered with bitter humor if that made her like the Marlovans after all.

No, it made her human. She knew that much as her thoughts whirled fruitlessly between betrayal—civilization—but then the moral act was always a choice. If it were unconscious, it would not be moral, would it?

She wrote back.

We both know that I am not a hostage. Once I've written to you, I will be detailing to the queen exactly what has been happening, including your convenient departure before your attackers attempted a wholesale slaughter. By the way, were we to die in that?

At the other end, Demeos sat beside his mother. Neither had slept since the word came back that half those expert assassins had died, without a single Marlovan suffering so much as a broken arm.

"Now she's writing to the Queen of Sartor," Demeos said uneasily. What good would it be to crown himself a prince if he could never return to Eidervaen again?

"Don't falter now." Lavais turned on him fiercely, cheeks mottled. "We are committed."

"But what's the queen going to do?"

"She can scarcely send an army by magic, can she? By the time she sends ships, this will all be over. And it's either us receiving them and graciously informing them that our internal troubles are our own business, or if the worst happens, the Marlovans are left with the chaos. But we will be successful if you Do. Not. *Falter,*" she enunciated, teeth showing.

Demeos could only think of beautiful Eidervaen, where nobody hired assassins. "But whatever happens, how can we return to Sartor?"

"Oh, you've kissed Sartor goodbye," Lavais said with pent-up venom. "Surely you've seen that by now? But we come out of this with the crown that is rightfully ours. Won't it be better to rule here than shadow-kiss in third-circle there? And by the way, watch them come courting us once we're successful. They have to marry those ugly princes and princesses off *somewhere.*"

And when Demeos just looked down at his hands, she tapped a jeweled nail on Seonrei's last note. "Anyway, just as well. It's clear that she is much too clever. She would have been immense trouble if you had married her."

Lavais considered, then at last wrote back, omitting the proper heading:

Whoever is using Princess Seonrei's notecase, be warned, we shall seek justice if anything happens to her.

She showed that to Demeos before sending it.

"I don't see what good that does, when we both know her handwriting."

"But others don't. We can now go out and report that the Marlovans are attempting to use her life in trade for their demands—after they executed a bloody takeover of the Artolei palace while we were enjoying our peaceful sled ride to see the falls."

In a blizzard? Demeos wanted to exclaim, but he kept silent. Sometimes there was little difference between Mother and Ryu.

So he rose, and bowed. "I'm going to retire. I think we could all use some sleep."

The Marlovans make a thorough search, rounding up all the servants remaining. Those among them who had the most to hide prepared to deliver their stories, until Iaeth and Fish came through, side by side, and one by one identified them—Iaeth confident that the spies would be summarily expelled through the gate.

Fish knew better.

The spies were searched down to the skin, then locked up.

Seonrei had put her head on her hand, slipping into an uneasy slumber while that was going on, guarded by her own staff. She woke suddenly, her fingers entirely numb, and the side of her face wet with drool when Iaeth knocked at the door.

"Enter." Seonrei straightened up, her neck shooting an agonizing pain straight behind her eyeballs. She reached for her besorcelled handkerchief to wipe her face as Iaeth slipped in.

"The Marlovan prince wants to speak to you," Iaeth said.

"Tell him I'll meet him downstairs."

Iaeth bowed and withdrew.

Seonrei had a private bath chamber, supplied by water from the river that could be warmed by a firestick adapted for the purpose—something common in Sartor but unknown in this kingdom, she'd discovered.

She bathed, dressed, and upon consideration took her golden notecase and Lavais's notes with her downstairs.

The prince was even prettier up close, except for that flat gaze. He said, without any social nicety, "We've locked up the spies. We can use them if we decide to communicate—if they shoot their own people, that's their affair."

He spoke slowly, in that slurry Iascan accent that Seonrei had been told was common to the north. But at least she understood most of it.

"There is no use in communicating with Lavais," she stated. "I've tried that. She's sticking to her lies."

"How?" Connar asked, then saw the little pieces of paper the princess held on her palm.

He remembered reading about magical communication in the Inda letters, and how Evred-Harvaldar had subsequently burned the means, as there was no way to guarantee they weren't intercepted by the enemy.

He listened as she translated the notes, and immediately understood Evred-Harvaldar's reasoning. Even with notes clearly written by the people themselves, claims could be made of falsity, because there was no runner serving as witness. There was no trail between sender and recipient, so Lavais Nyidri could claim that he was writing those notes, or that someone else was writing by his command, and not this princess.

Well, that sort of magic foolery was the Sartorans' problem. He said, "They'll be attacking soon, I expect. This palace is indefensible, but that wall out there isn't. Not with our bows along it. But we need more arrows. We're going through the place now, stripping out feather-stuffed cushions and pillows and the like, and gathering wood."

This was all beyond Seonrei. "Very well," she said, and because she sensed that something was amiss, her gaze strayed to Iaeth.

Iaeth said in an undervoice to Seonrei, "This is a siege situation. We should see what stores remain to us, and discuss their disposition."

Seonrei's gaze shifted to Connar. Military defense was entirely out of her realm of experience. Here was another: when it came to material things, she had always had exactly what she wanted, sometimes before she even had to speak an order. She reminded herself that she could still transfer away, which bolstered her courage. She said, "We must see what stores remain, and discuss how they are to be used."

Connar turned his palm up, which Seonrei reminded herself was assent, before commenting, "We still have travel bread. Or, does your magic extend to meals as well as letters?"

"It can, but only through the mages, who understand transfer magic," Seonrei stated, then, her vocabulary giving out, she murmured to Iaeth, who said, "We could get some things sent to us after we create a Destination, but overusing such a Destination has the risk of burning out."

"Burning out?" Connar repeated.

"No one truly understands how magic transfer works," Iaeth explained at a nod from Seonrei, who found the need for explanation of everyday things oddly steadying in this atmosphere that was the very opposite of normal. "Transferring items and people is safe in very few places in the world. One or two transfers are always possible elsewhere, the smaller the better. An animal such as a horse cannot be transferred, for example. Or a wagon."

"Understood. We can't use magic. The details don't matter. What does is establishing our defense." Connar turned his head. "Rat! Put the company quartermaster with them to inventory the food stores."

"Already done," Fish spoke up from his stance against the far wall, from which he could see everyone inside, and anyone approaching through the doorway. "What they couldn't take, they spoiled or outright destroyed."

"Even the fodder?"

"No. We have that area too tightly guarded."

"Then it's just us. Could be worse." Connar's mouth tightened as he turned back to Seonrei. "We do have some travel loaves left."

"As I began to say before, we'll see what we can contrive," Seonrei promised. "At least we have plenty of water."

"Do that." On the word 'that' he indicated Iaeth and Seonrei as a pair—a gesture that never would have occurred in Sartor.

Seonrei found the situation curiously exhilarating, though she was aware of an undercurrent of fear. She reminded herself that she could transfer away if she must, but instinct was strong to wait. To see if there was some way she could use her mind and skills to wrest a sense of civility and order away from the threatened chaos.

The first order of business would be to report to the queen, carefully arrange a Destination, and then see if a royal mage would have some suggestions as to what to do about stores.

The first attack arrived that night, as predicted. The Marlovans even predicted how it was likely to go—a noisy attack at the front gate, the major effort meant to take the back by surprise. That one was summarily dealt with in a rain of steel, an arrow to a man, before it retreated in scrambling haste.

The attack at the gate lasted longer, until the Marlovans began sending fire arrows—thin strips of oil-soaked cloth that splattered the oil and became difficult to douse.

That attack failed miserably as those driven from the back pushed into those at the front. A mob of struggling, angry people who'd believed they were safe as decoys turned into a mad scramble, causing many who slipped on the icy layer beneath the snow to fall under the kicking, shoving retreat.

Before dawn a sizable number of Ryu's army melted away, but that still left a considerable majority, who withdrew to the nearby village to lick wounds, and Disappear those dead they'd managed to bring back. Others were left where they lay, until a healer under white flag led a small party with a wagon to collect the fallen.

Those were gathered under the watchful eyes along the wall, arrows notched and tracking.

A mage duly appeared at Seonrei's invitation. Connar was there to witness the mage's arrival in a flurry of air that brought unfamiliar scents. The mage staggered, green-faced, as Iaeth helped him into a chair and pressed listerblossom steep into his hands.

Connar watched the man recover, his idea of investigating this magic for movement of an army vanishing at the sight of the man's reaction. Magic really was useless for war, he thought, as Iaeth chattered rapidly in Sartoran. She led the mage off in the direction of the kitchen, and Connar signaled for drill, leaving word that extra fodder for horses should be first if the mage really could bring food by magic.

The result of the mage's visit, Connar discovered when they all met that night in the dining hall, was a lot of jabber about how the presence of so much water nearby interfered with how magic worked, and so they would have to make Destinations at different points around the palace and bring in single items: a bag of rice, some vegetables, a basket of eggs.

Connar turned a meaning look toward Jethren when he realized there would be no relief here.

Jethren sent a glance at Moonbeam, his first runner, who grinned. His hands seemed to move slightly. In an eyeblink he held two thin-bladed knives, with which—still grinning—he slit the throats of the spies, ignoring cries and pleas. Then they opened the gates into a gale long enough to carry out the bodies, leaving them for Artolei's people to find.

The next two weeks trudged by, hour by hour. The Marlovans alternated drilling, serving on watch, and sleeping or getting what comfort they could.

The grinding march of hours was broken by three more mass attacks, two at the same time, at each gate, strike and run. The third was much larger, people carrying makeshift ladders along with sharpened tools and implements; Connar's archers picked them off unerringly, with devastating losses among Artolei's infuriated mob until, in the way of mobs, their emotion turned to terror and they retreated in a stampede, in spite of Artolei's and Ryu's determination to rally them.

Stalemate.

Inside the winter palace, everyone was on strict rations; Seonrei noted that Connar, Jethren, and Rat ate exactly what their runners and warriors ate, down to the same amount, in a way that seemed habitual. That left her glad that she had instructed her maid to let the cook know she expected no special treatment, a step she had felt deserved acknowledgment. But that withered when she walked among the Marlovans. Uncouth they were, but so far, the barbarianism seemed evenly divided between both sides, evidenced in the rust-stained snow after every attempt to breach the wall.

Seonrei began watching the drills, at first a glimpse, but gradually she stayed longer.

Iaeth joined her one day, after having disappeared on one of her expeditions. "The Nyidris have their foodstuffs too well guarded," she reported. "It would take too many to get there, and impossible to get past four rings of guards."

Seonrei didn't ask how she knew. Her gaze followed Jethren and Connar as they led the sword warmup, which was a dance in itself.

After contemplating her expression, Iaeth said, "So, Cousin?" in the intimate mode.

"I am contemplating the Dichotomies."

Iaeth let out a soft laugh, no more than a puff of air, which froze and fell. "You mean fire down below."

Seonrei grunted. "I hate war as much as I ever did. More, in fact. But watching them . . . it's the aesthetic appreciation of a thoroughbred's speed, or the free-wheeling drift of the eagle against the sun before it dives on some hapless little creature. That I do not want to see, though it, too, is a part of its nature."

Iaeth said slowly, "Aesthetic appreciation at a distance, yes. Astute. I don't want to get closer. Some of that is the quality of their silence. Prince Connar seems to have nothing to say beyond necessity. Captain Jethren . . . is more difficult to construe."

"Not so difficult," Seonrei said. "He watches Prince Connar. Easy enough to see the heat there."

"If it were mere heat, that *would* be easy," Iaeth retorted. She piqued herself on her ability to penetrate facades, but so far, he escaped her. "He doesn't give the prince the hot-eye when he's in the bath—yes, I saw them all once, while carrying in the towels, in hopes I would hear something useful. Jethren paid him scant heed there, but not when Prince Connar is fully dressed and fighting with two swords. Otherwise, Jethren turns his head for their women. Not our women, you'll note. But theirs, without so much as a drape of silk between them, hair in common braids, with that swinging stride and the feline arm muscles as they shoot arrows in practice."

"Actually, I see the attraction," Seonrei put in, dulcetly, her fan whirling in Rise of Interest. "You are observant."

A herald had to be, they both knew that.

Iaeth sifted Seonrei's words for clues. Was that an implied warning? Maybe not. Still, she decided to keep to herself the fact that the Marlovan ideal was someone she'd met nearly fifteen years ago, but his memory remained vivid. She'd caught him drilling like these men did, only in memory, at least, it was more lethal and yet more of a dance, with two knives, not a sword. But far more attractive had been his excellent manners, and the fact that he was as articulate as any Sartoran, with just enough accent to be interesting.

She laughed. "Enjoy. It seems there is little enough to entertain us, Cousin."

Seonrei snapped her fan tight, and walked inside to do the fan dance once more.

She was sedentary by nature, but she disliked the way she could feel bones beneath her flesh. She exercised to retain muscle, and to clear her mind that remained stubbornly cloudy . . . but after a few more days, she turned her travel mirror firmly face down.

TEN

Rat and Connar met each night to discuss the situation.

One night, after Rat reported on the progress of making arrows (the servants' cushions and quilting did not have useless down, as did that of the nobles, giving them a source of feathers) Connar said, "What's the state of the stores?"

"Low," Rat said. "But we haven't got to the leftover journey bread yet."

"What about their magic?"

"What they said about the air burning if there is too much of that transfer business, it's real. I smelled it. Very like an armory when all the fires are going, and the smiths banging out the steel. And the last bag arrived as ash."

Connar grimaced. "We can go to half-rations in the morning. Full for everyone on watch after an attack."

Jethren, thinking of West Outpost, said, "Do you think they'll bring a battering ram?"

"If they show up with one, let's ice the road below the gate. In fact, let's do that anyway, against the next attack. At least we have as much water as we want."

So they poured cauldrons of water over the wall in the dead of night, which froze into glassy smoothness by morning. Snow fell, a light covering. When the next attack arrived, the ice had as lethal an effect as the arrows from above, and once more the mob retreated at a fearful, angry scramble. This was supposed to be easy!

The third week, the winter palace went to half rations all the time.

Artolei appeared below them under white flag, dressed in glittering armor, a fine yeath cloak spread over his horse's haunch, and a plumed helm on his head. Connar climbed up to the wall, memories of the siege of West Outpost flickering in his mind. His mood was grim when he looked down at the supposed commander.

Before Artolei had finished the speech Ryu and Demeos had written—a mixture of promises and threats—Connar reached for the bow from the man standing next to him, but Rat, standing behind at shield arm position, muttered, "She'll make him into a martyr if you shoot him under a white flag."

Connar said, "I know. I want to shoot that damn plume off his head."

Rat grinned mirthlessly. "They'll be laughing about it clear to the border. Can you make that shot?"

Connar loosened his grip on the bow. "That's what I was trying to determine. I haven't practiced in months."

"Marlovayir," Rat called.

Pepper Marlovayir, first captain under Rat, whipped up his bow, and *twang!*

The plume exploded in a shower of feathers, Artolei let out a squawk of fear, and his horse bolted under him. Artolei got control—barely—and galloped away, shouting imprecations over his shoulder.

Seonrei was waiting when Connar climbed down. "They can't be sitting still out there."

"No," Connar said. "They aren't."

"The sun is higher in the sky every day. First thaw should be coming soon," she said. "There will not be ice. And there's the matter of food running out."

"We'll start quarter-rations today," he said. And because she had so far proved to be more of an ally than he had expected, "We're waiting on reinforcements."

Seonrei drew in a breath. "You think that young woman made it, then?"

Connar eyed her warily. Successfully identifying the question fast turning to suspicion, Seonrei said in careful, heavily accented Marlovan, "My servant Iaeth, she helped that redhaired maid to get away."

Connar's expression shuttered, but at least the suspicion seemed to have faded as he said, "We will plan as if she did."

When the Marlovans were alone, Connar turned to Rat. "You know the terrain. Estimate the time to Cassad and back."

"Already have," Rat said. "I thought the earliest she could return is yesterday."

Jethren said, "Even if they turn up, what are we going to do with a dozen Riders out of Cassad?"

"They will have spread the word," Rat stated with quiet confidence. "They'll all want in."

Jethren's eyes narrowed. He turned to his commander, but Connar seemed pleased as he rubbed his jaw. "Whatever number they have, they'll need to charge from the back. Let's run the old academy signal flag up below the eagle banner to make sure."

The food ran out the next week, and they started on the travel bread.

Seonrei eyed the brown loaves with trepidation. And when the cook cut off a piece no wider than the smallest joint on her little finger, she was hard put not to protest. She had never before felt hunger, but it was her constant companion now.

She managed not to say anything—her mouth was watering too much anyway—and retreated with her disc of bread. It was stale and dry. By the time she had gnawed a few bites, half an hour had passed. The taste was actually not as terrible as the thing looked—it was thick with honey, nuts, and raisins—but she knew she would be tired of that taste before long.

But it did fill the belly.

Another week, and they woke to find pools of snowmelt.

Artolei's mob rushed the gate once again. This time they had fashioned shields to keep over their heads, and they had put together bladed rams out of what had once been building support timber.

They lumbered toward the gates, slowed by the deep, slippery mud, and faltered at the gate under a steel rain from above. When they backed off, Rat signaled for the archers to halt, as they were dangerously low on arrows, and running out of wooden furniture to carve up.

The Feravayir army roiled around in the mud, formed up for another try, and another flurry of arrows sent them into retreat once more.

Connar ranged up beside Rat. "Ryu turn up?"

"No. But I imagine he was lurking in the background among those on horses."

He was, and rode back to the temporary headquarters his family had established by taking over the inn at Tinker's Turn at the north end of the town. They had expected to be there at most a week, long enough to establish that they had been innocently sledding to view the frozen falls when the Marlovans unaccountably went after each other as well as the Sartoran guests.

Bitterness welled in him as he braced to face the escalating argument with his mother and brother over what to do next. If only his mother would *listen* instead of yapping about how dangerous mercenaries were! At least she didn't know about the ones he'd secretly hired, and had planned to bring in as stonemasons to build a castle—until that damned Ivandred Noth sicced his brutes on the mercenaries' ship as it was entering the harbor. The other two ships hadn't even attempted to land. Cowards.

He rode in the back way, to avoid being harassed by the roaming rabble, of whom he was thoroughly tired. With his guards going before and behind he slipped along Weavers' Row and tramped across what in spring would be the inn's kitchen garden, to enter through the back door.

His steward was there, looking lugubrious—more fights were breaking out among his Perideth army, the result of wild rumors.

Ryu pushed his way through the inn to the front, and glanced out the window. His mother stood in the main square, surrounded by the household bodyguards. She was shouting promises and assurances. He didn't listen, but slipped around to the back again, past the squadron of armed guards keeping the rabble out of the inn.

By the time he'd warmed up again and eaten a meal, she returned. Her first words were, "You failed again." It wasn't even a question.

Irritated, he shrugged. "It was too soon. I *said* it was too soon. But they wanted to try, so why not? The good news is, the Marlovans look terrible. I watched them through my spyglass. They're a step away from starving to death."

"Is Seonrei still there?"

He shrugged again, sharper. "What does it matter? She can't do anything. I've been thinking. Let's give them three days. Apka should be finished with the rams by then, and the ramp to cover the ground."

"Three days," she repeated. "If we can keep everyone from going at each other's throats. You had better stop hiding here, and go among them. Promise whatever they want to hear. They'll forget it all once they get inside and kill everyone in sight. And maybe each other, when they find nothing of value," she added caustically.

Artolei, Ryu, and Demeos as well as the toughest of their captains went out to force people back to the makeshift quarters, promising everything would be over in three days, when they would be celebrating their victory in the palace.

They handed out extra provisions, and when it was clear that once again they'd managed to restore a semblance of order, a fourteen-year-old baker's apprentice slipped out of the crowd, carrying a basket of rolls. He perched on his third-cousin's supply cart, loaded with empty barrels and baskets. It was passed through the guards.

When they had traveled a sufficient distance from the town, he set out cross-country.

Before morning, he'd reached Colt Cassad, who was waiting at one of the gang's hideaways. The gang gathered around the apprentice. "The other four told me their reports. All five of us agree, rumor spreads faster about threats than about promises. Especially now."

"That's no surprise," Colt said. "Go on."

"The jarlan is promising all kinds of things. Beginning with loot in the Artolei palace, and so they quieted down. Especially after the order went out to do another handout of supplies."

Brief smiles flickered at the notion of Artolei losing another palace full of treasure.

Cassad propped fists on his knees. "Was Artolei there to hear about his place being offered as loot?"

"No. He was leading today's try against the gate."

"I hope someone tells him," someone commented.

The apprentice grinned. "Enkin said he'd make sure the rumor gets to Artolei."

Cassad grunted approval. Then frowned into the fire. "Unless a miracle happens, my guess is the Marlovans will fall. They have to've run out of supplies."

No one believed that Feravayir would improve as Perideth, at least with the Nyidris ruling. But Lavais's control of news had prevailed at the upper levels, despite the Tax Gang's efforts to spread counter-rumors at the lower levels.

Cassad said slowly, "I believe it's time for a new rumor to spread, one that might at least give the Nyidris some trouble. Get this one around everywhere, as fast as you can."

The apprentice ducked his head, skinny neck-knuckle bobbing.

Everyone turned to Colt expectantly.

Colt Cassad paused to consider his words. He'd reached the conclusion that Ivandred Noth had acted in good faith in sending Quill Montredavan-An to warn them. It was characteristic. Noth was a stickler for rules and regs, but he obeyed them as well, from all reports. While one might argue about the stupidity of some of those rules, a person whose deeds and words matched, and who further seemed to understand why Cassad chose to run outside the rules, was worth heeding, at least in this matter.

So it was time to return that good faith—and see what the Marlovans did with it. "We'll begin with the guilds . . ."

Inside the winter palace, the leaders met. "We're going to have to commence quarter rations once a day," Connar said to Seonrei. "If you want to go away by magic, now is the time."

She made a small circular gesture with one hand as she said, "I've come this far. I believe I will stay until . . ." She hesitated, then finished, knowing it was weak, "until I can't."

But Connar understood what she didn't want to say. So he said it. "They're inexperienced, but not stupid. Somewhere, someone is building a better ram. If they get firm ground under them, we'll lose the gate. Then it's hand to hand."

"I understand." She glanced away, her arms within the many layers of flowing silk sleeves pressed against her middle. "I think I might go lie down. One thing I've learned is that hunger seems to express itself differently from person to person. My chief maid has headaches. My herald-guard has the trembles. I am lightheaded."

So was everyone else.

That day, two men fainted during sparring. The next day, five. Connar changed the orders to only moving through the sword drill each morning. After the five were taken to the lazaretto, Connar led the way, looking strong and martial. Jethren worked even harder, until black spots swam before his eyes, lest he look weak before the true king, whose straight back and alert blue gaze demonstrated eagle clan's strength and leadership.

Every morning a scout climbed to the highest of those decorative spires. When Connar finished the sword drill, the scout returned from the long climb, to report as usual that there was no sign of anyone within a day's ride out there.

And so another grim day began. Connar and Rat were not talking to each other, except when necessary; Rat still believed that Lineas had won through, and the Noths would come. Connar struggled against ambivalence, his emotions mercilessly knotted. He wanted the reinforcements—desperately. But he couldn't believe—couldn't let himself believe—that Lineas would bring them. She was dead in a ditch somewhere, covered with snow. She was a prisoner, waiting to be dragged out and paraded below the walls. She was still riding, slowed by the weather . . . and late at night, when he roamed the tiled corridors of the palace without seeing their artful patterns, he imagined her holed up in some warm inn with Quill (who seemed to have vanished entirely), swilling and swiving.

He tried to smother resentment. Whenever Lineas surfaced in memory he recollected Nand of the Sword's talk about how heat was as unreliable as fire. That had been eminently sensible advice from a twenty-year-old to a teen—both unaware of the difference between the fire of limerence and the complexity of love. Connar only knew that to reveal his turmoil would be to make himself risible in others' eyes.

And so he slammed off to the practice yard to work himself into exhaustion. His purpose had narrowed to one goal: if he had to die, he was taking Artolei with him.

That night, Connar had fallen into another cold, sweaty, anxiety-broken dream full of images from the bloodbath at West Outpost, only it was he defending against shadowy figures as everyone he knew died in bloody ribbons around him, and he struggled to get his hands around Artolei's neck.

A voice punched through the tangle of images. It was Fish. " . . . wake up. There's a report."

Fury ignited in Connar at being dragged out of the relative oblivion of sleep, but it swiftly cooled. Report? Fish never woke Connar up for anything frivolous. He flung off the blankets and sat up in the dark room.

"The night scout swears he heard a whirtler," Fish said.

Connar leaped out of bed, then caught himself in the doorway as waves of blackness boiled across his vision. He gulped in air, then pushed away, irritably waving off Fish, who didn't look any better than he felt.

A short time later, he met the scout in the room they'd designed as their command center, which had a detailed map of the palace and its outbuildings, with patrols and watch changed chalked in.

"It was in the distance, but I know that sound," the scout reported, dragging his teeth nervously over chapped, much-chewed lips.

"Outriders," Connar breathed, and turned his face upward, as if he could see the spires beyond the ceiling, in the dark. "Rouse everyone. Let's divide up the rest of the stores. Whatever happens, we'll need our strength."

When the sun came up, Artolei's mob was already on the move, rolling wagons chained together, with hastily thrown together roofing to protect those dragging the ram suspended between the first and last wagon. Artolei, wearing a new helm, prudently rode at the back.

Connar was on the gate, his spyglass searching the crowd for Ryu. There he was lurking among the toughs some rows behind the eager attackers at the front, waving their pitchforks and sawblades and other tools sharpened into weapons.

Artolei yelled something.

Connar put his hand to his ear.

"It's a demand for surrender," Jethren said in disgust.

"Of course it is. I want to make him repeat it four or five times, sounding stupider with each."

Rat was paying no attention. He stood at the far end of the sentry walk. Jethren, jealously guarding Connar's left at shield arm position, turned his back on Rat—and jolted when Rat suddenly spoke up, "Look."

Jethren ignored him, but Connar turned his head sharply. And his eyes widened.

Jethren had to look. So the Noth rabble had turned up at last?

The horizon, made hazy by evaporating water in the slowly strengthening sun, seemed to have grown the world's longest hedge.

That was no rabble.

Below, Artolei was shouting the offer he and Ryu had worked on all the previous night, but when he came to the threat, "If you don't surrender . . ." He realized no one was paying attention, and looked around in irritated bewilderment, as his horse began to plunge and snort.

A murmur soughed through his force, and then they stirred, as if blown by a fell wind.

Artolei's horse, picking up the lightning change in mood, sidled, ears flattening. Artolei fought the reins, peering past the roof of the ram—and gasped. As he struggled to still the restless animal, winks and gleams of light resolved out of the haze into ghost shadows: Riders in gray riding in a line, banners furling slowly, horsetails wind-tangled.

On the wall, Connar drew a slow breath, giddy with wild joy.

Below, those who could see gaped, gasped, cried out, spreading their terror to those behind as that impossibly long line began riding slowly, the lances coming down . . .

Those closest to the just-beginning charge threw down their weapons, screaming "I surrender!"

"I quit!"

"Don't kill me!"

Some ran, hands over their heads to protect their scalps from being ripped off, others dropped to their knees. The chargers didn't waver—until a new figure detached from the westernmost line, and galloped toward them, two golds glinting on his arms: Ivandred Noth.

No one at the palace could hear what he roared, but the Marlovans understood the white and blue pennons borne by the Rider behind the commander: *Accept surrender.*

Noth turned toward the panicking army, shouting repeatedly, "Weapons down, and no one will be hurt! Weapons down!"

Crash! Clang! Horsemen surrounded the army, which immediately dissolved into terrified individuals. Keeping rigid order—while watching their leaders—the Riders forced themselves into groups, dividing the panicky army, as they whacked heads and backs with the flats of their wickedly curved cavalry sabers, which further scattered the former army.

Meanwhile Noth directed his army to thoroughly disarm those before the gate, to support the defenders (who were at that moment laboring to open the gates), and to restore peace to the adjacent town.

Up on the wall, Connar watched, emotions at a pitch. He drew in a shuddering breath. It was over now, but Artolei was trying to slither away. And he wasn't sure he had the strength to pursue him.

Connar slid a furious glance at Jethren. "Take him down," he muttered.

Jethren's teeth showed in a flashing, feral grin. He shouldered his way through the men crowding the sentry walk, then paused and looked back at the very same moment Connar was thinking past that puppet Artolei to his master.

Jethren mouthed, "Ryu?"

Pleased at that instant understanding, Connar opened his hand, and Jethren—though water-limbed with fatigue and hunger—enjoyed a resurgence of strength fueled by the thirst for vengeance.

ELEVEN

After his first real meal in weeks, Connar enjoyed another sensation even more rare: he slept through an entire night.

He woke feeling as if he floated in a pool under a summer sky—weightless, drained of thought, of emotion. At first he was content to lie there relishing the absence of that gnawing hunger and its resultant ache.

But the almost noiseless rustles and steps of Fish in the far room brought the previous day rushing back: the arrival of stores from the town, previously hoarded by a ferocious number of guards who melted away at the sight of armed Marlovans, and the subsequent meal as Ivandred Noth dealt with a steady stream of reports, while Connar pretended to listen.

All of it had been beyond him, except for the sweet, recurring thought: it was over. They'd won.

Now details began to emerge into his consciousness, beginning with the fact that Lineas *had* made to Old Faral and back. She was probably somewhere in the winter palace. He discovered he didn't care. Any sort of reaction right now felt as remote as the sky. He liked it that way.

But he couldn't lie in his pretend pool forever. Fish returned presently, with a tray of hot, fresh-ground and scalded coffee, a meal next to the cup. "Captain Jethren outside, wishes to report," Fish said.

His last order to Jethren returned to Connar, causing a spurt of curiosity. This quiet couldn't last. He didn't want it to last. He was in command. If he stayed in here, who was giving out orders?

That roused him.

When Jethren entered a short time later, Connar was dressed, halfway through a pile of jam-slathered oatcakes and shirred eggs covered with melted cheese.

Jethren glanced around, making certain no one was listening, and as he struck his chest in salute, he said, "Done."

"How?"

"Artolei, trying to escape. Two blows—from one of their cudgels. Before the mob trampled him. Cornered Ryu Nyidri in the town. We had to fight our way through his guards, though half ran when we carved through those at the door. He screamed about wanting a duel. I said fine. He had some

Sartoran weapons, the hilts made of gold and the like, the blade long, like a sewing needle stretched out. Worthless for anything but playing around."

Connar snorted. "And?"

"Twenty moves rather than two, most of 'em learning how to handle it. I cut him up before killing him."

"Witnesses?" Connar said, corrosive satisfaction burning pleasantly through him.

"None. Everyone was on the run. Including his own people. He was alone when we found him, trying to hide. We left him there. Noth's people were locking up the town."

And Jethren had fainted, but he wasn't going to admit to that. Never show weakness had been one of the earliest lessons beaten into him.

Connar indicated the door. "Go take liberty. Say nothing about it," he added, as the implications began slowly to occur to him.

Jethren understood. The eagle-clan king's orders had been repeated often enough: inspection, and if there was evidence of another plot, the jarlan was to be replaced with Ivandred Noth, whom most of the jarls recognized as jarl in some form.

Jethren didn't care. The one whose opinion mattered was Connar—and it had been so very satisfying to watch Ryu clutching his chest as he coughed up blood, before Jethren very nearly fell on top of him as faintness caught up with him.

Breakfast restored enough strength for Connar to seek out Noth, who had set up a command post in the main parlor, all the furnishings pushed back except for two tables of different design pushed together. The table bore a map and stacks of what looked like tally scrolls and books, with guild markings on the covers.

Runners came and went; Connar spotted Quill Montredavan-An standing behind Noth, hands behind his back, his robe muddy to the knees as he listened, and Connar suspected the royal runner had been tasked to write up everything he heard for a report to the king. On the side nearest the fire, the Sartoran princess sat, wearing what looked to Connar like all of her clothes, her shrewd gaze following everything, though she didn't speak.

As Connar entered the room, Lavais Nyidri swept in through the main door, trailing a riding of Noth's armed guards. She strode toward what Connar had learned was considered the principal seat in the room, and checked when she saw Seonrei there.

The princess gave her a brief glance, head to toes, then turned her head as if she were not present. Connar was not educated in Sartoran court etiquette, but he sensed the utter dismissal.

Lavais flushed, and Connar remembered the lies the woman had written. Yes, there were the scraps of paper, lying neatly in their own pile at a corner of that big improvised desk.

Lavais crossed her arms and threw her head back. "My son was murdered! I demand justice!"

"That is being addressed at this moment," Ivandred Noth said, unimpressed by her pose of moral outrage—her best weapon, he'd realized years ago. "I am in the midst of gathering evidence, with the outland princess you invited offering to sit in to witness justice." He opened his hand toward Seonrei in a gesture so ironic that everyone in the room could see how much he disliked Lavais Nyidri.

He went on in that dry, flat tone, "Royal Runner Quill Montredavan-An, in company with Princess Seonrei's herald-servant, personally inspected your son's body. The wounds were punctures, made by no weapon any of us carry. Your son was more likely murdered by one of your own mercenaries."

"We *never* deal with such trash," Lavais snapped.

"Hirelings, then," Ivandred said in a tone of such disbelief she gasped—and her eyes strayed to those notes lying on the table.

But she rallied. "It was all Khael Artolei," she stated. "He is *entirely* responsible for this reprehensible and tragic situation. We were merely guests at his winter palace. We were viewing the frozen falls when he sent his people to attack, and yes, my sons were seen with him, but they were there trying to remonstrate with him."

She paused there, chin lifted, a thin smile evident, and Connar understood that he had erred in siccing Jethren on Ryu and Artolei, which prevented Noth from interrogating them until they admitted the truth.

Jethren, listening at the back, cursed under his breath when he realized that he and the true king would certainly have gotten to watch that interrogation. Maybe even take part. But at the time, it had looked like the two would slither into the stampeding crowd and escape.

So here they all were, everybody in that room knowing that Lavais Nyidri was a lying liar. But she was getting away with her lies yet again. Connar's head throbbed with the sheer injustice of it—until he remembered his orders.

Triumph surged in him. He looked across the room at Lavais Nyidri. "The king said that if Feravayir proved to be inadequately governed, and I believe we can all accept your inability to prevent what has happened as evidence, then I was to remove you from the jarlate, and hand it off to Ivandred Noth."

"He wouldn't *dare*," Lavais whispered.

"I am the King's Voice, delivering his order. Any arguments against your replacement may be made at the next Convocation, but as of this moment, Ivandred Noth, you are now Jarl of Feravayir."

Shock rang through Lavais. Impossible. Her people would surely rise against . . .

Uncertainty caused her mind to falter. She had forced all the holders to furnish those supplies now being gobbled by the invading Marlovans. In the name of the faraway king, but it had been Nyidri guards who had smashed into storehouses and homes. It would take some work to win them back. But she had to be free to do it.

She turned a speculative glance toward Ivandred. On the surface, she'd maintained civility. She had always made certain of that. He was so dull, so ignorant outside of his endless marching and whatnot, surely she could win him again . . . But first she had better begin with Seonrei.

Ivandred Noth, who had been watching her closely, spoke. "Take her out. And see to it no one can disturb her. There are angry mobs still wandering around looking for someone to blame."

That stung. She worked to find a sufficient retort, but the runners were like huge ruminants, their breath smelling of cabbage as they herded her firmly out—just as Demeos was brought in by another group.

Demeos looked somberly at his mother, then turned away as he was thrust through the door into the chamber. He wondered what she had said, and the thought occurred to him that she might blame him, to save her own skin. It was a horrible thought, but he had heard her lie so many times, he was no longer certain what she would do or say. Except to present an innocent face to the world.

"Sit or stand," Noth said. "You will answer my questions freely, or after coercion, as permitted for investigation of treason. It'll either happen here or at the royal city. Take your choice."

Demeos still wore his Sartoran silks, and his fine brown skin had flushed with color, but he said evenly enough, "Ask your questions."

Noth did. Demeos began denying knowing anything—as everyone there expected.

Connar was so annoyed he walked out, to inspect the state of the palace as well as the perimeter patrols.

He stopped by the kitchen, ate a meal, then returned, to discover Demeos sitting in a chair, blanched as colorless as paper as Noth continued to shoot questions like arrows. Every time a piece of gathered evidence contradicted his lie, Noth read it out: reports from searches, inspections, and the slowly accreting reports of interrogations of the erstwhile army.

Over the few days, it became clear enough that Ryu had been the mastermind, Artolei his active accomplice. The only proof that Demeos had known about the conspiracy was testimony to his presence when Ryu or Artolei handed out orders. Nobody had heard him give orders himself—except about matters pertaining to entertainment and transportation in the carriages.

Lavais had been very careful to never be heard contradicting her pose of innocence, except for the damning conversation Lineas had first overhead. But even then, Lavais had not actually given orders that time: it was Ryu who had suggested the plot.

Meanwhile the defenders regained their strength as they worked alongside the rescuers from the far garrisons. Jethren shadowed Connar, determined to anticipate his orders and be seen carrying them out before Rat Noth could. Quill was still under Ivandred Noth's orders, mostly writing as witnesses were questioned, all to be sent to the king.

Lineas had seen at a glance the cost of the siege in Connar's sharp-boned face and tense expression. She made herself useful, but at a distance, making certain she never irritated him with a glimpse of her. She knew from meeting Quill at night that the king's report was being prepared, and so she went to Noth's first runner to volunteer to take it.

On a rainy morning Connar got to the interview room before anyone else—except for Noth, who didn't seem to sleep. "Are you going to dose Lavais Nyidri with kinthus?" he asked.

Noth said, "There isn't any of the white stuff to hand. It would have to be brought in and administered by a healer, is my understanding. And I'm not certain that is within the bounds of my orders."

"But you're now the jarl."

Noth looked up. His eyes were marked with tiredness. "I've been trying to determine if she gave treasonous orders. So far, no one testifies to that, which is no surprise. She knows that Marlovans obey orders or die. Which means those at the top bear responsibility in matters of treason and conspiracy. Her strategy all along has been to point blame anywhere else but at herself."

"But surely the truth herb would reveal how much she's lying, wouldn't it?"

"I suspect if we force that herb down her throat, all we'll hear is an ugly tangle of self-justification, all pointing at Ryu, whose bloodlust she conveniently ignored, if she didn't outright encourage it. I never understood how that boy came to be the way he was—his father was reputed to be lazy and comfort-loving. Doesn't matter now. The thing is, I don't know how much she's come to believe her lies in her own head."

Connar exclaimed, "You're not thinking of letting her go?"

The new jarl jerked his hand away, palm down. "No chance. If it were left to me, she would spend the remainder of her life in a one room cottage on a bit of isolated land, where she would have to grow her own vegetables. Cook her own food. Make her own clothes. Work to trade for what she needs."

Connar couldn't imagine the haughty woman knowing one end of a garden trowel from the other. While he relished the thought of an execution, that would be over fairly quickly. Whereas being forced to grub in the dirt like the lowest of her servants, or starve, seemed more fitting.

His recent intimate acquaintance with starvation prompted him to say, "I expect Da would prefer that. If there isn't proof that she gave the orders, proof he could present before the jarls." Now he really regretted killing Ryu, who of all of them deserved a formal execution in all its pain and gore as the jarls lined up to watch.

Connar's back twitched at that. But a glance at Noth made it clear his mind was still on Lavais Nyidri. "And I know Ma would approve that over an execution. She hates them," he found himself adding.

"What sane person doesn't?" Noth turned up his palm. "If you concur, let's put that in orders, then, and send her off right away. The king can always countermand the order if he wishes."

"What about Demeos?" Connar asked. "Are you going to turn him loose? You know he was part of it."

"The question is, how much. There are two of his and Ryu's riding mates yet to question. They should be brought in within a day or so, though I can guess what we'll find. But the royal runner Quill told me something that might provide a solution."

Quill? Connar's brows shot up. "What did he say?"

"It wasn't what he said so much as what he overheard Danet-Gunvaer saying, after my son and the princess were given permission to marry. That was, perhaps Starliss Cassad, who is right outside the gates on patrol right now, should be reassigned to marry Demeos, and someone else would be found for Ryu—assuming of course that the jarlan ever agreed to make those betrothals into treaty marriages."

Starliss Cassad. Connar's mind shot to the strikingly handsome new captain of a flight of skirmishers who had ridden down with Rat's brother Mouse Noth, senior captain at Hesea Garrison.

"I spoke to her last night. She says she's willing," Noth added, with a thin smile. "If you were to see your way to detaching her and her flight from Hesea Garrison, I believe that would solve the Demeos problem."

Demeos would spend the rest of his life as a hostage, thought Connar. Of course he'd be surrounded by Noth's most trusted men, but who could watch him closer than a wife, and runners she selected? He suppressed a laugh. "We can hold the wedding before we ride. Call it a peace celebration."

Two days later, under a sky full of patchy clouds moving slantwise, Seonrei invited Iaeth to walk the Purrad with her.

The briefest definition of the verb *napurdiav* is a ritual and meditative walk in a certain pattern, centuries old. Older. 'Walking the Purrad' is the idiom, often translated by outsiders as wandering a labyrinth or maze, though few Purrads are walled. The oldest were not built on one surface, though the centuries since those lost days reduced the Purrad to garden areas, designed for aesthetic refreshment.

Usually one walked it alone, but custom also permitted shared walks, usually for conversations upon matters of reflection.

There was no Purrad in the winter palace's back garden, but a lifetime of walking the fourfold intersecting triads imposed a palimpsest over that space, visible only in their minds, as Seonrei said, "Commander Noth received a messenger that a trade ship is at Parayid, preparing to sail for home. We will request passage. Once Demeos's wedding is over, I believe it will be time to depart."

Iaeth laughed. "Demeos seems a lot more amenable than I'd expected, for someone who expected to marry a princess and gain a coronet being reduced to what in any other land would be a hostage, and told to marry a warrior captain."

"It helps," Seonrei said dryly, "that she's so handsome. Donais heard gossip that she's related somehow to the Dei family."

Iaeth snapped her fingers. "That's right. There is, or was, a branch of the Deis right here somewhere. What an . . . odd thought."

"Odd because you can't imagine Deis dressed in dull-colored wool and wanding stables?"

Iaeth was surprised at the bite of sarcasm in her cousin's voice. "It was the opposite, in fact," she mused, ducking under a budding branch—their invisible pattern had at its center a great, spreading oak. "Odd that the Dei family wasn't mentioned in connection with the capital, or government, or some kind of potential trouble, as is customary in Sartor. In other words, the Marlovan Deis apparently lead quiet lives. I'm wrong?"

"You're not wrong. Forgive me for my assumption. Another of my many errors here. From what I've learned, this branch of the Deis has largely blended into other families, unlike the Sartoran Deis." (The context being their mutual awareness that the Sartoran Deis were careful to bring into the family only those as handsome and as clever as themselves—they married out their less prepossessing progeny, and they intermarried every fourth or fifth generation.) "But one can certainly see the Dei mold in that Starliss Cassad."

"True." Iaeth laughed as she sniffed the air, catching the aroma of fresh baking. She still didn't fit her clothes, and ate as often as she could. "And so, it has ended better than we dared to expect, though perhaps not with the aid of your diplomatic accord?"

To her surprise, Seonrei blushed to her hairline. "Ah-yah! I expect my arrogance about that is going to haunt my dreams for the remainder of my days."

"Eh? Cousin! We survived, and without the massacre we dreaded. All is settled to the prospective improvement of everyone, excepting perhaps Lavais Nyidri. But there, I see justice."

"Nothing is wrong with a peaceful accord. But everything was wrong with my arrogance in assuming that I would bring it about."

Iaeth said, "Ah?" And here they were on the Purrad; clearly her cousin wished to unburden herself, and so Iaeth assumed a listening attitude as their footsteps crunched, crunched, crunched.

Seonrei said slowly, "I thought I would sweep into this benighted land of barbarians where no one civilized dares go, and—demonstrating my own superior culture—on a tide of the awe that my name and lineage would surely inspire, gently shepherd the Marlovans into civilization."

"So." Iaeth's smile was more of a wince. "So."

Seonrei sighed. "I can't really penetrate the thinking of these Marlovans. Their language is a barrier, of course, but they are difficult to read for such . . . unsubtle persons. Prince Connar does not seem to be stupid, and he commands a vast army, standing second only to the king. And yet the Marlovan style of ruler appears to have little social hierarchy. Prince Connar eats what his stable hands eat. He wears what they wear."

"All true."

"I once attempted a conversation upon the theories of statecraft with Prince Connar, which perhaps I ought not to have done, our understanding of each other's languages being minimal. Once he comprehended my fumbling attempt at a question, he informed me shortly that such subjects belonged to his father. As if my question was some sort of trespass."

"Perhaps it was," Iaeth commented. "Which does not shed a very pleasant light on this unknown king, if even his son cannot discuss the verities of governance."

"I thought of that. But then he might have misconstrued my intent. That aside, if the king and queen in that far city do govern the way this Ivandred Noth believes they do, their rule cannot be as terrible as we have been told."

Iaeth said, "Overlooking the fact that so much of this kingdom is organized around the life of the warrior."

"True. What is a warrior to do but make war? And yet Ivandred Noth, who could have slaughtered that pack of rioters Ryu and Artolei had gathered, didn't. Because of his understanding of the wishes of this faraway warrior king."

Iaeth gestured with her hand in the fan pose for *dichotomy*.

Seonrei went on. "The more I ponder human nature, the less I seem to understand. But all questions of social covenant always come back to kings."

"Kings!"

"Every country has one."

"Not so!"

It was Seonrei's turn snap her hand in *Pardon my Protest*. "They do, whatever they are called. In Three Rivers, they are called Surveyors. In Hael Vendreon, chieftains. Across the water on the other continent, though both are old Venn colonies, I believe you might have heard of the country that calls their monarch Servant of the People."

Iaeth had not studied other lands to the extent that Seonrei had, for her life's work was bound to Sartor, but even she remembered reading about those bloody selections, so notorious for violence and bribery that trade shut down for increasingly long times beforehand, as each guild member or farmer over the age of twenty turned in a Counting Stick at the local Hall of Justice to select their ruler. And yet that colony had begun itself as a reaction to Venn rule, each who did the work of the country to have a voice in the running of it.

Seonrei's light, ironic voice went on, "No matter how much ritual they tried to add to insure fairness, people still coerced others, or bought them. Many didn't even go to the selection, but claimed sick and took to their beds until it was over, saying that one stick didn't matter. Until the scribe guild took things in hand. And so now they have a splendid ritual, in which everyone knows ahead of time who will win—coincidentally, always someone from the guild master's family."

"I concede that one, but—"

"The other old Venn colony calls their monarch Chief Counselor. I'm told these rulers wear the clothing of their commons, they use the language of the commons, but they are still monarchs descending from one of the most powerful guilds."

Iaeth pondered for a step or two, then observed, "The first lesson in history I remember is learning that we've gone backward since the days of Ancient Sartor, when we had a single queen, who had no power. Hers was an entirely symbolic presence."

"With immense prestige," Seonrei said, her upper lip curling. "Queens these days can be much the same as kings, though they still retain a higher status in Sartor and Sartoran-influenced lands, as princesses stand above princes. All is so very different from what we perceive of Ancient Sartor, in which armies were entirely unknown."

Iaeth sighed. "Our first lessons in such matters posit that humans need some sort of hierarchy, or there is a chaos."

"Correct. *Somebody* has to rule. We know that much from historical situations in which the ruling center, however you termed it, vanished. People did not settle down contentedly, each to their life—*someone* has to intervene if my neighbors' chestnut tree has grown so that it ruins the light during spring over my kitchen garden. I can try to talk my neighbors into trimming a branch, but what if they insist that their livelihood depends on those chestnuts? I cut the branch myself, she tears up my garden, and before we know it, the entire village is choosing sides and picking up rocks."

Iaeth folded her hands.

Seonrei sighed. "I know, I know . . . I've descended from discussion to lecture. But all my childhood lessons emphasized how government truly takes place in the minds of the governed, even in their acknowledgment of us as a ruling family, and how ritual and manners and fashion are the outer forms of authority and its implied responsibility."

"And," Iaeth stated, stamping on a slate rock in emphasis, "*my* lessons were in how those are infinitely superior to the use of force to impose order."

"Yes. Yes! So. I come back to the fact that Ivandred Noth did not loose his warriors to eradicate Ryu's rabble, and made it clear enough that mercy was expected from that king so far away. What we were told about the Marlovans seems, in fact, to have been fundamentally incorrect."

"Yet." Iaeth waved her hand to and fro in *What matter?* "No one is asking our opinion on their governance."

"But I need to understand what happened here. I'm beginning to wonder if it's the implied responsibility in positions of power, whatever they might be called, that is the first to erode. Look at Lavais, as greedy as she was ambitious. The worst of her was her sense of privilege, a sense I share because I grew up knowing that I am a Landis, descendant of the oldest ruling house in the world. I can walk into any house in Sartor and expect the principle seat—as long as my royal cousins are not present. Then I sit at their right. We all know it so well we move in an orderly manner on entering or leaving a room, each to her place."

Iaeth said, "And so?"

"That foolish Khael Artolei! In the time I spent with him and their court circle, before he and Ryu initiated their violent conspiracy, when he wasn't being goaded into talk about war by Ryu, he wasn't a bad person."

"Yes he was, unless you count murder on whim as not bad."

"I did not know!" Seonrei's gait faltered, then she struck out again, as if to leave the ugly realization behind her.

"I didn't tell you many things, as the knowledge was a burden and you already knew he was untrustworthy."

"I see we will have much to discuss before we wait on the queen."

"Yes. Please resume. I sidetracked you, for which I apologize."

"Thank you. I found Artolei very . . . unthinking, particularly in his belief that because he was born Artolei, it was not a mere matter of coming first socially, but that anything he did must be right. Ah, and that accords with your grim discoveries. His shadow-kissers, as the Colendi say, certainly reinforced his conviction that he did no wrong, but you notice they were the first to run when the Marlovans appeared on the horizon."

"Faster than Ryu's," Iaeth said grimly as they began treading the fourth triad. "But discerning, and avoiding, the lies and flattery of shadow-kissers is an old lesson."

"Yes. The new lesson for me—I come at last to my point—was my observation that all of them—Ryu, his mother, and Khael Artolei—were not emulating Marlovan barbarians. They were emulating *us*."

Iaeth did not deny it, and Seonrei's cheeks glowed brighter. But she gritted on, determined on this ramble into honesty, wherever it might lead.

"We do learn a sense of privilege, because it goes with authority, which we are taught must remain benign. I have to ponder, and will discuss with the queen, how *readily* our civilized, superior Sartoran style of government was being distorted into Lavais Nyidri's nightmarish semblance of a royal court. She was using what she learned from *us* against her own people, to rob them not only of their livelihood in order to increase her own wealth, but of their voices, to increase her power."

Iaeth sighed. "The obvious retort is that she was not *our* government. She was only adopting the trappings of social superiority."

"How dangerous are those, is my question?" Seonrei persisted. "Can they be considered as dangerous as all this steel surrounding us?"

"The obvious answer is that steel ends life. Falsity, greed, and pretense can be survived. There is no redress when you lie dead."

"Mm-mm. All right, from another direction. The Marlovans are definitely ignorant about magic. They lack amenities we assume are basic to life. Perhaps it is the word 'barbarian' that is the peccant notion, implying our social and cultural superiority, as it depends not upon deeds of war. Does the very idea of social hierarchy spell its own downfall?"

Iaeth cast her gaze upward as they made the turn to finish the last triad. "We need hierarchies because all us humans are barbarians at heart."

That, heralds were taught from the beginning. One had to become conscious of one's faults before they could be guarded against—and only then could one learn to truly guard others.

But she did not feel superior. She, too, had made grave mistakes.

They took the last steps and stopped, bowed to one another with palms together, and went their separate ways, Iaeth taking a roundabout path through the Marlovans' cottages, which perforce they still used, as quarters were extremely tight. But these past few days the Marlovans were seldom in the cottages during the day. They were either patrolling or performing their endless training maneuvers.

So she was not prepared to hear voices. From long habit she stepped sideways to the shadows, and peered around an archway carved with acanthus leaves. Though his back was turned, she immediately recognized Prince Connar. No one else had that long blue-black hair hanging down in a glossy river from its high golden clasp, bisecting powerful shoulders tapering down to a slim waist. Long legs flattered by those loose trousers and high-heeled boots. While they'd all been starving, she had gotten used to seeing him fighting for draining strength as they all had been.

But now he stood there fully armed, knife hilts gleaming at the tops of his riding boots, a sword strapped crosswise over his back—he had obviously just come from fighting practice—but his posture was still, as if he was a breath away from reaching for that sword hilt at his left shoulder as he faced—

Lineas?

And Quill!

The two runners stood side by side, both in blue robes. Quill had halted in the process of handing Lineas something.

Iaeth ducked back to remain unseen. The tension she perceived snapped her heartbeat into thundering against her ribs, faster than the rumbling drums of the Marlovans when they did that dance with steel.

Then the prince slid a foot back, and his hands dropped to his hips as Lineas said, "I've orders to ride for the royal city."

Connar's head turned minutely. Iaeth saw his profile as his gaze lit on the golden ring glinting at Lineas's heart finger, then flicked to the sealed scroll Quill held in his hands.

Quill cleared his throat, then said to Lineas, "I'm also to tell you that Digger ordered the cook to make you up travel rations, and Dandelion can be saddled whenever you wish."

Lineas took the scroll with both hands, her round gaze lifting to Connar, then away. "I'll leave at first light." She walked away.

Connar said to Quill, "And you?"

"I'm to stay with Noth until he readies the follow-up report." He laid his fist to his heart.

Connar gave one of those smiles that didn't reach his eyes, and as he turned away, Iaeth faded noiselessly, the hairs on the back of her neck prickling.

Behind her, Connar turned back as Quill took himself off. Connar gazed down at the place where Lineas had been standing.

It was the first sight he'd had of her in close to two years. She never had been beautiful, but those two years of very hard riding had left her looking somehow . . . more like herself.

What was that look she gave him? Not fear. Nor pity, at least. Something else—anything else but the welcome that had met him all those years on coming home, that smile that was not lust, nor possession, nor expectation—for he still did not comprehend the concept of tenderness. All he knew was, he had taken it for granted until it was gone.

He turned away again, throat thick with disgust. She wore a ring now. They both did. Sentiment, he told himself, was worthless, and he occupied himself with endless tasks until the nightwatch, when he found a professional who could match him in roughness—and then had the sense to steal away, leaving him sitting among the wreckage of the room with his head in his hands.

TWELVE

The first glimpse Iaeth had of Quill, she didn't recognize the polite, appealing young traveler named Senrid she'd met many years ago in that dashing figure galloping like a bolt from a crossbow toward the village where the Nyidris holed up.

Was he familiar? She'd turned her head, weary and giddy from hunger, but only saw his back, and the unfamiliar dark blue robe flapping in the wind, before he was lost among the armed warriors at his back.

She had been sent by Seonrei to find the Nyidris and stop violence if she could—and if she couldn't, to witness. "Whatever happens to them," Seonrei had said, "it's important that someone impartial see the truth. Even if they themselves have been living lies, that's no reason to stand by while the unthinkable is made everyday."

The second time she saw Quill was a short time later, when she got to the village, which was preternaturally still after the roaming, angry crowds of recent days. She no longer had to use stealth. Just as well, as her strength was about gone.

She was in a fugue when she reached that inn; later she could not recollect arriving, nor did she remember how she got back, but she did remember entering that chamber of death to find Quill kneeling over a prone figure, clearly dead: Ryu. He looked up sharply, and she blinked in surprise.

At first she thought he'd killed Ryu, but she saw in that stiffened body that Ryu had been dead for some time.

She looked away from Ryu to . . . *"Senrid?"* She recognized him then.

"Iaeth?" he said on a rising note of incredulity, recognizing her from his visit to Sartor what sometimes seemed a lifetime ago. Two lifetimes.

"Why are you here? Aren't you a scribe?"

He straightened up, one hand touching that dark blue robe he wore over a white shirt and riding trousers. "I'm a royal runner. People seldom use my given name. Permit me to re-introduce myself," he said, remembering that he'd let her believe he was a scribe student during his visit to Sartor's capital. Scribes could go most anywhere—including to the magic library, if sent by whoever they worked for. "I'm Quill Montredavan-An," he said, and to keep her mind off the exact circumstances of their first meeting so long ago, "Why are you here? Dressed like that?"

Iaeth had glanced down at herself from what seemed a remote height, remembering she had pinched a laundry attendant's shapeless, undyed clothes in order to disguise herself, but she was far too tired to explain.

But by then he'd put it together. "You're with the princess?"

"Yes. I accompanied her to this kingdom as her personal herald, to protect, of course, but also to investigate. Where are the rest of the Nyidri faction?"

"Under guard. I found Ryu Nyidri here, already cold."

She sank down onto a bench as they tried to piece together how Ryu had been killed from the scarce evidence before them.

The third encounter occurred late the night after her conversation with Seonrei. Following a heavy rain, she walked the outer wall of the winter palace, breathing in the chilly air as she looked out over the muddy expanse, here and there shallow pools reflecting the starry sky. Barely visible in the clear moonlight, patches of fuzz broke the dreariness of receding winter, though dirty snow churned up by many horses' hooves lay in the shadows of buildings.

And here came Quill, bearing a tray. "I was sent to find you." He spoke Sartoran in that intriguing accent. "Your princess commanded me to see that you ate this midnight snack."

Iaeth looked away, embarrassed when she recollected blacking out that first night, after they'd finished cataloguing Ryu's wounds. But so had many people, and more frequently.

He must have seen the wince she tried to hide for he said with cheerful sympathy, "I received roughly the same orders from Commander Noth. I thought I'd save us both a trip. And a fairly tense atmosphere." He tipped his chin back toward what she and Seonrei had termed the inquisitorial chambers.

"What's going on?"

"Just finished up the last of today's interrogations. Korskei, this time." She recognized the family name of the last of Demeos and Ryu's inner circle. "Insisted he thought he was protecting Feravayir."

"Of course he'd say that." She sat down right where she had been standing. He squatted down as well, heedless of the wet red stone, and set the tray between them: hot rolls, still steaming, a dish that smelled like pepper-cabbage over rice, and a little pot of some sort of preserve. Her stomach woke up as she broke open a roll.

"He might have been lying, as Areth clearly was, except that out came the most devastating testimony, every lie Lavais had been telling them. Beginning with the king's quadrupled taxes. All written out, plain as day. That, plus the fact that Jaya Vinn and Lemekith had abandoned Ryu and Artolei entirely, make it fairly clear—if the king decides to pursue it—what she and Ryu were really doing."

"Will he?"

Quill paused in the act of spreading jam on a roll. "He? Who, Ryu?"

"The king."

Quill laughed. "I can't speak for him. But I strongly suspect he'll leave it to Noth to deal with. He hates the mess of what could be called treason trials. That was made manifest during the Yvanavayir disaster."

"What was that?"

He told her, briefly. While she listened to the inside story of that northern war she'd heard references to, it occurred to her that this conversation was in her own language—that is, he spoke it as easily, as naturally, as she did.

He finished up, "Noth has already sent people to seize all Lavais Nyidri's holdings, and those of her pet guild leaders. All those warehoused goods under the pretext of kings' taxes will either go to the king, or else back into the trade towns, Noth is telling them. Watching him dismantle the Perideth myth is a pleasure."

"Perideth was a kingdom once," she observed mildly.

"True." Quill shot her a speculative glance, then returned to spooning up pepper cabbage. "But the Perideth Lavais Nyidri was building threatened to beggar the countryside so she could live like your royal Sartorans, with ten times the land and wealth."

Lay a criticism behind those words? Yes or no, the conversation had strayed in an unsettling parallel to that earlier discussion she'd had with Seonrei.

She flicked a glance to find Quill gazing off into the distance, as if leaving the implied question to her to address or not.

She was not about to defend Sartor's centuries of social structure to an ignorant Marlovan . . . so she shifted the subject. "I've scarcely seen Lineas since her return with Commander Noth. Only the once, when I told her how much I admired her for what must have been a rough ride. But she said it wasn't half the ride you made. What part did you serve in this—if you can say?"

"There's no secret," he responded. "I was sent here and there by those who do the sending. Briefly met the leader of the Tax Gang. He put me as bait for Ryu's initial trap at the beginning, after which I rode to Parayid, from which I was sent north again."

She shut her eyes, calling up a general sense of the map, then realized he had crossed the entire length of Feravayir—while no doubt dodging Ryu's assassins—and then back again.

He glanced skyward, took a bite, then added, "I reached Hesea Garrison just as Mouse Noth was facing what looked like a mutiny, with nearly everyone there trying to get leave on the flimsiest of excuses in order to ride with the Faral Noths, who had been summoned by Lineas as runner for Rat Noth. That's when I learned what was going on here."

He smiled briefly, his gaze so steady she could see the twin flickers from the Marlovans' torches in his eyes. Why torches, she wondered, when lanterns were less dangerous and gave just as much light?

The question vanished as he went on, "But my orders made their volunteer ride legal, so most of the garrison came down, leaving the rawest recruits behind to defend the walls. Though at their backs lies Darchelde," he finished cheerfully. "Our Darchelde Riders might not be able to leave the territory, but anyone coming from the south would have to ride through them to get to the royal city, which was probably Ryu's next grand plan. They'd have regretted it."

Iaeth finished off a roll, appreciating that Quill had delivered his strategic summary in Sartoran. Challenge? As she dusted crumbs off her fingers, her mind conjured up a similar situation in Sartor. Say, the province of Tandarei revolting, and neighboring Yostos desperate to take advantage, with the great duchy of Chandos defending . . . then she gave herself a mental shake. The entire point was that such a terrible uprising would never happen in civilized Sartor.

A challenge was ludicrous when all the advantages lay on one side.

He clearly saw something in her face, for he said, with raised brows, "Speaking of. If the princess and the rest of you don't carry transfer tokens on you, I'll eat this tray. Why *did* you stay?"

There was nothing accusatory in his wide smile or direct gaze, but she still felt stung, as if she and Seonrei had remained in order to witness the expected bloody spectacle. And his easy reference to transfer tokens made it clear he was acquainted with magic, at the least. "Her highness offered to let us return, but we came to serve and protect her. As for her highness, she stayed to do precisely what she is doing."

"A diplomatic witness," he said appreciatively, then looked up, and his face transformed. His smile had been friendly in a neutral way, but now his gaze softened to warmth as Lineas appeared, with the careful step of someone carrying hot liquid.

"Scalded coffee for all," she said.

She stooped. Both Quill and Iaeth reached up to steady the tray, as the welcome aroma of coffee reached them.

"Where have you been, wife?" Quill said in Marlovan. which Iaeth understood much better now. She glanced at his hand, and noticed the plain gold ring.

"Helping in the kitchens, husband," Lineas responded—and yes, she too wore a gold ring. "Keeping busy."

Lineas turned to Iaeth as she plopped down next to her. "I think having Princess Seonrei there is very good for everyone," she said in Sartoran. "I think . . . I think having her there was something the Nyidris needed to see."

Iaeth said, "They know that everything they say will be reported by the princess to the queen."

But neither Quill nor Lineas reacted to that, as if the Queen of Sartor were as removed as the stars.

Lineas continued, "He's also letting that one guild chief listen in, and he hasn't chased Korskei out."

"Witnesses," Quill said appreciatively. "Most effective way to end Lavais's lies, by having as many witnesses as possible, not only listening but seeing each other there. It's especially important for the guilds to learn that everything they were told by Lavais Nyidri was a distortion, if not an outright lie. And yet some seem not to believe it. Probably won't believe anything Noth says until the guilds are actually able to choose their new chiefs, and those chiefs survive traveling to the royal city and back, after brangling with—ah, interviewing—the king at Convocation. Heh."

Lineas said soberly, "I wonder how many of those who don't believe Commander Noth were benefitting in some way from the jarlan's corruption."

"Oh, most," Quill said. "But not all. Human nature being ridiculous more often than not."

Iaeth said, "Then you don't believe there is a very real fear about sanguinary reprisal from your king?"

Quill had been stacking his dishes. He sat back, the shadows in his face deepening the shadows under his cheekbones, and in the long dimples at either side of his mouth, turning his smile sardonic. "Marlovans," he said, "would know that sanguinary reprisal is the fate of those who gave the orders. And yes, I can see you about to ask if that happens. It does. A couple of generations ago, a lot. Though eventually the violence caught up with that king. I certainly don't advocate execution unless in extreme situations. But there are problems with every form of what's called justice. Your Gardens of Silence merely put off problems for another generation to handle—those who aren't harvested by Norsunder and taken beyond time, to be sent against us all."

Lineas said pacifically, "We're taught that the Sartorans also practice restitution, just as we do."

Quill looked up at her, and uttered a soft laugh. "I'm done. I'm done."

"Good," Lineas said in a quiet voice that Iaeth could scarcely heard. "I have to ride come morning watch . . . ." She left the sentence hanging.

But Quill obviously understood the implication. He got to his feet, picked up the combined trays, and he and Lineas walked away.

Iaeth retreated inside, where she found Seonrei folding a letter into her notecase. "I think," she said, "I've been put in my place by someone I thought of as a charming puppy."

"Puppy?" Seonrei repeated. "Where?"

"Oh, I met the royal runner Quill some years ago. Maybe ten? Anyway, he was not far from the voice-breaking stage. So polite. I thought him a visiting scribe, and took him around. He was so grateful. . . ." Another thought occurred, but flitted away—and here was Seonrei waiting for explanation, so Iaeth repeated the conversation succinctly.

At the end, Seonrei set her pen carefully down. "You might laugh, but you know, I find that quite disturbing."

"The fact that I still see people ten years younger than myself as puppies? Blame our system of putting herald-apprentices in charge of the new students. Anyone that much younger than I seems a perennial student."

"No." Seonrei negated that with a forefinger. "Do you know what the royal runners do? Aside from run messages, and act as bodyguards."

"Not really."

"I found out today. They are the ones who restore the water spells and the like. Marlovans seem to use very little magic for everyday use, but that which is used is maintained by these royal runners."

Iaeth thought back to her first meeting with young Quill—outside a magic library. Scribes often came and went, fetching texts for mage students, who in turn performed small spells in turn for copy services from scribes, whose scribal hand was very fast. She shook that thought away, as Seonrei went on, "What he said about Gardens of Shame, that is a debate at high levels."

"I know," Iaeth said. "No one wants the general public aware that Gardens of Shame can be breached by Norsundrians, for one thing. Are you saying that you think the Marlovans are . . . what? *Spying?* And we've never caught them with all our wards and tracers?"

"Not at all. Something far more serious. I wonder if they are somehow gaining access to magic—specifically what kind of magic—despite the guild recommending that Marlovans not be permitted to study the higher magics. They could be learning magic from anybody. Even dark magic. Yet, even that doesn't bother me as much as the idea of this young puppy of yours having mastered our language, and our history, and possibly some level of magic, as well as talking comfortably about state strategies—"

"—and choosing to remain a barbarian, is that what you're saying?"

"I don't know that I want to use that term. It doesn't seem useful anymore, as it so often implies ignorance, if not stupidity. *Dangerous* is more like it. I think your Quill is dangerous, he and his people. I have failed to reach a diplomatic accord, but this journey was not useless. I will at the end of my report recommend to the queen that we continue to keep the Marlovans at a guarded distance, because though I don't like to call them barbarians, I do think they are far from what we consider civilized."

Marlovan weddings were not known for extravagant preparations. The banquet was a little rougher than usual, but everyone accepted that the cooks had done their best so very late in winter, with scarce supplies.

There was plenty of good dark ale and beer, at least. The winter palace glowed with torches inside and out, and banners were hung up, along with fragrant cedar boughs. Everyone who had a drum brought it out, and the chief entertainment was dancing, spirits high on the part of rescuers and rescued. The few locals present forced a semblance of cheer, relieved the worst seemed to be over.

Connar led the men's first dance in place of Demeos, who didn't know it, then gave way for Starliss Cassad leading the women. After that it was dance as always, men trading off with women. Men did the sword dance in all its variations, and Starliss, who was very good at the Odni, brought out the old knife dance, which is lethally graceful; gradually the heat from the torches, good drink, and vigorous dancing warmed everyone to a cheer unknown in that place all winter.

Demeos sat isolated in the center of the festivities, wearing his fine silk and staring at the plaster-and-paint climbing roses on the wall as it sank in that Perideth, and a royal crown, had died with Ryu. His new household, all appointed by Noth, enjoyed themselves around him. He drank steadily, until the firelight gleamed in his unblinking eyes as he watched the whirling, stamping, and leaping dancers, steel flashing. So far he'd had little speech with his comely new wife. She'd said earlier that as a man grieving the death of a family member, no one would expect him to dance, and the prince would honor him by taking his place.

It was all false, in that he'd had no choice in the matter, but he recognized in her steady gaze that she meant it kindly. There was no smirk to her shapely mouth, no superiority in her summer-sky gaze. He had no idea what the future would bring. But life could be worse.

On the other side of the chamber, Jethren also drank steadily, his attention unwavering on Starliss's willowy form as she danced, so lissome with knives in each hand. Everyone assumed she would get a good wedding night. She was too handsome, and popular, not to. The question was, with whom. But Starliss had been raised by the Cassads, and knew what was proper and what wasn't. And so, when the festivities finally wound down, she went to bed alone.

From the ridge on the other side of the river, hidden by great, twisting trunks, Colt Cassad stood shoulder to shoulder with his beloved, surveying the winter palace glowing from the light of hundreds of torches. "And so. Ivandred Noth is now jarl. This can only be an improvement."

That sixteen-year-old stood nearby recognizing a lesson when she heard one. Yes, the royal runner had come in good faith, as it happened. At least the captain wasn't jawing a whole lecture.

The girl crossed her arms with a thump against her chest. "I don't believe they'll really use the Nyidri loot to fix anything. They'll just build another giant castle. How does that make life better?"

"We will watch and see."

THIRTEEN

As jarl, Noth felt obliged to accompany the princess to Parayid, where she would take ship for Sartor. Because they could only travel as fast as the Nyidris' once-prized Sartoran carriage (Seonrei did not ride, except at a decorous pace for short distances) news raced ahead of them.

That meant at every halt there were crowds waiting to plead, beg, demand, negotiate—ever larger crowds, as Ivandred Noth began the arduous process of undoing two generations of oppressive governing in the king's name. Not that he could do much. But at least he could gather eyewitness reports as well as interviews to be forwarded to the gunvaer, who he suspected would take immense pleasure in unraveling the corrupted mess the Nyidris had made of Feravayir.

Quill was there at Ivandred Noth's orders, to take note for the follow-up report to be sent to the king.

Until that night in the winter palace, when Connar suddenly walked in on Quill and Lineas discussing her orders to take Noth's report north, Quill had thought her over-scrupulous in striving to avoid Connar's notice. Quill never gave a thought to his own place in a gathering, beyond standing either against a wall with the other runners, or behind the person he was assigned to in order to assist them. That much was training. But after that encounter—somehow the worse for how little was said—he decided it might be prudent to do the same.

He couldn't understand Connar's attitude. Nor did he understand Connar's silence. Why not talk things out with Lineas? As he employed his old stealth training, avoiding Connar when he could, and taking care to stand out of his line of sight when he couldn't, he tried to imagine himself in Connar's place—if Lineas came to him and said her emotions had changed—but there imagination faltered. He'd be frantic to figure out why. And maybe that would be a terrible thing, to shadow her asking *what did I do, how can I change?* He knew from his own parents' broken marriage that sometimes there was no easy answer.

As for Connar, he was always aware of Quill, but at least the royal runner stayed out of his way—and when he and Rat Noth rode for Parayid Harbor Garrison, leaving Ivandred Noth behind to deal with the tangle of petitions, accusations, demands, and pleas, he lost sight of Quill altogether.

Connar admired everything he saw at Parayid Harbor and garrison. His mood lifted as Jethren's soured. Every sign of order rankled; Rat Noth now made a significant jump in the command structure. If the kingdom went to war, it would be Rat Noth and Stick Tyavayir seconding Connar-Laef, unless Jethren was able to find a way to leap ahead.

When the inspection was over, Connar said, "Everything is exactly the way the king wants it. We might as well ride for the royal city now. Get back before the hot weather."

Seeing Rat moving around with commander's gold on his shoulders, forced words from Jethren. "Is this a temporary appointment?"

Connar flicked a question his way. "What do you mean by 'this'?"

"Noth. Commander here. Father as jarl." Seeing Connar's brow furrow, he added in haste, "I thought the king didn't put sons of jarls at nearby garrisons." His throat spasmed on the words 'the king,' when he had been raised to only speak those words about the man standing before him now.

Jethren's heartbeat thumped as Connar's gaze narrowed. "If it's a problem, then Da will take care of it."

Summer had ripened all through the north when an outrider was spotted by the royal city's outer-perimeter riders.

Word relayed back to the royal castle, and spread from there.

Holly, Noren's personal runner, was carrying a load of sun-dried underclothes upstairs when Dannor Lassad, Bunny's first runner, skidded around the corner and nearly ran her down.

Dannor put out a hand to steady Holly and keep the clothes from falling. "Sorry, sorry," she said and signed. "They've been sighted!"

"They?"

"Connar-Laef is back! That means Rat Noth will be back, and Bun will be wanting to drink gerda-leaf," Dannor went on breathlessly, brown eyes earnest. "But your purple claypot is nearly empty."

Holly's hands clutched tight on the clothes. "Purple claypot?"

"Yes," Dannor said. "Ranet told me herself, that's the gerda-leaf Noren-Edli-Haranviar uses. Ranet didn't have any for us because she was pregnant, so I've been fetching it from the purple-glaze claypot. Isn't that right? Doesn't everyone share?" Dannor blinked, question widening her eyes.

Holly forced a smile. "Oh, *that* purple-glaze pot! For some reason, I was thinking of the *other* purple pot, you know, with the sweetgrass Noren likes strewn on her sheets." Dannor was too young, and too uncritical in her admiration of Noren's runners, to question. "Of course!" Holly exclaimed. "But I was just going to fetch more, after I finished the laundry here. I'll bring you some, shall I?" she babbled.

Dannor's face brightened. "Thank you! I have so much to do to get ready. Bun will want all Rat's things aired so his runners won't have to, and . . ." She ran off, enumerating all the tasks that had sprouted up faster than spring mushrooms.

Holly whistled softly as she let herself into the haranviar suite across from Noddy's. She spotted Noren sitting alone, writing home as she usually did on Restday. Ranet and Bun were nowhere in sight. Dropping the underthings onto the nearest surface, Holly caught Noren's eye, and her fingers blurred as she explained what had just happened.

Noren's face paled.

Holly flapped a hand outward, made Dannor's sign, and added, "I told her I'd fetch her some gerda. But should I put it in the old clay pot, or give her a new one? What should I do?"

Noren thought rapidly. "Poor Bun! No wonder she didn't get pregnant before they rode south. It certainly wasn't for lack of trying. We can't raise suspicions. Wash out the purple pot. Get real gerda in it. Give it to Dannor, and let her think we'll continue to share it. We'll keep my herb in here. That's safest."

Holly pelted off to do her bidding. Noren slipped out to alert Ranet that Connar was arriving soon, knowing that Ranet's back had been giving her trouble so late in her pregnancy. She liked a lie-down when she could get one.

The entire family had gathered on the wall to welcome Connar's company as they galloped through the gates. By now Connar had enough experience to be aware of the honor—and the family loyalty implied—of the king being on the wall to welcome him every time he returned.

His gaze swept over Bun, who tried to hide her sharp disappointment when she saw that Rat was not with them. His attention snagged briefly on Ranet, red-faced from the heat, her stomach huge. Connar raised his hand in salute to the women, his smile warming when he saw Danet looking tough as ever, though grayer.

By the time the company dismounted in the courtyard, Arrow and Noddy had come down to greet him. Connar clasped them both, saying, "I'll make my report now, so I can get it out of my head. I've been thinking of nothing else these past few days."

"You were brilliant, Connar. Brilliant!" Arrow said, falling into step beside him.

Connar sent him a quick look. Was that sarcasm? Connar was braced for the verbal trimming he deserved after his blunder, riding into the most obvious trap this side of the ten-year-olds in the academy, just because he'd assumed the Nyidris were too stupid to plot a trap within a trap.

But Da's tone and his smile were genuine. His and Noddy's both. As they walked out of the sunshine into the familiar dusty scent of the tower, Arrow rubbed his hands as he said, "I didn't understand exactly what happened with the Tax Gang. Noth wrote that you'd explain it. But using yourself as bait to draw that shit of a jarlan in, then clapping them all up with those reinforcements—which you'd already mustered—brilliant. And in the middle of winter!"

"What exactly did Noth say? So I don't just repeat what you already know."

Arrow flipped up his palm. "Not much. His reports are always on the short side: what he saw, what he said, what he ordered. Numbers. Since he wasn't actually there until the end, he said your report would carry the details. Since we knew you were all right, we decided to wait to hear it from you, rather than pester you to write it all out while you were finishing up down there."

Noddy opened his hand in silent agreement.

"Noth in place—which was what I always wanted—the Nyidris out. Everything perfect. Well, as much as can be expected. Your mother was sorry to lose one of her coming captains in the Cassad girl. She was surprised at her being married off to the Nyidri boy, I mean the one not dead. But your Lineas explained the strategy to her."

Connar's mouth tightened sardonically at that *your Lineas,* which went unnoticed by the king, who continued, "After your report, I want to talk to you about the academy. This is Andaun's last year as headmaster. Noddy's been up there with him, learning what to do. Noren, too, when she can."

Noddy spoke up earnestly. "I'm not trying to take your rightful duty. I wrote everything down that I learned, the way I did at Larkadhe. I can give you those reports."

Arrow broke in as they mounted the last few steps to the second floor. "But there's also the inspection in the northwest, a year overdue. The Nob has sent two insulting letters, as usual, pointing out that the treaty silver is overdue." He puffed, his voice husky. "But none of that has to be decided at this moment. Your report can wait a while. Go on. Your Ma and the girls want you first, then get a bath and something to eat. We can wait." He lifted his hand toward the door, and the queen's suite on the other side of the hall.

There they were, having followed up the stairs. They clustered inside Danet's interview room. Connar crossed the hall, to be greeted by a chorus of female voices and hands flickering.

Ma kissed him, told him she was proud of him, and then practically pushed him out the door again, into the arms of Ranet, sweaty and blotchy-faced from the summer heat, waddling with that gigantic belly. He didn't dare touch her. Would it hurt her?

She launched into a stream of talk, having considered for days and nights what to say. Only matters that would directly interest him. She began with what Iris had learned—how smart she was—and went on to possible baby names, and when he had nothing to offer, but agreed to everything she said, she moved on, talking faster, to how many of the girls from the queen's training had been sent to which garrison, which was something he already knew.

He stared haplessly during this stream. What was he supposed to be doing? She was already pregnant, so Ma couldn't be going on about that duty. Then he remembered his da's parting remark about duty.

This duty was done, but that one wasn't. As soon as she paused, expectantly, he said, "Those girls you and Noren have sent are great. Good as the new boys. Some better." And when she smiled, he said quickly, "I'd best get down to the garrison. I didn't give any orders."

He hadn't even asked to see Iris, napping twenty steps away. Her throat tight, Ranet stepped aside so that he could make his escape.

As he started down the back stairs to the garrison, he glanced around for Jethren, orders forming on his lips. But Jethren wasn't in his usual spot at his heels. Of course he wouldn't be there. Even Fish couldn't follow him to the king's rooms, or into his wife's, unless bidden.

Fish wasn't in Connar's rooms. Jethren wasn't lurking in his usual spot on the landing.

Hauth.

Was Fish still reporting to him? Connar remembered that Hauth spent a lot of his free time at the quartermaster's—that was where Hauth had yapped all that shit about dolphin clan and how Connar was supposed to knife his family in the back to become king. Jethren was also some sort of relation, as he recollected. Sneeze Ventdor had made that plain enough. And Connar remembered that silent salute in the stable annex.

It was all tied to Hauth.

He slowed at the first landing, and on impulse turned from the well-traveled route and ducked into one of the old tunnels that would put him on the back route to the quartermaster's. He jinked through an archway, and into a court stashed with winter shutters and other gear, where he chose a vantage from which he could see the tunnel door that emptied directly opposite the quartermaster's side door.

Fish was indeed on his way, partly to get it over with before his father sent someone to summon him. But this time he'd figured out what to say that should get this burden off his back, which meant he had to get there before Jethren did.

He used shortcuts that Jethren didn't know because he was too arrogant to ask. Sure enough, there was Hauth waiting. Fish repeated the gist of the official reports, adding, "Connar is as silent as ever. I can tell you what he did, but not what he said. Certainly not what he thinks. For that, you'll have to ask Jethren."

Hauth sat there, fingering the edge of the scroll that had become sacred to him, its meaning still pondered in the stillness of the night. "Kethedrend Jethren? Where is he? Get him."

Fish's lip curled, an expression he'd absorbed from Connar. "He won't come to *my* summons."

Hauth's one eye widened. "You don't discuss the best way to—"

Fish cut in. "I'm too lowly for him to notice. I'd better get back up to the suite," he added, and departed, smiling grimly. Let that shit Jethren deal with the interrogation and the jawing of worthless advice! Hauth never seemed able to understand that there was no telling Connar anything he didn't want to hear.

That was the smile Connar saw as he watched from behind a tower of stored baskets. Just Fish, still reporting to Hauth. As expected. He'd known that about Fish since the beginning. But no Jethren.

He waited where he was, just in case, but Jethren never appeared; finally Connar moved away, aware that someone from the garrison, if not from his family, would come looking for him if he stayed away too long. And he had learned enough.

Jethren had also been on his way to the quartermaster's, having dismissed Moonbeam to carry his things over to the garrison. He was moving through the stable to the back court along the winding public route. Mentally he totted up all the triumphs he had to report as he crossed the court, and was turning the corner to pass between the winter tack storage and the bootmaker's when white pain exploded across his head.

He reeled, hands coming up ready for battle, but before he could lash out, a familiar grip took his wrist.

He dropped his other hand. "Da," he exclaimed in protest. "What's that for? We *won*."

Halrid Jethren curled his lip. "Whining?"

Keth Jethren stilled, knowing from his earliest days that any tone of voice that could possibly be considered whining would only bring on more pain, along with *I'll give you something to whine about*. That was the core of Vaskad training: control of all emotions, everything focused on strength.

"We won," his father mimicked. "What's this 'we'? Where were you during this win? Holding the reins? Waving the wand over horse shit? All I hear is Noth here, Noth there, forever Noth, Noth, Noth. When I am going to hear *your* name, at the king's right hand?"

"I'm there." Keth Jethren knew better than to touch his jaw where the fist had landed, though the throbbing was insistent enough that his right eye was tearing. "As for the Noths, there's a lot of 'em. The new jarl. Rat. Mouse, at Hesea Garrison. Even the ones at Old Faral. They all got into it."

At Halrid's interrogative grunt, his son gave a succinct account of the winter palace action, prudently leaving out that they had ridden unknowingly into a trap. His father actually flickered a smile when he described killing Ryu Nyidri.

When he fell silent, Halrid flicked a glance at the other end of the narrow passage, at where Tigger, his brother, stood on watch, in case anyone strayed into the back court. His blond brows met as he considered the report, then he said, "You've got to tell the true king that Mathren's first lesson in strategy warns of anyone else being able to whistle up an army—"

Keth Jethren couldn't prevent the snort of derision. "Mention the name Mathren and see what you get." That stopped Halrid. "Why are you here? Why not wait until I reached the quartermaster's, like usual?"

Halrid's blond brows knit and his gaze shifted. "Fact is, Ret Hauth turned on us."

"What?" Jethren squawked in flat disbelief. Hauth would never turn against the true king.

Nor had he. Uncle Tigger spoke up from the corner. "Tossed us out."

Yeah, that sounded more like it, his da getting into it with Hauth, maybe trying to give orders. Keth Jethren squelched an almost overwhelming urge to laugh; his ribs actually throbbed briefly with the need to let it out.

Halrid hissed a sigh through his teeth. "Hauth seems to think he's the expert on these eagle-clan shits, but what progress has he made in putting the true king on the throne? None, that I can see. I told him it was past time to loose the Vaskad boy on the eagle clan, like he's been promised all his life. Give him half an hour. Quarter of an hour, he'll have them all dead before any one of these guards stirred a foot."

"And Connar would never rest until he hunted you down," Keth Jethren said grimly. "He'd cut you up himself, and he wouldn't make it fast."

Halrid's gaze shifted. "You'd think he'd be grateful. We will make him *king!* I know, I know, he's had his ears filled with poison from that shit Anred Olavayir. And for some reason he likes that bucktoothed rockbrain of an heir." His gaze returned, fierce with conviction. "It's your job to set him right. And help him to the throne he was meant to hold."

"And I will. But when I move up the chain of command. Which I would have done long ago if I'd gone to the academy with him."

Halrid's gaze narrowed, his fist tightening, but Kethedrend's tone was flat—observation. Halrid already suspected he might have made an error in refusing Jarend Olavayir's offer to send Kethedrend along with the Ventdor boys to the academy. But he hadn't wanted to risk his carefully raised boy being exposed to eagle clan poison.

He spoke forcefully, to convince his son—and himself—that he'd been right. "I told you then. Our training is better. Tougher. You're a leader. If you're good enough, he'll see it."

Kethedrend believed he was good enough. But he could be better than Inda-Harskialdna, and still not break that academy bond, which Connar wasn't even aware of. Resentment burned, a ball of fire behind his ribs, as his father went on, "Get it done, before the Vaskad assassin does something that draws attention to us."

"Moonbeam won't do anything unless I tell him to."

"For now," Halrid warned. "Crazy as he is, one of these days he's going to figure out that he's not only faster and stronger than you, but he's older, so why should he dog your shadow?"

Because I'm the only one who knows how to dose him out of seeing his ghosts, Keth Jethren thought, but out loud he said, "He understands chain of command."

Halrid gave a snort of disbelief.

Tigger turned his head. "Voices."

Halrid said, "We're going back home until Ret cools down. I've got my ears here. I want to hear progress."

He and his brother walked away, vanishing around the corner.

Jethren set out in the other direction, moving toward the garrison, gingerly working his jaw. But there was nothing he could do about the swelling; when he reached the garrison, and somebody said, "What happened to you?"

"Horse," Jethren said shortly.

Jarid Noth overheard, looked at the rapidly bruising side of Jethren's face, and said, "It happens. Especially at the end of a long ride, they'll kick out all of a sudden. Go to the ice house. Put some in a sock. Hold it to your jaw to keep the swelling down."

Jethren saluted, knowing the commander meant well. But nobody knew more about wounds and bruising than Nighthawk men.

FOURTEEN

The next day, Connar went over to the academy with Noddy for Firstday inspection.

At first it was fun to see the adulation in the boys' eyes, but that wore off fairly quickly. By the end of that long day, he understood that though he was the prospective head of the academy in name, he wasn't really in command. Andaun, the actual masters, even Noren, all made it clear that he needed to reread the Gand Handbook, and to listen to how things were done, lest this change or that lead straight to the days of Bloody Tanrid. By the night watch he was tired of hearing, "Oh they tried that in Year Whatever, and . . ." before moving on to a lecture illustrating the disastrous result.

Before the brothers parted for the night, Noddy brought the painstakingly written notes he'd promised, and held them out. Connar looked from the stack of closely written papers up to Noddy's trusting face, understanding that Noddy really liked this duty, the same way he'd liked sitting with all those babblers up at Larkadhe. But here he was, ready to give it up at a word.

"Noddy, why don't you take Andaun's place? That is, I know Da wants me as chief, just because I'm commander. But why don't we share it? Da won't mind that, I'm certain. You be in charge of these things." He indicated the papers. "I'll back you up. And sit with you at Victory Day, and whenever else you think best, if I'm not in the field. Like now. I should get on the road to the Nob before the season gets much later."

Noddy grinned happily. "Sure. If that's what you want."

That night, as rain roared overhead, Connar roamed the sentry walk under the canopies. He was alone for once.

Mindful of his father's exhortations, Jethren had been watching Connar from afar, and chose his moment to ask the only question Connar always accepted—and which sometimes elicited actual answers besides the obvious: "New orders?" Which was as close as he dared come to *What are you thinking?*

Connar muttered, mostly to himself, "Frozen Falls was a rescue. Not a victory."

Jethren said only, "Yes."

Connar flicked a glance his way, aware of conditional approval as Jethren watched a pair of sentries moving along the opposite wall, their silhouettes through the curtain of rain making the torchlight wink out then back in. Connar recollected that Jethren hadn't rushed off to the quartermaster's the way Fish had—he'd gotten kicked in the head by a horse, but reported to the stable anyway, to get orders. He followed orders. He fought hard. Didn't jabber.

Connar's attention shifted back to that near-disaster down south. Jethren had taken out Artolei and Ryu without leaving evidence, and hadn't said a word to anyone. To the end Noth had speculated about who might have killed them, from which side.

It was Hauth himself, long ago, who had said about Fish, *Make him loyal to you.* There might be something in that after all.

Connar said to Jethren, "Choose a reliable company to take on the inspection tour to the Nob. They don't need to be fast so much as good with all weapons."

Jethren looked as if he'd been given a year's liberty. "I'll have the list by morning," he promised.

And he did.

Two days before they were to ride for the northwest, Ranet sent her runner to fetch Connar, reporting breathlessly, "She's having birth pains."

Connar bit back the words, "What am I supposed to do about it?" Clearly he was expected to interrupt his tight schedule to go sit and wait, though he'd done his part of that particular duty last autumn. It was now her turn to do hers.

But the runner gazed at him eagerly, so he said, "I'll be there as soon as I can."

He thought he was reasonably fast, but it turned out Ranet's baby was faster. Connar arrived at her suite to discover that she'd had another girl. Not the prince everyone was waiting for.

Connar stared down at the blotchy baby-face, aware that he was actually relieved it was a girl. Rat Noth was safely tied down at Parayid. So far, Noddy hadn't gotten Noren pregnant. He felt a twinge of regret at that, solely on Noddy's behalf. He knew Noddy wanted children as badly as Ma, but as far as Connar was concerned princes could wait ten, even twenty years to be born. He'd barely begun the duty he'd always wanted. There was already Andas running around somewhere up north. Connar saw no need for ambitious princes to be crowding his back until he was old.

He smiled at Ranet and returned the infant as Ma, Noren, and their runners kept flailing their fingers and cooing. What can you really say about a baby except that it's there?

He made his escape for the garrison, oblivious to Ranet's long, thoughtful gaze following him out the door.

Danet saw. "Some people just don't know what to do with babies," she said to her daughter-by-marriage. "I was that way until I had my own. I think my mother was even more so. As I recollect, she had no interest in us until we were ready to learn how to do chores. I followed my older cousin around, and my sister followed me. Connar will take an interest when the girls start riding. You'll see."

Ranet buried her nose in the sweet curve between the baby's jaw and little round shoulder, snuffing up the ineffable infant smell. Tears prickled her eyelids. Connar hadn't been there when Iris was born, so she'd made excuses for him not knowing what to do with her when they finally met. But he'd shown an equal disinterest in Little Hliss's birth, which he could have attended if he'd wanted.

She said nothing to Danet-Gunvaer. That would only hurt her. But after the gunvaer left, Ranet poured out her bitterness to Noren, safe in the knowledge that no one could overhear them.

She finished up, her fingers snapping with emotion, "When Lineas gave me advice, she was too kind to say that what I felt was a mere heat, but it's the truth. How can you love someone you don't know? I don't know Connar. He doesn't talk to me at all."

She brushed her lips over Little Hliss's feathery eyebrows and along the contours of her soft, fragile skull, remembering how, after Connar had departed following their marriage, she'd gone into his rooms when no one was around to see her. At first it gave her such intense pleasure to catch his scent, how heat pooled deep inside her. Even seeing his old shirts packed neatly in a trunk spiked heat. But gradually that scent had faded, or else the heat had, and after he left last winter she'd come to see that she was trying to learn someone by standing in an empty room. It was far too emblematic of what marriage with Connar was like.

"Find a favorite," Noren responded when she looked up again. "Several favorites."

Ranet knew that was the practical solution. If only it was so easy! Nobody got her as hot as Connar. Not even close.

She looked down at Little Hliss. There were two other couples who could give the gunvaer that longed-for prince. It didn't have to be her. She had to be strong. Since she still found Connar attractive, if he came to her, she'd let him in. But she promised herself not to wait outside his door anymore. It only hurt her. At least until he demonstrated any interest in the two children they already had together.

Two days later, he was gone, and up on the third floor, Lineas and Quill were aware of a sense of release. Quill was already buried in tasks as head of the royal runners, thankfully handed off by Mnar Milnari.

Lineas had hoped to teach, and dreaded being sent off on another run, but it turned out she was to do neither. Arrow had handed off to Noddy certain state wing responsibilities he secretly found too onerous these days.

Noddy had plenty of helpers, but none of them quite fit the comfort of the routine he'd established with Lineas at Larkadhe. On her arrival back, he'd asked for her one day, then another, until it was understood through the castle that she was to be reassigned to Noddy in the state wing—where she, Noddy, and Vanadei settled back into their old routine.

Summer ripened to Lightning Season, then gradually waned.

The inspection at Larkadhe went well, as Connar expected. Same at Lindeth. At both places, Connar was warned about the Nob.

"Even if they know you're bringing the treaty silver, they'll still go for you," Nermand warned. "Attacking us seems to be the favorite sport of Bar Regren."

He'd replaced his father the previous year. Young Nermand was the same breezy person he'd been at the academy. Two or three years of enthusiastic sex play in the academy baths and at rec time lay between him and Connar, making it easier for Connar to talk to him than to most; Nermand's eye, and smile, made it clear he was quite ready to take up where they'd left off.

But Connar had resolved to stay away from anyone in his direct chain of command. He'd heard too many stories about the expectations of favorites. Sex he could get anywhere. Good captains were rarer.

So he remained oblivious to the lazy heat in Nermand's gaze and stayed with what mattered. "I expected them to attack an inspection company, but the Bar Regren will go for us even if we're carrying their damned treaty coinage?"

"Of course." Nermand flipped up the back of his hand toward the north. "They'll mask like bandits, steal everything they can carry, then send a messenger to the king, squalling that we still haven't done our duty. Learned that back in our great-grandfathers' day."

"We'll be ready for 'em," Connar said, thinking *Let them come.*

The Marlovans rode armed, ready and alert. They passed Chalk Hills, a vivid memory. No sign of anything except rocks and trees, but Connar could feel inimical eyes watching.

Jethren's scouts also rode armed, their numbers doubled. What they met was rockfalls at treacherous turns along the narrow mountain trail, and poison streams. The entire company had to halt to clear the rocks, and horses and animals had to line up to drink from the three ensorcelled buckets, which took an exasperatingly long time. Connar was certain he heard laughter drifting on the wind.

The ride up the peninsula, grueling even at the best of times, was torture during the heat of summer, slowed by these hostile actions to which the Marlovans could not respond.

They finally made it to the harbor called the Nob, dragging those the carts of coinage, which the Nob insisted on instead of other types of trade for their due. The harbormaster met Connar, and prolonged the tedium by speaking in some incomprehensible dialect before painstakingly spitting out one Marlovan word at a time.

Connar was soon wearied of the complicated economic life of the harbor town, whose supplies mostly came in by sea, paid for by Marlovan silver. In retaliation for the covert maltreatment, Connar insisted on the harbormaster's stringers accounting for every tinklet they spent, and also demanded to see the tally books. He retained just enough of his mother's lectures about such matters to know at least where to look on a page, but mostly he grimly kept them waiting before him, marinating in their own sweat as he stared down at those dull columns of numbers, every now and then pointing randomly to a line and asking for explanation, as he dreamed about setting fire to the entire town.

Jethren stood by, armed with at least six visible weapons, a smile as thin as a knife blade on his otherwise impassive face. Behind him lurked Moonbeam, lovingly whetting a knife. The sight of the three of them dampened some of the long-planned, exquisite insolence—but the locals got some of their own back again when the Marlovans departed, riding down the treacherous south coast to face more destroyed trails, rockfalls, and twice, fire. The locals knew their mountains to each rock and blade of tough grass, and managed to vanish entirely after every act.

When, at last, in the swelter of late summer, Connar reached Lindeth, as soon as he saw Nermand, he said, "Why are we doing this Nob run again?"

"Bad, was it?" Nermand asked, with the sympathy of one who'd been forced to do the duty off and on since leaving the academy. And, seeing that Connar wanted an answer, "It's the treaty."

Connar gazed out at the sunlight winking on the sea, and the ships bobbing gently on the water, bare poles inscribing slow circles. "Why did we make that treaty?"

Nermand opened his hands. "They talked about it enough when we had those history lectures our first year out of the scrubs."

Connar eyed Nermand, who looked merely puzzled, no accusation. "I didn't listen to anything about the sea," he admitted. "My future was the army."

Nermand accepted that with an indolent wave of his hand. "I probably would've done the same, if the king hadn't made it clear from my first day at the academy that he expected me to replace my da here at Lindeth. The treaty put us there as lookouts, back in the day. Mostly for the Venn. But also for pirate fleets. Our ancestors always dreaded the Venn landing big armies at the Nob and marching 'em down to take us here at Lindeth, then over at Larkadhe, and cut off the north from the south. Pirates burned the city at least twice."

Connar would just as soon they burned it again. "But the Venn are bottled up," he said out loud. "And I haven't heard of any big pirate empires except in old stories."

"True." Nermand flicked his fingers in agreement. "Also true that a fast tender is just as effective at keeping watch off the Nob, and is far faster than horseback in bringing bad news down the peninsula to us here. That's what we've been doing the past generation or two. But we still have to hold the Nob," he said reasonably—and unanswerably. "It's the treaty."

Three months later, "It's the treaty," Arrow said in exactly the same tone as Nermand had used.

Rain roared against the windows, which runners had pushed shut and locked until next spring. It was late autumn, and the entire castle was beginning the arduous task of preparation for Convocation at New Year's Week.

Arrow had already put on his winter coat, his body skinny beneath it. Connar hated seeing the signs of his aging—the thinning white hair, his bloodshot eyes. But those eyes were still alert. "It's what every king has said, and will say." He flicked a glance at Noddy, who opened his hand in assent. "Our ancestors made that treaty."

"To watch for the Venn. But the Venn aren't coming. They can't get past the Federation of Kingdoms blockage up north," Connar said.

"No. But there's also the Idegans," Arrow retorted. "You've only seen the south side of those mountains. I was never there, but my da told us how nasty that ride was, frequently along narrow cliffs. Well, the entire north side of that peninsula is different. Nice towns, even farmland in those valleys. The Idegans are in constant trouble with the mountain Bar Regren, but to them it's worth it to hold the north shore. They want the Nob so they can watch for trouble coming up from the sea on the south side. The truth is, we hang onto the Nob so they can't have it. I owe that much to my cousins who rode up there to find a bride and ended up dead." He looked away, not wanting to admit that while he thought Lanrid had been a horseapple, he still heard Sinna singing in his dreams.

"Ah," Connar said. "You think if we break the treaty, the Idegans'll take it?"

"I'm sure of it. I had to swallow that slaughter when Lorgi Idego broke off, and by the time I was strong enough to retake the north, I had a better idea of what we'd lose if I went after them. They fight like us. It wouldn't be easy, or fast. Your ma had plenty to say about the cost. So we trade, and the letters go back and forth nice. Hal even seems like a decent enough fellow. But I don't see any reason to hand them the Nob as a present. And half the jarls agree, which is why all the arguing."

"Do you think the Idegans would win against the Bar Regren?"

"Just like you did. Twice. From the report I got back from Camerend back then, the Bar Regren all go on about personal bravery and kills and the like. No notion of training other than hand to hand. You probably saw the truth of that. I know they saw it at Ku Halir."

Connar turned up his hand. Rat had reported much the same.

"But it would be a tough and bloody fight. Anyway, we're stuck with the Nob. So . . . we have that treaty silver to deliver, as stipulated in the treaty."

Connar sighed inwardly, and resolved that the next time the silver had to go north, he'd send someone else.

Arrow's mind ran along the same trail. "Might next time send someone you trust. No reason you have to do it, now you've done it. Seen what it entails."

Connar opened his hand in heartfelt agreement.

Arrow rubbed his thumbs along the upper edge of his eye sockets. "Right. Another thing. Happened not long after you left. Nearly forgot, what with one thing and another." It was close enough to the bell . . . he reached for his cup.

Connar noticed his father's fingers tremble a little. Arrow saw the direction of his gaze, snapped his hand into a fist, and sat back on his mat. "Braids Senelaec is the new chief of the Eastern Alliance. Old Amble Sindan, who has twenty years on me, is retiring to run a stud out of Dustdancer."

Connar remembered hearing that the Eastern Alliance horse studs started with some famous horse, often keeping the name long after the horse had died of old age. Dustdancer was reputed to be as fast as Rat Noth's Grasshopper.

Arrow continued, "He traded for some mares out of Algaravayir."

Connar's interest sparked. "That mare Noren was running when she first came to the Victory Day games?"

"Two mares. Her daughters," Arrow said. "Anyway, Braids being their new chief, I felt it in our best interest to shift him to detached duty, reporting to your Stick Tyavayir at Ku Halir."

Connar suppressed annoyance at this news of his carefully thought out command structure changed. But it was the king's right. Further, Connar knew he would have done the same. Braids as Eastern Alliance chief represented an enormous potential force. Not heavy, but fast. And more easily launched in any direction if Braids was roving in the area of possible trouble, rather than locked down at one or another of the garrisons. But.

Connar looked up. "I thought the Eastern Alliance chief was never a jarl. Not that Braids is a jarl. But he will be."

"I thought the same thing. Braids wasn't going to be the jarl until the Ku Halir battle, which also boosted his rep. Amble always wanted him, and the jarls had all agreed on him, clear back when he first got out of the academy. They seem to think it won't be a problem, his being a jarl, too. Now that he's married to Henad Tlennen, he'll be bringing in Tlennen cousins to help at

Senelaec. Anyway, the alliance always picks their chief. I'm not about to interfere with *that*."

Connar turned up his palms. "If they don't see a problem then there isn't a problem. I couldn't pick anyone better than Braids myself. Any other news?"

Arrow waved a hand, then fisted it when he felt the incipient tremble. "Nothing but the usual gabble about troublemakers up in the northern mountains, mostly from the Ghildraith."

That sounded promising! "Better go inspect myself."

"It was not much but rumor so far," Arrow felt obliged to add, seeing the flare of excitement widening Connar's eyes, the sudden, quick grin. He didn't remember Connar being one of those happiest riding hard toward blood and steel. But his expression was unmistakable. Arrow was thrown back in memory for a heartbeat. Lanrid had sometimes worn that same grin, usually just before he scragged somebody.

Strange, how expressions showed up in people who might be related, but hadn't met the other. When in certain moods, Noddy sometimes called Jarend to mind, the brother Arrow still sorely missed, though they hadn't seen one another since Jarend rode north in '60. And now they never would—unless Jarend turned up as one of the ghosts people insisted haunted the castle.

"No need," Arrow said quickly, smothering *that* thought. "Winter will be on us before you get there. Also, I told Braids to ride in for Convocation. Quill said I ought to have him report to you himself."

"Quill?" Connar repeated.

"Sensible. Like Camerend. When he's here, I always ask him to bring news he's heard on his travels. I can ask him things. He reads a lot. Like his father. I told you both, Camerend was the one who kept your mother and me from being scragged by Mathren's men after that bloodbath. I know I told you."

Connar opened his hand. It was true. Arrow had repeated the story several times, until they were tired of it. Connar and Noddy had grown up hearing "Camerend says" . . . and now he was hearing "Quill says."

"You can always ask us, Da," he said before thinking.

"What?" Arrow blinked, then slewed sideways to gaze at him.

"Us. Noddy and me. You don't need Quill." And seeing the confusion in Arrow's face, "When you were first king, you didn't have anyone except for Camerend. Now you have us. Not runners. Who are just runners."

Arrow thought, *Am I doddering?* He said slowly, "I'm not new to that damn throne." He said it in a joking tone, but his expression was not his joking expression. Connar wasn't quite sure how to interpret it.

But this he knew: he'd made a mistake. He said quickly, "What I meant was, you've taught Noddy and me, and now we're ready to help. Whenever you want us. Don't need to haul in the royal runners, like you did then."

Arrow saw Connar's shock of realization, followed by a flinch of regret, and forced a laugh. "Noddy says the same. Well, not about the royal runners, truth to speak. He likes having them at hand. You know how he is. He's made a scribe of that red-haired one, what's her name, used to be Bunny's first. You know who I mean, you and she were—"

"Lineas," Connar cut in dryly.

"That's the one. Anyway, Noddy keeps her and Vanadei doing scribe duty, because he likes to go over and over the reports, and then rehearse what he wants to say. And they don't get burrs under the saddle, because they know his ways. So since they're right there, I use 'em too, the way I did Camerend."

Connar sensed question in Arrow's tone, and decided to drop the matter. It wasn't as if the royal runners were any threat whatsoever. He just didn't want them around unless he had orders to give them. Then he had the satisfaction of seeing their backs.

He said, "I'm glad you told Braids to ride in."

Arrow thumped his fist on his knee. "Good. Thought you might. He'll come down with Wolf, who I'm told wants to be at Convocation. Though I don't know how, considering he still can't stand, much less sit a horse. Damn. Convocation! Half the castle is already scrambling about, starting to get ready. Seems like the last one just ended."

Connar remembered the previous Convocation, and all that jawing he'd endured from the jarls in a single day. Once again spoke without thinking. "Why not go to every five years? Or longer?"

Arrow grunted. "It would be . . . comfortable. But Danet is right when she says discomfort is our tax."

"Tax?" Connar repeated, as Noddy opened his hand in agreement.

"When I was your age, I thought I'd be randael in Olavayir. When I blundered, all that'd happen was my da would give me a jawing. My brother would be jarl. Then Mathren's murdering everyone right and left me the only man standing, and I got stuck as king. Though I was still the same man, it meant that, when I blunder people die. Convocation is my tax."

He squinted at Connar, headache panging at his temples. He longed for a drink, but time was crawling. It was far too early. The healer had scowled at him before going on at length about drunkenness. Arrow was *not* a drunk. He couldn't afford to get drunk. He was very careful about that. He drank just enough.

The problem was, the day seemed to get longer and longer before the mid-watch bell at five, when the day was nearly done and he could relish that first sweet sip.

Sometimes when he almost got the shakes like this, his head aching and his mouth dry, it helped to move around. Cool off. "Come on. Let's go down to the yard. Noddy's got the new boys from the academy seniors doing lance evolutions around this time. You might as well see how they're shaping up."

FIFTEEN

Maddar Sindan-An, Cabbage Gannan's wife, stood back and eyed the fine House tunic Kendred, Cabbage's first runner, had finished sewing. Then she turned to Cabbage's current favorite, Fnor-Tailor (differentiated from Fnor-Beekeeper), who had selected the fabric and supervised the dyeing.

Old Stalgoreth's colors had been green-edged gold, but only Marlovan kings could have gold. Cabbage hadn't wanted to use his family's colors of purple-edged green—they were supposed to be Stalgoreths now, not Gannan, anyway—so Maddar had suggested the opposite.

But purple was a very tough dye to sustain through a lot of fabric, so Fnor-Tailor had recommended compromising on a purplish blue with green edging, with no device as yet. Cabbage was afraid to choose one without the king's approval.

Cabbage eyed himself in the polished steel, scowling. "Does it make me look false? Like I'm pretending, or something? Who wears green on blue? Or maybe you're right about the device, and we should go back to the old Stalgoreth, what were those flowering things? At least this looks much better than that moth-eaten old tunic Da wears. As it should, as my jarlate is more than twice the size of Gannan. But what if Connar makes me last of all the jarls, stuck sitting in the back . . ."

Maddar listened to the tone, not the words. When he started talking like this, dithering then bragging, always coming back to Connar Olavayir, she knew he was going back to his old anxious self, the Cabbage lurking under his brother's and father's bullying fists.

"I think this will do. Fold it up," she said to the waiting runners. To Snow, she canted a look.

"And I'm going to make certain they packed that pot of strawberry compote I made," Snow said, following the runner and the servants to the door. "You'll be glad of it long before you reach Ku Halir."

"Cabbage," Maddar said when she and Cabbage were alone with Fnor-Tailor.

Fnor put her hands up on his shoulders, digging her thumbs into the thick muscle there and rubbing in a soothing circle. Maddar looked on approvingly as she considered what to say, and how to say it.

Cabbage was big and strong and brave. The women who got fire for men said he was handsome. Maddar saw in his quick, uncertain temper and his tendency to brag when he was most uncertain, the boy who had been cruelly bullied by his dreadful father and brother. She didn't know if the fact that Cabbage was a terrible judge of character and situations other than fighting was a result of that bullying, or just him. She was glad that he listened to her, but she knew he would listen to anyone who was consistently nice to him. Which made her all the more grateful that he seemed to pick good-hearted women as favorites.

While Fnor expertly rubbed his shoulders, and the tension began to ease from his posture, Maddar said, "You are an excellent jarl. You are also Nadran-Sierlaef's chosen, Commander of his First Lancers. He will be the next king. Connar will take orders from him. It doesn't matter what he thinks of you. You're a jarl now, a king's man."

Cabbage's forehead wrinkled again and he muttered fretfully, "If there's a war, I'll be under Connar."

"And he'll give you the same orders you had at Tlennen Field, when you broke the enemy lines. And when you broke that West Outpost. And wasn't he the one who sent Keth Jethren and his men to you to train in lance tactics? Not to anyone else. To you."

Cabbage sighed. "Yes." He grinned a little. "I tried to recruit him. He'd be great."

Maddar was done with the subject of Keth Jethren, who had reminded her a little too much of Lightning Season in human form. Maybe it was that first runner of his, the one they called Moonbeam. Nobody would tell her what his real name was, and he didn't, or couldn't, speak.

That wasn't what bothered her about Moonbeam. Nor the scars on the visible parts of his body. She'd seen the signs of bullying in him, too. You didn't dare raise your hand inadvertently on the periphery of his vision, for example, or touch him accidentally. But unlike Cabbage, who flinched—and even Jethren, if you came up behind him—Moonbeam would get this crazy look, like he was a breath away from gutting you with one of the knives he always wore. Then other times he'd sit with a flat stare, looking through you, through the walls, as if he watched the sun beyond the world. She had been glad when they left Stalgoreth, and she hoped that Cabbage wouldn't be successful in recruiting either of them back, no matter how good they were with lances.

Shaking off the memory, she said, "You and Connar-Laef might not get along at rec time, but he knows your worth. We all do."

Cabbage began to relax a little at that. But he still fretted. "I don't see why Connar hates me," he mumbled. "He looks at me like a dog turd on the carpet."

"That's his problem. Nobody here looks at you like that. The king thinks highly of you, or he would have put someone else here. Nadran-Sierlaef also thinks highly of you."

Fnor spoke up, adding her fluting voice to Maddar's. "It's true! Just the other day I overheard Cook while putting up the bread telling the steward how good you are to go out weeding the kitchen garden on Restdays, when the kitchen staff gets to sleep in. The people think a good jarl is great on the battlefield, but the *best* jarl is one who cares about them in little ways."

Cabbage's sulky mouth eased, and he muttered, "I like weeding. Clears my head." His voice lightened. "The people in the northern trade towns salute me when I ride by. And nobody made them do it."

"That's right," Maddar said encouragingly. "They know your reputation, one you've earned. So ride down to the royal city and take your place among the jarls. You won't even have to look at your father if you don't want to. Have a good time. Go out with Nadran-Sierlaef to your favorite spots. Drink, dance, sing."

Fnor whispered in his ear, "Visit the Sword and get laid. If you learn any new good tricks, bring them back for us to try."

And when Cabbage grinned, Maddar finished, "If there's exhibition riding, tell the boys how great they are, because some of them will want to ride with *you* one day. Have fun, and bring back all the news."

Cabbage Gannan rode out with Riders from the First Lancers—men he'd been with since his days at Lindeth. The few with families had moved them to Stalgoreth, and two of the single men had found local wives. As Cabbage rode away from the enormous castle that the king had bestowed on him and his progeny to come, he smiled past the new banner, streamers snapping in the wind, to the Riders. His father hadn't let him have anyone from Gannan, not that he needed any of them. He was building his own clan. Well, he would as soon as he and Maddar had children. She'd said they would do that after they turned thirty. Too much to do before then. Weird to think thirty wasn't all that far off. *Thirty!*

That buoyant sense of pride and satisfaction carried him down the south road through increasingly sharper weather. At the great crossroads, where the north-south road met the east-west, Cabbage spotted the Senelaec heir's crimson and black pennant outside the posting house. Inside he found Braids loitering, waiting out a storm boiling over the eastern mountains. Braids hailed him with a grin, and Cabbage hosted them to dinner, over which they decided to ride together down to Senelaec, and thence to Convocation.

Cabbage worried about his place in the jarls' hierarchy, and of course, he worried about encountering Connar. Braids worried about his da insisting on going, when he was still so weak. Of them all, the only one with unalloyed anticipation was Kendred, Cabbage's first runner. As a boy at Gannan, he'd found life something to endure. Getting away on Cabbage's army assignments had been good, but there was always the dread of a return to Gannan.

All that had vanished at Cabbage's appointment as jarl, and now Kendred was finally getting to really see the royal city, not just the royal garrison, as had happened on their last, brief stay, before the jarl promotion. Maybe that would include a tour of the famous academy (he suspected Cabbage would not be able to resist bragging, if no other opportunity presented itself), but one thing for sure, he expected to visit pleasure houses he'd only heard about through endless reminiscences for ten years.

The weather continued to be fretful, at best, encouraging as fast a ride as the horses could manage. Braids knew Cabbage of old. An afternoon of enduring the bragging alternating with complaining brought the usual reward. Cabbage settled down, in his own mind having established himself a step higher in hierarchy. Since Braids didn't give a spit for rank, they jogged along amicably, Cabbage falling in with all Braids' carefully worded suggestions (usually preceded by "Do you think we should . . ."), which brought them to Senelaec.

Wolf had never regained his ability to walk. The Senelaec runners and carpenters had experimented with different types of chairs and carts on wheels, finally coming up with one that was small enough to carry Wolf inside and out. It had pegs worked into the frame at the back so it could be raised and lowered into notches.

For this trip to Convocation, they had rigged up a rope-hung raft suspended from a frame, pulled by two powerful horses. It jounced and swung unmercifully, but Wolf insisted that the ropes took the sting out of it —and he kept calling for more speed.

And so they arrived at the royal city at the tail end of a sleet storm, their spirits high at the prospect of being dry, warm, and given hot food they didn't have to watch their runners struggling with in wind-battered tents.

And the royal castle complied. At the first sight of those blue clouds that morning, grizzled Tam, still reigning over the kitchen, had ordered extra spice-wine to be prepared.

Lineas, assigned to welcome duty at the stable that day, had time to reflect on how many in the castle had performed the exact same duty Convocation after Convocation, and so could predict for others what to expect. But her life, which she had thought would follow a similar linear line through the years, had bent and jinked so much that each Convocation since her arrival at age twelve had seen her at a variety of duties.

This year, she alternated with two others in directing new runners. She waited in the summer tack room, which smelled dusty, but the air was marginally warmer than that outside. When the horns for a jarl tooted, she pulled on her gloves and slipped to the stable door.

Keth Jethren had been assigned to welcome jarls. The royal castle had reports from outer perimeter riders, but welcome duty still involved waiting around for the guests to arrive. Jethren hated sitting around. At least his father had gone back to his mining town weeks before. Jethren passed the time waiting by working on double-stick fighting at the nearest court, with a young runner posted at the royal castle stable to warn him as soon as the arrivals were sighted on the horizon. He ran across the length of the castle, arriving as the horns trumpeted the chords for two jarls.

Lineas ducked back as he shot through the courtyard entrance to the tower, and ran right through the Evred ghost that he obviously couldn't see.

Not Evred, Lineas reminded herself. At least, according to Fish, who had said someone recognized the drawing she'd made so badly. The ghost was Lanrid, another Olavayir from the old generation. That was less interesting to her than the question of light: the low clouds made everything gray and dreary, but the ghost was clear as a summer morning. Yet that ghost-light, wherever it came from, cast no shadows.

Hooves and cart wheels clattered through the gate, mud splashing everywhere.

Cabbage Gannan spotted Jethren, and leaped down from his horse. "Jethren! Thought about joining the First Lancers?" Cabbage asked, warm in his conviction that his question would be heard as the compliment he intended. "Offer still open."

Jethren had endured a full season of Cabbage Gannan's bragging; one day he had counted how many times the walking turd had begun a sentence with *When I was in the academy*. The same academy Jethren should have gone to, to train with the future king. He said neutrally, though it hurt him to the back teeth, "I'm under orders."

Cabbage never knew when to let go—not that he, or anyone, could read Jethren. "I could speak to Connar."

"As you will," Jethren said, and turned away before he could drive a fist into that smug, superior face. "I'm to direct you. The jarls are here, along the first floor." He indicated the tower behind him. "Courtyard entrance. Your Riders will be up in the southern wing, there." He pointed along the wall to his left, to crenellations barely visible.

Cabbage glanced around. "Kendred will see to that," he said unnecessarily, with a peremptory gesture. "Where is everyone gathered?" He could scarcely wait to see his banner bestowed in the throne room.

"They're all over the castle. If you want something to drink, your first runner can bring it, or if you want it still hot, there's the captains' mess over garrison-side."

Before Cabbage could prolong this inane conversation by asking for a list of who had arrived, Jethren turned to Wolf and snapped his fingers to his chest in salute as Wolf was eased out of his travel cart by his devoted runners, and into his push-cart.

Cabbage blinked at Jethren's broad back, then decided of course the greeters had to make a fuss over old Wolf Senelaec, who couldn't even stand up without help.

And so Cabbage left, as Lineas, in a quieter and much friendlier manner, was answering Cabbage's first runner's questions.

Kendred had immediately recognized Lineas as the skinny, freckle-faced girl who had put him down hard that day so long ago, before Cabbage's first assignment at Lindeth. He remembered it not because of that (though he still didn't know how she'd done it, as it certainly wasn't superior strength, she being half his size) but because the aftermath had been so very unlike everyday life in Gannan.

At first he'd feared that the food and things waiting outside his tent when he woke so painfully were some kind of threat, or maybe a reminder who'd gotten the best of that fight, but there had been no follow-through. Even stranger, no one else seemed to know about it. He'd waited for the expected chaffing about being dropped by a girl built like a twig. But nobody seemed to know what had happened, and right about the time he could walk without pain, the strange gifts had ceased.

After reaching Lindeth, he'd forgotten her as he got used to a very different life—but she'd come to his notice again not long ago, when runners' gossip brought word of the Lineas with sponge-colored hair whose grass run had brought Rat Noth to Ku Halir just before disaster. There were plenty of Lineases—his grandmother was one—but not with that red hair.

Here she was again, much the same, except that hair had darkened to the color of iron rust. His single question—*Where do I go*—turned into a flood in the face of her easy manner and clear explanation, until one of Braids' runners punched him in the arm, saying, "Come along! I'll show you our digs."

She watched him go, wondering what in her responses had changed him from that tight, wary face and almost surly tone to something like friendliness.

She still wasn't certain what 'friends' meant. That is, she knew what they were. She saw people pair and group so naturally they seemed to have some sense she didn't. Neit was a friend. She had said so. Was it picking people? Neit had picked her.

As she walked alone back inside the stable to finish out the watch, she wondered what people saw when she walked through the world. She'd begun assuming she was mostly invisible, especially when that pairing off happened. Perhaps it was because she forgot she was a 'me' moving through the world, rather than the 'me' observing everyone else and reporting it in detail in her journal, in hopes of understanding.

Another thing she and Quill could talk about—though they never seemed to catch up with all they wanted to say. At least she didn't. And she could ask Neit, when they next saw one another . . . .

In later years no one remembered that Convocation as anything out of the ordinary. Lineas's usual stream of observations did not include anything she found alarming or even remarkable.

Convocation was a list of unending jobs for her, as well as for the other royal runners. Now that Quill was back, Mnar Milnari relinquished the burden of running both training and the constant demand of Convocation. Danet observed with approval the way her daughters-by-marriage helped with second-floor demands. From her perspective, the royal castle hummed with good will as well as order; Arrow whisked Ivandred Noth and those of the jarls he liked up to his rooms, where he could drink as much as he liked.

He and Wolf Senelaec ended up alone on the last day of the year. Well lubricated by spiced wine, Wolf gave Arrow a grim, detailed account of the battle of Ku Halir, until Wolf broke down entirely, and Arrow with him, reflecting that no parent should ever have to lose a child. They drank themselves into insensibility, and woke up to thundering headaches.

Both moved with wincing care through New Year's Firstday as the jarls gathered, Arrow finding the Jarl of Gannan's loud, accusatory voice nearly unbearable. At least Gannan didn't yap as much as usual. He lost his breath fast, for which everyone, even his followers, were grateful.

Cabbage Gannan had expected a warm welcome from Noddy, but he was surprised and delighted to find an equal welcome from Tanrid Olavayir, first of the jarls—who liked anyone Noddy liked. On entering the throne room earlier that Firstday, he gestured, saying, "Come sit with me. I'll be glad to explain anything that's new to you."

With Noddy looking on with a beaming smile, and Arrow indifferent to how the jarls sorted themselves, Cabbage found himself lofted to second place in the hierarchy. The older jarls and their riding captains accepted this as his due as Commander of the First Lancers as well as jarl of one of the largest territories, whatever it was called.

The two new jarls gave their first oaths. Arrow's speech went over well, ending as it did with his much-hailed promise to drop the king's tax back to the usual fifth, now that they had peace. In high moods, they all left the frigid throne room in search of warmth and refreshment. The younger jarls and their first runners or riding-captains-to-be discovered that Cabbage, in a good mood, liked spending freely, which meant convivial evenings in town at which they didn't have to disburse a tinklet.

And so the week passed.

Cabbage avoided his father so assiduously he never heard the praise the jarl heaped on his second son, referring often to hereditary Gannan bravery. The Jarl of Gannan—once he got over the shock of his second son being promoted almost over his head—had come realize how much prestige there was in Cabbage's reputation, and the fact that the royal heir favored him.

That bragging irritated Connar, who already found Convocation useless. He avoided the jarls as much as he could, which made it more difficult to find Braids Senelaec, until he finally sent Jethren for him on Fifthday night.

Jethren located Braids, a slight figure a head shorter than he. Braids and a few riding captains were clowning around in one of the courtyards, Braids sitting on their backs as they did pushups and bet on the number before they collapsed laughing on the icy cobblestones.

Braids was perfectly ready to come at a summons, reminding Jethren of their first meeting, before the trip over Skytalon Peak, when Braids greeted him—then said with obvious regret, "Oh, sorry, sorry, I keep forgetting to salute. I was only at the academy a couple of years. Before that I was a girl. I still don't remember saluting."

In Jethren's mind, Braids' brief academy tenure separated him out from the invisible chain binding Connar together with those academy captains he'd grown up with, a chain he had yet to link himself into.

The two walked up to Connar's suite, where Fish had hot spice wine, last year's darkest ale, and freshly scalded coffee waiting. Braids asked, "Was it your boys doing that lance evolutions exhibition today? My dad said that alone was worth jolting over every pothole in the kingdom, just to see that."

"Half," Jethren said, amused. "The other half were last year's seniors, on fire to impress Nadran-Sierlaef and the Commander of the First Lancers. I take it you don't do lance evolutions over there in Senelaec?"

"Look at me," Braids said, hands out. "Most of us are too light for the lances. Heh, I wanted so badly to try 'em I could taste it, when I got to the academy that year. Until my first practice, when I got knocked clean out of the saddle. And it never got much better," Braids said as Connar indicated with a flick of his eyes for Fish to come forward.

"What'll you have?" Connar asked.

"Whatever everyone else is drinking." Braids flung his hands wide. His cheeks glowed from the two cups of spiced wine he'd already taken aboard. "Me and Pepper Marlovayir, and a couple of others, were pretty much the same as the straw targets after that. I don't think I actually held a lance twice more. We were too valuable being whacked right and left by you heavies. You missed that fun," he added, indicating Jethren. "Though I suspect you had plenty of fun over there at Olavayir."

"Being knocked out of the saddle by Tanrid-Jarl—in those days, Tanrid-Laef," Jethren said with a brief grin as he lifted his tankard of dark ale.

Braids remembered the massive young man sitting at Noddy's right hand at the Firstnight banquet. Someone had pointed him out as the new jarl of Olavayir. "He was never sent to the academy?"

"Uncle Jarend wanted him at home," Connar said, and leaned forward. "Tell me about these rumors up north."

"That's just it. Rumors. Mostly of mercenaries hired by Elsarion, who ran north. Could be real, could be the usual sort of blather. I sent a pair of good scouts up there to poke around. Between 'em they speak several tongues. Including Idegan."

Connar's brows shot up. "You think it's Idegans causing trouble?"

"Nah." Braids put his tankard down. "Why would they? What I told the scouts to find out is first, what's going on. And if there really are organized raids in the far north, who's the target. And do the Idegans know about it."

"That's the north end of Yvana—of Stalgoreth," Connar commented. "Up above the river?"

"Well, even beyond there, actually," Braids said. "The flatlands are definitely Stalgoreth. But north of that, Stalgoreth's borderland, it's rocky and hilly, and there are all kinds of wild legends about those high mountains—winged people—caves with jewels that talk. Whether or not any of that is true, one thing's for sure, the people are stubborn up there. Keep themselves to themselves. Have their own lingo, barely understandable if you know Iascan. They insist the border starts below their hills, and they don't owe allegiance to anyone."

"Then it's not our problem." Connar sat back, arms crossed to hide his visceral reaction to "high mountains." Even starving to death watch after watch was preferable to the repetition of the Skytalon trek.

"Stick Tyavayir said the same."

No surprise there. Connar caught a glance from Jethren, whose mouth had thinned. Yeah, they all felt the same.

Braids turned his palm in the direction of the throne room. "I told the king what Stick said, and *he* said, if raiders smash them and set up housekeeping, then it becomes our problem. But there's nothing more than rumor right now. Which brings me to our idea, that is, my Da and me, well, we've begun training at Senelaec—"

A knock at the door, and Vanadei poked his head in. "King sent me with a summons," he said. "He's with the Jarl of Feravayir. Wants you there to talk about garrison assignments."

Connar rose, but said to Braids, "Report whatever you find out about the north. If there's a threat to our land, you'll be a part of whatever expedition is necessary."

Braids lifted his tankard, then realized belatedly he'd just received an order. The clay vessel sloshed as he switched hands and saluted.

Connar walked out, and the door shut on Jethren's bark of a laugh. "You really don't salute, do you."

Braids mopped ineffectually at his good crimson and black House tunic, smearing ale all over. "Half my company is girls, and the queen never required saluting. Neither does anyone in the Eastern Alliance. And most of my boys were never in the academy. You hear an order, you go do it. I understand the necessity," he added hastily. "It's just, remembering."

Jethren accepted that. It was much the same in Olavayir. He'd had to train himself to remember ordinary saluting. The fist to the true king had been a different matter.

Braids leaned forward. "What I started to tell him was this. Da has this idea, since we're the first line of defense against the eastern border, we ought have our own training. Not just riding and shooting as individuals."

Jethren's eyebrows lifted. "You'll train your own captains?"

"No! The academy does that. There's Connar-Laef, come up through the academy with Rat Noth riding shield for him, Stick Tyavayir and Ghost Fath behind them. Even though I was only around them one year before they were promoted on to the garrisons, I could see they'd been worked into a chain of command we'll have for the rest of our lives."

Jethren's eyes narrowed, and Braids wondered if he was explaining wrong. "What we're doing at Senelaec is drilling the ridings to *be* commanded. Everybody who can't go to the academy can come to us. Everyone says my da is a great teacher. And it's something he can do, now that he can't ride himself."

For the rest of our lives echoed in Jethren's mind. But he rallied. Braids Senelaec did not give orders any more than people came to him for predictions. This was merely drunk talk, enthusiastic drunk talk. "Will your da train lancers?" he asked, reaching for the easy mood of earlier.

"Nah." Braids flat-handed that idea away. "I expect Noddy, that is, Nadran-Sierlaef, will send them all to Stalgoreth for that. The way they did with you."

Jethren understood then, cold running along his nerves. This babbling skirmisher spoke for them all. In their minds, no matter how hard he worked, he was just another lancer under Cabbage Gannan, because he had never been at the academy. The captains Connar-Laef turned to were those he'd been raised with.

The realization lay in his chest like a stone of ice.

He fought aside the reaction as Braids talked on. " . . . big boys get snapped up by everyone else. We go for the fastest, not the strongest. Girls *and* boys, now that the queen is putting the best of her girls in training as skirmishers at the garrisons."

When Braids stopped for breath, Jethren said, "Time to turn in. I've got duty come morning. I don't know about you."

Braids sat upright. "Oh! I think we're riding out." He got up slowly, his head swimming, and made his way out, memory of the conversation fading with the effects of drink.

Jethren followed him, hearing an echo of Braids' voice, *the chain of command we'll have for the rest of our lives.*

Then his mind emptied when he saw the door to the opposite suite open. He slowed, stealing a look inside—and there she was, Connar's wife, perfect in face and form. The rightness of the true king having so perfect a gunvaer . .

. he tried to make that his conscious thought, but desire overwhelmed him, his hot gaze following every curve that Connar's hands had caressed, until she, sensing it, turned and caught it.

Heat flashed through him. But not through her.

It was *him* again. His stare annoyed her. There was too much hunger in it.

She opened her hand in a polite gesture and turned away, addressing the other women he hadn't even realized were in the room, and he went away.

Noddy's Name Day celebration was over except for eating up the leftover tartlets when Danet received a letter from Feravayir. When Noren, Ranet, and Bunny came to her suite as they often did in the long autumn evenings, she said, "Starliss Cassad had a boy."

"Already?" Bunny exclaimed, not without envy.

"She says that she and Demeos have reached a good understanding, and if she's expected to have children, she might as well get it done now than wait. She's Noddy's age," Danet reminded them. "You're back on your feet faster at thirty than forty."

"Demeos is still popular," Noren signed.

"Very, according to other reports," Danet said drily. "As long as he isn't plotting, that's fine. It seems his friends have been busy spreading the rumor that he had nothing to do with his brother's treason—thereby also distancing themselves." She sniffed.

Noren commented, "Lineas says the new Feravayir guild chiefs were all elected by their members, for the first time in many years. The Nyidris had told them whom to elect, before."

Danet leaned over her low table and patted one of her ledgers. "What they really like down in Feravayir is paying their proper fifth tax, after years of Lavais Nyidri apparently gouging them and blaming it on *us*. They still haven't caught her tax guild chief," she muttered darkly—which Noren already knew, Ranet had only perfunctory interest, and Bunny none at all. The only thing about Feravayir that caught her attention was any discussion of when Rat would return.

Danet intuited enough of that to shift the subject. "One thing I do know. Prices shot up and down as a result of certain guild elections being hotly contested. That had better smooth out soon, or they will be receiving some letters I've already begun."

No one had anything to add to that, but she was content with it. Everything was peaceful. She was grateful, oh yes she was.

Peaceful but not *perfect*. Perfect would be a prince or two growing under her eye. Well, the young people were still young people, and it wasn't as if there wasn't an heir, Jarend's grandson they called Cricket, up in Olavayir. But Danet had never laid eyes on the child. Jarend, who she remembered hated change, hadn't wanted his only son to attend the academy, and had kept his Riders' boys close as well. So Danet didn't know any of the rest of the family. Tanrid's visits at Convocation had been sporadic, and when he did attend, he spent his time with the men. When she'd asked Arrow about him, all she got was a typically vague answer, "He reminds me a lot of my brother."

Well, Noddy had barely reached thirty. The rest were still in the galloping twenties. She reassured herself with the comforting thought that there was plenty of time, and she knew they were doing their best.

Which was in part true.

Noddy could see how genuinely unhappy the subject of children made Noren when it came up, so he always changed the topic to something like expected arrivals. Bunny of course was eager for Rat's return, and could speculate endlessly about it.

As Ranet and Noren walked out before retiring for the night, Ranet glanced both ways along the hall before signing, "I'm sorry. Every time the gunvaer looks at me in that way, I know she's thinking about children, and I feel guilty that it has been so easy for me."

Noren winced, and looked away, which was odd. She usually watched everyone. But then she signed, "I feel most sorry for Bunny. It's cruel. She waited so long, but once she and Rat got together, they only had a few weeks before he was sent south."

"At least they don't seem to want him down there permanently," Ranet signed back.

They parted outside the heir's suite, Ranet walking on down to her own, across from Connar's. For once light streamed out Connar's open door, and she heard men's voices, all recognizable: Noddy's deep one, Connar's golden one, the husky one belonging to that tall Jethren who looked at her with such hunger.

If Jethren hadn't been there, she might have gone inside, but she quietly slipped into her own chambers. It wasn't that Jethren wasn't handsome. It was that unwinking stare of his. That and the flat, almost contemptuous way he glared at Noddy made the back of her neck grip.

She was completely unaware that he organized his day as often as he could so that he could watch when she and Noren exercised their horses, especially when—three or four times a week—they rode and shot. They were both far better than the teenage girls they taught. Either of them could have ridden with the army skirmishers if they'd chosen. Neither of them ever missed the mark, shooting right hand or left.

He'd also tried to watch her Odni drills, until he discovered that there was a coterie of castle guards ardently fond of early morning sentry walks in the area overlooking the court below the queen's suite. He held himself above them. Anyway, knife drills were not as hot as the sight of her riding like a bolt from a crossbow across a field, slamming arrows into targets at either side.

He tried to catch her eye whenever they were in range of each other, but her attention never strayed his way. Well, Connar's wife. Of course no one else would be on her mind, he believed.

Connar took Jethren as honor guard when he rode to Ku Halir, and then to East Garrison. Connar could have sent someone, but he was restless—riding, inspection, overseeing drill were at least *movement*.

Ranet resigned herself to not seeing him at all, except on Restdays, when he always came to the family gathering in the gunvaer's chamber. He invariably sat with Noddy, and though he smiled at the girls, and let them climb all over him, Iris shrilling "Look at me! See what I can do?" as she made faces or poses, he didn't seem to notice them any other time.

Or Ranet herself.

She kept her promise to herself, and stayed behind her door. He knew where she was.

A few days later, the Restday after Noddy's Name Day, Ranet felt Noren's touch on her forearm as she was about to leave her chamber for the nursery down the hall in order to get the freshly bathed girls.

Instead she backed into her room, waved her runner to fetch Iris and Little Hliss, and faced Noren, whose serious expression made her heart thump.

"I think Connar still has feelings for Lineas," Noren signed.

Ranet stared back helplessly, then, "Has he told you that? Or told Noddy?"

Noren snapped the words away with a quick gesture. "He doesn't talk to me at all. Whatever he says or doesn't say to Noddy stays between them. But ever since you and I spoke after Little Hliss was born, I've been watching him. It's how he always scans a room when he enters."

"He's looking for her? How can you tell?"

"It's . . ." Noren's clever, sensitive hands paused, suspended in air, then fluttered quickly, "It's something perhaps I notice, and others don't. When he looks around a room and she isn't there, his attention goes to whoever's mouth is moving. But the rare times she is there—usually when she's with Noddy, and we all gather for some reason—he . . ." She mimed stilling. "And his gaze goes straight to her, then he never looks her way again. Even if her mouth moves. I've watched. It's consistent."

"Feelings . . . do you think he's still in love with her, then?"

"What does 'in love' really mean? Was he ever 'in love' with her? Didn't you tell me once she said he wasn't? No matter. What I see could be anything. Including hate. But there's something there. Feelings." Her palms flattened after the word.

"She made a ring marriage," Ranet said.

"That might be the problem," Noren replied with a sober look.

That night, as most of the castle slept except for the night guards patrolling ceaselessly, a soot-black shape drifted along the deep shadows of the second floor.

Moonbeam went walking, always to see the targets. Keth promised him when the wrong king and all his kind were dead, the ghosts would be real again. Soon, now.

Most often Moonbeam found his way to the king's chambers, the most difficult to breach. He stood staring down at the snoring figure while caressing one or another of his knives, imagining where to place the first cut. How long before the second.

Next most often, the huge rockbrain they called heir. Moonbeam would take his time with that one if he was as good a fighter as he looked.

From time to time he slipped into the rooms where the eagle clan women slept, for they were targets, too. He didn't know if any would give him a good fight, and Keth wanted the beautiful one. The two children, he would make it quick, *slash slash,* before they even woke. They were no threat. There was sweetness in a win only if there was risk.

Back again to the king's suite, where the true king would lie.

Another peek, another carving scheme.

But Keth said, not yet. Not while blame would surely point toward him. And so Moonbeam stole out again, a shade deeper than the shadows, and left them sleeping.

SIXTEEN

Vior Mat Cingon was not distorted by someone else's vision into what he became, and I want to spend as little ink and time on him as I can.

The vagaries of heredity had brought out a Venn ancestor from way back, shaping him tall and strong, with light brown hair. He was born with good looks and a good home, but a weakness for gambling and an insatiable taste for luxury caused him to run from a promising career in the Coast Patrol at the other end of the continent, leading him to be snapped up by a particularly vicious pirate who tended to run through crew faster than they could be lured to join.

Ten years of bloody fighting on decks had hardened a lazy, lying oaf into an indifferent killer before he and a few cronies got the drop on a prize crew and landed, with the stolen ship and its booty, in a notorious harbor. As pirates tend to have long memories for those with the temerity to steal from them, he turned his back on the sea and caroused his way inland while the booty lasted.

Three more years of bloody infighting had brought him to the captaincy of a mercenary troop that turned brigand against trade caravans when they couldn't get hired. He'd never quite lost his taste for gambling, but he no longer trusted the chance of markers or cards: he was always on the lookout for the quickest, surest way to wealth.

Having heard of the whispering jewel caves which yielded single gems each worth more gold than the rare dragoneye stones of the far north and far south, he and his followers had been tramping the mountains of Ghildraith, following a very old map one of his followers had killed someone to get, when they ran across Jendas Yenvir the Skunk.

Some negotiation with steel inspired Cingon to join Yenvir—until events made it more profitable to shift loyalties to the richer prospect, Thias Elsarion. But at Tlennen Field, when it became clear that Elsarion was shortly to go the way Yenvir had, Cingon and his band deserted the field and bunked north to resume their search for the jewel cave.

Winter and hunger brought them to a tidy little valley, sufficient unto itself. Some quick and bloody work in the quiet of the night replaced the village chief with Cingon and his band.

From there, one valley led to the taking of another, bringing us to the present time.

Cingon had proclaimed himself king of the mountains, but he was a king living in a stone cottage, among people who spent their entire summer getting ready for winter. The yearning for the elusive jewel cave began to seem a mirage . . . and meanwhile there was all that wealth in the south.

When a party of his roving thugs captured a pair of Marlovan scouts tending to a horse that had slipped on ice and injured a leg, they elicited the fact that the blue-eyed Marlovan commander who had scythed his way through Elsarion's force and destroyed the entire pass below Skytalon had gone down south to make more war.

All the way south? That was practically Sartor!

Cingon told his followers, "A little quick work, and we're the kings of Stalgoreth. We can be in the stronghold tight before the Marlovan prince gets all the way up from the Sartoran Sea to face us."

Braids' two scouts, who had been promised their lives if they cooperated in providing information, had seen no harm in lying about where Prince Connar was. They didn't live long enough to find out what Cingon would do with the information; the thugs kept the injured horse, recognizing a prize when they saw one, but the other escaped before they could catch it.

Cabbage Gannan's perimeter patrol found the still-saddled scout horse grazing alongside a river, and brought it to the jarl castle. Everyone knew scouts never abandoned their horses, especially still saddled.

Cabbage sat down straight away to compose a message—which Maddar intercepted. In the kindest way possible, she said, "You really can't send this to Connar-Laef."

"Why not?" Cabbage demanded, his voice rising as his gaze shifted away. "He hates me. He'll blame me if I do *anything*. But this is *my* jarlate, and I have a *right* to investigate and protect my border."

"Strictly speaking, that horse was found on the other side of the river that we regard as the border, but in any case, I don't think anyone, including Connar-Laef, would argue about your rights. It's this first part, where basically you're saying that you know you have to report it or he'll blame you. Please consider leaving that off entirely. The only part that matters is your patrol finding that horse, and here you are letting everyone know, just as you ought. Unless he gave you special orders at Convocation?" she amended, eyeing him.

"Never said so much as a single word to me. Only talked to Braids. Who was to investigate," Cabbage muttered.

"That's all right, then. You found a horse that had to belong to one of Braids' scouts, and according to standing orders, you're reporting it before you send someone to look into it."

Cabbage balled up the paper he had labored over, and wrote two lines: what they'd found, and that he was going to take a force to investigate, dispatching copies to Braids, and to the royal city.

Braids, having heard the two trumpet blasts announcing an arrival at Tlen, where he was temporarily staying, left mid-conversation, hoping it wasn't just another runner from Ku Halir. When he reached the stable yard and recognized the newcomer's mud-splattered pennon as Cabbage Gannan's new colors, his heart beat sharply.

"Found a horse," the runner said hoarsely as he dismounted, and fell against the hard-breathing animal. Braids nicked his chin up in permission, and stable hands ran to take care of the horse as two more of his people steadied the Gannan runner. "Still wearing a saddle pad. Up against the northwest corner, along the river."

Silence fell.

"Damage?" Braids asked.

The runner made a vague swipe at his own belly, saying, "Galled."

Which meant the horse had tried to scrape the saddle off, which had chafed its skin. "Galls weeks old," he added.

"Second scout?" Braids forced out the word, "Bodies?" One scout was a distant Tlennen cousin, the other Trot, who he had grown up with. She'd been promoted to scout after the Tlennen Plain battle. Neither were inexperienced—but weather was harsh in the mountains, and their experience was on the plains.

"Searched, two days," the runner said soberly, "Nothing. Horse could have gone a long distance."

They would have to assume at least one scout was dead. But by whose hand? Braids thought of those rocky hills, and wondered if it was accident. He wasn't certain which would be worse, lying on a hillside with broken bones, or a brigand's knife.

Meanwhile Cabbage's runner had drunk from the ladle thoughtfully brought, and in a less raspy voice added, "Gannan-Jarl said to tell you, he's sending the First Lancers north."

Braids grimaced. "They won't be much use in the hills."

"Said that. Said it'll be a warning to anyone on the watch, but he'll spread everybody out. Searching first."

Braids turned to Henad Tlennen. "We'd better ride north. We'll be a lot more effective in rocky hills than those heavy horses."

"All of us?" She jerked her thumb toward the stable.

"No . . . Hound Company, with all the scout dogs for start. Send someone to fetch something from Trot's and Sand's gear, and bring it along for the dogs to sniff. We'll send the rest of their things to their homes. If we leave by tomorrow, we can reach Cabbage in two weeks, three at the outside, with remounts. First, let's put our fastest on the road to the royal city to report."

The runner eyed him uneasily. "Gannan-Jarl sent one of us to the royal city."

Braids clapped him on the shoulder. "I'm sure he did. We'll send another to report our Hound Company going north. And it won't be you. You've earned your liberty," he added to the runner's immense relief.

Arrow had given orders that any runners bearing Senelaec crimson and black be brought to him wherever he was, and his sons notified.

Down at the sword court, Jethren beat back Connar's attack, swords sending up sparks. The circle watching them skidded back as Connar faded back a step, then charged at Jethren, who spun and sidestepped after shifting his sword to the left hand to beat off a furious attack.

His eyes stung with sweat and his breath rasped in his throat, but he fought on. He had to win. Too many losses and Connar lost interest. There were very few he chose to fight with—all as strong and fast as he was, but with the precision control that kept serious wounds to a minimum as they fought full out with bare steel. There were few headier senses than a genuine win, rare as those were, but Jethren strove to beat his way inside that invisible barrier.

As Connar backed away and wiped the sweat off his face, Jethren wondered—not for the first time—why swords. From what he'd heard, Connar had picked up a lance on his very first day of training, and had nailed the target. Maybe it was another of those deferences to his buck-toothed dolt of a brother—

From the other side of the castle, at the city gate, the great bell clanged sourly once. That meant a runner spotted at the gallop.

Connar lowered his sword as he said to Jethren, "That has to be Braids. Come on."

Jethren had avoided being in the usurper Anred-Olavayir's vicinity as much as possible. It was easier to pretend he didn't exist, until the time came when the true king rid the world of eagle clan altogether. But this was new, Connar insisting Jethren follow him up to the royal castle's second floor, an invitation he'd cut off his right arm rather than refuse.

He tossed his blade to Moonbeam to clean and put away, and followed Connar. Sweaty as they were, with dust from falls imprinted on their clothes, they ran up to the state wing.

Jethren had never been this close to the so-called king, and was disgusted to see at first glance that the rumors about drunkenness were no exaggeration. The king's nose was red with even more broken veins than Hauth's. His hair was thin, sparse at the sides, turned white, and he looked like a collection of slats inside his loose clothes.

Jethren was so busy trying not to glare at Arrow that he missed the subtle stiffening of Connar's shoulders, the brief flex of his hands at the sight of the red-haired royal runner kneeling behind the scribe table against the far wall.

"Connar," Arrow said in greeting, then his eyes narrowed at Jethren. "Who's this—no, you're one of my brother's boys, aren't you? Tanrid sent you along?"

Sodden the false king's brain might be, but he wasn't oblivious. Jethren forced his hand into a proper salute, but inwardly aimed it at Connar's back as he moved to the wall.

Lineas and Vanadei had been transcribing their shorthand notes for Noddy after the long, tiring interview with the new guild chief in charge of the stringers, or money changers, at Parayid. They exchanged glances of silent question, her heartbeat in her throat as she studiously avoided looking at Connar. Vanadei indicated the door and began to rise.

Arrow lifted a hand. "Wait. We might need to write letters, and you two are as fast as scribes, so you may as well bide tight."

Hands to heart, they sat back, Lineas lining up her already straight pens and touching her perfectly squared blank sheets of paper that still smelled a little of the paper-press, as she did her knife drill breathing to calm her juddering heart.

Connar dropped down onto the floor beside Noddy's mat. Arrow watched in approval as both his boys took seats on their mats opposite him. He was secretly relieved that this so far had been one of his good days. He'd been debating whether or not to admit to the irascible old healer about the occasional lapses, even what you might call blackouts. He knew what he'd hear: no more drink. But every time he tried to stop drinking altogether, he felt as if his body had been beaten by heavy rocks, and his thinking was worse than ever as the hour glass dropped a sand particle with the speed of melting snow.

He simply had to have a drink. At least one. *He* knew his own body best, and as for all that blather about aging, Amble Sindan had been riding the plains past eighty, and Wolf Senelaec had told him on that visit to Senelaec long ago that the old fart drank everyone under the table every New Year's Week. Arrow wasn't even sixty! He fisted his hands to control the tremble fluttering in the joints and turned his attention to the waiting runner, who turned out to be from Cabbage Gannan. Not Braids.

But the report was about Braids' scouts after all.

After the man finished, "It could be nothing beyond an accident," Noddy said hopefully.

Arrow grimaced. "Then the second scout would have reported. Two scouts vanished, a single horse, still saddled . . . it would take more than a brigand or two to bring down two experienced scouts. Braids wouldn't send someone new."

"Right," Connar said. "I'd better ride north." He paused, remembering those magical letter things the Sartorans had used in Feravayir. A strong desire to have instantaneous news was followed promptly by distrust. What if the enemy got hold of them, and sent false news to lure them into ambush? Runners were *always* best. There was nothing to be done about the wait—but an enemy would have an equal wait.

"Do it," Arrow said. "If you're fast, you can get whatever is going on up there done before winter sets in hard. My guess is, you'll meet Braids Senelaec somewhere on the road. Between the two of you and young Gannan, that should settle the matter."

Connar was mentally reviewing the map. "The more I think about it, the more I hate having Rat Noth stuck clear down at Parayid. He's been there a year. Things are settled down there. Time to bring him up here to run shield in any direction if needed. Mouse Noth, or Dognose Eveneth, or even Pepper Marlovayir, if Rat wants to promote him, would be fine down at that harbor. Mouse grew up at Parayid with Rat. Dognose knows the coast. The Marlovayirs have a coast, though I don't know that they do anything there."

Arrow grunted with approval. "You could put Rat Noth in at Hesea Garrison as permanent commander. It's time to replace old bones with new. Which places him right in the middle of the kingdom. We might have to expand that garrison, though."

Jethren listened, doing his best to remain effectively invisible, but inside he exulted. If Rat was permanently stationed at Hesea, then that cleared the way to Connar's right hand—

Connar turned Jethren's way. "If we promote you to Battalion Commander of the Third Lancers, you could be at Hesea under Rat, along with his skirmisher commander. And if there was major action that didn't require lancers, you could hold Hesea while Rat runs shield to me."

"Good thinking," Arrow exclaimed. "Then we could move . . ."

As the two exchanged names of captains, commanders, and companies, Jethren sat as still as ice.

All year the image of that army, riding in perfect order, as seen from the walls of Artolei's winter palace, had been gnawing at him. That and his father's words, *Mathren's first lesson in strategy warns of anyone else being able to whistle up an army. . . .*

But it seemed Rat Noth could do anything. No one blinked an eye at his being able to summon an entire army, as if he were the king's commander. No one thought anything of Braids Senelaec effectively running his own academy at Senelaec. And here was Jethren, about to be relegated to the midlands, maybe for the rest of his life—forever under the command of Rat Noth?

They're untouchable, he thought. Because they were in the academy. Braids wasn't even in it that long. But it seemed that all it took was a year.

" . . . right?"

Jethren glanced up, to find Connar looking at him expectantly. He reached for the context, and vaguely recollected the previous few words, *but we'll have to postpone promotions for now.*

"Right," Jethren said, and saluted for good measure, fist to heart—then panic closed his throat when he saw himself facing Connar with that telltale fist there.

"Good," the false king declared. "Go to it, boys," he said, and Jethren let out a shaky breath. The old drunk hadn't even noticed.

Jethren walked out in a daze, his mind only able to grasp one thing: he had this new action, whatever it turned out to be, to prove himself. Vaguely aware that drill was over, he wandered in the direction of the garrison.

And so for once he was not shadowing Connar's steps—which left Connar free. For he'd noticed Noddy pulling Vanadei aside for some task with their piles of papers, as Lineas slipped out the old, rarely used servants' side door.

So that was how she managed to vanish all the time.

But he knew all those old ways. He and Noddy had explored them all when they were small.

He turned to Arrow. "I'll give the orders to ride out in the morning," which his Da accepted with a smile of approval.

Connar exited and headed for the back stair.

His calculation of relative speed was precise. He emerged from a deep-inset archway just as the old wooden door to the servants' entry creaked open, and there was Lineas, her freckles stark against her blanched face. Eyes wide and black.

Connar cast a fast glance around. They were alone, with stacks of barrels and a shed full of garden tools waiting for spring.

"You've been avoiding me," he said.

Lineas looked up. "You seemed so very angry with me," she said, almost too low to hear. "I . . . don't deal well with anger. I think I hurt you, when I, how I . . ."

"Lineas, I'm not made of glass," Connar said impatiently. "I thought we were good, then all of a sudden we weren't. You should have told me long before that you were running with someone else."

He'd forgotten how straightforward, how honest her gaze was. Never angry, accusatory, or worse, haughty, pretend-cold and coy. He'd seen the entire range in all his various encounters, but rarely had he met with the tranquility that was inherently Lineas. He didn't even have a name for it, only that she was like a summer stream.

"You were my first," she said. "So much I didn't understand. Still don't, really. I'm sorry—"

A thin rain began falling. He was distracted by tiny beads of water dotting her high forehead; she was aware of him standing before her, tall, so very well made. All the features she had once loved, had caressed, were still as fine. Finer. And the heat was still there, but underneath a complexity of layers more important.

"I didn't come here for that," he said, still impatient. "I want to know what I did wrong. Why you hate me."

"You didn't do anything wrong," she said. "And I don't hate you. How could I? I don't hate people, though many frighten me. You . . . I still care about you."

"If that's true, come back to me." He held out his palm.

She opened her hand in a gesture part negation but part plea. The gold glinted on her heart finger. "I can't."

"Once," he said, low as a whisper. "Once, and then it's goodbye. If you insist. If you do really still care about me."

Lineas looked down at her palms, wet with rain, then up. "I'll talk to you any time, and gladly. I'll sit by you if you have a nightmare. But we will never share a bed again. That part of me—I made a promise."

His eyes narrowed, which seemed somehow to make them bluer. "So this care of yours, it's really pity."

She had gone over their last conversation so many times it had almost become threadbare in her mind, devoid of color and texture because she mulled so many possibilities. But this much she was sure of: they had parted after that same word, pity.

"Not pity," she said quickly. "If you're hearing that as some sort of judgment. How could *I* judge *you?* I would do as much for anyone who asked, but for you there's all that we shared." She put her hands to her heart. "I'd like to be your friend, your helper, but I can't be your lover—"

Her reasonable explanation died on her lips when she saw his face tighten.

Exasperation eddied through her. "Connar, you can't possibly find me better looking than Ranet, much less all your other lovers, and as for sex, I'm sure you have better every day. You were my first. I had *no* experience. If you think all the friendship and care and empathy I have to offer you is merely *pity,* what do you really want from me?"

"I don't know," he said, but not loud enough for her to hear as he turned abruptly and left.

She stood where she was, arms wrapped tightly around herself as she stared at the rain-washed stones where he had stood, until the sick sensation clogging the back of her throat eased.

She forced herself to examine the conversation. Perhaps it was impossible to have handled it better.

While she stood there, up on the third floor, Quill oversaw the daily flow of duties, but he was aware that something had happened. Camerend had taught him how to evaluate the flow of life in the castle. He had heard the bell, and knew that the king had been sitting with the heir in the state wing, which meant that Connar would go there. He knew Lineas attended most days on Noddy, which meant that Connar and Lineas would come face to face, after she had put herself to great trouble to avoid him.

Before that—months ago—he had helped her to broom down the cobwebs and sweep out some of those old tunnels, the ones no longer in use because of the current patterns of movement. He'd also renewed the glowglobes in those passageways, after a brief, unsuccessful attempt to reteach her what to him was simple magic, and he saw for himself that magic seemed to cascade through her fingers rather than shaping properly.

He didn't think she had to go to such lengths. It was a false semblance of peace of mind, to be on the watch all through the day to avoid someone. Doing that was still thinking about them. But she hadn't asked what he thought.

So that rainy night he watched and listened, and knew by the wakes of runners when Jethren, then Connar, moved back over to garrison-side. He waited, and finally Lineas appeared, looking damp, cold, and distraught; she closed herself in her room, where, he knew, she would pull out her journal and dissect memory, emotion, and conversation in code, because she had told him so. She had never shared the actual journal—and might never.

The watch change bell rang, the day closed in, and people went off to the evening meal, but the light remained glowing under Lineas's door, so he confined himself to his room, door open, and occupied himself with such matters as he could while he waited.

It was late when her door opened softly, and she peeked out. Seeing him beside his desk, door open, she crossed the hall, closed his door, and sat down on the bed, hands crossed over her chest to grip her shoulders. "I was always told," she said plaintively, "there is never just one person, that love doesn't last."

"I was told there is not one kind of love," he said. "But it successfully seems to require all participants sharing at least some of the varieties. Right now I love it when you come to me and talk things out."

The stress eased from her face, and she told him what had happened.

At the end, she said, "You're right about kinds. People say 'love' but what do they mean? He never once said he *loved* me, even today. Wait, did I? No, I don't think I did. I said I cared for him, which of course I do. But what does he really want? I wonder if he just wants to go back to when we were young. But that doesn't make sense. He'd had that horrible experience at the academy, and now he has everything. *Everything*."

It was out before he could think, "I believe he wanted you to break your vow."

She looked up, startled. "Really? Why? To hurt you? But he doesn't know you."

"I don't think it's me, except that I'm in his way." Quill stopped, and thought back to some of the odd, tense exchanges he'd had with Connar. He dropped his hands to his knees. "I don't really understand it, for I don't understand his relationship with you, which, so far, he doesn't seem to have reproduced with anyone else. You mattered to him in a way he might not understand any more than you do."

"That's so odd," she breathed. "Most people think I'm boring. Or weird." Her voice dropped on the last word.

"You are emphatically, entrancingly you. But what does Connar see in you? Or is there something else galling him. Making me wonder, if you broke your vow, would it enable him to break one of his own?"

"To whom? I really am confused now."

"So am I," he admitted. "It's probably me seeing castles in clouds."

SEVENTEEN

If Connar had been asked, he would have retorted that he'd never made any vows to anyone, other than his oath before the jarls when he was made commander. And he would cut out his tongue before betraying Da, or Marlovan Iasca.

His marriage with Ranet was a treaty marriage, no vow exchange either way, other than those pertaining to duty to family and kingdom. She was free to find favorites; he did his part when she came to him. It was admittedly a relief that she had not come for a while, but he assumed she was busy with the girls, who were clearly happy and healthy growing under Ma's eye, just as he and Noddy had. His early childhood, in memory, was a time of endless summer days roaming about the castle having fun, and he assumed Iris and Little Hliss would be doing the same as they got older. They would even go to the academy together, as the academy girls were coming along just fine. More of the first or second years went back home than boys did, but those who remained were clearly marked for future skirmisher captains. The boys' archery had improved noticeably from his day, in speed as well as precision. Maybe it was a matter of competition, but it worked.

As for Lineas . . . Connar refused to think about her, or that exchange, until he was galloping northward, banners snapping behind him. "Pity." She'd actually sounded affronted.

What *was* it about her? She was right in that it certainly wasn't her appearance, which was nothing extraordinary, or the sex, which he could get anywhere, and much hotter. But he hadn't been able to bring himself to admit out loud that it was the nights with her curved gently against him doing nothing more than breathing that made it possible for him to sleep. And his dreams were good. The rare times they weren't, she was right there.

That sounded pitiful put into actual words.

He simply had to keep busy and put her out of mind the way everybody else did with past lovers. That's all she was, merely a past lover.

Castle life faded behind him and anticipation sharpened as they encountered runners posted to wait for them. And so he learned that one of the freakish ice storms that roared over the mountains in autumn had driven all living things to ground until it was over, except for the broken tree branches and a thousand streams and drips.

The next runner posted farther along detailed discovery of the abandoned bodies of the two scouts, which caused a search spiraling out until the finding of a string of valleys between two great peaks having been taken by mercenaries.

And finally, there was Braids, bringing the news that caused Connar to smile: they'd found the mercenaries themselves.

"You were fast," Braids said, belatedly smacking his fist to his chest when he noticed the rest doing so. "We only got here six days before you."

Connar grinned. "Because you left us all your remounts. Thanks, Braids. For those, and for the runners with the reports. Tell me everything."

Braids' grin hardened. "About that." He turned his head. "Squeak!"

A short, round girl no older than seventeen ran out from the mass standing in the middle of Braids' camp, in no particular order. Most of them were female.

Squeak had a high voice. "Braids sent me'n my cousin ahead to scout. Careful, because of what happened to Trot and Badger. No wearing our coats, that was our orders. We just reached Igreth, a village on the other side of the river, a day before the enemy came in, some riding, most running, and took the town before we knew what happened." Her gaze dropped, and everyone there knew that "taking the town" meant violence.

"My family owns an inn at Wened, so I put on an apron and offered to help at the tavern for a bed, when really I wanted to go to ground. The enemy took over everything, demanding food and drink, without paying, and this one with diamonds at one ear, he said their captain is the new king of Stalgoreth." She repeated all the bragging she'd overheard in a night of serving Cingon's mercenaries, then finished, "The more they drank, the more they blabbed. They think Connar-Laef is still in Feravayir."

"We'll have to convince them differently," Connar said. "Where are they now?"

Braids brought from inside his grubby coat an equally grubby map. "Gannan—Stalgoreth, that is—said we should take them by surprise, so he's kept everyone back of the Reth River, here." Braids jabbed the roughly east-west line across the map of Stalgoreth.

"Did Gannan send you to meet me?" Connar asked.

Braids' gaze shifted at the name "Gannan." He hesitated, not certain what to say. Cabbage Gannan absolutely had the right to defend Stalgoreth, no one said otherwise, but he'd talked so much about chain of command that Braids had volunteered to ride south to meet Connar. How much of that to say?

But his hesitation was enough. "We can ask him," Connar said easily. "Lead the way."

The first thing they saw on entering Cabbage's camp were all the Stalgoreth banners. These were huge, with the long streamers called swallow-tails. Jarls carried similar banners, but seldom more than two when a jarl rode in column, or to Convocation.

There were eight visible.

Connar and Braids dismounted, and as runners took the horses to the picket, Cabbage came out of the command tent to meet them, his darting gaze picking out Connar and staying there.

"Did you think we wouldn't be able to find you?" Connar asked.

Cabbage had readied a speech, but this unexpected question threw him. A snicker, no more than a breath, reached him, and he flushed, as Connar said conversationally, "All these banners."

It was on the surface an even tone, but it was completely wrong for the situation—as if it wasn't serious. As if Connar didn't take the Jarl of Stalgoreth and Commander of the First Lancers seriously. Two lightly spoken sentences stung Cabbage like a lash on raw flesh, and emotionally he was back in the academy.

"We had different companies searching," Cabbage said in the defensively belligerent tone that set Connar's teeth on edge. "We had to send them all the way to . . . ." The more he babbled, the more it sounded in his own head like he was covering up, when he really had just wanted a reminder that this was *his* jarlate, and jarls had the right to defend their own land.

He cut himself off, and gritted, "I have a plan."

A brief silence, no sound but the wind flapping through the closest banners, then Connar said, "Let's hear it."

They walked into Cabbage's capacious new command tent, and sat on mats as runners brought freshly scalded coffee and pan-biscuits stuffed with sharp cheese. Cabbage began to explain his plan with a lot of justification that grated on half his listeners, and made his partisans wince on his behalf.

Finally he noticed the flat line of Connar's mouth getting tighter, and hastily outlined the latest observations from his scouts, who had remained out of line-of-sight of the enemy. These, identified as mercenaries, were coming in a widespread line, no order or discipline. Cabbage then outlined his plan, which was the standard defense they'd all learned back in their academy days: deflecting charge, draw the enemy, hit them on the flank, surround and destroy.

What he couldn't quite bring himself to say was that he wanted to be in command—and by the time he was at the end of his words, and Connar had remained silent the entire time, arms folded, Cabbage backed down, saying, "I can ride front-line with the First Lancers and draw them."

"Let's do it." Connar turned his head. "Braids, you'll run the flank. We'll back you up along the riverside, in case any of them decide to turn and run."

Cabbage Gannan had chosen excellent ground.

The enemy was two days outside Stalgoreth's huge castle and its adjacent trade town. They knew they were close, and decided to surprise the Marlovans by setting out before sunup. They forded their last river, sash-high in the bleak gray of pre-dawn, so that when the sun briefly rimmed the distant mountains to the east, it silhouetted the line of lancers ahead of them, shields high, the steel of the lance blades briefly throwing back blood-red glints before low, advancing clouds swallowed the sky.

Cingon's force wavered, shock dousing the comfortable belief that the real enemy was at the far end of the subcontinent.

Cabbage gloried in giving the signal. Horns blared, and his First Lancers trotted in deliberate slow speed, then began the gallop, thundering over the marshy land as the eerie *Yip! Yip! Yip!* soared—

They smashed through the mercenaries, whose loose command structure had been sufficient for villages and caravans. Those who had been at Tlennen Field had all run early on, talking of being vastly outnumbered until they'd come to believe it.

Rain slanted down in showers as the horses galloped the last few paces, and then in torrents, limiting visibility to gray shapes. Braids' skirmishers lost speed in movement and in shooting, but the closer they had to ride, the more lethal their shots, no one wasting an arrow.

Cabbage shouted with savage joy. For him all the nerves had been in the wait, and the agonizing what-ifs. Action forced his attention to focus to one goal: he had to be the one to bring down the enemy leader, and that leader, the scouts had all reported, wore a weird-looking half-helm made of the gold he had wrested from his victims, studded with gems, that left the top of his head bare. Though anyone could tell you, gold was too soft to ward a blow—to Marlovans, the words "crown" and "coronation" were names for the oaths a new king made at midnight at Midsummer or New Year's Firstday. Nobody had ever seen an actual crown.

Cabbage gestured to his first runner Kendred to stay tight in case he needed his lance or his remount, and his honor guard to stay behind him, and charged again, straight at the thickest knot of enemies—who began to scatter.

"Get them! Get them!" Cabbage roared, and the honor guard obediently began chasing the scattering mercenaries, dispatching them one by one.

As Braids' skirmishers were hampered by the mud fast turning to liquid brown, Connar waved his company in among them, and made certain his two sword hilts were loose and ready at each side of his saddle. He never felt more alive than when galloping toward the enemy, tucking the reins under his right knee, and drawing his swords—

They cleaved through confused mass of Cingon's mercenaries. Half tried desperately to form up, hampered by those who were wheeling about, seeking escape.

A few tried to surround their leader, whether to protect him or seeking protection will never be known. Cabbage Gannan rode down on them, striking to either side with sword and shield, leading a deadly arrowhead of steel until thunder cracked right overhead, and the torrent abruptly turned to punishing hail.

Visibility dropped to scarcely a horse length in front or to either side as Cabbage's First Lancers went about decimating the mercenaries, and Connar's men swept the perimeter to make certain none got past. Cabbage lost sight of his target and charged on, unaware that Cingon had swerved toward the river with the intent of escaping—where he met, and did not survive, Jethren's third riding.

Cabbage rode on, shouting orders that Kendred couldn't hear. Kendred, in turn, had lost sight of the honor guard, and Cabbage couldn't hear him. He urged his mount to come up alongside Cabbage—and his horse slewed sideways in the mud, causing Kendred's cold hands to slip on Cabbage's lance. He twisted in the saddle, shifting his weight so as not to drop it, just as the horse leaped over a body. Kendred made a neat parabola over the horse's left hindquarter, arm clapping the lance to his side—and he landed hard, one leg twisted around the lance so firmly the snap of his knee shattering nearly drowned the roar of hail.

He lay where he was, head thrown back—and upside down saw Cabbage nearly plunge into Connar, coming from the right, with Jethren at shield position.

"Oh, *you,*" Cabbage snarled, completely caught up in the chase. He kicked his horse's sides and yanked the reins to one side, presenting Connar with his back and his horse's rump as he looked for more enemies to cut down.

Connar was a heartbeat faster in seeing only their three horses—his, Jethren's, and Cabbage's now moving away. His horse sidestepped to avoid a dead mercenary whose double-handed straight sword had landed in the mud hilt up.

Instinct was faster than thought.

Connar bent in the saddle, grabbed up the sword with one hand, and hurled it with all his considerable strength.

It caught Cabbage square in the back, severing his spine. His head rocked back, his hands flew up, and he fell dead to the mud, his horse racing off riderless. Fierce, red-hot joy flashed through Connar—then the consequences caught up with his mind.

He shot another glance around, then met Jethren's fierce grin.

Elation glowed in both faces as hail roared around them, stinging bare skin. Both mistook that shape of that elation: Connar saw completely loyalty at last, though he'd had it since the first time they met, and Jethren saw that at last he had crossed the magic barrier to Connar's inner circle.

Moonbeam caught up as they rode on in search of enemies.

Kendred, indistinguishable from the mud around him, tried to rise, but pain flashed through him in such white agony he passed out.

EIGHTEEN

Connar rode in a zigzag so that never more than one person could report having seen him retreating in a line from where the former Jarl of Stalgoreth lay in the mud not far from the riverside.

His mind raced ahead as the possible consequences set in. Always he came back to that wide grin of Jethren's—the unquestioning approval of loyalty. That, and the thought of being rid forever of Cabbage Gannan infused Connar with buoyancy, though beneath it—far below—he waited for guilt to smite him; he kept imagining the shock in Lineas's face. No. Betrayal.

To that he said mentally, *What you think no longer matters.*

The hail lifted briefly, and in that moment as a shaft of sun slanted down before being swallowed again, he saw that only Marlovans remained upright riding in every direction, those on foot taking weapons, or cutting scalp locks: by now there was an understood rule that you could only take a trophy after a man to man win, or if you were an archer, five kills.

As Jethren's men caught up with him, he shouted over his shoulder, "Muster."

The trumpets would restore order to those riding every which way. There were the horses to see to, some badly cut about the face by the hail, then the reports to monitor as runners and servants dispersed to collect animals, weapons, wounded, and dead.

He rode southward, toward those dripping banners, and dismounted before Cabbage's great tent. Slowly the reports came in: the one with the golden helmet definitely dead. All the mercenaries dead, their horses captured. Reports of Marlovan dead—at first no one, then one, then five, then twenty, but that turned out to be the same five counted by three separate people. There were another five badly wounded and unconscious, one of those Kendred, Cabbage's first runner. No one recognized any of the unconscious fallen, anonymous in their mud.

Cabbage was brought in on a cart, laid out with the foreign weapon beside him at the left, and his own sword at the right. His runners closed in around him to take him away to be cleaned up, along with the other dead. Connar felt gazes on him, not accusing, but evaluating. His heart thundered against his ribs, and he was aware that he still did not feel guilt. His worry was at getting caught, which would forever ruin his standing in men's eyes. In Noddy's eyes. In Da's.

In his captains' eyes, and the jarls.

"Send word ahead," he said, raising his voice. "Full memorial at the castle. Midnight. Everything done right."

Approval eased faces here and there, sober acceptance in others. General exhaustion everywhere. Later, the exhilaration would be back, but for now they were filthy with mud and other people's blood, exhausted, and covered with mercilessly stinging ice cuts.

Two days later, they reached the castle, to find it waiting to receive its dead hero. And he was a hero to them. Riding at the front of the cavalcade, Connar had set himself to expect an exercise in hypocrisy because of course everyone would feel the same about Cabbage as he did.

But that was not the case, which he found unnerving, however briefly: there was genuine grief in Cabbage's pretty wife, the popular and highly admired Maddar Sindan-An. A couple of other women spoke as well, obviously favorites. Connar couldn't imagine Cabbage having favorites, but maybe he had been different in the bedroom. For that moment, as he stared at the still, cold body lying on the bier waiting for the Spell of Disappearance, regret seized him: never again would either of these women lie next to a warm man, but then the thought of Cabbage Gannan in the throes of sex disgusted him so viscerally he rallied, and confined his thoughts to the threatening weather, the still-stinging cuts and the bruises he hadn't noticed as he scythed through the enemy.

When those who wished to speak had finished, he knew what they needed to hear. "I will leave Maddar Sindan-An as jarlan until the king appoints a new jarl. As for the First Lancers Battalion, that belongs to my brother, Nadran-Sierlaef. He will choose your next commander, and where you will be stationed. But Poseid, you were with Gannan the longest, so you stand in as interim commander."

A murmur of approval raised a susurrus around the ring of torchlit mourners, and Connar stepped back, as the Jarlan of Stalgoreth waved the torch over Cabbage's body three times, murmuring the Spell of Disappearance.

With Cabbage gone, Connar's guts eased. It was over, all except for the private, family memorial, reserved to those closest to Cabbage and his commanders, as they chose among his personal possessions and then burned the rest.

Connar never noticed Kendred, Cabbage's first runner, who listened from the side from a rolling chair brought out by his fellow runners.

Kendred had woken up halfway to the castle to a devastating headache matched by the pain in his knee and in his heart. Memory had eluded him until the pain began to recede. His head still throbbed, but as he stared across the great parade court in the castle that he now recognized as a copy of that at the royal city, Connar's voice rang through nerves into memory, and cold sweat broke out all over him.

If that was not a dream—he still wasn't completely certain—then the Commander of the King's Army had murdered Cabbage Gannan, from the back. The commander who had all the power, and who had hated Cabbage. Everyone knew that.

As voices around Kendred murmured about how the second prince was paying proper tribute, and so forth, Kendred wanted to yell, *Murderer! Traitor!* But would he be believed?

Worse than that, would that Jethren, or worse, his crazy first runner, kill him, too? If only he was certain, but the memory was so blurred, so gray . . .

He shut his eyes, and when the steward whispered, "Do you need listerblossom?" Kendred whispered back, "Yes."

He had to think it through.

Jethren's exhilaration carried him from the aftermath of that grim slaughter, slogging through pools of red-stained mud in order to restore order, to their return to the royal city. Connar never spoke of what had happened, even when the rare times they were briefly alone, but after all, what was there to say? The obstacle trying to crowd up next to Connar in chain of command was gone in one stroke. But that was the action of a true king.

Jethren, in attaining that circle of trust at last, would proceed more cautiously. As soon as he could get liberty, he visited Hauth, who was eager for the usual report.

Jethren had decided to keep the cause of Gannan's death to himself, at least until Hauth and his father reconciled. It was a powerful secret—the means by which he had entered that new level of trust. He didn't want Hauth part of it.

But that didn't mean he couldn't use him. "With Gannan dead, there are two obstacles to my moving up the chain of command," he said. "Senelaec is one, and Rat Noth the other."

"What do you mean to do about it?" Hauth said.

Jethren had thought about it the entire ride back to the royal city. He liked Braids Senelaec. What's more, Braids was an excellent commander. It would harm the defense of the east if he suffered an accident. But, "I just need Senelaec moved down the chain of command. What is his weakness?"

Hauth scowled. "None, really. I only had him for two years, but I never saw anything like Holdan and his penchant for drink, or Khanivayir quarreling over imagined slights. Zheirban constantly in trouble with hothouse women. The Senelaecs are notorious for sloppy discipline, but they're formidable in the field. Though terrible as land governors," he added.

"Usually short at harvest time, often needing royal stores to get through the end of winter. And of course there's that ridiculous feud with the Marlovayirs."

Jethren grinned. "I think I've got enough."

Restday morning, a runner came up to the royal castle's second floor. At first, the family let out cries of relief that the invasion had been thoroughly routed. But when the short list of dead was headed by new Jarl of Stalgoreth, Danet stamped across her chamber and back, dashed her wrist across her eyes, and because the interweaving of Marlovan order across generations was never far from her mind, she began fiercely, "If Maddar Sindan-An and that boy had done what I told them, and started a family, at least there'd be —"

Then she remembered who was in the room with her, and whirled around. Noddy sat still on his cushion, head bowed, and Danet wished she had her knife at her wrist so she could cut out her tongue.

She struck her hands together, hard, then said as she signed, "I've heard many good things about Lefty Poseid, young Gannan's cousin. Everything will settle out."

It was a desperate attempt at a save, but Noddy just sat there, unable to eat. The sight of his pain hurt Noren, a pain she accepted as her burden. Whenever she began to waver for Noddy's and Danet's sake, she had only to think of her sister Hadand, who could not bear any deviation from the invisible chains of her rituals, to harden her resolve.

Noddy had mourned after losing his Uncle Jarend, only met briefly once as an adult. Seeing his father's devastation had overwhelmed him. His grief at losing Cabbage Gannan was worse. Not that Noddy railed or shouted or slammed about. His grief turned inward, his mouth downturned at the corners, calling his father's "arrow" sharply to mind.

He was so stricken he could not concentrate. Sad on his behalf, Lineas was deeply remorseful because her most vivid memories of Cabbage Gannan were her clashes with him when she was twelve, though in their brief meetings over the years since, his indifference toward her made it clear he'd forgotten. She threw herself into extra labors, meticulously writing up the guild and army supply reports as they flowed in, so that Noddy would find them easier to deal with when he was ready.

Noddy's work sat for a day, two, days. As the days slid into a week, Lineas and Vanadei decided to get through as much of the labor side as possible, until Noddy was ready again.

They worked long into the nights writing out painstakingly what ordinarily they explained out loud. Lineas was vaguely aware of the rest of the world moving on as New Year's Week came and went—just as well there was no Convocation, as no one had the heart for it—and winter settled in beneath an ice-blue sky, the ground iron hard.

As the weeks dragged by, she was vaguely aware of mild bumps in the grind of routine: the gunvaer speaking irritably of "those idiot Senelaecs;" Quill at work even longer hours than hers.

The snow came, days and days of it. Noddy returned to work at first just mornings, always apologetic, especially when asking for them to go over things with him repeatedly. The king joined them now and then, which Lineas found unnerving until she began to understand his exasperated orders for repetition: he was having trouble seeing what they wrote. (And he was having trouble retaining the lists of numbers, but he was not going to admit to that.)

"I spoke to the healer," the chamber runner said in a low voice after a very trying day. "We have rounds of glass made the way field glasses are made, that can help sharpen things close up, but the king insists he'll look weak and stupid before the guild chiefs, and they'll argue even more."

Noddy spoke up in his deep voice, "Those chiefs *like* details. He doesn't. I'll come every day now. I just wasn't sleeping well."

He kept his word. The atrocious weather bought them time and slowly the piles of unfinished business began to diminish as the tray containing outgoing messages waiting for a decent thaw began to grow.

That first thaw brought Neit striding in among the messengers who had been pinned down all along the roads. She was a welcome sight, coat skirts swinging slantwise in opposition to the roll of her hips, her deep chuckle heard along the hallways like the first breath of summer.

"I did my stint at East Garrison," she said to Lineas. "I'm back for reassignment."

Danet appointed her adjunct runner to the second floor, which made Neit happy. That brightened everyone's mood.

Not that the winter was easy. Toward the end of a cold, stormy month, Quill was missing when Lineas trudged up to the third floor after a long day of labor. She was too tired to ask what crisis, or even crises, he was dealing with. They preferred his room for winter, as hers let in icy drafts that beat the eastern walls. She fell asleep as soon as her head hit the bed. That became a pattern—she fell asleep alone, and woke up with him beside her.

One evening very late, as spring rains brought the smell of green through the windows for the first time in what always felt like years, Lineas trudged upstairs late once again, weary from an acrimonious brangle between a messenger from the Nob and stringer representatives of Lindeth and Parayid, to discover Neit and Quill deep in conversation. Quill was dressed in city clothes.

She checked on the threshold of his room, wondering if she ought to have knocked, though they had dropped that habit long ago. Flashing through her mind were so many reasons why she would find these two handsome persons sitting there in apparent intimacy. But trust, she had come to realize, was not a one-time thing, though celebrations like ring vows before one's loved ones and friend circles might make it seem that way. It was an everyday thing, decision by decision.

Trust. Mistrust, distrust. Her inner eye gave her Connar, standing in the courtyard with drops of rain glistening in his black hair. She broke that image by walking in.

The two looked up. Neit rose, saluted Lineas with finger to heart, then was out the door in three quick strides.

Quill sat back, reading Lineas's expression. "Ferret affairs," he said. "I assumed you had enough to occupy your mind over in the state wing. Do you want to hear it?"

"Is it something I would like?" She sank down tiredly onto the bed, hands clasped between her knees.

"Not at all."

"Do you need me to listen?"

"Maybe later. But I just finished bringing Neit up-to-date before sending her on a run, so I'd rather not go through it twice."

"Then I am going to soak my hands in hot water, and crawl into bed." She sighed. "We're nearly caught up—despite that snake from the Nob—and then Holly came in with a question about getting the bedding shifted out of storage to the academy. Already."

He paused, slanting a glance down at her. "Have you eaten?"

"Oh. Forgot. That before the bath."

"Shall I bring you something?" he asked, pausing in the doorway.

She spread her hands. "No, no, if you have to go do ferreting in the city, I'll be fine."

He came back in, folded her into his arms, and murmured into her hair, "I love you."

"And I you."

He went out, stopping to ask the night duty fledgling to bring Lineas a hot meal because he knew she would forget, and was gone.

NINETEEN

It seemed to Lineas that suddenly one day they woke up and the world was green. Spring flourished in dramatic suddenness, and the western windows of the royal castle, open to the air, brought in the high, shrill voices of ten-year-olds, counterpointing the adolescent honk of the bigger academy seniors.

Among the new arrivals was Jarend Olavayir, Tanrid's son—who refused on his tenth Name Day to respond to the name "Cricket." He was already tall, though not nearly as huge as his father, uncle, and grandfather; the bucked teeth were less pronounced. He looked at the world through critical eyes, for he was orderly by nature.

It was also clear that he was going to be a problem.

The ten-year-olds had a housemaster for the first weeks, then a senior who slept in a tiny alcove off the dormitory with its two rows of beds. The housemaster named Faldred (Baldy to the youngsters) was a mild man who also instructed the academy in reading, writing, and mapping. A steady man, not given to wild punishments or coddling.

He was up talking to Danet, Noren, and finally Connar, every night of the week after the academy had its first inspection and began the routine that would carry them through to Victory Day.

"The Olavayir boy has been carefully taught," Baldy Faldred said. "Ahead of his group in reading and writing, very meticulous. Good skills on horseback, and knows how to shoot correctly. But he seems . . . " A hesitation, a shifted glance to the side, then, "I will say that the Mareca girl in particular teases way too much. So did her two brothers, coming through here. All three of them get the consequences. She's up at the mess hall washing and stacking dishes now. The other girls are also quick. Well, all children are generally quick when it comes to chaffing one another, but these girls tend to run in packs. And young Olavayir has yet to make friends. It could be said that he was born without a vestige of a sense of humor. He's constantly on the watch for the slightest deviation from the rules, and of course obeys them himself."

"He's a prig," Noren signed.

"I didn't want to say it, but yes."

Connar—nominally co-headmaster of the academy—sat back, arms crossed. Thinking that he had relinquished this duty to Noddy ages ago, he intended to keep silent.

Noren said, "Can you pair him with another child, one from whom he might learn better how to get along?" That was what her mother had done for her sister Hadand, to ready her for their separation when Noren moved to the royal city.

"I can try that, but then the others might squawk about special treatment."

"Then pair everybody up. Say it's new," Danet said. "Tell them the first lesson in command is to watch out for one another."

Faldred saluted. "I'll try that," he said, since obviously nothing better was being offered.

Connar walked out, found Jethren waiting in the hall, and gave a terse summation.

Jethren cracked a laugh. "If he were under me, I'd know how to discipline him."

Connar slanted a sardonic glance over his shoulder. "I'll suggest you replace me in co-running the academy." Let him get an earful of *But we've always done it THIS way . . .*

Jethren, still heady with success, heard that as a promotion, and said, "I'd be honored." He recollected how coddled Cricket Olavayir had been from infancy, and relished imagining him under Da's hands. Just for a day.

But then Connar changed the subject. "The armorer still waiting?"

"Yes. He's put together a new helmet. That is, it's the same helmet, but it has a raised piece up here on the back, with this sliding ring that moves up to permit more hair to be added, then slides down over it to lock it in place. He wants to show you."

Connar was indifferent to the helms. He couldn't stand wearing one, as it limited his vision, and made his head sweat unmercifully. But he knew that the sight of those scalp trophies was effective on enemies.

Jethren began cautiously, "Were there any other orders we ought to know about?"

Connar snapped his hand away as they started down the stairs two at a time, recollecting the conversation in the king's chambers before he got yanked in to listen to academy problems. "What do you know about these rumors accusing the Senelaecs?"

Every muscle in Jethren's body clenched. "I hear . . . there's talk in the taverns . . . something about Senelaec in effect running his own army."

Connar paused between steps, slewed around, and Jethren took the full impact of that angry blue gaze. "Who is stupid enough to say *that?*"

Jethren restrained the impulse to back away, and gestured, hands out. "It's gossip! People blab all the time! Their point being, the king," (he swallowed, nearly choking on the word) "passed laws years ago against the jarls having private armies."

Connar began walking again. "That was the old days, coming off that shit Mathren and his private army."

Jethren bit back the exclamation *But that was to put your father on the throne rightly his.*

Connar went on sardonically, "Not to mention the sort of private army Artolei and Ryu had last winter in Feravayir. The Eastern Alliance has trained together ever since my Da was a boy. And they don't train captains, but Riders." A fast look. "I didn't know about this yapping. What I meant was, rumors they're going to expand into Marlovayir, to make up for their shortfall in harvest. Even more stupid! Da sent a runner, suggesting that Marlovayir come over to Senelaec for their summer games. That should take care of that."

Jethren grimaced inwardly. His plan had failed—after he'd used up all his and his two captains' pay in buying rounds of drinks for his volunteers to spread the rumors in every tavern in the city.

He'd have to think of some other way to take Braids Senelaec out of the chain of command. Assassination was impractical. Even if he sent Moonbeam—who alone of all of them was likeliest to achieve it without being seen—Connar would order a ferocious investigation.

Jethren was still sweating when they reached the armorer's.

The royal summons came suddenly, six weeks later, as summer's first heatwave ripened berries and currants. Danet was in the last, most exasperating part of sorting out the monstrous mess of the Nyidri treasure, to be distributed through Feravayir in order of need. Her door opening and Sage saying, "The king sent for everyone," made all the calculations she had been juggling splinter like dreams when one is suddenly woken.

"Damn," she snapped, startling Sage.

Danet didn't bother explaining. Numbers, to most people—even to certain of her otherwise superlative runners—were something that happened to someone else, preferably far, far away. People only wanted to see the result.

"Tell him I'll be right there," she said, and bent over to jot quick notes as she tried to recapture the most important ones.

Connar had just ridden in from lance practice. He threw the reins to a stable hand, leaped down, to find Vanadei standing in the courtyard. "I was sent to find you," Vanadei said, fist to heart.

"On my way," Connar said, wondering what could be amiss that he hadn't heard about. He glanced around the courtyard, his gaze snagging on the Gannan pennon hanging near the gate, and spotted a line of horses in the guest stalls. A runner accompanied by an entire riding. That was odd.

Noddy and Lineas were already on their way from the state wing, Vanadei having been the first to be alerted by the king's hall runner. "Wants you both. And quiet," Vanadei had added before heading down to the stable to wait for Connar.

Quiet indeed. Not even Noren and Ranet were summoned.

Arrow sat in his interview chamber, exasperated. He'd given orders for Jarid Noth to take care of the Riders the Jarl of Gannan had sent, which was code for "Stash them somewhere and don't take your eyes off them."

Gannan's runner was just a runner. He would not have chosen to come on this expedition unless he was a madman. But Arrow still took fierce pleasure in totally ignoring the man left to stand inside the door. Arrow sat still, fists tight on knees as he watched the slight ticking in the shank buttons on his coat. He'd never noticed that before, the little bump, bump, bump of the shanks in time to the whoosh in his ears, and wondered if others ever observed that on themselves. Most were too busy. Heh.

Then the door opened, and in they streamed—the last one Quill, who saluted, then retreated to the wall opposite Lineas and Vanadei, who stood behind Noddy. Connar watched with narrowed eyes, wondering why three royal runners were necessary.

Arrow flashed a glance at Lineas. "Redhead! I keep forgetting your name. You take notes. I know you won't blab, unlike that pack of scribes over there in the other wing. I don't want any of this getting out."

Lineas dropped to her knees at the little side table where Arrow's runner in charge of messages usually sat. His ink was fresh, the quill sharp, and plenty of paper of various sizes waited, all of it smelling press-fresh. The king as well as the scribes got the best batches as a matter of course.

Lineas dipped the quill and waited as the king snapped his fingers and waved at the Jarl of Gannan's runner, without a glance in his direction. "Read it out for them."

The runner, his fingers shaking, picked up the paper the king had thrown down, and in a voice only slightly quavering, read out nothing short of an indictment, couched in the most pompous language imaginable, backtracking and restating *rumors from more than one trusted source* and *my family has been known for its loyalty ever since the founding of the kingdom* until it got to the point: "My son Senrid Gannan, Jarl of Stalgoreth, was not killed by the enemy but murdered."

Shock brought all the royal runners' heads up.

Connar stilled, arms tightening. Excuses and counter-accusations whirled through his mind as nausea churned in his gut. Of course Cabbage would poison him even from beyond death . . .

" . . . by Ranet Senelaec, otherwise known as Braids, Commander of the Eastern Alliance. While his father, the Jarl of Senelaec, is raising a private army, forbidden under the present king the first year of his reign, in order to invade a neighboring jarlate."

"Braids?" Noddy said, looking around bewildered. "Did I hear that right?"

Arrow thumbed his temples. "You did."

" . . . we, the undersigned, demand a hearing before the jarls."

And, clearing his voice a fourth time, the runner read out the names of four jarls and five captains of Riders.

The first to respond to the stunned silence was Danet. She sighed sharply, and got up from the mat beside Arrow. "The Senelaecs again?" she said, quite unfairly—and she knew it was unfair, but she had been yanked away from important work just when it was most ticklish. "I do *not* have time for this idiocy. It's yours to deal with," she said to Arrow, and walked out, the door shutting behind her with a decisive thump.

"You. Out," Arrow said to the Gannan runner. "Tell Denard in the hall to show you to the rest of your party. I'll send for you when I'm ready."

The door shut again, this time soundlessly.

Arrow drew in a breath. Then another, hating how short they were. "I can understand how angry that old jarl is. A handful of deaths, his son one. But every one of those who died has parents. None of them are throwing around wild claims."

"The Jarl of Senelaec was not even there," Noddy said. "He cannot ride a horse. Why would he invade Stalgoreth?"

"Gannan's saying it's a conspiracy," Arrow said. "And the invasion is supposed to be Marlovayir. Of course it's all fart noise, but he's got Zheirban, Eveneth, and Khanivayir backing him. We all know why, because it's not their sons getting the promotions. Jarl families, rank and birth, that's all those old shits bark about, every time I have to lay eyes on their damn faces at Convocation. I can't even confirm the Fath boy at Halivayir because he's not from a *jarl* family. Zheirban wants that worthless second son of his there so bad he can taste it. Him and his harem! Everyone knows he runs through money like water, over at the Sword. Those girls have him trained—and who can blame them, if an idiot is ready to throw down silver just to get his wick dipped ten times a night?"

Noddy—predictably—rumbled, "He's not that bad. It's just, he falls in love a lot. He thinks."

Arrow snapped his fingers. "Never mind Zheirban. Gannan's lies are the problem here."

Noddy said soberly, "Braids wouldn't kill Cabbage."

"Of course not," Arrow snapped, as Connar covertly watched Quill, wondering why he was there. "It's all noise. But deliberate noise, is what I'm learning. Camerend, report."

Camerend? It took a heartbeat for everyone to realize the wrong name had come out. Arrow, seeing their confusion, reddened. "Camerend—Quill—you know who I mean." He pinched fingers to the bridge of his nose.

Quill remained standing against the wall. "You may be aware of rumors noised against the Senelaecs during winter. Whenever rumors last more than a few days, especially if there's anything that touches on military matters, we report them to the king. He asked us to investigate."

Connar's head came up. He'd grown up hearing reports of various rumors, but until now he'd assumed they floated around the royal castle, and the king's runners brought them in. But he had never thought of deliberate investigation . . . by the royal runners?

Yes.

Quill went on, "We began to suspect that these rumors were generated inside the royal city here. Not at Senelaec, or even Marlovayir. We sent two runners to do nothing but listen at taverns in all three locations. Until the second thaw, when carters started moving out, carrying the usual load of gossip, there was no evidence of any such rumor in either Senelaec or Marlovayir. Therefore we assume that someone began them here in the city."

"The Jarl of Gannan, you think?" Noddy said unhappily. He did not like the jarl, but he could understand his anguish at losing his son. "But why? Didn't the letter say that Kendred, that is, Cabbage's first runner, is missing? They don't think *he* did it? But no, then why would they accuse Braids or his da of, well, isn't that *treason?*"

"Yes. Note that Gannan didn't quite say the word. But he dropped enough bricks around it so that even *I* could catch what he meant." Arrow sighed sharply. "My guess? Because Braids is the new Eastern Alliance Chief —notice Gannan called him a 'commander' although he knows very well that the Alliance chooses a chief, who is completely outside our chain of command. But what galls Gannan is that Braids will also be a jarl one day. That'll boost him in one jump from one of the smallest jarlates to the most powerful jarl of them all. Even though he's the backbone of northern defense, those sour old shits will be up on their hind legs barking about him sitting on the first bench. Because *that's* what matters to them." His voice sharpened,

Connar watched Noddy turn to Quill, who said quietly, "I can't speculate. We only deal in evidence."

Connar's heart thrummed sharply. The accusation against Braids was almost laughable. Almost, because clearly somebody somewhere had said something to raise suspicion. He didn't remember any first runner in the hailstorm at that riverside. Cabbage had been alone, or Connar wouldn't have acted—

He shut down that thought. "How will you go about investigating?" he asked.

Quill glanced his way. "We've been collecting eyewitness records written by observers who were with Alliance Chief Senelaec. We've got to find Gannan's first runner Kendred. Find out where he was, and what he saw. So far, all we know is that he was among the wounded carried off the field.

Broken leg—badly broken. But he managed to move some time after the various companies rode out of Stalgoreth. Or someone moved him."

Arrow said, "Quill, you go up to Stalgoreth yourself and ferret around until you find out. I think all Cabbage's people are still there." He cocked his head, as thumber rumbled in the distance. "Not tonight. Leave in the morning."

Quill saluted.

Arrow rubbed the sides of his head. "I have some sympathy. Some. Old Gannan lost a son. But I still think the man has rocks for brains." He waved an impatient hand. "Murder of a jarl's son . . . we'll have to grant his hearing, unless we can find proof that he's wrong. Until we do, we'll have to consider sending out notice to all the jarls." His voice rasped. "Maybe as well set the hearing for Victory Day, when a lot of 'em will be here to get their boys and girls."

The questions he could see in all the faces were just that, unanswerable all. He didn't want to hear those useless questions. The entire subject made his stomach ache and his head feel like it was stuffed with hot stones. He waved them all out, longing to eat something, to settle his stomach. Lie down for a while. His limbs felt heavy, which annoyed him the more. He was not an old man!

But he *was* a man with a headache, so he decided to let himself have a single cup of bristic early.

His rooms emptied, and he retreated to the bedroom, which was somewhat cooler. Then he took out his jug and poured half a cup. He'd stop there.

He sipped, and cursed. Even the bristic tasted bad, like iron. He was in the worst mood. What could Gannan be thinking? He still had a son, who would inherit Gannan! What use raising a fuss over Stalgoreth?

He took another sip, then spat it out. "Get me another jug. This one went bad," he said—and fresh irritation burned through him at the confusion in his chamber runner's face. "Don't you hear me?" He never bothered with Sign in his own rooms, but brought up his hands to reinforce the order, except the right had the shakes bad, and the left one felt odder by the moment, like a glove stuffed with sand.

He worked his dry mouth. Now his tongue felt like another glove filled with sand.

The runner moved abruptly away, and Arrow lay back, relieved not to be bothered with anyone. But then the runner returned with Danet, who dropped to her knees beside the bed. Twin anxious faces stared at him. He tried to demand what the trouble was, but that sock in his mouth muffled the words.

"Arrow, don't try to talk. Just . . . stay still." To the runner, "Summon the healer. No one else."

Arrow tried to say, leave that old nag alone, he's useless, but Danet laid a cool, dry hand across his brow, and said softly, "Just lie still. Don't talk."

Arrow found it easier to obey. He stared up at the face he knew so well. So many lines. Hadn't noticed before. His was probably far worse. But they were not quite sixty!

Then the healer was there, and reaching for his hand to take his pulse—which he never let him do. He hated that kind of fuss.

The healer's white brows drew together, but all he said was, "Anred-Harvaldar, get some rest. I'll send some medicine right away." And to the runner, "See that he drinks it all."

Arrow wanted to roll his eyes, but it was easier to close them.

Danet got up, her knees watery. As soon as they reached the outer room, she turned on the healer. "What is it? Apoplexy?"

"Yes. But so far, not devastating, and chances are good it won't be, if we can keep him quiet. I will prepare some willow steep with berry juice. That's all he is to drink, along with as much water as he wants, for now. Listerblossom if he complains of headache. Don't let anyone in who can fret him. He shouldn't talk, but if he gets upset at that order, let him talk himself out. He needs sleep most of all."

She found her mouth too dry for speaking, so she signed agreement, and the old man bustled away.

Danet turned to the waiting runners. "You heard. No one in. No one. I'll deal with the family. You keep everyone else out. Send them all to me."

She turned to the door, and then she was inside her suite, standing over her desk, feeling as if her head floated above her somewhere. But she had to think. So she sat down, and said to Sage, who was the duty runner at present, "Get Mnar Milnari—no, she's not here."

Danet remembered that Mnar had gone to Darchelde to see her family, after her crotchety old mother had finally died at age ninety-eight. It was the first time Mnar had been away from the royal castle since her arrival as a twelve-year-old. She'd never had but a day or so of liberty now and then in all those years.

Me either, Danet thought. But then, gunvaers don't get liberty. And if you bring that up, everyone will just say it's whining, who wouldn't want to be gunvaer and have everything you want?

What she wanted most of all was peace.

"Quill," she said to Sage. "Get Quill."

And when he was there, she explained what the healer had said, finishing, "I'm countermanding the king's orders. Send someone else to Stalgoreth to talk to those people, if you like. I'm convinced it's all a lot of noise, but Arrow will want to know something is being done. I need you to remain here . . ."

She didn't finish, but he struck hand to heart in understanding, privately resolving to brace himself for magic transfer as soon as he could be sure of a few hours.

TWENTY

Danet called Noddy and Connar in first. Mindful of Noddy's easily bruised feelings when someone was in pain, she told them what had happened, stressing that the healer felt that their Da would recover if left in peace.

"What do you want us to do?" Noddy asked soberly.

"I asked Jarid Noth to send the Gannan party back to their jarl, promising that a royal communication would follow soon. I told him not to give them any travel food—they can buy their own," she added acidly.

Not even Noddy argued with that.

Danet turned to him. "I think Arrow would want you to continue at the state wing. Set aside any affairs that absolutely must be decided by him, and take care of everything else. The more that gets done, the easier he will be. Anything you can't decide, we can go over together before pressing it on Arrow, until we know he's improving. Connar?"

He had been staring at the wall, and started at the sound of his name. "Yes?"

"I've told Quill what's going on, as he's the leader of the royal runners, and oversees runners going in and out. Since I believe that the Jarl of Gannan's idiocy is exactly that—as if Senelaec could afford even a *tiny* army and me not know about it—I asked him to lay aside investigating on his own. I know he's the best, which is why we need him *here*. He can send one of his eager young runner students up to Stalgoreth. We'll have to have interview papers to counter Gannan's lies. But that wasn't what I meant to say." She rubbed her eyes and dropped her hands, guilt oppressing her. She could not help but think that Arrow's apoplexy was her fault for stalking out and telling Arrow that it was his mess to deal with.

Well, now she had to take the consequences. Including never letting herself indulge in private spites again.

"Connar . . . you'll be making all military decisions, until your da recovers. I can't help you there. But I do suggest you send someone you trust up to Senelaec, maybe even to Marlovayir, for a friendly visit and a tour around, which becomes an official search only in the extreme unlikelihood anything is amiss. I'd believe the moon is made of cream before I'd believe

Wolf Senelaec intends to invade anything outside of his bed at the end of a long day."

"Sure," both her sons said.

Noddy walked out, determined to get right to work.

Connar went straight to Jethren, who saw in a heartbeat that there was trouble.

Connar gave a brief summation, then, "I never saw that first runner. He should have been there, though I didn't think of it in that moment."

"Visibility was bad, that I do remember. I'll send Sleip and Punch to find out. They're my two best scouts."

Connar met his gaze straight on. "Do they know what to do if there's any question about what this Kendred saw?"

They are Nighthawk men, Jethren wanted so very badly to say. It was too soon—though the day was coming, he was sure of it now. With a ring of conviction in his usually flat voice, he said, "They're trained to be quiet and effective."

Connar left to think through alternate plans.

Jethren said to Moonbeam, "Summon the scouts. And we'd better pass the word to everyone else, heads down, be ready for anything." Jethren eyed Moonbeam's grin, and the tension in his hands as he played with a knife. "Are the ghosts bothering you?"

Jethren had learned as they grew up that when Moonbeam began honing his knives obsessively, he would soon be using them to test whether his "ghosts" were real or not, and it would be inconvenient if he stabbed someone important by mistake. It was time for a dose.

Connar threw himself into overseeing the plans for Victory Week—a tradition he loathed—as well as the tedious task of sorting for assignment the seniors who had finished their last year of the academy, as days, then weeks slipped by.

The news that the king had suffered an apoplexy leaked out slowly at first, as news does—but when it got to runners not enjoined to silence, it spread as fast as a horse could gallop. Danet was able to control it to the extent that the rumors were mitigated by assurance that the king was fine, recovering nicely.

However, the truth was not as clear. Danet went to see Arrow every morning after she woke and each evening before she retired. His entire left side had paralyzed, slowly worsening. His speech was gone except for two words that seemed random, *no* and *yes.*

"Do you want some coffee?"

"No, no, no, yes, no, yes, yes."

If she held a cup next to his right hand, he would paw vaguely at it, but they discovered they had to be very careful when letting him drink—his chamber runner said liquids, even water, choked him. They gave him liquids with a little spoon, and boiled his food into soup or pottage.

A few weeks in, his oldest runner said apologetically, "We think we know what he's trying to tell us when we bring in cups and mugs."

Danet sighed. "Drink, of course."

"The healer said on no account may he have any strong drink, including small beer. We're supposed to get the willow infusion into him three times a day, but he, well, he . . . ."

"Show me."

Danet sat by, and watched Arrow frown then spit out the bitter medicine, as if he were a small child. Sick fear chilled her. She took his face into her hands, and gazed into his eyes. "Are you in there, Arrow? Tap my hand twice. Or kick me, if that's easier."

"Yes, yes, yes, no, no, no." He made vague motions with his right hand, fingers clumped together. Memory struck hard—the strength in those hands holding Noddy high above the river waters when they crossed Olavayir's border thirty years before.

She turned away, her throat aching. "I'll be back after the night watch changes," she said huskily, determined to speak to him like an adult. Maybe, maybe, he heard her. If he was asking for drink, surely that meant that Arrow was still inside that poor head.

Noddy came in when he knew his father was sleeping, as he couldn't bear to see him struggling one-sided, and babbling that incessant no/yes. He sat by Arrow, sometimes late into the night, holding his curled left hand and gently smoothing the fingers flat, then kneading the muscles with his thumbs as Arrow's breathing deepened. When his own fingers tingled from the time spent gently working at those cruelly stiffened tendons, he slipped away silently again.

Connar came by twice, but it disturbed him so deeply to see Arrow helpless, uncommunicative, that he told Danet, "If he wakes up, or asks for me, I'll come at once wherever I am, whatever I'm doing. But I can't look at him like that."

Connar ordered his day by thinking *Da would want this done* before each task. His reward was Danet's tired smile when he stopped by her rooms to report. But countering that was the pain in Noddy's oft-expressed, "When do you think he'll be better?"—as if Connar would know.

When he was away from the second floor, that invisible knife prick goaded him with memories of Cabbage: in the kitchen garden, at the academy, at Tlennen Field.

At Stalgoreth.

Oppressing them all was the matter of Gannan's demanded hearing. It was the king's prerogative to call in the jarls, and none of them wanted to do it for him—undiscussed, but on all their minds, lay the question, what if the king got no better? Victory Day was not that far off. The most distant jarls would have to ride the very day they received the summons, if they were to reach the royal city in time.

Danet, Noddy, and the family told each other they needed proof that the accusations were false, so the whole thing could be made to vanish.

Connar remained silent.

One hot summer morning a few days before Danet had mentally promised herself to resolve it one way or another, Connar was seeing off a company of academy seniors and first-year garrison warriors to run a ride-and-shoot out on the plains below the south river, the winners getting liberty to play in the water and the losers having to tend the horses and pick up the arrows. As they were mounting up, calling insults and challenges back and forth, from the city gates in the distance two trumpet blasts beat on the somnolent air—jarl reversed, which meant a jarlan was arriving.

Connar mentally shrugged as he watched the columns form up then ride out. Jarlans were the women's business.

In rode a party that had drawn aside for ride-and-shoot company to pass through the castle gate. A Rider bore a single crimson and black pennon: Senelaec. The mass resolved into two women among a lot of senior-age boys, these boys wearing colorful clothes of rose and yellow and contrasting blues, greens, and silver, instead of Rider gray or brown.

Sartorans? No. The garments, not quite coats, were tight-waisted, but with fluttering sleeves, and the skirts long, slit high at the sides and back, revealing trousers in bright colors, and riding boots made of different shades of dyed leddas, with tassels swinging at the top. The boys drew attention away from the woman in the robe so faded that its crimson was no more than pale pink, rose at seams. And every one of them, including the jarlan and her runner, carried swords at their saddles, and bows.

The boy who immediately who drew the eye had the Olavayir short upper lip, but on him it was an attractive curve, revealing just the tips of two white teeth, in a beautiful face dominated by limpid brown eyes.

"Connar-Laef!"

Connar's attention went to the thin pink-robed woman, her face lined face under sun-bleached light hair. He knew her. She was Calamity Senelaec, met the last time he rode through Senelaec on the way to Ku Halir, back when they were chasing Yenvir the Skunk.

He approached the party as they reined in. "Did we know you were coming?"

"You did not. I hope to find your mother free," the jarlan said as she dismounted, and then, coming closer, "How is Arrow?"

Connar gave the answer everyone in the family gave while in public hearing, "He's better."

Calamity's face brightened. "Good! I'm to bring him Wolf's greetings, if he'll see me."

By then Fnor, Danet's first runner, had appeared. "Jarlan." She saluted.

Calamity looked from one to the other of her party. "I'll leave you to it," she said, and followed Fnor inside, her first runner at her heels, carrying the jarlan's gear.

Connar turned to the group of teenage boys, dominated by that attractive blond one, who gazed at him with a quirk of humor.

"And this is . . ."

"Don't recognize me, Brother?"

The clothes looked Idegan, but that voice was pure Marlovan. "No," Connar said.

The boy chuckled, a happy sound. "Well, no surprise there. I'm sorry to report that Grandma, whom you never met, died at the turn of the season, so I'm free—it being much too late for me to run in your academy."

"Andas?"

"In the flesh." Andas turned his hand in an airy circle, indicating a thin redhead with slanting brows and a crooked mouth, "Evred Tyavayir. His Uncle Stick is at Ku Halir." And he went on to introduce the rest of his party—all connected to Halivayir, Tyavayir, and a few from freeholds like Farendavan.

"Come inside," Connar said, gesturing to Fish to take charge of the other boys. "Noddy will be glad to see you."

"I know," Andas said. "He wrote so many letters to Grandma begging her to let me visit just once. I don't know what she expected would happen to me here. It doesn't look all that threatening. Or maybe she thought I wouldn't go back." He chuckled. "She probably thought I'd be lured away from business."

"Business?" Connar repeated.

"Farendavans are drapers." Andas flicked one of his rose-dyed sleeves. "You knew that, surely—"

"Is that really Andas?"

Noddy appeared at a lumbering run, and promptly enveloped the boy in a massive hug that threatened to squash him. But Andas only chuckled, and the two started talking over each other so fast that Connar left unnoticed to get back to his day.

Calamity forgot them all as she followed the runner upstairs. So many years had passed since the jarlans rode to Convocation, though sometimes it seemed only a year or two ago. Danet's letters ever since had been in response to Calamity's—who had recognized with that vague sick sense that no matter how hard she tried to be funny and sisterly in those letters, with long descriptions of everybody, Danet's replies had been courteous, you could say friendly, but they could have been read in the middle of a town square. The private Danet had gone behind the gunvaer door and locked it.

So Calamity had no idea how this visit would be received, but for Wolf's sake—for them all—she had to make the attempt.

Danet had received the news of her arrival with surprise, then consternation, remembering all those wild rumors about invasions. As she ruthlessly cleared her schedule, sending every runner on the second floor dashing in all directions, she pictured some combined force of Gannan and Khanivayir heavies marching on Senelaec to . . . to do what? Help with the farming?

Shutting down her chattering mind, she ordered the chamber runner to fetch cold water, fresh fizz, and whatever the cooks had prepared for midday, and then sat behind her low table, hands gripped in her lap, as the sound of quick women's footfalls preceded the appearance of Fnor escorting Calamity.

The two women studied each other, each shocked at how much the other had aged. Calamity had practiced her salute and made it now, then began her prepared speech, "I know this is a vast intrusion, Danet-Gunvaer, but for the sake of—"

"Sit down, Calamity." And because of her own stupid surmises, she added, "Is Senelaec being invaded?"

"No!" Calamity dropped on the guest mat as if someone had turned her knees to water. "Horrible thought. We lost far too many people at Ku Halir. I don't think we could fight off a gaggle of granddas with one leg and one eye between them."

Food and drink appeared then, and both waited until Danet sent the runners out again with a glance at the door.

Calamity was hungry and thirsty, but she had to get this out first. "We know all about Gannan's threats. He tried to get Knuckles Marlovayir to join! I never thought I'd be grateful to him—he *still* talks about the Night of the Moons as if it was the funniest thing that ever happened—but that's far different than Gannan and his poison. Anyway, I needed to get here before Braids does. He's going to offer to relinquish his command—"

"Of the Eastern Alliance?"

"*All* of it. Everything. If that's what it takes to shut up Gannan and those other old farts."

"No chance. Connar wouldn't let him go."

"That's what we tried to tell him, but I think he feels terrible that he wasn't somehow able to prevent Cabbage's death. He chokes up if the young man's name even comes up. As if Braids could save everyone on the field!" Calamity sighed, then said, "Wolf sent me to you to propose this: that Braids be left as he is, and nothing will change on the surface. Except when Wolf dies, the jarlate can die, too. That is, it can go to whoever Arrow thinks best. So many of our best died on that road that day . . . we've always been short on farming, but now it's worse than ever." And Calamity recounted sobering, even shocking numbers.

Danet grimaced. She had skimmed the reports numbering the dead after that nightmare at Ku Halir, confining herself to what she could deal with, which were the numbers pertaining to supply and rebuilding. But deep down she had not wanted to know how much the Senelaecs had sacrificed.

"Old Tdan Tlennen said when she came out for the wedding New Year's Week—though everything was iron hard, under black frost—she could tell by what grows and what doesn't that we have more sand than soil in places. One look, and she knew! *I* didn't know that, and I've lived there since I was ten! She said it has something to do with how the rivers used to be long, long ago. I don't know how much of that is true, but, well, one thing I do know is, you're always having to come to our rescue from the royal harvest storage, even though Arrow forgave our taxes twice."

Danet winced as Calamity glanced up, clearly trying to keep the suspicious gleam along her lower eyelids from brimming over.

Calamity continued with determined cheer, "It was so very good to have a wedding, instead of memorials. Thank you, by the way, for agreeing to let them marry."

"I told Braids years ago he could pick his wife. And I know Henad's first betrothed was killed at Halivayir, which left her without anyone."

"They were so very close, too. Grew up together, knowing they'd marry one day. We thought she'd never get over him, but there she was, fighting alongside Braids, and, well, somehow the two of them . . . ." She thumped her heart, her mouth crooked.

Danet had the sudden thought that Calamity was like a bird. It was ridiculous on her own part to resent a bird for being true to its nature. Even if Calamity lived to be old, she was always going to be flighty.

"Calamity. Drink some of this fizz," Danet said, and now she sounded like the Danet of old. "Or the cook will be insulted."

Calamity blinked down at the purple liquid, tasted it, then sat back, her lips rimmed with red. "That's *delicious!* What's in it?"

Danet talked about fermented berry juice recipes, and from there they went on to catch up on family details until the meal was over, then she sent Calamity off to enjoy a bathe and a rest while she walked down to the garrison side to find Connar.

As soon as he saw her, he broke away from the knot of men he was talking to, and advanced quickly to her side. "No change," she said in an undervoice. "But I've something that has to be discussed. I would like you there. It concerns you, and you might be able to see something differently from me."

Together they went up to the king's suite, where they found Arrow lying on his bed in fresh clothes, his hair braided loosely to keep it from snarling around his neck and face, as no one likes lying on a pillow with his hair clasped high. One of the runners had brought in fresh herbs whose acerbic scent Arrow liked, and set them between the bed and the open window. Arrow's eyes were open, and his head turned to track them.

Danet sat down by the bed and took Arrow's right hand in hers. The fingers twitched. She squeezed them gently, her throat tight, but she spoke steadily, restating everything Calamity had said.

Connar frowned when she reached Braids offering to give up command, but then his expression smoothed when Danet got to Calamity's and Wolf's counter-offer. "This is a royal decision, Arrow. We need to know what you want here. Senelaec lost more than I realized." But she would make up for that. Her guilt was not his burden to bear. "They seem at peace with the idea of releasing the jarlate on his death. Which no one can claim is a traditional one. In fact, its creation was the beginning of that stupid feud. There might even be some oldsters alive who can remember it. But Calamity assured me that the Marlovayirs are not any part of Gannan's allegations."

Arrow stirred, and out came a stream of nos and yesses as he looked to the side. Danet let go his hand. He groped, the yesses rising in frustration.

"What do you need? Water? Are you hungry?"

"No, no, no, no, yesyesyes . . ."

The word slurred as Arrow turned his head again—and Connar understood: that was the cabinet where he always kept the jug of bristic he'd secretly shared with the boys on some Restday evenings, after the queen had gone to bed. "I think he wants a drink," Connar said. "From the cabinet."

"Well he can't," Danet retorted sharply.

"Not even a taste?" Connar asked, as Arrow's voice rose, *yesyesyesno!*

This was the first definite response either of them had seen that Arrow's mind was indeed present. Danet sighed. "Arrow, this is not me denying you, it's the healer. If he thought it would do you any good, I'd sit here and hold you while you drank as much as you liked. But he said that *any* of it might kill you. We had the runners take it all away. We've got fresh-made fizz in your jug now, if you don't want water."

Arrow collapsed back, closing his eyes.

Danet firmly suppressed tears, and spoke gently. "So, about Senelaec. Are you agreed that Wolf remains jarl until his death? After that, Braids stays commander of the Eastern Alliance, but he won't become a jarl as well as head of the Alliance, which I suspect is the real sticking point."

She sighed. "As for Braids killing Gannan's boy, Quill brought me three separate testimonies from Cabbage Gannan's own people. These three rode the entire battle with Braids, who was never anywhere near Cabbage Gannan. All three offered to be questioned under white kinthus. I can write up a formal response to Gannan refusing the hearing, including copies of all these things, if you agree."

Arrow's fingers groped, and when she took his hand, he gripped hers.

"That's agreement?"

"Nononononoyesyesyesss."

Connar met Danet's eyes. "I think he's saying yes."

"I do, too."

Arrow pulled his hand away, frustrated that his mouth wouldn't say the words that he wanted: he didn't see any need for Wolf to make such a promise, or for Braids to resign his command, and old Gannan was a lying pile of road apples.

But as usual, no one understood him. Disgusted, he gave up. It was good to see the family, but except for Bunny, it was always a relief when they left, for they always tried to get him to talk.

Maybe it was all her years of tending to animals, large and small; Bunny never tried to make him talk, but softly combed out his hair in a way that felt so good on his scalp, and rubbed his feet so that they didn't jerk and twitch, and she crooned nonsense words in a small singsong. It wasn't a beautiful voice. He still had not found anyone whose voice matched his memory of Sinna, lost so long ago, but he liked to listen to her until he drifted into dreams.

Connar didn't see either of the visitors for the remainder of the week. He'd forgotten about them until he nearly ran into Andas, who had wandered over to the garrison court to watch the castle guards at morning drill.

Andas looked up at Connar, and grinned. Today he wore plum and light blue, with those absurd sleeves that would get in the way of everything.

"Did you want something?" Connar asked.

"Just watching," Andas said, and added in a way typical of seventeen, "That drill is so easy. I learned it by the time I was thirteen, when I first rode with the Faths on perimeter runs." He smothered a yawn, then admitted, "Anyway I ran out of coins. I thought when we came I couldn't possibly spend everything Uncle Brother gave me. But I've never been in a city before."

Amused, Connar said, "What did you spend it on? Surely not clothes—I've never seen that kind of thing you're wearing anywhere in the city."

"These are Idegan fashions," Andas said, shaking out his sleeves. "I go up there twice a year to sell our linens. Most of us, except Evred Tyavayir, have family on both sides of the mountain. And no, I wouldn't buy anything here. Except maybe those boots you all wear. Ours look good, but one season and they sag at the ankle, or have to go back to the cobbler for soles and heels. But I don't have enough coin left to order any. The boys at the Sword are *expensive*."

"So are the girls," Connar said appreciatively. "There are a lot of Marlovans up in Idego? I thought they all spoke that mush-mouthed type of Iascan."

"Mush-mouthed." Andas snickered. "They all think it's descended from real Sartoran. But no, only the old people sometimes speak Marlovan. Like, those over thirty, and even older. Everybody else up there speaks *Idegan.* They dress like this, but their drills are tougher than that." He canted a thumb toward the whirling swords in the courtyard. "And the riding is like what we do."

"So no one seems to want to reunite with the south?" Connar leaned against an archway, crossing his arms.

Andas pursed his lips, gazing upward, then turned his wide brown gaze to Connar. "Why would they? Business is better, the old folks all say, Tax is completely different, and nobles don't pay *any* taxes, because they defend the harbors when the king calls. We get more for our linens up there, because they like colors, so it's worth the hire of caravans. My cousin—well, he's a fifth-cousin, the second prince. He told me that Idego is twice as wealthy as it ever was while part of Marlovan Iasca."

"Do they regard you as a prince up there?" Connar asked.

Andas snorted. "Grandma said only to use that to buff the price of linens, which sell to the best. Grandma told me all the time that being a Farendavan was better than any king." He turned a shrewd gaze to Connar. "Are you asking, do I want to ride down here to be third in line for king? No. I've heard all the stories about all the Olavayirs fighting each other over the throne. Grandma made sure of that. But if someone attacked Noddy, I bet I could raise all Lorgi Idego to back him."

It sounded like seventeen-year-old bravado, but his gaze was steady.

Connar said, "Backing Noddy is my job."

Andas's quick grin returned. "That's what Noddy says. I don't know you, but Noddy's letters always bragged about you. So did Da's," he finished soberly. "I hate seeing him like that. Can't talk. I blabbed a lot, but I couldn't tell if he understood a word I said. Except he held onto my hand like I was towing him in a lake, and when the healer brought out the willow steep, he made a face like he was going to puke. I hated watching him try not to drink it, and how they talked to him as if he were a little child."

"The healer is doing his best," Connar said. "He believes that a diet of willow infusion and the berry draft somehow makes his blood flow better."

Andas turned up his palm. "I offered to bring Da some dark ale—he used to write to me about how much he liked that—but the healer landed all over me, and that's when I came away. I didn't ride all the way here to get jawed at."

"The healers say it would kill him," Connar stated.

"Oh. He could have said that, instead of jawing all over about how thoughtless I am, and laloo haloo. If he isn't going to change, I guess it's better we're riding out after Restday."

A step on the other side of the arch, and there was Jethren. "The lancers want to know if you're riding out with them," he asked, Moonbeam at his shoulder.

Connar turned. "Tell Needle to saddle my horse. Andas, want to watch?"

"Will you do targets or just evolutions?" Andas hedged. "Evolutions are boring—lances going in circles—but if you're charging targets, and the lances might break, that's fun!"

"We can arrange that."

Moonbeam's restless hands stilled, then his thumb stroked along the blade of his knife, stroke, stroke. The time had come, at last.

Purpose.

"But there can be no knife," Jethren had said over and over. "Understand? You can't lay a finger on him. If you do, they'll know it's us, and if we're dragged to the flogging post for treason, then who'll be loyal to the true king?"

Moonbeam understood that, and so he had continued to visit them all at night, in preparation for the day when Keth Jethren said, *It's time.*

Except that Keth Jethren was too busy worrying about the scouts and the search for Kendred, and his daily orders, and Moonbeam suspected he had never been able to see the ghosts. That false king's pain was brighter than the breathing part of him. It was time to free him from pain and let him join the ghosts.

Moonbeam knew all about pain, every kind, from white-hot to dull blue.

Extraordinarily quick and nimble, by age four he'd been his father's pride until the night Anderle Vaskad killed the boy's family before his eyes, one by one, as a lesson in who held the power of life and death.

After that his memories splintered, and stayed splintered as Vaskad began brutal training to make him into the world's best assassin as a gift for Mathren Olavayir.

But that dream ended the Night of Blood, when Keth Jethren as a little boy crawled into Moonbeam's hiding place, and held his hand until the screaming died away.

After that Moonbeam had two purposes: the one Keth's father trained him to was to kill Mathren's murderer. The one he chose was to protect Keth Jethren, the little boy who shared everything with him, who brought bandages when Moonbeam was bleeding, who kept his secrets after the bad days, who didn't laugh when Moonbeam signed about the ghosts. Who never tried to make him talk, because Moonbeam had learned early that the wrong words were so very, very painful. Better never to speak at all.

Jethren was the one who found the medicine that made the ghosts—who Moonbeam didn't want to see again until they could become real—turn into smoke.

Moonbeam was very good at moving about without anyone knowing where he was. He stole a jug of the very best bristic, and carried it back to the royal castle.

The false king glowed pain-red and yellow, blue only after they forced the bitter drink down his throat, if he didn't cough it up. He said the drink hurt his stomach, and Moonbeam saw the way he curled around it while glowing with the orange pain of fire. Moonbeam had watched for days, until he heard the way to free him from the pain. And there would be no knife, just as Jethren said.

It was time.

Moonbeam drifted along the shadows to wait until the hour past midnight, when he saw the golden light snuff in the tiny window next to the big open windows that belonged to the king.

Then he moved noiselessly to the second floor, and into the king's chambers.

Moonbeam poured out the bristic very carefully, and as gently as a nurse with a newborn, put one strong, scarred hand under Arrow's head and with the other hand helped guide the cup to his lips.

Arrow was beyond wondering who this shadowy figure was in the dark. His head sank back as the longed-for, sweet fire lit up his veins.

Oh, the burn was so very, very good.

It was so good, so very good to just lie in the warmth of that fire, and think back to when he was a second son, riding around the three hills of Nevree. His heart pumped hard as if he were galloping and his limbs turned to water, but that was all right as memory surged and billowed around him, impossibly bright. The wind had never smelled fresher, the sun warmer, and even riding no longer hurt. The horse's gait was so gentle, slowing and slowing, and as he reached farther into those long sunny days of boyhood oh! There he was at last, Sinna singing.

TWENTY-ONE

Connar was in the bath when Fish appeared with neatly folded clothes. "You'd better come," was all he said.

"What?" Connar barked, surging out of the water.

Fish looked away, his throat working. "The king—" He stopped, as all through the castle the great bells began to toll in steady rhythm.

Connar thrashed into the clothes then ran up the stairs four at a time. He noted armed guards at every landing, for the first time in memory, and raced past them. He burst into the king's chamber, still barefoot, his wet hair slapping his back. Armed guards had blocked off the landing at both ends, put there by Jarid Noth, who stood just inside the king's interview room, not far from where Danet leaned against a table, blanched of face.

Connar pushed past a couple of runners and walked into the bedroom, the old healer bent over Arrow lying on the bed, at first glance peaceful, but Connar had been around the stillness of death long enough to recognize it.

He turned away. "What—when? Was no one on duty?" he snapped, whirling about to glare.

Poor old Nath stood by, looking as if he'd been gutted. "I went to bed at midnight. Same as always. He lay peaceful, like every night. He drank his medicine. Everything the same—"

The old healer straightened up from the bedside. "Not the same. There is a strong scent of drink here. Bristic," he added.

"Impossible," Nath whispered. "There was no bristic in this room. You can ask Aldren, who helped me change the king's sleep shirt for the night. We checked everything before he went to sleep, and I never left the outer chamber until I retired."

All eyes turned to the far cupboard, which Arrow could not possibly have reached—even if it had contained any liquor.

Connar bit back the words *Why was there not a close perimeter guard?* He knew no one had been stationed to watch all night on the landings. Arrow himself had said it was a cruel, stupid duty. The night guard patrolled, and the halls were not empty for long between circuits.

As if reading his mind, Jarid Noth said, "The night patrol reported nothing out of the ordinary. After midnight, everyone moving about is noted down. Everyone. I can bring the chalkboard, but I assure you, all looked exactly as usual."

Connar's memory brought an image: drill court, and Andas's bright head as he talked about—

"Where's Andas?"

"They're having breakfast," Danet said, brows meeting. "Why?"

"Something he said yesterday—no. The day before. He might . . . he might have meant well."

Danet snapped, "Fetch him. No one else," she added, and runners ran.

Andas ran in a short time later that seemed unconscionably long to those still standing there. His wide eyes turned in question from one to the next, then at last to the still figure, and rounded in starkness. "Is he—what happened?" He whispered, as if speaking too loudly might disturb that figure on the bed.

Connar fought to keep his voice even. "Did you bring Da a little gift last night? Meaning well?"

"Gift?" Andas repeated.

"Bristic. Did you give him a little?"

The old healer spoke up, voice dry as corn husks. "From the smell, this was not a little. There's a pool of it still in him."

Andas's mouth rounded. "No! I only came over with Noddy yesterday, after Restday drum. Then we went out riding. And I was with Evred the rest of the day, until we went to sleep—wasn't even late, because we had to rise early for the road—"

Danet lifted her hand and the babble shut off. "Go sit in there. Wait. Do not move."

And when Andas moved like a figure in a dream, she shut the door and turned to Connar and the runners. "Who else would do this to him? If there's that much in Arrow, then it's deliberate."

Fnor said quietly, "Assuming Andas Farendavan would want to give the king this drink, is he good enough to bypass all the patrols?"

"Boys," Danet said heavily, "can do anything if they put their minds to it."

No one pointed out that girls could be just as sneaky. There was no use in that. Absent of clues, they had absolutely nothing to go on.

Danet shut her eyes. "Let him go. Even if it turns out he's lying, what could we prove except teenage stupidity? Andas loved Arrow. He would never have wanted him dead. I'd stake my own life on it. Let him go." At last the tears she'd been fighting began to spill as she said, "Someone has to tell Noddy. I think it had better be me." To Jarid Noth and then to Connar, "The word will spread fast. You two make sure everything is orderly. No one speak of bristic. Including to Noddy. Let him get over the worst of the shock first, while we try to figure out who is responsible."

Connar could not bear to look at that frail figure on the bed again. He pushed his way out, then another thought occurred:

Hauth.

He yanked his hair into its clasp, pulled on his boots, and left his chamber. As soon as he got downstairs, he was surrounded. In that mysterious way of astonishing news, by the time he had crossed the castle to the military wing, moving at his fastest walk, somehow word raced ahead of him and shock radiated through the castle.

Strictly controlling his own upset, Jarid Noth dealt with the castle sentries and guards. Connar faced a crowd of King's Army lancers, Riders, and boys a year out of the academy. "I want a triple perimeter patrol," he said in his field voice.

"Is there . . . danger?" an eighteen-year-old forgot himself enough to say.

Connar glared. The boy stood rigid, eyes down, face red. The king was dead—they all knew it—they were excited, but under that, he saw the signs of fear, the same signs he saw before a charge.

"No," he said. "No danger. Because there is no danger, we're going to patrol to demonstrate that all is in order. Understood?"

This time the thud of fists against chests and a resounding "Understood!" echoed up the stones.

He meant what he said, but the motivation was to clear out all these staring the eyes, the busy mouths. It was too easy to imagine Hauth sending one of those old Olavayir Nighthawk men to sneak into the king's bedroom.

The urge to hurl guards at the man was nearly irresistible, but his own culpability required a personal visit: he should have confessed Hauth's idiocy to Arrow years ago. But he hadn't. For so many reasons that made sense at thirteen, and then sixteen, and then he'd tried not to think about it for years.

Noddy had Ma, and Noren, Ranet, Vanadei and all the second floor and the third floor as well to surround him. Right now it was important for Connar to take care of the dirt before he could face Noddy.

But even with the king's army battalions out riding around the city, there were still so many people coming at him from all sides, each with urgent questions to be dealt with. All day he labored until Fish appeared, silently holding a tray. Only when he smelled coffee and saw the wine-braised fish and tartlet did Connar permit himself to become aware of the headache pounding his temples, and his gnawing stomach.

Jethren appeared behind him, silent, clearly waiting for orders. Connar glared his way, then at Fish, who he knew regularly reported to Hauth. He was fairly certain Jethren no longer did, but he was one of those Nighthawk men.

He slammed down the coffee cup. "Where were you last night at midnight?" he rapped out.

Fish's head moved back, his eye wide with surprise. "You gave me liberty yesterday after the watch change," he reminded Connar. "I was with Hibern," naming his lover in the city. "Came back at the clang."

The "clang" being the single bell one hour before the dawn watch. Which was as usual. Connar picked up the mug again, knowing he could question Fish's lover—who might or might not tell the truth, but Fish's clear astonishment, and the question in his face, made the suspicion die down. They all knew the king had died, but not about the bristic. Fish seemed totally bewildered instead of guilty.

Connar turned his narrowed gaze to Jethren, whose brow furrowed in unspoken question. "You gave us liberty. I was at the Sword with Sholt and Iceheel."

Connar pinched his fingers to the bridge of his nose, wishing the headache would lift. It was so easy to throw suspicion at these men who all were connected with Hauth. He needed to deal with Hauth himself. That was the source of his distrust.

"Fish, go see if my brother wants me, but if he's buried in the entire family pack—"

"Connar-Laef!" Jethren and Fish were violently thrust to either side. "You'd better come," Vanadei whispered, terror making him almost unrecognizable.

This time Connar ran up the stairs five at a time, skidding around the corner, and bolted down the hallway faster than he ever had as a boy.

He nearly ran down Noren, who was just then coming out of the heir's suite, her eyes red and puffy, her expression ravaged. Ranet stood behind her, but Connar scarcely gave her a glance as Noren signed, "He won't talk to me." Her hands stiffened so that the tendons stood out, and her eyes closed, tears leaking from beneath her lashes.

"Where is my mother?"

"She was with Quill. She wants him to drop everything and investigate . . . ." She twirled a finger in the air, the sign for *Bristic.*

Vanadei opened Noddy's door, and gestured for Connar to enter. "He's in there."

Connar bushed past.

Bunny crouched directly outside Noddy's bedroom. She looked up with red-rimmed eyes. "He won't let anyone in but you."

Connar pushed open the door and looked inside the bedroom, which at first seemed empty, the bed neatened, everything in order. It was lit by a single candle. But then what looked at first like a shadow in the far corner shifted, and he saw Noddy sitting in the corner, his knees drawn up.

Never in either of their lives had Connar thought his brother small, but Noddy looked small, somehow, with one arm thrown around his head, his face turned into his elbow as he wept.

Connar crossed the room in two strides, and knelt down. "Noddy."

Noddy gave a great, shuddering sob. "I can't do it, Connar. I can't."

Connar smelled blood. He frowned, eyeing Noddy twisted up, and said in a different key, "Noddy? Did someone hurt you?"

The wakening anger roused Noddy enough for him to straighten slightly, revealing a wet, dark patch over his left shoulder, seeping downward. His right hand still clutched a blood-streaked knife. "I tried . . . I tried, but I can't get past my ribs."

Shock reverberated through Connar. "Noddy, give me the knife."

"Don't make me be . . . in there," Noddy sobbed.

"I'm not making you do anything." Connar forced his voice low. Quiet. "Noddy. Please. The knife first." As he spoke, he closed his hands around Noddy's blood-slippery fingers, and gently loosened the hilt.

He set the knife well behind him, and clasped Noddy's huge hand, sticky as it was, and said, "Talk to me, Noddy. Who tried to make you do what? I'll kill them—"

"They said I have to go into Da's room." Noddy's voice was husky with horror. "I can't do it. I can't."

"You don't have to do anything right now," Connar said. "I'm here. I won't let anyone in until you want them. But you have to tell me, what happened here?"

Noddy just wagged his head, lost in grief, until Connar said, "Noddy, the first thing people are going to say is that I stabbed you."

Noddy's head jerked up at that. He roused, mouth working. Then his face crumpled. "It hurts so bad. And when they said I have to . . . I thought . . . Kill the *pain.* I can't take Da's place. I can't be in that room."

Connar got it then. Noddy had taken the knife to himself.

He let out a breath, then another, the hammer in his head relentless. He tried to gentle his voice. "Noddy, you've been Sierlaef all your life. You knew that one day you would be king, the way Da always wanted."

"I can't do it. I just can't." He sobs. "I don't even have any children, but you do. You've got the girls, there's a chance of a boy. Or maybe Bunny will have one and . . . ."

"The children don't matter right now," Connar said. "You're young. We're all young. Children will happen, just as you said."

Noddy reached for the knife again, and when Connar blocked him, Noddy gulped in a shaky breath. "I thought, if I killed myself, then *you* can be king. And I don't ever have to go in Da's room. I can't do it, Connar." He broke into deep, convulsive sobs.

"Noddy, we can wait. The castle is quiet. The city is quiet. There is no enemy at the gate. You don't have to face anyone now."

Noddy looked up, wiping his blood-smeared sleeve across his face. "I won't feel different tomorrow. I don't even want tomorrow to come."

Connar gritted his teeth, recognizing the old, immoveable Noddy.

Then Noddy's forehead creased, and his voice rose, pleading. "Connar, it can be like Da and Uncle Jarend. You know. Da let Uncle Jarend go home. He knew how to be jarl. Uncle Jarend said for Da to be king. Second brothers inherit. It happens all the time."

"But I don't know how," Connar said. "You've sat in with Da all these years. I'm your commander. I don't know the first thing about what you do up there in the state wing."

"That part I know," Noddy said, wiping his eyes again. He sat up a little, which Connar thought a good sign. "I *like* doing it. You can do the rest. You stay in Da's room. You sit on his throne. You talk to the jarls at Convocation. And if there's trouble, it'll be like the first kings, who commanded the army. Please Connar. Please."

Connar began to see the possibility. This was not Hauth's bloodbath—not even close. "You want to divide the duties? We can do that," Connar said, trying to think past the first trickle of relief, now that Noddy wasn't reaching for that knife.

Then he heard a rustle behind him as Danet entered.

Noddy said before Connar could frame words, "Connar says he'll be king. I don't have to be in Da's room. I can stay where I am."

"All right." Danet's shoulders sagged. "If you boys are agreed, then that's what matters." And when Noddy looked up hopefully, she said slowly, encouragingly, "As long as you both agree, I don't care who's king. However, this much I know from experience, tradition is as strong as law. When we summon the castle to the throne room, Noddy, you have to be king long enough for people to see you hand the sword to Connar. If that's truly what you want."

Noddy said fervently, "That's what I want. Just like Uncle Jarend. Then I can stay in my own room."

"That's right," Danet and Connar said at the same time.

Danet sighed with relief as Noddy slowly got to his feet, swaying, for he had also gone without food since the previous day.

"We'll summon the castle now, so that people see order. Then, Connar, I suggest you declare the memorial for tomorrow night. I don't think any of us can face it tonight."

Connar understood "Noddy" for "any of us." He turned up his palm in agreement.

Danet went on, "While we assemble the castle, you boys get something to eat. Clean yourselves up. You don't have to wear the formal House tunics until tomorrow, but it's important to change your clothes, and to look like you mean what you say. People need to see you being firm. Both of you."

When the nightwatch bell rang, the entire castle save the night sentries gathered into the throne room, where the jarls' benches had been moved to the walls by the household runners.

The royal family walked down to the state wing in silence, Connar gritting his teeth against the urge to strike Bunny, who kept sniveling. One fast look sent Noren and Ranet stepping to Bunny's side, and holding hands with her.

The three women walked in together behind Danet, who followed her sons into the throne room. They lined up in a row before the empty throne, Noddy—bandaged under his best day coat—looking at Connar and Danet for reassurance before he stepped to the edge of the dais, gripping Arrow's sword.

Those old enough to remember the events of thirty years ago found it eerie, how much Nadran-Sierlaef resembled Jarend Olavayir, but there was no slim, bucktoothed figure standing next to him. Instead, there was Connar, a tall, magnificently built young man so strikingly handsome it was difficult to notice anyone else in the room.

Noddy began in a soft mumble. People in the front leaned forward, turning their heads to hear. "The king died during the night. In his sleep." In his distress he held tightly to Arrow's sword, forgetting Hand, but Ranet took care of that with suitable grace. As most of the castle was fluent in Hand as well as speech, Noddy's words reached farther than his voice.

Noddy stepped back, handing Arrow's sword off to Connar. "My first and last act as king is to appoint my brother Connar in my place."

Whispers whipped through the gathering in a susurrus as Connar stepped to the edge of the dais in front of the throne. "We'll hold the memorial for Anred-Harvaldar tomorrow night."

More whispering—it was traditional for the memorial to happen at midnight the day the king died, but who was going to complain?

Jethren stood in the back, exalted and worried by turns. What had happened? Connar was angry, that much was clear.

Then, as Connar raised the sword, Moonbeam's breathing changed. Jethren shot him a look. The mad, ardent grin caused his blood to chill: Moonbeam had been crazy all day, signing constantly that his ghosts were still not real, why weren't they real? Since morning, Jethren had already given him more doses than he had for a year. Moonbeam was going to need a new target, that much was clear.

On the other side of the room, Lineas pressed her palms together, grieving for Bunny, whose silent tears gleamed in the torchlight. She grieved for the king, who had reminded her of Lightning Weather—warm and bright, though dry and sometimes fiery.

She grieved for Noddy and Connar, though she couldn't say why, except that she feared the burden they shared. As she watched Lanrid Olavayir's bright ghost walk through the walls, cross the room through the whispering crowd, and then vanish through the west wall, she shivered, then saw that the royal family was walking out. People began to disperse, now talking loudly as everyone speculated to his or her neighbor on the scarcest of actual facts.

Connar accompanied Noddy upstairs and to his rooms. Noddy wandered to his bedroom, and Connar slipped out, handing the sword to Fish to put away. He saw the women in the gunvaer chambers, Danet peering anxiously out.

Connar walked in because he must, though everything felt unreal. Impatience mounted inside him, and he fought it as the inner voice whispered, *king*. "Everyone is tired," he said. *King*. "I want to settle a few things, then get some rest. Tomorrow will be difficult." *King, king, king.*

He walked out, and to his room down the hall, aware that runners were already tidying the king's suite. Outside his chamber, he found Jethren, and inside Fish. There was nothing about either of them to suggest they had been speaking. Good.

But they were Nighthawk men, or related to Nighthawk men. *King*.

Connar entered his bedroom without giving orders to either, so perforce they waited in place. He opened his trunk, slipped knives into the inside loops of his boots, then exited. "Both of you. With me."

He led the way down the hall to the back stair that led to the baths, and then took the passage off the halfway landing. Everyone who had gathered in the throne room had had plenty of time to disperse.

Of course Hauth would have followed Pereth back to the quartermaster's, where he usually sat holding court. Connar remembered that vividly.

Hauth was indeed there, exalted and garrulous, celebratory drink at hand. At last, at *last*, justice had been served. Not completely—there was still that lump of a Sierlaef—but the rest of eagle clan were all women, who could chatter all they wanted but would never hold a throne.

Now, for the king to turn to those who had been loyal from the very beginning. So when Connar walked through the door, Hauth laughed. "We were just talking about you, how very fine you looked! And how much better you will appear when you take the throne tomorrow—"

"Was that you?" Connar said.

The lance master stuttered to a stop. "What?"

"Someone slipped bristic to my father. It killed him. Was that you?"

Fish stared, shocked. Jethren's breath hitched, terror slamming his heart as he thought, *It couldn't have been Moonbeam?* And he remembered his father's warning.

Another dose, definitely—and keep him dosed.

Hauth drew everyone's attention with an exultant laugh. He snapped open the roll of paper he had carried every day, saying, "Connar-Harvaldar, I wonder if your father was there."

It was Connar's turn to exclaim, "What?"

Hauth smoothed the paper with worshipful strokes of his fingers. "This is Lanrid Olavayir. Your real father, your true father. He is following you around. He might be in this room with us now!"

Connar stared down at that wrinkled, smudged scroll, which he recognized as the sort of paper Fish carried for the occasional times he had to write messages for Connar. He took a step forward, saw the drawing, and memory struck him, sharp. Clear. Chalk Hills. Lineas acting strange, drawing the ghost she claimed to see, though she had a broken arm.

"We *all* recognized him," Hauth went on in that ringing, jubilant voice. "She even put in the chipped tooth!" Hauth brandished the paper so it rattled, holding it higher, almost in Connar's face. "Do you understand? That girl drew a perfect likeness of Lanrid. It's clear proof that his spirit has been following you around, Connar—it was time, past time, but here you are, king at last—"

On that *past time*, Connar's fingers found the knife hilt. He straightened up and with all the strength in his body stabbed the blade through that obscene paper, straight into Hauth's heart.

Retren Hauth's eye widened in shock, pain, betrayal, then rolled upward as he fell heavily.

Quartermaster Pereth screamed, "What have you done! What have you done!"

Connar snapped, "Which one of you acted for him? I *know* it was Nighthawk. No one else would have crept into my father's room to drown him in bristic until he died."

He gazed from the quartermaster's stark, staring eyes to Fish's open-mouthed shock. Could he be wrong?

No. He was not wrong. Hauth might have used one of his relatives, or one of the other Nighthawk shits, but he was very certain he was not wrong.

He pointed to the knife. "I'm king now. And I will fly the eagle banner. Dolphin clan is *dead.* If I ever hear the words 'Nighthawk' again—*ever*—I'll have every one of you flayed at the post for treason."

Connar's hands shook. He gripped them behind his back. "Jethren." He shot a fast glance at the blond man by the door, his face impassive, except for the vein beating in his high forehead. "Make this go away." He pointed at Hauth's fallen body, then walked out.

He didn't get ten steps before he spotted a tall blue-robed figure framed in the archway leading to the supply wing.

"Quill." The word came out on an exhaled breath.

Quill said, "I was sent to find you by Commander Noth. Someone said they saw you coming this way."

King, said that inner voice.

Connar's lips curled in a smile. Despite the headache still hammering at his skull, he drew in a deep breath. *King.* Another word for "investigate" was "spy." Quill's name had been spoken far too often lately, always in reference to state or military affairs.

"Quill," he said, his teeth showing in a smile that caused Quill's muscles to tighten to readiness. "Just in time to take me on a tour of the third floor."

King. The word was unspoken, but it lay in the air between them.

Quill laid his fist to his heart. "As you wish."

Fish, without further orders, stayed behind Connar as the other two walked in silence through the castle byways. Neither spoke until they reached the second floor landing in the royal wing.

They started up the stairs, Quill saying conversationally, "Of course we haven't had time to clean for an inspection, but you should find everything in order. Mnar Milnari—who is presently on her way back from Darchelde, after attending her mother's memorial—would not tolerate anything but scrupulous neatness."

As he mounted the stairs at a leisurely pace, he went on in that pleasant voice, discussing the layout of the third floor. " . . . and the fledges' study area is the same room as the old royal nursery," he was saying as they breached the top stair.

Connar glanced around. The usual royal runner lurking at the top was missing. Neat it might be, but discipline was clearly lax. He laughed to himself, as Quill began the tour. "To your right here is the library, with the study materials for the students. You'll find these are copies of what the scribes over in the state wing use . . . ."

And so it went. Room to room. Desks, pens, paper in every state of preparation, draped to dry, cut and stacked, rolled into scrolls waiting to be sent. Royal runner students of all ages peeped curiously out, hands going to chests as Connar walked by.

The living areas were various sizes, some reflections of the rooms on the second floor. The masters each had rooms that looked small to Connar. Students shared rooms, two or more to each.

He could not tell which room was Lineas's. She had not appeared.

In one large chamber, a map on the wall, with runners' roads marked. On the other side of the room lay a book with what Quill said was the spells the students with an affinity for magic studied from, and there on a table lay buckets and fire sticks for practice.

It was all in order. Even boring. But when they had returned to the landing, Connar said, "Very fine. I'll review your drills in the morning, along with Fish here."

Connar indicated Fish, still at his heels.

"Fish will take over as chief of the royal runners, as of tomorrow. Quill, you may show him everything again tomorrow, then you will join my brother over at the state wing. He's going to need the extra scribes, and I understand you were very helpful to my father."

Shock rang through the listeners all up and down the hall.

"As you wish," Quill said.

TWENTY-TWO

Shendan Montredavan-An had put together what the royal runners called the invasion plan. That meant Bloody Tanrid or one of his minions coming up to the third floor to "inspect." Often enough those inspections had included pawing through people's trunks and shelves to look for weapons, as runners were not permitted to carry weapons unless going for a run outside the gates. Letters and messages were also seized and read in the hunt for conspiracy—no one dared to tell Tanrid-Harvaldar to read a few of his own royal histories, which would have made plain that those of his predecessors most tireless in hunting conspiracies tended to generate them.

There were some quiet years, and then Mathren's grip on the royal city had reinstituted the surprise raids. During Arrow's reign, "inspection" had slowly dwindled to a drill once a month. The younger fuzz and fledges were thrilled if they were on duty at the top of the stairs and they heard the word "inspection" in the middle of some otherwise innocuous talk.

Because of this, they grew up knowing to avoid that word while coming up the stairs. So as soon as the duty runner at the top of the stairs heard Quill's genial voice carrying up the stairwell, "Of course we haven't had time to clean for an inspection . . ." he thought, practice? Real? Didn't matter.

He grabbed the nearest person, made the sign for inspection, and so it went. By the time Quill and Connar had come halfway up the steps, all the magic books had been flung into a trunk and the waiting transfer token slapped against it. Soon followed the royal runners' archives, and finally, the matched pairs of wrist knives used in the Fox drills.

The royal runners kept silent through the tour as their chief talked on and on, and the handsome, seldom-seen prince—soon to take the throne as king—looked about appreciatively. On the surface, everything was pleasant, polite, friendly. And it wasn't as if the second floor hadn't been upstairs plenty of times. The gunvaer was seen a lot when Mnar Milnari was present. But they all felt the tension underscoring that *inspection*. Quill didn't do things without reason.

Then, just before he left, the new king delivered the stunner: Quill was no longer chief. What was worse, they had a total outsider catapulted to the top.

When the royal runners were alone again, and Quill had dispatched a transfer token to the Darchelde Destination as an all-clear, he said, "Everyone into the lair."

A puff of air from the inner chamber indicated a magic transfer. Quill stepped in and found Lineas, her hands clasped to elbows, her face greenish as she swallowed convulsively.

"Trunks all right?" Quill asked, coming forward, arms open so she could lean against him.

"Fnor sent me first, as I was right there. Someone had to drag those trunks off the Destination," Lineas said.

One of the first lessons in magic was that two objects cannot occupy the same space. The heavier they were, the harder the incoming object would shove against anything in the spot where things appeared. Trunks could explode into splinters, sending the contents scattering. "I heard Connar and, well, I know he hasn't said a word to me since he got back from Stalgoreth. But I felt such tension."

"Yes," Quill said, soberly. "Listen. The first thing you should know is that I've just been replaced by Fish Pereth."

"Fish? But why him? He's not one of us."

"I suspect," Quill said with gentle irony, "that's why Connar placed him here."

Lineas lifted her hands, palms out. "Do you think he wanted it?"

"He looked just as shocked as you look right now. The gunvaer asked me to investigate who might have given the king that bristic. I was there combing the night guard report until the summons to the throne room. After that was over, I headed straight back, meaning to copy that report to compare to our list of movements seen last night, when Noth asked me to find Connar. Someone had seen him heading toward the quartermaster's. When I got there, I found Connar and Fish, and I swear I smelled blood. I also saw Fish's face. He looked like a man whose bowels had gone cold."

She said, "Something must have happened! I know the new runner at the supply desk. Do you want me to ask her—"

"No." Quill gripped her hands. "It might only be reaction to the king dying. But whatever it was, I'd rather your name not be associated with anything at the quartermaster's."

Lineas remembered the shocking news that the king hadn't just died in his sleep. Speculation right now was worthless. So she said, "People are going to miss the king."

Quill smiled sadly. "I miss him, and I scarcely ever saw him, except to be sent off to the far corners of the kingdom. But Arrow was a good man, and a good king. The two don't always go together," he added, and there was the wry Quill she knew. But then the sardonic quirk at the corners of his mouth, not quite a smile, vanished. "I'll find out what happened at the quartermaster's. Without drawing notice." He passed a hand over his eyes. "Right now, we've got a night to transform this place for Fish to run."

Lineas rubbed her hands up her arms. "Fish. I don't know what to think. I do remember that you older boys didn't like him."

"There was little to like in those days. His older brother was worse, far too ready with his fists, especially toward us younger ones. But the past is immaterial. For everyone's sake I need to extend a genuine welcome. I want Fish to be able to ask me questions. Maybe even to ask my opinion. Insulting him is not going to gain me anything but him wanting to get rid of every sign of me. That's human nature." Quill opened his hands.

Lineas knew he wasn't willing to speculate farther, not while so much had changed so rapidly. Not with Connar at the center of it.

So she forced her mind to practicalities. "What about Fox drills?"

"Everyone will do fuzz drills for now. No double knives. The fuzz drills are enough like the garrison drills that Fish will be able to lead them. All magic studies will have to be resumed at Darchelde, which means more transfers."

"They'll hate that."

"As do I. Can't be helped."

"Will you have to move rooms?" she asked.

"Probably. May I move my trunk over to your room for now?"

"Of course." Lineas flexed her hands. "I just . . . feel . . ."

He didn't want her to sense the incipient threat that he was aware of. There was nothing they could do except be vigilant. He said quickly, "It's been a strange night, but the royal family just lost Arrow. Grief grabs people differently. You were the one who pointed that out to me. Anyway, everyone is waiting. Probably full of questions."

She accepted that, and followed him to where the royal runners all sat on the floor mats, fuzz at the front. Lineas looked at those solemn young faces, the tight, childish shoulders, and knew they were not far from fear.

"A change of king always brings other changes," Quill said to the group. "But one thing that doesn't change is our responsibilities."

Voices rose.

"Why an inspection? Is there danger?"

"Why did the new king demote you?"

"Why an outsider?"

"What's wrong with how we—"

Quill snapped his fingers and turned his palm out. Then—mindful of anyone who might be lurking in the hall or on the stairwell, listening—he said, "Inspecting the third floor is traditional when we have a new king. Camerend called for 'inspection' the night the previous king found himself with an empty throne. It turned out he didn't want to come up here, but we were ready in case he did. As for why I was reassigned, I don't know. I also don't know why none of you were appointed to my place. So let's talk about what we do know, which is altering the schedule to make things easier for your new chief . . . ."

In Hand, he said, "We will speak to you one by one."

Back at the quartermaster's, for a long, excruciatingly suspended moment everyone stared down at Retren Hauth's body.

Finally the quartermaster wiped a shaking hand across the icy sweat on his forehead. "Just like Mathren," he whispered. And then, with an accusing glance at Jethren, "We kept warning him. How much Connar hates dolphin."

Jethren said, "Moonbeam and I will take care of Hauth. But I don't know what to report, and where, to make it go away."

The quartermaster slumped, his face so distraught he seemed to have aged ten years in less than an hour. "I'll handle that." He still spoke in a whisper. "Ret was solitary. The dispositions are easy enough. He'll have retired for his health. And that's what we'd better tell the family in the city. Connar is now king, so Ret retired." He wiped his face again. "I'll clean up the floor myself." His mouth crimped as he looked down at the bloodstained drawing, mostly ruined. "That goes into the fire first thing."

Jethren had no argument with that.

He and Moonbeam straightened Hauth out, and did the Disappearance Spell. Then they left the rest to the quartermaster, and walked out.

As soon as Jethren got Moonbeam away from any possible lurking ears, he said, "You did it, didn't you. The bristic."

Moonbeam stared back, pupils pinpoints in his ice-pale eyes. He signed: *They still are not real yet.*

Jethren's heart hammered. He said forcefully, "That's because you acted without orders. You *know* you have to act on orders."

Moonbeam stilled, one hand caressing one of his knife hilts. How many was he wearing? Jethren knew he couldn't take Moonbeam in a fight, and added quickly, "But you didn't use a knife, so you can have another dose."

As he dug out the precious bellflower root, he wondered how much longer he could control him. But he was far too useful to kill. As Moonbeam drank down the dose, Jethren let out a breath of relief.

"Fish Pereth?" Danet said the next morning over breakfast. Noddy was still sleeping, but all the women were there. "Isn't that your first runner, a garrison runner? Does he even know how to write?"

"Of course he writes. Who do you think copied out my reports?" Connar said, and reached for more coffee.

He was in a good mood, the best he could remember. Hauth was dead. They'd kept the guards at the landings for now, but Connar was certain Hauth was responsible for that bristic. He'd clearly gone insane, the way he was waving around that soulsucking drawing and ranting about ghosts. But even if he hadn't given the order, Connar was convinced that Nighthawk lay behind the murder. They now knew what would happen if any of them tried to touch Noddy.

"There was nothing amiss with the royal runners," Danet went on, her brow creased in question. No, in dawning worry.

Connar suppressed impatience. "As I told Quill last night, his name always came up when Da talked about someone helping him. I figured Noddy will need him, especially now. Fish can direct the royal runners. Actually, they seem to pretty much run themselves." He added, "Everything else will stay the same."

Danet's expression eased. "All right, that makes sense. You might have waited, but, no, I'm not going to start squabbling with you over your decisions. Arrow and I talked things out. I hope you and Ranet will do the same, and I'll confine myself to handing off my tasks to her."

"No," Connar exclaimed. "When I said things will stay the same, I mean it. What you do—what Noddy has been doing—what the rest of you do, it's all good the way it is. Why mess with it? I'd rather not even move rooms, except that Da's map room is there, and his interview chamber is big. I think he'd like us using it all, instead of leaving it empty. But no one else needs to move, and you know I promised Noddy he could stay put."

He expected her to be pleased, but Danet said slowly, "All right, that makes sense, too." She cast a glance at Ranet.

Connar did as well, and met a gaze like a blow.

Danet said, "Why don't the two of you take this chance to discuss details. I have to go over to the scribes to oversee how the records get changed."

Noren got to her feet, hands flashing. "I'll help Noddy. He's still . . ." Her face reflected sorrow, and she walked out."

Bunny followed silently, used to being ignored by Connar. Danet gathered the runners with a sharp glance, and the door shut behind them, leaving Ranet and Connar alone.

Before he could speak, she clasped her hands together. "The gunvaer means well, but I expect there isn't really much for us to say. I understand that I'm a duty to you instead of a partner. And I'm willing to do any work that needs doing."

She waited, calm. Her gaze steady and cool from eyes shaped like Braids's. They were cousins, he remembered. The adoration he was used to seeing—used to feeling caged by—had vanished, leaving her appearing very much older, without any of the sag of aging.

"What do you want?" he asked.

She stirred, opening her hands and looking at them as if invisible words had been writ across her palms. Then she turned them down loosely on her thighs—shapely as always under the loose folds of her linen trousers and her summer robe. A spark of desire twitched low, but he suppressed it. Lying in bed and fending off chatter was the last thing he needed to be doing right now.

Then she spoke. "If you mean, what do I want *to do,* I'm content doing exactly what I've been doing," she replied. "However, if you are actually asking what I *want,* that would be for you to somehow find time for our children. I had to teach Iris that Noddy was not his da, nor Uncle Jarid, nor Grandda. Now I'm having to go through the same with Little Hliss."

His first reaction was irritation. This was not something immediate, like Da's death. But he knew what Lineas would say, that few things were more important than the bonds of love and family. Irritation sharpened; why remember what she said? She was a hypocrite, her so-called bonds as self-serving as anyone else's. Loyal as long as it was convenient, then find someone else.

"Right," he said. "But you couldn't bring it up any time during the last six months, when things were quiet?"

"I don't see you," Ranet replied in that calm, even voice. "When I do, at Restday drum, I always made sure the girls are there, for them to see and talk to you. But you don't stay long enough for me to get your attention."

His arms tightened and he suppressed the retort that the children didn't talk, they climbed all over him with fingers sticky from jam tarts or honey biscuits, and Little Hliss slobbered. At least Iris knew the Waste Spell, but Little Hliss always seemed to smell of diaper.

That was another hypocrisy. It was all right to say you didn't like children, but you were not supposed to say it about your own. "I'll be better with them when they get a little older. When we can have conversations," he said.

"When they go off to your academy." It was not a question.

"That, too. That's what I know," he added, hating how defensive he sounded.

She heard it, too, and saw the signs of the annoyance he was trying to suppress. Neit was another who didn't like children. All right, she'd said her piece, and would have to accept whatever he chose to do with it.

She got to her feet and shook out her robe. "We will continue on as we have, then, until you say otherwise."

He rose as well, and left, aware that he felt off-balance, as though he'd missed something. But he hadn't. Everything was settled—most particularly Quill, who would not be riding to Stalgoreth.

He walked out, and Noren, who had been waiting, emerged from her room and came to Ranet's. "Any changes you two worked out that we need to know about?"

Ranet's lovely face was smooth as ice. Noren knew Ranet fairly well. She would once have said really well, until the visit from the lively woman who insisted on being called Aunt Calamity.

The Jarlan of Senelaec had been cheerfully loquacious, one subject being her sister, the former intended gunvaer. Aunt Calamity had said that Ranet was a great deal like her mother Fuss, who was now living deep within the Eastern Alliance territory—quiet until pushed to the limits, then her emotions would be like summer thunder.

Noren knew that to be true. That is, she had seen Ranet upset. But she'd rarely seen her angry. She'd assumed that gentle Ranet didn't get angry, though she could be very strict with the girls in the queen's training.

"Wolf and Fuss are a lot alike," Aunt Calamity had said earnestly. "Braids as well. You really don't want to see them angry. Well, you've heard about Braids on the battlefield, I'm sure. If Ranet had been at Tlennen Fields, or Ku Halir, she would have been riding right beside him."

Noren looked for signs of that anger now, but perceived a face as cool as snow as Ranet said, "There appears to be nothing to work out. We're to continue as we were."

Noren signed acceptance, and left. When she was able to get the gunvaer alone, she repeated the conversation.

Danet noted that Noren had waited until they were alone with the tallies. She sighed. "I confess my first reaction was relief. Only because I'm not ready to be kicked up to the tower as a senior gunvaer, though I know it's coming. It should be coming." She paused, fingers stiff, then signed slowly, "This is my fault. I once told the boys that whatever they worked out would be fine. As long as they were both agreed. What I meant was, I didn't want to see them fighting."

Noren smacked the back of her fingers against her palm in emphatic disagreement. "No blame! Nobody wants that."

"I should have foreseen that Noddy might feel the way he does . . . but yes, I see what I missed: Ranet is left with a title and little else, as you are training to replace me. Do you want to train her?"

Noren gazed at the wall, then replied slowly, "She has no head for numbers. But she is better than I am with the girls. And for that matter, with the boys over at the academy." She looked up. "Now that Connar is king, he probably will not want to remain co-headmaster of the academy. We've all seen how reluctant he is."

"No, he has enough to contend with, armywise. So you're saying Ranet ought to be head on her own?"

Noren responded, "I'll ask Noddy, but if he's taking over all state matters, I know he'll be relieved to hand it off to her."

Fish Pereth was very well aware of the irony of his present position.

All night he'd listened to his father and brother go round and round about that bristic. Pereth suspected that Jethren was behind it, but one thing he was certain of, if Connar found out, there was no telling what he'd do. Fish still dreamed about Cabbage Gannan's death.

So now he was suddenly in a place he'd wanted badly when he was a boy. But he was no longer a boy. He'd gotten used to the danger of the battlefield, but this unasked-for promotion felt like a different quality of threat.

As the day passed, he felt as if he glided along the ice on a deep lake. Quill had been an obnoxious know-it-all when young, but Fish remembered his own penchant for sneaking and tattling. Since Quill's return from going around the country renewing baths and buckets a few years back, he'd been affable in their few encounters, doing his job competently and then getting out of the way. That same affability was there when Fish reached the third floor the next morning and found Quill waiting. As Quill took Fish through the routine of study, practice, and the rota for message-running, he was patient and attentive.

The tedious explanations dragged on, always coming back to the complicated chalk slate on which each day was organized, and Fish began to feel more isolated than he ever had in his life. But there was no one to complain to. He'd spent all night with his terrified father, assuring him that if Connar wanted them dead, it would already have happened. His brother had avoided him at pre-dawn mess.

When the bell clanged for the night watch, and it was time to get ready for the memorial, Fish—after a full night and day with no sleep—felt he'd fallen into one of those miserable dreams in which he'd lost an important message, his horse had escaped from its stall, and he tried to run, but he couldn't move faster than a crawl, and Connar was somewhere in the distance, very angry.

Fish faced the waiting royal runners, all waiting to be dismissed to ready themselves for the memorial, and forced himself to give his first order. "My name is David Pereth. I realize there is another David here. Pereth is fine, but I *hate* Fish." And, palms turned up, "I guess we all ought to get ready."

They put two fingers to chests and dispersed.

Quill started to move away. Fish—now Pereth—turned to Quill, and desperation drove him to say, "I didn't ask for this change."

Quill's eyelids flickered. He stilled, his profile bland as carved stone. Then he turned, smiling. "I'm always around if you have questions. And of course the others will give you whatever help you ask for."

Pereth tried again. "I'll ask him to put things back the way they were."

Quill said, lightly, with sympathy, "I expect it's too late for that."

Pereth stared—then heard his own words, *back the way they were*, and remembered that the king was dead. Quill had taken the larger meaning: nothing would ever be the same.

The inescapable reminder was the king's body laid out before the throne as torches along the walls leaped and flared, giving the banners on the high walls a semblance of moving in the wind.

The royal family lined up, impressive in their blue and gold House tunics. Pereth, standing against the wall in his borrowed royal runner robe, and isolated among the rest of the royal runners, didn't listen Connar's speech past the announcement that as it was too late in the year to summon a coronation Convocation at New Year's, it would be called for Midsummer, after which it would be put off for three years.

Convocation. Pereth would be expected to organize the third floor's part. He'd seen how hard the royal runners worked during Convocation. After he left Quill he'd gotten down to the second floor to find his personal things neatly packed up by Cheese Fath, his former assistant, and the chamber runner Pereth had appointed to deal with laundry, meals, and the like. Apparently Connar had promoted them to chamber runners.

The last thing Pereth did before readying for the memorial, wearing the blue robe that Cama Tall, one of the royal runner masters, had loaned him, was to move his things into the empty room they'd shown him. It was twice the size of his chamber downstairs, and it even had its own fireplace. His small trunk looked absurd in that great, empty space, which he suspected had been Quill's room.

While Pereth's thoughts turned inward, Lineas's turned outward. She watched the torch flames flicker, throwing shadows over the watching faces as Connar passed a lit brand three times above the silent figure on the bier. The room had filled with more ghosts than normal, or maybe it was just that she saw more of them.

She turned her head, seeking among them—and yes, there was Lanrid, who everyone had thought was Evred. The ghost faded and brightened like a flame; she watched, rapt, until it dimmed to liminality, and through it she beheld a tall pale-haired man gazing straight at her: it was Jethren's first runner, the one with the odd name. What did they call him, Moonlight?

His hand moved, almost too fast to follow: *You see.*

Her lips parted as she signed back, *You see them too.*

Voices rose in the Hymn to the Fallen as the Healer said the words of Disappearance, distracting her. Tears blurred the dais. She wiped her eyes, and Anred-Harvaldar was gone. The new king staring down at that empty stone, as behind him, Danet-Gunvaer wiped her eyes repeatedly. Noddy and Noren stood holding hands. At their other side stood Ranet, holding her two children, one asleep in her arms, the other a little figure pressed against her side, eyes huge.

Ranet's face was a mask. Bunny, next to her, could only see her profile, but sorrow poured ice water through her veins.

Connar lifted his head. "Tomorrow is a day of liberty for all, sentries to serve half-watches."

It was over.

The royal family walked out to the courtyard below the king's suite, where Arrow's runners waited with Arrow's very few personal effects. Bunny's heart overflowed with tears when she saw them, and she chose her da's oldest robe, hoping it would retain his scent longest.

Noddy, suffering in a silence broken by an occasional deep sob, took his father's cup because Da's hands had handled it, and he also took Arrow's hair clasp to send to Andas. Connar already had the sword. He picked up Arrow's knives, unused these long years.

Danet chose nothing from that pile—she already had piles of reports and notes scrawled in Arrow's impatient slashing hand. Noren, who hadn't known him well, preferred to keep her memories, rather than things, and Ranet picked up Arrow's writing materials with a mind to saving them in case there was ever a prince to come. The girls already had little gifts Arrow often brought back from the city after he'd visited his favorites at this or that pleasure house.

A couple of Arrow's favorites from the pleasure houses had also come. They stepped forward, and one took a sash, the other Arrow's comb.

That left the runners, who either chose something or did not, then the few remaining items were placed in a pile and set on fire. They stood in a circle, flames lighting their faces: rank had ceased to mean anything in that moment. Young, old, male, female, all distinctions diminished, leaving them people in grief.

TWENTY-THREE

The city settled into its routine, business excellent. They had a handsome new king, famous for his prowess. He had an open hand with largesse, and the pleasure houses competed to draw his attention whenever he came into the city.

For a time Connar expected Braids to show up and offer to resign his command, as Calamity Senelaec had said he would, but when the weeks sped by and there was no sign of him, he figured that the jarlan had managed to reach him with the news of the compromise.

There was no response to Danet's letter from the Jarl of Gannan. She and Connar, talking about it, figured that if he was going to raise a fuss, it would be at the Midsummer Convocation when Connar took the jarls' vows.

"We'll prepare for that," he said. Softly spoken, but his smile, the tone, was a threat.

"Good," she retorted stoutly. She had to get used to Connar's style of ruling. Just as well he looked so intimidating. That old fart Gannan needed intimidation.

Noddy didn't like change, but within a matter of days he felt as if Quill had always been a part of the state wing routine. Noddy liked Quill. He was as patient as Lineas, and as clear in his ideas. He listened to all sides. Noddy did not know that Lineas and Vanadei had been discussing difficult issues with Quill long before the king was stricken, only that his ideas fit what they had been talking about. Noddy especially liked how much Quill knew about Marlovan history, past decisions, and mistakes. His suggestions were always good.

The state wing was the civilian side of Marlovan government.

Every village in Marlovan Iasca was within a week's ride of a military outpost. Every town had an outpost. Every region had a garrison. Each decision they made over civilians was recorded by scribes, who funneled those letters by the regular runners to the state wing, where they were examined by the archive scribes, and separated out according to a complex table that had been evolving ever since the first Marlovan king. The fundamental understanding was that jarls dispensed their own justice, but people did have recourse to the king, even if getting their grievances aired was labyrinthine and time-consuming.

Quill had always liked Noddy, but he was impressed by both his comprehension of the labyrinth, and his patience. He began to comprehend through Noddy's anecdotes, related in that slow, deep voice, that he had learned governing in Larkadhe, when he saw the people whose petitions came before him. That had convinced him that no problem was ever too small for him, because these were not small problems to the people behind the petitions.

Quill was acutely aware of how conditional happiness was. He relished these daily gatherings, talking and laughing with people he loved, as they got glimpses into the lives of Marlovans everywhere. This was the heart of government, he believed—though no one wrote songs about finding compromises between apple pickers and beekeepers, or discovering ways to get air into mines without endangering the miners. But he still sensed unseen shoals, and so he and Mnar Milnari kept the royal runners in inspection mode, outwardly cooperating with Pereth (who was doing his best to run a complicated branch he only partially comprehended) but keeping magic studies, and ferreting for the truth, to a very small number.

Quill knew everyone in service throughout the royal castle. In the days after the memorial, at the midday break or in the sweltering evenings, it was easy to visit his friends among the staff—usually carrying a jug of fizz, or some fresh biscuits—to ask how everyone was, and make a request for examples of certain types of records for teaching purposes. Like how Supply finishes up records for those who have moved, been promoted, or died.

Will I like it? Lineas had asked.

Not at all.

By tacit agreement, each night after they finished up in the state wing, Lineas walked Noddy back to his suite, joining him and Noren as often as not as they talked over their respective days. Then she continued up to the third floor.

That left Quill and Vanadei back in the scribe chamber, which had a single window high above the parade ground. No one could listen in.

"What is this MNA next to Retren Hauth's name?" Vanadei asked, when Quill brought from his sleeve the copy he'd made of Retren Hauth's supply and disposition records. "This looks like one of the gunvaer's abbreviations."

"It is," Quill said. "MNA means Mathren's Nighthawk Army."

"Ah." Vanadei laid the paper down, and Quill snuffed the lantern, so no one in the parade court below would see the lit window. They sat in the dim starlight, each scarcely more than a silhouette to the other. "The infamous private army. But surely with Mathren dead, that died, too."

"It did, and it didn't. The survivors of their struggle for power after Mathren's death ended up in Olavayir at Jarend-Jarl's invitation. They had families. Before he retired, Sneeze Ventdor was pungently forthcoming about

Kethedrend Jethren and his company being Nighthawk men, while talking to Stick Tyavayir. Neither paid attention to Fnor busy copying reports in the corner as they talked."

Vanadei turned up his palm; Fnor was one of their best young ferrets.

"Here's what concerns me. Fish Pereth might be explained away as Connar's first runner, but Jethren was there at the quartermaster's the night that Retren Hauth suddenly retired from nearly decades of blameless instruction at the academy—without even waiting for Victory Day, which he had helped run for years. I know I smelled blood that night. And those faces, that was the shock of sudden death. Even in Jethren, who is about as bloody-minded an individual as I've ever met."

"You think they killed Hauth?"

"No, I think Connar did."

Vanadei started at that. "Why?"

"Mmmm." Quill got to his feet and leaned against the wall so he could look out at the sentry walk, torches winking ruddy red as the silhouettes of guards passed back and forth in front of them. "Considering that Connar is now king, which makes seeking justice for Hauth somewhat complicated, I think there are three more pressing questions. One being, is Nighthawk still an entity—which implies a goal—and second, is this goal related to those two spies of Jethren's nosing around Stalgoreth, asking after Kendred, Cabbage Gannan's first runner."

Vanadei fell silent. Earlier that day, Quill had received a note from one of his ferrets in Stalgoreth that two of Jethren's scouts had been asking questions—

> *. . . but the healer who packed Kendred into the cart for the trip down into Alliance territory returned to Ku Halir. He's known as Moss Toraca. He's actually a farrier, but he was serving as field medic for that battle.*

"Vanadei, when you go back upstairs, I want you to contact Fnor in Ku Halir to spread the word to be on the watch for Jethren's ferrets, who might appear and be searching for Moss Toraca." Quill handed Vanadei the note, with descriptions of Sleip and Punch.

"All right," Vanadei said. "But what about this Kendred?"

"That," said Quill, "I think I have to investigate myself. But it'll have to be Restday, when Noddy is with his family."

"You mean to go by magic?" Vanadei asked, grimacing.

"Can't be helped," Quill said, though that method had its risks and limits. Besides the transfer reaction, there was also the matter of a Destination. He did not dare use Braids as a Destination, as he would never be able to explain away suddenly appearing right next to him.

He also had no idea where Braids was, so he couldn't find a familiar place nearby to use as a Destination, risky it itself. And even if he did, assuming he could make up some excuse for being in the area, he was no longer a royal runner. Anyone could innocently comment on having seen him in Tlennen, or Sindan-An, or Senelaec, or Wened Lake, when he was supposed to be copying reports in the state wing. "No, on second thought, I'd better contact Lnand. She really isn't needed in Parayid anymore."

"Bringing me to your third question. You didn't say what it was." Vanadei packed his scribe materials together by feel, and got to his feet.

"Right. That being, what do we do with the answers?"

"I think Lefty Poseid is a very good idea as replacement for Cabbage," Noddy said to Connar over breakfast one morning. "Did you know the Poseids are Iascans from that part of the north? Righty told me that once. The people there like Lefty. I saw that on my visit."

He looked away, the way he invariably did when mentioning someone gone. Then he said, "Connar, would you like to come to the state wing? See what we do there?"

Hit by an image of his utter boredom in Larkadhe, Connar was about to refuse. Then the thought occurred that it might be worth the time to see exactly why Noddy needed three royal runners, rather than scribes. Vanadei made sense, as he was a first runner who could do scribe duties. Quill, Connar had assigned to Noddy to tie him down. But why was Lineas there?

After an interminable session that was exactly as tedious as he'd expected, the only answer he could come up with was that Lineas had become a habit at Larkadhe. And everyone knew Noddy liked the comfort of habit.

When the midday watch change bell rang, Noddy said, "Let's break. Quill, will you ask my mother for the new customs tallies from Parayid?"

"If she won't let it out of her sight, I'll copy the relevant pages," Quill said, hand to heart.

Noddy's somber face eased to the lopsided grin that Lineas found endearing. He turned to Vanadei. "If you'll explain one side of the Wheelwright accusations, and Lineas, you the other—"

Connar spoke up from the wall he'd been propping. "Vanadei, your skills are equal to both sides, no doubt. Lineas, I want a tour of the archives."

Lineas started. She'd actually managed to forget Connar was there. She swallowed. He watched her throat working. "Very well," she said, on a faint note of question.

Outside the door, she tipped her chin up, giving him a considering glance. "The scribes can give you a better tour than I can."

He snorted. "I doubt that. Somehow it seems you royal runners know everything better than anyone else. Why else would you end up over here so often?"

She said softly, "We go where we're told to go." The flatness of her tone made him hear the unspoken *As you very well know.*

"Don't tell me you wouldn't welcome a break from wheelwrights squabbling."

"They came all the way here from Feravayir," she replied in that same even, soft tone. "Their petition is important to them." She didn't look up, but she was intensely aware of him walking at her side. The sound of his breathing, even his scent, which her body still responded to.

"More important than my time?" he retorted.

As he contemplated her bent head, her face hidden by her frizzy, rust-colored hair, she tried to calm the thud of her heart, wondering what was in his mind. She knew it was not a matter of thwarted lust. For that matter, she didn't understand her own reaction; while the attraction was still there, it was a thin thing, a guttering candle compared to the sun of her youth. She had no words for the tangle of emotions still existing between them. Maybe only the faraway Colendi did, they with their thousand terms for the vagaries of human passion.

To business, then. "What part of the archive did you wish to see?"

"Everything," he stated. "Yes, I know we were given tours as boys, but I raced through as fast as I could. Noddy and I both did. Now it seems to me that I ought to find out what my predecessors did and didn't do, don't you think? Start at the very beginning."

"That isn't in Marlovan," she warned. "Though the scribes have been working on translations, most of the oldest records are in Iascan. First the Cassadas. What's left of those."

"I can read Iascan," he said, smiling. "Noddy and I were tutored by no less a figure than the legendary Camerend when we were small."

She knew he was mocking her, though there was no sign in face or voice. Her own face heated, and she turned away. "The gunvaer can show you the royal archive, which I have never seen. It's what the kings and queens wrote themselves. Mainly letters, I understand, but other things as well. And of course there are all the legal archives, and garrison ledgers, and I'm certain you've seen the academy records." She pointed in three directions.

"Thank you," he said. "I may as well start at the beginning." He opened the door to the oldest archive, which had no windows, and had been purposely located deep within the building, away from the changing airs of the seasons.

She left. Connar strolled along the shelves, sniffing the complexities of the air, identifying only dust and a whiff of mildew. He didn't see the scrolls and bound books as he reflected on how much life had changed.

Everything seemed settled. He considered Jethren's report, brought by his second runner: No one had found Kendred, Cabbage's first runner. He might even be dead. He definitely had been wounded. And as Cabbage had been riding alone when his horse blundered into Connar's, Kendred was likely to have been a distance away. And visibility had been rotten.

But Connar wasn't *certain.*

He looked around the quiet chamber, undisturbed for years and years. So very far from the noise of castle life.

He turned away. He had research to do . . . but he didn't have to begin it today.

He left, retreating to the garrison, his own comfortable domain, relishing the signs in all those fisted salutes that he was now truly the one who made the rules.

And so it was time to get on with that, right? He spotted Jethren leaning on the low wall behind the water butts at the army's own court, separate from the guards'. Jethren was watching a single-stick match, but turned his head at Connar's approach, then straightened, fist to heart.

Always predictable. Connar laughed inwardly, but he was not displeased.

"Any orders?"

"No. Not now. Everything is as it should be." Connar was in a good enough mood to share his thoughts. Jethren had done what he'd asked, and Hauth was gone forever. "I'm thinking ahead. Nothing changing before we get through Convocation at Midsummer. The jarls will be barking at me about this and that, and old Gannan will certainly howl the loudest. Once that's over, I'm thinking that it's time to get rid of the Nob."

Jethren's head turned sharply, the feral grin Connar had seen on Skytalon flashing. And his mind went right to where Connar's was: "Did you want the north shore mapped? If so, I volunteer."

Pleased, Connar said slowly, "That sort of expedition is usually for scouts. Not captains or commanders. You really want to go? I was going to promote you to command the Third Lancers under Rat Noth."

"No one maps as well as I do." Jethren amended, aware that he dare not leave Moonbeam behind, "Well, actually, Moonbeam does better drawing."

"He can draw?"

"Really well," Jethren lied. "We can assess every castle and its defenses. The territory around them."

Connar turned unseeing eyes to the two men sweating in the court as they strove to catch his attention with their prowess. The kingdom was quiet. But there was the north, effectively yanked from under Da as a new king at his weakest. Connar knew it had still rankled, all those years later. And now he was dead, and couldn't do anything about it.

But Connar could.

He could send scouts to assess the north, but who could he trust not to blab about it? The exhilarating idea of restoring the kingdom was merely an idea, one that depended on so many factors. First, getting rid of the Nob, as a lure to Idego. Then waiting to see if Idego took the bait and rushed up the north shore of the peninsula . . . and even then, his map of Lorgi Idego was at least a generation out of date the further it got from Andahi Castle.

Then there was the strategic concern: Marlovans trained to defend their castles, and to face enemies in the broad plains.

"Do it," Connar said. "Once Convocation is over, we'll have three years until the next, giving me three years of respite from the likes of Old Gannan and Zheirban. A lot can be accomplished in that time."

Jethren saluted sharply, grinning as if he'd been given a promotion. "We'll be on the road by sunup."

Two weeks into his new rule, Connar summoned Royal Runner Chief Pereth down to the king's suite. Pereth looked around, finding it mostly unchanged. All the same furnishings.

Cheese Fath, Pereth's replacement as first runner, went out and left them alone. Connar said, "Are you settled in?"

Knowing Connar of old, Pereth gave the correct answer: "Yes." Although "settled in" was debatable. He still felt that odd sensation of skating over ice, with all the waters and lake life invisible below.

"They follow your orders?"

Pereth gave in to impulse and said, "I haven't given orders yet. Their rota is smooth. I still don't understand it. I wasn't trained up to it. But they all know it."

"Do you read the reports that come in?"

"There's no time. And a lot are sealed."

"What happens to a sealed report?"

"It gets taken to the roost's scribe desk. Noted who sent a message, and to whom. Who on the rota is taking it. Mnar Milnari mostly tends to that. She explained to me that if a message goes astray, they can start from there to track it. She said that the outpost scribes also note who arrives, and where they're going." Pereth saw signs of impatience in Connar, and finished, "There's a lot more."

"I'm sure there is. You'll get used to it. But right now I want you to make this a priority: to learn their magic."

Pereth bit back a *What?*

"I want to know exactly what they can and can't do," Connar said. "How they do it. How long it takes to learn it. Mostly I want to know if any of it can be used in the field. Quill told me it was impossible, but the royal scribes aren't trained to think in military terms."

"But they start those lessons at twelve!"

"You surely can learn what a child of twelve can," Connar retorted, brows rising.

Only one possible answer to agree, salute, and get out of there.

Pereth did, giving vent to his frustration by smacking his hand against a stone wall as soon as he reached the stairwell to the third floor. He had skimped reading history when he was a young runner in training, but even he knew that magic was mostly useless in war. It was unwieldy, and spells could be negated.

However, Connar had not asked for an opinion. He wanted facts.

So, as the rest of the season streamed past, Pereth began magic lessons with carefully chosen youngsters, memorizing nonsense sounds and words. It was tedious almost beyond bearing, and the more frustrating as he saw what he was building toward: repeating spells over and over in order to make fire sticks and glowglobes.

The sun began arcing northward, and the weather changed from one day to the next, one day hot and sunny, the next full of thunder and stinging rain, as the prevailing winds fought one another high over the mountains.

By the time the east winds won, bringing cold off those eternally snowy peaks, the hole that Arrow had made in life gently but inexorably closed in. Danet still found herself watching the opposite door, sometimes even getting up to go over with the intention of sharing a thought, then she'd catch herself.

Not that she couldn't talk to Connar. Of course she could. But the door to the king's suite was rarely open. Connar didn't like people walking in on him. If he came to breakfast (which he often did) then Danet knew he was in a ready mood for conversation. Even better, she saw Connar on Restdays making an effort to pay attention to his girls, who were very much in the trying puppy stage, their minders constantly chasing after them.

One morning as winter drew near, when everyone had finished and gone off to their chores, Danet put out her hand to Ranet. And when they were alone, "I like seeing Connar with the girls. That has to be your influence."

Words piled up unspoken behind Ranet's lips. The gunvaer had lost too much this last year—her mother, her husband. She seemed as tough as ever, but Ranet knew she could be hurt. "I asked him to."

"Good. He isn't a natural with small creatures the way Bunny is. I notice the girls are always slipping off to her rooms if they think they can get away with it."

"Kittens," Ranet said succinctly, smiling.

Danet uttered a short laugh. "Well, it doesn't come naturally to Connar, I can see. Any more than it did to me. But he's making an effort. Maybe that will help Iris be a little less shrill for attention, now that she's getting some from her Da."

Ranet agreed and left to get started on the day's labors. She started down the hall to her room, which now had an empty suite across from it. She sometimes looked at that closed door, finding it emblematic of her life. Marriage was a treaty. Everyone grew up knowing that. It was the weft to the warp of family and work, but what gave it color was the relationship the people built. Hers was a neutral thread spun out of silence.

She turned her back on Connar's old rooms and began to reach for the latch to her door when movement at the periphery of her vision caused her to look up. She saw Quill at the stairwell. He'd paused.

"Looking for me?" she asked.

"If you have a moment."

"Certainly. Come in."

He covered the distance quickly, and followed her into her room. "Do you need privacy?" she asked, as her runners were in the bedroom straightening things up.

"Not at all. I merely wondered if you've heard from Braids lately. I'd thought he was coming into the royal city, but if he did, I didn't see him," Quill said.

"Braids?" she repeated, wondering what Quill would want with Braids, especially now that he was no longer a royal runner.

Quill looked apologetic. "While I'm no longer on the third floor, I pass through when I'm with Lineas for the night, and people still have a habit of asking me things. Like, updating locations of various people. In case we—they—have to run a message. It seems that these days Braids could be any number of places that are weeks or even a month or two apart. He must live on horseback."

Ranet laughed. "I think he does. And he always liked it, too, when we were young. I expect right now, this time of year, he and Hendan are running the perimeter as the studs release the horses for winter grazing. They'll be completely out of contact, probably until New Year's Week, going by how things were when I grew up."

"Oh, that's good to know. I'll pass that on," he said. "Thanks!"

They parted, Ranet forgetting completely about Braids as she struggled not to envy Lineas. She knew that Quill, as Noddy's scribe, would have been given a room with the scribes at the other end of the state wing, which meant he crossed all this distance to be with Lineas, and they weren't even trying to have a child—not that she'd heard, anyway.

She glared at that closed door opposite, slammed hers, and firmly turned her attention to how much cloth to requisition from the weavers, for the academy next spring.

Quill moved swiftly back to the stairs and down, relieved that he hadn't been seen. Not that there was anything overtly wrong with his question, but he very much wanted to stay unnoticed as much as he could.

Lnand, the most experienced of all the ferrets, had transferred to Ku Halir, and had spent fruitless weeks ever since hunting Kendred, Cabbage's first runner. She'd met bewilderment—*Wouldn't he be sent back to Olavayir?* She met ignorance. *Who? Oh, well, why aren't you asking at Stalgoreth?*

Why would one of their runners be down here in Tlen . . . in Sindan-An . . . And she met question. *Why are all these people looking for him? Did he steal something?* It was the question increasing to suspicion at a trade town in Sindan-An that caused her to report failure to Quill: She couldn't find Kendred, she couldn't even find Braids, and asking was beginning to draw attention.

Every time he decided to give up, he remembered those ferrets of Jethren's searching—and the fact that Jethren himself, with his first runner, had vanished abruptly not long after Connar became king. But no one seemed to know where.

Vanadei, as yet, was the only person Quill had discussed the matter with. Every time he thought about sharing it with Lineas, he remembered that he'd have to begin with that night at the quartermaster's, and forbore. His argument with himself went like this: It would be mere selfishness to drag her into the quagmire of questions without answers. There was nothing she could do, and she would have to hide her reactions from Noddy, who could be very observant at unexpected times.

But underneath all that lay the subject of Connar, as volatile as fire.

TWENTY-FOUR

Midsummer 4090 AF

The throne room in Choreid Dhelerei's royal castle was originally a gathering hall and retreat for the entire trade town, which was poised on the middle hill of three, divided off from the other two hills by rivers to either side. As the town spread mostly southward, the castle was enlarged to the north. By the time the Cassadas family came to rule Iasca Leror, the castle had been rebuilt four times. The gathering hall had been elevated to a throne room with the dais added, as well as the Sartoran-influenced clerestory windows high up, to bring in more light and add a hint of grace.

The Cassadas family made that chamber beautiful. During their rule, that vaulted ceiling had hundreds of glowglobes hanging down at various sizes and lengths, resembling a starlit sky whose magic could generate warmth in winter, and be reduced to cool, tiny lights in summer. The bland sand-colored stone was hidden behind fine carving, exquisite plaster and tile and tapestry, designed to lead the eye upward, to convey airy lightness and aesthetic harmony.

When it became clear that the Marlovans could not be defeated, the Cassadas prevented a wholesale slaughter by surrender, marrying one of their daughters to the Marlovan chieftain—but before they left, they stripped the castle bare.

The conquering Marlovans moved from tents to castles, finding nothing but stone. As castle life was new to them, they remained unaware of the silent commentary on their lack of civilization; they affixed iron sconces to the walls of the throne room, and hung up banners and weapons taken in battle as decoration. The second king (mindful of how he had replaced the first king) added a good, sturdily built throne with an assassin-proof raised back and winged sides, thus engendering the first (and some will maintain, only) Marlovan fashion: raptor-footed wingback chairs. Mats on the floor were eventually replaced with benches.

All the coronations since those days took place in this nearly bare chamber, the only pageantry the drums rumbling in galloping counterpoint from the gallery below the windows, as new kings strode to the dais between the jarls and their captains, the commanders, and the guild chiefs. If the new king had married a suitable fighting queen, she was the one who gave him the two swords—one the old king's, one his own sword—sometimes in a display of skill of her own, after which he performed the sword dance—a ritual before battle—with three chosen men.

Then came the oaths, king to jarls, and jarls to king, after which all would retire to the secondary hall across the way, for a huge feast. That was it for ritual and pageantry.

So it was this year. Connar and Ranet made an astonishingly good-looking couple. Since winter Ranet had been practicing handling two swords, for though she was only gunvaer in name—as she was a wife—she knew what she owed both families, the royal Olavayirs and her own. Wolf Senelaec had dragged himself back to the royal city, and he was out there whooping the loudest as she tossed the swords spinning high into the air, then caught them by their handles before turning them over to Connar.

Their fingers touched briefly—hers warm, his cool and dry—and that was all the physical contact they had had for a year.

She backed up between Danet and Noren, and watched as Connar, Noddy, Stick Tyavayir, and Rat Noth (there in his father's place, before transferring to Hesea) performed the sword dance with athletic grace. Up on the dais, Ranet gazed out over the gathering, her expression serene, her emotions in a tumble; from the front, in the place of Captain of the Honor Guard, Kethedrend Jethren observed through narrowed eyes, burning with regret that he had not been asked to make one of those three with Connar. But he would get that place, he vowed silently, his gaze straying to Connar's beautiful wife, who had tossed those swords so spectacularly.

After that came the innovation that was received with enthusiastic popularity: It seemed that Keth Jethren, Commander of the new king's honor guard, had gone all the way up north to bring back . . . a dance troupe, to perform for the jarls at the banquet.

"How did he even think of that?" Knuckles Marlovayir asked Camrid Tyavayir, who had inherited Tyavayir this past year.

Camrid shrugged, his eyes on the floating draperies worn by the female dancers. "The Olavayirs used to have some connections up over the Andahi Pass, that's what I heard. He had leave, went to visit, and met up with these dancers. Brought them back for the coronation."

Knuckles grinned as the lissome women twirled and leaped, the draperies revealing, and concealing, enticing curves. Low-slung belts made of tiny coins jangled, drawing attention to the dip between rounded hips, watched raptly by men from eighteen to eighty. Marlovan women just didn't dance like that. And why ever not, grizzled old Captain Basna muttered to his jarl.

Male dancers were a part of the troupe. At first certain jarls, on discovering these foreigners didn't carry any steel, shrugged, wanting the women back, until the dancers brought out fire.

"Now *that* is worth watching!" Old Zheirban said to Mareca as a pair of men tossed whirling torches back and forth.

Mareca, who was very much enjoying the men for themselves, concurred, and added, "A good way to begin a new reign, I think. Very good."

Everyone seemed to agree—except of course for the Jarl of Gannan, wheezing purple-faced in ill-concealed fury. But there was no gainsaying the three witnesses who had been with Braids Senelaec during the entire clash with the mercenaries. The older jarls who had gone along with Gannan despite his dubious accusations, because it was always a good idea to put reins on a king, especially a young one hot to gallop, privately agreed that the old wolf was barking at the moon.

"As for young Connar," Khanivayir's Riding Captain said, his gaze dwelling appreciatively on the handsome young king currently watching the dancers and smiling, "unlike some sons, he hasn't been ordering up a lot of rock-headed changes just because he can."

Grunts and palm-up gestures of agreement from the oldsters met this: they were all aware of jarl sons who had, on inheriting, thrown all their fathers' ways to the winds, which struck very close to home.

The following day, they were equally entertained by watching the academy boys and girls compete in riding, shooting, and weaponry.

Connar invited Rat Noth to sit beside him. Rat enjoyed the clear, warm sunlight. He was in an excellent mood. He was finally reunited with Bunny, who would ride to Hesea with him, Danet-Gunvaer had promised. The Nyidris were gone except for Demeos, but he was a follower, currently trotting after his new wife. And with this transfer to Hesea Garrison, Rat never had to see him again.

As the ride and shoot commenced, Connar said to him, "I'm glad you'll be at Hesea. That puts you in reach."

Rat glanced sideways in question. "For?"

"Next summer I want to try something new. Instead of the academy seniors pitted against each other, I want a better challenge. You bring up a company of seasoned warriors. They'll be facing seniors out with something to prove, so it shouldn't be too boring."

Rat was surprised, but not displeased. Everybody loved wargames. Much more fun than drill, and no one got killed. He foresaw a good winter, as everyone competed to get picked for the wargame company.

"What kind of games are you thinking?" he asked.

The new king looked up and away, as if considering. He didn't seem to notice the youngsters working so hard on the parade ground, every so often looking up expectantly at the royal family. "Different things," Connar said finally. "Different terrain. Different problems. We've seen a few in the past few years."

"That we have," Rat acknowledged.

The last competition finished, and covert glances were sent toward the king—who raised his fist in approbation, and a pleased shout erupted from the stands and the field alike, sending birds squawking. Rat hadn't thought Connar was watching but he clearly was, watching everything everywhere. Great commander, great king. Rat left smiling.

And he was still smiling two days later as he and his escort rode for Hesea, Bunny with them.

Danet stood on the wall, her feelings sharply ambivalent. She'd always dreaded sending Bunny south, but these circumstances were so much better than what she'd dreaded in the past. Bunny was happy. She was only going as far as Hesea Garrison. And, Danet thought , determined to find something good in this situation, the Noths were known for almost always having boys. She adored her granddaughters, but it would be good to have next generation's heir growing up under her eyes.

She knew Arrow would have agreed.

With the jarls and their captains gone, Connar at last had leisure to sit down with Jethren and his map.

It was an extraordinarily detailed map. At first glance it was overwhelming. "How did you get this close without raising suspicion?" Connar asked.

"It was the dancers," Jethren responded. "Found them early on, at the far end of Andahi. Their caravan leader had quit on them. They were looking about for someone to manage the animals and their carts. They were glad to hire Moonbeam and me, and when I found out they were traveling the length of the coast, and that military camps tended to hire them as entertainment, we stuck to them all winter and through the spring. At Ghildraith, they were arguing about whether to cross the strait and risk one of those pirate-infested harbors, or go back along the north coast, competing against all the other troupes, when I got the idea of telling them to come south. As cover."

"Cover," Connar repeated. "Not just for the Idegans."

"And it worked. Everyone who asked why I was gone, when I told them I'd brought that troupe back for the coronation, not a one argued. The queen told me yesterday when she saw me down in the stable that the troupe is taking over some old building in the city, that has a raised platform, like a stage. Rumor has it, it was for plays, back in the old days."

Connar already knew that Noren had hired the male dancers for a gathering she'd given the night before to the female masters in the queen's training and in the academy, as a reward for their efforts during the Convocation.

Connar was not tired of the dancers—far from it—but he was tired of them as a subject. "I sent the Nob runner back empty-handed. We're done with the Nob. I told Fish to put a couple of royal runners to shadow him up the peninsula, ones who know something about boats. They can go doggo up there. Listen. If Lorgi Idego strikes, the royal runner scouts are to sail for Lindeth, as Nermand said it's far faster than taking horses back down the peninsula. Then a grass-run to alert us. I'm gambling on it not happening right away."

Jethren considered that. Distances, how long it would take to muster once the decision was made. Then that journey up the north coast of the peninsula. That side might be marginally easier, but no one would attempt it in winter, with no shelter and a long supply line.

The surface of his mind turned these facts over, but he was aware of the high moral ground. Surely it was time for a reward.

And Connar said, "Excellent map. Everything I wanted."

Here it was!

Then: "Didn't you once say you wanted to run the academy?"

Jethren hesitated, expecting almost anything but that. Then his mind arrowed straight to Ranet, who his Nighthawk men had reported was now the academy headmaster. "Yes." But the word had a rising inflection—question.

Connar's brow furrowed. "You said once the training you had at Olavayir was tough."

"Yes." Amazement seized Jethren. Was it possible that he could bring in the Vaskad training already?

"That's what I want at the academy. If it takes the Bar Regren a year to harass the Idegans into striking back and taking the Nob, so much the better. That gives you a year with the seniors. Get them ready for the games."

"Games?"

Connar smiled.

Ranet found out midway through winter, when Danet asked Connar if he wanted to meet with them all, as had become habit, to plan the new academy year. It was no more than a courtesy question, because he was now king, and he'd handed off headmaster duties. But to her surprise, he said to set up the meeting. He'd be there.

He was—with Jethren. "Everything you do with selection and logistics is excellent. Don't make any changes. But I want Jethren to oversee the training," Connar said, aware that no one would gainsay him now.

Ranet didn't argue. She said, "I can see that you'd want one of your captains training your future captains." And she was the first to leave.

She walked to her room, determined to get her emotions combed out. Connar didn't hate her. But that wasn't the relief she would have expected. Hatred seemed preferable to indifference.

When winter showed its first signs of relenting, it was time to haul the academy's furnishings out of storage, and begin the logistical toil of readying for another season.

One of those tasks was meeting with Jethren.

Ranet decided the meeting ought to be held in the headmaster's building, which during the past couple of years had only been used for overflow supplies.

Jethren arrived, with words ready on his lips. This was their first face to face, and he felt like a boy. "I'm to tell you that Sindan Monadan will be the master in lance training," he said.

Ranet retorted easily enough, "And you're the fifth person to inform me. Pass along the chain that I have been duly informed." She pointed to the chalkboard, where the name "Monadan" had been written in among the other masters' names.

He laughed, a sudden sound that made him look a lot younger. Her incipient distrust eased somewhat. Laughter could do that, she knew. She said, a shade more cordially, "What changes did you have in mind? If it's complicated, we'll need to call meetings with the masters."

He opened his hands. "Begin with a single rule change for the seniors. The rest can come. The rule is this, the last in any exercise gets a beating."

She frowned. "What kind of beating?"

"Nothing that lays them up." Jethren gave a short laugh, more a bark, and she felt the dislike returning. "What use is a barracks full of wounded? At Olavayir, we got five across the shoulder blades. Incentive to work harder."

Ranet bit down on a protest. Danet had absolutely forbidden beatings for the queen's training. Serious troublemakers had been sent home. The same had held true in Senelaec.

But beatings were traditional in the academy. And anyway, this seemed to be what Connar wanted.

She said, "If that's all, then I don't think we need to call for extra meetings. You can explain when the masters meet for schedule discussion."

Which meant they were done. He left, disappointed, but not surprised.

When the masters met, once they'd covered the schedule, Jethren explained the new rule. Ranet watched the masters accept it with mild expressions of interest, question, and a couple of downward glances of doubt. But no one complained. They were too used to obeying orders.

Jethren said, "Once they get used to it, train them to handle it themselves. It becomes the riding, or flight, captain's responsibility."

"Ten-year-olds hitting each other?" Baldy Faldred, the writing and mapping master, asked.

"Seniors only," Jethren said. "This year. And remind them they'll be going up against a garrison company at a wargame this summer."

Spring arrived stealthily. There was still snow in the shadows when the academy began filling up. Up in the gunvaer's suite, Danet reflected on how the idea of a new year could vary so much. They counted the year change from when the sun was farthest north, but the farmers—and in the city, the academy—regarded those winter months as part of the old year.

The new year began for half the city when the academy bells tolled for the first time, calling the youngsters to inspection. Sometimes she watched through Noddy's windows, enjoying the fresh young faces below. Arrow would have liked seeing how his academy had become so much a part of Marlovan life.

Noren stood beside Danet, awareness extended to everyone busy outdoors again after so long between walls. Spring light and work one liked were so simple, but so powerful in creating happiness.

Ranet was too busy with the unending stream of demands to think about such things. Everything seemed to be satisfactory. But there was that one new change.

As the first month came to an end, and the spring rains lightened up for a brief period, Noren and Ranet went out riding together. It had occurred to Ranet that when one wished for private conversation with a hearing person, going outside where one could see who was within listening range was preferable to trusting in walls and halls, where anyone might be lurking. But with someone who relied on sight and not sound, outdoors was not necessarily private—then, the walls and halls served best.

Noren knew all the spots where trees or land obscured them, however briefly, from the scrutiny of sentries on the city or castle walls. She reined up under the branches of an old tree, and signed, "You've been worried about that new rule."

"It's . . . not what I thought would happen. At first they thought it was funny. Then—maybe it was those two weeks of rain—they seemed, oh, grim. At the same time, the masters had to land on the ten- and eleven-year-olds because they just had to mimic their elders, taking it upon themselves to begin smacking around their slowest."

"That's annoying."

"Yes, but not surprising. And the masters said it was no different than breaking up fights. So, nobody's questioned this new rule." Ranet stroked her horse's neck to keep her hands busy, glanced at Noren's waiting face, then snapped her fingers together. "Some even love it, Jarend Olavayir being one of them."

"He relishes rules, that one," Noren responded. "And I suspect he likes seeing the Mareca girl get thwacked when she's last in the obstacles runs because she's so short."

"True," Ranet said. "But she shrugs and declares her mother is ten times harder at home. And she's always first in the ride-and-shoot, which means more to the youngsters than running obstacles. Anyway, they're adjusting.

I'm not sure whether to be relieved or not that they all seem to think it one more rule."

"They're warriors," Noren reminded her. "They have to be harder than the enemy."

Noren sighed, thrown back to early childhood. It had taken reaching adult age to realize that her mother had foreseen from the beginning that her daughter would likely be called upon to replace the false Ranet that Braids had been until he was nearly sixteen. There had been no words spoken, except—Ranet understood now—there had been expectations.

But Ranet had been a child, with childish boundaries, which didn't extend any farther than Sindan-An castle—and her worst enemy, a Keriam cousin named Gdan, whose sarcastic teasing had caused many fights.

Ranet remembered her mother talking repeatedly about the difference between self-defense and sneakily starting a fight, then claiming to be a victim. Finally, when Ranet was ten, her mother had taken her onto the walls, where no one could hear them. *When you're around Gdan you are never your best self,* she had said. *You are only your angry self, thinking this time you have to win. But there is no real win, there is only the next time.*

I hate her, Ranet's own voice echoed in memory—sounding a lot like Iris.

Feelings are feelings. Sometimes you can't change them. But you can change how much you see her. Stay away from Gdan, so that you can be your best self.

Ranet explained that. Noren watched with her serious face as Ranet finished, "I struggled so hard to be my best self. Two years later Aunt Calamity came, and asked if I wanted to go to Senelaec, and I—oh, never mind that. My point is, does hitting the last person in an exercise truly bring out the best self?"

Noren swatted at a fly buzzing around her mare's ears, then responded, "I think whoever you ask will give you a different answer."

Ranet laughed, turned the subject to Bunny's exuberant letter from Hesea Garrison—which she found the most fascinating place in the world, mostly because it was not the royal city—and the conversation sank into the back of both their minds.

Summer ripened and the earliest leaves began to wither in the dry glare of Lightning Season when it was time for the seniors to depart for the wargame. Jethren was to command them. Ranet reasoned that it made sense. If he was in charge of training, then he should be the one to ride at their head to see how that training did in the field. She would never go into the field.

So Ranet watched from the walls as the seniors trotted out behind Connar and Jethren, banners fluttering in the hot, dry winds, their blue as intense as the sky.

The seniors rode southward, camping along the way and drilling industriously in anticipation of meeting Hesea Garrison's best under the famous Rat Noth in a mock battle, with the king watching! So much more fun than those poor babies back at the academy, with their silly Victory Day games!

TWENTY-FIVE

Everyone knew about the new senior wargame, of course. There was even a flurry of wagers among the royal castle guards and in the city.

The rest of the academy still had Victory Day games to look forward to, and the city, of course, would celebrate whether or not there was an academy.

Victory Day meant extra work for the castle staff, except up in the state wing, as few wanted to be away from home for Victory Day.

Almost three weeks passed, and the festival was two days off when among the celebrants and merchants streaming into the royal city came a dust-covered couple dressed in wagon-driver dull green. The man wore an eye-patch, his head down as though to protect his single eye from the glaring brightness of Lightning Weather.

The woman drove the wagon, and the man rode in back with the baskets of jugged sage honey, which identified their origin only if you knew that the right sage for this honey grew on the slopes of the eastern mountains.

They made their way to one of the inns popular with the market regulars, and while the man stabled the horse and stayed with their goods, the woman made her way among the festival crowds to the royal castle, where she asked the duty runner to find Lineas the Royal Runner.

Lineas was up on the third floor, helping with tedious chores such as list-copying when word was passed along. She went down to the stable, where a woman her own age waited, someone Lineas had never seen before.

When Lineas stepped from the shadowy archway into the bright light, she was distracted by the luminous quality of the Lanrid ghost she had assumed for so long was Evred, king for a day. Lanrid's coloring was jewel-toned and clear, from his bright hair to the deep blue of his tunic and the shimmering gold thread of the leaping dolphin on his chest.

Lineas blinked past that to the tense-looking woman standing in the yard, licking her lips.

Lineas said, "You asked for me?"

The woman shifted her gaze to one side and then the other, licked her lips again, then said, "You wanted some of our sage honey?"

Lineas blinked. "What?"

The woman's lips tightened, and she said, "I have some for you. A . . . a gift." She turned away, walked a few steps, then turned back expectantly.

Lineas had only the copy duties, which anyone on the third floor could do. Curious, she followed the woman out the castle gate, and down the broad street leading toward the city center.

The woman walked fast, head bent, in silence. Lineas followed, curiosity intensifying. When they reached the main street, the woman's pace faltered, and she halted. Turned. Said, "So . . . someone told us—me—you are with the king. A favorite."

"No." Lineas didn't hide her surprise as she held up her hand with the ring on it. "That's in the past."

The woman's lips parted as she gazed at the ring. Then she crossed her arms. "I was told you're kind. That you don't blab."

"I'm glad," Lineas said, amusement bubbling inside her. "To whom do I owe these compliments?"

Another surprise. That seemed to be the wrong question, for the woman's face lengthened in panic. Then a blink, and her expression shuttered.

Lineas sighed. "I walked away from some very tedious work that I don't like leaving for someone else, so if you've nothing else to say, I'll return to work."

"No!" The woman snatched at the air, licked her lips again, and squared her shoulders. "If—someone—wanted to talk to you. And didn't want that blabbed around. Would you heed their wishes?"

Lineas sighed again. "If someone is not causing anyone harm, I certainly would respect their wishes for privacy. If that's what you're asking."

"You would?" The woman stepped closer, her voice dropping, her pupils huge in staring eyes. "You *promise?*"

Lineas held her hands out. "I promise."

"Good." The woman stood there, lips compressed, breathing heavily. "Good, good." Then she turned abruptly. "Come."

The woman walked fast, pausing at each intersection to look about intently until they crossed the square toward the huge, rambling inn where tradespeople and caravanners usually stayed.

She ducked around a corner, then under an archway into a tiny court. They crossed that and squeezed around stacked baskets to a door under an overhang. Another long, desperate glance back at Lineas, then she seemed to come to a decision, and opened the door to a room with a tiny window that was tightly shuttered in spite of the stifling heat.

Lineas stepped warily into the thick gloom, the air pungent with the sweat of desperation. A man sat on a mat next to a tiny table, bedroll on the other side. The man was big, even hunched over, his lineaments somehow familiar.

The woman lit a candle. Lineas was going to protest against the added heat, then paused when recognition came: "Aren't you Kendred? First runner to Cab—ah, to the Jarl of Stalgoreth?" Who was now dead.

The woman backed to the closed door, looking terrified.

Kendred, who had been wearing an eyepatch, lifted it up. "I guess my disguise wasn't so good," he said slowly. "Spring, close the door. It's all right. I called her here, right?"

"Why would you need a disguise?" Lineas asked.

Kendred and the woman named Spring exchanged looks. Then she darted forward and sat down close to Kendred's side.

Kendred said, "You didn't know that people have been searching for me?"

Lineas opened her hands. "I've been working as a scribe for Nadran-Sierlaef. My duties concern lists and petitions."

At Noddy's name, Spring whispered something and made a quick urging motion with one hand.

"He can't do anything," Kendred whispered back fiercely enough that Lineas heard it easily. Then he turned to Lineas. "I'm going. Out of the country. The healers did what they could for my knee. But the way it shattered, I can barely walk. It's said that healers down south over the sea can fix anything. So we'll work our way across. But first . . . I think honor requires me to say something."

Spring keened under her breath.

Kendred's voice hardened. "I have to. I don't know what you can do. That is, if you don't sic the king's men onto me. I know he's had Jethren's spies sticking their noses all over, but nobody liked them in Stalgoreth. Them and their Olavayir superiority."

Spring keened again.

Kendred muttered, "I'm going to say my say. If she rats, she rats." Then back to Lineas. "You didn't. At Gannan."

Lineas said, "I won't promise if someone is going to be harmed in any way."

Spring said fiercely, "The only one't'll be harmed is *him*." And to Kendred, "Give it to her. Do it the way you pledged."

Kendred sighed, then held out a much-folded paper, sealed. "If you'll promise me to wait a week before you read it."

"I need my own assurance," Lineas said gently.

"The harm has already been done," Kendred said so bleakly that alarm tightened the back of Lineas's neck. "The threat is only to me. Give me a week, then read it. Do whatever you think is right after that. Just give me that week. No one will take any hurt of it, any more than's already happened."

Lineas agreed, took the paper, and slid it into her robe pocket. Spring jumped up, dashed to the door, then came back with a jug of honey. "Here."

She pressed it into Lineas's hands, her dark eyes pleading. "It's good. Some say, the best."

"Thank you," Lineas said, more confused than ever, and left, the jug cradled against her side, the paper a weight in her inner pocket.

The academy seniors under Jethren and Rat Noth's chosen company met at Old Faral, which had been warned well ahead of time that it would be the site of this game. Amid much anticipatory ribaldry, the companies camped, half outside the walls, half in the courtyard of the old castle.

Connar met with Jethren and Rat Noth. "The problem is pretty obvious, one army attacks the castle. The other defends. If it ends too soon, we'll run it again, swapping the armies."

"Can the inside force come out on the attack?" Rat asked.

Connar opened his hands. "Would a castle ride out to the attack?"

Rat grinned. "Most commanders I know would, if they thought their lancers could hit the siege company hard enough."

"Let's see what they do," Connar said, and opened his hand toward the two commanders.

The academy seniors were the first defenders. Despite the loud talk among the boys, and Jethren's unspoken determination to win, Rat's company broke in before morning was over; they attacked front and back gates as expected, but while the two attack parties roared and repeatedly raised their ladders and sent showers of jelly arrows over, in pairs covert teams slipped along the walls between the sparsely posted sentries (who were all gazing out cursorily while mostly craning to see the action at the gates). Clamber up, jump the sentry, and they were in.

After that, defeat was swift. As Jethren had predicted, the seniors weren't desperate enough. They fell apart quickly, and didn't surrender so much as stop, as was their habit on their own games. Vaskad would have flogged them all himself, Jethren knew—one of his earliest memories was all the blood—but he kept his teeth shut. Discipline would come, but the initial failure was his own.

The next day, Rat's defenders let the seniors try to break in all day, then came roaring out in two noisy groups, a third having sneaked out, crawling through the sun-dried weeds until they encircled the seniors. Then, as night began to fall, they took them utterly by surprise. Almost the same strategy, and Jethren had fallen for it yet again.

When the commanders met that night, Jethren held onto his temper. Rat didn't look his way as he said, "This is good for the boys, but we could have foreseen how fast they would go down."

Connar turned his way. "You have a suggestion?"

Rat shuffled his feet. "Split both companies in half. Let the boys mix with my company. It's what they'll be doing anyway when they get their garrison assignment next year."

"True. Do it," Connar said. "Between the two of you, divide them up tonight. Let's see if tomorrow is better."

Jethren walked off with Rat, trying to figure out how to take the lead without demanding it. But Rat started in with very accurate evaluations of the seniors, garnered after two days of watching. Since his suggestions balanced the strong and the weak, that left Jethren with nothing to say except agreement.

Rat sent him a company from Hesea, under Captain of Skirmishers Plum Noth—who was the focus of all eyes the rare times he spoke. Just about every one of those utterances began with "Rat usually says," or "Rat often does . . ." and Jethren could see the conviction in all the listeners—even the seniors.

He wanted to command, but the need to win was greater. And so he accepted Plum's suggestions.

This time the challenge took days. Connar rode around smiling at the combatants who, in their turn, worked harder under the king's eyes, and unnoticed by them all Moonbeam drifted along the perimeter watching, watching.

At the end of the week they officially called a draw, the king praised them all at a last night banquet at which ale flowed freely, and they parted, promised another game—a different one next year—before they separated.

Connar often rode ahead alone, but on this return journey he beckoned Jethren forward on the first day, and rode ahead with him, until the column was out of earshot.

"Rat's trickery aside, we aren't much better than Artolei," he commented.

Jethren forced out the words, "Rat Noth was better."

"Oh, for a game." Connar flattened his hand. "All he did was adapt his usual two-prong flank attack. That foolishness with sending his insertion team flat against the wall to the midpoint would never happen in a real siege situation. The sentries would be looking down constantly. Those boys stuck midway along the wall were trying to see the fun at the gates."

"True."

"A setback." Connar's voice deepened with dissatisfaction. "Not the only one. I wasted all last winter and most of spring pawing through moldy records to find out exactly how our ancestors took the Iascan castles in the first place. I assumed they had siegecraft that had been forgotten, but from what I could tell, there were two fairly bloody assaults, led by the first king."

"We have so many ballads about Anderle Montreivayir," Jethren said. "He must have left records."

"We seldom sing the Hymn to the Beginnings anymore." Connar slanted a sardonic smile at Jethren. "But you should remember that he was not the first king. That was Quill's forefather, Savarend Montredavan-An, who lived long enough to conquer Iasca Leror. He might have planned to write his memoirs in his old age, but Anderle's knife ended that."

Jethren mentally shrugged. Ancient history was, well, ancient.

"According to the Iascans, I discovered, the rest of their nobles negotiated treaties or surrendered outright. And those castles mostly seemed to have been outposts. It was Anderle Montreivayir who started building bigger castles, presumably to keep the Venn from coming after our ancestors. Setback. We'll try again next year."

Jethren said nothing, but inwardly resolved that he had a year to learn everything there was to be known about siege warfare.

At the royal city, Victory Day arrived, passed, and faded into memory as the academy youths started home and the academy itself had to be readied for winter—which meant emptying it down to the stone.

No matter how busy Lineas was, awareness of that sealed paper tucked into her journal never ceased. Lineas was curious, but there was also a sense of burden. Kendred's and Spring's anxiety and even terror had made that clear.

After she had helped inventory the academy furnishings and weapons, she donated the jug of honey to the always-ravenous, grateful fuzz in the roost, then went to Pereth to tell him she was going back to the state wing.

"Thanks," he said tiredly. Then he gave her a considering look. "Listen. About this magic. Someone said you studied it once. The others here don't explain very clearly. I think they know it too well, so it becomes like trying to tell someone how to walk. Do you understand the difference between what they call first level, and whatever the second is?"

Lineas said, "I studied magic, but I failed at it. I was never even able to manage first level spells. However, from what I recollect, second level incorporates such things as healer magic. The Beard Spell, and so forth."

Pereth's brows met. "But that's simple. I remember that much."

Lineas said, "It actually involves changing things on bodies. The Beard Spell could go so very wrong if done wrong. Think of losing all your hair, or worse, having it grow from your eyes, or something."

Pereth made a warding motion with his hand. "I get it. Yes, I guess I can see that. Thank you."

She left, regretting what was after all only a partial lie. Second level magic did incorporate healer spells, though much more complicated ones than the Beard Spell. It also incorporated magic transfer in all its forms. But orders were orders, and she had that letter to read. Putting it off only meant more thinking about it.

With it tucked in her inner pocket, she picked up her writing tools and walked over to the state wing, aware that the farther she got from the royal wing, the less tense she felt.

When she reached the inner chamber, she found it empty, as she'd expected—Quill would be finishing Fox drills in the winter storage extension, and of course Vanadei would be with Noddy.

She sat down on the nearest mat and opened the letter.

This is what I saw when the invaders came into Stalgoreth. I was in the mud. Leg broke. Alone on the field. Then I saw Connar-Laef throw the foreigner sword into my jarl Senrid's back. Senrid, everyone called Cabbage. Senrid fell off his horse. Keth Jethren rode shield to Connar-Laef. I blacked out. My head was bad after I woke. I forgot for a time. When I remembered I told Braids Senelac. He took me to Sindan-An. My sister in Stalgoreth sent a message Keth Jethren's ferrets searched for me. I have to fix my knee. I can't ride. So we will go over the sea. Braids said he can't ride against a king. It will be a war. Not against enemies. Against us. Spring said tell someone you trust. That is you.

Lineas lowered the letter, her fingers trembling. Why had Kendred given it to her? He was not around to ask—he was a week away, and no doubt traveling as fast as he could.

"Lineas, what's wrong?"

She looked up, startled. Quill crossed the floor in three strides and dropped down beside her. Lineas first crushed the paper into her fingers, then she recollected Kendred's last spoken words to her, in effect entrusting her with this revelation.

This burden.

Instead of answering, she held out the paper, and watched as he scanned rapidly. Twice. Then he lowered it. "How did you get this?"

She explained.

He grimaced. "A lot is now clear."

"I would be glad for clear." She folded her arms across her churning stomach and leaned into them. "Like?"

"Why Braids has not returned to the royal city. Why Lnand was effectively blindsided by him and Stalgoreth, and Jethren's ferrets were as well. The ferrets seem to have given up entirely, I'm glad to report: three of our people spotted them along the road to the Andahi Pass, though the royal runners were not informed, and so there is no record of their mission."

"Not even Pereth knew?"

"He might have received spoken orders, which included not logging the runners or the message. But that's guesswork. Going back to Kendred's letter here, I suspect we also now know why Gannan leveled that accusation against Braids. I'm wondering if a message to Cabbage's father got garbled along the way, and of course Gannan would interpret it whatever way suited him best."

Lineas rocked back and forth. "How many people do you think know about it?"

"Hard to guess." Quill looked upward. "Maddar Sindan-An, almost certainly, and those closest to her. We now have firsthand testimony that Braids knows. We can assume those closest to him."

"But they haven't said anything."

"I feel certain they're all aware that bringing an accusation like this against a king is far different than it would have been against Connar when Arrow was alive. They hesitated then, and now it's probably too late."

Lineas's stomach knotted with tension. "I know Connar always hated Cabbage Gannan. And yet I'm wondering how clear Kendred's sight was. His head was injured."

"And this occurred in the middle of a hailstorm," Quill said. "But I'll warrant Braids, at least, interrogated Kendred thoroughly. And this line about 'throwing the sword into Gannan's back' is fairly specific. The healer who examined him said that his spine was severed by a single blow."

"Why . . . ?" Lineas whispered.

"It might not have been calculated. Call it a fit of petulance, the heat of the moment, even the chaos of battle. That has covered many questionable acts in our history. However, that's all speculation, and we finally have a witness. Which is better than we have with Retren Hauth."

"Retren Hauth the lance master?"

Quill said gravely, "I'll ask you again, how much of this do you want to hear?"

Lineas knew from his tone that she would hate anything she heard. But . . . "It seems I have to. Quill, the more I think about it, the more I believe Kendred thinks I can somehow get justice for Cabbage."

"Yes," Quill said, handing back the letter. "But getting it from a sitting king is . . . difficult. I suggest you store that somewhere safe, for now."

And then he told her what he knew.

Connar returned in time for his brother's Name Day, and life settled into autumnal activities, centered around harvest and tax season.

There were still bad moments. One morning, a biscuit crumbling in Danet's hands threw her back to breakfast with Arrow as he impatiently slathered jam on biscuits, half-crumbling them as they talked out kingdom affairs. Sometimes they argued, but it had never been bitter.

Her stinging eyes turned toward the hallway and the closed door opposite. *How* that closed door hurt, reminding her with the implacability of stone that there would never again be crumbled biscuits slopping down

Arrow's front, or his snapped fingers, or his impatient prowling around the room.

His voice.

She shut her eyes, but knew that closed door was still there. She could knock, of course. Connar always made time for her, but there was that sense that she was interrupting him. At least he continued to come to breakfast, but when he did, the conversation was much as it was when he was young: trivialities. She heard about decisions when the evidence showed up in the ledgers.

Such as the abandonment of the Nob.

She brought the subject up one morning, after the word came in that the silver usually bound for the peninsula had been sent to furbish Old Faral castle.

"That caught me by surprise," she said carefully. "Of course it's your decision to make. But I would like to hear your reasoning."

"That treaty was pointless." Connar jerked one shoulder up. "A dead loss, everything about it. Da held onto the Nob to keep it from the Idegans. I don't care if they're stupid enough to try to take it." He smiled, his eyes as bright and clear a blue as ever, but she sensed in his tone that there was nothing to discuss—that he didn't want to discuss it.

There was no more partnership, that is, not with her. And that was the way of the world, she told herself. She was aware that she had been granted more of a say in governing Marlovan Iasca than most any other gunvaer, possibly even the great Hadand. It was reasonable and even proper for Connar to share government with his brother. She still handled the kingdom's tallies, but she no longer controlled where it was spent, or how. Again, that was to be expected with a new king. Nothing wrong.

But it hurt.

Connar saw something of that hurt, and left, puzzled. She couldn't really be regretting the Nob. Maybe she was just missing Da. Noddy still talked sadly of what Da might have wanted.

Connar crossed over to his suite, to find Fish Pereth waiting with Cheese. Oh yes. He wanted to be called Pereth now.

"Problems on the third floor?" Connar asked, impatient to get down to the courtyard.

"No. Everything is fine." Pereth was bitterly convinced he could drop dead and the royal runners would carry on smoothly and efficiently around his stiffening corpse. But he'd long ago learned not to share opinions unless Connar asked. Which had happened so rarely he could still recollect them all.

Because of that—because of many things—Pereth actually had two items, but he'd decided after weeks of rumination that broaching the second one depended on what he heard in response to the first. "Since I'm no longer a first runner, I'd like to get married. I realize that royal runners only marry among themselves, but that's easily adjusted, Hibern's a scribe over in the city. We could use her on the third floor, especially with New Year's Week coming—"

"No. Is that all?"

"No?" Pereth was so taken aback he forgot old habits.

Connar sighed. "Can we get into this another time? They're all waiting on me down in the courtyard."

Pereth remained silent. They both knew very well that Connar could keep them waiting half a day and no one would say anything.

Connar's eyes narrowed as he studied Pereth's face, then he said, "Look. We're both young. Barely thirty. There's plenty of time for a wife, who will be wanting your attention, and probably a family, which demands more time. Right now I want your focus on magic. I need to know what I can use, and you're the only one I can trust to find out."

Yes, well, that was the second item Pereth had on his mind. He was now able to complete small spells, and had been experimenting on his own. Magic was dangerous. It burned if you used it too much. But given that, there were all kinds of possibilities—if you were willing to take the risk.

Pereth had figured Connar might say what he'd said. And being right in that indicated he'd be right in guessing that Connar would require, even demand, that Pereth take every risk to learn what he wanted.

Maybe someday.

Like, after he was married.

"As you wish," he said, fist to heart, and left.

TWENTY-SIX

Early in spring of 4092, the initial spate of messengers after first thaw brought the unsurprising news that the Nob had fallen to the Bar Regren.

Connar had already received word through his royal runner scouts, who had (with the rest of the Marlovan contingent there) escaped to ships, those with foresight having managed to reduce their holdings to precious metals.

The two whose goods could not be spirited out spread oil over everything, and set fire to their buildings in the teeth of the Bar Regren.

There was little reaction in Marlovan Iasca. Life went on as usual.

Jethren had begun the academy season with another setback, when Connar told him no siege equipment. "This game's goals are strategy. Timing. Logistics. Remember, we are talking about defense." But he soon overcame it. The entire academy was lusting to be chosen for the garrison game, as it was now being called. The returning seniors from the year previous had, in time-honored manner, inflated the report of their experience, heightening the sense of competition.

Jethren used that competition to tighten the consequences of being slow, clumsy, unskilled. Discipline at the academy was much harsher, resulting in more injuries. The riding master who had replaced Bunny resigned, saying to Danet, "It's ridiculous to take a switch to children whose riding skills are all about the same, whoever is last depending entirely on the animals."

Two of the senior girls had separately gone to Ranet and asked to be sent over to the queen's training. As one girl said, "I know the academy trains captains. But if being a captain means beating my sixteen-year-old sister bloody, I'd rather ride under Henad Sindan-An. We all know her wings are the fastest in the kingdom, and she's never used a stick on anyone, not that I've heard."

The girls were transferred, scorned by those who stayed behind. Jethren made it clear that only the toughest as well as the fastest and deadliest would be chosen for this year's garrison game.

And so it was.

It was a rainy summer when Rat arrived at Hesea Springs, where Connar, Jethren, and the academy seniors were waiting.

While the seniors drilled until exhausted under the hard eyes of Jethren's two captains—finally captains of their own companies—Connar called them together, saying, "The game will begin here. You are invaders, and your goal is to attack Ku Halir and Tlen at the same time, or as near as you can."

Rat Noth hated returning to Ku Halir, which still featured in his nightmares, but before he left, he admitted to Bunny that Connar's plan made sense. Of course he'd want to find ways to better defend the city in case Elsarion did come back.

Connar went on, "I asked Ghost Fath to bring down some volunteers from Halivayir to harass your supply lines on your way east. Let's make it a challenge," he finished, smiling.

Rat grinned. He hadn't seen Ghost Fath for what felt like a lifetime. Same with Stick Tyavayir. "I received a runner from Braids Senelaec," Connar added, as Cheese Fath brought in a tray of braised trout and fresh-steamed cabbage. "He'll provide some defenders at Tlen. So you decide between you who will attack Ku Halir and who Tlen."

Early the next morning, in the royal city, Lineas woke to find a silhouette at the end of the bed, outlined in weak blue light. "Quill?"

His head turned. "I just heard from Camerend." He lifted the paper, which curled at the ends. "He heard from Uncle Vanda."

Lineas remembered that the man Quill called "uncle" was a former royal runner, and a longtime friend of Camerend and Mnar Milnari, though as far as she knew, no actual relative of either. Why he had lived in Lorgi Idego for decades she didn't know, but she'd learned while at Darchelde that this Uncle Vanda was close friends with the King of Lorgi Idego, one of the reasons there were good relations between the two kingdoms.

She sat upright. Letters at dawn were seldom a good sign. "Is something wrong?"

"It seems that the Bar Regren have attacked Andahi Castle twice since they took the Nob. Prince Cama is trying to convince his father to let him lead their defensive force up the peninsula to retake the Nob, and settle it as an Idegan harbor. No one was surprised when regular trade began refusing to land at the Nob, as the Bar Regren predictably began charging fees that are outright piracy. But now that trade is also wary of landing at Andahi because of the fighting. That would be very bad for our spice trade."

Lineas shut her eyes, calling up the map. "Why don't they just sail to Lindeth?"

"It has something to do with currents and winds. The better half of the year—which would be anything not winter—the islanders can easily reach Andahi, then go on down the strait. Sailing to Lindeth instead means rounding the peninsula against currents and winds. They'd lose months of the strait trade before the winds turn against them again."

Lineas's response was more polite than interested, and he knew that to her the situation was remote. He tucked the letter away until the end of the day, when he and Vanadei could speculate as they copied out the day's records.

Which they continued to do over the next few days, as a series of thunderstorms crashed through, heading for the plains to the east.

Then came another note in Quill's golden notecase, from their ferret in Ku Halir. The three were alone that morning, as no petitioners had turned up, and Noddy had gone up to the tower to watch a truly spectacular storm, leaving them to finish up some copywork in anticipation of a free afternoon.

Quill took the note from his case, and read it out to Vanadei and Lineas: Connar and his wargamers had been sighted. This year, not only Ku Halir was to defend itself against attackers, but also Tlen! Everybody was looking forward to the fun.

"Another castle defense," Vanadei commented when Quill was done reading. "And Rat Noth leading the attack!"

"Last year was castle defense as well," Quill said as he pulled a fresh sheet of paper toward him.

Lineas said soberly, "It doesn't surprise me, after that dreadful winter at Frozen Falls."

"True." Vanadei jabbed his penknife in the air. "Whew, it's still hot in here. When will these storms stay long enough to cool things off?"

Quill's pen scratched rapidly across the page. When he'd finished a line, he muttered, "Why two castles at once?"

Vanadei sat back. "More fun? There's no threats, right? Elsarion still crowned with bird droppings in his Garden of Shame?"

Thunder crackled and boomed overhead. Lineas watched the windows glow blue-white, leaching the world of color. She wondered if she should go see if the Lanrid ghost was at its usual post near the stable, and how it would look in the lightning's glare.

Vanadei continued to carve his nib, until he noticed Quill sitting very still, his pen slowly forming a round drop of ink, which splatted onto the page.

"Damn," Quill said softly.

He wasn't looking at the page.

Lineas, always sensitive to every subtlety in his voice, forgot ghosts and turned to face him. "Quill, what's wrong?"

"Nothing—maybe—I don't know." He threw the pen down. "Where's the map?"

Noddy kept a rolled map in the little room next door, for he liked to see exactly where petitioners came from. Quill sprang up, fetched it, and spread it out on Noddy's empty desk. The other two set aside their writing tools and turned on their mats, eyes shifting from Quill to the map to Quill again.

He glanced up, his body taut. "What if . . . this is not practice for defense?"

"What else could it be?" Lineas asked.

"Where are you going with this question?" Vanadei asked, drawing his sleeve over his high forehead. "It's stifling in here."

Quill said, "I was trying to figure out why Connar would put everyone through the logistical nightmare of defending two castles at the same time. There aren't two castles that close together that would need defending at the same time. Except . . . look here. Where do you see two castles that could be attacked at the same time, thus preventing the other from coming to its neighbor's defense?"

Lineas and Vanadei crouched obediently over the map, one red head and one dark.

"Halivayir and Tyavayir are fairly close, but there are now regular patrols up that spine of forested hills behind them, that could be called in as reinforcement," Vanadei said.

Lineas added, "There's Tenthen, the capital of Algaravayir, near enough to Marthdavan, both very small castles in the middle of farmland. Neither is a city like Ku Halir. Hills between them."

"Look again," Quill said gently. Softly. "Wider range."

Lineas's gaze worked rapidly over the familiar markings on the map. The closest castles to one another were in the middle of the kingdom, far from where any invader—

"Shit," Vanadei muttered, white-lipped. "No. No chance."

Quill bent down and swept his hand over the north shore, from Andahi to Trad Varadhe and back again. The two harbor-cities were not that far from one another.

"No chance, right?" Quill asked. "I'm putting two and two together and getting twenty-two, right?"

Lineas said, "I still don't get it."

Vanadei wordlessly traced his forefinger from the royal city up through Olavayir, to the Andahi Pass, then right, to Trad Varadhe. And from there in an oval along Idego's mountainous border.

Lineas's brow furrowed. "You think Connar will have to defend Lorgi Idego?"

"Not defend." Vanadei thumped his fist lightly on the table. "Attack."

"That's impossible." Lineas spoke fast, as if urgency could banish the idea. "We've had no trouble from them, ever. Quill, you were saying a few days ago that your Uncle Vanda helps keep relations friendly. Why would Connar attack the Idegans?"

"To reunite the kingdom," Vanadei said. His voice sharpened with irony on the word *reunite*.

In the distance, the departing thunder boomed. Outside the open window, rain hissed in a cataract.

Quill rolled up the map again, speaking fast. "We already know he's been sending out his own runners, Jethren's ferrets. He has to know that the Bar

Regren have been attacking Andahi since the first thaw of spring. He surely knows that Prince Cama wants to take the Nob, and drive the Bar Regren out to sea for good."

"But he would have *just* found that out," Vanadei argued. "He doesn't have golden notecases. He couldn't have known about Prince Cama begging to lead a force against the Bar Regren. You just heard it by magic notecase."

Quill stared down at the rolled map. "But all that is predictable. What if," he said, "that was Connar's plan all along?"

"What?" Vanadei's and Lineas's voices clashed, and were drowned by another rumble of thunder.

"I kept wondering why, after all these years of treaty, he'd let the Nob go. Especially when everyone knew the moment we didn't send the silver up there, the Bar Regren among the locals would sell out the rest of their neighbors in a heartbeat, especially if they saw the Marlovan guards depart."

Vanadei said, "After which the Bar Regren would turn their eyes down the rest of the north coast toward Andahi."

"Which has happened," Quill said. "But Lorgi Idego isn't huge. To push the Bar Regren right back up the north coast, then secure the Nob, the Idegans would have to strip their garrisons at the harbor cities down to holding staff. Which effectively leaves them open for an invading army to come up the Pass, while Prince Cama is busy chasing Bar Regren up the peninsula."

Vanadei pushed his flattened palm away. "Connar wouldn't. Would he?"

Lineas was rocking on her mat, arms across her stomach. "He would," she whispered. "I think he would. If he thought he could win." She drew in a shaky breath. "What should we do? What is . . ."

She didn't want to say the word *right.* It seemed so horribly ironic.

Quill thumbed his eyes. "Before she died, Shendan made me promise, whoever was king, to do my duty as if oath-sworn to someone I could respect. I wonder what she saw, or thought she saw?" He clapped his hands to his thighs. "Speculation. This is —"

And Vanadei quoted, "'Let your choices follow the right road, even if the road seems to be invisible to the world around you.' The last class she taught, she made us translate that into five languages."

The three looked at one another.

Quill scrambled to his feet. "I've got to talk to Rat. Help me think of some urgent reason for Noddy to send me to Ku Halir."

Vanadei said, "Should we take this to him? Or to the gunvaer?"

"No," Lineas and Quill said together.

"Right." Vanadei sat back, grimacing. He knew Connar hadn't already discussed it with his brother. If he had, Noddy would have been moping anxiously. Noddy hated fighting. He still suffered from the occasional nightmare caused by the Chalk Hills attack all those years ago, and what he'd seen when defeating Yenvir, as well as Tlennen Plain. Also, Noddy always agreed with Connar, not the other way around.

All three knew the gunvaer would be horrified. She would exert all her strength to talk Connar out of throwing away lives, as well as livelihood, on invading what had been acknowledged as another kingdom. But she wouldn't win.

And Connar didn't seem to talk to Ranet. They all knew the two led separate lives.

"I've got to go," Quill muttered.

"What can Rat do?" Lineas asked.

"I don't know, but I believe he'll hear me out. And if he laughs me out of the room because I'm so wrong, all to the good."

Unfortunately, Noddy could be very acute. Finding a reason to disrupt what he regarded as their comfortable foursome, even during a period when actual state business was slack, was far more difficult than they'd thought. Noddy, in his way, had far too many questions, each more uneasy than the last, as though he sensed something amiss. One day, two, then three passed, Quill ever more impatient.

He was debating whether he should risk magic when Victory Day dawned, clear for once, the air pure and clean. The royal family, except for Connar, gathered to watch the academy games held for those left behind.

The first horse race had barely begun when Vanadei, standing behind Noddy, overheard Ranet saying to the gunvaer, "I do wish Braids would at least answer my letters, if he's too busy to visit. I've sent both my runners into Sindan-An, but they can't find him."

"He's probably with Connar," Noddy said.

Ranet turned to smile at him. "Ah, I didn't think of that! But Weed just got back, and Neit's up there as well—"

Vanadei said quickly, "Send Quill."

The royal family all turned surprised faces to him. Ranet said, "But isn't he your scribe now, Noddy?"

Vanadei so rarely spoke unless spoken to that Noddy and Ranet were startled. He said quickly, "He is. But we have so little to do these days. And I know he sorely misses riding. Remember, that's what he trained for."

Noddy's brow cleared. "I didn't think of that. Of course we can send Quill, if he really wants to go."

"You can ask, but I'm certain he'd thank you for the chance to ride in this excellent weather."

Ranet looked doubtfully at the thunder line already purpling the western horizon, but Noddy clapped his hands. "Quill never asks for anything. If he wants to ride, then he can take Ranet's message to Braids. The three of us will manage in the state room, just as we did at Yvana Hall."

Vanadei agreed with enthusiasm, and Quill was gone before the horse events were halfway finished.

The first night Quill stopped, he arranged for a private room, and with the door locked, used magic to transfer to Ku Halir's secret Destination, laid down years previous. It was in an old storage room.

He emerged cautiously, fighting against sneezing from the dusty air, so different from the mud of the royal city, and checked around until he discovered that the siege was still very much in progress. Not wanting to risk being seen, he braced for the wrench of the return transfer, and the next day, continued riding north.

The bands of storms that had been boiling up out of the southwest seemed to follow him northward, then passed him, leaving his road adrip. When he reached Ku Halir, it was to find the siege over, the city full of roistering academy seniors.

Quill made his way to the area over the stable where runners invariably were kept. Here he found Neit, the sun-browned smile lines around her eyes crinkling when she saw him. "Quill! I thought they'd chained you to a desk!"

"Everyone was on a run, and Ranet wanted a message taken to Braids," Quill said.

Neit's brows shot upward. "He's somewhere between here and Tlen, last I heard."

"I'll get on the road to find him after I eat something," Quill said. "How did it go here?"

"Great. Well, mostly." Neit laughed. "The gunvaer sent me to be liaison for the handful of senior girls, but they didn't need me. I spent most of my time watching, until the runs between Tlen and here broke down, nobody finding who they were supposed to find."

She paused to chuckle. The room was empty, everyone preferring to leave its stuffy air for entertainment. Quill sank down onto an empty cot, hoping to draw Neit into conversation.

She was clearly ready to chat. She perched on the wooden footboard of the bunk across from his, and said, "Nobody asked me, but I wonder why Connar had them attacking two castles at the same time. Both sieges went really well, but they could have been in different years, on opposite sides of the kingdom, as far as message-running and supply was concerned." She laughed again. "What's the need for such complication?"

"Who won?"

"I was only briefly at Tlen, toward the end, when the messages were going awry. Rat and Stick Tyavayir stalemated until yesterday, when Rat broke through. Keth Jethren won both sieges, as defender and attacker, no surprise there."

"No?" Quill prompted.

Neit snorted. "I've known Keth since we were brats scrambling in the mud at Olavayir. The only games I ever lost when I had to captain the enemy were to him."

"What's going on now?"

"Half want to have another go, Jethren against Rat, and half want to go home. Until Connar makes a decision, they're on liberty."

"I may as well give my greetings to Rat while I'm here," Quill said. "Where can I find him?"

He'd said it casually, easily, as if the idea had just occurred, but Neit shot him a speculative glance as she said, "He's up in command with Connar."

Quill smiled, hands open. "They won't want to be interrupted. Stick is with them, I take it?"

"All the commanders." Her unblinking gaze shifted between his eyes, and she said, "What's on your mind?"

"Why?" he hedged, remembering yet again that most of those commanders were friends from youth, academy mates.

Neit shifted her gaze away. "Stick was talking, over ale. You know, how you do after action. Said they could be running games on attack as well as defense, ha ha." Her teeth showed. "Then they started joking about who they'd be drilling to attack. Ha ha. If it was old Gannan, everyone wanted to volunteer. Ha. Ha."

"Ha. Ha," Quill repeated, and, remembering that Lineas had trusted Neit utterly, he lowered his voice. "What about the entire north shore?"

Neit's mouth dropped open. Then she shut her teeth with a click. "But . . ." She wiped her hand across her face. "They were uneasy with the idea of attack instead of defense. Thinking that Connar might go down to Parayid again, though Rat's da has it well in hand. Or he might ride against Gannan. Or even the Nob, to retake it. But . . ." She whispered, "You're talking about a *war*."

Quill explained his thinking, to which Neit listened in silence. Then Quill said, "I should run my message. But if you should see Rat . . ."

"I'll talk to Ghost Fath," Neit breathed. "He went down to the lazaretto to visit the wounded. We had a few." She added, "Tlen had more."

Footsteps pounding up the stairs caused their heads to turn. "There you are," Henad Tlennen said, tall and mud-splashed. "We've been looking for you! The king wants everyone there. You, too. You might have to replace me. I need to get back down south," she said to Neit, who groaned.

Quill slid by. "I'll be on my way, then."

"Wait!" Neit's hand stretched out, then fell. "Never mind. Uh, give my best to Braids. If you find him."

Quill's gaze shifted to Henad, who was married to Braids. But she only smiled brightly, until Quill said, "I was sent by Ranet-Gunvaer."

Henad's smile vanished as if struck off her face. She said, low, "Try Wened."

Quill was soon on his way.

Within a few days, after various encounters with runners and outposts, most of them in the environment of Tlen, he began to build a mental picture of confusion instead of the regular relays he was used to. A day out of Wened, he was fairly certain the confusion was deliberate. Someone was mucking up the communication stream.

He stopped to change horses and to refresh his water flasks at the last outpost. Midway between that and Wened, he heard hoofbeats. There was no reason to hide. He urged his horse to the side of the road to let the party pass —but instead they reined up, and he found himself surrounded by armed skirmishers, Braids at their head.

Quill blinked away the sudden memory of Colt Cassad and his gang surrounding him. Surely this was a different situation.

Between their last meeting and this, Braids had hardened. All his round-faced boyishness was gone, leaving a blond, wiry man with a gaze like a crossbow bolt above an unsmiling mouth.

"Ranet sent me," Quill said, when Braids didn't speak first.

"So I heard."

Venturing a shot of his own, Quill said, "Kendred met with my wife in the royal city. He felt he had to confess before he vanished."

At that, the Riders sidled looks at one another, and a couple whispered. Braids looked skyward, then clapped his hand to his forehead—and there was a glimpse of the old Braids, never far from laughter. "He would, of course." Then an accusing look. "Where is he now?"

"Probably somewhere between the south coast and Sartor," Quill said. "At least, I think he said he was going there. To seek a healer for his leg. You understand, I didn't speak to him. Only Lineas did."

"Lineas," Braids repeated, his expression easing again. "She tell anyone?"

"Only me. And Vanadei. We haven't told Noddy. It would grieve him so very much."

Braids expelled his breath, and Quill noted hands moving away from weapons, and shoulders easing. "Do you need to go into Wened?"

"Not at all. This journey was entirely to find you."

Braids wheeled his horse after a glance at the low, fast moving puffs of clouds. These usually meant rain. "Then we'll ride south as we talk."

They left the road entirely, and again Quill remembered his anomalous position with Colt Cassad, somewhere between guest and hostage.

Braids ranged up alongside Quill's horse, as the rest of the Riders formed in pairs ahead and behind. Braids looked across as he said, "I haven't been able to face Connar since Kendred told me what happened. And I believe him," he amended. "The details were too specific. And Kendred had no reason to lie. He admired Connar. Maybe still does, though Connar sicced Jethren's wolves on him, and smeared my name all over the kingdom, getting old Gannan to blame me for Cabbage's death."

Quill flattened his hand. "I don't think that was Connar."

"No? Why not?"

"I was investigating it, by royal order, before Connar heard about it. The rumors started in the royal city, at a point when Connar wasn't there."

"He could have had Fish spread 'em."

"He could have, but I never once got a description that would match Fish Pereth. Whose looks are fairly distinctive, and he's known in several pleasure houses, where he and his mate go when he gets liberty. But one of the descriptions of these strangers that was consistent was of Rock Alca, one of Kethedrend Jethren's captains, a man with a scar down the side of his face and a nick in one ear. Alca was spreading around money, buying everyone drinks, talking for a few weeks, then he was gone."

"Jethren could have sent Alca on Connar's orders."

"Possible. But it seems unlike Connar, don't you think?" Quill said. "He's more direct." And, because they'd come this far, "For example, right after the king died, I'm fairly sure he killed Retren Hauth."

"The lance master?" Braids asked, eyes wide. "What for?"

"No one knows. Officially he retired. That's what the records say. No rumors were spread, nothing was said. But he vanished suddenly, right before Victory Day. When I went down to the quartermaster's to seek Connar, I think it was directly after it happened. I'm sure I smelled blood."

Braids gave an explosive sigh. "Yeah, that sounds more like Connar." He looked upward again, but this time Quill caught the gleam of moisture in Braids' eyes as Braids rasped, "I couldn't figure out why he would slander me. Why my father had to throw away the title over lies, especially after what he went through at Ku Halir." He coughed, then, with a semblance of normalcy, "Does Ranet know?"

"We haven't said anything to anyone in the royal family. No one is sure how to proceed. Or even if we should."

Braids said, "I know. I'm the same. I just haven't been able to make myself face Connar, knowing he murdered Cabbage. Not even a duel. Stabbed in the back. And there is no justice for him. Justice," he repeated with disgust. "What even *is* that, when it comes to murder? Especially when you accuse a *king?*"

"I'll need to take some sort of message back to Ranet," Quill said, having decided not to say anything about the possible invasion of Lorgi Idego. That was still entirely speculation. Braids had enough to contend with. "She says all her messages to you seem to have gone astray."

"I've been avoiding them. Don't know what to say to her. She has to live with him. Sleep next to him. What good would it do her to know he murdered Cabbage Gannan, then lied about it? And presided at the memorial! When I think of that I want to puke." Braids' voice rose, sending a bird squawking in protest from an old, wind-twisted oak at the left.

He went on to talk about his first year at the academy, which was Cabbage's last year, how good Cabbage had been in the field, how at least Lefty Poseid was a decent jarl. Someone Cabbage would have picked himself. And so he finally he talked himself around to a less bleak mood.

"Even though it changes nothing, I'm glad you came. I guess I can face them all now. There's no use in saying anything," Braids added. "Connar's the king. He can do or say anything he wants, and nobody can do anything. Also, I know how bad it would be for Noddy. He thinks his brother perfect. And who wants to be the first to tell him different?"

He spat into a patch of weeds.

In Ku Halir, Connar gazed out at the lightning branching over the lake, then turned to his row of captains. "Seems we're in for a siege by weather. Next year." He smiled.

They saluted, and dispersed.

Later on, in Stick Tyavayir's quarters, with his trusted runner Snake Wend posted outside the door, Neit shared everything Quill had said. She met a profound silence, until Rat muttered, "I wondered if we were preparing for an attack. But I couldn't figure out who. Unless it was old Gannan, though he hasn't done anything outside of being a horseapple."

"If it's true," Ghost began, then shifted his feet, and looked away. "This is still all guesswork. Connar hasn't said a word about Lorgi Idego. He's only talked about defense."

Stick's mocking smile had twisted. He crossed his arms. "And if the worst does happen? We all remember what happens to commanders who refuse orders. I hope that Quill is crazy, but if he isn't, and I never saw him do anything crazy, we've got to think up an answer, or we'll find ourselves riding up the Pass next spring. And the first ones under our sword will be some cousin of the Faths, or the Farendavans, or half a dozen other jarl families with relatives over there."

Silence gripped them all, so heavy they could hear one another's breathing.

"I have to think." Rat got heavily to his feet. "I have to think."

At the same time, as rain roared overhead, Connar sat with Jethren, who had ridden in from Tlen that day. With a triumphant smile, he threw down the note his grass-runner had brought in the night before, sent straight from Larkadhe.

"As I thought, the Idegan army is drilling to go up to claim the Nob. Of course they won't leave before next spring. It would be suicide to attempt those mountain trails in ice, and winter comes fast up there. It's already too late even if they had them all mustered."

Jethren grinned back, euphoric. All his work through spring had paid off. He'd won twice. He hadn't been able to go against Rat, but apparently Rat had said himself that Jethren's wins were faster.

Connar went on, "Rat will second me. We'll take Andahi. Ghost Fath can deal with Trad Varadhe, and Henad Tlennen will run the skirmishers. You've proved to be good at everything. I want you fourth in the chain of command, running logistics."

Jethren's blood turned to ice.

TWENTY-SEVEN

As Connar's entourage gathered in the stable yard for departure, Rat Noth approached him. Squinting a little against the morning sun, he said, "We know enough about defending castles. Storming them."

Warmth shot through Connar at the image of Rat leading the attack that broke Ku Halir's formidable defense. "That, you proved," Connar said genially. Rat was a prince now, but no hint of presumption. Straightforward as an arrow, and Connar's fond smile acknowledged it, observed with corrosive jealousy by Jethren a few paces away.

Rat said, "Next year. Let's run on the plains, eh? We've got good charging grounds at Hesea."

Connar laughed. "Perhaps." He hoisted himself into the saddle.

Rat squinted up at him, a tough, rangy figure, his forehead high as his hair thinned above his temples. "I'll fight to the death against an invader," he said.

Connar gazed down at him, knowing that Rat spoke the truth. He always spoke the truth, and had since they were small. He was utterly loyal—and utterly without vision. "I know," he said. "You've proved that. With captains like you, the days of heroes are not over, whatever our fathers say."

Rat wiped the back of his hand under the jut of his chin as he glanced away at the riders forming into column, banners stirring in the rising wind. "My da said that heroes only emerge in terrible times. And most of 'em are villains to other people. I've no wish to be a hero."

"Too late." Connar laughed. "There are already ballads about you." Another chuckle at the sight of Rat's lean cheeks reddening, and he lowered his voice. "There will be more ballads, after we reunite the kingdom."

He clucked to his horse, leaving Rat standing there staring after him. "Get used to it," he called over his shoulder, laughing again.

Ghost Fath and Stick Tyavayir, standing a pace behind him, flicked glances at one another. Neit, behind Stick, looked down at the rain-wet gravel below her feet, muttering, "Oh damn. Damn. *Damn.*"

Jethren mounted, keeping a correct horse length behind his king. He waited until the brassy royal fanfare echoed from tower to tower as they trotted through the gates. No gallop, not at the beginning of a long ride in the humid summer weather.

Once they reached the open road, Jethren said, "I don't think Rat Noth likes the idea of the kingdom reunited."

Connar had seen it, too, but his confidence in Rat's steadfast nature sustained his ebullient mood. "He'll follow orders."

"Until he doesn't," Jethren muttered, but under his breath.

Connar's mood stayed sunny as they rode fast through the warm summer days. The nights had begun to cool, refreshing riders and horses alike, and the journey to the royal city was quick.

Connar lifted his hand to those gathered on the walls and lining the main streets on the way to the castle as the fanfare reverberated between stone walls and shivered on the air. He relished the heart-stirring sound, the lines of smiling faces, some singing ballads, others banging drums and pots and pans, drowning each other out. It was sheer noise, but then music had always been noise. They were doing it for him, and he knew he would never tire of it.

The horses clattered into the royal stable yard. As they dismounted, he said to Cheese Fath, "Arrange a banquet for the captains." Pleased as he was, he didn't want to listen to either speculation or questions that he wasn't going to answer, so he added, "Summon the dancers."

When you were a king, there was no worry about schedule conflicts. After the first runner carried out this order, the troupe's chief, a woman nearing fifty, who now only danced in the background and otherwise choreographed and managed their finances, called everyone together. "The king is giving one of his banquets."

"Ah-ye," someone exclaimed happily from the back. The king giving a banquet usually meant largesse.

"We still have this evening's performance, remember. So those who want an after-hours romp get ready for the royal castle. The rest, we'll set aside *Shendoral Lost Time* and do *Three Couples In Search of a House.* One good thing about these Marlovans, they don't know the difference between something new and dances so old our grandmothers thought them out of fashion."

Laughing with anticipation, dancers scrambled to change places, led by those who wanted a crack at a king. Especially that king. They were already familiar with him and his ways—he rarely went with anyone twice, and always months apart—but many, both male and female, had hopes they'd be the one to dazzle him and take up the easy, lucrative life of a king's favorite.

The evening was a spectacular success, carried on the king's expansive mood. The food appeared and the captains enthusiastically got outside of it; the dancers danced, eyes meeting eyes with question and promise; those who wished to pair off did, but the king walked away alone.

When he got to the royal wing, he heard voices and laughter spilling out of Noren's chamber across from Noddy's. Ranet was just leaving, light gilding her fair hair and outlining her slim silhouette as she glanced down the hall, noted Connar, checked, then continued on toward her room.

She was about to enter when the quick ring of heels caught up, and Connar reached past her for the door latch. "What were you celebrating?" he asked. "Victory Day is well past, but we're not yet at Noddy's Name Day."

Ranet extended her hand toward Noren's suite. "Do we need a reason? As it happens, Noren wanted to salute the first cool day in what feels like years. We had hot spice wine." Maybe a little too much spiced wine; looking up into Connar's smiling blue eyes ignited fire in her veins lightning-quick, negating all her hard work to cool her heart to indifference.

Then he extended his hand. "Why stop now?"

She laid her fingers in his warm, strong hand marked with hard calluses across the palm, and drew him inside her chamber. And once again it was sweet passion and fire, falling down and down into the glowing embers of contentment, then slumber, to wake up alone.

But, for the first time in so very long, at peace.

She had caught his good mood, though she wasn't quite ready to trust it. The next weeks gave them a last, unexpected burst of summer warmth, cool in the evenings, which lifted everyone's spirits. Connar came each day to breakfast in Danet's chamber.

As it was tax-gathering season, Danet had plenty to do, but she was used to keeping her labors to herself: The columns of numbers she found so revealing and fascinating were random dullness to everyone but Noren. But Connar asked, and showed interest in her observations. Noddy was happy to see Connar smiling, and sitting next to Ranet instead of across from her; Noren, with the sensitive nose, sniffed for the gerda herb that women must ingest in order to become pregnant.

But there wasn't any.

Ranet had decided there was plenty of time. Right now Connar seemed to be coming for her rather than to make a child, and she wanted to see if that would last.

Even after the weather abruptly turned vile, voices and laughter rang down the second floor, mixing with the shriek of giggling girls as Iris and Little Hliss gamboled in and out. All that autumn Connar spent time with his family, worked harder than ever in the captains' drill court, and formulated his plans, discussing them privately with Jethren, which exhilarated the latter. But there was still that threat of being demoted to logistical support for the reunion of the kingdom to gnaw at him.

Winter began to threaten, scarcely noticed amid the bustle of autumn. The first blow, softer than the first tentative snowfall, went entirely unnoticed, so busy everyone was: Neit had yet to show up. Though Danet had sent her to keep an eye on the first-year senior girls among the academy students at the Ku Halir/Tlen game, and those girls had long gone home until spring.

The second blow was equally misconstrued at first: Ghost Fath wrote to Connar, resigning his captaincy in the army as of the New Year.

According to the old king's rule, we're to serve ten years. No more than that expected of those of us with other responsibilities. Even if I am not yet declared a jarl, I have a jarl's tasks, including helping Leaf with our boy now that he's gone from crawling to running.

Manther Yvanavayir is also resigning, as he has never recovered from the chest wound that makes him cough every winter. But if the kingdom ever calls for defense against invaders, we will count ourselves among the first tenth.

Anderle Fath, "Ghost"

Connar read it through twice, fighting the sharpness of disappointment. But Ghost had the right. He'd served ten years as a captain—more than ten years, if one counted the garrison apprentice years between the academy and his first captaincy at Larkadhe.

At least losing Ghost didn't upset his chain of command for the spring campaign too badly. He'd just swap Ghost with Stick Tyavayir. Surely he could convince Ghost to command Ku Halir while he took Stick Tyavayir up Andahi Pass in his stead. Their command styles were nearly alike, after working together for ten years.

But a few weeks before New Year's Week, another letter arrived, under a jarl's banner, making it an official communication from jarl to king. It was from Camrid Tyavayir, Stick's older brother, and new jarl as of last Convocation, writing a formal letter withdrawing his brother from the army now that his ten years were up, stating jarlate need.

The crucial line being:

. . . while today's army furnishes plenty of capable captains to command garrisons, I have no uncles left, and I only trust my brother to patrol the Spine east of Tyavayir, where the Bar Regren once came on the attack, and could again now that they hold the entire peninsula.

Whether intended or not, Connar saw in that a jab at him for abandoning the Nob. He didn't know Camrid, who had never been at the academy. But everything Camrid said was true, and inarguable. Including the fact that younger brothers did have two chains of command, one being familial. And Arrow had always permitted the jarls to withdraw their sons at need, which he'd regarded as compensation for getting those sons into the academy instead of training at home.

Connar tossed away the letter, cursing as he prowled his chamber. Of course he had "capable captains," but they were all right where they should be. He'd have to shift everyone around, which meant a lot of explaining away his real reasons, if he didn't want word somehow reaching the Idegans. He had no doubt they had spies salted in the royal city at least, if not in the lower ranks of the army, as he himself now had two of Jethren's men up in Lorgi Idego.

He couldn't pull in Braids, who guarded the kingdom's eastern border, and anyway Braids was entirely a skirmisher captain. Henad Tlennen as well. Cabbage Gannan was dead.

Connar gazed out at the sleet-wet courtyard below, and considered yanking Neit from runner duty. He knew from Rat Noth's and Braids' reports after Ku Halir that she was good; he remembered that she had been the only one to think of sending for reinforcement when the Bar Regren ambushed them at Chalk Hills. But during the short time she'd been a captain, her companies had been small. Whereas Plum Noth might have a larger command, but he had yet to prove himself in battle.

"It'll have to be Mouse Noth," he said aloud, which meant getting a runner all the way to Parayid and back with Mouse well before winter ended and he could muster the army. And that meant sending a runner *now*.

He summoned Jethren, who hid the sharp elation that burned through him when he understood that Stick Tyavayir was also out of the chain of command above him.

"Sleip is back, right?" Connar asked.

"Both scouts are back." Jethren struck fist to heart in corroboration.

"Send the fastest one down to Mouse Noth at Parayid. Replace him with Pepper Marlovayir. I want Mouse running shield to Rat Noth when we attack Andahi."

It was out before Jethren could stop it: "What if Rat Noth doesn't want to come?"

"What?" Connar rapped sharply, jerking around to face him.

Jethren had been holding repeated conversations in his mind ever since summer, over and over. His campaign to smear Braids had failed utterly. Rat seemed unassailable.

But Jethren had seen what he'd seen, that day in Ku Halir's courtyard. "Not Mouse Noth. I don't know what he thinks. It's Rat Noth, as fine a commander as ever was found, and loyal," he added in haste as Connar's expressive black brows drew down. "But when you talked about the kingdom reuniting, he didn't like hearing it."

Connar made an impatient movement. "He didn't like gaming at Ku Halir, either." Connar hadn't noticed Rat being more silent than customary on the ride from Hesea Spring to Ku Halir. It had been Pepper Marlovayir who'd chattered about how grim Rat's memory was of the battle, and how much he probably hated being back. "But he follows orders."

Jethren had imagined this conversation in infinite varieties over the months since they left Ku Halir, always leading to this same point, which he had wanted so very badly to say to Connar. But there had to be the right context.

He decided that was now. "Just as well he's so loyal." And forced a laugh. "For a man who can wave his hand and raise an army all on his own."

Connar's mouth twisted. "What are you talking about, 'wave his hand.'"

"At Frozen Falls. He sent a runner off, who came back with an army. Which is good," Jethren amended, seeing the irritation tightening Connar's features. "Or we'd be dust."

Connar said, "I'm the only one who waves a hand and raises an army. And Rat knows it."

"Right. Right. Just a thought."

Jethren got out as fast as he could, cursing under his breath. Always, always he had imagined Connar looking shocked, exclaiming, *That's right!* Or, *I never thought of it that way,* and demoting Rat, then promoting the most dedicated and loyal . . . .

What was the use of air-dreams?

Jethren slammed back to work, trying to avoid Connar as much as he could, while Connar thought with disgust how much he loathed hidden jealousies among his captains. What did you expect from someone who'd been trained by the likes of Retren Hauth, seething with secrets and lies? Everyone trained as an assassin, from stable hands to captains?

He was just as glad not to see Jethren over the next few days. The man was meticulous, useful, and an excellent sparring partner, but Connar wouldn't tolerate slander among captains. Maybe Jethren should be the one left behind—

Every time Connar's thoughts ranged in that direction, he came up against the fact that two of his most trusted commanders were no longer available to him, unless he forced the issue by calling up the King's Tenth, which meant one of every ten men in the kingdom coming to his call. But to do that, by the treaty forced on Bloody Tanrid, he had to have Convocation agree to it. And Convocation was a year off.

The timing was exactly as he'd planned. Cama Arvandais was surely going north this spring, leading the Idegan army, and Connar was certain he'd be far beyond reach at the Nob by the end of summer. Leaving Lorgi Idego wide open. It had only taken a season to clear the north back in Inda-Harskialdna's day, so surely he could do the same.

He didn't have long to brood.

The first thaw occurred, bringing the inevitable flood of runners, including Neit, finally returned. To Danet, she gave a sheaf of letters that she'd picked up at outposts along the way, and delivered a verbal report that mostly repeated what Danet already knew about how well the academy girls had done in the wargame at Ku Halir.

Then, the moment she was free, she went to Ranet, and handed her a letter. "From Henad Tlennen," Neit said tersely. "To be given to you by my hand, with no one around."

Puzzled, wondering, Ranet began to read.

In her chamber, Danet was also reading the guild tallies she received every quarter —and then rereading them.

Sage and Fnor were startled when Danet yelped, "Damn!" and surged to her feet. She slammed open her door, then caught herself up when facing the closed door opposite.

Connar's chamber, not Arrow's.

Forcing her voice to neutrality, she said, "Sage, will you request Connar-Harvaldar—" No, you didn't summon a king, even your own son. "That is, find Connar-Harvaldar, and request a moment of his time? I'll go to him wherever he is."

Her scruples were unnecessary. As soon as he recognized Sage, Connar ran up to Danet's chamber. "Ma? Something wrong?"

Danet had been pacing back and forth, rehearsing her words to herself. It was so important not to seem like she was interfering with his governing; and while she was glad that he and Ranet seemed to have repaired whatever had gone wrong between them, she suspected that Ranet had no more an idea of what Connar was planning or doing than she did.

So she held out several pieces from the sheaf of papers Neit had brought. "I have to get all this into records, and I don't know how to account for these very large orders for what appear to be military supplies, including bandages and various healer concoctions, to go to Larkadhe."

Connar had been very careful in dispersing those orders over a wide area, but he saw at once that he'd underestimated Danet's ability to translate numbers into a strategic map.

And so he lied. "It's preparation for the next garrison game. Which will be early, this year, and up north. I've seen what the south has to offer. We've twice met in the midlands. I haven't been north in years." He was aware he was talking too much, and shut up.

But it worked. Her expression cleared. "Ah! Your father would have approved. If you want my help, I'll always be glad to pull these things together for you. And I know how to balance our demands against local need."

Connar leaned forward to kiss her bony cheek, the sagging skin soft. Worry crowded his heart at how she was aging. But she still worked hard, and she wanted to help. "Thanks, Ma. I'd thought to spare you extra labors, but I'll remember what you said."

"I like doing it," she answered, smiling wider, to hide the curl of question in her heart.

He walked out, and straight past Ranet's closed door.

Behind that door, Ranet sat behind her low table, her arms around her knees, which she hugged up against her as she stared down at Henad Tlennen's letter. Neit sat across from her, concerned at her stricken expression.

"Braids didn't want to tell you about Cabbage's murder," Neit finally said, to break a silence that had tightened to painful. "But Henad felt you had to know. I was to answer any questions. As for the rest of it, Stick said to remember that the plans to attack Lorgi Idego are still speculation, until Connar gives actual orders."

Ranet looked up, her huge pupils making her eyes look dark. It was unsettling, in her too-pale face. "Who else knows?"

"About which part?"

"Everything."

Neit considered. "About Cabbage's death? Besides Henad, Stick, Ghost, and Braids? Maddar Sindan-An almost certainly. Kendred was with her before Braids took him south. As for people here, I'd say Quill knows everything. Probably more than anyone. The king—Arrow-Harvaldar, I mean—before he died put Quill onto investigating the accusations against Braids."

"Quill . . ." Ranet repeated.

"The royal runners go everywhere, they collect reports, they interview. They carry out royal orders, and they are careful to differentiate between eyewitness and secondhand reports. I learned that much from Lineas, when we were up at Larkadhe."

Ranet's lips curved in what was almost a smile. "Then we can assume that what Quill knows, Lineas also knows."

"I'd expect so. Especially with respect to Kendred's witness to Cabbage Gannan's murder. As I said, she was the one Kendred went to. Oh, and of course there's Fish Pereth, who would have been riding in Connar's wake with the remount and extra arrows, but you know first runners are oath-sworn to keep their masters' counsel for life, so I wouldn't try him, even if he has been shifted over to the roost. If nothing else, his life wouldn't be worth spit if he blabbed. As for who suspects Connar's plans to invade Lorgi Idego, the same—except for the Stalgoreth people. I don't think anyone's sent any runners up there with pure speculation."

"Thank you," Ranet said.

Neit knew a dismissal when she heard it. She took her leave, aware after years of running all kinds of messages that Ranet was struggling against extending her dislike of what she'd heard to the bringer.

But Ranet had already forgotten Neit. *You might even approve of this invasion,* Henad had written.

I don't know what is in your mind these days. We haven't talked, you and I, since we were girls. If you were already aware of all these things, I beg you to help me to understand. If you weren't, Braids said your life would be easier for you to remain ignorant as long as possible. But I thought you would want to know.

Ranet read it through again, then went about her normal activities. That night, she dismissed her runners, opened her door, and waited. When Connar came up the hall, he saw her outlined there, still in her day robe, trousers, and boots, he stopped, surprised.

She held out a hand to invite him in.

He noted the open palm, the sweep of her hand into the room, rather than reaching for him. Her lovely face was inscrutable, the rise and fall of her breasts fast beneath the robe, the breathing of suppressed emotion.

Intrigued, he followed her into the room.

She shut the door and stood with her back to it. "Henad Tlennen wrote to me. She says, among other things, that she thinks you intend to invade Lorgi Idego."

Connar's brows rose. "I told Rat Noth that I'm going to reunite the kingdom. Stick and Ghost were there. Word seems to have spread fast."

"But you haven't told any of *us*." She snapped her hand out toward the rest of the second floor.

"I've only told those necessary. I don't want word leaking to the Idegans. The family, I haven't told for different reasons. Noddy will worry. You know how much he hates fighting. It seems to be in his nature. Ma will also worry. Easier on them to find out after I'm successful. Or dead." He laughed, confident.

"It'll be a slaughter," she stated. "On both sides."

He continued to smile, clearly amused. "The Idegans'll be a challenge." She could see in his stance, the quirk of his eyes, that he liked it that way.

She gazed at him, so many emotions surging wildly that she held herself tightly against screaming with frustration.

But she could see that none of it mattered to him. He was big and strong and he was now the king. All the power was in his hands.

Though that didn't mean she couldn't try. "Why not wait for Convocation?" she asked. "Then you can call for the King's Tenth."

"Because I know what they'll say, after they take days and days to say it. The south doesn't care about the north. Khanivayir and Zheirban, possibly Marlovayir and Gannan, will be all for it. Olavayir—my cousin—will support us. He has no reason not to. There's so much trade between Olavayir and the north, reunion would spare us those stiff tariffs we've been paying."

Ranet knew that all that was true.

"I won't get all the jarls behind me, so why trouble with them? I can manage without the tenth. The whole plan hinges on coming in behind Cama Arvandais when he takes his army up to clean out the Bar Regren from the Nob. He'll come back to find us there, and if he's reasonable, he'll accept the new rule, the way Da had to accept Hal Arvandais's cowardly declaration of separation at a time when Da had no army and no treasury. I know it bothered him all his life. He mentioned it again not long before he died. Call it justice."

But he's dead now, Ranet wanted to say. She didn't. It would be needlessly cruel. She knew this "justice" was an excuse, not a reason, for this war.

She gazed up at Connar's charming smile, his steady, watchful blue gaze, and her questions about Cabbage Gannan withered. *I don't know you at all,* she was thinking. She had regained that precious intimacy with him, but that was body with body. She did not have a true meeting of minds, much less hearts. Those remained as distant as Lorgi Idego and Marlovan Iasca: two entities with all that insurmountable mountain in between.

And it wasn't she who'd failed. That mountain existed between him and everyone. It occurred to her then that in all the years she'd known him, he had *never* asked, "What do you think?" or "Why don't we talk it out?"—even though he'd grown up in a family that was always talking.

Her throat ached. "All right," she forced herself to say neutrally. "I'll keep silent."

He rewarded her with a kiss, which she submitted to, though the heat had utterly gone from it, drowned by a cataract of sorrow.

TWENTY-EIGHT

Neit went straight to the state wing. Noddy lit up with pleasure when he saw her, and as there wasn't much business anyway, he invited her to join them.

"I probably won't be here long," she warned.

Noddy swung heavily to his feet. "I'll go get Noren, and send for a meal."

Vanadei—whose job that was—leaped up and moved toward the door. "I can do that."

Noddy waved a hand. "No, I will. I've been sitting too long. You know how my back gets if I don't move around." With a beaming smile at Neit, he left.

Neit turned to the others, her own smile dropping. "Henad wrote to Ranet. Told her everything. I could see she was upset."

Lineas gripped her hands together. "Of course she would be. Wolf's daughter Marend is a sentry at Andahi, the Jarlan of Senelaec told us when she was here with Andas."

Neit opened her hand. Having gone up the Andahi Pass to Andahi Castle, she was very familiar with how the Idegans had resumed old customs, female archers on the walls to defend the castle, men riding out. "Marend Arvandais is there, the Faths have cousins over there, the Farendavans also—and speaking of families, the entire Arvandais clan used to be Tyavayir four generations ago. There are a slew of second and third cousins having visited, and even married, back and forth. They stopped when the Idegans divided off from us, but all the old people still know each other."

Quill had been leaning against the wall, arms crossed. Neit couldn't remember ever having seen him angry, but he was now, lips a white line, red across his cheekbones. "I can't get away," he said, low and savage. "Without raising question. I'm convinced the only chance there is of halting Connar is to disrupt his command chain, beginning with Rat Noth."

"How?" Neit asked. "I know Rat hated hearing that about reunion. But he follows orders. He knows refusing orders gets you killed."

"There's resignation," Quill reminded them. "What if all the Noth captains resigned? They at least ought to know what Connar plans."

Neit whistled. Then said doubtfully, "But won't Connar run his war himself? He seems so determined on it."

Quill said, "His command style is consistent: He likes to plan carefully beforehand, then lead from the front. He fights, but he doesn't seem to command in the heat of battle the way Rat does, and Braids can, if pressed."

Neit said, "There's something I *could* do, which is to suggest Rat have a family convocation. Give me a message from somebody in the royal family to run to Hesea Garrison, and I can be on the road today. Then I don't have to face the gunvaer again, and lie. Or Noddy." She frowned. "Has anyone sounded *him* out on the possibility he might support Connar's attack?"

Vanadei said, "Oh, yes. We did that while Connar was at Ku Halir. Even getting close to the subject raised a lot of anxious questions. Noddy is observant in his own way. There's no possibility he'll favor us invading Lorgi Idego."

Neit turned to Lineas. "Could Noddy talk Connar out of it?"

Lineas looked away, her expression wistful. "I'm afraid not."

Vanadei said, "She's right. Connar has always made the decisions between the two of them. The rare times Noddy won't go along with Connar's lead, Connar accepts it and goes on alone. Here's my fear. I think this plan will destroy Noddy, whoever wins. He really liked the Idegans he got to know so well up at Larkadhe."

Neit slapped her palms to her thighs. "All right, then. I'm mum. I'll cheer him up for a little while, but you'll have to find some reason to send me southward."

Lineas had been thinking. "Why don't we talk to Ranet?"

Neit bit her lip. "Good idea. Though she's mighty sore. I don't think I want to go back to her quite yet."

"I'll do it," Lineas offered.

And so, when Noren and Noddy reappeared, Lineas excused herself and ran back to the royal wing. She seldom saw Ranet, as their lives had completely diverged, so she had no idea what to expect.

She found Ranet sitting in a welter of papers, as she began the process of figuring out barracks arrangements for the coming academy year. Her beautiful face reminded Lineas of carved stone as she looked up with polite question. "Lineas?"

Lineas stole a look sideways, and seeing Ranet's first runner busy brushing out a riding coat in the far room, used Hand to ask, "Could you invent some sort of message to send with Neit to Rat Noth?"

Ranet stilled, her face lowered so that Lineas could not see her expression, but her tight shoulders betrayed emotions held in.

Ranet's first thought was that the royal runners had definitely known more than the royal family. Why hadn't they told her? Then she remembered Henad's letter. No one seemed to want to tell her anything, because she was the gunvaer. No, that wasn't it. It was because she was so close to Connar.

Close to Connar. What a howling mockery *that* was!

Ranet looked up at Lineas's freckled face, seeing the worry there. She asked, testing, "First, what is the real message?"

Lineas said readily, "To encourage Rat Noth to consult his entire family. Maybe if they all unite, they might be able to talk Connar into not attacking Lorgi Idego."

"Good." Ranet could accept that. "I will. But in trade, will you do something for me?"

Lineas struck her palm to her heart. "As I am able."

"Two somethings. First, will you and Quill inform me when you come across things like Kendred's confession?"

Lineas's mouth rounded. "Certainly. We didn't . . . we thought . . ."

"You thought to spare me, of course you'll say. I don't want to be spared. I don't want decisions made for me. Second, will you tutor Iris?" And to Lineas's clear confusion at the leap of subjects, "She is . . . difficult. The nursery minders can't cope with her refusal to have anything to do with numbers, writing, or reading. She wants to draw. And lately she's been in a pelter about learning to dance the way the foreigners do, though I think she just wants those colorful garments that look like they would shred in the first brisk wind."

"I don't know how to dance like that," Lineas said earnestly.

"Learning to dance can be left to others. You royal runners seem to be trained with what could be called a royal education. And I know you are patient and kind."

Lineas saluted gravely. "I would be honored."

She ran back to the state wing to report her conversation with Ranet.

The others listened in surprise, then Neit said gravely, "It sounds a bit like she's punishing you."

Lineas looked puzzled. "Punishing? Me?"

"Siccing that brat on you without warning."

"But Ranet did warn me that Iris is difficult."

"All right, I guess that's fair. And you might not find her as wearing as I do. Every time I see her, she's interrupting the adults by prancing around the room flapping her hands at the wrist and squealing, 'Look at *me*, I'm a *pony!*' or some such, and if she doesn't get enough attention doing that, she finds something else to shriek about that you can hear clear down to the landings."

"Pereth has had to send down three different tutors," Quill admitted. "And I tried as many before I was booted from the third floor. The problem with our royal runners is, they usually tutor those eager to learn. Or are at least well-behaved."

Lineas considered difficult people she had dealt with all her life, and said, "I'll find a way."

Neit grunted as she got to her feet. "Better you than me. All right, I'll go collect my urgent message and be off."

Winter set in hard. Between brief thaws, thick snow blew against walls in slanting drifts, sparkling a fierce blue-white in the low northern sun.

Lineas spent her mornings with Iris, who looked so disconcertingly like her father, but whose personality could not have been more different. Iris never stopped talking, except to draw. She covered sheets and sheets with galloping and rearing horses, manes and tails flying. As Lineas was very deft at drawing, she gained Iris's conditional trust by demonstrating tricks of perspective and shading, and soon drawing became a reward for getting through tedious lessons.

As for the tantrums, Lineas did not try to cajole, scold, threaten, or bribe. She did what her father had done when she was very small and tried raging at the world: She walked out saying, "I guess we're done for the day"—even if it had only been a quarter hour, as happened once. There were fewer tantrums after this unvarying response.

Toward the end of a long month of cooped-up castle life, a flurry of excitement spreading from mouth to ears through the royal castle's garrison was the first notice Jethren had that a new arrival had appeared out of the whirling snow.

"Rat Noth is here!" The news carried as fast as the wind.

Connar, at the other end of the castle, heard some of the excitement, before a wide-eyed young runner appeared. "Commander Rat Noth just rode in!"

"Bring him up," Connar said.

And shortly after, Rat walked in, looking exactly the same as ever, though maybe the V at the top of his temples had broadened and his horsetail was a little thinner.

"I wasn't easy in my mind," Rat began abruptly, as always. "So last month I sent around to my cousins. Uncles. We met in Algaravayir." No mention of the very hard riding in the teeth of winter this must have entailed, but Connar had traveled enough to recognize it. "Talked it over. Plum said he'd write up what we said, and we'd all sign it if we had the same mind."

He handed off a grubby, much-folded piece of paper.

Connar ran his eye swiftly down the pompous, almost tortured attempt at formal language that those who seldom wrote anything seemed to assume necessary at such times. His gaze came to rest on the list of names below the screed: Aldren Noth of Algaravayir, Ivandred Noth, Mouse Noth, old Lemon Noth, the Rider Captain in Marthdavan, Plum Noth from Telyer Hesea, and Flax Noth in Darchelde, which wasn't even supposed to be involved in kingdom affairs, though Connar knew his father had ignored that old treaty.

All had signed their given names, some of which Connar didn't even recognize. The important point was, these represented nearly all the Rider and mid-level army captains from the entire south, saving only Jayavayir's. The only Noth in command missing from that list was Vandas Noth, up at Larkadhe, who was obviously too far too reach.

He could wave his hand and raise an army, spoke Jethren in memory.

"I don't want to resign," Rat said plainly. "The army is my life. It's the only thing I know. I'm good at it. So I'm coming to you now, before any orders have gone out. Ask you to wargame here, there, anywhere. Not to ride into Lorgi Idego."

"But we'll win," Connar said. "With you riding shield. There's no one better."

Rat turned away, head bent, callused hands propped on his skinny hips. "Yeah," he said finally. "Could be. But I'm thinking about after. Riding around for years, having to search castles and cottages for weapons, while they hate the sight of us. Rounding up resisters. Executing them. And you know it won't just be men. It'll be their sisters. Mothers. Granddas." He shifted from foot to foot. "Think of how *we'd* be, if Elsarion had managed to take us. It'll be the same over the mountains. They train like us. Enough of 'em think like us. A lot of 'em have relations on both sides of the mountains. Including the senior gunvaer. Those'll be the first ones we'd have to cut down."

Connar stared in disbelief. "So what you're saying is, you will refuse to obey orders?"

Rat reddened to the ears. "I'm saying, I'm trying here to talk to you, before any orders have gone out. Nobody's moved a foot. I'd rather resign than go up north against the Idegans, and I don't want to resign. You can put me anywhere else. Even demote me to stable hand or riding master. I'd be good at either."

"It's *reuniting the kingdom,*" Connar said, stunned.

Rat shuffled his feet. "I'm not good at politics. But it seems to me it would only be reuniting if they sent Cama Arvandais down to Convocation, asking us to take them back. They aren't. With Cama riding up the Prick to the Nob, what we'd be doing is a sneak attack, against people half the northerners know. And spending southern lives when they don't see any benefit. They still complain about their taxes going to northern wars from a century ago, as well as the more recent ones."

When your horse throws you, or your opponent gets in a smart blow, there's that heartbeat or two when you don't breathe, you just stand there bewildered. But then the pain hits.

The stun had worn off, and the pain struck, deepened by the anger of betrayal.

Connar had had a lifetime of practice in hiding anger, which he'd believed since early childhood made him ridiculous, because he'd found other children's loss of control risible. So he said, "When you get back to Hesea Garrison, hand off command to Pepper Marlovayir."

Rat Noth blanched pale, then his face reddened to the ears. But he said nothing. He saluted smartly, turned with a flare of muddy, wet coat skirts, and though it was snowing again, the sun already setting, he rode right out.

Connar dismissed the runners with a wave of his hand, and stood staring down at that grubby paper as if it were a poisonous serpent until startled by a knock at the door, and Jethren's voice, "Connar-Harvaldar. Someone said Rat Noth was here, but gone again?"

"Come in."

Jethren heard the shortness in Connar's voice, and his heartbeat accelerated. When he walked in, Connar tipped his chin down at the paper, resting like a dirty, wing-crumpled butterfly on the otherwise tidy desk.

Jethren read it, then looked up as the implications set in. Infuriated—for it looked as if their carefully laid plans were being summarily thwarted—he couldn't keep back a corrosive, "Seems to me you knew exactly what to do about idiots up in Stalgoreth."

Connar's chin jerked up sharply.

Jethren's heartbeat throbbed in his temples. Clasping his hands tightly behind his back, he added, "And in the quartermaster's."

Connar stared unblinking at him for what seemed an eternity. Then he turned away. "Do what you want."

He crushed the paper in his fist and pitched it into the fire. Then he walked out, leaving Jethren there with tacit approval. He walked to the landing, up the stairs. Royal runners parted like waves as he stalked into the roost, halting when he discovered Pereth and Mnar Milnari amid a welter of chalk boards and papers.

"Send runners to the jarls. Cancel Convocation." Connor paused, his mind sifting reasons. Then he remembered that he didn't have to give a reason. He was the *king*.

He walked out.

As soon as Connar was gone, Jethren sped out, elated with triumph. He passed the landing guards and raced downstairs. He had a fair idea of the trajectory of Connar's temper by now. Connar at that moment would cheerfully see Rat Noth dead at his feet, but he'd cool off. Maybe even send someone after Rat to try to woo him back. Keth Jethren had proved he was capable, over and over again. But still, as long as Rat Noth was alive, Connar would always reach for him first.

Do what you want.

What Jethren wanted was to be rid of them all. As he ran downstairs, he envisioned those Noths forming an army and riding against Connar to force him to give up riding into Lorgi Idego. If he refused, would they force him to abdicate? They even had a prince in Rat Noth, thanks to his marriage with Connar's sister. They could put Rat on the throne, and who would be able to stop them?

He found Rock Alca drilling at the garrison, and grizzled Hanred Leneit over at the armorer's, looking over the slowly building stockpile to be taken north.

A quick lift of the chin, and they followed him to his quarters at the army end of the garrison barracks, where Moonbeam sat staring out at the snow, honing a knife.

"Our chance is here. But we have to act fast. Get the scouts," he told Moonbeam. To the captains, "You're riding out tonight."

Connar's temper stayed hot. He rode into the city seeking obliteration, which as usual only lasted as long as lust did, then returned to the usual fitful sleep.

At breakfast, Noddy said, "I heard Rat Noth was here yesterday. But he didn't stay."

For once Connar was impatient with Noddy's habit of stating the obvious. He reined it in hard, saying, "He rode back to Hesea with some changes in command."

"Oh." Noddy passed on to other things, but Connar felt Ranet's gaze.

When he left, she followed him to his room. "Did he resign as well?" she asked.

Connar's temper flared white hot. "We can restore the entire kingdom with relative ease. Why is that so difficult to understand? Why do we have excellent captains frightened to do what they trained all their lives for? Is it because the army is full of women? The Noths are thinking like *women!*"

Ranet's lip curled. "How do women think?"

Connar threw up his hands, fingers flexed and stiff. "You tell me! Tell me why you, a gunvaer, are not full of excitement at the prospect of regaining the kingdom we had a century ago. Is this what Tlennen-Harvaldar had to deal with when he sent his army up there?"

"I don't know. If he wrote down his thoughts, apparently the first Olavayir king saw fit to burn them," she retorted. "But this much I can tell you, the Idayago of those days was rotten with corruption. People starving. Nobles fighting the king. We gave them all a better life, yes, but there were still people resisting our rule as conquerors and invaders all through Cama One-Eye's life, and his sons'. That much is in the archives. I can show you where." Annoyed as she was, it occurred to her he was at least *talking* to her.

Or was. He shot her a look of acute disgust. "What possible use are old records? I'm reestablishing the kingdom, and doing it the quickest way possible, spending the least number of lives."

She wanted to yell *Why do it at all?* But she knew if she did she would lose him altogether. He was determined, and what's more, she knew that at least some of the jarls would be delighted. The army as well. Battles meant glory and promotion.

So she forced her voice to a semblance of normal. "I hope that means Rat and Bunny will be back. I miss her."

She walked out, leaving him aware of the fact that he had essentially given Jethren permission to get rid of Rat Noth entirely. He turned toward the door, seized with doubt, even remorse. He trusted Rat, a lot more than he trusted Jethren, who had always been jealous, that much had become clear recently.

He *had* trusted Rat. Who'd gone behind his back to his entire damn family.

Connar scowled at the map. Well, if Rat was going to abandon him in this treacherous way, then he was utterly useless. Might as well be dead.

Rat Noth was subliminally aware of a tail, but he was moving too fast to do anything about it. When he had to be, he was as fast as the best grass runners. Traveling hard tended to make his chest get congested, stuffing his nose so he couldn't smell rain on the wind. Usually a good sleep helped, but he couldn't sleep, tired as he was. Angry, frustrated, worried, he could not prevent his mind from returning to that confrontation with Connar and reimagining it. But he always came up against his own failure. He was coughing hard when he clattered into Hesea Garrison and slumped wearily off his horse.

As soon as she'd heard the fanfare announcing the return of the commander, Bunny got up and proceeded down the stairs as if walking on eggs, her fingers stiff at her sides.

"Bun?" Rat croaked, ignoring the waiting runners. "Why are you walking like that?"

She was about to speak when she remembered that he got embarrassed easily, talking about intimate things. She didn't understand it, but she respected it. She drew him inside, signaling in quick Hand for hot drink and dry clothes, and as soon as they were alone, said, "Remember, just before you rode to Algaravayir, I told you I wasn't sure . . ."

He blushed all the way down to his high collar. "Then it's true?"

"Third month." She swallowed quickly. "And I seem to have inherited my mother's touchy guts. Though if I don't move fast, and stay upright, and watch what I eat, I can keep it down."

Rat was going to throw his arms around her but halted, then fell into a fit of coughing. Bunny patted his hand, then snatched it back. "You're cold all the way through! Let's get you changed."

Digger and Jugears, his first and second runners, had warm clothes and hot food waiting by the time he got upstairs to the two rooms that he and Bunny shared.

He coughed his way through the meal, listening to one report after another, before calling in Pepper Marlovayir. With him, Bun, and the two runners present, he said, "I've been demoted. Pepper, you're commander, as of now." Pause for a cough. "But you'd better be ready for a possible summons to ride against Lorgi Idego."

Pepper had been wrestling mentally with the idea ever since Rat had warned him why he was riding for the capital as fast as a grass runner. Pepper's private feeling was, if Connar was going anyway, why not with the best? But if Rat wouldn't do it, he wouldn't do it. Pepper would if ordered.

Rat saw much of this in the side glances and subtle shifts in Pepper's stance. He accepted it. People were going to do what they were going to do.

"So, I may's well get in some bunk time while you take over."

Pepper saluted a last time and withdrew, leaving Rat sitting tiredly, waves of exhaustion weighing his eyelids.

Bunny leaned down to kiss him, but he fended her off. "No—I really am sick. You've got a child in you. I don't know if they can get sick off someone and I don't want to find out."

Bunny was torn between wanting to stay with him and longing to be horizontal and quiet. She paused at the door. "Did you tell my mother what we suspected?"

"Didn't see her," Rat croaked. "Rode in. Talked to Connar. Rode out."

It was then that Bun realized how upset he was, so she held her breath, bent down to kiss his clammy forehead, then backed away. "You get some rest in our bed. The lazaretto is empty. I'll bunk there. It's closer to the kitchen, so Dannor can bring me ginger-steep. It seems to help. We can talk it out tomorrow."

Rat stretched out his hand, clasped her warm fingers, and let go.

He woke with a gasp, aware that he was not alone in the room. The near total darkness was broken by a sliver of moth-pale light between the shutters. That line was partly broken by the angle of a masculine shoulder.

With senses honed by years of danger, Rat knew that whoever was in the room with him was male, and big. Rat's fingers groped beside the bed for the knife he kept in the loop in his right boot. His fingers closed on the handle and he surged out of bed, the hammer of a headache nearly dropping him.

A breath, the scrape of a foot, then a faint line of light glinted along the edge of steel. Rat crouched, mind floating free: so this was it, then. A familiar feeling from the midst of battle, as his body reacted faster than thought. He had killed too many people to count, people he might have liked if he had not met them in the ferocity of war; he had always thought, the rare times he let himself think of such things, that he would probably die by violence. He'd assumed it would be in battle, not in his bedroom.

If it was to be, he would still go down fighting.

Moonbeam respected Rat Noth as a great warrior. Only orders had brought him here. He had even waited until Rat Noth had seen his wife, and had slept a little, for Moonbeam had gotten close enough in the chase to see that his target was ill.

But he had orders, and he had to do everything right before the ghosts could be real again.

Rat whirled and struck—air.

Thin blades scythed with lethal precision out of the darkness. Icy heat struck the inside of Rat's wrist, and when the boot knife fell from fingers that had lost their grip, the cold blade sliced across his throat. His headache diminished in beats, drowning in lassitude as he fell to his knees. But he scarcely felt the impact for he was blinking against the fulgence of dawn, only it was brighter than the summer sun, far too bright to see.

The scent of spring was so subliminal Quill could not have identified what it was, except that it breathed into his dreams until urgency worked its way through the image of Pereth poking him insistently with a lance.

The pokes finally brought him up through the layers of dream into wakefulness, Lineas's shadowed face bent over his, her fingers gentle but insistent on his chin.

She leaned on an elbow, the rest of her half-pinned under him, their legs tangled. "Your notecase," she whispered.

The dream-lassitude and the insistent warmth of morning withered. He sat up, rummaging under the pillow. "I slept through it."

"You were tired."

Sometimes it was comforting to say the obvious, he reflected as he flicked the case open. Lineas had slid out of bed, and crouched before the fire to light a candle, which she brought, shivering, back to bed.

"It's Camerend," Quill said after a glance at his father's handwriting. Then a hissed intake of breath. "Better read it."

Senrid, I am sorry to report that someone murdered Flax Noth two days ago, while he was riding back from the winter pasture. The patrol found him yesterday, and I waited to investigate, knowing you would have the same questions I did—and still do.

He had no enemies, nor was there any sign of a duel. The murder was certainly accomplished by a trained assassin, footprints were blurred by brush. . . .

It went on to state that the memorial would be that night. Lineas scanned rapidly through that, sorrow closing her throat. Flax had been popular. He was Lineas's mother's cousin, well-liked by all.

She wiped her eyes and read the remainder of the note:

At first we assumed it was random, but I sent a runner to Hesea Garrison to report to Rat Noth, in hopes he would order the roads watched by his patrols.

But I was just now woken by our outer perimeter patrol, who escorted Itch Noth in—he had ridden all night. Rat Noth was murdered several days ago. Runners are on the way to the royal city to report.

"Murdered?" Quill breathed, looking up. "Rat? *Dead?*" He rubbed his face violently, then sprang out of bed and began pulling on his clothes. "I've got to . . . Wait. Wait. Where first?" He scowled at the fire, then up at Lineas, who was also dressing as fast as she could get her trembling fingers to work.

"Lineas, what exactly did Ranet say happened with Connar the day Rat arrived and left?"

"The gist of Connar's speech, according to her, was that the Noths resigned and that they were thinking like women. The way she said it, without looking at me, I suspect she thought that Connar was aiming that at me in some way."

Quill's breath hissed out. "Rat and his cousins must have resigned. Over the invasion of Lorgi Idego, which Connar would know your opinion of. I don't think she's wrong."

The idea made Lineas uncomfortable. But it was after all only guessing, so she finished, "Connar told her Rat left with orders for a change in command."

"Which Noths?"

"She didn't tell me."

Quill reached behind the bedding for his knives. "But we know who commands where. I just need to think—the map. Where's the map. Calculate distances—"

Lineas was already sketching the map into a page of her journal. She blobbed ink at the approximate sites of each garrison or jarl castle where a Noth served as captain or commander. Then both looked at the horrible truth: assuming the assassins had all set out from the royal city, and Rat at Hesea Garrison was already dead, then . . .

"Parayid," Quill whispered as he shoved his feet into his boots. "The only one they *might* not have reached yet."

"But—"

He whispered the transfer spell. The faint burn of hot metal singed Lineas's nostrils as the ribbons of color weaving through the air coruscated wildly, and he was gone, the flames in the fireplace stirring.

He had sketched a Destination at Parayid on a previous visit. Magic propelled him violently into a stack of brooms and buckets, sending him crashing painfully. He kicked his way free and bolted out of the storage cubby into a castle full of flickering torchlight, shouts, and running feet.

Quill dodged a patrol running with bare steel. The leader checked, looked at his blue robe, and ran on, the patrol streaming past, their footfalls drowning out his "What happened?"

Quill shut up and dashed for the scribe station, which was where runners usually gathered. Sure enough, he found it full of people in various states of dress.

"What happened?" he asked the nearest.

"Quill?" an older runner declared. "When did you ride in?"

"Just now. Nobody noticed me. What happened?"

"The jarl is dead," the runner stated, red-eyed with fury and grief. "Throat slit in his sleep."

"Mouse?"

"Alive. Barely. He woke when they came in, fought. He was losing—he was naked, and there were three of them—but his favorite, who'd gone out for hot steep, came in with the mugs, saw the fight, threw the steaming steep at the assassins and screeched as she pegged them with every bit of furniture she could lay hand to, waking everyone in earshot. One of the killers tried to go for her, but the runners came in, there was a fight, and the assassins got away."

"Any description?"

"Yes," a woman spoke up. "Desi said that they all had dark clothes, and scarves covering their faces, but when she threw the hot liquid into one's face, he yanked the covering off and she got a fast look. She said he had a white scar here." The runner drew a line down the side of her face. "And a piece missing out of his ear." She tapped her ear above the scar.

One of Mouse's runners said dubiously, "That sounds like Rock Alca, one of Jethren's captains."

"Jethren! Isn't he captain of the king's honor guard?"

"I thought Alca was a lance captain. Why would he be in Parayid, trying to kill Mouse? It's got to be some other man all scarred up. Or you saw wrong."

Quill half-listened, his mind reviewing a mental map. With sick conviction, he realized that distances and travel times roughly matched up: these assassins could very well have been sent the day Rat Noth confronted Connar.

"Never mind the guessing!" The first runner spoke sharply. "We're on lockdown, with a triple perimeter out beyond the city. We'll find 'em."

Quill hoped so, but trained assassins knew egress as well as ways of dealing death. His mind leaped to the mystery of the king and the bristic—still unsolved—as he said, "I guess I won't be able to deliver my message to Ivandred-Jarl."

"Turn it in at the command center," the chief scribe said somberly.

Shock, Quill was aware as he made his way down to the command center, had iced over the well of grief, but it was thinning rapidly. How many deaths? Already Ivandred's hurt like a knife dipped in poison.

The reek of sweat and the sharp barks of helpless fury warned him of the chaos in the command center. He stood outside, listening. As expected, the captains under both Noths knew little more than the runners, and were doing their best to cope by sending out a stream of orders.

Quill exited without them ever noticing him except as another runner in blue. He found his way to an isolated spot, and braced himself for the agonizing wrench of the return transfer.

Lineas had been busy. Vanadei was in the room with her, and on the table waited a mug wafting the welcome herbal scent of listerblossom steep. Quill drank it down, but as the transfer reaction faded, the grief branched through him and he wiped his eyes as he reported.

Lineas wept silently. Vanadei, who had only briefly met Noth, waited while his two companions recovered, then said, "Riders are on the way. The news will be official in a month. What do we do until then?"

Quill's hand slid to his sleeves, and gripped over the hilts of his knives. "I'll wager my life that was Alca. I so want to go after Jethren and choke the truth out of him."

Vanadei's voice flattened. "But what if he was acting on orders? From everything I've seen, he doesn't scratch his ass without Connar's approval."

Lineas whispered, "It might not have been Connar. Sending assassins doesn't seem like him."

Quill sighed heavily. "Yes, he seems to attack people himself. Whereas everything I've been able to glean about Nighthawk made it clear they were trained in all ways to kill. Mathren Olavayir certainly relied heavily on assassins."

"Back to Jethren," Vanadei said.

Quill squeezed his eyes shut and his head dropped back. Then he gave a tired sigh. "But even if I challenge him to a duel in the style of the old days, what would it change? Connar's entire honor guard is Nighthawk men from Olavayir. *If* Connar ordered these assassinations, then nothing can touch those men. It'd be treason. Which I'm angry enough right now to accept, because then I could witness to the jarls before Connar has me flayed at the post. But even confronting Jethren might make you a target for the rest of Nighthawk." He turned to Lineas.

"They don't notice me. Except for Jethren's first runner," she amended.

"Moonbeam?" Quill and Vanadei said together, startled.

Quill said slowly, "You never told me he was stalking you. That man is dangerous."

Lineas flickered her fingers in *Stay, stay*. "No stalking. Just brief encounters, like in the royal hall when I go to tutor Iris, and he's outside the king's chamber, waiting. I doubt very much he's going to attack me there!

And he always asks the same thing, do I see them? And then the number. Of ghosts, I mean."

"Ghosts?" Quill repeated.

Lineas briefly summarized her first encounter with Moonbeam at the memorial for Arrow-Harvaldar. Then, "The strange part is, where I usually see one or two, sometimes he'll say four, usually six, and one time eight. Except for the time he said none, with this strange smile, and his eyes were completely black."

"Eyes all black? That sounds like the effect of bellflower root," Vanadei exclaimed.

"A regular assassin's tool." Quill grimaced. "To see in the dark. But it's very poisonous. It isn't just the eyes, but the heart affected, according to my mother, who studied plants and herbs."

Quill's downturned mouth, his averted gaze, hurt Lineas to see. To distract him from the immediacy of his distress, she said, "He's been most consistent in saying six. The last time, it was when I had to go over to fetch—no, that doesn't matter. He was there. The wind was bad that day, and it made my eyes tear. You know how light is strange when there's liquid in your eyes, it can almost be like looking through a prism. Well, I blinked, and I am very sure I saw a crowd of ghosts around him. But another blink and there was just the blobby one that I often see on the second floor."

Quill made an effort and mastered himself. Mourning could wait. "That *is* strange." Then, lower, "I thank you for sidetracking me. I needed that moment." He kissed her.

Vanadei said, "I don't see the worth of revealing magic transfer now. And a lot of danger."

The morning watch bell clanged. It was time for the royal breakfast, after which Lineas had tutoring.

Quill said quickly, "Let's go. Maybe it'll be useful to observe how Connar reacts. But until then . . ." He tapped the wrist sheaths beneath his loose sleeves. "I'm going armed. I suggest the both of you do it as well." To Lineas, "You might be beneath Jethren's notice, but not Connar's."

Alca and his team had gone to ground, after two more tries to get into Parayid to finish off Mouse Noth. Each time they got no nearer than a sight of the castle, and were nearly caught. Security might have been lax before for trained assassins, but it wasn't now.

So Alca, furious at having failed half the assignment, gave the order to return to the royal city.

They wisely avoided the main roads, but miscalculated how fast word might have spread in all directions, not just northward to Choreid Dhelerei. And, believing themselves the elite of the elite, they never considered that there were highly trained warriors who knew every bend in the smallest stream, every fold in the ground, every stand of trees.

They'd reached a dip in a trail skirting the forest of Telyer Hesea when steel-armed figures seemed to spring up from the ground to surround them. The three of them faced ten or twelve dark-clad warriors.

Alca said, confident in his skill, said goadingly, "At least give us the chance to fight one on one."

Colt Cassad's soft tenor held no mercy. "The way you did Ivandred Noth?"

He led the attack.

Alca was the first one down, but took the longest to die.

TWENTY-NINE

Connar hesitated to give the order to muster and proceed to the north. Winter still held the kingdom in an icy grip, with endless ranks of snow clouds sailing over the eastern mountains.

They *could* start riding. Connar's temper had cooled enough for him to wait anxiously to find out the result of Jethren's mission. He didn't want Rat Noth dead. He wanted him obedient. But he had said *Do what you want.*

So he set the army and the garrison guards against one another in various attack and defense scenarios around the city. Slopping and mucking about in the slush kept them busy and tired, until Jethren presented himself, head back, lips curled in triumph.

When they were alone, he began the list.

"Old Aldren Noth of Algaravayir?" Connar interrupted, appalled. "The man has to have been eighty!"

Though Alca hadn't returned yet, the rest had had the success Jethren expected of them, proving that they truly were the elite. "Your orders were to do what I wanted. I wanted a quick, sharp strike, or you know they all would have been popping up with demands, refusals, and even the old could've summoned the rest to back them."

"They might anyway," Connar muttered trying to grapple with the fact that the Noth captains were *gone.* But they had loyal followers. Relief—regret—then the gut punch of conviction that there would be consequences.

Jethren, watching him carefully, said simply, "You're the king."

That was reassuring until the day that the runners from Algaravayir, Darchelde, and Hesea Garrison showed up in an angry, aggrieved clump, most of them having straggled into the Hesea Plains outpost to hide from the latest storm. Then they rode together into the royal city, a solemn, even nervous bunch.

And Connar arrived at supper to find the family regarding him with shocked eyes, Danet's reddened from grief. "The Noths were assassinated. Did you know? All of them except Ivandred Noth. So far! Who knows what happened in Parayid?"

Connar reflected that he should have known. Far as Parayid was, still Alca ought to have been back by this time.

It was Noddy's shocked gaze that cooled Connar's roiling emotions to a knot of ice. He shifted his gaze away, and lied. "Assassins," he said. "I believe it was the Bar Regren. Or even the Idegans."

"Idegans," Danet repeated. "Why ever for?"

"We know that they're going after the Nob. They might want Larkadhe at the other end, or even Lindeth, and everyone in the kingdom is aware that Rat Noth was my best commander. Short of coming after me, which is very difficult, he'd be relatively easy."

He saw the expressions of shock furrowing to uncertainty. It was certainly plausible.

"I'm sending scouts to investigate," he added, and strangely enough, he added with the ring of truth, "I'm going to miss Rat. He was my right hand."

Ranet had seen that alone of the family, Connar was not shocked by news that she would have thought would render him incandescent with rage. But she said nothing.

Later that night, she permitted Little Hliss to climb into her bed, something the child was always begging for, as she tended toward bad dreams, especially if she sensed tension around her. Ranet arranged words in her mind to avoid Connar if he came to her, but no one disturbed them.

Two days later, Mouse's long runner turned up—with Bunny, whom he'd found collapsed at an outpost, sick. Quill braced for mention of his presence in the south. This would be the worst time in recent history for the secret of royal runner transfer magic to be exposed. But as it turned out, his brief appearance had been utterly forgotten.

Iris had been given Bunny's rooms after Bunny left for Hesea Garrison. Even if they'd been empty, at first Bun only wanted to be with her mother.

Danet was thrilled with the only good news she'd heard in weeks, but Bun's pregnancy resulted in Danet's anxious grandmotherly exhortations to take better care of herself and think of the baby. Bun did not want to think of the baby right now; all she could think about was Rat, and how she'd refused to let him into her room that horrible day.

After a night with Danet, who had never been good with the kind of tenderness Bunny needed right now, Bun moved into Noren's side room. "He'd still be alive," she sobbed, over and over.

Noren's strong hands repeated firmly, "No, you would both be dead. All three." Then returned to stroking Bunny's hair until she finally slept.

Ranet could not sleep.

She tried for a worthless hour or two, then got up and stood in the weak light of a new moon, looking down at the sweet, pure curve of her daughter's slumbering face. What kind of world was she growing up in?

Grief and anger harrowed her as she paced around the chamber. Finally, an hour before dawn, she dressed and waited, her door open a sliver, and when she heard the king's door down the hall open and close, she walked out and confronted Connar.

He halted, Jethren and that weird Moonbeam at his heels. Connar gestured for them to move on, and Ranet said, "In here."

Connar stopped in her doorway.

Ranet said, her tone sharp with disbelief, "Is it true, the Bar Regren assassinated the Noths?"

Connar's gaze shuttered. "It's true if I say it is." At her recoil, he grimaced. "Look, Ranet. Everything I do is for Marlovan Iasca. Everything. All you need to do is run the academy, and wait for everything to work out." He said it softly, coaxingly.

She wanted to believe him, but between that soft, musical voice and her belief was the image of Bunny's ravaged face.

He leaned down to kiss her; her head turned instinctively, so that his lips landed on her cheek. His breath caught as he stilled, then he stepped back and was gone.

The morning watch bell rang.

Little Hliss woke, and the minder appeared to get her bathed and dressed. Iris was already up, dancing around impatiently. Ranet, dry-eyed, collected her daughters and went to breakfast, where everyone did their best to cheer Bunny.

When Lineas came down the hall, Ranet sent Iris into her room to get her writing tools, and faced Lineas. "Is there anything new I should know?"

Lineas looked down at her hands, hating the situation. Hating what she had to say. Hating the tension she sensed in Ranet, who had always been so thoughtful, who had seemed from a distance to be happy. There was no vestige of that happiness now.

But a promise was a promise. "The runner from Parayid reports that the single witness to Mouse Noth's attack gave a description that fits Captain Alca of the honor guard. But no one has been able to corroborate it," she added scrupulously.

"Thank you for telling me," Ranet said as Iris reappeared, impatient to get the lesson over so that Lineas could teach her more drawing.

Ranet wrote a series of letters until the midday bells rang. She summoned her runner, and handed the letters to her. "Dannor, you are the only one I trust to ride straight to Henad Tlennen."

Dannor was flighty, and often silly, but she wasn't stupid. Her round face sobered.

"Henad can see to distributing the letters. Just take them to her. Over winters, she's either at Tlennen or Sindan-An. So when you go downstairs, and anyone asks, just say you're carrying another letter to my cousin Henad. All right?"

Dannor blinked, gulped, and repeated, "Another letter to your cousin Henad."

And she departed.

When the bell rang, and Ranet saw Lineas depart for the state wing, Ranet went to Iris's room and held out her hand. "Want to learn to dance?"

Iris's sulky expression vanished, and there was her charming, dimpled smile. "Yes!"

"Come on. Put on your practice jacket. No, not your good cloak. We're going in practice clothes. See? I have my old gray riding coat on."

Iris flounced into her room, but didn't argue.

And hand in hand they walked out of the castle, into the main street.

Between storms, Jethren's scout Sleip slipped into the royal castle from that blind spot in the back that Connar had once shown Jethren. Sleip brought Jethren the welcome news that Prince Cama of Lorgi Idego was indeed mustering his army to ride up the peninsula at the first hint of spring. Fierce pleasure radiated through Jethren—there was no question now who would ride shield with the king. And at last, his captains would also be promoted to commander. As promised.

But later that day, a scout belonging to the Nighthawk captain who'd killed Flax Noth reported word of a contingent of jarls intent on riding up in spring to demand a Convocation. These were being led by Adamas Totha, cousin to the Iofre Linden-Fareas Algaravayir and now Adaluin of Algaravayir, as the Iofre had laid down her title on the death of Aldren Noth.

And that night, another scout reported word going through the local guilds that three brigands dressed in black had been found dead and left to rot on the outskirts of the forest of Telyer Hesea: murder with intent. "Cut up bad. But one of them matched Alca's description," the scout said, flicking his ear.

"Give the order to muster," Connar told Jethren, once they were alone.

"There's a blizzard out there."

"It'll be gone by week's end." Connar turned up his palm. "I want to be well up the Pass before Adamas Totha turns up. He's a veteran pirate fighter. He was defending the coast all during my father's reign. No mere snow will stop him or his Iascans."

"I don't care how strong they are," Jethren stated. "We can take them."

"Then we're attacking our own people," Connar retorted. "They're coming to demand justice for old Noth. How's it going to look if our campaign begins with scything through our own people? They think the Noths were assassinated by Bar Regren, remember. We'll ride. My brother can listen to them, and sympathize, and promise them peace. When we return with victory, it'll give them a newer, bigger perspective on peace, all of Halia ours again."

Jethren bit down on protest. At last he had what he wanted. Camping in ice and snow would have to be endured.

So he gave the long-expected orders.

Connar kept himself busy, avoiding the family. But late one night, he found Ranet waiting outside his door when he returned from the garrison "I see a lot of preparation," she said, and he was glad to see her smile again. "Are you riding out soon?"

"Yes."

"When? I'd like to host a banquet to celebrate your campaign. I'll even hire the dance troupe. I know how popular they are. Bring Commander Jethren and your entire honor guard. Even the runners. They work as hard as anyone."

Connar smiled back, taking her by the shoulders. If Ranet had accepted matters, the rest of the family would follow. "That would be excellent. Thank you. And when we return, let's you and I try for an heir, shall we?"

"Absolutely." This time she kissed him back.

The week sped by, everyone busy. Ranet, the meticulous planner, oversaw the furbishing up of the academy for another year, and at night, she attended to the plans for her banquet.

When the day dawned, wet and cold, the banquet hall across from the throne room was as festive as possible with extra torches and lamps, and cedar boughs brought in to add their scent to the air. Many beeswax candles glowed around the perimeter.

When it was time, Ranet kissed her girls as they slumbered peacefully in bed, and dressed in her best House tunic. She brushed out her hair and braided it up into shining golden ropes.

Then she left the silent royal floor, nodded to the pair of guards on duty at the landing, and trod down to the banquet hall, where Jethren and the honor guard, from captains to Riders, plus their runners, began to drift in, wearing their best coats.

Ranet stood by the door, greeting each warmly as she poured warm spiced wine and pressed it into his hands. Even the scouts found themselves treated like commanders by the king's beautiful wife in her summer-blue and gold robe.

The hall was soon packed, filled with laughter and bawdy jokes. The food was excellent, the drink plentiful, and as promised, here were the dancers, the women wearing skimpy outfits that sparked a roar of approval.

Drums rumbled a slow, sensuous beat as the dancers began to perform, weaving their way seductively along the tables. On the dais, male dancers tossed flaming torches back and forth, and leaped, flipped, and tumbled.

No one noticed that the royal family had not shown up after all, though they had certainly been invited. Up on the second floor, Danet had found herself yawning, heavy-lidded, over her afternoon coffee. Noren and Noddy had fallen asleep, she at her desk, arms cradling her head, and Noddy had lain down for a moment, and dropped into dreams.

Only Bunny was awake, taking Maddar Sindan-An on a tour of the city, Maddar having ridden in with Henad Tlennen the day previous, along with Snow, her lifemate. "We've never been in the royal city before," she'd said to Bunny. "You know it best of everyone."

Bunny still was in deep mourning, but Cabbage Gannan's wife deserved her making the effort—and Snow's constant stream of comments and jokes managed to make her smile, when Bunny had thought she never would again.

It was a relief for Bunny to get away. She showed the two all over the stable, then at Maddar's request, they rode through the empty academy, which was in the process of being furnished for spring. On the way back, they paused on a slight rise and Bunny looked up at the gold-lit clerestory windows on the west wall of the banquet hall, and breathed with relief that she didn't have to be there at all. "The healer won't let me have wine, and anyway it tastes bad right now. But I know the best place to get chocolate in the entire city."

Snow and Maddar exchanged glances, then Snow exclaimed, "I never get enough chocolate. Especially if it's island stuff, with spices in. Lead on!"

They rode into the city.

In the banquet hall, Connar sat in the gilt-edged wingbacked chair reserved for the king, Jethren at his right. Ranet circulated the room, returning long enough to toast them, and to ask if they wanted anything more.

The dancers' wild gyrations got wilder. The drumbeats pounding as the wine flowed. One by one the dancers whirled out, to be replaced by pairs of new dancers in shrouding layers of filmy material, who floated along the perimeter. One was very tall, but what drew the eye was the swing of her generous hips as a coin belt slung low clinked and jingled. Another had swathed fabric around a very large, round belly; she was maybe a month or two from childbed. Their dancing left much to be desired compared to those in the flimsier garments, but the wine was flowing freely by then.

Unnoticed, the men in the troupe withdrew, to find Kit Senelaec, Braids' sister, waiting at the door with a hefty bag of gold.

"I know the gunvaer already paid you," Kit said as she handed the heavy bag to one of the four. "But this is extra. Your leader will explain."

And she did, when they got to the stable yard, shivering under their cloaks. "Get into the wagon," the troupe leader said, as she nodded to the driver.

"What? What's going on?"

"I'm afraid we're done here," she said in Dock Talk, which was the only language all the dancers had in common. "But we'll travel nice up through the east pass, and try our hand at Shiovhan. They say the nobles there throw jewels on the stage if they like you."

They rolled out of the royal castle, unnoticed by Bunny as she, Maddar, and Snow returned, Bunny yawning and apologizing. "I don't seem to be able to stay awake much after dark these days," she admitted.

"That's all right," Maddar said. "The chocolate was wonderful. Snow and I will walk you upstairs ourselves."

Watching them go was Quill, from the slit window of the tower adjacent to the stable yard. All his instincts hummed with danger, though on the surface the gunvaer's party seemed like a festive occasion. But the second floor was suspiciously quiet, and Ranet had sent the kitchen staff back to their wing, which was unheard of during a banquet. Though the sounds coming from that direction were convivial, he was convinced that *something* was about to happen.

He said to his picked team of royal runners, each armed with two wrist knives, "Surround all the doors to the banquet room, in case the gunvaer calls for help. Weapons only for self-defense, as a last resort, of course."

Vanadei said, "Are you sure we shouldn't alert Commander Noth?"

Quill thought of the commander sitting in his office devastated by the news of the Noth assassinations, the rumors whispering through the garrison, the ugly looks toward Jethren and his men, and flattened his hand. "I'd like to spare him if I can."

Vanadei's mouth twisted; no need to remind anyone that Jethren and his men were now untouchable, whatever rumors were flying. And they knew it.

Quill said, "There's too much tension. Be too easy for an argument to turn into a bloodbath between the honor guard and the rest of the garrison."

"What you mean is, you don't trust Jethren as far as you can spit into a wind," Cama Tall muttered.

Quill didn't deny it. "But we're civilians, and trained to moderate situations," he reminded them. "And though Jethren's men might like to mix it up with the rest of the garrison, to them, we're not worthy targets. So, if the gunvaer is planning some sort of confrontation after the entertainment, let's let her have her say, and stay within call."

They slipped through the back way, and took up their stations as back in the banquet room, the masked dancers began moving among the tables, trailing gauzy, perfumed ribbons over shoulders and arms, but their eyes—hidden by veils—tracked Ranet unwaveringly as she made a last circuit of the room.

Amatory jokes turned to outright invitation. Wine passed from hand to hand. The dancers' musicians had slipped out with the men, leaving only drummers, which was fine with the Marlovans. A couple of raunchy ballads led into "Owl Jarend's Last Charge," that bawdy favorite.

Ranet didn't even hear it. She was watching the level of drink; they had just about reached the stage where they would notice there was no more food, wine, or bristic, and no servants around to fetch more.

Enthusiastic if tuneless voices bellowed the line, *He dropped his pants and whipped out his lance,* as Ranet stepped three paces from Connar, and turned to face him.

"My first true act as gunvaer," Ranet said bitterly, took a miniature crossbow from her sleeve, and shot Connar in the heart.

The women threw off the shrouding fabric they had bought from the dancers. Each closed with her target, pulled daggers from under their draperies, and struck.

Men cursed and bellowed with rage. Some screamed. A few fought, but surprise and drink worked against them.

Connar's wide, startled blue eyes met Ranet's. He jerked back against the chair, clutching at the bolt. His mouth filled with blood, and he choked, and slumped over the table, his beautiful black hair fanning over the ancient wood.

Uttering a deep, wrenching sob, Ranet crashed to her knees beside his chair, and—still clutching the crossbow in one hand—threw her arms around his legs as the rest of the room erupted into chaos.

Jethren—who hadn't been drinking because Connar wasn't drinking—whirled out of his wingbacked chair and flung himself toward Ranet, who had not planned to live beyond that moment.

Henad Tlennen had been on the watch. She signaled a pair of women who closed in, knives flashing as they blocked his way. He dashed hot wine into one's face, leaped over the table, and booted the second in the chest, sending her crashing over a chair. Then, poised on the table, he swept his gaze at the dead and dying, and bolted, bending long enough to pick up a knife dropped by a woman curled over a broken arm.

He vaulted over two of his men, now dead, and swept the exits. At least two figures at the south door. At the north, for some reason, that royal runner Quill stood alone.

Quill stood there in shock, until he saw Jethren coming at him with knife upraised.

Before Quill could speak, Jethren grinned, bloodlust fueled by anger. Everything destroyed, everything he'd worked for so hard—he would *kill* anything that got in his way. He struck.

But the royal runner was like water, impossibly fast, impossible to pin down. Rage made Jethren wild, until he shifted to avoid a stab at his eyes, then felt ice flower just below the arch of his ribs. He looked up, his oddly numb lips struggling to curse, but the third blow went straight to his heart, and he was dead before he hit the ground.

Breathing hard, Quill looked up, to see Vanadei and Cama Tall running toward him from the direction of the south door.

"What—*why?*" Vanadei asked breathlessly.

"He wasn't going to back down," Quill began.

"I saw that," Vanadei cut in. "If you hadn't, I would've. But what's going on in there?" He stared through the open doorway. "Wait, is that the king . . . ?"

The three stared in at the carnage as the women went from one to the next, making sure they were all dead.

"What do we do now?" Cama Tall asked faintly.

Dannor Basna appeared in the doorway, filmy mask hanging, a spray of blood marking her face. She pointed to the inner door then said hoarsely, "Moonbeam got out. He cut up four of Henad's Riders." She wiped her face with shaky fingers, smearing the blood. "I don't know if he left them alive."

"Moonbeam?" Quill repeated.

Vanadei blanched as he glanced across the banquet hall to that inner door. "That's where we stationed Cama Basna . . ."

A young runner appeared in the hallway behind Quill. "There are dead sentries out beyond the throne room! Where's the king?"

"Where? Which direction?" Quill snapped, ignoring the question.

"Toward the royal wing," the runner keened, eyes stark.

Vanadei and Quill spoke together. "The second floor."

Where Lineas had been stationed, in case any of the royal family woke from whatever it was Ranet had slipped into their afternoon coffee.

Quill said, "Run."

In the banquet hall, Henad Tlennen sent one compassionate glance Ranet's way, then said to the rest of the women, *"Go."*

Once Bunny was safely seen to bed, Maddar and Snow disappeared down the stairway to the stable to ready the horses, leaving the royal floor quiet once more.

Unaccountably, to Lineas it smelled like lilies.

Quill had asked Lineas to watch the second floor, just in case, though there were the two guards at either end. She watched Maddar and Snow go as she drew in a slow breath, trying to recollect where she had smelled that before. It had been a long time, that's all she remembered. Had Bunny been wearing scent? But she never wore scent. Yet it was impossible for lilies to be growing while spring had barely fuzzed the trees.

Lineas walked a little ways along the hall, then halted when noise from the two guards at the far stairwell alerted her: a shout, followed by a cry, then a gurgling moan that ended with a choked-off yelp.

Lineas's attention shifted to the tall, pale-haired man in night-assassin black who walked toward her, blood-dripping knives in both fists: Moonbeam.

Moonbeam stopped a couple of strides away and regarded her through pupils round and black as holes cut out of the night sky, then sheathed one of his knives, nasty as it was, and signed: *How many?*

She breathed in as she made an effort to still her trembling fingers, then signed as she said, "Too many to count. Do you smell lilies?"

At that moment, from the far landing behind Lineas, footsteps as the other pair of guards came at a run.

Moonbeam's hands moved so fast she was only aware of a dark blur and the glint of steel pinwheeling past her head on either side, reflecting the torchlight above her. Then the nasty sound of knives striking flesh: a groan, a cry, and the heavy fall of bodies.

Lineas froze, her heart thudding frantically against her ribs as Moonbeam reached behind him and brought out another knife with his left hand.

With his right he signed, *Six*.

"Which six?" Lineas was aware of her voice sounding high, childish. Trembling—then, because she would be scrupulously honest until her last breath, she blinked rapidly. Was that a flicker to his left, and on his other side? "Wait. Wait."

Moonbeam took a step toward her. He could see her gaze shifting to points around him. He signed, *How can you make them real?*

"Real as in living?" Her gaze was stark.

"Yes," he whispered. "Yes."

At that moment Quill, who had been advancing in utter stealth, reached for Moonbeam, who had been concentrating so hard on the one person who seemed to understand him, he neglected his surroundings until the hiss of cloth reached his ears.

He began to spin, knife arcing—but Quill was faster, one blocking, the other slicing gently, inexorably, across the beating artery at Moonbeam's throat.

Lineas wailed as she leaped forward. Moonbeam dropped the knives, pressing one hand to his spurting throat, but already he was weak. He fell to his knees, fighting to use the last of his rapidly diminishing strength to turn anguished eyes to Lineas, desperate to understand. To be understood.

Her stinging eyes filled with tears that acted like a prism, and she perceived them all: the pale-haired mother, the father in a warrior's coat. A small sister, and three others who blended in shifting panes of light, the resemblance achingly clear.

"I see. I see. These six, they're your family," she whispered to Moonbeam, throwing herself down beside him. She took his hand, bloody as it was, and leaned down into his fading gaze. "They are here with you. You are *not* alone —"

The scent of lily blooms strengthened as the ghosts around her melded into a glow like starfire. In its light the castle walls appeared as insubstantial as smoke. Lineas turned her head, enthralled, for now she could see a multitude of ghosts, bright and faded, some still retaining human shape, others blobs of pale light.

Far below and away to the south Lineas beheld the familiar blond ghost in the blue tunic with the golden dolphin leaping across his chest, visible in a slow ripple of light like the sun over water, intermingling with the brightness of a new ghost, hair dark, eyes bluer than the summer sky. The two blended until the starfire expanded in coruscant rings to envelope them all, and then they winked out, leaving the fresh, heady scent of lilies until that, too, faded, and was gone.

Lineas laid Moonbeam's lifeless hand on his breast, tears running in a silent cataract, bouncing off her robe in splotches.

Vanadei, who had come up at Quill's left as shield, spoke urgently. "What now?"

Quill tried to claw sense out of the chaos of the last hour. "I don't have any authority to be giving orders."

"Someone has to," Pereth spoke up from behind. He and a host of royal runners approached, dark blue robes flapping, some of them pulled over night gear. He glanced at Moonbeam lying in a pool of blood, and said flatly, "Who else is dead?"

"Jethren and his captains, scouts, and runners," Quill said. "And the king."

Pereth's expression remained unchanged. "In that case, I'm free. As of this moment, I resign." He held out his hand in an ironic gesture toward the royal runners clustered behind him, and pulled off his robe, revealing he was still wearing a sleep shirt over his trousers. He dropped the robe down beside Quill. "Far as I'm concerned, they're all yours."

Quill cast weary, distraught glances at the five still figures in the hallway, one of them dead by his hand. The numbness of shock protected him, but he knew that would not last. In the space of an hour he had killed two people. One of them the king's right hand . . .

But Connar was dead.

He squeezed his eyes shut against the sudden image of Ranet deliberately raising that crossbow as she said something too soft to be heard.

Then Lineas's voice broke through his fugue. "I truly hate to disturb Commander Noth, but shouldn't we raise the guard?"

"The night duty captain," Vanadei said, snapping his fingers.

Cama Tall came up behind them. "Cama Basna is still alive, and one of the sentries. They should be taken to the lazaretto immediately. I've sent—"

At that moment squads of guards emerged from both ends of the stairwell, having been alerted by a wall sentry who'd spotted the three royal runners dashing along the halls, weapons in hand. Shouts echoed as they encountered the bodies left behind by Moonbeam on his way to the second floor, then they spread out, weapons bare, to check the royal rooms, where the family slumbered under the effects of sleep herb.

A captain approached, looking down at Moonbeam in his blood, knives beside him, then to Quill, still holding his own blades. "I take it you stopped him?"

"Yes," Quill said tiredly. And, to Lineas, "Let's go."

Still trembling, she sent one troubled glance back at Moonbeam, then took Quill's arm. They retreated to the now-deserted third floor, leaving the captain to restore order over the crowd of runners and guards moving around as if to shed tension in the aftermath of violence.

When they reached Lineas's room, Quill shut the door and turned around. "Not that I could have done anything. But I really thought Ranet and those women were going confront them, or argue, or even hold the men hostage until they promised to see reason. We were going to back them up in case Nighthawk turned on them. I *never* thought she would walk up to Connar and shoot him dead. How is that going to be anything but treason?" He dropped his blades on the floor, sat down heavily, and muttered, "I feel sick."

Lineas pulled him against her, and for a time they held tightly to one another, finding comfort in the sound of each other's breathing, and beating heart.

Finally he let out a sigh. "What next?"

"Let's get a bath. It's late. If the castle is locked down, that means no one will be doing anything more until morning, when the royal family wakes up."

"Right," he breathed, and forced himself to his feet, then as the great bell began tolling, sank down again. "Who's going to tell the family?"

"Morning," Lineas said firmly, though she didn't feel firm at all. "Everything can wait until morning."

"Very well," he said wearily, knowing that he owed it to Noddy and Vanadei to be there when Noddy heard the news. He and Lineas both.

She picked out clean clothes for them as he wiped his knives on his ruined robe. Then they went down to the bath.

Quill could not relax. Too much was poised on a pinnacle, and a breath of wind either way could cause a rock fall. *Skytalon.* He winced, surged out of the bath, dressed, and found Lineas waiting.

When they got upstairs, they found Pereth standing against the wall outside Lineas's room. "I think," he said, as the last clang of the great bell died away, "there are things you should know."

Sleep was decidedly not going to happen. Lineas silently opened her door, and for the first time, Pereth stepped inside. "It's going to be long," he warned.

And it was. Knowing that Quill would tell her anything she hadn't heard, Lineas went out to fetch hot steep for them all, as Pereth began with how Retren Hauth had been secretly training Connar at the academy—and why.

It was soon evident that Pereth had not been trained as the royal runners were in recounting events in order. Either that or he was too unsettled to remember the forms as he skipped forward and back in time. Some things he summarized, others he described in detail, such as how badly Connar had reacted to that Victory Day conversation his Uncle Retren forced on him, and the realization that he had not been picked for his talent, but entirely because he'd been the product of—as he put it—as stupid a pair of shits as had ever been born, and the grandson of a worse shit.

Then Pereth leaped to the secret Vaskad training that the Nighthawk people had been so very proud of, and Jethren's goal to win Connar the kingship, after which he jumped to the story of Cabbage's murder at the riverside, with Jethren as witness.

"But that doesn't explain *why* he killed Cabbage Gannan. Or was that whim?"

"It might have been premeditated. Don't know," Pereth said. "All I can tell you is that he hated Gannan since the day he started calling him Cabbage, if not before. But that's when I saw it."

Lineas—who had slipped back in unnoticed—murmured, "I think I remember that time. But it wasn't Connar there, surely. It was other boys."

Pereth signed his thanks as he took a sip, then he said, "What you remember is the day Gannan got assigned kitchen duty. Connar and his brother came to gloat on another day, and I remember it because my brother told me to tell Gannan what seemed to be a big secret, that Connar wasn't a real prince, and that the king would replace him with the Chief Weaver's baby, if it was a boy. Later, much later, I figured my brother got the orders from my uncle, as his first attempt to cut Connar off from his family . . ." And he went on to relate what had happened between Connar and Cabbage Gannan.

At the end, Quill said skeptically, "I can see that causing a squabble. We squabbled over everything in those days. But I can't believe Connar would even remember it all these years later. He had to have known he was adopted. We all knew upstairs that it was no secret. And it certainly didn't divide him from his family."

"All I can tell you, from my experience, is that Connar never forgot anything, especially if it humiliated him." He finished off the steep in three gulps.

Quill glanced at Lineas in mute enquiry, and she said, "I don't know how he felt. We rarely talked about anything except immediate matters."

Pereth sighed. "Right. He didn't talk to anyone but his brother, if he could avoid it. So I had to learn to watch him for clues." He turned the empty cup in his hands. "Any more questions?"

"Yes," Lineas said, when Quill didn't speak. "What can you tell me about Moonbeam?"

Pereth flinched at the name—a common reaction, Lineas had become aware. "Almost nothing. Uncle Ret told us only that, as a boy he survived the fight between Mathren Olavayir's commanders at the Nighthawk castle, following Mathren's death. He was already crazy when the Jethrens took him into their family. Could hear just fine, wouldn't speak. He grew up with Kethedrend Jethren as his bodyguard and runner combined. Halrid, Keth's father, kept up the assassin training. Kethedrend kept him leashed by giving him assassin-root, which supposedly made it impossible to see the ghosts he claimed were always around." Pereth shrugged. "I did say he was insane."

Lineas did not try to explain how the dangerous dose must have altered Moonbeam's vision enough to suppress his ghosts. She hid the sorrow she felt for him, a once-loved child, fractured by the pain she had seen beneath all the physical and psychic scars.

But the other two hadn't seen it, and she knew Pereth emphatically did not believe ghosts existed. So she shifted the subject. "What do you want to do now?"

Pereth opened his hands. "Don't know! I just did what I was told, and kept my head down."

Quill said, "You've got to have more military experience than most, following him through all those battles. You were certainly with us every step of the way on that wretched march up Skytalon."

Pereth lifted a shoulder. "It got so that I could usually predict what orders were coming next, and ready things so he didn't have to ask, which he liked. But when I spoke orders, it was always in his name. *I've* never held any position of command. I certainly was no good up on the third floor. I know the other runners went to Mnar Milnari behind my head. Can't say I blame them." He glanced furtively up, but neither Quill nor Lineas betrayed the contempt or disgust he dreaded. They just looked tired and unhappy. "Can you tell me what happened?"

Quill said, "I wasn't in the banquet hall, but outside of it, so I had a confused view. No doubt there will be an investigation, and more details will emerge."

Pereth accepted that, and went to his room, where he lay awake staring at the ceiling.

Lineas shut her door. She and Quill lay down together, exhausted but unable to rest. She dreaded the dawn, which would bring the royal family to wakefulness—and the discovery of yet another royal death. She couldn't imagine Connar, so vital, so intense, lying lifeless. It hurt to try.

So she turned to Quill, who lay with his arms crossed behind his head, his gaze wide open, reflecting the pale stars of impending dawn through the open window opposite the bed.

"You can't sleep either?" He smiled her way, then sat up. "Sunrise soon. We may as well go see what's happening instead of fretting about it."

They walked out to find Vanadei coming up the steps to the third floor. He turned around to join them. "They're awake."

"How bad is it?" Quill asked. They all remembered how devastated Noddy had been after his father's death.

"Bad." Vanadei looked down. "But he wants to see you."

Quill started down the steps, then paused, saying in Sartoran, "Those women. I recognized a lot of them. Like Neit. Henad. I thought their dressing like the foreign troupe was odd, but maybe part of the entertainment."

"Same. But I've said nothing, because I didn't see any faces, except for Dannor's. And I'm not going to speculate. What I can tell you is, apparently they all got out before the lockdown. I heard that right before I came up here."

Lineas's eyelids flashed up. "Ranet, too?"

"No. Still there, according to the report." Vanadei's mouth twisted. "Alone. Nobody knows what to do with a gunvaer in this situation. The guards seem to believe she tried to defend Connar. So they've ringed the banquet hall as protection."

Quill said, "Let's get this over with."

Quill worried about what he should say if Noddy asked him about what he'd seen in the banquet room, but it turned out Noddy's mind was entirely on the secret invasion plans, and the Noth assassinations. Quill told him what he knew, adding what David Pereth had informed him.

Noddy sent Vanadei for Pereth, who repeated everything he had told Quill. By then, Danet had woken, and Noren as well.

When someone said that Ranet was still in the banquet room, the entire royal family decided they had to go downstairs. "You come," Noddy said to Vanadei, an appeal. "Quill, you too. And Lineas."

Danet, always so capable, was dazed with leftover sleepweed and shock; Sage hovered anxiously at her left, hating how the gunvaer trembled, pausing hesitantly before going down the stairs she had descended countless times before.

Danet felt rotten, but she scarcely noticed her physical discomfort. She was locked inside her head, aware that she had not wanted to believe Connar was lying to them about his invasion of the north, about the Noth assassinations. But whenever she'd tried to convince herself that the Bar Regren had killed the Noths and were plotting an invasion, her mind had always returned to Connar's reaction at the news of Rat Noth's death. There had been no sign of anger. Instead, he'd been watchful, even though he'd said all the right things.

Noddy had also sensed this anomaly, and he had been nerving himself ever since to confront Connar. But he hadn't, because he was afraid of what he might hear.

And now he'd been forced to hear it. Guilt burrowed deeply into Noddy. "It's all my fault," he muttered, too disconsolate to use Hand. "I made him be king because I was a coward when Da died."

Noren didn't hear, as she was a few steps ahead and didn't see him talking. Danet slid her arm around her big son's waist. "Not a coward. Grief isn't cowardly. It just is." Her husky voice suspended, and Noddy choked down a sob.

When they reached the banquet hall the guards parted, and they walked in.

The bodies had been removed—Connar to the throne room, where his runners were tending him—the furniture righted, and most of the blood mopped up. Ranet still sat on the ground to the right of the big gilt wingchair, her elbow on the seat where Connar had been before they carried him away. She leaned her head on one hand, the crossbow on her lap.

She had sat there in a sick daze through the night, sometimes dozing off briefly, her thoughts like captured fireflies, until the force of memory jerked her awake again: her hands releasing the bolt. Connar's wide, shocked blue eyes. The pain, the disbelief, the betrayal in his gaze before all the life, the light, was gone and he crashed face down.

At the sound of footfalls, she looked up and winced against the cramp in her neck.

Then she stood and laid the crossbow on the table. "Noddy, I planned it all. I hired the dancers, and told them what to do. I shot Connar myself. Because of the blood on his hands. Because it was only going to get worse, and no one would stop him . . ." Her face twisted, but then she made an effort they could all feel, and threw her head back. "I'll go to the lockup. Whatever you do to me is only right."

Noddy stared in shock. Until that moment he'd clutched at the idea of unknown assassins disguised as dancers, taking her by surprise as well as Connar and his honor guard.

He choked on another sob, but everyone there knew he would do what he thought right, even if it destroyed him in the process.

Noren's sudden clap startled them all. Heads turned as she signed, "No."

She paused, acutely aware that if Ranet had engineered the death of someone Noren loved instead of a man she had worked hard not to dislike, she would probably feel differently, but then is true neutrality even possible when judging human actions?

However. During that long walk she had been thinking over what Vanadei, Quill, and Pereth had told them.

She flexed her hands. "If Connar had ridden north with his army and attacked Prince Cama Arvandais and his captains while they were celebrating in a tent, nobody would have argued that it wasn't a preventive strike in war. What happened last night was a preventive strike."

"But it wasn't against any enemy," Noddy said slowly, his gaze naked with appeal. "Was it?'

"It was," Noren stated. "The worst kind of enemy, the enemy from within. Those Nighthawk people conspired in secret, and this is the result. Do you really think that Connar would send assassins against Rat Noth, who he'd known and trusted since they were ten? But Jethren was jealous of Rat, even I saw that. As for Connar killing Cabbage and the lance master, he didn't do that kind of thing before he had his ears poisoned by Mathren Olavayir's evil through that Jethren."

This new idea shook them all. Danet shut her eyes, struggling against conflict: her growing fears this past two years; and beneath that, the incandescent rage of a mother who could not protect her child.

"Yes," Noddy whispered. "That's right. It was a preventive strike."

Danet turned his way, words trying to work past her tongue. Then it struck her that Noddy had given his first order as king.

It was done. *She* was done. "Whatever you say," she whispered, too distraught for Hand.

But Noren read it in their lips.

Noddy scarcely heard. He was trying not to look at Ranet, who saw his averted gaze, and anguish clawed her heart once more.

The royal runners still stood behind them. Quill watched (and Lineas that night recorded), as authority settled around Noddy and Noren, a perceivable yielding from everyone there, making them harvaldar and gunvaer as definitely as if they stood on the dais in the throne room on the other side of the north wall.

And so, bit by bit, the royal castle from new king and queen down to the kitchen helpers worked to restore a semblance of order.

The memorial for Connar was held that night, Noddy speaking the few words Noren chose for him. He hated the thought of being king, but guilt forced him to accept that as his penalty. No one could move him from his conviction that he'd failed their father by being weak after Arrow's death, and thus had failed Connar, who had only learned how to be a military commander—a great one, Noddy insisted, with the ring of sincerity in his voice. But he hadn't had the chance to sit with Arrow through all the seasons, learning the peaceful side of kingship.

Ranet was not at the memorial. She had gone from the banquet hall to her room, where she drank down the potion Sage brought her, without asking what was in it. If there was poison in it, so be it.

It was only a dose from her own stash of sleepweed, for Noren had seen from her dark-circled eyes the sleepless nights Ranet had endured.

Ranet slept all through that day, and the night.

Early the next morning, Noren went to her. Ranet's two remaining runners withdrew in silence, worried eyes betraying their anxiety over what was to happen to them, though they had been asleep with Ranet's girls.

"I came to discuss what's to be done," Noren signed.

Ranet gripped her hands behind her back. "Is it prison after all?"

"No."

Ranet let out a slow breath, then turned a sober gaze to Noren. "If it was anyone else but you and Noddy, I know I'd be in prison, waiting for the jarls to show up to watch me be flayed at the post."

"Right now, all I can think about is the cost of secrets," Noren replied. "No accusations here. We all have secrets. But Noddy and I are agreed, the fewer the better."

At Ranet's confused look, she went on, "Pereth told us a lot about Connar that we didn't know. Mostly how that Nighthawk company had as one of its goals turning Connar against the rest of us. I don't think even Tanrid Olavayir knows the extent of the Nighthawks' plans. They prided themselves on secrecy. As for the rest of the kingdom, rumors are already flying outward. We'll correct them in time, even the ones that will make us all look very bad."

"Worse than Connar was as a king?" Ranet's voice sharpened, a brief return of her anger. "*He* gave the orders to Nighthawk."

"I don't want to say anything about Connar right now," Noren responded. "He's gone. We have now to deal with. And there are many who believe he was a great king. They probably will continue to, even when the truth of the Noth assassinations—that it was not Bar Regren, or Idegans, but us, Marlovan against Marlovan—reaches the far corners of the kingdom."

"Do you believe he was a great king?" Ranet asked, her face taut with tension.

"Maybe he was a great warrior king." Noren's fist rose then flattened to emphasize *warrior.* "But, as we all know, a great warrior king has to make war."

Ranet said slowly, "And Noddy?"

"Noddy has talked himself into believing that Connar was corrupted by Kethedrend Jethren. Whether or not that is true, Jethren is going to pay for assassinating the Noths by losing his reputation as a loyal captain. He will become the traitor who hired the female assassins to kill the king, who then turned on him."

"And so . . . what is to happen to me?"

"And so you have to disappear," Noren replied, her hands firm. "For Noddy's sake. For Danet's sake. Every time they see you, they will remember Connar lying dead before the throne. As for the rest of the kingdom, word will go out that we've sent companies of searchers on both the east-west and north-south roads to find the assassins," Noren continued, having contemplated how very meticulously Ranet had planned to protect the dancers as well as the women who had helped her in her bloody work.

Everyone protected except herself.

Two stable hands had confided to a blank-faced Vanadei that they'd know Thunderpup anywhere, the bay horse that carried Henad Tlennen to victory so many times. One of the servants who'd delivered spice wine to the banquet hall whispered to cronies that the tall one with the swinging chain belt around the best hips in the palace could only be Neit; Kit Senelaec's fluting voice was instantly familiar to a Senelaec Rider-daughter whom Ranet had placed with the bakers; Maddar Sindan-An had vanished with the rest of them.

But those who shared these confidences fervently acknowledged that every one of those women was connected to someone who had been murdered by the Nighthawk gang, and, well, just was just. Those Nighthawk men, keeping themselves to themselves because they thought they were better than anyone else, of course they were a pack of treachers.

So Holly, Noren's runner who always knew what was going on in the palace almost as it happened, had reported to Noren late the night before.

Noren suspected the dancers were escorted by Henad-Sindan's archers—if not Henad herself—which meant they would be going over roads only known to those from Sindan-An, on the other side of the hills behind Choreid Dhelerei. No doubt the dancers would emerge at Lake Wened as part of some trade caravan, whereupon they would vanish over the eastern pass to Anaeran-Adrani.

Nighthawk taking the blame is the best justice we can contrive, Noren thought, thoroughly aware of the irony.

Time to shift the subject. Ranet had accepted effective exile, as Noren had expected she would. She raised her hands. "Danet-Gunvaer hopes you will leave the girls. They are still princesses."

Ranet gave her a pained smile. "And that's another problem, at least for Iris. She reminds me far too much of the descriptions of the infamous Fabern of a century ago. She even seems to look like her, beautiful, black hair, though I know that's incidental. I want Iris to not be a princess until she reaches a steadier age. So . . . if I'm to live after all, I think I need to take them to my mother at the Keriam holding. That should satisfy both conditions. It lies in a tiny valley in Sindan-An, and my girls will learn good, useful lives there, without the—" She had been about to sign *taint,* but she caught herself; the meaningless title she had borne so briefly had been willingly picked up by Noren. And she would be excellent. "—the expectations of titles."

Tears filled Ranet's eyes. She smiled crookedly. "I know Danet-Gunvaer will hate it, and I half-wish I could leave them with her. But they'll be back to see her, I promise. In the meantime, she'll have Bunny's baby close by, and of course you and Noddy are still young. Surely you'll have children."

As always, Noren accepted the invisible knife that Ranet had no idea she was stabbing into Noren's heart. But that guilt would never be spoken aloud. "Of course," she said.

"And for that matter, Bunny might remarry."

"She says she won't, but it's early days."

Their eyes met again, and Noren signed, "You are alive. Not even thirty. Go and make something of it."

Ranet saluted, palm to heart, and Noren left.

Ranet opened the inner door, and addressed her wide-eyed clump of runners. "Pack everything," she said. "The girls, too."

They saluted, flat hand to heart. Meaningless maybe, but how that salute hurt! The last time, she thought, and turned away. She would be gone soon, leaving such things as titles and salutes utterly behind.

She walked out to her main room, struggling to fight down the tight throat of grief, then became aware of movement on the periphery of her vision. Noren had left the door open, as she often did—sound meant nothing to her—and there was Lineas, looking in, puzzled. "I couldn't find Iris," she began.

Ranet stiffened. "The girls are with Bunny right now. And . . . tutoring is ended. We will be leaving today." A hissing breath. "I guess I ought to be grateful for your telling me the truth . . ." Her voice suspended when Lineas looked away, the unmistakable sheen of tears in her eyes.

No moral superiority, no pity. Certainly no triumph. All these Ranet had expected. And she knew she would see them in others, as she had in Henad Tlennen and Maddar Sindan-An, who had been utterly convinced of the rightness of their act.

But Lineas gazed back, grief flattening her mouth, as she said, "Please. No 'ought to.'" She looked away, then back. "Gratitude. Like hope. So strong." Her thin hands clasped at her equally thin chest and widened outward. "But can become such terrible weapons. When hope is gone. When gratitude becomes an obligation."

And Ranet said, "You did love him."

Lineas was about to say that what she had been feeling recently had been closer to anger and even dread whenever she and Connar met. And she could see anger and resentment but also question in him. But she heeded the impulse to rein hard on admitting it; she sensed that it would only hurt Ranet, who had through no fault of her own received only indifference from him.

So she said what she could say, "I cherish the memories of those early days. Though they didn't last."

The taut skin in Ranet's face eased. Then she said, "Do you condemn me?"

Lineas thumbed her eyes. "I . . . could never do what you did. But I understand why you did it." *And I know you will carry the burden for the rest of your days.*

Eyes met eyes in complete comprehension.

As for Ranet, she had decided not a quarter hour ago to make a clean break, but because Lineas was the only other person who could truly understand her anguish of love, grief, and guilt, she asked, "Will you write to me? "

"I will," Lineas promised, stepped back, and softly moved away.

AFTERMATH

Nighthawk Company was gone. Those remaining, such as Kethedrend Jethren's father and uncle, went to ground when word of the Night of Knives began to spread—they absolutely believed that the Idegans or the Bar Regren, or even the few surviving Noths, had sent those dancing assassins in a retaliatory strike, and would seek to finish the rest of them off, because that was what they would have done. And so their secrets eventually died with them.

A fresh set of runners went out to cancel Connar's cancellation of Convocation. Neit became personal runner to the king, with it understood she would continue to serve in various capacities. There was no tying her down to a desk any more than she could be yoked to command.

No one was surprised when Jarid Noth resigned as commander of the castle guard and moved upstairs to the south tower with Danet. Everyone was surprised when Noddy appointed David Pereth to the post. This turned out to be an excellent choice, all agreed—except for his disgruntled older brother, who disliked having his former target catapulted over him in the chain of command. Pereth was able to marry at last, and on his father retiring as quartermaster, he got his wife Hibern—who had spent ten years keeping the ledgers at the city guild house—the position, which she served in for Noddy's entire reign.

That spring, fewer than half the youths returned to the academy, but Noren and Noddy decided to begin as they would go on. "If they show up, we'll teach them," Noren promised.

Noddy added, "And no more beating anyone who's last. I always hated that."

The jarls convened at Midsummer to see Noddy crowned as Nadran-Harvaldar. At the time, still reeling from the whispers of assassins and a near-invasion from the north (*Was that them invading us, or us invading them?* some asked, but no one was ever quite sure), the jarls were relieved to find themselves with an easy-going gentle giant of a king.

But human nature being what it is, suppressed injustices erupted at the prospect of a king who invariably opted for compromise and mercy.

First it was Algaravayir, after Linden-Fareas died that autumn. Adamas Totha declared Totha independent from Marlovan Iasca, citing the Olavayirs' history of depredations to what had once been Choreid Elgaer, and to the Algaravayir family—which included the murder of old Aldren Noth. The Jevayir cousins to the Cassads declared Telyer Heyas a separate state as well, like Totha, going back to its Iascan roots.

With the examples of Totha and Telyer Heyas before them, Demeos Nyidri, who had stepped forward as jarl on the death of Ivandred Noth, declared himself King of Perideth.

To stem further erosion of Marlovan Iasca, Noddy embarked on a tour of the kingdom, patiently listening to complaints and accusations alike. Unnumbered Marlovans came angry, and went away heartened, assuaged, at least neutral.

Meeting the three leaders in the Hesea Plains between two of the great rivers, Nadran-Harvaldar signed the Treaty of the Rivers, officially recognizing Totha and Telyer Heyas as allied realms, and Perideth as well. Though in after-years, once Starliss Cassad's progeny took up the deep-rooted Sartoran inclinations of the Nyidri family, that alliance was more of a wary truce on Perideth's part.

Mouse Noth, embittered over the utter betrayal of his family who had served loyally for generations, ran Perideth's defense, in tandem with Colt Cassad, whose people were legitimized as border Riders, with their own chain of command. Mouse Noth and Colt Cassad shared their resentment against the Olavayirs, who had proved yet again to be terrible kings, a resentment so fierce it not only outlasted Noddy's reign but was passed down the generations afterward.

Starliss made an excellent queen, her only stipulation being that Lavais Nyidri be left where she was. By that time Demeos so enjoyed his life that he had no intention of putting himself under his embittered mother's poisonous rule once again, and so, though she lived to see Perideth restored as a kingdom, and her son as king, Lavais herself spent the rest of her life tending her vegetable garden. But she'd gotten pretty good at her loom.

Bleak as Noddy's kingship began, it did not continue all regret and resignation.

Directly after signing the Treaty of the Rivers, Noddy confirmed Ghost Fath as Jarl of Fath, a decision hailed by all those in the north. Wolf Senelaec outlasted the Jarl of Gannan by a year, after which Senelaec was absorbed into Tyavayir, except for the once-hotly contested westlands returning to Marlovayir. Braids Senelaec remained chief of the Eastern Alliance, and though he was not a jarl, he was as powerful as a king. The horse thieving trade dried up during his lifetime, and trade along the southern pass flourished. Stick Tyavayir became commander of the King's Army for Noddy's lifetime.

Bunny's daughter came in due time, and proved to be the delight of Danet's life. Bunny continued to live at the royal castle, and though eventually she had the occasional lover, she never married again, or had another child.

Danet, who'd insisted on moving up to the old senior gunvaer tower, remained a welcome part of the family.

Ranet kept her promise and sent her daughters when Iris turned sixteen. Iris was gorgeous, with her father's blue eyes, and her singer's voice, which she used often. Little Hliss was horse-mad, and would later marry into the Sindan-Ans. But under her grandmother Fuss's strict upbringing Iris had settled into a bewitching mixture of her unknown grandmother Fi's charming wickedness mitigated by Ranet's clear vision.

So, when the somewhat unprepossessing Adrani second prince came over for a diplomatic visit (to look around and make sure the Marlovans were staying put, and not boiling up another war) he fell hard for Iris. Whether she fell for him or for his title, the world will never know: She played fair, becoming a loyal princess to her prince once she moved to Anaeran-Adrani at age twenty, where she reigned with grace and charm over the Adrani court.

Noddy ruled for thirty quiet years, broken only by occasional troubles, mostly dealt with by Braids and Henad until they were able to raise capable commanders again. It has been pointed out in later times by those most ignorant of their own history that the Olavayir kings ranged from bad to mediocre, claiming Noddy the worst of them because he lost so much land. Those with more foresight observe that few write ballads about the peaceful times: Arrow and Noddy together gave the kingdom sixty relatively peaceful (Danet would have said *unheroic*) years, broken only by outsiders bringing trouble.

Meanwhile Jarend Olavayir, Noddy's heir, assumed more and more responsibility in the northwest.

Jarend became jarl after Tanrid died. Five years later Noddy slipped away in his sleep, and Jarend inherited the throne.

Jarend was by nature the most rigid and rule-bound of the Olavayir kings. Within the first five years of his reign, he not only reinstituted the "last in line gets beaten" rule, which he had relished during his academy years, but he carried his grudge against women—and his distorted memory of women sneaking in to murder the king he'd admired above all others—to close the academy, and the army, to women.

Back in 4095, Camerend had, after the kingdom had been peaceful for an entire year, admitted that the one wish of his heart was for the Montredavan-An line not to die out.

Savarend was born in 4095, Isa in 4096, and Noren in 4098. Noren Montredavan-An had wanderlust, and ended up sailing the coastal patrol out of Lindeth. Isa was a scholar, leading magic studies as a royal runner.

The third year into Jarend Olavayir's reign, late one night Quill found Lineas up in the tower library she loved best, which looked westward over Darchelde. She stood before the fireplace with one of her journals, tossing it lightly from hand to hand.

"What are you doing?" Quill asked, coming up to put his arms around her. "I take it you finished another one? There are plenty of fresh bound books down in the scribe chamber."

"I'm considering whether to chuck this, and the rest of them, into the fire," she admitted.

He peered into her face, startled. Disturbed. "Why?"

She looked away, her profile unhappy. "Who could possibly want to read my ravings?"

"I don't know what you write in there, but I'm very sure it's not raving."

She met his worried gaze, then tossed the book at him, closely covered pages flapping. "See for yourself."

Quill looked down at the tiny, coded hand, then up at her, trying to intuit what prompted this mood. "I would like to very much, but it'll probably take time to learn your code. I think I'd appreciate revisiting the past through your eyes, written in your wise and compassionate words."

"Wise." She snorted, more like a girl of sixteen than like a middle-aged mother, soon to be grandmother. "I have never in my life felt wise. Especially as I scrambled to understand what everyone else seemed to know." She smiled reluctantly. "It seemed life never let me be still long enough to sit and try to be wise."

"Camerend once told me that wisdom is not a lake, but a river. Unlike a lake, which can become stagnant, a river is forever reinventing itself as it moves along. So flows knowledge through time, gathering strength until it becomes the wisdom of the sea."

He cocked his head. "The wisdom of the sea. I do love that image, though I don't know how wise the sea is. More relentless, I should think." He pulled her back onto the settee they often sat on to watch the sunset together, and leaned over to tap the worn-edged journal. "*You* are wise, my Lineas. You proved it by raising kind, long-seeing children."

"It seems to me you had a part in that." She shot him a wry glance. "Why the flattery? Are you trying to jolly me out of burning this thing? It's not the decision of a moment of pique. I've been thinking it this past couple of years, as we watched Jarend Olavayir undo many of Arrow's more generous laws, and all of Danet-Gunvaer's changes. I am so glad she didn't live to see that. It's as if all her—our—hard work has come to nothing."

"But it hasn't. Remember what Noren said in her last letter: Women always remember, because they write. To each other, to their descendants. And what they remember, they can bring back."

Lineas sighed, and leaned against him. "Well, as for that, I still don't know if it was a good or a bad thing to have women in the army."

"I think it was a thing. Neither good nor bad. Like anything else."

And—inevitably—both their minds turned to the expected grandchild. She mused, "If Savarend and Dannor have a boy, that dreadful treaty confining the family here will be lawfully concluded."

"And?"

"Well, for one thing, jarlans will be looking for marriage treaties."

"We're used to that with the girls."

Lineas turned to gaze into his eyes. "My dear, you and your father put a great deal of effort into giving our son a prince's education."

"Ah. That. I see where you're going, and you're right. The older generation always believed we'd regain the throne. Savarend and I have talked about that. He doesn't have any more ambition than I do, but at the same time, can't help but think we'd do better than Jarend Olavayir."

It was a joke, but went awry. When he saw the tension remaining around her eyes, he added, "It's only talk. Though I've no idea what our grandchildren will be like, I have confidence that Savarend will raise them well, and if one of them should marry a king, or end up as one, it will be lawfully. But the best education in itself is never amiss."

"True." She leaned against his warm shoulder and gazed out the window at the golden fields of autumn. "I don't know how wise it is. It seems to be too obvious, maybe even fatuous to say it, but peace will only happen when *everyone* wants it."

"And does the work to keep it," he agreed, hugging her. "You can teach me the code tomorrow. Right now, come away to bed."

Who's Who

The Eastern Alliance

Tlen, Tlennen, Sindan-An, and Sindan, with the Senelaecs over to the west, were the primary horse breeders of Marlovan Iasca. The Sindan-Ans were the primary family among them, closely seconded by the Tlennens. The Tlens were by this time a much smaller jarlate, and the Sindans never held land at all—their many branches were spread among their cousins as Riders.

Not only were these clans constantly intermarrying, their family names were often given as first names, so new boys at the new academy could be expected to meet identical-looking blondes named Tlen Sindan and Sindan Tlen—until they got a nickname.

The Eastern Alliance jarls elected a chief among them who dealt with outsiders, and commanded the alliance when the whole needed to be raised. At the time of this record, that was Amble Sindan.

The Noth Family

There were three main branches of the family.

The Algaravayir Noths descended from Senrid (Whipstick) Noth of Choreid Elgaer, who features prominently in the chronicles about Inda-Harskialdna.

The Noths connected with Parayid Harbor in Faravayir descended from Whipstick's second son.

Then there are the Faral Noths, plains riders and horse masters connected to Cassad, Darchelde, and southern points. They are descended from Flatfoot Noth, Whipstick's cousin.

Because the Noths were scattered all over the kingdom, they are listed under the various clans and garrisons where they lived, **their names bolded.**

* signifies encountered in Book One.

Narrator

The same narrator who oversaw the Fox memoir detailing the history of Inda Algaravayir, known as Inda Harskialdna. (Subsequent details in later records.)

Marlovan Jarl Households and Rider Families

Individuals connected to jarl households listed under that household. For example, Farendavan, under **Tyavayir**.

Arvandais (of Lorgi Idego)

Jarl: Hastrid [deceased]
Jarlan: Starand
*Daughter: Hadand "Hard Ride" [deceased]
*Son: Haldren "Hal", present king
First cousin: Ndiran Arvandais. (Married to Wolf Senelaec 3 years, took daughter Marend on dissolving the marriage)
*Third-cousins: Farendavan family [see Tyavayir]
Anderle Vaskad: [see Nighthawk below list of jarls]

Algaravayir

*Iofre: Linden-Fareas
***Aldren Noth,** stable chief, guard captain
*Daughters (by Aldren Noth): Hadand, Noren (future gunvaer)
Adamas Totha (cousin to Iofre on mother's side, the Iofre's heir)

RIDER FAMILY: NOTH

Runners:
*Pan Totha (runner to Noren)
*Holly (runner to Noren)

Cassad [see Telyer Hesea]

Darchelde (family name Montredavan-An: confined within their own borders for ten generations by old treaty)

*Jarlan: Shendan, secret mage chief [deceased]

*Son: Savarend-Camerend "Camerend," former chief of royal runners, co-chief of royal runner training, now jarl

*Son: Savarend-Senrid "Quill" by Camerend's wife Isa Eris, adopted by Frin Basna, married Lineas Noth

Daughter: Danet "Blossom" by second wife, *Hliss Farendavan

"Flax" Noth: guard captain

Tanrid Stonemason: hereditary stonemason for Darchelde castle

Tdor Noth: runner

Daughter: Lineas Noth: royal runner

Eveneth

Sons: Camerend, Keth "Dognose"

Daughter: Fnor

RIDER FAMILY: MARECA, BASNA

Sons: Barend, David

Daughter: Dialen

Farendavan (see Tyavayir)

Feravayir (family name Nyidri)

*Acting jarl Commander **Ivandred Noth**

Sons:

***Ganred "Rat," Vandas "Mouse"**

"Digger": first runner

"Jugears": second runner

"Salt": third runner

"Itch" Noth: long runner, scout

*Jarlan: Lavais

Sons by Lavais and former jarl: Demeos m. to Starliss Cassad, Evred "Ryu"

Plix: kitchen steward under Lavais Nyidri, spy for Ivandred Noth

Areth: noble friend to Nyidri sons

Korskei: noble friend to Nyidri sons

Lemekith: noble friend to Nyidri sons
Jaya Vinn: noble heir, friend to Nyidri sons
Holder Nireid: holder, formerly duchas generations ago, friend to Lavais Nyidri

RIDER FAMILY: NOTH, PARAYID BRANCH

Gannan

*Jarl: Evred
*Jarlan: Fareas
Sons: Indevan "Blue" m. Lnand Sindan
*Senrid "Cabbage" m. to Maddar Sindan-An [SEE YVANAVAYIR]
Daughter: Ndand

RIDER FAMILIES: STALGRID & POSEID
*Sons: Lefty and Righty Poseid, twins

Runners: Kendred (Cabbage's first runner)

Halivayir

Jarl: Indevan
Son: Kendred "Bendy"
Daughter: Hadand "Thistle"

RIDER FAMILY: DORTHAD
Leaf Dorthad, betrothed to "Ghost" Fath
Steward: "Goose" Banth
Nanny

Jayavayir, also known as Jayad Hesea (family name Jevayir)

Jarl: Indevan "Iron Spear"
Grandsons: Hana, Ivandred, Senrid

Holder Khael Artolei: holder of a border territory, maternal second cousin to Nyidris of Feravayir, friend to Nyidri sons

Khanivayir

Jarl: Barend

Jarlan: Mran
Sons: Tanrid "Squeak", Retren "Snake"
Daughter: Shendan

RIDER FAMILIES BASNA AND MONADAN

Marlovayir

Jarl: Indevan [deceased]
Jarlan: Ndara (moved back to family in Eveneth)
*Son: Tanrid "Knuckles"
*Sons of Knuckles: twins, Salt and Pepper (captain under Rat Noth)
Wim: recruit under Pepper
Daughter: Tdiran

RIDER FAMILY: STADAS

Marthdavan

Daughter: Lis
Sons: Jarend, Chana (once "Chelis")

RIDER FAMILIES: BAUDAN, NDARGA, and **NOTH**
Dannor Ndarga
Lemon Noth, Riding Chief

Olavayir

Eagle-branch
*Grand Gunvaer: Hesar [deceased]
*Jarl: Indevan [deceased]
*Jarlan: Ranor
Randael: [deceased]
*Randviar: Sdar
*Sister: Hlar (born Halrid, third brother), chief potter
Sons: Kethedrend [deceased], Tanrid [deceased]
*Jarend (married to Tdor Fath)
Son: *Tanrid, married to Fala Nermand
Tanrid's son: Jarend "Cricket"
Daughter: Ranor
*Anred "Arrow," married to *Danet Farendavan
Sons: *Nadran "Noddy" m. Noren Algaravayir,
Connar [see dolphin branch] m. Ranet Keriam, adopted into Senelaecs

*Hadand "Bunny" m. Ganred "Rat" Noth [see FERAVAYIR]
Connar and Ranet's daughters: Daughter: Fareas "Iris," Little Hliss

*"Sneeze" Ventdor, second cousin to Jarend and Arrow (Rider captain, Cmdr. At Ku Halir)
Barend Ventdor, (cousin to Sneeze, third cousin to Arrow)
Runners: *Gdan (runner to Ranor-Jarlan)
*Nand (Olavayir border Rider)
*Tesar "Tes" (Danet's long runner, niece to Gdan)
*Nunkrad "Nunka" (in charge of nursery)
*Loret (Danet's First Runner)
*Shen (Danet's second runner)
*Sage (Danet's third runner)
Fnor (Danet's fourth runner)
*Halrid "Floss" Vannath (Tanrid's first runner)
*Neit Vannath (Jarlan of Olavayir's long runner, later captain of skirmishers and liaison between garrisons)
*Nath (chamber runner to Arrow)
Aldren (second runner to Arrow)
*David "Fish" Pereth (Connar's first runner)
*Vanadei (Noddy's first runner; royal runner)
"Cheese" Fath (runner under Fish Pereth)
Dannor Lassad (Bunny's first runner)

Dolphin-branch
Garid [deceased]
*Kendred [regent; deceased]
*Mathren [Commander of King's Riders; deceased] m. Fnor Marthdavan [deceased] [for details of secret army, see NIGHTHAWK, below]
Sons: *Lanrid [deceased],*Sindan "Sinna" [deceased]
Lanrid and Fini sa Vaka son: *Connar [adopted by Arrow and Danet, **see eagle branch**]
Runners: Thad (Mathren's third runner
Tlen (general castle runner)
Kend (second Runner to Mathren)

Senelaec

*Jarl: Hastred [deceased]
*Jarlan: Ndara (returned to family in Eastern Alliance)
Jarl's brother: Tanrid "Tana"
Sons: *Hastred "Wolf,"*Tanrid "Yipyip"

Daughters: *Fareas "Fuss," *Carleas "Calamity" (adopted from **Noth** relations)

*Mardran "Cub," son of Wolf and Ndiran Arvandais

Marend, (daughter of Wolf and Ndiran Arvandais, taken to Arvandais by Ndiran)

*Ranet/Ran "Braids," son of Wolf and Calamity, raised as a daughter chief of Eastern Alliance, m. Henad Tlennen

*Fareas "Kit," daughter of Wolf and Calamity

*Ranet, adopted from Keriam family, to replace Ranet in betrothal to Connar Olavayir

Runners: *Pip
*Ndara
*Young Pan
*Ink
*Trot (becomes a scout under Braids' command)
*Fnor

Sindan-An

Jarl: Tanrid "Rock"
Jarlan: Ranet
Son: Evred "Baldy"
Daughter: Fnor
Daughter: Maddar m. to Cabbage Gannan

RIDER FAMILY: SINDAN (related to the Sindans of Sindan-An and Tlen
Daughter: Pandet Tlen
"Snow" Baker (daughter of bakers, lifemate of Maddar)

Telyer Hesea, combined with Faral (family name Cassad)

*Jarl: Handas
*Jarlan: Carleas Dei
Sons: Aldren, *Barend "Chelis" (for a time)

*Daughter, later son: Carleas "Colt," adopted from deceased sister Hlar Dei, leader of partisan gang

Jarl's sister's daughters: Chelis m. Eaglebeak Yvanavayir,
Starliss m. Demeos Nyidri

RIDER FAMILY: NOTH, FARAL BRANCH

"Plum" Noth: captain under Rat Noth, second-cousin

Tlen

Jarl: David "Tuft"
Jarlan: Tdan
Son: Garid
Daughters: Hibern, Chelis "Owlet"
Pandet (second cousin)

RIDER FAMILY: SINDAN & HOLDAN
Son: Senrid "Rooster" Holdan
Daughter: Shen Sindan

Tlennen

Jarl: Garid
Jarlan: Hibern
Son: Mardren "Marda" adopted sister's boy
Daughter: Henad (commander of skirmishers) m. Braids Senelaec

RIDER FAMILY: SINDAN
"Amble" Sindan: Eastern Alliance Chief
Lnand Sindan m. to Blue Gannan

Toraca

Jarl: Nadran,
Jarlan: Faral
Daughters: Fala, Gdir
Sons: Indevan "Horseshoe," Nadran

RIDER FAMILY: TUALAN
"Moss" Tualan, army farrier, field medic

Tyavayir

Jarl: Halrid, Jarlan: Han
Sons: Camrid, *Tanrid "Stick" (captain under Connar)
Camrid's son: Evred

RIDER FAMILY: FATH

Sons: Tlennen, *Anderle "Ghost" (captain under Connar)
Daughter: Genis

Runner: Askan (runner to Stick)
Runner: Keth (runner to Stick)
Runner: "Snake" Wend (long runner to Stick)

TRADE FAMILY: FARENDAVAN
Father: Hasta, captain of riders sent by Tyavayir to Olavayir to fulfill treaty
*Mother: Hadand, chief weaver
*Son: Hasta "Brother" m. to Tialan Fath, mated with Hanred Basna
Daughters: *Danet, m. to Anred Olavayir
*Hlis, later Chief Weaver
Son: *Andas, by the king and Hlis
Daughter: *Danet "Blossom" by Camerend Montredavan-An and Hlis

Yvanavayir/Stalgoreth

Jarl: Ganred
Jarlan [deceased]

Sons: Aldred "Eaglebeak," Manther
Daughter: *Fareas "Pony"
Runners: Fenis (Pony's runner)
Pan
Mlis

RIDERS ALL FAMILY CONNECTIONS

AFTER CHANGE TO STALGORETH

Jarl: Senrid "Cabbage" Gannan
Jarlan: Maddar Sindan-An
Snow, baker/scribe, lifemate to Maddar
Fnor-Tailor favorite to Cabbage

Zheirban

Jarl: Anderle
Jarlan: Maddar
Sons: David, Camerend
Daughter: Gelis

RIDER FAMILY: LENNACA

Nighthawk

Mathren Olavayir's private army

Anderle Vaskad [deceased]: Swordmaster and war trainer, first under former king Tanrid Olavayir AKA Bloody Tanrid; had early training of Jarl of Arvandais and Mathren Olavayir.

Surviving the massacre after Mathren's death:

*Retren Hauth, maternal second-cousin to Mathren, sent to Nevree as lance master

"Tigger" Jethren: brother to Halrid Jethren, also of Nighthawk Company, then Olavayir Rider

Halrid Jethren: Lance Captain Nighthawk Company/Olavayir Rider

Son: Kethedrend "Keth" Jethren: Lance Commander under Connar

"Moonbeam": Keth Jethren's first runner, kidnapped by Anderle Vaskad from Arvandais, trained from early childhood as an assassin

Hanred Leneid, (Rider captain under Keth Jethren, assassin)

"Rock" Alca, (Rider captain under Keth Jethren, assassin)

Sleip, (scout and assassin)

"Punch"(scout and assassin)

Royal Castle, Royal City, and Academy Staff

***Jarid Noth**: City Guard Captain, promoted to Garrison Commander, interim King's Army Commander

Indevan "Toast" Basna: Captain of Garrison Training

*Amreth Tam: Kitchen Steward

*Vnat: kitchen help, greens

*Liet: buttery

"Old" Chelis: potter

*Evred Pereth: Quartermaster

Sons: *Halrid (guard-in-training), *David "Fish" (runner-in-training, Connar's first runner)

*Hlis Farendavan, Chief Weaver [see Farendavan]

*Evred Andaun: Academy Headmaster

*Retren Hauth: Lance master, brother-in-law to quartermaster

Evred Stadas: archery master

"Baldy" Faldred: mapping teacher, housemaster

Halrid: head mason

*Spindle (castle runner)

*Mard (runner to Evred)

*Tarvan (runner to Evred, then to Jarend Olavayir)

*Liet: castle runner

*The Captain's Drum, pleasure house (closed after Evred's death)
*The Silver Shield, pleasure house
*The Singing Sword, pleasure house
Branid (worker at the Singing Sword)
Liet (worker at the Singing Sword)
Nand (worker at the Singing Sword)

Royal Runners

*Shendan and Camerend Montredavan-An, chiefs in charge of the runners, and (first one, then the other) co-chiefs of the royal runner training [see **Darchelde**]

*Mnar Milnari, co-chief of the royal runner training
*Senrid "Quill" Montredavan-An
Lineas Noth
*Fallon (referred to only) chief trainer of long distance runners
*Branid (ferret)
*Ivandred (long runner, ferret)
*Hlar Dei [deceased] (sister to Jarlan of Cassad)
*Lnand (long runner, ferret)
*Dannor (assistant master, in charge of fledges)
*Cama "Cama Tall" (long runner, ferret)
Cama Basna (master)
*Fnor (scribe, ferret)
*Vanadei (Noddy's first runner)
*Liet
*Ndand

Adranis

Sarias Elsarion: duchas of Elsarion
Mathias Alored Elsarion: brother to Sarias

Brigands and Mercenaries

Jendas "Skunk" Yenvir
Barnat, son of Aiv
Adzi
Vior Mat Cingon, mercenary formerly hired by Elsarion

Bar Regren

Ovaka Red-Feather (chieftain)
Ovaka Mol, chieftain's second son
Oba, grandson of Ovaka Red-Feather
Ewt
Thiv
"Finger"

Ku Halir Garrison and City Denizens

*Commander: "Sneeze" Ventdor, kin to Arrow
Captain: Barend Ventdor, kin to Arrow
Scribe: Ndand

Castle Inn: Enka Kiff, owner
Son: Retren (army recruit)
Daughter: Ndara "Jam"

Three Sails Inn: Tolvik, owner

Weaver: Var
Wim: scout under Pepper Marlovayir

Larkadhe Staff

Steward: Keth "Steward" Dei
Healer's Assistant: Indevan "Inda" Janold
Court scribe: Barend

Sartorans

Seonrei Landis: a princess of Sartor
Iaeth: maternal second-cousin to Seonrei, herald-scribe
Donais: personal tailor to Seonrei

ABOUT THE AUTHOR

Sherwood Smith studied in Europe before earning a Masters degree in history. She worked as a governess, a bartender, an electrical supply verifier, and wore various hats in the film industry before turning to teaching for twenty years. To date she's published over forty books, one of which was an Anne Lindbergh Honor Book; she's twice been a finalist for the Mythopoeic Fantasy Award and once a Nebula finalist. Her YA fantasy novel *Crown Duel* has been in print for over twenty years.

She reviews books at Goodreads and blogs intermittently at Dreamwidth. Find her website at Sherwoodsmith.net.

ABOUT BOOK VIEW CAFÉ

Book View Café Publishing Cooperative is an author-owned cooperative of over fifty professional writers, publishing in a variety of genres including fantasy, romance, mystery, and science fiction.

Book View Café authors include New York Times and USA Today bestsellers as well as winners and nominees of many prestigious awards, including:

Agatha Award
Campbell Award
Gaylatic Spectrum Award
Hugo Award
Lambda Literary Award
Locus Award
Nebula Award
PEN/Malamud Award
Philip K. Dick Award
RITA Award
World Fantasy Award

Book View Café, since its debut in 2008, has gained a reputation for producing high-quality ebooks. BVC's ebooks are DRM-free and are distributed around the world. The cooperative is now bringing that same quality to its print editions.